Praise for The Demon Child Trilogy by Jennifer Fallon

Medalon

"A warm and intriguing book with all-too-human characters who draw you in more deeply with each page."

—L. E. Modesitt, Jr.

"*Medalon* is an intriguing, intelligent, and fun read with a refreshing take on female characters so often not seen in the genre." —Elizabeth Haydon

"A gripping tale of warring ambitions, politics, and *real* people. The characters (and even the gods!) spring to vivid, believable life, making *Medalon* a great read. More please!"

—Ed Greenwood

"I read *Medalon* by Jennifer Fallon and am impressed. This is a powerful, solid, imaginative, sometimes brutal fantasy novel with a splendidly worked-out cast of characters. I like the way the gods are less than omnipotent, and dragons are magical constructs; this seems realistic in terms of magic, no oxymoron intended." —Piers Anthony

Treason Keep

"A well-executed fantasy with complex characters and entertaining style." —*Kirkus Reviews*

"Intrigues, rivalries, and romance provide an entertaining tangle in the second book in Australian fantasy author Fallon's Hythrun Chronicles (after *Medalon*). Accompanied by a large cast of compelling characters . . . new readers will be well rewarded; fans arriving straight from book one can dive right in." —*Publishers Weekly*

Harshini

"As in *Medalon* (2004) and *Treason Keep* (2004), the capricious gods are part of the mix, and now intrigue and counter-intrigue become even more complicated. The battles are fierce, the losses heartrending in Fallon's beautifully created world, whose disparate inhabitants are once again completely convincing, making *Harshini* a chilling, thrilling conclusion to the trilogy."   —*Booklist*

"For fantasy fans comes another title from an Australian author highly rated in this field. This is the final volume of the Demon Child Trilogy and it lives up to the entertaining action, imagination, and power of its predecessors. . . . Prepare yourself for a non-stop adventure and romance. A good getaway read."   —*The Australian Woman's Weekly*

"One of the better Australian Fantasy books this year . . . With Jennifer's first trilogy under her belt I expect to see great things in the future. Jennifer isn't only a writer to watch but she may become one to emulate. *Harshini* is a good book."   —*Altair*

WOLFBLADE

Book one of the Wolfblade Trilogy

JENNIFER FALLON

TOR®
fantasy

A TOM DOHERTY ASSOCIATES BOOK
NEW YORK

This is a work of fiction. All the characters and events portrayed in this book are either products of the author's imagination or are used fictitiously.

WOLFBLADE

Copyright © 2004 by Jennifer Fallon

Originally published in 2004 by Voyager, an imprint of HarpeCollins*Publishers*, Australia

Excerpt from *Warrior* copyright © 2006 by Jennifer Fallon

Map by Ellisa Mitchell

A Tor Book
Published by Tom Doherty Associates, LLC
175 Fifth Avenue
New York, NY 10010

www.tor.com

Tor® is a registered trademark of Tom Doherty Associates, LLC.

ISBN-13: 978-0-765-34869-2
ISBN-10: 0-765-34869-1

First U.S. edition: January 2006
First U.S. mass market edition: September 2006

Printed in the United States of America

0 9 8 7 6 5 4 3 2 1

For Glennis,
and, as always,
Adele Robinson

PART ONE

THE END
OF INNOCENCE

CHAPTER 1

It was always messy, cleaning up after a murder. There was more than just blood to be washed off the tiles. There were all those awkward loose ends to be taken care of— alibis to be established, traitors to be paid off, witnesses to be silenced . . .

And that, Elezaar knew, was the problem. He'd just witnessed a murder.

A slight, humid breeze ruffled the curtain in the alcove where the dwarf was hiding, the tiled floors of the mansion echoing to the sound of booted feet. The faint, fishy smell of the harbour lingered on the wind, rank and uninviting. Or perhaps it wasn't the nearby bay Elezaar could smell. Maybe the decay he smelled was here. Maybe the swords of his master's killers had opened a vein somewhere and the stench came from the moral decay that seeped from the very walls of this house and permeated everything it touched.

Still trembling at the narrowness of his escape, Elezaar moved the curtain a fraction and looked into the room. His master's corpse lay across the blood-soaked silken sheets, his head almost severed by the savage blow which had ended his life. On the floor at his feet lay another body. A slave. She was so new to the household Elezaar hadn't even had time to learn her name. She was only twelve or thirteen; her slender, broken body in the first bloom of womanhood. Or it had been. The master liked them like that—young, nubile and terrified. Elezaar had lost count of the number of girls like her he had seen led into this opulently decorated chamber of horrors. He'd listened to their screams, night after night, playing his lyre with desperate determination; he provided the background music to their torment, shutting out their cries for mercy . . .

This was no subtle assassination, the dwarf decided in a conscious effort to block the memories. This was blatant. Done in broad daylight. An open challenge to the High Prince.

Not that the attack was entirely unexpected. Elezaar's master, Ronan Dell, was one of the High Prince's closest friends—assuming you could call their bizarre, often volatile relationship "friendship". In Elezaar's opinion, his master and the High Prince shared a passion for perversion and for other people's pain rather than any great affection for each other. There were few in Greenharbour who would lament the death of Ronan Dell. No slave in his household would miss him, Elezaar could well attest to that. But even if the slaves of Lord Ronan's house stood by and cheered the men who had stormed the mansion—was it only an hour ago?—their change of allegiance would do them little good. Slaves, even expensive, exotic creatures like Elezaar, were too dangerous to keep alive.

Particularly when they could bear witness to an assassination.

Wiping his sweaty palms on his trousers, Elezaar stepped out of the alcove and made his way cautiously through the chaos of shredded bedding and broken glass to the door. He opened it a fraction and peered out. But for a toppled pedestal and a shattered vase, the hall was deserted, but there were still soldiers in the house. He could hear their distant shouts as they hunted down the last of the household staff.

Elezaar waited in the doorway, torn with indecision. Should he stay here, out of sight? Out of harm's way? Or should he venture out into the halls? Should he see if he could find anybody left alive? Perhaps the assassins had orders to spare the innocent. The dwarf smiled sourly. He might as well imagine the killers had orders to set them all free, as imagine there was any chance the slaves of the house would be spared.

Perhaps, Elezaar thought, *I should stay here, after all. Maybe the soldiers won't torch the place when they're done. Maybe he could escape. Maybe Crys had found somewhere* to hide. With their master dead, perhaps there was a chance to be truly free? If everyone thought Crysander the *court'esa* and Elezaar the dwarf had perished in the slaughter . . .

I have to get out of here. I have to find Crys.

Elezaar froze at the sound of footsteps in the hall, hurried yet fearless. He shrank back against the wall, holding his breath, his view of the hall beyond shrinking to a slit as he waited for the danger to pass. A figure moved in his limited field of vision. His heart clenched . . .

And then he almost cried with relief when he realized who it was.

"Crys!"

The tall *court'esa* turned as the dwarf called out to him in a loud hiss.

"Elezaar?"

"Thank the gods you're still alive!" Elezaar cried, looking up and down the hall furtively as he emerged from behind the door.

"It's a miracle *you're* still alive," Crys replied, apparently unconcerned about the danger he might be in. "How did you get away?"

"I'm small and ugly, Crys. People either don't see me or they think I'm stupid. How come you were spared?"

For a moment, Crys didn't reply. Elezaar looked up at him curiously. The brothers had always been close, even though their status as slaves had seen them separated more often than not since childhood. In fact, this was the first household they had ever served in together. Both played down the relationship, however. It didn't do to give a master any more leverage over you than he already had; particularly a master like Ronan Dell. Crysander was such a handsome young man, with his dark eyes and long dark hair. He was also blessed (or cursed) with the slender type of physique that so appealed to masters who wanted their slaves to have all the skills of a well-trained *court'esa* and yet still manage to give the impression they were an adolescent boy. Crys had suffered much in Ronan Dell's service; almost as much as Elezaar. But in different ways. And for different reasons.

The young man glanced down at Elezaar, smiling apologetically as he saw the dawning light of comprehension on the dwarf's face. Elezaar stifled a gasp. *No wonder Crys looks so unafraid. He wasn't in any danger from the assassins. He's one of them.*

"You betrayed my master." It wasn't a question, or even an accusation. It was a statement. A simple fact.

"Not at all," Crys said. "I've been faithful to our master all along."

Elezaar suddenly remembered the breastplates of the soldiers who burst into Ronan Dell's bedroom. The eagle crest of Dregian Province. He'd not had time in all the excitement to think about it before.

"We belonged to Ronan Dell, Crys."

"*You* belonged to the House of Dell, Elezaar. I have always belonged to the House of Eaglespike."

"And how does the old saying go? Beware an Eaglespike bearing gifts?" Elezaar stopped abruptly as the sound of footsteps grew louder. "We must find a better place to hide!"

"There's really no need—" Crys began, but before he could finish, a troop of soldiers rounded the corner. Elezaar began to panic, wondering if there was any point trying to make a run for it. There wasn't, he realized quickly. Crys might escape but with his short, stumpy legs, the soldiers would run him down in a few steps. The dwarf glanced up at Crys again, but the young man seemed unafraid. He simply shoved Elezaar back into the room, out of sight, then turned to the captain of the troop as the invaders approached. His heart pounding, Elezaar leaned against the wall, wondering how long it would be before he was caught. Crys might betray him in some misguided attempt to prove his loyalty to Lady Alija. Crys might betray him to save his own neck.

Or he might not. He was, after all, Elezaar's brother.

"Did you find them all?" Crys asked as the soldiers stopped in front of him.

Elezaar's heart was hammering so hard, he was sure they must be able to hear it in the hall. Through the slit in the doorway, he watched the officer in the lead sheathing his sword as he neared Crys.

"Thirty-seven slaves," the man confirmed. "All dead. There should be thirty-eight, counting the dwarf. We didn't find him."

"And you won't," Crys told them. "He's long gone."

"My lady wanted nobody left alive," the captain reminded him.

"No credible witnesses," Crys corrected. "The Fool could stand on a table at the ball tonight in the High Prince's palace, shouting out what he'd seen here, and nobody would believe him. You needn't worry about the dwarf."

The soldier looked doubtful, but Elezaar guessed they were running out of time. And it was easy to believe some strange-looking, half-witted dwarf was too stupid to bear witness to their crimes. Assuming he even survived long on the streets of the city.

"I suppose," the captain agreed doubtfully. "What about you?"

Crys shrugged. "My fate has been arranged for days. I've been sold. With the Feast of Kaelarn Ball going on at the palace tonight, by the time your handiwork has been discovered, I will have been safely under lock and key at Venira's Emporium for hours."

"Then we're done here," the captain agreed, his hand moving from the hilt of his sword to the dagger at his belt. Elezaar saw the movement—he was eye-level with the captain's waist—and opened his mouth to cry out a warning . . .

Then he clamped it shut again. To utter a sound would cost him his life. If Crys was in danger; if he couldn't see that Lady Alija would never allow a *court'esa* to live when he could testify to her direct involvement in the assassination of Ronan Dell—well, brother or not, Elezaar had no intention of sharing that danger with him. Besides, the man may simply have been moving his hand to a more comfortable position . . .

The captain's blade took Crys without warning. Elezaar's brother didn't even have time to cry out. The soldier drove the dagger up under the slave's rib cage and into his heart with businesslike efficiency. Elezaar bit down on his lip so hard it bled and turned his face to the wall, unable to watch something he had known was coming and had been power-less to prevent. He heard, rather than saw, Crys fall. Heard the creak of leather as the captain bent over to check that Crys was dead; heard the fading stamp of booted feet and the scrape of sandals against the polished floors as the soldiers retreated, dragging Crysander's body behind them.

Elezaar stayed facing the wall for a long, long time.

It was dusk before Elezaar found the courage to move. In that time, the room full of death where he waited had filled with the buzz of hungry flies, attracted to the feast laid out for them.

Immobilised by fear though he was, Elezaar had not wasted his time. His body was still but his mind had been rac-ing, formulating and then discarding one plan after another.

The first thing he had to do was find somewhere safe, and for a *court'esa* bonded to a house that had just been wiped out, that was not going to be easy. The slave collar he wore would betray him if he tried to flee into the city. Even if Elezaar could find refuge among the homeless and the un-wanted on Greenharbour's streets, they were too hungry and too desperate to shelter him for long. Particularly if there was a profit to be made by turning him in.

No. If he wanted to survive this, he needed protection. And Elezaar intended to survive this. He had a score to settle. His brother may have been a misguided fool, thinking he could betray one master for another, but his life had been worth more than a swift knife to the belly, just to keep him quiet.

Protection. That was what Elezaar needed. But who would protect a slave? More to the point, who would protect a Loronged *court'esa*? A dwarf *court'esa* at that?

Someone who will profit from it, Elezaar realized. What had Crys told the captain? *My fate has been arranged for days. I've been sold. With the Feast of Kaelarn Ball going on at the palace tonight, by the time your handiwork has been discovered, I will have been safely under lock and key at Venira's Emporium for hours.*

Elezaar finally found the courage to move.

Venira. The slave trader, he thought, as he opened the door. He stopped and looked down at Crys's blood pooled on the floor. Tears misted his vision for a moment. Elezaar wiped them away impatiently. He was too hardened to grieve for his brother. There was too much pain down that road. The dwarf looked away and forced himself to keep moving. It was almost dark. If he was caught on the streets alone after the slave curfew, he'd be in serious trouble. Or someone might come looking for Ronan Dell. He was expected at the ball tonight. The High Prince might send someone to fetch him if he didn't show.

And Venira's slave emporium closed at sunset. If Elezaar couldn't get to the slave quarter before the slaver left for the night, he ran the risk of a night in the streets, one he was quite certain he wouldn't survive.

Safety lay, Elezaar knew, with the slave trader. He'd already bought and paid for a Loronged *court'esa* from Ronan Dell. Elezaar would see that Venira got his merchandise. As arranged.

Just not the *court'esa* he was expecting, that's all.

chapter 2

From the balcony overlooking the great staircase of the Greenharbour Palace, you could see tomorrow. At least that was what Marla remembered thinking when she was a small child. That was back in the time she thought of as Before. Before, when everything was certain. Before, when she was safe. Before she was sent away. Before her father died.

Before her brother became High Prince.

But I'm back now, Marla thought with satisfaction, although her memories proved something of an exaggeration. You couldn't see as far as tomorrow, but you *could* see right across the hall, and get a very nice view of the handsome and smartly dressed young men who had come for the ball this evening.

The hall was massive. Sixteen glorious cut-crystal candelabra showered warm yellow light over the numerous guests as they arrived. The musicians in the corner were tuning their instruments. Bare-footed slaves hurried back and forth from the kitchens, piling the long tables with exotically displayed foods and countless flagons of fine imported Medalonian wines. Thirty-two fluted marble columns that looked as if they could support the weight of the entire world reached up towards the gilded ceiling that even here on the first-floor balcony was far above her.

Marla pushed her hair off her face, wishing she had thought to tie it back before escaping from Lirena's eagle-eyed care. Somewhere down there, amid the sea of faces, polished boots and slicked-down hair, was her future husband. She had no idea who he was just yet, but he was sure to present himself at some stage this evening. He was bound to be handsome, undoubtedly wealthy and, of course, the son of one of the many noble houses her brother would approve of. She sighed contentedly. Tonight was the start of something wonderful. *This is the night destiny will step forward and offer me his hand . . .*

"Marla Wolfblade! What are you doing out here in your underclothes gawking like a fresh-bought slave?"

With a last wistful look at the sparkling spectacle unfolding below, Marla turned to face her nurse. "I am *not* in my underclothes!" she corrected. "This is a *dressing* gown. For goodness sake, stop fussing, Lirena! I just came down for a quick look. It won't take me long to get dressed."

"Bah!" the old woman scoffed. "Since when did you master the art of getting dressed in under an hour?"

Marla looked up and down the wide balcony with a frown, hoping nobody had overheard the old nurse scolding her. It was so unfair that her aunt hadn't given her a proper lady's maid and quite embarrassing that she had come to the Convocation of the Warlords accompanied by her nanny. Marla understood things had been difficult lately. She knew the wealth of the Wolfblades had been devoured by her late father's many (and ultimately futile) wars and their ongoing legacy. But surely there was enough left for her to be properly attended? Appearances, she knew well, frequently meant more than the facts.

"You come away from there, my girl, before somebody sees you!"

"Lirena, you *must* address me as 'highness' while we're here in Greenharbour!" she hissed, although she did as she was ordered and moved back from the marble balustrade.

"Then you come away from there, *highness,* before somebody sees you!"

"Don't take that tone with me!"

"Don't *you* take that uppity tone with *me,* missy!" the old woman retorted with a disturbing lack of respect for her mistress's rank. "You get back to your room right now, or you'll be making your first official public appearance with a tanned backside. You're not so old you can't be taken over my knee to teach you some manners, you know."

Marla opened her mouth to object, and then clamped it shut as a door opened along the hall and three figures emerged, deep in conversation. She turned to Lirena in a panic, pulling her pale green gown tighter around her slight figure. The men walked toward them, engrossed in their discussion. The oldest of the three had closely cropped grey hair and wore the black robes of a sorcerer. The younger men were dressed in unremarkable dark trousers, boots and plain linen shirts which meant they were probably servants, she decided, dismissing them immediately as beneath her notice.

The older man looked up and nodded to them politely, barely diverting his attention from what his young attendant was saying. Lirena curtsied as low as her old bones would

permit as they passed. Marla followed suit, hoping her graceful (and much practised) curtsey, was sufficient. The sorcerer
and his companions walked on for a few steps and then
stopped suddenly. The grey-haired sorcerer turned back to
study Marla with a quizzical eye.

"You're Lernen's sister, aren't you?"

"I am the *High* Prince's sister," she replied with another
curtsey, and just the slightest emphasis on the "high".

"You look younger than I thought you would."

Marla swallowed down a moment of panic, wondering
why this man would be thinking about her age—or anything
to do with her for that matter. She smiled, hoping her expression was as sophisticated as she imagined it to be.

"I am almost sixteen, my lord. I would hardly call that
young."

The sorcerer studied her for a moment with dark, in-
scrutable eyes.

"*Almost* sixteen? I do beg your pardon, your highness," he
said with a faintly mocking smile she didn't much care for.
"Are you enjoying your return to Greenharbour?"

In truth, Marla was quite overwhelmed by her sudden and
unexpected removal from the quiet mountain retreat where
she'd been hidden away for the past ten years, but she wasn't
going to admit it out loud to anybody. "It is a pleasant change
of pace, my lord."

The sorcerer smiled. "I'm sure you'll find it even more so,
once the party begins."

"Will I see you there, my lord?"

He shrugged. "Perhaps for a short while. Several thousand
people crammed into a confined space isn't my idea of a good
time. But I'm sure Wrayan and Nash will find it entertaining."

Marla glanced at the young men. They were both staring at
her, rather rudely in fact. The tall one was quite handsome,
with thick brown hair and nice hazel eyes. In contrast to his
companion, the other young man had laughing eyes and thick
dark hair that Marla thought might be very nice to run her

fingers through. The unexpected thought made her blush. But his smile seemed infectious and she couldn't help but respond to it.

"Perhaps you'll be serving us," she said, in a generous attempt to give the poor lads some encouragement, although they didn't really deserve it for gawking at her like that.

"Wrayan is my apprentice, your highness, not my servant," the sorcerer informed her. "And this is Nashan Hawksword, son of the Warlord of Elasapine."

Lirena hissed softly in horror. Marla said nothing for a moment, hoping the balcony would open up and swallow her. When it refused to cooperate, she was forced to smile apologetically at the young men.

"I'm sorry, my lords. I had no idea—"

"There's no need to apologize," Wrayan assured her generously. "I'm not wearing the robes of the Collective. It's a common enough mistake to make."

Common enough for country rustics who don't know any better, she wailed silently in despair. "I hope you took no offence, my lord. I mean, I . . . I didn't really mean to imply that . . ." *I'm babbling! Oh, the gods take me now!*

"I promise, Princess Marla, neither Wrayan nor I are offended," the Warlord's son reassured her. He really was *very* handsome.

"It's my fault," the older man said. "I suppose I should have introduced myself and my companions before attacking you like a Karien inquisitor. I am Kagan Palenovar, and this, as you have already discovered, is my apprentice, Wrayan Lightfinger. And this is Nash Hawksword of Elasapine. And it is I who should be apologising, your highness. It's just I've heard your name mentioned a great deal recently and I always like to put a face to a name."

Marla stiffened with alarm. *Kagan Palenovar? The High Arrion himself? Why wasn't he wearing his diamond pendant, so she could tell?* Then she noticed the silver chain around his neck, the edge of the pendant denoting his rank hidden in the folds of his black robe. She swallowed the hard lump in her throat, nervously assuming what she hoped was an air of innocence. "I can think of no circumstance that would bring my name to the attention of the Sorcerers' Collective, sir. I trust it was in a pleasant context?"

Kagan seemed amused by her question. "I believe the discussion had something to do with an offer for your hand, your highness. As the most recent offer came from someone in whom I have a great deal of interest, I was curious about you, that's all. Now, if you will excuse us, I have several things to take care of before the ball begins."

He bowed politely and, followed by his apprentice and the young lord, turned away, heading down the long hall until they were swallowed by the gathering darkness. Marla stared at their retreating backs, numb with shock.

"Marla! Come on, lass! You've embarrassed yourself enough for one evening—standing here chatting to the High Arrion in your underwear."

"Did you hear what he said?"

"Aye."

"He said he was discussing my betrothal. He said the young man in question was of great interest to him."

"Aye."

She turned to the nurse, eyes glittering with excitement. "Don't you see, Lirena? He said the offer came from some-one *in whom he has a great deal of interest*. Oh, by the gods, Lirena, do you think I'm going to marry a *sorcerer*?"

"That's not what he said, Marla."

"But what else could he mean? Wrayan is his apprentice, and sorcerers only ever take one apprentice at a time."

"Sorcerers don't usually marry," Lirena pointed out.

"Then he must have been talking about Nashan Hawksword." She smiled shrewdly, thinking there was an op-portunity here she would be a fool to ignore. Marla was des-perate not to be sent back to Highcastle. If everyone believed she was happy with the marriage her brother was negotiating on her behalf, the chances were good she would be allowed to stay in Greenharbour. A bit of enthusiasm might be prudent . . . She sighed dramatically. "His eyes, Lirena. Did you see his eyes? They were so blue . . ."

"What I saw was a foolish girl standing in her underclothes chatting to the High Arrion like a common streetwalker," Lirena snapped. "And if that girl doesn't get her backside straight back to her room this minute, she won't be getting anything other than spanked."

Marla tossed her head and gathered up the folds of her dressing gown, refusing to dignify Lirena's crass threats with a reply. She turned her back on the old slave and flounced along the hall to her room.

I'm going to marry a Warlord.

It couldn't have been more perfect if she'd planned it herself. She would have a townhouse here in Greenharbour, she decided, and another in Byamor, the main seat of Elasapine. In Byamor she would no doubt reside in one of the vast, magnificent palaces belonging to the Hawkswords and have countless slaves to do everything for her, *court'esa* to amuse her, a sorcerer-bred horse that nobody would tell her she was too inexperienced to ride, and a handsome Warlord for a husband . . .

I'm going to marry a Warlord. I'm going to marry a Warlord.

She would have to write to her cousin back at Highcastle immediately. That horse-faced bitch, Ninane, would be green with envy. They didn't let just anybody marry a Warlord. You had to be *somebody* and she was the only sister of the High Prince of Hythria, after all. One didn't come much better credentialed than *that*. You had to be beautiful to marry, and clever, and sophisticated . . . all the things Marla hoped she was. She reached her room and ran straight to the mirror.

Nashan Hawksword. Marla Hawksword. Lord and Lady Hawksword . . . it had such a nice ring to it.

"Look, Lirena, already my skin is glowing with the first bloom of love!"

"You're red-faced from running up that damned hall," the

old woman corrected crossly as she closed the door behind them. "Now you finish getting dressed, my girl, or you won't be goin' nowhere."

Marla smiled brightly, feeling suddenly generous toward her old nurse. *She'll be able to retire, once I'm married. I'll see she's given a small estate and enough to live on comfortably. I may even free her if she wants it. Lernen should be able to afford it now. With his only sister married to a house as powerful as the Hawkswords, the other Warlords will give him anything he wants. I will be a grand lady, with jewels, and carriages and all the power I want . . .*

Because I am the only sister of the High Prince of Hythria and I'm going to marry a Warlord.

ChAPTER 3

Wrayan Lightfinger poured his master and the young lord of Elasapine a generous cup of wine each and crossed the sitting room of the High Arrion's suite to hand the cups to them. Kagan was staring out of the window at the torch-lit dock, watching the guests' barges wait their turn to tie up and disgorge their passengers. Lernen had treated everyone to a harbour cruise for the afternoon. Another extravagance he could ill afford, and probably done solely to impress his visitor from Fardohnya. The High Arrion took the cup and turned to look around his apartment. The rooms were sumptuous here in the High Prince's palace. Every painting was a work of art, every piece of furniture crafted by a master. Kagan kept rooms here for convenience. His own palace was less than a mile away.

"So, what did you think of the Princess Marla?" Kagan asked his young companions.

"I think I'm in love!" Nash declared, accepting the wine from Wrayan. "She's gorgeous."

"I'm not surprised Lernen's been swamped with offers for her hand," Wrayan answered, much more careful of his opinion than Nash. Kagan rarely asked idle questions. Until he was sure why his master wanted his opinion, he would not elaborate further. In truth, Marla Wolfblade was quite simply the most stunning creature Wrayan had ever laid eyes on. In his mind's eye, he could still see her standing out there on the balcony in her pale green dressing gown, as if by holding it so tightly closed she was protecting her virtue. He could still clearly picture her long blonde hair, tousled and in disarray, and her large blue eyes wide with excitement. She was funny too—all puffed up with her own self-importance, which did nothing but draw attention to her innocence.

"You think she's gorgeous, Nash?" Kagan said, taking a sip of wine. "Now there's an opinion you'd be wise to keep to yourself. Until she's safely married, Lernen will treat anybody who even looks crosswise at his sister as a threat. The same goes for you, Wrayan."

Wrayan frowned. "He's never treated me like a threat. For that matter, he actually made a pass at *me* once."

"Did he really?" Nash chuckled. "I thought you'd be a bit old for the High Prince's tastes, Wrayan."

Kagan wasn't nearly so amused. "You sound like a Patriot, Nash."

"Well, you have to admit, the Patriot Faction does have a point. Our venerable High Prince Lernen really is a disgrace to his throne."

"And any attempt to unseat him would be treason," Wrayan reminded him.

Nash looked unconcerned. "I didn't say I *supported* the Patriots, necessarily. I just think they might have a point, that's all."

"Well, our High Prince's rather disturbing sexual preferences notwithstanding," Kagan shrugged, "Marla has spent the last ten years safely out of sight at Highcastle. He's never had a reason to feel threatened about her until now. But she's reached a marriageable age and suddenly she's the most valuable thing he owns." Kagan took a good swallow from his cup and frowned. "I foresee interesting times ahead."

"Oh, so now you think you're a prophet, I suppose?"

They all turned towards the unexpected voice. Lady Tesha Zorell stood at the door, as tall and effortlessly elegant as always, her long black formal sorcerer's robes soaking up the lamplight as she moved. Ranked second only to Kagan in the Sorcerers' Collective, the Lower Arrion's dark hair was arranged to perfection and she wore a look of vast disapproval.

"Pity your newly discovered seer's gift didn't extend to the fate of Ronan Dell."

Wrayan looked at his master, wondering if Kagan had any idea what she was talking about.

"Ronan Dell?" Kagan repeated in confusion.

"He's dead."

"When?" Nash asked in surprise.

"Earlier today," Tesha informed them. "The assassins took out Ronan and every slave in the household. It was a real bloodbath, by all accounts. I'll have one of those," she added, pointing to the wine Kagan held.

Wrayan hurried to comply. Tesha Zorell was the second most important member of the Sorcerers' Collective. Although not nearly as well connected as Kagan, what she lacked in family connections, she more than made up for by the sheer force of her personality. While not exactly afraid of her, neither was Wrayan anxious to incur her displeasure. He filled another cup and handed it to her with a small bow.

"He even has manners," Tesha remarked, as she lowered herself gracefully onto the cushions without waiting for an invitation to be seated. "He certainly didn't learn those from you, old man. Or that slimy little pervert, Lernen Wolfblade."

"Yes, well, sometimes they just pick these things up of

their own accord," Kagan sighed. "I'm not sure where I went wrong."

"Do we know who was responsible for the assassination, my lady?"

"I'm guessing someone in the Patriot Faction," Tesha suggested, sipping her wine. "Lord Ronan was a close friend of Lernen's, after all. But with all the slaves dead, there's not much chance of proving it."

Nash downed his wine in a swallow and handed the empty cup back to Wrayan. "Forgive me for being rude, but I really should be attending my father. He'll want to know about this. You will excuse me, won't you? Lord Palenovar? Lady Tesha?"

"Of course," the High Arrion replied. "And please give your father my regards." When Nash had bowed hastily and fled the room, the Lower Arrion faced the High Arrion with a suspicious frown.

"Do I want to know why you seem to be so friendly with the only son of Charel Hawksword these days?"

"Nash is Wrayan's friend, Tesha. That I enjoy his company on occasion is simply a pleasant consequence of his acquaintance with my apprentice."

"And you still have one, I see. I'm astonished. I was certain you would have managed to dispose of him by now."

"He's proving to be rather more resilient than I anticipated," Kagan replied with a shrug. "But never fear. I'm sure I'll manage to get rid of him, eventually."

"Sooner, rather than later, I imagine," she said with a frown. Tesha sipped her wine and studied the High Arrion thoughtfully. "This is starting to get out of hand, Kagan."

"And what do you expect me to do about it?"

"The factions are resorting to assassination to resolve their differences. You're the High Arrion of the Sorcerers' Collective. Don't you think *some* of the responsibility is yours?"

"I haven't been idle, Tesha."

"Yes . . . I hear you've been meeting with Hablet of Fardohnya and the prince."

"*High* Prince," Kagan corrected, in a fair imitation of

Marla. Wrayan was certain Tesha had no idea Kagan was mocking her.

"And?"

"And what?"

"Don't try my patience, old man. What happened?"

"Hablet made an offer for Marla," he said.

"Why?"

"It's no great secret, my dear. The Fardohnyans want to stitch up the hole in the royal line they lost when Hythria first separated from Fardohnya twelve hundred years ago. Our venerable High Prince of Hythria, on the other hand, is flat broke, terrified of his own Warlords, under threat from a pretender who's backed by an entire faction who opposes him—to the point where they're openly murdering his friends—and he has no real desire to govern his country, particularly if it's at war with his neighbour."

"Then Lernen will accept the offer?"

"That remains to be seen."

Tesha took another thoughtful sip of wine. "Our influence in Fardohnya has been eroded considerably since Hablet took the throne. Perhaps you could arrange the release of those members of our order he imprisoned when he was crowned King."

"Well, don't get too excited just yet. In his moments of sobriety, even Lernen can see the danger in the idea of his sister becoming queen of a neighbouring country that's just as likely to turn on him without warning."

"Traditionally, the King of Fardohnya has no queen."

"Up 'til now."

"This could be the start of something very promising," Tesha decided. "You've done well, Kagan."

"Don't thank me. Thank the gods Lernen has a sister of marriageable age. There won't be any deals without that."

"Then you had best see she remains safe, hadn't you?"

"I'll keep Marla safe and sound," he promised. "Just you make sure you keep an eye on the Warlords. And your dangerous little protégé, Alija Eaglespike."

"Are you implying Alija might have had something to do with the attack on Ronan Dell?"

"I'm not implying anything, Tesha; I'm saying it outright."

Tesha shook her head. "You're wrong."

"Without her pushing the notion of her husband as a viable alternative to the High Prince, the Patriot Faction would have no focus. They're not going to be happy if they think Lernen has found a way to keep his throne."

Wrayan listened to the conversation with interest. In all the years Wrayan had been apprenticed to him, Kagan had done as little as possible to fulfil his duties as High Arrion and then only begrudgingly. He had continued to profess his abhorrence of all things political right up until the current High Prince, Lernen Wolfblade, ascended to the throne. Since then, Kagan had been acting just like a real High Arrion and Wrayan had been hard pressed to keep up with him.

"I'm curious, Kagan, as to your sudden change of heart," Tesha said. "The last time I asked you to aid me in settling a dispute, you told me to . . ." She hesitated and glanced at Wrayan before she continued. "Well, suffice to say, you suggested I perform an anatomically impossible feat upon myself."

"And how do you know it was anatomically impossible? Did you try it?"

The Lower Arrion reddened with embarrassment. "Kagan, if you continue in this vein, I will move to have you expelled."

Kagan looked unimpressed by the threat. "You'd have me expelled for being crude? Here's an idea! The Patriot Faction, led by the Warlord of Dregian Province and aided by his sorcerer wife—in direct contravention of our rules—is actively plotting to take the crown of the man we're sworn to protect. Why not bring *that* up at the next Convocation?"

"If we had a High Prince with half a brain, or even one located in his head rather than his nether regions, none of this would be happening, Kagan," Tesha pointed out testily. "The Patriots were nothing more than a clutch of whining old men until that pervert you're so determined to prop up took the throne. And as you are his chief advisor—"

"So it's *my* fault Lernen is a useless prick? Fine! The Convocation of Warlords is only a few days away. Once we've confirmed Laran Krakenshield as the Warlord of Krakandar, I'll have the High Prince declare war on his cousin in Dregian Province, shall I? We'll find out who the Royalists and the Patriots are then, won't we?"

"Don't be ridiculous—"

"Here's a lesson for you, my young apprentice," Kagan cut in. "What the Lady Tesha is trying so hard not to say is that it doesn't matter how dangerous the threat to the High Prince gets, the Convocation of Warlords wouldn't lift a finger to stop the Patriots. Now why is that, do you think?"

Wrayan knew it wasn't a rhetorical question. Kagan rarely forced him to study, but he was always questioning him and his observations. It was the way Kagan liked to teach, which was to say he would rather not be teaching him at all.

"Because damn near half of them have *joined* the Patriot Faction?"

Kagan laughed aloud. Tesha wasn't nearly so amused. "What are you teaching him, Kagan?"

"As little as possible," Kagan admitted honestly. "I'm trying to make him learn for himself. It's a lot less work for me and a lot better for him in the long run."

Tesha wasn't really listening. Wrayan felt a tickle against his mind as she tried to probe his thoughts, but he shut her out with ridiculous ease. Kagan noticed the push too. Tesha was almost, but not quite, an Innate, which meant she was very good at giving the impression she had real magical talent, but didn't have much skill when it came to actually putting it into action. Kagan, on the other hand, was a master of reading other people's body language, which made many people *think* he was a magician when in fact, he had no magical talent at all. It was simply his quite astounding skills of observation.

"You've not a chance of cracking *that* boy's mind, Tesha," he laughed.

"I know the boy's potential, Kagan. It's why the Collective sent him to you for training."

"And all this time I thought it was my charming personality."

Tesha rose to her feet and placed the empty wine cup on the low table. "It is times like this when I truly grieve the loss of the Harshini. It is a sorry state of affairs indeed, when the choice of apprentice-master for a boy of Wrayan's ability is a lazy, cynical old fool." She lifted her chin and departed the room, her back straight and unrelenting.

"Ages come and ages go," Kagan noted as he watched her leave, holding out his cup to Wrayan for a refill, "but that woman never changes."

"You couldn't have felt anything. How did you know she was trying to probe my mind?"

"She had that look on her face."

"What look?"

"That constipated look of intense concentration she always gets when she thinks she's using magic."

Wrayan shook his head in amazement. Even after all this time, he couldn't quite believe Kagan could have such a level of disrespect for his peers and still get away with being their leader. "You really are a troublemaker, Kagan. You know that, don't you?"

"I do," the High Arrion sighed. "I am a bad, bad man. If they had a Troublemakers' Collective I'd probably be High Arrion of that, too. Shall we go to the party and upset a few more important people?"

Wrayan shook his head. Kagan was incorrigible. "What about Ronan Dell?"

"What about him?" Kagan shrugged.

"Shouldn't we be trying to find out who killed him?"

"I know who killed him, Wrayan."

"Shouldn't you be trying to prove it, then?"

"Probably," the High Arrion conceded. "But right now, all I can think of is that the world is rid of a monster who preyed on the weak and the helpless, and fed the sick appetites of our esteemed High Prince. The world is well rid of him, Wrayan. I might despise the Patriot Faction and everything they stand for, but sometimes I have to admit they do have excellent taste in their victims."

chapter 4

Marla was finished dressing and pacing her royal apartment impatiently by the time her brother arrived to escort her downstairs. A tall, gaunt man, although still only in his early thirties, Lernen had aged visibly since Marla had seen him last at his coronation. The responsibilities of High Prince had begun to weigh on him. His hair was dyed black this week, his cheeks were sunken and rouged and his brown eyes were dull with worry. This Convocation was his last hope, Marla knew. If the sorcerers wouldn't aid them, the Wolfblades might soon be nothing more than a memory.

But the sorcerers have *helped us,* she reminded herself. *I am to marry Nashan Hawksword and, once the sister of the High Prince of Hythria is allied in marriage to the Warlord of Elasapine, not the Patriots, not Barnardo Eaglespike, not even the Fardohnyans, will dare challenge us.*

"Marla, you look lovely," Lernen told her as she presented herself for inspection, twirling around in a small circle in a swish of lavender silk. The dress had belonged to her cousin Ninane and had been re-sewn by Lirena to make it more fashionable.

"Is it really all right?" she asked, a little concerned. "It's the feast of Kaelarn, the God of the Oceans, after all. I thought maybe I should be wearing blue."

"It's a lovely colour. Didn't cousin Ninane have a dress the same shade last year when she was here for the Feast of Kalianah?"

"Lirena!" Marla wailed in despair, her eyes filling with tears.

The old nurse rolled her eyes at the High Prince. "You really don't think before you open that big mouth of yours, do you, Lernen Wolfblade?"

Lirena had nursed all the Wolfblade children and treated none of them as a slave should. Marla always wondered if Lernen was just a little bit afraid of his old nurse, a suspicion that seemed more than justified as the High Prince took a step back from the slave, apologising profusely.

"I can't wear this!" Marla complained. "If Lernen noticed it's a hand-me-down, everyone will!"

"Nobody will notice anything of the kind," the old nurse assured her. "Your brother's just more observant than most about that sort of thing, that's all."

"You truly are a vision," Lernen added hurriedly. "Nobody will notice a thing, I promise. Now dry your eyes or you're going to look all red and blotchy when you go downstairs."

She sniffed inelegantly. "Are you sure nobody will notice?"

"Positive." Lernen smiled at her encouragingly. "And if anybody does say something, then I'll order him beheaded! How's that?"

"Now you're teasing me."

"You'll be fine, Marla."

"I suppose . . ."

"But there is something we must talk about, my dear," her brother continued with a frown. "Things are happening which affect you . . . danger all around us. One of my friends was murdered today . . . and now . . ." The High Prince's voice trailed off helplessly, as if he couldn't bring himself to add to her woes by telling her the rest of his news.

Her recycled dress forgotten, Marla brightened considerably when she realized what her brother was trying to say. "Oh Lernen, don't look so distraught. I'm sorry about your friend, but I know what you're going to tell me, and I couldn't be happier."

"You *couldn't*?" Lernen glanced at Lirena with a puzzled look. The old nurse shrugged, as if to say, *who could fathom the fickle mind of a teenage girl?*

"I couldn't be happier," she repeated firmly.

"And you don't mind?"

"Of course I don't mind. I've always known I would have to marry someone you chose, but Lernen, I swear if I'd chosen him myself, I couldn't have done better."

"But you'd be so far away . . ."

"It's not that far, silly. I'll visit you as often as I want."

"Are you sure you don't mind, Marla? Really? He's a little older than you, I know, and certainly not what I envisaged, but this alliance would mean we could do something about Barnardo—"

"Shoosh, big brother," she said, placing her finger on his painted lips to silence his apology. "I understand, truly I do. It's a sound political decision. And I honestly, truly, positively don't mind a bit."

"I don't deserve such a sister," he told her, with obvious relief. "But how did you learn of it? It was to be kept secret until the negotiations were completed."

"We bumped into Lord Palenovar," Lirena explained as she tidied up the chaos Marla had left in her wake. "He let it slip that an offer had been made."

Lernen nodded. "Kagan is the mediator for the negotiations. An interesting man, if somewhat disrespectful. I keep meaning to chide him for it, but I'd be lost without him. And his rank allows him some leeway, I suppose."

"His rank?" Marla asked. "You mean because he's the High Arrion?"

"He's not just High Arrion, Marla, he's a member of one

of the oldest and most powerful noble families in Hythria. And the most ardent supporter of the Royalists in Greenharbour. I wouldn't have a throne if not for him."

Marla's eyes narrowed thoughtfully. "Then his apprentice—and his friends—would be of a similar political persuasion?"

"I suppose. I never really thought about it."

So Nashan is a Royalist, she concluded with satisfaction. "Oh, Lernen, you've made me so happy." Impulsively she threw her arms around his neck and hugged him. Lernen held her stiffly, never comfortable with overt displays of affection from his sister.

"Yes, well, we should be getting downstairs," he said, peeling her arms from around his neck.

"I'll make you so proud of me, Lernen," she promised.

"I'm proud of you already, dearest."

"How long will it be?"

"How long will what be?"

"How long will it be before I'm married?"

Lernen shrugged. "Not until you turn sixteen. In the spring, perhaps. Your intended is a devotee of Jelanna, so he may want to hold the wedding on her feast day. We haven't got that far in the negotiations, in truth. And you'll need to be trained first. I suppose I shall have to buy you a *court'esa* or two now."

"Just you make sure you pick a good one," Lirena advised with a grunt as she bent over to pick up another towel Marla had dropped.

Lernen smiled nervously. "It won't be me who picks Marla's first *court'esa*, Lirena. Gracious! What a terrifying thought. Anyway, it's usually a female relative who accompanies a girl on her first trip to the slave markets."

"Oh, Lernen!" Marla cried in alarm. "*Promise* me I don't have to go shopping for a *court'esa* with Aunt Lydia!"

"Sounds like a grand idea to me," Lirena grumbled. "At least you'd wind up with one that's more than just a pretty face and a well-shaped backside."

"If I let Lydia pick my first *court'esa* I'll wind up with an old man who wants to teach me accounting!" Marla complained. "Anyway, who asked you for your opinion?" She turned to her brother and smiled sweetly. "Please, Lernen, promise me you'll find someone else."

Her brother shrugged helplessly. "I suppose. Although I've no idea who."

"Don't worry. We'll think of someone." She hugged him again and then laughed delightedly. "I'm so glad you sent for me. You will let me stay here in Greenharbour until I'm married, won't you?" Lernen had seemed unwilling to commit himself on that point for days now. Marla thought it might be prudent to extract a definite promise while he was feeling so kindly disposed towards his sister.

"Didn't you hear what I said earlier, Marla? Our enemies are everywhere! Ronan Dell was murdered today. In broad daylight!"

"Yes, but you have lots of guards here in the palace. And the Sorcerers' Collective is on our side, aren't they?"

"Well, yes, of course, but—"

"Then I'm as safe as you are. *Please* let me stay."

"We'll see."

Marla chose to take that as an answer in the affirmative.

"That's settled, then," she announced happily. "Now we can go to the ball!"

ChAPTER 5

Exhausted and fearful, Elezaar had to pound on the door of Venira's Emporium for quite some time before anybody came to investigate. The façade of the slave emporium was impressive. Tall marble columns flanked the polished brass-sheathed doors. During the day, two slaves stood either side of the doors, ready to assist customers from their litters or coaches, but at this hour, they were long gone. The street was deserted and Elezaar's voice was hoarse by the time the door was opened by another slave, who looked the dwarf up and down then smiled briefly when he recognised him.

"I thought your soul would be looking for its way to the underworld, by now, Fool."

"It very nearly was, Dherin. Is Venira still here?"

"He's still here," the slave confirmed. "He was waiting for your brother to show up."

"He's not coming," Elezaar informed him flatly. Dherin waited for Elezaar to elaborate, but when the dwarf offered no further explanation, he simply shrugged and stood back to let him enter. After he bolted the door, Dherin led the way through the dim halls and empty showrooms to the slaver's private quarters out the back. Elezaar shuddered as he walked through the interlinked courtyards, wondering what had possessed him to come back here.

Protection, he reminded himself.

But it was a very temporary sort of protection. Venira might sell him tomorrow to the enemies of Ronan Dell and all Elezaar would have achieved by coming here tonight was a stay of execution. But there was a chance, however slender, he might not.

And that was the risk, the gamble, Elezaar had taken.

It was well after dark before he was shown into the slaver's presence. Venira was a grossly fat man with an expansive belly, chins so numerous they looked like gills, and the garish bad taste of a self-made millionaire. He wore rings on every finger and the body-weight of a small child in gold chains around his neck. Too fat for trousers, he favoured long, tent-like robes of rich brocaded silk which were so hot he was followed everywhere by a slave with a large fan whose only function was to cool his master down. When Elezaar was admitted into his presence, the slaver was lying on a pile of overstuffed cushions on the floor, a low table laden with food before him, and the ever-present slave standing over his master wearing a bored expression as the fan moved through a slow arc, doing little to cool the humid air.

"I was expecting Crysander," Venira announced, picking at the fruit bowl on the table. He popped a grape into his mouth, quite deliberately crushing it with his teeth to send a spray of juice across the landscape of his chins, before deigning to turn his gaze on the dwarf.

Elezaar shrugged, glancing around the room. It had changed little since the last time he stood here several months ago. That was just before he had been sold to Ronan Dell. "He was unavoidably detained," he explained. "He sent me in his place."

The fat slaver seemed unimpressed. "I could sell your brother a dozen times over for the number of offers I'll get for you, Fool."

"I can't be held responsible for things beyond my control, Master Venira," he shrugged with an ingenuous smile.

Venira picked up another grape and treated it to the same torment as the first one. "I hear there was trouble at Lord Ronan's place today."

"Really?"

"They say he's dead."

"What a shame."

Venira studied Elezaar closely. "They say the assassins killed all the slaves in the house, too."

"What a pity."

Venira's eyes narrowed. "Including your brother."

"I'm heartbroken."

"I can tell." The slaver leaned back on his cushions. "Who did it?"

"Who did what?"

"Who murdered Ronan Dell?"

"I have no idea, Master Venira. Lord Ronan sent me on an errand early this morning and by the time I got back to the house they were all dead. Crysander had enough breath left in him to tell me to come here in his place. That's all I know."

"You're lying."

"I don't know who killed them, Master Venira."

"And even if you did, you'd never admit it." The slaver smiled slyly. "You may prove to be worth more than I first thought, Fool. Perhaps I'll hold an auction for the last remaining survivor of the Dell massacre. I wonder what will bring the higher price? Your testimony or your silence?"

"I have nothing to tell, Master Venira. I saw nothing. I know nothing."

"So you claim," Venira scoffed. He shifted his bulk on the cushions and waved another slave forward. "Take him to the compound. See he's fed, bathed and clothed appropriately. Get rid of that Dell collar he's wearing and put a plain one on him. The little man may actually be worth something this time."

"You got a fortune selling me to Ronan Dell the last time," Elezaar pointed out.

"And you'd better be worth even more now, Fool. I'm sick of all the trouble you cause me."

"Perhaps next time my master and his household are butchered, I could arrange to be one of the victims," Elezaar suggested helpfully. "So you're not put to any more trouble."

"You do that," the slaver agreed and then he waved his arm and Elezaar was taken away.

The slaves at Venira's Emporium were not mistreated. Although left in no doubt about their status in life, Venira was too aware of the value of his merchandise to risk damage by beating or starving them. They were quite well catered for, in fact, one of the reasons Elezaar had decided to risk coming here. If this night was to be his last, at least he would spend it in relative comfort.

After his ablutions he ate a plain but nourishing meal of meat, cheese, bread and watered wine, and then he was led into the slave cells. Dherin locked Elezaar in a bare cell separated by bars from his neighbours. In the cell on his right was a handsome boy of about twenty with smooth olive skin and dark eyes who looked him over with interest.

"I'm Lorince," the *court'esa* announced, walking to the bars to examine Elezaar more closely in the gloom. The only light in the cells was provided by a torch in the hall and its flickering light was mediocre at best.

"Elezaar," the dwarf replied, offering the young man his hand through the bars. "You been here long?"

"A bit over a month. Venira says the market's slow this time of year."

"What brought you here?"

"Same old story," Lorince shrugged. "I was the *court'esa* of the youngest daughter of Lord Caron's House in Meortina. She got married. Her new husband only trusted his own slaves. Happens all the time."

"Mine fell in love," the slave in the cell on Elezaar's left remarked. The young man was lying on his bunk, his hands folded behind his head. "It's a real bitch when that happens. Nothing you can do about it, either."

"You're not from Greenharbour," Elezaar remarked, looking at the lad's pale skin. He was long-limbed and handsome, with dusky eyes and thick brown hair tied back in a leather thong. It was the fashion these days among the *court'esa*. Elezaar had never really warmed to it though. He found it much easier to keep his hair short.

"Bramster," the young man confirmed. "It's up in the mountains. In Elasapine Province. My name's Darnel. You're the Fool, aren't you?"

"You've heard of me?" For a moment, Elezaar forgot his woes, rather flattered to think he might be famous.

"There aren't too many Loronged *court'esa* like you, little man. What are you doing here?"

"My master was assassinated."

Darnel smiled sympathetically. "Bitch when that happens, too."

"It's always the way, though, isn't it?" Lorince pointed out unhappily. "Just when you think you're settled, something happens and you're right back where you started."

"You have to find a reason to make them want you," Elezaar said, clambering up onto the bunk. The mattress was filled with straw but it was clean and dry and he was exhausted from the events of the day. For this one night, he was safe. It might well be the last safe night Elezaar ever spent. It wouldn't take them long to work out where he was. He knew that. And even if they didn't figure it out for themselves, Venira was just as likely to announce he had a certain dwarf for sale. Right now, Elezaar was more valuable than he had ever been in his life before. Venira—a merchant, first and foremost—understood that. But it also meant the slaver would endeavour to keep Elezaar alive, simply because there was no profit to be made from his death.

Darnel smiled languidly. "Trust me, little man, I know how to make them want me."

Elezaar shifted himself on the bunk and looked across the gloomy cell at the dark-haired *court'esa*. "It's not about sex, Darnel. Any *court'esa* worth his collar knows how to make a man or a woman want them. It's what they train us for. But to be safe, *really* safe, you need to be indispensable. That takes more than sex."

"Were you indispensable?" Lorince asked.

"He wouldn't be here if he was," Darnel pointed out with a cynical laugh.

"I was working on it," Elezaar sighed, settling back on the bunk. "I'd almost convinced my master that life without me was bound to be intolerable and then *wham*! Along come a whole bunch of assassins and ruin everything. Six months' work down the drain and nothing to show for it."

"You're lucky you survived," Lorince sympathised. "I've heard they often kill the house slaves during an assassination."

"They do," Elezaar agreed. He closed his eyes, and then opened them again abruptly when his vision filled with images of blood-splattered corpses, severed limbs and his brother Crys lying in the hall with a look of utter astonishment at his betrayal on his deathly white face.

"Next place they send me, I'm going to become so indispensable, they'll never let me go," Lorince announced, leaning against the cool bars.

Elezaar saw the faraway look of hope on the young man's face and smiled. He'd been that naïve once. Secretly, he still was, in the depths of his soul. Somewhere deep inside Elezaar lingered the same hope—that he would be sold into a House where his talents would be recognised. Somewhere they wanted him for more than the entertainment value he offered. Only then was any *court'esa* truly safe from being sold over and over until they were beyond usefulness. Most wound up in the general slave markets, unwanted, worthless and just as likely to be sold as hunting bait for a jaded lord, or perhaps to a gaming house, to end up facing a rabid dog or some tormented bear for the entertainment of the patrons who wagered on how long it would take for him to die.

On the bright side, Elezaar thought, *that's not likely to be my fate. They'll find me. Eventually. If not tomorrow, then the day after. And then they'll kill me for what I know. Like they killed Crys. Quickly. Mercilessly. And painlessly.*

When all was said and done, Elezaar mused, for a *court'esa* who had witnessed a murder, that wasn't a bad way to die.

CHAPTER 6

Marla walked down the great staircase on her brother's arm, surveying the scene like a newly crowned queen. She scanned the crowd below for any sign of Nashan Hawksword but couldn't spot him immediately.

"There's the High Arrion," she said, spying Kagan's grey head and dark formal robes amid the sea of people below.

"Don't point, Marla," Lernen scolded. "I can see him."

Clinging to her brother's arm, Marla pushed her way through the throng, nodding a greeting here and there to a familiar face. The greetings were returned cautiously, as if the other guests feared that by associating with her brother too closely, some of the Wolfblade family's ill luck would rub off on them. That would change soon, she consoled herself. *When I'm married to the heir of Elasapine, they'll be tripping over each other to curry favour with us.*

As they neared the sorcerer and his apprentice, Marla discovered Lord Palenovar deep in conversation with another man dressed in an elaborately embroidered sleeveless coat. His thick arms were hairy and his ears pierced with small gold trinkets. *A Fardohnyan,* she thought with distaste.

"They really shouldn't let those thugs into civilised gatherings," she whispered to her brother.

Lernen looked at her in surprise, but had no chance to answer her. The Fardohnyan spied them, his bearded face breaking into a huge smile. "Lernen!"

Although younger than her brother, the man was built like a bear and was almost as hirsute. The Fardohnyan shoved his way forward through the curious and disapproving stares of the people around them. He gathered her brother in a crushing hug, slapping him on the back so hard Marla expected to hear Lernen's spine cracking.

"Your majesty," the High Prince replied.

The Fardohnyan let him go and held him at arm's length for a moment before laughing loud enough to be heard across the vast hall. "Enough of this 'your majesty' nonsense. Call me Hablet. We'll be family soon."

Like that *would ever happen*, Marla scoffed silently. She looked around for Nashan, but there was still no sign of him. Wrayan was smiling at her encouragingly. Then Marla caught sight of her future husband over by the food tables. She fluttered her eyelids coyly in his direction and smiled ever so faintly.

"She's a healthy-looking heifer."

With a start, Marla realised the Fardohnyan king was referring to her. "I *beg* your pardon?"

"Feisty, too, by the look in her eye," the beast laughed. "I like that in a woman. I'll need a wench capable of keeping those other catty little bitches on their toes."

"I'm sure the Princess Marla will prove adequate to the task," her brother remarked uncomfortably.

"Lecter! Lecter, come meet my bride!"

Shaking her head in confusion, Marla glanced at her brother, then the Fardohnyan king and finally her gaze swung around to Wrayan. The awful truth dawned on Marla at the same time as Kagan stepped forward and placed a firm hand on her shoulder. Marla opened her mouth, but whether to object or scream even she couldn't say for certain.

The world suddenly swayed beneath her and Marla felt herself falling. Before she could utter a sound, Kagan slipped his arm through hers, holding her upright. "Just walk forward, Marla," the High Arrion hissed. "As if there's nothing wrong."

The panic filling her mind left her beyond the ability to protest. The noise of the crowd around her became a blur of white noise. She could hear someone making excuses. She felt herself propelled forward through the vast hall. Her body was following the commands Kagan gave it, but her mind was screaming. *A Fardohnyan! I'm to marry a stinking, smelly, disgusting Fardohnyan.*

"I want to die!"

"Don't be absurd, of course you don't want to die."

"Let me go," she begged, as Kagan propelled her through the crowd. "Let me die!"

"Are you always this melodramatic?" Kagan sounded calm and faintly annoyed. They pushed through the press of people, her brother close behind them. She had no idea what had happened to Hablet. Or Nashan.

When they reached a small anteroom off the main hall, Kagan pushed her through the door before letting her go. Lernen hurried in close behind, confused and concerned as she staggered on the exquisitely patterned rug.

"My lord, what is the meaning of this?" he gasped as he closed the door on the crowd. The silence was startling after the noise of the ball.

"You didn't tell her," Kagan accused, turning on Lernen. Marla had never seen her brother cower before, but the sorcerer's tone would have made a whole battalion turn tail and run. "You didn't even warn her!"

"But she knew!" her brother protested. "She said you told her. She told me she was thrilled!"

Kagan turned to look at Marla. He shook his head ruefully. "On the balcony earlier this evening," he concluded after a moment. "You thought I meant you were to marry Nash Hawksword."

Marla nodded dumbly, not trusting herself to speak.

Kagan cursed softly and walked to the table by the window. He picked up the nearest decanter, pulled out the stopper and took a long swig directly from the cut-crystal bottle. Then he walked across to Marla and thrust the decanter at her.

"Here, you look like you could use a drink."

"Kagan, if you would just explain why you bundled Marla out of the hall so abruptly. If we have offended Hablet—"

"Your precious sister was about to offend the King of Fardohnya a damn sight more than our departure," Kagan informed him.

"But she said she was pleased. She said she was—"

"She assumed you had arranged a marriage with Charel Hawksword's son, Lernen. Your little princess here isn't nearly so accommodating when it comes to the Fardohnyan king."

"I want to die," Marla muttered miserably. "I would *rather* die than marry a Fardohnyan."

"Oh, *enough* with that," Kagan snapped. "Get a grip on yourself, girl."

"I won't do this," she wailed, tears welling up in her eyes. "Please Lernen, don't make me do this."

"Marla—"

"Lernen, get out."

"But . . . my lord—"

"Out! Marla and I need to have a little chat, and you don't need to listen in. Go out there and tell Hablet your sister was so overcome by the sight of her handsome future husband she felt the need to recover herself before meeting him. He'll like the sound of that. And tell Wrayan I need him."

Lernen did as the sorcerer commanded without so much as a flicker of protest. Kagan turned his attention to Marla. He glared at her for a moment, then pointed to the small chaise in front of the window.

"Sit."

Marla did as he ordered, still clutching the unstoppered decanter.

"Have a drink."

"Ladies don't drink strong liquor."

"What rubbish! The only person who ever drank me under the table was a lady of the finest breeding. Drink up."

A little reluctantly, Marla lifted the decanter to her lips and took a swig of the dark brown liquor. It burned all the way down and left her spluttering.

"Feel better?"

"No!"

"Good. Then you've learned your first lesson. Drinking doesn't solve anything."

"I never suggested it did," she retorted.

Kagan smiled and took the decanter from her, placing it on the table beside the chaise. He dragged another beautifully carved and polished chair across the rug and placed it in front of her, kicked his robes apart and straddled the seat, folding his arms across the back. The High Arrion studied her for a long moment in silence, but if he was reading her thoughts, Marla couldn't tell.

"You nearly got yourself killed out there tonight."

"I never said a word!"

"No, but that's only because I intervened. And it wasn't any magical mind-trick that tipped me off to your impending gaffe. It was written all over your face."

"I'm not an idiot, Lord Palenovar. I wouldn't have said anything to embarrass my brother."

"I beg to differ, your highness. You looked like somebody had just thrust a week-old dead fish under your nose. And one word, one hint to Hablet that you fancied another man and it's likely he'd want both your heads."

"I don't care! Who does he think he is, anyway? I can't believe some greasy, uncouth foreigner can demand such consideration of my brother. Or the High Arrion."

"That greasy, uncouth foreigner is the most powerful man in Fardohnya, my girl, and the only man with an army sufficient to aid your brother in making the Warlords of Hythria toe the line."

"Then why can't my brother just *buy* his cooperation?"

"Because the only coin Lernen has left to trade is you, Marla," Kagan pointed out gently.

Marla sniffed back the tears that threatened to undo her. "It's not fair."

"No, it's not. Actually, it's barbaric."

"Then why are you helping to arrange for me to marry *him*? Married to Nashan Hawksword, I could—"

"Don't be stupid, girl! You met Nash for less than five minutes and wove an entire fantasy around a misunderstanding. You don't know him; you don't know anything about him. Trust me, Marla, where you're going, a look, even a wistful sigh in the wrong direction and you'll be putting your life in grave danger. Forget about him. He has no more say over who he'll eventually marry than you do, so he's not free to indulge your little romantic whimsy, even if you were."

"Did you *see* him? He's a brute!"

"How can you tell? You saw Hablet for half a heartbeat, and even then you weren't really looking at him. You were too busy swooning over Nash."

"I was not *swooning*. And I happen to be an excellent judge of character."

"Ah, yes. The lady who decided she was in love based on a conversation consisting of two whole sentences."

"You mock me, my lord. You have no concept of my pain." She looked away, refusing to meet his eye. "And I never said anything about being in love."

"You're the one with no concept of pain, Marla. You have been coddled and protected all your life. The fact is you're a spoiled, wilful child who needs to grow up a whole lot more before you step out that door. The deal is almost done and your future is very close to being decided. Whether you suffer it or enjoy it is entirely up to you."

"*Enjoy* it? How can I enjoy it? I'll be living in a harem with a bunch of strange women who don't even speak the same language."

Kagan shook his head at her. "You can't fight this, Marla. Learn to accept it."

"He's really old!"

"He's twenty-six. The same age as Nash Hawksword, actually. I notice Nash's age didn't seem to bother you."

"But he's a barbarian!"

"By whose definition?"

"You're not being fair!"

"I'm being more than fair. I am trying to save your foolish neck. More to the point, I'm trying to save your brother's throne."

"Why do I care about that?"

"Because if the Patriot Faction wins their current push for the throne and your brother is removed, they'll take out anybody else in his line, to prevent any problems in the future."

"Take *out*? You mean they'd kill me? Just because I'm Lernen's sister?"

"In a heartbeat."

"How do you know?"

"Ronan Dell was murdered today, Marla, for the crime of being your brother's friend."

That put rather a different light on things. "Oh."

Kagan smiled sympathetically. "Right now, you have two choices, young lady. You can accept your fate while those of us who *don't* fancy seeing you skewered on a sword try to do something about it. Or you can continue to act like a spoilt child and doom your brother to certain conquest by his enemies."

"Why should it be up to me to save Lernen?"

"Because you had the misfortune to be born the daughter of a prince."

"A *High* Prince," she corrected absently.

Kagan sighed heavily. "Marla, we all have to do things we don't like. I've no more desire to sit here lecturing you about responsibility than you have to listen to me. I know you're disappointed, particularly in light of the rather fanciful plans you had for Nash, but you do me a great disservice by jumping to conclusions. Your life is not going to be the torment you imagine."

"How do you know?"

"Because if I can possibly find a way to prevent it, you *won't* be marrying Hablet of Fardohnya. Right now, that solution is yet to present itself. But we need to buy time. And

Hablet is that time. So until a better option comes along, I don't need you complicating things by acting like a spoilt brat."

She sniffed inelegantly and wiped her eyes. "And Nash? What will become of him?"

Kagan cursed softly and savagely for a moment. "Dammit, girl! Haven't you heard a word I've said?"

"I was just asking," she said defensively.

"Stop asking. Stop even thinking it."

Marla stared at him sceptically. "Are you really going to try and prevent it?"

"Only if I can find a way that doesn't involve a lot of people dying. Including you. And it's not as if you have to marry him right away. You've still a great deal to learn before you're fit to be anyone's wife."

Marla looked down at her hands, and then she took a deep breath and raised her eyes to meet the sorcerer's. Suddenly, she felt very certain of what she must do.

"Could I have a moment alone?"

Kagan studied her suspiciously. "You're not planning to kill yourself, are you? Or do anything else stupid?"

"No," she promised. "I'd just like a few moments to get used to the idea. If I must do this thing for Lernen, I will," she declared selflessly, with a heavy, dramatic sigh. "I will put aside my own feelings. For my brother. And for my family. For Hythria. My sacrifice will be my gift to Hythria's people."

"Oh, *please*," Kagan moaned, rolling his eyes. But he rose to his feet and did as she asked, leaving her alone in the anteroom to contemplate her fate.

And what a fate it was. Lernen had married her off to a Fardohnyan. *What was he thinking? Surely it would have been better to pick a Hythrun consort for his only sister? Were things so bad that he needed Fardohnya's help?*

Before she could come up with a satisfactory answer, the door opened again. Marla sighed, thinking she was never to be left alone. But it wasn't Kagan returning, it was the Lady Tesha Zorell.

"Lord Palenovar asked me to keep you company." She smiled as she closed the door behind her.

"I'd really rather be left alone, Lady Tesha."

"Indeed."

Marla had no intention of being stuck with Tesha Zorell for any length of time so she forced a bright smile and rose to her feet. "On second thought, I'd like to return to the party."

"Are you sure, your highness? Lord Palenovar mentioned you were a little upset over the news of your upcoming betrothal."

"I was," she admitted, with an unconcerned shrug. "But I'm over it now. And the night really is quite young. This may be the only chance I get to enjoy myself before I'm formally betrothed."

The Lower Arrion studied the princess for a moment, clearly suspicious, but in the end she shrugged and allowed Marla to head for the door and back to the party.

ChAPTER 7

Alija Eaglespike halted on the top step of the ballroom and surveyed the hall, her worst fears solidifying into reality as she picked out King Hablet of Fardohnya's pet eunuch, Lecter Turon, in the crowd, accompanied by the High Arrion's apprentice, Wrayan Lightfinger. Nothing could have confirmed the rumours that Kagan Palenovar was brokering a marriage between the Fardohnyan king and Lernen's young sister, Marla, more than seeing those two underlings together.

Kagan is going to hand over Hythria to Fardohnya without a whimper, she thought. *Gift-wrapped.*

And the wrapping will be Marla Wolfblade.

She let her gaze linger on Wrayan Lightfinger for a moment, let the power swirl around her as a silent warning. Kagan's apprentice was, perhaps, the only other living sorcerer who could challenge her magically. Kagan certainly couldn't. The problem was, Alija didn't really know how powerful Wrayan was. He was very good at shielding his ability.

As if he knew she was thinking of him, the young man glanced across the hall and met her eye. His expression didn't change, his gaze didn't waver. His confidence was disturbing.

"Here comes Kagan," Barnardo remarked, breaking her concentration. Alija looked at her husband, fighting back the urge to scratch at her arms where the formal robes of the Collective were making her itch. She rarely wore them. Hardly any of the sorcerers in the Collective did. *You would think with several thousand years of magical experience behind them, someone could come up with a robe that didn't make you itch.*

"Say nothing," she warned. Barnardo could be an idiot at times. On public outings such as this, she was afraid to let him out of her sight.

"If he says anything to me about Ronan Dell's murder—"

"He won't," Alija promised. "He knows better."

"Lady Alija. Lord Eaglespike." Kagan stopped just below the bottom step and bowed, if you could call such a perfunctory nod a bow. "How nice of you to join us."

"Lord Palenovar." Alija responded with a bow just as disrespectful as the one Kagan had treated her to. Kagan had no idea how much Alija would have preferred *not* to be here this evening. Certainly not with her husband. She was desperately trying to convince the Warlords of Hythria who were leaning towards the Patriot Faction that Barnardo was a viable alternative to Lernen as High Prince. A task much more easily accomplished when Barnardo wasn't around. But if they hadn't shown up tonight, people might think they'd had something to do with Ronan Dell's murder. "Surely, you didn't think we'd miss something as important as the Feast of Kaelarn Ball? Whatever would the court gossips have made of our absence?"

"I can't imagine," Kagan replied. "Perhaps you could leave and we would find out?"

"You can't threaten us!" Barnardo snapped, his petulant whine making Alija wince.

This all would have been so much easier if I'd not been so impatient, she realized. The chance to take the throne had seemed so easy once. Back when Lernen had just become High Prince and there wasn't a soul in Hythria who didn't know him for what he was. Nobody had expected him to last the year out. He had no heir and was not likely to get one. All it needed was the right man to step forward and the High Prince's seat was his for the taking.

The right man, Alija had been convinced, was Barnardo Eaglespike. He was Lernen's cousin, so he had a blood claim to the throne. He was a Warlord with the resources and— significantly—the army of a rich province behind him. He had allies. He had everything needed to step into the breach when Lernen failed.

Alija was a Patriot. She cared too much about Hythria to let it rot in the hands of a despot. So she had calculated the odds and gone with the favourite. For the sake of her country, Alija had turned her back on a man who loved her and chosen the route to power instead, privately convinced that only she could steer Hythria through the coming crisis and back to greatness.

And where had it gotten her? *Nowhere.* Somehow, Lernen had clung to his throne. Barnardo Eaglespike had all the necessary qualifications for kingship except one—a brain. Her Innate power frightened her colleagues in the Collective, so instead of winning the post of High Arrion as she should have when Velma retired a few years ago, they had appointed that old fool Kagan Palenovar instead. Not because he was powerful—Alija had more power in her little finger than Kagan would ever command. No, he'd won the post because he was from an old and trusted noble family, his sister had been married to not one, but two Warlords, and he was notoriously uninterested in politics. Those spineless fools in the Collective considered him by far the safer candidate. They had weighed up Alija's ambition against Kagan's total lack of it and she had lost badly in the comparison.

And the irony? Kagan was running the damn country, just as they'd feared Alija might, and nobody seemed to realize it. Had she done nothing; had she simply bided her time, married the man she loved and spent the last few years steeped in happiness instead of intense disappointment, she'd be in exactly the same position. Laran Krakenshield was going to inherit Krakandar Province in the next day or so. He would be Warlord in his own right, richer and probably more powerful than Barnardo, and a far better candidate for High Prince, given he was articulate, well-educated and he commanded enormous respect from the other Warlords, who considered him to have conducted himself with nothing but honour in the manner he had waited for his inheritance.

Still, Alija didn't lose much sleep over the route she had chosen. There wasn't any point. She had played her hand and it hadn't worked out quite the way she'd expected. She consoled herself with the thought that even if she'd married Laran Krakenshield, the chances were he would never have agreed to make a play for the throne. He was too damned honourable for that. This way, she had power, limited though it was. And wealth. And her boys. They were young yet, still babies really, but she was driven by ambition for Cyrus and Serrin as much as herself these days. And all was not lost. Not yet. It wouldn't be lost until the moment Hablet of Fardohnya took Marla Wolfblade as his wife.

And that was something she was willing to go to almost any lengths to prevent.

"I didn't come here to threaten you, my lord," Kagan told Barnardo with a sly smile. "I came merely to suggest you try the oysters. They're fresh from your own province, I believe."

"You think we came all this way to eat our own oysters, Kagan?" Alija asked with a thin smile.

"You'd better not have come for any other reason, Alija," he replied softly.

Alija didn't miss his meaning. Barnardo, however, took umbrage at his tone and puffed his chest out, looking mightily offended. "My Lord High Arrion! If you think you can stand there and tell us what we should or shouldn't be doing—"

"The High Arrion meant no offence, my dear," she cut in soothingly. "I'm sure he merely wanted to point out the success our trading delegations have been having."

"Naturally," Kagan agreed, with that same oily smile. Alija knew what he was thinking. She knew he enjoyed watching Barnardo make a fool of himself. The High Arrion might be a lazy old drunkard, but he wasn't blind to her husband's failings. It was probably why he still supported Lernen. In Kagan's eyes there probably wasn't enough difference between the leadership abilities of Lernen and Barnardo to bother changing the status quo.

"Then we will make a point of trying the oysters as the High Arrion suggests," Alija said with an oily smile of her own. "One can tell a great deal about the surrounding environment from the taste of an oyster, and I believe tonight is as good a night as any for testing the water."

"Then be careful you don't wade in so deep you drown, my lady," Kagan replied. "I might find it a little difficult to throw you a lifeline."

"You're assuming I would accept one from you, Kagan Palenovar."

"When one is drowning, my lady, one rarely has a choice."

"Then it's a good thing I'm not drowning, isn't it?"

"Not yet," Kagan conceded. Then he grinned. "But the night is young."

Alija slipped her arm through Barnardo's. "I believe, my lord, we are keeping you from your social obligations. Come, Barnardo. I think I see Lord Foxtalon over by the orchestra. We must thank him for the present he sent when Serrin was born."

Alija didn't give Kagan a chance to respond. She tugged Barnardo away from the High Arrion. He turned to her as they descended the steps, followed by their entourage, demanding to know what present from Lord Foxtalon had been so impressive it required a personal thank you. Alija wanted to slap her husband for being so dense.

Kagan stepped back to let her pass, his gaze barely wavering. *He thinks he's won,* she realized. *Even with Ronan dead, he thinks that with Marla's marriage, Barnardo has no hope of claiming the crown.*

And he's right. If Marla married Hablet of Fardohnya, all Alija's dreams became just that, nothing more than idle dreams. The fear that Ronan Dell's murder should have sparked in the High Prince was all but wiped out by the false sense of security he would acquire with the King of Fardohnya for his brother-in-law.

But as Kagan had pointed out, the night was young. And until the marriage happened, the greatest asset Alija had was the other Warlords' fear of what an alliance with Fardohnya meant.

The battle was far from over.

CHAPTER 8

"This should be interesting."

Laran Krakenshield glanced over his shoulder at the young man who had spoken, following his gaze to the entrance of the ballroom where Barnardo Eaglespike and his wife Alija had just entered. He also noticed his uncle, the High Arrion, quickly moving to intercept them. Many other eyes turned towards the sorcerer and her Warlord, no doubt wondering the same thing as Laran: what would happen when they confronted the High Prince and his new Fardohnyan ally?

"That's one situation we'd do well to stay clear of," Laran advised.

Nash grinned. "You're not even a tiny bit interested in what your uncle is saying to your former lover?"

"Alija and I were never lovers," Laran corrected, turning to the ice sculpture on the table which he'd suddenly decided required his undivided attention. The frozen water dragon was melting rapidly in the humid closeness of the ballroom.

"You'd have to be the only male past puberty in Hythria she *hasn't* slept with," Nash chuckled.

"Really? And when did you sleep with her?"

"Well, I didn't," Nash conceded. "Not yet, anyway."

"There you go, then," Laran cut in. "Now shut up and mind your own business."

Nash smiled knowingly, still watching the commotion at the entrance, while Laran studiously ignored it. Alija was Barnardo's wife now and there was no point in thinking about her. No point in wondering what might have been. Besides, she had brushed him off like an annoying insect when she realized what Barnardo could offer her. Laran was unproved and unknown, caught in limbo until his thirtieth birthday and the time when he could take charge of his wealth and his province. Barnardo was a much safer bet for an ambitious woman like Alija—a powerful and wealthy Warlord and cousin of a weak and easily manipulated High Prince. Alija was many things, Laran thought. Sentimental definitely wasn't one of them.

"Are you going to speak to her?" Nash asked.

"Who?"

"Alija, of course."

"I've nothing to say to her."

"You'll have to say something eventually," Nash suggested. "I mean, she's bound to want to congratulate you when the Convocation votes you your province in a few days."

"*If* they vote me my province," Laran corrected.

"They will," Nash promised. "They have no choice. You're the only man in Hythria who actually wants to live so far from the capital. I really don't know what you see in Krakandar, myself. Far too close to those vicious sluts running Medalon, if you ask me."

"The Sisters of the Blade don't give us much trouble," he shrugged. "They're too busy trying to rid their own country of pagans to worry about the pagans south of the border."

"Yes, but one day those nasty bitches may actually *succeed* in ridding themselves of their own pagans," Nash said. "And then you know what they'll do, don't you?"

"Invade Karien?" Laran suggested with a faint smile, taking a sip from his glass. The wine was too sweet and he winced at the taste of it, trying very hard to give the impression that he had no interest in what was going on between Alija and Kagan across the hall.

"Now there's a thought!" Nash was saying, oblivious to the direction of Laran's thoughts. "I wonder who'd win that little skirmish? What are there—a few thousand Defenders to take on a few *hundred* thousand Kariens?"

"I'd back the Defenders any day," Laran said, forcing himself to look away. There was nothing between him and Alija any more. And no point wishing there was. He fixed his attention on Nash. "One well-trained Medalonian Defender is worth a hundred reluctant Karien conscripts."

"You sound like you actually admire them!" Nash accused, looking a little alarmed at the thought.

"I do," Laran agreed. "I mean, I've no time for the Sisterhood, but their Defenders are trained better than any other soldiers in the world. Including ours."

"You know, that's bordering on sacrilegious, Laran."

The future Warlord smiled. "Maybe Zegarnald created the Defenders to give us a worthy opponent?"

"What's this about the Defenders?" a voice boomed behind them. "I turn my back on you two for five seconds and now you're planning to declare war on Medalon!"

Laran and Nash turned to find Laran's stepfather, Glenadal Ravenspear, the Warlord of Sunrise Province, standing behind them. He was a big man with a broad grin and a voice that could decalcify a man's spine at fifty paces when the mood took him. Laran liked him a great deal, not because he was a powerful Warlord, or a clever one, but because he had made Laran's mother happy. After a lifetime of misery brought on by a series of unhappy arranged marriages, she deserved some small measure of peace.

"How did you get in here?" Laran asked. "I thought this ball was restricted to civilised people?"

The big Warlord laughed. "They let Hablet of Fardohnya in, didn't they?"

"I heard a rumour he's made an offer for the High Prince's sister," Laran said.

Nash's smile faded. "It's no rumour. And her son will be heir to Hythria, some day."

"Not if Lernen has a son."

Nash shook his head unhappily at the thought. "Since I can't recall the last time a young male slave gave birth, that's not very likely, is it?"

Laran looked at his two companions hopefully. "Look, I know what he fancies—gods, the whole country knows it—and I agree it's not very healthy, but surely he realizes he has a duty? They only have to find him a wife with the right bloodline. After he gets her with child, who cares what he does? Or who he does it with?"

"A sound plan if you could get him to cooperate," Glenadal agreed. He lowered his voice and glanced around before adding, "The problem is—Lernen isn't interested. If what I hear rumoured is true, Hablet is offering him a fortune and the chance to get an heir without having to sully his hands by laying them on a woman. I don't think he cares what happens beyond that."

"It won't happen," Laran said, shaking his head. "The Convocation of Warlords will never countenance a Fardohnyan-born heir to the High Prince of Hythria's throne."

"Hence the Patriots' seemingly acceptable suggestion that we abandon the current bloodline," Glenadal pointed out. "To those who don't want to be ruled some day by Hablet's get, Barnardo Eaglespike is an eminently reasonable alternative."

"He'd strip the country bare in five years," Laran said.

"But he's Hythrun," Glenadal reminded them. "A lot of people would rather be raped by one of their own than a foreigner."

"Raped is still raped, Glenadal."

"Why can't we just marry the High Prince's sister to a Hythrun then?" Nash asked.

"Who?" Laran scoffed. "Any man foolish enough to make an offer for Marla Wolfblade needs an army the size of Medalon's to back him up and more wealth than any one province owns. That's what makes Hablet's offer so attractive to Lernen. The Fardohnyan king is richer than a god and has access to a standing army bigger than the population of Green-harbour."

"Besides, the only unmarried Warlord in Hythria is you, Laran," Glenadal reminded them. "And you're not even sure they're going to let you have Krakandar yet."

"Perhaps *I* should make an offer for her?" Nash laughed. "I'll be a Warlord soon. And she's really quite stunning, you know."

"Don't you think your father might have something to say about that?" Laran suggested. "He was looking pretty hale and hearty earlier this evening. I'm not sure he'd be too pleased to hear you announcing that you're soon to replace him."

"Well, maybe *soon* is a bit of an exaggeration," Nash conceded. "But it's kind of tempting for a patriotic Hythrun, don't you think? The chance to father the next High Prince? Particularly if all it requires is a brave man willing to take a beautiful, well-trained princess to his bed."

"A sacrifice a noble and selfless Royalist such as you would be more than willing to make, I suppose?" Laran asked with a wry smile.

"Of course," Nash agreed. "I'm renowned for my selfless devotion to the cause."

Glenadal smiled. "I'd not joke about it too loudly, if I were you, Nashan Hawksword. Nobody has much of a sense of humour when it comes to the succession."

"It's probably a foolish notion," Nash sighed. "Besides, I'm waiting for Riika to grow up."

"You'll be waiting a long time before I let you near *my* daughter," Glenadal chuckled, slapping the young man on the back. "Anyway, she hates you."

"Did she tell you that?"

"No. I decided it for her."

"Help me, Laran!" Nash begged, turning to his friend for support. "He's not being fair!"

"Help you get your hands on my innocent little sister?" Laran asked with a wink at his stepfather. "Are you forgetting how well I know you, Nash?"

"I would treat her like a queen!" Nash promised.

"Isn't that what you told that *court'esa* last night?"

"*Laran!*"

The Warlord laughed. "Keep trying, Nashan. I like you. One day I may even let you stand in the same room as Riika without an armed escort. But don't hold your breath."

Nash opened his mouth to object but the words never came. Over his shoulder, a door to one of the anterooms opened. The movement caught his eye and they all turned to see what was happening. A young girl dressed in a swirl of lavender silk emerged from the room followed by an elegant, black-robed sorcerer.

"Ye gods," Laran breathed in awe. "Who is *that*?"

"That," Nashan replied, "is Marla Wolfblade."

"You weren't joking when you said she was stunning."

"I know. I think I'm in love," Nash declared, clutching his hand dramatically over his heart.

Laran shook his head and looked at his stepfather, rolling his eyes. "He said *that* to a *court'esa* last night, too."

ChAPTER 9

The first thing Marla saw when she emerged from the anteroom was Nashan Hawksword staring at her with open admiration, his hand on his heart. Behind him were two older men. One she recognised as the Warlord of Sunrise Province. The other man, she didn't know. Nash took his hand from his heart, picked up his wine and raised his glass in her direction.

She thought her heart might shatter into a million fragments at the sight of him.

"That's Nashan Hawksword," Lady Tesha explained. "The son of Lord Hawksword, the Warlord of Elasapine. It would be rude not to acknowledge his greeting."

"It's rude to farm me out like a prize brood mare," Marla retorted petulantly. "That doesn't seem to bother anyone."

Tesha ignored her comment, taking her arm to lead her forward to greet the Warlords.

"Lady Tesha," the Warlord of Sunrise said with a gracious bow as they approached. "How lovely to see you again. And with such a charming companion."

"Allow me to introduce her royal highness, Marla Wolfblade," Tesha said. "Marla, I believe you already know Glenadal Ravenspear. This is Nashan Hawksword, son of the Warlord of Elasapine, and Lord Laran Krakenshield, the Warlord of Krakandar."

"I had the honour of meeting her highness earlier," Nash said, taking her hand. He kissed her palm, sending a shiver down her spine, then handed her over to Laran Krakenshield.

Laran bowed politely, taking Marla's hand, kissing her palm also, although far more properly than Nash had done. He was very tall, with dark hair, blue eyes and features too stern to be called handsome. "Lady Tesha exaggerates, your highness. I'm not actually the Warlord of anything yet."

Marla smiled, trying to give the impression she cared. She had no interest in Laran Krakenshield.

"Surely your appointment as Warlord of Krakandar is a mere formality, my lord?" Tesha asked.

"Nothing in Hythria is a mere formality," Laran replied. "As you should know, my lady."

The comment caught Marla's attention. "What do you mean?"

"Just that nothing is ever certain until it's done, your highness. Not in this country, at any rate."

"But Krakandar is your birthright, is it not? What could go wrong?"

Nash laughed, amused by her innocent question. "Any number of things could go awry, your highness. It's the nature of life to be uncertain. That's what makes it so interesting."

Maybe he was right. Maybe nothing was certain, after all. Maybe there was some hope for a future that didn't involve a loveless, lonely existence in a foreign country, far from everything she knew and loved.

"If uncertainty is your guiding principle, Nash," Lord Ravenspear chuckled, "I wonder how you manage to get anything done."

"Well, mostly it's just luck, I think."

"You're a follower of Jondalup, Lord Hawksword?" Marla asked, hoping she didn't sound like she was simply fishing for any pathetic excuse to stand here and talk to him. "The God of Chance?"

"Actually, I've always fancied myself a follower of Kalianah first, your highness," Nash told her with a mischievous smile. "I tend to pray to the other gods as the need arises."

"Which would account for why they seem to ignore you so regularly," Glenadal remarked. "Pay no attention to him, Marla. Nashan Hawksword is a rogue and I'll not let him or my stepson corrupt you any further. Come!" he ordered, offering her his arm. "Walk with me. My wife is back home in Cabradell so we'll get all the gossips talking about what you're doing hanging off the arm of an old beast like me."

Marla liked Glenadal Ravenspear. He had always been kind to her and was one of the few who ever bothered to visit her at Highcastle. Her cousins' estate was located within the borders of Sunrise; her Aunt Lydia was married to Frederak Branador, one of the vassals of the Ravenspear family. Marla took the Warlord's arm and smiled hopefully at Tesha.

"Is that all right with you, Lady Tesha?"

"I suppose you're as safe with the Warlord of Sunrise as any other man in this hall," the sorcerer remarked. "You will keep her safe, won't you, Glenadal?"

"Like she was my own child," the Warlord promised.

"I notice you didn't actually bring your *own* child to Greenharbour for the Convocation," Tesha pointed out—a little annoyed, Marla thought.

"Riika will make her debut into society when I deem her ready, Lady Tesha. Never fear. In the meantime, I have a princess to escort and a great number of dirty old men to turn green with envy."

Without waiting for Tesha to reply, Glenadal led Marla away, holding her arm. He escorted her from the tables, through the crush, towards the balcony doors at the far end of the hall.

"Thank you."

"For what?"

"Rescuing me from Lady Tesha."

"Did you need rescuing?" the Warlord asked curiously.

Marla sighed heavily. "You have *no* idea."

"Actually, I think I do. You've heard the news about the Fardohnyan offer, I take it?"

She nodded mutely, afraid that if she said anything she might start to cry. Nash had been swallowed by the crowd. She couldn't even see him in the crush.

"It's a tempting offer, lass."

She forced herself to stop searching the sea of faces for another glimpse of Nash and concentrated on what Glenadal was saying. "What? Of course."

"Your brother's going to find it hard to refuse."

"Can't *you* speak to him?"

"And tell him what, child? They're murdering his friends in broad daylight now. Hablet's offer is just what he needs to hold off Barnardo's push for the throne. You don't think he's going to turn his back on an opportunity like that for the sake of his sister's feelings, do you?"

"It's cruel," Marla insisted. "And inhuman."

"It's politics," Glenadal shrugged.

"But . . . what if I love someone else?"

The Warlord laughed. "Love's got nothing to do with it, child. You're a princess of the blood royal. You don't have that luxury. If it's romance you want, buy yourself a handsome young *court'esa* to keep you amused." When he noticed Marla's scowl he smiled. "Come, lass, it's not that bad. By the time you've been married five years, Hablet will have a score of wives, anyway. You probably won't even need to visit his bed once you've given him a son."

"I'm not going to give him a son. I hope he never has a son. I hate him."

The Warlord glanced around nervously. "Be careful what you wish for, Marla. Careless curses can come true."

"Good."

He shook his head sadly. "It's a hard thing, Marla, when you learn who it is that you have to marry. I remember wanting to kill myself when I was presented to my first wife."

"Why?"

Glenadal chuckled. "Because she was so damned self-righteous. And ugly."

"Why didn't you?"

"Kill myself? I had a duty, lass. A duty to my family. To my province. My vassals. To my people."

"I hate duty. I hate being a princess. I wish I was like Lady Jeryma. At least she got a choice."

"You think so? Shows how much you know! When I married Laran's mother, I was forced to keep her away from anything sharp for quite some time after the wedding."

Marla was shocked. "You did not!"

"I swear it on my only daughter's head."

"I always thought you and Lady Jeryma were really happy together."

"We are now," he agreed. "But it took time. And sometimes it never happens at all. I hated my first wife right up until the day she died giving birth to my only legitimate son who lived for about three breaths longer than she did. I hated her for that, too."

Marla smiled thinly. "Are you telling me this to make me feel better, Lord Ravenspear? Or worse?"

"I'm telling you this to remind you how futile it is for you to fight this, lass. Lernen needs you married to someone who can prop up his very shaky position. You might as well accept that and move on. There is no other choice for you."

"Lord Palenovar promised me he'd try to find a way out of it."

The Warlord shook his head. "That was a foolish promise Kagan knows he can't keep."

"But he's the High Arrion."

"Aye. But he's a sorcerer, not a miracle worker. Still, he's a Royalist at heart, and I suppose he doesn't want you married to a Fardohnyan any more than I do. I suspect if there was some other way, Kagan would have found it by now. Don't cling to false hope, Marla. It'll just hurt more in the end."

"Can't the two of you get together and do something? I mean, he's your brother-in-law, isn't he? Surely, with the most important Royalists supporting the High Arrion, if you spoke to Lernen—"

"Marla, there's no point," he said, with a squeeze of her hand, dashing her hopes with his sympathetic smile. "Unless a miracle on the scale of the Harshini suddenly returning from exile after a hundred and fifty years happens in the next week or so, you'll be married to Hablet of Fardohnya by the end of the year, and there's not a damn thing you can do about it."

ChAPTER 10

The ballroom of the High Prince's palace in Greenharbour could comfortably accommodate two or three thousand people. It did not make it a large room. It just meant the inevitable meeting between Alija Eaglespike and Laran Krakenshield took a little longer than either of them expected.

Alija would have preferred to speak to Laran alone, but she couldn't risk letting Barnardo out of her sight. A conversation with Laran was long overdue. She'd not spoken to him alone since the day she'd accepted Barnardo's proposal of marriage. In five years she had never once had an opportunity to explain her actions to him. It was probably too late now. And even if she had the opportunity, would Laran understand? He was a staunch Royalist; one of those people who believed you supported the High Prince, even when it was wrong. If Lernen Wolfblade was the legal successor, then Laran Krakenshield would support him, even if he knew the man was a perverted fool with no interest in ruling his country.

Of course, there were others who supported Lernen Wolfblade because they quite *liked* the idea of a High Prince who was a perverted fool with no interest in ruling his country. Alija despised them for it, although she well understood the reason. The High Prince's inaction left the Warlords with a free hand to do as they pleased.

"Lord Krakenshield!" Barnardo bellowed when he spied Laran, making Alija wince. Barnardo had no inkling about her previous relationship with Laran. He'd been too blinded by the idea that a beautiful young sorcerer was interested in him to enquire too closely about any rivals for her affection.

"Lord Eaglespike. Lady Alija." Laran's tone was polite and neutral.

"All ready to become a Warlord, then?" Barnardo chuckled, slapping the taller man on the back. "I should threaten not to support you at the Convocation and make you offer me a bribe, eh?"

Alija closed her eyes for a moment, wishing the ground would open up and swallow her. Or better yet, swallow Barnardo. She knew he was joking. Laran probably knew it, too. But he was talking loud enough to be heard halfway across the ballroom. Alija had spent months trying to sell Barnardo to the other Warlords as an honest man; a man with a much higher level of personal integrity than the incumbent High Prince. Jokes like that did nothing to aid her cause.

Laran smiled politely. "It's a good thing I know you're only teasing, Lord Eaglespike. I'm not sure what I could offer as a bribe to a man who has everything." He looked at Alija pointedly, daring her to react.

She didn't flinch from his gaze. "I'm sure my husband would be mightily offended by the mere suggestion of a bribe," she replied, also loud enough to be overheard. "He

will support you, Lord Krakenshield, because you are the
legal heir and, more importantly, the best man for the job.
To support you for any other reason would be unconscionable."

Before Laran or Barnardo could reply, they were disturbed by the arrival of Nashan Hawksword, who barrelled
into their midst with no inkling of the discussion he was interrupting. On his arm was a fair-haired girl, no more than
fifteen or sixteen, her face flushed from dancing, her blue
eyes aglow with excitement every time she glanced at her
companion.

"Come on, Laran!" he laughed. "Find a partner! They're
about to start the *Novera*!"

The *Novera* was a peasant dance that had recently become
popular among the young nobility of Greenharbour. It involved a great deal of foot stamping, hand clapping, partner
swapping and laughter. Alija had seen it performed at a number of functions this year and been rather amused by the
scandalised matrons who considered the whole thing raucous
and unseemly.

"Oh! Hello, Alija!" Nash said, suddenly noticing Laran
was not alone. "And Barnardo! This is Marla."

He pulled the young woman forward as he introduced her.
The girl curtsied, a little awkwardly, and giggled. She appeared to have consumed rather a lot of wine. Alija stared at
her in shock. "Marla *Wolfblade*?"

"That's right," Nash declared. "I forgot, she's your cousin,
isn't she, Barnardo? There you go, your highness! You said
you wanted to meet them, and here they are! Lord and Lady
Eaglespike!"

"You're not what I expected, Lady Alija," Marla said with
another giggle, clinging to Nash's arm possessively.

"Neither are you," Alija replied, still shocked to meet Lernen's sister like this. She was a pretty little thing, all doe-
eyed innocence and come-ravish-me charm. Alija guessed
Marla had yet to be trained by a *court'esa*. No young woman

with the benefit of a *court'esa* education would act so foolishly in public. And certainly not with a young man who could be considered a serious contender for her hand when there were negotiations well underway to marry her to a foreign king. Where were her minders? Where were the people who should be watching over her, making sure something like this wouldn't—*couldn't*—happen?

"We shall have to get together soon, Marla," Alija suggested with a friendly smile. "We are cousins, after all, if only by marriage. I suppose you don't have many female friends in Greenharbour."

"Hardly any," Marla admitted. "Well, none . . . actually."

"Then I shall see your brother and arrange for us to go shopping, perhaps? You really shouldn't miss out on all the fun of the city just because you don't know anyone here."

"That would be . . . nice." Marla seemed a little uncertain. Lernen had probably convinced the poor girl that Alija was the demon child, or something equally frightening. It amused Alija to make friends with the princess. And it would irritate the hell out of Lernen and Kagan Palenovar.

"Well, you two can plan shopping trips later," Nash announced. "Right now, you need to find a partner for the *Novera*, Laran. What about you, Alija?"

Nash was smiling at her, fully aware of what he was suggesting. Barnardo might not know of her relationship with Laran, but Nash certainly did and he was enjoying the opportunity to work a bit of mischief.

Alija sighed regretfully. "I couldn't possibly, Nash—"

"Yes, you can, dearest," Barnardo assured her loudly. "It's all the rage, I hear, but far too boisterous for me. Here, Laran, dance with her!"

"I've no wish to force the Lady Alija into anything she doesn't want," Laran said gallantly as Barnardo thrust her into his arms.

"Nonsense!" Barnardo laughed. "She's just saying that so I won't feel bad."

He smiled cheerily at his wife, delighted he was able to arrange this opportunity for her to let her hair down.

Idiot.

"Off you go, my dear. Have a little fun. I'm sure your reputation will be safe with Laran."

In the end, there seemed little point in objecting. With some reluctance, Alija allowed Laran to lead her onto the dance floor in Nash and Marla's wake. As they took their places, the princess was staring up at Nash as if there was no other person in the whole world. *Interesting*.

"I never thought I'd find you in my arms again," Laran remarked as they found room among the lines of dancers.

Alija turned from Marla and Nash and looked up at Laran. He had his arm around her waist and she could feel the lean strength of him through the itchy black robes she wore.

"Don't get too used it, Laran. My husband might object."

Laran smiled briefly, but it never reached his eyes. "Ah, your husband . . . I hear you recently bore him another son."

"Serrin," Alija confirmed, thinking her children a safe topic. "He's nearly six months old."

"You've really outdone yourself, Alija. A respected member of the Sorcerers' Collective. A Warlord's wife. Mother of two healthy boys. Now what? Are you planning to be the next High Arrion? Ah, but that's right! You're planning to be the next High *Princess*, aren't you?"

"At least we'd *have* a High Princess," she retorted, a little hurt but not really surprised by his scathing tone. "That will never happen while Lernen sits on the throne."

"And you think that gives you the right to unseat him?"

"Is that what you think?" she asked curiously. "I'm doing this because I want to be High Princess of Hythria?"

"Is there another reason? It surely can't be because you think Barnardo is a better man than Lernen."

"Your average beggar on the streets is a better man than Lernen Wolfblade, Laran. Don't insult me by pretending you don't know it."

"That doesn't give you the right to replace him, Alija. Lernen Wolfblade is the legally anointed High Prince. To take any action to change that, either by assassinating him or replacing him with his cousin, would be wrong."

"And leaving such a reprobate on the throne is *right*?"

"In the short term, perhaps, it may be difficult," he conceded. "But Hythria's security in the long term is threatened more by what you're trying to do than anything Lernen is up to."

"You think a Hythrun heir spawned by Hablet of Fardohnya isn't a long-term threat to this nation? What world do you inhabit, Laran? It can't be the same one I'm living in. In my world, we're on the fast road to oblivion, either by the hand of the fool who currently claims the title of High Prince, or the deal he's about to do with a man we know we can't trust. Where exactly in all *that* is the long-term security of Hythria you're so determined to protect?"

Before Laran could answer, a loud voice bellowed from the podium where the orchestra was ensconced. "Lords and ladies! Take your places!"

There followed a great deal of good-natured pushing and shoving as the dancers found themselves a place in the lines. Alija and Laran were separated briefly and then pushed together again as the orchestra struck up the lively *Novera,* putting an end to any further meaningful conversation.

Alija joined in the clapping and the stamping, the laughter and the dancing, with one eye on Laran, one eye on Marla and Nash, and a feeling of deep foreboding at the thought Barnardo might be embarrassing himself while she was not there to prevent it.

CHAPTER 11

I t was quite some time before Wrayan was able to escape the Fardohnyan delegation. He didn't like diplomacy; liked his unofficial role as a diplomat even less. The Sorcerers' Collective was supposed to be above partisan politics. They were supposed to treat all people the same, without fear or favour. It wasn't supposed to matter what nationality you were or which faction you belonged to.

The reality, of course, was quite the opposite. Since the disappearance of the Harshini over a hundred and fifty years ago, only the Sorcerers' Collective was left to ensure peace among the nations of the world. And they had failed dismally. Karien in the north eschewed all gods but Xaphista. Medalon had hunted its pagans into extinction. Fardohnya had made it increasingly difficult for any sorcerer to live or work within its borders, the suspicion being that because the Sorcerers' Collective maintained its headquarters in Hythria, it was—by definition—a Hythrun organisation. Hablet's first act as king when he took the throne (after he'd systematically disposed of any rivals, of course) had been to either imprison or banish all members of the Collective from Fardohnya.

As for Hythria, it was—in Wrayan's opinion—on the brink of self-destructing. The only reason Alija Eaglespike and the Patriot Faction were having any success in their campaign to remove the current High Prince and replace him with Alija's husband was the gradual decline of the Wolfblade House. Four generations ago, the Wolfblades were being hailed as the reason for Hythria's prosperity and stability. Now they teetered on the edge of ruin, their scion nothing more than a spoiled, perverted man-child with no thought for the long-term consequences of his actions. All that was left of the Wolfblades, the only hope for their redemption—and with it the redemption of Hythria—lay in the hands of an unsuspecting fifteen-year-old girl with no training in politics, no experience at court and no idea what was about to happen to her.

"We're doomed," Wrayan said aloud to no one in particular. It was very late, the first tentative rays of dawn were just feeling their way over the horizon. His walk had taken him away from the palace and the noise of the party still going on in the ballroom and along the deserted jetty where the High Prince's barge bobbed gently on the turning tide. He smiled in the humid darkness. "I should have stayed home and been a pickpocket like my pa."

"Yes," a voice declared peevishly behind him. "You should have."

Wrayan turned to find a fair-haired boy of about fourteen or fifteen perched precariously atop one of the pylons behind him. He was dressed in a ragtag collection of cast-off clothes. The lad must have been sitting very still when Wrayan walked past him. He hadn't noticed the boy at all.

"I *beg* your pardon?"

"You should have stayed in Krakandar. With your pa."

"How do you know I come from Krakandar?" Wrayan asked. He'd spent a lot of effort trying to lose his northern accent. Apparently, to no avail.

"I just do," the boy shrugged. He untangled his legs and jumped down, making no sound as he landed on the wooden decking of the wharf. "You've got a bit of Harshini in you, too, I reckon."

Wrayan smiled. This was Kagan's work, no doubt. "Do I now? And how do you figure that?"

"Well, you can see *me*."

"That's probably got something to do with the fact I have eyes," Wrayan pointed out, wondering what Kagan was up to. His master had suggested on a number of occasions in the past (usually when he was drunk) that Wrayan's power came, not from any human talent, but from some unknown Harshini ancestor.

Does he think I'll believe his wild theory if someone else says it too?

"Well, it's proof you have *Harshini* eyes," the boy conceded. "You knew I was there as soon as I spoke. For that matter, you heard me, too. That doesn't happen with humans normally. We have to make it happen with them, or they can't see or hear us at all."

"Us?"

"The gods."

Wrayan laughed outright at that. "So you're what? A *god*?"

The boy drew himself up, looking mightily offended. "Well, what did you think I was?"

"A rather poor actor, if the truth be told."

The boy stamped his foot impatiently. "What *is* it with you mixed-bloods? You're all so disrespectful it actually hurts."

"I'm sorry I hurt your feelings, Divine One," Wrayan replied with a grin, quite impressed by the boy's petulant scowl.

"Don't you *Divine One* me," the child pouted. "You're only saying that to appease me. You don't mean it."

"Then prove you're a god," Wrayan said with a shrug.

"You're supposed to have faith. I shouldn't have to."

"Tell you what," he suggested. "Ask one of the other gods to appear, right now, and I'll believe anything you want."

"Why should I? I know I'm a god. I don't need to prove it to anyone."

"Then I really should be getting back to the party."

"Jelanna's in there," the boy told him. "And Kali. Zeggie's floating around somewhere, too. He can smell blood from a year away."

Wrayan stared at the boy. "You want me to believe the Goddesses of Love and Fertility and the God of War are wandering around the High Prince's ballroom, mingling with the guests?"

"Of course not, stupid! Nobody can see them. Well, nobody except you."

"And what are they doing here?"

"Are you serious?"

"*You* seem to be."

The boy sighed heavily, speaking to Wrayan as if he was more than just a little stupid. "Jelanna and Kali are here because any time someone holds a big do like this they can draw power from it."

"How?"

The boy grinned impishly. "Free-flowing alcohol and dancing. The two things guaranteed to lead humans off the path of celibacy and into the arms of the Goddess of Love. Jelanna and Kali hang around together a lot at parties."

"They do, do they?" Wrayan remarked, biting back his smile. "Why?"

"Kali ploughs the field and Jelanna gets to reap the crop, I suppose. She is the Goddess of Fertility, after all."

"And the God of War? Why is he here?"

"Because Hythria is Zegarnald's playground," the boy shrugged. "You lot would rather fight than eat. He likes that in his humans."

"And Kaelarn? The god for whom this extravaganza is being staged? Where is he? Holding court in one of the palace fountains?"

"I dunno," the boy shrugged. "Back in the Dregian Ocean, I suppose, where he usually hides out. He couldn't care less about what humans get up to."

"Then this is all a bit of a waste. Which god are you?"

The boy looked shocked. "You have to *ask*?"

"Well, if you make me guess and I get it wrong, you'll probably turn me into something disgusting. I thought it safer to ask."

"You know, it's really rude to mock a god, Wrayan Lightfinger."

The boy knew his name, confirming Wrayan's suspicion that his master had something to do with this. Kagan had probably worded the lad up before the party, just waiting for the right moment to get his apprentice alone and convince him of his magical origins. Wrayan wondered where Kagan had found the time to organise such a prank.

"Forgive me, Divine One," he begged insincerely.

"Only if you honour me."

"And how would you like me to honour you, Divine One?" he asked, thinking that, with his luck, Kagan had this lad posing as the God of Music. Honouring Gimlorie would probably require Wrayan to walk back into the ballroom to sing some bawdy and entirely inappropriate ditty at the top of his voice in the middle of all those important guests. Kagan did things like that when he'd had a few too many ales.

"Actually, here comes somebody who already has," the boy replied, suddenly and unaccountably amused by something which escaped Wrayan entirely.

"What?"

"I do believe your friend has managed to honour both me and Kali in one go," the boy chuckled. "Not a bad feat for a human."

Footsteps sounded on the wharf behind him. Wrayan glanced over his shoulder to discover Nash Hawksword and Princess Marla hurrying along the jetty, apparently unaware he was there. He turned back to the boy. "What are you babbling about?"

The would-be god laughed delightedly. "Your friend there has stolen a heart."

"This way!" Nash called softly, his voice choked with laughter. "Quickly! Or someone will see us!"

A little panicked at the thought of Nash Hawksword fleeing into the darkness with Marla Wolfblade, Wrayan glanced over his shoulder at them and then turned back to the boy. But the motley-dressed youth was gone. Wrayan turned back just in time to discover a rather inebriated Marla throwing herself into Nash's arms, oblivious to the fact that Wrayan was watching them from the shadows.

"Are you sure we won't get into trouble?" the princess asked. "Coming out here without a chaperone?"

"Not if we don't get caught," Nash assured her. He peeled the young princess's arms from around his neck and held her at arm's length. "Besides, I think you might benefit from the fresh air. You really have had a little too much wine, your highness."

"I don't care! My life is over anyway!"

"That's a bit extreme, don't you think—"

"Don't you understand?" Marla cried, shaking herself free of Nash. "I have to marry that Fardohnyan pig!"

"I know, but—"

"Help me, Nashan, *please,*" Marla begged, throwing her arms around him again. "I'll die if I have to go through with this!"

"Oh, if only I could, your highness," Nash declared, with all the sincerity of a young man concerned only with the girl in his arms and not in the least bit interested in what she had to say. It was at that point that Wrayan decided, for the sake of Hythria, he should probably make his presence known.

He coughed loudly, emerging from the shadows. "I do hope I'm not interrupting anything, my lord."

Marla squealed with fright. Nash pushed her away as if she had suddenly turned white-hot, although his panic receded a little when he realized it was Wrayan.

"Er . . . no . . ." Nash stammered guiltily. "Her highness and I were merely . . . admiring the barges . . ."

"Might I suggest you admire them from the balcony, Lord Hawksword? In the light. Where everyone can see you?"

The young man glanced at Marla and nodded. "That's probably a good idea. I mean, people might get the wrong idea . . ."

"People might," Wrayan agreed.

Marla glared at them for a moment, rather put out, it seemed, by the suggestion that she was involved in anything untoward.

"Why *should* we go back inside?" she demanded. "To save my precious reputation? Well, I don't care about it! I don't care if everyone thinks I'm ruined." Her voice was rising steadily. Wrayan glanced back at the palace nervously. They weren't so far away that she couldn't be overheard. "In fact, I think it's a wonderful idea! Then that Fardohnyan pig won't want me, and I won't have to be sold off like a prize brood mare to—"

Marla never got to finish her complaint. Wrayan froze her mid-sentence with a simple wave of his arm.

For a moment, the silence rang loudly in Wrayan's ears. Then Nash turned to him with a look of alarm.

"What have you *done* to her?" he hissed.

"Saved her neck, probably," Wrayan told him, trying to maintain an air of confidence he didn't really feel. Despite the fact Marla was temporarily silenced, he wasn't sure what he'd done to make it happen and really had no idea how to undo it. He turned on Nash, covering his uncertainty with impatience. "And your neck, too, incidentally. What were you *thinking*, Nash?"

"We were dancing and she said she wanted some air," Nash explained, full of wounded innocence. "How was I supposed to know she wanted to lure me down here and beg me to save her from an unwanted marriage?"

"Oh, like you didn't notice it's the only thing everyone has been talking about in Greenharbour for the past week?"

"Will she be all right?" he asked, peering at Marla's frozen form in the gloom. "She doesn't appear to be breathing."

"She'll be fine. Why don't you go and do something useful like find her nurse. Or help me get her back to her rooms before she can do anything else to harm the negotiations. Or herself."

"Are you sure she'll be all right?"

"Yes! Now go!"

Nash finally did as Wrayan asked and fled the wharf, heading for the palace at a run. Wrayan stared at Marla for a moment, fascinated by her pose, frozen halfway between words, her hands raised, mouth open, eyes blazing with indignation, caught between one moment and the next . . .

Then he let out a remorseful sigh and sent a thin thread of thought towards his master.

Kagan, he thought, with the mental equivalent of a heavy sigh. *I'm afraid we have a problem . . .*

CHAPTER 12

Dear gods, Wrayan! What have you done?"

Kagan straightened up and stared across the bed at his apprentice who was flanked by Nash Hawksword and Marla's nurse, Lirena. They all looked confused, with the exception of Wrayan who managed to add guilt and a touch of remorse into his rather bemused expression.

Marla Wolfblade lay on the bed of her royal apartment, limp and unmoving, bathed in the warm pink light of the coming morning which streamed through the east-facing windows. Were it not for her warm flesh and healthy colour, Kagan might have pronounced her dead.

"I just . . . waved my arm," Wrayan told him hesitantly.

"You just *waved* your arm? Gods, don't even think of jumping up and down!"

"What's wrong with her?" Lirena demanded. "Should I fetch the High Prince?"

"No!" Kagan ordered. "Nobody needs to know about this. Marla will be fine."

"But you don't know what's wrong with her," Lirena accused, hands on her hips. "Do you?"

"She's just caught in a spell, that's all."

"What sort of spell?"

"The sort that does this to you, obviously," Kagan snapped at the old nurse.

"You're a fraud, old man. You have no idea *what* sort of spell she's under," Lirena concluded in disgust. "You're just guessing."

"Perhaps you could go and find some warm compresses, my lady?" Kagan suggested. "It might help revive her."

Lirena looked reluctant to leave her mistress's side, but the chance to be doing something even remotely useful was tempting. She hesitated for a long moment before nodding and stalking off towards the door, muttering about the dangers of playing with magic and interfering in something that should have remained the province of the gods.

"Do you think the compresses will help?" Nash asked anxiously as Lirena slammed the door behind her.

"I have no idea," Kagan shrugged. "But they'll keep Lirena occupied for a time. What are you doing here, anyway?"

"Nash helped me carry Marla up here," Wrayan explained.

"Does anybody in the palace *not* know about this?" He didn't even want to think about the trouble ahead if someone had witnessed Wrayan and Nash carrying the unconscious princess to her room.

"We were careful," Wrayan insisted. "Nobody saw us."

"And you have *no* idea what you did?"

Wrayan shook his head helplessly. "It all happened so quickly. Marla was getting all worked up about ruining her reputation and she was shouting and—"

"Why was she shouting about ruining her reputation?" Kagan cut in anxiously. *Dear gods, could this get any worse?*

"Well, after she asked Nash to save her from Hablet—"

"Why was she asking you to save her from Hablet?" Kagan demanded of the young lord. "More to the point, what were you doing down on the wharf alone with the High Prince's sister in the first place?" He quite liked Nash, but trouble seemed to follow him around like a faithful puppy. Not serious trouble as a rule; more the trouble one usually attributed to youthful high spirits than to deliberate malice, but it was still a matter for concern. Particularly when it left members of the High Prince's family in a catatonic state.

"She wanted some air," Nash told him, wounded by what Kagan was implying. "And we weren't alone. Wrayan was there."

"And what were *you* doing on the wharf?" he demanded of his apprentice. "I left you watching over Lecter Turon."

"He'd retired for the evening. And Hablet had gone to bed, too. Anyway, you must have known I was there. That's where your prankster found me."

"What prankster?"

"That boy you had waiting for me down there claiming he was a god. The one you arranged to convince me I really am descended from the Harshini."

"For pity's sake!" Kagan exploded. "You just waved your arm and look what happened. I don't need to hire pranksters to convince you of what you are! What I should be doing is hiring an assassin to have you taken out, you idiot boy, before you do any more damage!"

"But I didn't mean to hurt her!"

"Is Wrayan a Harshini?" Nash asked, suddenly more interested in that little snippet than the fate of the princess.

"No!" the young sorcerer declared emphatically.

"He's apparently got some Harshini blood in him," Kagan admitted, paying no attention to Wrayan's denial. "Not enough to be called Harshini, but enough to be an issue. Enough to do something like this."

"Who'd have guessed," Nash said, thoughtfully.

"Get that look off your face, young man."

"*What?*"

"Only three people in the world know about my suspicions—you, me and Wrayan. If I hear so much as a *whisper* back from anybody else about it, I'll cast a spell on you, Nashan Hawksword, that makes only women over eighty irresistible to you and you'll spend the rest of your days salivating over sagging breasts that hang somewhere down around the knees."

Despite the fact he had no hope of ever performing such a feat, Kagan delivered the threat with sufficient effect that Nash seemed quite sure he meant it.

"I'll take the secret to my grave," Nashan hurried to assure him. "I promise."

"You'd better," Kagan snarled, then turned his attention back to Wrayan.

"I'm *not* Harshini, Kagan," Wrayan sighed. It was perhaps the ten-thousandth time he'd said that to his master since becoming an apprentice sorcerer. Kagan had been meaning to tell him that repeating a thing didn't make it a fact.

"Of course you are," Kagan said.

"If I was, Kagan," Wrayan pointed out. "I'd be able to do a lot more than I can."

"Do a lot more?" Kagan repeated, with a shake of his head. "You just waved your arm and look what happened to the princess!"

"Um . . . I may not be an expert on anything magical," Nash ventured cautiously. "But . . . I mean . . . how would you know what a Harshini is, Kagan? Unless you count the rumours that keep cropping up about the Halfbreed still being around, there hasn't been a Harshini seen or heard of in a hundred and fifty years or more."

"Exactly!" Wrayan agreed. "When did you ever meet a Harshini to make a comparison?"

Kagan knew it wasn't that Wrayan minded being a sorcerer, even an apprentice one, but he didn't want to be earmarked as Kagan's successor. In this city, where the Assassins' Guild was so powerful it openly conducted business in its own headquarters barely five hundred feet from the entrance to the High Prince's palace, it was never a good idea to be marked for greatness too early in life. Such notoriety inevitably meant one had only a small chance of living long enough to fulfil one's destiny. Still, he had one surprise up his sleeve.

Kagan smiled smugly at the two young men. "I've met Brakandaran."

Wrayan eyed his master sceptically. *"Really?"*

"Truly."

"You never did," Nash scoffed.

"I swear it's true," Kagan insisted. "It was on Marla's seventh birthday."

"How did you meet him, then?"

"Marla's father was tied up with one of his many little wars so he sent me in his place to deliver her birthday present. Brakandaran was visiting Highcastle at the same time."

"Brakandaran the Halfbreed was a guest at Highcastle," Nash repeated, shaking his head. "Just popped in for a visit, did he?"

"He wasn't there openly," Kagan explained, a little exasperated that both Nash and Wrayan refused to believe him. "He was posing as an itinerant farm worker."

"Then how do you know it was Brakandaran?"

"Garel's present to his daughter was a sorcerer-bred stallion," Kagan explained. "A stupid present for a seven-year-old girl, but then the late High Prince was never renowned for his wisdom—"

"Bit like the current one, actually," Nash cut in.

Kagan glared at him before he continued. "It was a devilish beast. Nobody had a chance of controlling it, certainly not a girl who'd just mastered riding her pony. But she insisted on riding him, and of course he bolted. I don't think I've ever felt so helpless. We just stood there and watched as the High Prince's only daughter clung to the saddle, screaming at the top of her lungs, while the horse headed at a dead gallop towards the fence line and the cliff beyond it. Then out of nowhere this farmhand appeared and stepped in the path of the beast. I felt his power, Wrayan, even as far away as I was. I could actually *feel* it. For a man with no real talent of his own, that's saying something, let me tell you. It sent a chill down my spine. The horse suddenly slowed, and then stopped. Then it turned around and followed this stranger back to the stables, meek as a lamb."

"Did he say anything?" Wrayan asked incredulously.

"Not much. He refused all offers to reward him for saving the princess. Just helped her out of the saddle, patted her on the head and told her she was a brave girl, and simply walked away."

"Didn't you go after him?"

"Of course I did."

"And . . . ?"

"I begged him to tell me who he was. Told him I'd felt him drawing Harshini magic. He laughed at me and told me I was imagining things. So I pointed out that I was High Arrion of the Sorcerers' Collective and that I wasn't imagining anything; that I'd been around magic long enough to know it for what it was and that everyone could feel him touching the source from halfway across the paddock, I was simply the only one who knew it for what it was. I was awestruck by the idea, as you can imagine. It was the first time in my life I'd felt true magic at work. I think I was on my knees by then. At that point he just smiled and shrugged, told me to stop grovelling and asked me to keep the news that I'd just met a Harshini to myself."

"Did he say anything else?" Nash asked.

"When I called him 'Divine One' he told me he wasn't and that I should simply call him Brak."

"And you never said anything about meeting him? To anyone?"

"I promised him I wouldn't."

"So why are you telling us?"

"Because I've felt the touch of a true Harshini, Wrayan Lightfinger. Don't ask me how it happened, or how far back in your ancestry it goes, but somehow, a pickpocket's son from the slums of Krakandar has Harshini blood in him. It's more than being an Innate. You can actually touch the source."

Wrayan shook his head. "That's absurd. And even if it was true, how come you've never mentioned meeting Brakandaran before now?"

"Because I don't think it ever really occurred to me what makes you so different. Not until you waved your arm and froze the High Prince's sister."

"It's not possible, Kagan."

"On the contrary, my boy. What was your father? A thief?"

"A pickpocket," Wrayan corrected. "There's quite a difference."

Kagan shrugged. "Well, I don't see the distinction myself. But don't you see? With your rather dubious ancestry, it's more than just possible. Nash can tell you his family history for the past thousand years. How far back can you trace *your* family? One generation? Two at a pinch? You've no idea of the blood running in your veins."

"There was a time when halfbreeds were common enough," Nash reminded Wrayan, obviously warming to the idea of his friend being Harshini. "Until the Sisterhood wiped them out, at any rate."

"Exactly!" Kagan declared. "It's not hard to imagine a halfbreed spending the night with a Krakandar whore who went on to become your great-great-grandmother, or something."

"So now you're calling my grandmother a whore?"

"She was, wasn't she?"

"Well . . . yes . . . but that's not a very nice thing to say, Kagan. And it doesn't actually help us much."

Kagan's shoulders slumped in agreement. The lad was right. Knowing it was probably Harshini magic that had caused Marla's state wasn't a great deal of help in solving their dilemma. "Can you remember *nothing* of what you did?"

"I recall wishing she would stop. I just wanted her to quiet down." Wrayan shrugged. "I just remember thinking *if only she'd stop.* And then she did."

"So why can't you undo it by waving your arm and thinking *if only she'd start up again*?" Nash asked.

Kagan shook his head in despair. "Out!"

"Don't you need my help?"

"Not unless you've become a magician in the last hour. Or can come up with a better suggestion than that."

"Actually, he might be right," Wrayan suggested. "Something like that might just undo the spell."

"It might not, either," Kagan warned. "And I'd rather you didn't experiment with your uncontrollable powers on the High Prince's only sister."

"So what are we going to do?"

"Nothing, for the time being," Kagan announced. "For all

we know, this is simply temporary and it will wear off on its own in a few hours."

"And if it isn't temporary?" Wrayan asked nervously.

"Then we scour the libraries, Wrayan," Kagan told him. "If what you've done is a result of using Harshini power, perhaps there's something, somewhere, that explains how this works."

"I'm truly sorry, Kagan. I never meant any harm."

"I know." The High Arrion sat down wearily on the bed and took Marla's limp hand in his. There was no pulse at her wrist, but the flesh was warm and sprang back readily when pressed. She was definitely alive, but nobody had been confronted with genuine Harshini magic for more than a hundred years. Not unless you counted his own encounter with Brakandaran the Halfbreed. But that was nearly nine years ago and there was little chance of Lord Brakandaran magically appearing to save the day this time.

Kagan was at a loss. Nobody remained alive—certainly nobody Kagan could contact—who could explain what had happened to Marla. He couldn't begin to imagine what it would take to restore her.

"Is there anything I can do?" Wrayan asked.

"You could try praying, Wrayan," Kagan suggested heavily. "You could pray."

ChAPTER 13

One of the advantages of being an Innate sorcerer was the ability to go without sleep for extended periods of time. Alija wasn't sure why this was so. She just knew that simply reaching for the source revitalised her and allowed her to carry on as if she'd had a full night's sleep. It was frustrating, though. There was so much more she should have been able to do, but with the Harshini gone, there was nobody left to teach her.

Innates had always been rare, even when the Harshini were still around. Before Alija, the last recorded Innate discovered by the Collective was over sixty years ago. And now there were two of them, if you believed the rumours about Wrayan Lightfinger. That meant there were at least two people in the Sorcerers' Collective who could actually wield real magic. The rest of them got by working spells (which were unsuccessful, often as not) and dabbling in politics, which was the reason most sorcerers gravitated towards the Collective.

Power was power, whatever the source.

Alija considered them all abominations. They were not what the Harshini wanted, not what the Harshini intended. Not the reason the Collective existed.

Back in the old days, before the Sisters of the Blade in Medalon turned on the Harshini and effectively eradicated them, the Collective had been a centre of learning. Magical learning. The magic wielded by the Sorcerers' Collective had been real magic in those days, not the tricks and illusions they used now. The High Arrion had been chosen for his or her strength, not family connections. Time had robbed Alija of the opportunity to reach her full potential. She was born a couple of hundred years too late.

But that wasn't going to stop her fulfilling what she saw as her mission in life. She would see the Collective restored to its former power. She intended to make certain future generations of sorcerers were chosen because of their ability, not their political ambition. And she was going to ensure Hythria remained a strong and independent nation, a situation unlikely to occur while that idiot Lernen Wolfblade was High Prince. She was a Patriot, after all.

Alija walked to the window and looked down over the bay. The palace was visible across the harbour, the last of the party lights being put out by the slaves as dawn approached. They could have stayed at the palace, but Alija preferred their townhouse. It was more private. She trusted the slaves here.

Dawn's early light had not yet washed the darkness from the sky. From the gauzily curtained bed behind her, the soft rumbling snores of her husband indicated that Barnardo was still sound asleep, and likely to be so for several hours yet. He was always a late sleeper. And a heavy one. Alija, on the other hand, enjoyed the mornings. Perhaps *because* Barnardo was a late sleeper and she knew, for that time, she was guaranteed a few hours' peace each day.

Looking to the east and the softly brightening sky, Alija thought of her boys, back in Dregian Province. She didn't like bringing them to Greenharbour. There was always the risk of assassination. Always the risk of something. Like most noble houses, Alija followed the practice of surrounding her sons with a number of companions of a similar age and appearance, in the belief that should an assassin manage to get close to her children, he could not be certain which was actually the heir and which were the companions, but she didn't put much faith in that solution. Alija had always thought, were she the assassin, the simple solution to such a dilemma was simply to put all the children in the nursery to death, but apparently the Assassins' Guild had some unlikely ethic about killing innocent bystanders. They would take out the contracted target and not a soul besides, erring on the side of caution if there was any doubt.

She smiled grimly. That's what she'd ordered the soldiers who assassinated Ronan Dell to do. There had been no innocent bystanders in *that* household. And it was the reason she had risked using her own troops rather than hiring the Assassins' Guild. Alija wasn't nearly as squeamish as they were. It had all gone just as she planned, too, except the dwarf was missing. She wasn't sure if she should worry about that or not. Ronan's deformed little pet might simply have been out of the house during the attack, in which case, Alija couldn't have cared less about his fate. But if he'd witnessed the attack . . . if he could identify the killers . . .

Alija froze as the faintest prickle of magic washed over her. It sent an unfamiliar chill down her spine. It was too faint to guess the source, or even the direction it came from.

Was it Wrayan Lightfinger? He was the only other person that Alija knew of who should be able to touch the source like that. Or was there another, yet-to-be-discovered Innate out there somewhere on the streets of Greenharbour? It wasn't such an unlikely scenario. Wrayan had been found in the marketplace in Krakandar using his untrained gift for telepathy to extort money out of unsuspecting gamblers.

Alija's own talent had also been discovered by accident when she'd unwittingly informed her mother about her father's new lady friend and the games she'd heard them playing down in the boathouse by the lake. As the lake house belonging to Alija's family was located some fifty miles from the family seat in Izcomdar, her revelation had been disbelieved at first. She was only five years old, after all. Everyone put her stories down to a child's wild imagination. A brief smile flickered over Alija's face as she recalled the moment her mother had finally taken her seriously. They'd been down by the kennels, inspecting a new litter of hounds, when a ruckus distracted them. Everyone had looked up to discover two of the other hounds copulating in the next cage. Fascinated by the odd sight, and paying no attention to the Kennel Master who was explaining the benefits of crossing those two particular bloodlines to her mother, Alija had laughed delightedly and announced, "Look! They're playing the same game as Daddy and his lady friend!"

Although she could see the funny side of it now she was a grown woman, Alija still remembered the horrified silence that had descended on the kennels. And the incessant questions her comment provoked after everyone had gotten over their initial shock. Finally, when she couldn't get a satisfactory answer from her daughter, Alija's mother had made a surprise visit to the lake house, where (Alija learned later) she had discovered her husband in the arms of Lady Lyana, wife of the Baron of Shalendor.

Alija was much too young to understand the scandal at the time. It was considered perfectly all right for a man or a woman to keep any number of *court'esa* for amusement. They were possessions, after all, not real people. One kept them for pleasure, the same way one kept works of art hanging on the walls or bards to perform at dinner parties. But it was totally unacceptable to entertain oneself with another member of one's class, particularly when that person was married to the ruling lord of a neighbouring borough.

Being the wronged party, Alija's mother had been able to demand all sorts of concessions from her husband and his family for the humiliation she suffered, and Alija saw her father only rarely after it happened. Fortunately, she was much older before she made the connection between her visions and the visit to the lake house that had resulted in so much crying and screaming and recrimination.

Once the fuss had died down, however, her mother's attention turned to her daughter and *how* she had seen what was going on in the boathouse, rather than *what* she had seen. There was a trip to Greenharbour and a lot of meetings she didn't understand between her mother and the High Arrion, and then she was informed that she was to be taken into the Sorcerers' Collective and apprenticed to be a sorcerer. She was an Innate, they told her. The first one they'd found in decades. She was special. She was destined for great things. One day, she might even be famous.

As the youngest of five children and the only girl, Alija had always felt rather more put upon than special. She embraced the notion of her destiny with enthusiasm, waved goodbye to her mother and her brothers and turned her back on the outside world, determined to fulfil her unknown destiny in the Sorcerers' Collective the best way she could.

By the time she reached her teens, Alija was certain she had discovered what that destiny was. Hythria was slowly being destroyed by corruption. It had infiltrated the ranks of the

Collective and reached right up to the High Prince's throne. The Sorcerers' Collective was a mockery of what it had once been. Hardly any of the sorcerers had the faintest idea about magic. Most didn't even pretend to learn. They were interested in political power and were simply using the Collective as a way to secure it.

Alija was determined to stop it any way she could and her first step was to rid Hythria of the Wolfblade family, whom she considered the root of the problem. Garel Wolfblade had been a fool and a spendthrift. His son, Lernen, made the former High Prince look like a statesman. They had to go and Alija was resolved to make it happen. Then, when she took her rightful place as High Arrion—there was nobody else who could even come close to her power—she could sort out the Sorcerers' Collective as well.

She had continued to believe it was her destiny until Tesha Zorell marched into the Sorcerers' Collective ten years ago clutching the collar of a ragged, fair-haired boy of about thirteen, claiming he was an Innate, too.

Tesha had found Wrayan Lightfinger in Krakandar, she claimed, while visiting the city to check on the administration of the province for which the Sorcerers' Collective was responsible until its young heir came of age. Alija's first reaction to Wrayan had been unreasonable jealousy. *She* was the special one and it simply wasn't fair that some pickpocket's bastard from the slums of Krakandar could be blessed with the same ability. But over the years, her anger had changed to cautious hope. Wrayan's ability had never been in question, but he was still an apprentice ten years later, indicating that he was having a great deal of difficulty mastering his magical ability. Alija had been studying the texts left behind by the Harshini since she was seven years old. They'd had to teach Wrayan how to read at thirteen before he could even begin to learn anything. He had power to burn and no way of mastering it, which meant perhaps his arrival was part of her destiny, too. She had certainly redoubled her efforts to learn after they brought Wrayan to Greenharbour, so in a way, she had him to thank for her high level of skill.

And she could use his power, Alija had discovered.

There were a number of Harshini techniques for amplifying your power temporarily. Alija had found the text just before she'd left Laran for Barnardo. She hadn't finished working the method out yet, but she would one day, and then she would be able to achieve pretty much anything she wanted just by willing it to happen. The catch—there was *always* a catch—was that even simple mind-reading took intense concentration and only seemed to work if she was in physical contact with her subject. How much easier life would be if she could simply seek out the mind she wanted from across the room and sift through its contents without her victim being any the wiser. Unfortunately, unless Alija could manage to brush against her target, or find some innocent reason to touch them, she had little hope of learning anything useful.

Barnardo mumbled something in his sleep and turned over with a grunt, but he didn't wake. The sky was considerably lighter than before, but there had been no further feeling of magic.

Was it Wrayan? she wondered. *What was he doing?*

And now there was the problem of Marla to add to Alija's woes. Lernen had managed to surprise the Patriot Faction with his sudden move to marry his sister off to the Fardohnyan king. It was unclear who had first suggested the idea, but the notion had caught on quickly and it seemed they were only days away from an agreement.

In some ways, that actually helped their cause. Barnardo had begun to look a lot more attractive to the other Warlords since the alternative might be a Fardohnyan-born High Prince some day. Perhaps they should let this fiasco develop as it would. Kagan might actually be playing right into their hands. Perhaps it had been unnecessary to eliminate Ronan Dell. Maybe Barnardo didn't need to move against Lernen at this Convocation after all. With the threat of a Fardohnyan ruling them in the future, the Warlords might finally be goaded into doing something about Lernen and actually approach Barnardo to take the crown, instead of the other way around.

But without reliable eyes and ears in Lernen's camp, Alija

was only guessing. Reading minds took time and concentration, and she couldn't wander around the palace all day, clutching at people while she sifted through every mind surrounding Lernen, trying to figure out what was going on.

Alija needed something a little more reliable. A little more traditional.

She smiled as the solution came to her. Marla was almost sixteen and about to be married. It was obvious she'd not yet been *court'esa* trained. The young princess would need to purchase her own *court'esa* soon to teach her the arts of love, before heading north to Talabar and her new husband. That Lernen would consider sending his sister to Fardohnya without such training was unthinkable.

If Alija worked things right, she could place her own eyes and ears in Marla's entourage and nobody would ever know. It was perfect.

Barnardo stirred on the bed again. She glanced over at him with a frown. *If only,* she lamented silently, *there was such an easy solution about what to do with you, my dear*.

But Alija could only work magic. Miracles were out of her reach.

CHAPTER 14

By mid-afternoon on the day following the ball, Wrayan was beginning to panic and suspected Kagan was, too.

Marla's condition had not changed. She lay on the bed caught in a frozen moment and showed no inclination to emerge from this state. The compresses had had no effect. The nurse was beside herself. Lirena was demanding the High Prince be told and threatening to do it herself if

Kagan didn't do something to immediately restore her mistress.

In the end, Kagan had sedated Lirena with a powerful soporific, leaving Wrayan to watch over the princess while he settled the old nurse into her bed and a nice long sleep that would hopefully keep her out of the way until Marla recovered.

Wrayan paced the princess's room anxiously, trying to recall what it was that he had said or done to bring about this disastrous turn of events. He could think of nothing but his own approaching doom if the situation couldn't be resolved. His thoughts grew ever more morose until he was beginning to wonder if Lernen would demand his life in retribution for this terrible thing when a noise by the window startled him. Wrayan jumped at the sound of an unexpected voice.

"Boy, you've really gone and done it this time, haven't you?"

He turned to find the motley-dressed boy from the wharf sitting on the windowsill, studying him with a smug, supercilious grin.

"How . . . how did you get in here?"

"I'm a god," the boy reminded him. "I can go anywhere I want."

Wrayan glanced at the closed window, wondering how the lad had managed to climb through. They were on the third floor and the only thing outside the princess's window was sheer drop to the water in the harbour below. "Kagan let you in, didn't he?"

"Kagan? Oh, that fat old fellow with the white hair, the diamond pendant and the really bad poetry?"

"Poetry?" Wrayan asked in confusion.

"What do you call it? Not poetry. Something else . . . something even sillier . . . That's right! Spells!"

"Spells?" Wrayan repeated blankly.

"You *know*. Those awful verses sorcerers use when they want to call on us to help them." The boy climbed down from the windowsill and began to walk around the room, picking up objects as he went, like a thief casing the place for a burglary.

Wrayan watched him carefully, wincing as the boy up-ended a priceless crystal vase to check the maker's mark on the base. "I can't remember whose idea it was that they had to rhyme, though. Zymelka's probably. *Calling on all gods divine, make this grape fall off the vine . . .* or something equally ridiculous. He makes all this noise about being the noble God of Poets and how he's above the petty games of the rest of us, but he's really just an Incidental God when all is said and done, although as cunning as an outhouse rat when you get to the truth of it. Anyway, I mean it's not as if we can't hear humans speaking."

"Who *are* you?"

The boy carried on inspecting the room as if Wrayan hadn't spoken. "Still, I suppose it helps sort out the real requests from the idle musings. And it's not as if Zymelka can get his honouring from many other sources, poor chap. He plays up to Kali when he's really desperate, trying to get her to make people fall in love, 'cause humans are notorious for spouting bad poetry when they're lusting for someone. And I suppose it would get a bit mucky if we thought every rhetorical question uttered by a human was a call for assistance, wouldn't it? You'd have unexplained stuff happening all over the place."

Wrayan, by now, was completely lost. "What *are* you talking about?"

The boy rolled his eyes. His inspection had taken him around the room until he reached the bed. He glanced down at the unconscious princess laid out on the silken coverlet and then looked at Wrayan with a cheerful grin. "Never mind. Did you want some help fixing your little princess?"

"You know what's wrong with her?" he gasped.

"Don't *you*?"

"Well . . . not really . . ."

"You've suspended time around her. Anybody can see that."

"Any*body*?"

"Any god, then," the boy conceded. "Why did you do it, anyway?"

"I didn't. Well, not on purpose."

The boy laughed. "My, my, aren't you going to have some fun now you've stumbled over the source."

"What source?"

"The source of the gods' power," the boy explained. "You don't think you did that just by waving your arm, do you?"

"Actually, that's exactly what I did."

"No, what you did was tap into the source, my friend, the same way the Harshini and the gods do. Not a skill owned by many humans, let me tell you. In fact, can't think of a single human who can do it. You have some Harshini in you."

"That's absurd! At best, I'm an Innate."

"Innates can only skim the surface of the source. You dipped into it."

"I did no such thing!"

"Fine," the boy shrugged. "Bring her back without my help, then."

Wrayan hesitated for a moment and then sighed. "I can't."

The lad smiled. "Then you've got a problem, haven't you?"

Wrayan closed his eyes, beyond confused, almost beyond hope. "Are you really a god?"

"Yes."

"Which one?"

"I am wounded beyond words you have to ask that, Wrayan Lightfinger."

"Dacendaran," Wrayan concluded with a resigned sigh. "The first time we met you said I should go back to Krakandar and be a pickpocket like my pa. Only the God of Thieves would encourage a sorcerer to become a pickpocket."

"Yes, well, I have a problem with this whole 'sorcerers should worship all gods equally' philosophy myself. It's not really fair. Especially when Zymelka manages to make every sorcerer say a poem any time they want to invoke our power. Nobody objects to *that*. If there had to be some great act to differentiate a spell from a prayer, why couldn't they steal something and honour me? Or kiss someone and honour Kali?"

"Why not kill someone and honour Zegarnald?" Wrayan suggested.

Dacendaran sat himself down on the edge of the bed, treating Wrayan's suggestion as if it was serious. "We thought about that once. Forever ago. Zeggie was rather fond of the idea, as you can imagine, but in the end we decided it might get a little messy. And Voden didn't like the idea much, either. Zegarnald bosses the rest of us around, but even he doesn't mess with Voden. The God of Green Life is way too strong and has absolutely no sense of humour when it comes to things like that."

"Can you really bring her back, Divine One?"

"For a price."

Wrayan sighed. "How much?"

"How *much*?" the god repeated, looking hugely offended. "I'm a god, you fool. What do I care about money?"

"Then what must I do?"

"I want to be honoured."

"I will build a whole temple in your name, if you want," Wrayan promised. "Just bring her back."

"What do I want with a temple?"

"What *do* you want, then?"

Dacendaran smiled mischievously. "I want you to steal something."

"Fine. What?" For the son of a pickpocket, the request hardly bothered Wrayan. Before he'd left Krakandar and come to Greenharbour to be an apprentice sorcerer, he had honoured Dacendaran plenty of times—often on a daily basis.

"Nothing big. Just a trinket really."

"Which trinket?"

"*Trinkets,*" Dacendaran corrected, emphasising the plural. "You don't think I'm going to let you get away with just one measly little theft for something as important as restoring the High Prince's sister, do you?"

"What *trinkets,* then?"

"Anything you want, really. I just want seven of them."

"That's all you want me to do? Steal seven trinkets from anybody I like?"

"That's not what I said. I said I want seven trinkets. I didn't say you could choose your own marks."

Gods, Wrayan thought impatiently. *This is worse than haggling in the markets with a fishmonger.*

"I heard that," Dacendaran snapped.

"I'm sorry. Who must I steal these seven trinkets from, Divine One?" Wrayan asked, forcibly containing his impatience.

"The seven Warlords of Hythria."

Wrayan stared at him. "You're out of your mind!"

"*I'm* out of my mind? I don't have a princess caught between one moment and the next lying on the bed awaiting discovery, boyo. Just watch who you're calling insane!"

"But how am I supposed to steal something from each of the Warlords?"

"That's your problem. If I tell you how to do it, you're not honouring me. You'd just be cheating."

"But, even if I could do it . . . it could take months!"

"That's fine by me. I mean, it's not as if she's going anywhere, is she?"

"I need to bring her back now! This minute!"

"Sorry. It doesn't work like that."

Wrayan's mind raced desperately, wondering how he was supposed to bargain with a god. There was nothing he'd ever come across in the vast Harshini library of the Collective that gave any instructions. Were there rules he didn't know of? Things he couldn't ask for? Concessions he'd be a fool not to demand?

Then Wrayan remembered one vital fact that gave his negotiations a rather pressing urgency. "But . . . but if I don't restore her right away, the High Prince will have me put to death and I won't be able to honour you at all, will I?"

That seemed to give the god pause. "Oh."

"Oh, indeed," Wrayan agreed, desperately running with the idea, even though he was making it up as he went. "On the other hand, if you were to restore her right away, then . . .

then . . . I could devote my time exclusively to honouring you, Divine One, without the awkward inconvenience of my execution getting in the way."

Dace glared at him suspiciously. "How do I know you'll keep your promise?"

"Because . . . if I don't . . . you can have . . . um . . . *me!*"

"What do you mean?"

"If I fail to deliver your seven trinkets in a reasonable time, I'll come over to you," Wrayan promised. "I'll leave the Collective and return to Krakandar. I'll follow my father into the family business and become the greatest thief in all of Hythria just to honour your name."

"And what do you call a reasonable time?" the god asked.

"A year," Wrayan said. "Give me a year, and if I haven't stolen your seven trinkets by then, I'm all yours."

Dacendaran thought about it but before he could answer Wrayan, the door opened and Kagan walked in with Alija Eaglespike at his side.

chapter 15

Kagan wasn't sure what he expected to see when he opened the door to Princess Marla's bedroom. At best, he hoped she'd merely appear asleep so he could convince Alija that nothing was amiss. He didn't know how Alija had learned about Marla's condition. Someone might have told her, although Kagan was reasonably sure she'd not heard about it that way. Wrayan hadn't left Marla's side; Nash had been sworn to secrecy. Perhaps Lirena had let something slip while she was fetching the compresses? Slaves gossiped the way other people breathed—unconsciously, regularly and without it, they would probably die. Or it may be that Alija—being an Innate herself—felt the prickle of magic in the early hours of this morning when Wrayan had accidentally worked his will and frozen the princess down on the wharf.

But however she found out, Alija knew something was amiss and was not going to let go of it until she had seen Marla for herself.

The relief Kagan felt to discover Marla coming awake as they entered the room, rubbing her eyes in confusion, was indescribable.

"My lord!" Wrayan declared, looking rather startled.

"Ah!" he said, covering his relief well. "I see her highness is awake."

Kagan was desperate to ask Wrayan how he had managed such a thing, but wouldn't dare such a question with Alija in the room. She was as good as any sorcerer he'd ever met, better than most. Had it not been for the discovery of Wrayan and his almost unheard-of abilities, she might be considered the most powerful sorcerer alive. He'd heard her name bandied about as his successor on a number of occasions. And unless Wrayan started to demonstrate a previously unsuspected talent for politics, she may yet succeed Kagan. But even if Alija didn't have Wrayan's magical potential, she was by far the most astute and certainly the most ambitious politician in the Collective. That she had defied years of tradition by marrying a Warlord was proof enough of that.

"Lady Alija," Wrayan said, smiling at her innocently. "How nice to see you again."

"I'll admit to being a bit surprised to find you here, Wrayan. Are you *still* only an apprentice?"

"I'm afraid so, my lady."

"You're not holding him back, are you, Lord Palenovar?" she asked with a slightly raised brow. "The way they spoke of Wrayan's potential when he first came to us, one could be forgiven for thinking he was our greatest hope for the future. Yet here he is, ten . . . or is it twelve years later? And still only an apprentice?"

"He's a slow learner," Kagan shrugged, having no intention of discussing Wrayan's progress with Alija Eaglespike. Her question was motivated by little more than jealousy, in any case.

"What happened . . . ?" Marla muttered from the bed, her eyes fluttering open.

"The excitement of the party was all a bit much for you, I fear, your highness," Kagan told her. "You fainted. Fortunately, Wrayan and Lord Hawksword were on hand to rescue you. They brought you back to your room and I've had Wrayan keeping watch over you ever since. I just packed your faithful nurse off to bed. She was exhausted, poor thing."

"I don't remember—"

"Well, of course you don't," he cut in, before the princess could go into too much detail. "You've had us all quite worried. See, even Lady Alija felt it necessary to check up on you."

Marla smiled wanly. "I didn't mean to cause so much trouble."

"Think nothing of it, my dear," Alija assured her. "But I think I should stay with you, now you're awake, just to make certain you're fully recovered."

"That really won't be necessary, Lady Alija," Kagan told her in alarm. "Surely, your husband is expecting you to attend him?"

"Barnardo's more than capable of looking after himself for a few hours while I see to the welfare of our cousin." She bustled past Kagan and looked around the room with her hands on her hips. "Good grief, look at this place! Wrayan, open those windows, would you? It's like an oven in here. And you, my lord! What were you thinking? Fetch a slave immediately and have a bath drawn for her highness." Alija smiled at Marla and shrugged helplessly. "Men! Truly, it doesn't matter how much power you give them, they still haven't got a clue when it comes to the little things in life."

Marla smiled, obviously amused and perhaps a little overwhelmed by Alija's commanding presence. Wrayan opened the windows as Alija ordered, but he seemed to be looking for something, or someone, who clearly wasn't there.

"I've no wish to put you out, my lady," Marla said, pushing herself up on the bed. "I feel fine."

"No thanks to these two," Alija snorted. She turned on the men and pointed to the door. "Out! Both of you! Marla needs to change and doesn't need an audience during her ablutions."

Kagan's first reaction to Alija's presumptuous order was to defy her. His second thought was to give in. Marla had no idea what had happened. Kagan's suggestion that she had fainted was probably all the girl needed to hear. She certainly had no reason to suspect anything was amiss. Alija obviously wanted to question the princess, but as Marla knew nothing, there was nothing incriminating she could tell the sorcerer, even if Alija tried to read her mind. And while Alija was trying to pump the princess for information, Kagan could get Wrayan alone and find out what had really happened while he was gone and how his apprentice had so miraculously restored Marla.

"Come then, Wrayan," Kagan ordered. "Let's leave the women to their incomprehensible women's business. It's past breakfast time, in any case. I need some ale."

Wrayan nodded his agreement absently, still looking around the room as if he had misplaced something.

"Come, lad!"

They left Alija fussing over Marla like a broody hen. Kagan grabbed Wrayan's sleeve and dragged him through the sitting room and into the hall.

"Kagan—"

"Not here, boy," the High Arrion ordered.

He headed down the hall towards the stairs and took the flight leading upwards two at a time, not slowing his urgent pace until they were out on the roof garden of the west wing. Kagan quickly looked around the area to ensure they were alone before he turned to Wrayan.

"What did you do?"

"Nothing."

"*Nothing?* The spell just wore off then?"

"Not exactly."

"Don't toy with me, Wrayan. I'm not in the mood."

"Well, I had some help . . . I think."

"Help? What sort of help?"

"I think one of the gods helped me."

Kagan threw his hands up impatiently. "Don't play the fool with me, boy! You've no need to convince me you're a worthy supplicant of the gods! What did you really do?"

"I'm serious, Kagan," the young man declared, looking hurt that his master doubted him. "I swear to you, Dacendaran appeared and offered to restore Marla. He said she was caught in time, or suspended in time, or something like that."

Kagan shook his head in disbelief. "You expect me to believe you spoke to the God of Thieves?"

"Well, I certainly didn't bring Princess Marla back on my own."

"The gods don't just appear to people, Wrayan."

"I know that."

"And yet you expect me to believe—"

"He said you're right," Wrayan cut in.

"About what?"

"About me having some Harshini blood in me. He said that was the only reason I could see him."

Kagan stared at the young man as it began to dawn on him that perhaps Wrayan really *had* spoken to a god. If the young man could inadvertently call on their power, there was no reason to think he couldn't speak directly to the gods themselves. That's what being Harshini was all about, after all. They were the bridge between the gods and ordinary mortals. Although the link would be tentative at best—the Harshini ancestor Wrayan knew so little of must be five or six generations in the past—there was enough there, it seemed, to give him a toehold into that magical realm that no longer existed in the real world.

Kagan sighed, wishing he had some idea how to handle

this unexpected situation. "Well, I'll give your god one thing, Wrayan. His timing is impeccable."

"What am I going to do, Kagan?"

The High Arrion shrugged. "I don't know, lad. I suppose you should start by not waving your arm around again."

CHAPTER 16

Are you sure you're feeling well enough to get up?" Alija asked, hurrying over to the bed as Marla swung her legs around.

"Truly, my lady. I really do feel fine."

"Very well, just don't stand up too quickly."

Marla stood up slowly as the sorcerer suggested, but more to appease Alija than from any real need for caution. She felt just the same as she had at the party: a little bit drunk, and rather bemused by events.

"There! You see! I'm quite steady."

Alija smiled at her. The sorcerer was a very beautiful woman. Marla had heard stories about her from her cousin Ninane, most of which involved dark magicks and even darker secrets, but they seemed rather silly in the cold light of day. In reality, Marla decided, Alija Eaglespike was actually rather nice.

"I'm glad to see it, little cousin," Alija said with a smile. "Now, let's see about a nice long soak in a lovely cool bath. I find that the only civilised way to deal with Greenharbour's humidity."

"I forgot what it's like down here on the coast," Marla said, thinking a cool bath was just the thing. "The weather is quite different at Highcastle."

"Mountain air is thinner," Alija explained. "And you don't

have this damnable humidity to deal with. Still, you'd better get used to it. I hear Talabar is even worse than Greenharbour during the rainy season." '

Marla sank down on the side of the bed at the reminder of her dreadful fate. "I know."

Alija looked at her curiously for a moment then came to sit beside her on the bed. "Is something wrong, my dear?"

"Not really."

"Surely . . . I mean . . . it couldn't be possible that you have no wish to honour the alliance your brother is proposing with Fardohnya, could it?"

"No," Marla told her miserably. "I know my duty, Lady Alija. I will do as Lernen asks."

"But . . . ?" the sorcerer prompted gently.

Marla wiped away a stray tear, suddenly feeling very alone. "It's nothing."

Alija placed a comforting arm around her and drew her close. "There, there, cousin, you mustn't let it get you down. Is something bothering you? Has someone done something to you? Did something happen last night, perhaps?"

Marla shook her head with a sniff. "No. It's nothing like that."

"Then what is it, my dear? Come, you can tell me. I promise it will go no further."

There was a palpable warmth radiating from that contact and Marla began to relax for the first time since she'd learned of her dreadful fate.

"It's just . . ."

"Yes?"

"Well, I think I might be falling in love with someone else."

Alija didn't react immediately.

"I know it's wrong of me, my lady, but . . . I just can't help it!"

Alija hugged her close for a moment and then smiled. "It's not wrong of you, Marla. Whatever gave you that idea? It's perfectly natural for a young woman to fall in love."

"And perfectly awful when she does it the same day her brother sells her off to the Fardohnyan King."

"I can see that it would be," Alija agreed. "Does the object of your affection return your feelings?"

"I don't know . . ." She shrugged helplessly. "I haven't had a chance to find out. I think so. He seemed . . . attentive."

"And does he have a name, this lucky fellow who has inadvertently stolen your heart?"

Marla nodded, not certain if she should name him. Lord Kagan had been angry at her for even thinking about him.

"You won't be mad at me?"

"Of course not!" Alija assured her. "I would never condemn a person, man or woman, for honouring Kalianah."

"Lord Palenovar told me I shouldn't hold out false hope."

"Well, until I hear the name of this paragon of love and devotion, I've no way of knowing if you harbour false hope or not, my dear."

"You won't betray my secret?"

"Of course not."

"It's . . . Nashan Hawksword."

Alija was silent for a moment before she spoke. "Did Lord Hawksword do anything to encourage your affections, Marla?"

"Not really. It was one of those 'eyes across the room' things, I think. You know, like in the stories, when you just see a person and know, right at that moment, they are going to be the love of your life?"

Alija smiled. "Have you spoken to Nashan about it?"

"I was going to . . . but then I fainted."

"I see." Alija stood up and began to pace the room in thoughtful silence.

"Do you think me a bad person, Lady Alija? For being so wanton?"

"Wanton?" Alija asked with a small laugh. "My dear, your behaviour has been nothing but exemplary. If anyone has been wanton, it's your brother for brokering such an untenable arrangement without taking your feelings into consideration."

"I wish the High Arrion felt the same way you do," Marla sighed. "He just told me to put up with the arrangement until he can find a way out of it."

Alija's eyes sparkled at the news. "You mean the High Arrion is brokering a deal with the Fardohnyans he has no intention of honouring?"

"I don't know," Marla shrugged. "Lord Ravenspear said Kagan was just saying that to keep me happy. He told me to grin and bear it, too."

"You poor thing! To be torn this way and that by men who have no care for the feelings of a tender young girl. The way they treat the daughters of our noble houses is disgusting."

"But you weren't made to marry someone you hated," Marla pointed out.

"I was fortunate enough to have some magical talent. As a class, it is the noblewomen of Hythria who have the least freedom. Less than slaves, in many cases."

"Can you help, my lady? Could you speak to my brother?"

"I'm not sure if that would serve or hinder your cause, my dear," Alija told her. "As you may be aware, there are some fallacious rumours doing the rounds claiming my husband has designs on your brother's seat. Even rumours that we were somehow involved in that tragic business with Ronan Dell. It's inevitable, I suppose, for that sort of talk to crop up when there is no clear heir to the throne. I mean, Barnardo is your cousin, after all, so people see him as the natural successor, should Lernen be unfortunate enough not to get an heir. However, it means any words from me championing your cause might be . . . misconstrued."

"But what am I to do?" Marla cried. Every avenue for redemption seemed to collapse as soon as she stepped on that path.

"You could . . . do both."

"What do you mean?"

"I mean, what's wrong with marrying Hablet and taking a lover?"

"In Fardohnya? It would be a death sentence!"

"Yes, they're not as open-minded about those things as we

are, I suppose. They have no problem with Loronged *court'esa*, though. You may have to settle for that."

"What's that? A Loronged *court'esa*?"

"A male *court'esa* guaranteed sterilised," Alija explained. "The drug they use is a poison called loronge. It has a rather high fatality rate, unfortunately, but those men who take it and survive are guaranteed sterile. They are the most expensive of all *court'esa*. There is a huge demand for them."

"Why?"

"Because, despite the herbs *court'esa* use to prevent accidents, most noble houses wouldn't consider allowing their women anything else. In the question of bloodlines, there can be no doubt about who fathered an heir."

"I suppose that will be the next thing," Marla grumbled. "Some pretty boy *court'esa* to teach me how to keep Hablet happy. I used to think I couldn't wait until I got my first *court'esa*. Now I'm dreading it."

"If you use your head, Marla, your *court'esa* will become your greatest asset. Especially if you can find one who is totally loyal to you. I've still got the very first one I was given; he's proved very useful over the years. And they can be rather enjoyable, you know," she added with a faint smile.

"I don't care, Lady Alija. I don't want to marry Hablet. I don't want to know how to make him happy."

Alija came to sit beside her on the bed again. "Would you like my help?"

"Can you stop my marriage to Hablet?"

"I was thinking more along the lines of helping you choose your first *court'esa*. It's a tricky business, you know."

"I suppose," Marla shrugged. "I don't really care any longer."

"Of course you do!" the sorcerer scoffed. She stood up and clapped her hands decisively. At her summons, several barefoot house slaves, who must have been waiting in the other room, hurried in to prepare her bath. "We will attend to this immediately. You shall have your bath, and I shall speak to the High Prince and inform him that I will be escorting you to the slave markets tomorrow to select your first *court'esa*."

chapter 17

The slave markets were busy as the litter carrying Marla and the Lady Alija pushed its way through the crowd towards the exclusive area at the far end of the vast marketplace where the *court'esa* were on display. There were several firms who specialised in *court'esa*, Alija explained, the best of which was undoubtedly Venira's Emporium, which had been in business longer than anyone else and served the most exclusive clientele. For a Hythrun princess, according to Alija, there was simply no other place to shop.

As they dismounted, two well-oiled slaves, wearing little more than welcoming smiles and very short loincloths, hurried out to help them out of the litter. They followed the slaves into the dim coolness of the entrance, where they were immediately served tall glasses of cool mint tea, while other slaves hurried forward with damp towels to wipe their hands and feet.

"My Lady Alija!" a voice declared joyously from the gloom. A few seconds later the owner of the voice appeared. He proved to be a short man with a vast belly that wobbled whenever he spoke, wearing a brocaded gown, a fortune in gold and followed by a fan-wielding slave. "What a delight it is to see you here again!"

"Hello, Venira. You've not gotten any thinner, I see."

"Ah, my lady, you wound me to the quick. I have simply starved without your patronage."

"I'm sure," Alija agreed. "Allow me to introduce my husband's cousin, her royal highness, the Princess Marla."

Venira's dark eyes lit up. "Marla *Wolfblade*? The High

Prince's very own sister?" Venira looked as if he might swoon. "Oh, Lady Alija! You do me too great an honour to allow me to serve a person of such distinguished lineage!"

"I'm sure *you'll* manage to put a price on it," Alija remarked, with a wink at Marla. She smiled back, thinking the slave master the most outrageous character she had ever met.

"My cousin is in search of her first *court'esa*, Master Venira," Alija explained. "I thought we'd glance over your pitiful stock before moving on to somewhere more likely."

"My lady, there is no other slave house in Greenharbour, nay, in all of Hythria, with a better selection of *court'esa* than the House of Venira." Marla noticed with interest that it took a few seconds after he stopped speaking for everything to stop wobbling.

"So you say, Venira. But I think we shall be the judge of that. Lead on."

With a bow that was considerably hampered by his bulk, Venira led them through another set of etched double doors into a courtyard shaded by thin muslin sails. There, a dozen or more young men and women lounged about, all wearing short, almost transparent costumes designed to display their assets to the best effect. Alija cast her eye over the group and shook her head.

"We want only male *court'esa*, Venira. Loronged males."

"Of course, my lady. If you would follow me?"

Venira led the way through the courtyard. The *court'esa* watched as they walked through, their eyes following the two women curiously. Marla felt uncomfortable and rather overdressed compared to the statuesque young men and women who posed for her as she passed.

"Pay no attention to this lot," Alija warned as they walked through. "Damaged goods, every one of them. You really don't know where they've been. We'll find you one that has a proven record of service."

Marla nodded warily and hurried on in Alija's wake.

The next set of doors opened to reveal another courtyard. This one was much more opulently decorated. Amid the sheaths of muslin and the potted palms a number of men and women sat, draped on display over silk-upholstered couches. This lot looked at them with a level of uninterest that bordered on condescending. They moved on to another set of doors and into a room sectioned off into alcoves, each discreetly hidden from the next.

"This is Lorince," Venira announced, approaching the first alcove. "Formerly in the service of Lady Caron of Meortina. He is an accomplished musician and dancer, in addition to his more . . . erotic skills."

"Why did she get rid of him?" Marla asked. He was a handsome boy, no more than twenty, with smooth olive skin and eyes so dark they seemed to devour her soul when he looked at her. He moved on the couch to better display his assets, which, as far as Marla could tell, were quite substantial.

"Alas, Lady Caron recently perished in childbirth, your highness. A sad moment for her husband, but a happy chance for me to acquire a rare piece of merchandise."

"Died in childbirth?" Alija enquired with a raised brow. "Odd. She seemed quite well when I spoke to her at the Feast of Kaelarn Ball two nights ago."

Venira smiled, apparently unconcerned that Alija had caught him out in a lie. "Please forgive my dramatic licence, your highness. I thought it more romantic than the truth."

"And what is the truth, Venira?" Alija asked.

The fat slaver shrugged. "The daughter of the house got married and her *court'esa* will now be provided by her husband's family. It's an everyday occurrence, my lady."

"True. But he's much too young for Marla," Alija declared. "She needs something with a bit more experience."

"Perhaps this will please my ladies?" Venira suggested, moving to the next alcove. "Recently acquired from Lady Rena of Bramster. He belonged to her eldest daughter, who married Lord Aryn of Baronnlae. It was a love match, you know, so the young lady no longer felt the need for . . . *profes-*

sional . . . entertainment." He winked at Marla and chortled.
"One wonders how long it'll be before the shine has worn off
romance and she's back here looking to make another purchase, eh?"

With a disdainful frown, Marla took a step back from the
slaver and turned to look at the *court'esa*. He was long-
limbed and handsome; fairer than his companion, with
smouldering eyes and long brown hair. His muscles had
been oiled to perfection, his body was as perfectly sculpted
as one could hope for. But his expression was vacant and
empty. It was as if there was no soul inside the flesh and
blood exterior.

"What do you think, my dear?" Alija asked, apparently
finding this one satisfactory. "Would you like a closer
look?"

Marla shook her head. She was in no mood to purchase this
slave. Or any *court'esa* for that matter. Since she was old enough
to understand what it meant, Marla had been looking forward to
this day. Now it was here, she discovered she wasn't the least bit
interested. There was a certain finality in the act of purchasing a
court'esa. She suspected it would seal her fate forever. While
she was an untrained virgin, she was worth hardly anything, but
court'esa-trained she became more than the alliances she
brought with her to the marriage. She became a real wife.

And that was an idea she was not prepared to entertain.
Not with Hablet of Fardohnya, at any rate.

"Can we keep looking?"

Venira led them past several other alcoves. Some contained men, but Alija waved them on, declaring them too
young, too old, or simply not handsome enough for her
young cousin. A number of the alcoves were occupied by
women. One held a pair of identical twins; in another, was
the most exquisite young woman Marla had ever seen.
The *court'esa* was slender and statuesque, her thick fair
hair tumbling past her waist in a cascade of carefully
arranged coils that somehow managed to give the impres-

sion she had just climbed out of bed. Her eyes were heavily made up with kohl, giving her a sultry, exotic appearance. Marla stared at her, wondering if she would learn that come-hither look once she had her own *court'esa* to instruct her.

"The princess would prefer a female *court'esa*?" Venira enquired curiously when he saw that Marla had stopped. "If that's the case, then I have—"

"No," Marla said, staring at the *court'esa*. "I was just wondering about her, that's all."

"Her name is Welenara, your highness. She's here among the Loronged *court'esa* because she's just been sold. To your brother, actually."

"The High Prince bought a *female* slave?" Alija asked in surprise.

"As a gift for the Fardohnyan king, I believe, my lady."

Marla frowned. News that Lernen had made a gift of the exquisite *court'esa* to her future husband did nothing but depress her more. What hope would she have of gaining any sort of status in a Fardohnyan harem when Hablet had creatures like Welenara at his beck and call?

"The High Prince's own tastes are rather more . . . exotic," Venira added with a knowing leer.

"What about that one?" she asked, pointing to the next alcove. She wasn't really interested in the next slave, but was desperate to change the subject before Venira decided to start telling her exactly what he meant by Lernen's "exotic" tastes.

"Ah, the young lady has an eye for quality, I see," Venira declared, moving to the next alcove. "And for a lady such as yourself, I have been saving this one. Allow me to present Corin!"

A young man stepped forward from the next alcove and bowed gracefully. He was tall and slender, with thick fair hair that fell to his shoulders. Alija smiled when she saw him. "Ah, now this is more promising. What does he do?"

"He is a poet, my lady," Venira assured her. "He speaks Hythrun, Fardohnyan and even a smattering of Karien, I'm led to believe. His verse is said to be sought after from one end of Hythria to the other."

"Said by you, no doubt," Alija snorted.

"They claim his tongue is coated in silver, my lady, making him useful in more ways than one."

The young man said nothing while Venira sang his praises. He did, however, spare Marla a conspiratorial wink, which made her blush.

"Who was his previous owner?" Marla asked, guessing that was the sort of thing one needed to enquire about if one wished to give the impression she was at least making an effort to select a *court'esa*.

Venira hesitated, glancing at Alija before he answered. "Why, I believe it was one of Lord Eaglespike's vassals, your highness. Lord and Lady Garkin of Kinsae. Lord Garkin's gambling debts left him somewhat ... financially embarrassed, shall we say? I was fortunate enough to be able to assist him by purchasing Corin."

Marla cast her eye over him disinterestedly. He was all right, she supposed, but not really to her taste. She looked around the courtyard and spied something in the far corner. "What's that?"

"That is Elezaar the Fool, your highness."

"The Fool?" Marla asked. "What is it?"

"A rare and expensive creature," Venira told her, although he was looking at Alija whose eyes had narrowed suspiciously. "A Loronged *court'esa* who doubles as a Fool."

"There'd not be many of those around," Alija remarked.

"The only one in existence," Venira confirmed.

Marla stared at the slaver and her cousin curiously. It seemed as if there was another, unspoken conversation going on between them. "Can I see him?"

Alija shook her head, but did not deny the princess. "Some half-witted dwarf is not why we came here, Marla."

"I know. But he sounds interesting."

"Bring him out, then," Alija sighed. "The sooner she sates her curiosity, the sooner we can get back to the business at hand."

"As you wish, my lady." Venira hurried off and returned a few moments later with the ugliest creature Marla had ever laid eyes on. He stood no taller than Venira's waist and his back hunched unevenly, forcing his neck forward which made him appear to be begging simply by looking up. He walked with a rolling gait that seemed quite painful and one eye was clouded white and obviously blind.

"This is Elezaar the Dwarf, your highness," Venira announced.

"How much do you want for Corin?" Alija asked, dismissing the dwarf with a glance.

"Perhaps you would care to join me over some tea, my lady, and we can discuss the price?" He smiled indulgently at Marla. "I am sure her highness will be entertained by the Fool while we're engaged."

"You go on ahead, Lady Alija," Marla said. "I'll just keep looking."

"Very well."

Marla waited until Alija and Venira had disappeared through the double doors before she turned to the dwarf.

"What do you do?"

"Teach the art of pleasure, your highness," the dwarf explained. "Both your own and the pleasure of your future husband."

Marla was shocked that the creature had dared to answer her so bluntly. She glared at him. "For your information, worm, I have no intention of bringing any pleasure at all to a husband. Or letting a creature like you lay a finger on me."

"That is your choice, my lady. I am here to serve you. Or not," he added with a bow. "As my lady wishes."

CHAPTER 18

The sight of Alija Eaglespike stepping into Venira's Emporium almost brought Elezaar undone. Two days without being discovered had begun to foster the false hope in him that he might just survive Ronan Dell's massacre. But as soon as the Lady of Dregian Province caught sight of him he knew he was done for. Nothing could save him now.

Except perhaps, he realized at that moment, the High Prince's unsuspecting little sister . . .

Elezaar bowed as elegantly as he could, his mind racing. There was nothing obvious he could offer this woman-child. She obviously found his physical appearance repulsive. At such a young age, she wasn't at Venira's Slave Emporium looking for something to tempt her jaded palate. Like everyone else in Greenharbour, Elezaar knew the High Prince was trying to broker a deal with the King of Fardohnya. Ronan Dell had been talking of nothing else to his cronies in the days before he was murdered. No, Marla Wolfblade was here because she was after someone like Lorince, or Darnel. Someone to teach her the skills she needed in the bedroom before she married Hablet of Fardohnya. Someone like the newcomer, Corin.

The dwarf glanced over at the handsome young *court'esa* suspiciously. Corin had arrived just this morning. Venira had hurried him through the building and placed him in the showroom without so much as checking him for fleas. That wasn't like the slaver. He was jealous of his good reputation and would do nothing to risk it.

Still, even if Princess Marla wanted Corin for her bed, Elezaar had to find a way to make her want him as well. To be purchased by the High Prince's sister would do more than protect him from Alija. It might well put him right out of her reach.

"How did someone like you get to be a *court'esa* anyway?" the princess asked. Elezaar quickly revised his opinion of the young woman. She wasn't repulsed by him. Merely curious. "Aren't you too ugly? Too short?"

"There are some who find my short ugliness appealing, your highness. Even arousing. Those people who like things that are . . . a little . . . different."

"So what are you trained in? Besides perverted sexual practices?"

The dwarf smiled. "There are no perversions, your highness. Merely different perspectives."

"I'll bet you cling to that philosophy. But you must do something else. Do you tell jokes?" The princess seemed amused by him. It probably wasn't enough, but it was a start.

"I am trained as a historian, your highness," he informed her, wondering what Alija and Venira were talking about. Was Alija arranging to buy him as they spoke? Demanding that he be handed over to her? Was he to be taken from here and delivered straight into the bowels of hell?

"And what else?" the princess asked.

Elezaar treated her to his most charming smile. "I play the lyre, tell jokes, and speak several languages fluently. My real skill lies in a less tangible area, however," he added, desperation making him bold. "And it's that which makes me so valuable to you."

Marla smiled at his nerve. "What special gift? Do you have a cock as long as your forearm, or something?"

"Alas, it is Lorince who has been blessed by the gods in that area. I have a talent for politics, your highness."

Marla was disappointed. "Is that all?"

Elezaar was genuinely horrified. "Is that *all*? Have you no concept of the power I can bring you, your highness?"

"What power?" She laughed sceptically. "You're a *court'esa*. And a short, ugly one, at that. You have no power!"

Elezaar had so little time. His palms were sweating as he struggled to maintain an outward air of calm while Alija was probably arranging his death in the next room while that fat slug, Venira, munched grapes and spilled the juice down his chin.

"I can show you how to manipulate men, your highness," he told her, dropping his voice conspiratorially. "I can show you how to make them do as you desire, not the other way around."

"Any *court'esa* can teach me that," Marla pointed out with a shrug.

"I don't mean just in the bedroom," he told her, almost whispering now. "I mean *anywhere*. Any place. I can show you how to rule even a king or a prince, if only—"

Elezaar cut his words off abruptly as Dherin approached. The older slave coughed politely before bowing low to Marla. "Your highness, the Lady Alija asks if you have decided on the slave Corin yet, or if you wish to see more."

Marla looked across at the *court'esa* in question, eyeing him up and down thoughtfully.

"He's very handsome," the slave added, hoping to push her into a decision.

"But to say 'yes' is tantamount to giving in," Elezaar said quietly behind her.

Marla turned to him in surprise. "What did you say?"

"Selecting a *court'esa* is tantamount to agreeing with the fate the High Prince has in store for you, isn't it?" he suggested. Elezaar was only guessing, but at this point he had nothing to lose. Alija was probably buying him right this minute. He had only one chance to impress the Princess Marla or his life was over anyway.

"How do you know what my brother has arranged for me?" she demanded suspiciously.

"The whole of Hythria knows about the offer for your hand from the Fardohnyan king, your highness. And I'm sure you don't object to the principle of being *court'esa* trained," he said, taking a wild stab in the dark about the reason for her obvious reluctance to pick a *court'esa*. "But it's one thing to be taught the art of love so you can come to the bed of a man you love to give him pleasure all night long. It's quite another to agree to learn the same skills to entertain some foreigner who, in the normal course of events, you wouldn't have spared the time of day."

Marla stared at him in astonishment. She said nothing. Elezaar couldn't tell if he'd impressed her or merely hastened his demise by insulting a member of the royal family.

"Your highness?" Dherin prompted.

"Tell Lady Alija I will take the dwarf."

Elezaar almost fainted with relief at her words.

Dherin was aghast. "Your *highness*?"

"I want the dwarf."

"But your highness," the slave ventured cautiously. "For a young lady such as yourself to be taught by such a . . . creature—"

"Are you questioning me?"

"Of course not, your highness," he hurried to assure her with a grovelling bow.

"Then go and tell the Lady Alija I have made my choice and I want the Fool."

"As you wish, your highness."

The slave backed out of the courtyard, bowing as he went. Marla turned to stare at her newly acquired chattel, shaking her head at the folly of what she had just done.

Elezaar gave her a lopsided smile. "I am yours to command, your highness."

"Then I command you to—"

"Marla! What is this nonsense about buying the dwarf?" Alija demanded before Marla could add anything further. The Lady of Dregian Province strode back into the showroom with Venira on her heels, a look of intense displeasure marring her lovely face.

"I want him," Marla shrugged, as if that was all the explanation she needed.

Alija stared at the young woman for a moment, as if debating something, and then, inexplicably, she smiled.

"Then we'll take them both."

"*Both,* my lady?" Venira gasped.

"The High Prince can pay for the Fool. You may send the account for Corin to me. Barnardo and I will make a gift of him to our cousin. As a birthday present."

"There's really no need," the princess assured her, as the sorcerer deftly sidestepped Marla's plans to prevent being *court'esa* trained. "Besides, I couldn't possibly accept such an expensive gift."

"Nonsense, child!" Alija scoffed. "You're a princess and soon to be a queen. Nothing is too good for you."

"But, my lady—"

Corin is Alija's spy, Elezaar realized, as she insisted that Marla accept her offering. *I'm not out of the woods yet . . .*

"See to it, Venira," Alija commanded. "Have them sent to the palace. Today."

Without waiting for the slaver to reply, she took Marla's arm and linked it through her own. "And now that's taken care of, my dear, I think we should visit my dressmaker. We really should take this opportunity to see about buying you some more fashionable clothes."

Elezaar watched them leave then looked over at Corin. Venira had claimed he was a poet. Was he an assassin, too? He didn't wear the raven ring of the Assassins' Guild but that didn't mean he wouldn't kill if Alija ordered him to.

"So it seems we're to be housemates," the young man said with a knowing smile.

"So it seems," Elezaar agreed cautiously, wondering if Corin's apparently harmless statement was actually a threat.

I may have just stepped out of the pot and into the kiln, he realized with despair.

But he had confronted Alija Eaglespike and was still alive and that, in itself, was nothing short of a miracle.

PART TWO

BROKEN PROMISES, SHATTERED DREAMS

CHAPTER 19

Despite the Convocation of Warlords approving his inheritance, Laran Krakenshield's thirtieth birthday was an occasion for celebration for very few people. His mother, Jeryma, was pleased, no doubt, and probably his youngest half-sister, Riika. His other half-sister, Darilyn, hadn't stopped lamenting her own woes for long enough to notice her brother was having a birthday. His half-brother Mahkas was, more than likely, already making a list of the titles he thought he deserved as the only brother of Krakandar's Warlord.

The vassals and the people of Krakandar province, however, probably weren't rejoicing at the prospect of Daelon Krakenshield's son stepping up to take his place.

Krakandar had been under the protection of the Sorcerers' Collective for almost twenty-eight years. Those who remembered the last Warlord recalled a savage, brutal, hot-headed young man whose folly cost him his life. Nobody was particularly anxious to have history repeat itself when his son inherited the throne.

The Collective's governance of Krakandar had been both benign and astute during the years they had held it in trust for its heir. Consequently, Laran had inherited a province that was in a much healthier state than the one left to him when his father was killed in a drunken duel. He was now one of the richest Warlords in Hythria.

But his good fortune had a downside and Laran knew he would need every skill he owned to secure his newly acquired lands and position. Every move he made would be watched by the other Warlords. The nature of Hythrun politics was such that instability tended to prevent any one Warlord from rising to dominance. But nearly three decades of stable rule by the Sorcerers' Collective meant Krakandar was enjoying an unprecedented level of prosperity. Rarely had a Warlord commanded so flourishing an empire. Laran privately wondered if he would live to enjoy his birthright for long. Ronan Dell had been murdered for the crime of simply being close to the High Prince. Some nervous Warlord would probably have him assassinated long before he could wield any sort of real power.

It was a sobering thought.

But constantly looking over your shoulder for an assassin can be a tiring thing. Laran tried to forget about it and immersed himself in the day to day running of his vast province. Like the other Warlords, Laran commanded the loyalty of seven vassals who in turn administered their own smaller estates, made up of seven boroughs each. Laran was so busy dealing with *them,* that thoughts of assassins, factions and the distant politics of Greenharbour were pushed far back in his mind.

But midwinter, two months after his arrival back in Krakandar following the Convocation in Greenharbour and the formal assumption of his inheritance, brought news which both shocked and saddened the young Warlord.

Glenadal Ravenspear, the Warlord of Sunrise Province, his mother's fourth husband, was mortally injured in a riding accident. His uncle, Kagan Palenovar, the High Arrion of the Sorcerers' Collective, brought him the news himself, arriving unexpectedly on his golden sorcerer-bred mount with his apprentice, Wrayan Lightfinger.

Laran quickly ordered the palace into action, and then set out with just a handful of guards on the hard ride to the city of Cabradell in the southern province of Sunrise, some eight hundred miles from Krakandar, where his mother lived with Glenadal.

* * *

"Laran! Thank the gods you came so quickly."

It had taken just under eleven days and several changes of horses to get to Cabradell. Exhausted from the forced ride, Laran took a moment to collect himself before he embraced his mother. Always a small woman, Jeryma had gained weight since he saw her last, no doubt the result of middle-aged contentment as Glenadal Ravenspear's wife. There was a smattering of silver among the gold of her hair, too, these days. She was dressed in red, not mourning white, which Laran took as a good sign, although her expression was grim.

"I came as soon as I heard," he told her, taking in her weary face with concern. "He still lives?"

"Barely," she agreed. "He's been asking for you."

"I'll go to him. You should get some rest."

Jeryma smiled. "There will be time for rest soon enough, Laran. Go see your stepfather. Kagan can look after me."

The High Arrion nodded his agreement, offering his arm to his sister. Laran spared his mother a concerned glance then strode down the walkway to Glenadal's chamber.

The Cabradell palace was more a villa than a fortress, nestled at the foot of the majestic Sunrise Mountains, for which the province was named. Built of white stucco with a red tiled roof, the palace sprawled over the peak of a small rise which gave it a commanding view of the city below. The air was cooler here, closer to the mountains, and the breeze that snatched at Laran's cloak as he traversed the walkways connecting the various wings of the palace had the taste of distant snow upon it.

When he reached Glenadal's suite, the guards on duty opened the carved doors without question, recognising Laran on sight. He stepped into the gloom and the heavy scent of lavender, which was smouldering in oil burners placed around the room. The Warlord lay on a low, exquisitely carved pallet in the centre of the dimly lit room. On her knees beside him was a girl with long fair hair and a tear-stained face. She sobbed silently as she applied a cool compress to Glenadal's forehead, her tears staining the silk sheet covering the Warlord.

The girl looked up at the sound of the door closing. When she saw who it was she scrambled to her feet, ran to Laran and threw herself into his arms.

"I'm so glad you're here!" she sobbed, clinging to him.

Laran held his sister close for a few moments and let her cry, not saying anything. In truth, he wasn't sure what to say to her, anyway. It was hard to imagine what she was going through, sitting here watching her father die. Riika was just fifteen and beginning to fulfil the promise of her mother's beauty.

"Why don't you go and get some rest?" he suggested gently, when her tears abated a little. "I'll sit with him for a while."

"No. I can't leave him, Laran. If something happens . . ."

"Then it won't be your fault," he assured her. "Now go! Get some rest! You're not going to be able to help anyone if you collapse, are you?"

She hesitated, glancing back at her father. "I really shouldn't . . ."

"Consider it a big-brother order then."

Riika sighed in defeat. "Promise you'll call me if anything changes."

"I promise."

Riika glanced back at her father with a frown. "Maybe I should go to the temple first. I could ask Cheltaran to aid him."

"The God of Healing will hear your prayers wherever you are, Riika," Laran promised. "Rest is what *you* need."

She smiled hopefully. "Maybe . . . now that you're here . . . he might perk up a little. He's been hanging on for so long, Laran. I can't believe the gods could be so cruel as to take him from me now. Not after all this time."

"Go, Riika," Laran urged, walking her to the door, certain that was the only way she was going to leave. There were dark circles under her eyes and her face was haggard. There was no telling when she'd last slept. Kissing the top of her head, he held her close for a moment then opened the door. "I'll stay with him until you get back."

She nodded, squinting a little as she stepped out into the light. Laran pulled the door shut before she could change her mind and walked back to the bed where his stepfather lay. Glenadal's breathing was laboured and a drop of blood-flecked spittle rested on the corner of his mouth. As if sensing the change in the person watching over him, the old man's eyes fluttered open. It took them a moment to focus on Laran and then he smiled.

"You'd think," he rasped painfully, "that at my age . . . I'd have more sense than to try breaking a horse by just climbing on its back."

"Is that what happened?" Laran asked, taking a seat on the floor beside the pallet. "Kagan said it was a riding accident."

"He's just being kind. Probably trying to . . . protect my reputation as a wise . . . old statesman."

"Does it hurt?"

"Damn it, boy!" Glenadal gasped, "I've got a couple of infected ribs poking through my lungs! What do *you* think?"

Laran smiled. "Is there anything I can do?"

Glenadal took a couple of painful breaths before he answered. "Promise me you'll take care of Riika."

"You know I will."

"And your mother. Take care of her, too."

"Of course."

The old Warlord closed his eyes for a moment, breathing shallowly, while he gathered his strength. Even from where Laran sat, he could smell the sickness on Glenadal's breath. The infection that had turned a simple punctured lung into a life-threatening injury had a firm grip on the old Warlord now. When he opened his eyes again, he reached for Laran's arm. The grip was frail, but determined.

"This . . . accident is a great opportunity for you, Laran."

"You're going to die on me, old man, and leave me a sister and a mother to take care of," Laran said with a smile. "I've seen the way you spoil them. I'll be bankrupt in a month."

Glenadal smiled wanly. "It's good you're here, Laran.

Everyone else has been tiptoeing around me . . . like I'm too stupid to know I'm dying."

"Have you considered the possibility that you may actually survive this, you old fool?"

"I thought about it," he said, shaking his head painfully. "But I know my time is up. I can feel it. I can feel Death sitting at the foot of my bed, waiting for me to falter."

"And this great opportunity you speak of?"

"My death will save Hythria."

Laran smiled at the old man fondly. "You just can't help yourself, can you? Just have to think you're the most important person in the world."

"I mean it, Laran. I have no legitimate son."

"Then whoever Riika marries—"

"No!" Glenadal gasped, gripping his arm with desperate strength. "I promised her mother . . . *your* mother, I'd never force our daughter into a marriage she didn't want. You must swear to me you will honour that promise."

"I swear, Glenadal," Laran agreed doubtfully. "And it's a noble sentiment, but realistically—"

"I have drawn up my will, Laran. I have named you as my heir."

Laran stared at him, shocked beyond words. "But . . . but you can't! I already hold Krakandar. The Convocation will never grant me lordship over Sunrise as well. Gods, Glenadal, that would give me control of a third of the whole damn country."

"I know."

"This is insane!" Laran said, shaking his head. "Who else knows about this idiotic idea?"

"Only your mother."

"And she agreed to it?"

"As you will. When you've had time to think about it."

"When did you get time to cook up this ridiculous scheme between you?"

"We didn't *cook it up*. At least not the way you're thinking." He had to stop to catch his breath before continuing. "We just discussed how you were the only unmarried Warlord . . . and how, up until now, no Warlord was in a strong enough position to make an offer that could counter the Fardohnyan offer for Marla Wolfblade's hand." Glenadal smiled wanly. "And don't look at me like that. I didn't seek my deathbed deliberately. Circumstances have . . . conspired to aid us, lad. Don't be a fool. Take the opportunity and run with it."

"You're denying Riika her birthright."

"She won't *have* a birthright if Fardohnya overruns us, Laran. Take the chance. For me. For Hythria."

"What about Chaine?" he asked cautiously.

The Warlord shook his head. "It's just a rumour, Laran."

"One that's never let up in all the time I've known you."

"Still nothing more than a rumour, though. And even if I was willing to admit to such a thing, it would cause too much pain to those I love . . . to acknowledge a bastard on my deathbed. It would embarrass your mother. It would kill Riika."

"That's not a reason not to do the right thing by your son, Glenadal."

"I have no legitimate son, Laran. If it will make you feel better then I give you leave to do the right thing after I'm gone. Right now, I am only concerned about Hythria." Glenadal closed his eyes, exhausted by their discussion. He said nothing more for a time, simply lying there, his breathing laboured, clinging to life.

Laran watched him draw each painful breath, wishing his stepfather wasn't dying, because he would dearly like to throttle the old fool.

"Glenadal," he sighed, trying to word this as carefully as he could. The man was on his deathbed, after all; he really didn't want to upset him. "You're the closest thing I've ever had to a father, and I hold your opinion above all others. You know that. But in this, you're being completely irrational. You can't expect me to agree to it. You can't ask it of me."

Glenadal smiled and turned to look at him.

"And that, Laran Krakenshield," the old Warlord mumbled through his pain, "is why it *must* be you."

CHAPTER 20

Jeryma led Kagan inside to a low couch in the main reception hall and signalled a slave for refreshment. It was a long room with an intricately patterned black-and-white tiled floor. The palace at Cabradell had changed a great deal since Jeryma first came here nearly two decades ago. Room by room she had stamped her personality on the place until it felt as if this was the way it had always been. As they sat down on the beautifully embroidered, brightly coloured silk cushions, his sister glanced at Kagan's companion, waiting for an introduction.

"This is Wrayan Lightfinger."

"Your apprentice?" Jeryma asked with a slightly raised brow before turning to Wrayan and offering him her hand. "I've heard of you, young man."

"Nothing too sinister, I hope, my lady," Wrayan replied. He raised Jeryma's palm to his lips and bowed elegantly. Wrayan's skill at court etiquette always surprised Kagan. The boy had grown up in the slums of Krakandar, but he seemed to have an instinctive ability to turn on the charm whenever it would do the most good.

Jeryma smiled. "He certainly didn't learn those manners from you, Kagan."

"Well, you know how it is with the young," Kagan shrugged. "They just seem to pick these things up on their own." He turned to Wrayan then, and for the benefit of his sister, added, "Why don't you see to the horses? Glenadal's people probably don't know the first thing about sorcerer-bred mounts."

"And do a sweep of the surrounding countryside," Jeryma added.

"My lady?"

She smiled. "I've heard of your special talents, Wrayan," she explained. "And I'm glad you're here. With Glenadal at death's door, the vultures will be circling soon."

"I take it you don't mean the feathered kind, my lady?"

"I most certainly do not."

"Then it will be my pleasure to aid you in any way I can, Lady Jeryma," Wrayan informed her as he took his leave of them with a small bow.

"He's very polite," Jeryma remarked as they watched him leave.

"Irritating, isn't it?"

Jeryma took his hand and squeezed it fondly. "It will be all right, Kagan. I've already buried three husbands. I'm getting quite good at this."

"I doubt that," Kagan replied, studying his sister closely. "You buried three husbands you barely knew. You and Glenadal have been together a long time."

"I suppose," she sighed. She straightened an imaginary crease from her skirt. Jeryma had a distant expression on her drawn, pale face. "Have you arranged many marriages as High Arrion?"

"A few. I get a lot of requests, but I don't allow many of them."

Kagan thought of one marriage he would never have allowed had anybody bothered to consult him—Alija's to Barnardo Eaglespike. But he hadn't been High Arrion then. It wasn't his decision.

Jeryma nodded approvingly. "Things are different now. I remember hating Glenadal when we first married."

"Never," Kagan scoffed.

"I did," Jeryma assured him. "I thought him the rudest, most uncouth creature I'd ever met. Velma was still High Arrion, then. She ordered my marriage to him only a month af-

ter Darilyn's father was killed. I was ready to kill myself
when I heard. Glenadal brought me here to Cabradell after
the wedding, took away all the sharp instruments in my room
and left me there for a week before he came back."

"Why?"

"He knew I was frightened. He knew what Jacel had been
like. He knew I needed time to heal. Remember, I was still
only in my mid-twenties. My entire experience of men had
been Daelon Krakenshield, who was a hot-headed fool, Phylrin Damaran, who was more a father than a husband, and Jacel, who was more animal than man."

"But you love him now?"

"I suppose," she said with a shrug. "I don't really know.
I've never felt a rush of longing for any man I've been mar-
ried to. I've never met one I couldn't live without, at any rate.
I hope my daughters do better in marriage than I."

Kagan smiled. "So do they, I imagine."

"I shouldn't be burdening you with my woes," Jeryma said
with a sigh. "You have enough to concern you. Are Darilyn
and Mahkas coming, too?"

"I spoke to Darilyn before I left Greenharbour. She had
some affairs to wrap up in the city before she could leave.
She should be here within a day or so."

"Her social calendar, more likely," Jeryma suggested with
a frown. "And Mahkas?"

"He'll follow in a week or so. He was on a border patrol
when I arrived in Krakandar. Laran had to send somebody to
find him."

Jeryma smiled thinly. "Knowing Mahkas, he's probably
managed to 'patrol' all the way into Medalon. I suspect
they'll find him in a Bordertown tavern, having most of his
adventures over a barrel of ale."

"He's a good lad, Jeryma," Kagan said. "At heart."

"I know. Perhaps marriage to Bylinda will settle him down
a bit."

"Perhaps. But what of Riika?" Kagan asked, suddenly realising that he had not yet seen his youngest niece. "How is she bearing up?"

"Not very well," Jeryma admitted. "I'm hoping you and Laran can console her somewhat."

"I'll do what I can. Is she with him now?" Kagan rose to follow Laran into Glenadal's chamber, but his sister caught his sleeve.

"Before you see him, there's something else I must tell you."

Kagan sat beside her, patting her hand comfortingly. Jeryma looked very worried. "I have seen men on their deathbed before, you know."

"I'm not concerned for your tender sensibilities, brother. We have another situation to deal with."

"Exactly what do you mean by a *situation*?"

"Glenadal intends to name Laran as his heir, since he has no son of his own."

Kagan's eyes widened. "The other Warlords will not allow it. You must convince Laran to refuse! It will mean his death if he accepts. Especially now, when he's only just taken possession of Krakandar. No one has ever held two provinces."

"I tried to convince Glenadal he was being foolish when he first suggested the idea to me," Jeryma admitted. "But after a time, I came to see that the idea has merit."

"I'll *make* Laran refuse, Jeryma! I have no wish to bury my nephew alongside your four husbands." Kagan was too shocked to be tactful. If he accepted this bequest, with the death of his stepfather Laran Krakenshield would control almost a third of the Hythrun landmass.

"Think of the possibilities, Kagan."

"I am thinking of them!"

"And you think it's a bad thing?"

"I think it's a *dangerous* thing, Jeryma. Even if Laran agrees to this—and I suspect he'll not have a bar of it—he still wouldn't be strong enough to do what you want of him."

"Not without help," his sister agreed cryptically.

"What's *that* supposed to mean?"

Jeryma refused to answer. She simply smiled and patted his arm as if he were a small child being distracted from a toy his big sister didn't want him to play with.

"Go," she said. "Say your farewells to Glenadal, brother. There'll be plenty of time to speak of politics later."

chapter 21

He says you know about this insane idea!"

Jeryma glanced up with an innocent smile as Laran stalked into the main reception room where she was enjoying a rare moment of solitude. With a silent wave she dismissed the barefoot slave who was pouring her tea, waiting until he had left the room before answering her son. "He told you then?"

"Yes, he told me. I won't accept."

"Don't be foolish, Laran. You have to accept it."

"Actually, mother, I don't have to do anything of the kind. I will simply ask the Collective to assume responsibility for Sunrise Province, the way it did with Krakandar when I was too young to rule. The Sorcerers' Collective can manage the province until Riika marries someone suitable."

"Which would be a wonderful plan, my dear," Jeryma replied calmly. "Except for one small detail. The Collective will not support you. The High Arrion agrees with us."

"Kagan would never agree to this!"

"Kagan has just spent several months very reluctantly hammering out an arrangement that will deliver us into the hands of Fardohnya within a generation, Laran. He is far more sympathetic to the Royalist cause than you give him credit for."

"And you know I'd support the throne with my life," he reminded her. "But we'd be mad to buy into a faction fight,
Mother. Let Riika marry someone capable of ruling Sunrise
and leave it at that. Nash Hawksword would marry her tomorrow if he could. I know Riika is fond of him. Please, for
all our sakes, forget any foolish notions you and Glenadal
have about manipulating the succession."

"Nashan Hawksword is the heir to Elasapine. If you don't
think yourself fit to rule two provinces, Laran, where, in the
name of all the Primal Gods, do you get the idea that Nashan
Hawksword is?"

That was something Laran hadn't given much thought to.
But there had to be a way out of this. He didn't want the responsibility. He didn't need the problems this bizarre idea
would inflict not just on him but on all of Hythria. "Perhaps
someone else then . . . Have you thought that Chaine might
make some claim?"

"Chaine Tollin has no claim on the Ravenspear House,"
Jeryma said coldly. "And I'll thank you not to encourage him
by letting him believe that he does."

Laran eyed his mother quizzically, wondering at her tone.
"Do *you* think he's Glenadal's bastard?"

"Even if I was certain of it, Laran, it makes no difference.
Glenadal has never acknowledged him, which means Chaine
is simply a captain in the employ of the House Ravenspear. A
competent captain, I'll grant you, and one of above-average
intelligence and resourcefulness, but rumour does not make
an heir. And now, if you don't mind, I'll hear no more on the
subject."

Laran shook his head, thinking his mother's refusal to
even discuss the matter was only going to add to his woes.
As Jeryma said, Chaine Tollin was a competent captain, of
above-average intelligence and resourcefulness. And he
enjoyed the loyalty of Glenadal's army. It was foolish in
the extreme to simply brush him aside as if he didn't matter. But there was little point in pursuing the matter at the
moment.

"Has Glenadal no nephews? No cousins? Not even a distant relative you can marry Riika to?"

"There is no one else. Besides, Riika is much too young to be thinking of marriage."

"She's the same age as Marla Wolfblade," Laran reminded her sourly.

"Which is unfortunate but unavoidable," Jeryma replied uncomfortably.

Laran studied his mother, looking for some hint of reluctance. It seemed unbelievable that she would go along with this. Jeryma's face was set in determined lines. If she felt any remorse, she was hiding it well.

"You would have me do to Marla Wolfblade what was done to you," he accused.

That struck a chord. For the first time, Jeryma couldn't meet his eye. "It's not the same thing, Laran."

"It's exactly the same thing, mother," he said, seating himself on the cushions opposite. "You want me take control of a third of Hythria, kidnap and marry a girl damn near half my age . . . and don't look at me like that. She's been promised to Hablet of Fardohnya. There is *no* way to secure her participation in this little escapade of yours without using force. Then you'll expect me to get an heir to the Wolfblade House on her—having spent most of my life listening to you threaten to have me castrated if I ever did to another woman what was done to you—all the while trying to keep my own head on my shoulders fighting off the inevitable attack from Fardohnya and probably a coalition of all the other Warlords—Royalist and Patriot alike—on the off-chance Lernen will name his sister's son his heir. Assuming she obliges us by actually *having* a son, that is. Have I missed anything?"

"You always did have a gift for getting straight to the heart of the matter, Laran," Kagan announced as he walked into the room. When he reached the square of cushions in the centre of the large hall, he leaned forward and kissed

Jeryma's cheek. "He's resting as comfortably as he can. Ri-ika's with him."

Jeryma nodded, glancing across at Laran as Kagan took a seat beside her. "Laran is not very enthusiastic about our plan."

"*Our* plan?" Kagan asked. "When did it become *our* plan?"

"See!" Laran exclaimed, certain Kagan would have none of this. "I told you he'd never agree."

"I didn't say I don't agree with Glenadal's plan, Laran. I just don't think I deserve any credit for its conception."

"Then take the credit for its destruction. Tell her what folly this is!"

"It is folly," he agreed. "But not necessarily a folly we should dismiss out of hand."

"Kagan!"

"I've been trying to find a way out of this nightmare since Lernen first told me he was seriously considering Hablet's offer, Laran. This is the first time I've had even a whiff of a plan that might have a chance of succeeding. This gives us a chance for a Hythrun-born heir to the High Prince's throne. It keeps Hythria in the hands of the Hythrun without placing it in the hands of a Patriot. I know there's an element of risk. But with both provinces under your control, you'd have the resources you'd need to fight off any threatened retribution from Fardohnya."

"Not if Hablet made a serious incursion through the Sun-rise Mountains," Laran warned. "There's more than one pass through the mountains from Fardohnya into Hythria."

"You would need allies," Kagan conceded.

"And who would ally with me, uncle?" he asked. "What Warlord would stand back, watch me take control of Sunrise and Krakandar, and then offer to help me? I'm more likely to be a target than an ally."

"Every Royalist in Hythria would back you, Laran."

He scoffed at the suggestion, shaking his head.

"If it is done quickly," Jeryma suggested. "And quietly . . .

it could be a done deal before any of the others even realize what is going on."

"Ensuring we have no way out of this," Laran suggested sourly.

"If we go down this path, Laran, there's no point in wishing for an escape route. There will be none."

Laran turned on his uncle angrily. "*We?* What do you mean, *we*? Aren't you supposed to stay out of this sort of thing? What happened to the famous neutrality of the Sorcerers' Collective?"

"I *am* looking after the Collective's interests," Kagan announced. He clutched at his diamond-shaped pendant, looking rather offended by his nephew's accusation.

"Since when did the Collective's interests involve starting a war with Fardohnya? Or a civil war in Hythria?"

"Since I realized that it doesn't matter what I do, Laran, that Fardohnyan tyrant intends to rid Fardohnya of every member of the Collective he can get his hands on. When Hablet assumed the throne there was a bloodbath in Talabar. I don't fancy helping his cause along. Or giving him a chance to wreak the same havoc in Hythria."

"Then shouldn't you be doing something about Hablet? Why pin all your hopes on me?"

"Because we trust you, Laran," his mother said simply. "Glenadal trusts you."

Laran shook his head. "That's not enough."

"It will have to be," Kagan said flatly.

Laran stared at his mother in surprise. "I can't believe you, of all people, have agreed to this. All those stories you told me when I was a boy, all those dreadful anecdotes about how demeaning and degrading it is to be the daughter of a noble house of Hythria, married off for her bloodline like a particularly valuable slave. What of them, mother? Are you so enamoured of the idea of being the grandmother of the next High Prince that you suddenly find your many and much publicised objections to arranged marriages inconvenient?"

"That is unfair, Laran."

"I'm sure Marla Wolfblade will agree with you."

"She won't suffer the way I did," Jeryma explained. "You're a good man. I know you won't hurt her."

"Are you so sure of that?" he asked pointedly.

She met his gaze evenly, almost defiantly. "Yes, Laran. I am."

"I'm twice her age."

"Marla is sixteen, or so close it barely matters. You are thirty. That's merely fourteen years. In a few years, your age difference will mean nothing to either of you."

"What if she wants to marry someone else? And I don't mean Hablet."

"Marla Wolfblade is the High Prince's sister. She will have been raised to understand this is not her choice."

"Suppose *I* want to marry someone else?"

"Do you?"

"That's not the point."

"Well, as you obviously don't have another candidate in mind, *I* don't see the point in discussing it."

"I will not have anything to do with your plans to overthrow the rightful High Prince of Hythria, mother."

"Nobody is asking you to overthrow him, Laran. I'm as staunch a Royalist as ever there was and I'm offended you would think otherwise. All I'm asking of you—all Glenadal is asking of you—is that you ensure the next High Prince of Hythria is a Hythrun, not a Fardohnyan."

"I could do that by joining the Patriots and backing Alija's plan to have Barnardo overthrow Lernen."

"That's not funny, Laran."

"Are you so certain I'm joking?" He shook his head, at a loss as to how he was going to get out of this. And wondering if he should try. Glenadal was right about one thing. This plan would ensure a suitable heir to the throne. And it would stop Alija and her cronies in their tracks. That was a more tempting reason than any other he could think of. But he still wasn't convinced. Not completely. "The whole idea is madness. And without the backing of any other Warlord it will never work."

Before his mother could respond, a sudden cry echoed through the palace. It was a tormented keening that tore through Laran's soul.

"That's Riika," he said, on his feet and already halfway across the hall at a run as he spoke. Jeryma and Kagan were close on his heels as he ran towards Glenadal's room, knowing with sick certainty that the only thing which could cause such a mournful cry was the passing of the Warlord of Sunrise Province.

chapter 22

Highcastle was aptly named, perched atop the ragged cliffs of the southernmost coastline of Hythria. From high on the battlements, Marla watched the pounding waves surge and crash against the base of the cliff, throwing up curtains of glittering spray. The high mountains in the southern reaches of Hythria had always fascinated her. The world seemed to lose its colour here. The pristine snow from last night's fall had settled serenely over the black trees and the entire horizon was cast in a monochrome still life. Huge pines blanketing the mountainside stood tall and proud, their heavy boughs tipped in pure white. Even the overcast sky had taken on the same shade of colourless grey that the rest of the world had assumed.

Marla walked around the tower, hugging her fur cloak tight, lost in a morose fugue that had dogged her ever since Lernen had sent her away from Greenharbour after arranging for her to marry the Fardohnyan king. She barely spoke to anyone. Wasn't eating, wasn't sleeping. Suicide suggested itself as an option occasionally, but she wasn't quite ready for so drastic a step. *Perhaps I'll do it on my wedding night,* she thought. *That would be dramatic. Not to mention tragic. And painful. And probably messy . . .*

With a mournful sigh, Marla ran a gloved hand over the ice-rimmed stonework and studied the icicles that stuck to her glove.

"Cold enough for you?"

She started at the sudden intrusion on her solitude. "What do you want, Fool?"

Her *court'esa* shivered and stamped over to the edge, standing on tiptoe to look down with a shudder. "Lirena sent me to find you. What are you doing up here, your highness? It's freezing!"

"Just admiring the view," she replied with a shrug.

"Aren't you cold?"

"Yes."

He smiled, squaring his twisted shoulders manfully. "Well, if you can stand it, so can I."

Without being asked, the dwarf fell in beside her and walked with Marla as she finished her circuit of the tower. On the other side, the view stretched away into the distance over the white-capped black waves of the Bay of Mourning. A castle sat on the other arm of the bay, white and slim-spired, like a sketch of an enchanted kingdom. Its owners had built it to be as graceful and pretty as Highcastle was cumbersome and dull.

"I wonder what's happening in Fardohnya this morning," Elezaar asked, easily guessing the direction of her thoughts as she studied the view.

"You know, until now, I don't think I ever realized how close to Fardohnya we are here."

"It's not that close really," Elezaar said. "There's quite a few miles of impassable mountains between us and them."

"Couldn't they sail across the bay?"

"I suppose they could, but it wouldn't do them much good. There's nowhere to land down there. Does that place have a name?"

"Tambay's Seat they call it."

"Ah," the slave replied, as if the name held some meaning for him.

"Who is Tambay?"

Elezaar knitted his brows as he looked up at his mistress. "Not is. Was. He was only one of the three most famous figures in both Hythrun and Fardohnyan history. Don't they teach you princesses anything?"

Marla shrugged. "They might have, but I probably wasn't listening. I never put much store in lessons."

Elezaar shook his head. "A woman who can't read or write would hide in shame in my profession."

"But noblewomen don't need an education," Marla pointed out petulantly. "Noblewomen are for looking decorative and making babies. I don't know why the gods even bothered giving us a brain. I mean, it's not as if we ever get to use it."

"Ah, so that's what's eating you up."

Marla turned her back on the view and leaned against the chilly wall, hugging her arms close to her body. "It's not fair! Lernen sent me back here simply to shut me up. And to learn how to be a good wife to . . . that . . . that Fardohnyan brute! Well, it won't work!"

"Hence the reason you have yet to call on my services. Or Corin's. Your highness, may I offer you a small piece of advice?"

"Why not? I'm just as much a slave to my brother's whims as you are."

"Then learn from a slave. Open defiance is rarely profitable unless you can back it up with force. You have no force, therefore your defiance does nothing but alert others to your discontent."

"I don't care if Lernen learns of my discontent! I want him to know about it!"

"You might find your cause better served by working in the shadows rather than the light, my lady."

"What do you mean?"

"Why don't we go down to a nice warm fire? Perhaps I can educate you over a cup of mulled wine."

She stared at the slave suspiciously. His head was far too large for the body it rested on. "Why do you keep following me around, offering to help me?"

"Because I have no more desire to go to Fardohnya than you, your highness."

She glared at the *court'esa*. "Well, if you want to do something useful, little man, find a way to prevent it."

"You are a princess, your highness, and, in your own way, just as much a chattel as I am. What separates us is the price they demand for our services. I may not be able to stop your wedding, but, if you let me, I can show you how to play the game so that you gain some measure of control over your life. You have a great deal of power at your fingertips."

"If I had any power, Fool, I wouldn't have to marry Hablet."

"You have power, your highness," Elezaar corrected. "Your son will be the heir to the High Prince's crown. Have you thought of that?"

Marla couldn't believe she was having such a discussion with a slave. She ought to call for a guard. Have the Fool disciplined for talking out of turn. But there was a ring of truth in the voice of the hideously deformed *court'esa*. She found herself unable to deny it. "Don't be ridiculous! Lernen's son will be High Prince, not mine."

"Your brother will never father a child, my lady," Elezaar warned. "The only children to get close to him will be the ones he takes to his bed."

"Don't you dare repeat that heinous nonsense!"

"Why not?" he asked with a shrug. "It's the truth. Every slave in Greenharbour can relate a story or two about your brother and the slaves he amuses himself with. Few of them have a happy ending."

"It's not true!"

"Are you so blind, your highness, to think that a man cannot be so base?" the dwarf asked. "Or is it because he's your brother that you find the truth so hard to stomach?"

"You have a nerve, slave, to speak to me so."

"I live to serve, your highness, and I can do you no better

service than make you see the truth. The whole of Hythria knows your brother is concerned only with his own pleasure. He cares nothing for the lives he destroys in the process. And that includes your life."

"Even if it's true, I still don't see how it makes me powerful."

Elezaar smiled. "Then it will be my honour to instruct you, my lady. You have need of friends, I think."

Marla shook her head, puzzled by the dwarf's comment. "I have plenty of friends."

"You have no friends, your highness," Elezaar warned. "You have family who see you only as a tool in their political ambitions. Everyone else around you is either a slave or paid to be with you. Even Lirena, whom you trust implicitly, is the servant of your brother, not you. There is not a soul in your company you can rely on." The Fool hesitated for a moment, then added carefully. "Except me."

"Except you?" she scoffed, wounded by his words, the more so because she realized they were true. "Why should I rely on you?"

"Because you are the first master or mistress I have ever had who doesn't treat me like a circus animal, your highness. I wish, with all my heart, to stay in your company. For that, I would do anything to ensure you are free to keep me around."

"I haven't done anything but ignore you, Fool."

"When being the centre of attention means torment, my lady, being ignored can be a gift more valuable than freedom."

"What about Corin?"

The dwarf hesitated before he answered. "Use Corin for his intended purpose, your highness. He's very good at what he does. Make him teach you everything he knows. But don't get attached to him."

"Are you saying I shouldn't trust him?"

"I'm saying he was a gift, your highness, from the woman who belongs to the faction trying to engineer your brother's downfall. It would pay to be cautious around him."

"How do I know *you're* not a spy?"

"You don't."

"Then I shouldn't trust you either."

The dwarf nodded approvingly. "That is the Fourth Rule of Gaining and Wielding Power, your highness. Trust no one."

"The Fourth Rule?" Marla stamped her feet against the cold. "What are you babbling about? I swear you've more cheek than any slave I've ever met. I should have you whipped."

"You'd not be the first mistress to order that, your highness," Elezaar shrugged. "Some even did it to discipline me."

"And the others?"

"Pleasure comes in many forms, your highness. Some of it is painful."

"What are you talking about?"

"I mean some people—more than you might expect—find pain arousing."

"That's absurd!" Marla scoffed. "Why would anybody enjoy pain?"

"Because pain, if sustained for a sufficient length of time, can bring on a state of euphoria."

"You're making that up!"

"It's true. I swear. Mind you, it's not a sport for amateurs. It is a precarious game finding the pain threshold that triggers the euphoria, but for those who hunger for the feeling, well worth the effort."

"I can't imagine ever wanting to inflict pain on somebody I love."

"What makes you think arousal has anything to do with love, your highness? You don't love King Hablet." Suddenly, the dwarf smiled. "In fact, one can, without using too much imagination, see your highness gaining a great *deal* of pleasure from inflicting pain upon her new husband."

Marla laughed delightedly. "You are a wicked little man, Fool."

"But I'm *your* wicked little man, your highness," he reminded her with a courtly—albeit awkward—bow.

"What else can you teach me?"

"Anything you want to know. I can teach you about love. And hate. And I can teach you the Thirty Rules of Gaining and Wielding Power." Then he added with a cheeky grin, "Provided we do it downstairs. Near a nice warm fire."

"I suppose we should go in," she agreed. "I'm just so sick of Lirena and Ninane and Aunt Lydia. They're driving me mad."

"You have nothing to worry about for the next few hours, your highness. Your aunt and Lirena are currently engaged on an inventory of the pantry, and your cousin . . . well, she is easily taken care of."

"How?"

"Send Corin to her."

"You want me to let that horse-faced bitch have my *court'esa*?"

"It's not as if *you're* interested in using him, your highness."

"I know . . . but it's . . . well, it's the principle of the thing. Why should she get to enjoy him?"

"Because it will give you power over her."

"How?"

The dwarf smiled mischievously. "I promise you, Princess Marla, if you instruct him correctly, Corin will see to it that your cousin will do anything you ask of her in the future, if the reward is the promise of another visit from—what did Venira call him?—your 'silver-tongued' *court'esa*."

"That is a truly evil plan, Fool."

"You don't like it?"

"I love it."

"Then might I offer you my assistance, your highness? Those stairs are icy and quite treacherous."

Marla let the dwarf take her arm, thinking it was the first time in weeks that she hadn't felt the gloom of depression weighing her down like a winter fog. *Perhaps the Fool was right.* Maybe, if she used her head instead of moping about like a lost child, she could do something about her future.

At the very least, she might get rid of her cousin for a few hours and would not have to seek the battlements to find a few moments of peace.

"If this works, Fool," Marla announced as they descended the icy stairs, "I will have to find a way to reward you."

"You could start by calling me Elezaar," the Fool replied.

CHAPTER 23

Riika Ravenspear saw her father laid to rest in the Ravenspear family vault through a haze of unbelieving tears. She had never, in her short life, been forced to confront the death of a loved one; had never even contemplated the notion of living without her doting father watching over her like an indulgent guardian angel. She knew she was shamelessly spoiled; knew Glenadal and Jeryma had protected her from many of the harsh realities of life.

And she knew, with certainty, life would never be the same again.

Shivering in the cool wind coming off the high peaks of the Sunrise Mountains, Riika stood beside Laran, clutching her half-brother's arm for support as her uncle, the High Arrion, beseeched the gods to watch over Glenadal's soul. Almost the entire population of Cabradell had turned out to watch. The hillside around the family crypt was crowded with people; a silent, curious mob, come to see the ruling family in mourning and a great man laid to rest.

Laran glanced down at her every now and then, to see how she was holding up. Aware that she was being watched by so many people, Riika was trying very hard to be strong. She would have given much for even a fraction of her mother's dignity. Even Darilyn's dry-eyed composure was better than the blubbering wreck Riika had been since her father finally succumbed to the simple infection that had robbed him first of his strength and, eventually, his life.

Riika glanced at Darilyn out of the corner of her eye. Her sister had arrived two days after Glenadal's death, complaining endlessly about the state of the roads in the provinces and demanding to know why nobody did anything about them. For once, Riika envied Darilyn, who managed to appear both regal and suitably grief-stricken at the same time. Dressed in widow's white, her veil embroidered with delicate gold flowers, a hand resting on each of her young sons' shoulders, Darilyn was still making much of her own husband's death while on a border raid into Medalon with Laran and Mahkas nearly two years ago. Darilyn enjoyed being a widow, Riika thought uncharitably. She liked the attention it got her. She liked the sympathy. And Darilyn thought she looked rather becoming dressed in white.

Kagan finished his prayers and stood back to allow Jeryma access to Glenadal's shrouded figure. Her mother laid the Warlord's sword on top of the shroud, then stepped back, her lips moving silently beneath her veil in a prayer to whatever god she thought best equipped to guide her husband through the afterlife. Zegarnald probably. The God of War was a favourite of Riika's father.

Laran gently let go of Riika's arm and stepped up to place her father's dagger beside the sword, followed by her half-brother Mahkas who placed Glenadal's favourite goblet on the funeral bier. Although three years younger than Laran, Mahkas was by far the more handsome of the brothers, a roguish charmer who relied on charisma as much as skill to get what he wanted out of life. A captain in the Krakandar army, he wore a beaten silver breastplate embossed with the kraken of his home province and a long blue cloak against the chill breeze. Mahkas had arrived only yesterday, full of apologies for being late and lamenting the fact he'd not been able to speak to Glenadal before he died.

And full of questions about what would happen next.

Riika wondered if Mahkas thought her father had named *him* the heir to Sunrise. He would not think Laran a likely candidate, already being a Warlord in his own right. And Mahkas knew of Glenadal's promise to Riika that she would never be forced into a marriage against her will. Did he think that made him the only likely successor? Mahkas had got along well enough with his stepfather and with no independent wealth of his own—Mahkas's father had been a penniless aristocrat whose marriage to Jeryma had been arranged to repay a political favour—he was certainly well placed to take advantage of his stepfather's generosity.

Poor Mahkas, Riika thought. *He'll be devastated when he learns the truth.*

Darilyn and her boys stepped up next. Her sister placed a delicate posy of blue mountain roses—the tiny wildflowers that grew prolifically throughout the Sunrise Mountains and were the symbol of the House of Ravenspear—on the shroud. Each of the boys then placed a small carved horse, representing Glenadal's favoured mounts, Nofera and Thunder, beside the flowers. When they were done, the boys returned to their mother's side and it was Riika's turn.

She hesitated, reluctant to step forward, reluctant to perform this final, irrevocable act of farewell. Bright sunlight, robbed of its warmth by the wind, beat down mercilessly, making her a little light-headed. Perhaps, if she didn't take this last, fateful step, Glenadal would still be alive. Perhaps she'd wake up from this nightmare to find her father standing by her bed, holding a candle that illuminated his jovial features, laughing at her foolish nightmare, promising he'd live forever, just as he'd done when she was small. *Don't you worry about me,* he used to say. *Death will take one look at me and run the other way, screaming in fright.*

He'll hear one of your jokes is what you mean, her mother would respond with a smile, as if the ritual was some time-honoured tradition between them. *They're enough to make anybody run screaming in the opposite direction, even Death . . .*

"Riika," Laran whispered in gentle reminder. "It's time."

Riika shook herself, forced her limbs to move. She stepped forward, clutching her father's shield. It was heavy and cumbersome and her arm ached from carrying it, but it bore the crest of the Ravenspear House and as his only child she felt she deserved the honour. Mahkas had advised against it, offering to carry the shield for her. The weight might be too much for her, he claimed. He sounded genuine in his concern, but she did wonder for a moment if Mahkas had offered to bear Glenadal's shield because he thought it would be a good thing for all these spectators (or more specifically, all these citizens of Cabradell) to see him holding such a potent symbol of her father's lordship over their province. If he thought himself the only logical heir, then it was possible. On the other hand, Mahkas may simply have meant exactly what he said. The shield was very heavy and at the funeral, with the whole of Cabradell watching, it wouldn't do for her to stumble or falter. Laran had thought the same thing. But he didn't offer to carry it in her place. He had simply taken her aside, just before they joined the long procession up the hill to the family crypt, and shown her the best way to hold it and the safest way to lift it up onto the bier. That was the difference between her brothers, really. One was all substance, the other all show.

With a small grunt, Riika lifted the heavy metal shield and placed it atop her father's shrouded body, the way Laran had shown her. The act itself did little to ease her grief. She didn't feel any sudden sense of closure. The only weight she was relieved of was the physical weight of her father's shield. Riika felt let down. Wasn't this supposed to make it easier? Wasn't the whole point of a funeral to give the family a chance to say goodbye? Wasn't it supposed to alleviate the pain, somehow? What was the point of a funeral, otherwise? Death had already taken Glenadal away. This ceremony was for the living, really, not the dead.

Oh, Papa! Why did you leave me? Did I do something wrong? Am I being punished for something?

"It's all right, Riika," a voice told her soothingly. A strong arm encircled her shoulders and drew her gently away from the bier. It was Laran, she realized. She'd been standing there like a fool, sobbing shamelessly. *What must people think of me?*

What do I care?

What will happen to me now?

Laran handed her over to Jeryma and then stepped forward with Mahkas and the other pallbearers honoured with placing Glenadal's body in the tomb. The two men who took position at the front were her father's most loyal confidant, Orly Farlo, and his most senior captain, Chaine Tollin.

Riika had objected loudly to the captain's inclusion in the funeral party. There was a persistent rumour around Cabradell that Chaine Tollin was Glenadal's baseborn son, a completely unfounded and malicious piece of gossip that Riika refused to acknowledge. Nobody with half a brain believed it. He didn't look a thing like Glenadal. He was too tall, too dark and far too irritating to be her father's son. Besides, Riika already had two half-brothers. She was sure that if she shared any blood-bond with Chaine, she would have felt something in his presence, other than the urgent need to slap him for the insolent way he spoke. Far from putting paid to his delusions of grandeur, letting him take part in the funeral procession gave the rumours credence. Nobody would think Chaine was included because he was the captain of Glenadal's personal guard. They would all assume some deeper, more significant motive.

The other pallbearers were Haril Guilder, her father's closest vassal, the Earl of Valcan Pass and Kahl Pendagin, the Baron of Tyenne, the man who had sold the Warlord of Sunrise the stallion that would eventually kill him. Riika had not thought him deserving of such a place of honour, either, but had been overruled by her mother. Jeryma considered the on-

going need for Lord Pendagin's support more important than
placing blame for what had been—even Riika was willing to
admit—a tragic accident.

On an almost inaudible count from Laran, the six men lifted
the stretcher from the bier to their shoulders and marched
slowly towards the crypt where Riika's ancestors were interred. Although the small marble building was elegantly designed, its ageless architecture reminiscent of the Harshini,
the tomb terrified Riika. It was customary to come here every
year on the Feast of Death during the month of Corlio, to enter the tomb and pay one's respects to one's ancestors. She had
done everything, including faking illness in the past, to avoid
being made to pay homage to all those dusty old skeletons.

And now Glenadal was to become one of them.

It just didn't seem fair.

They waited in silence for the pallbearers to emerge from the
tomb. Riika surreptitiously tried to blow her nose, fearful of the
sound carrying across the silent slopes. She was spared the embarrassment by one of Darilyn's boys. Bored with this grown-up
ceremony he didn't understand (and obviously bribed into good
behaviour by his mother) Xanda squirmed out of his mother's
grip and turned to stare at the silent crowd before addressing
Jeryma, rightly assuming she was in charge of such things.

"Can we please go home, Grammy?" he asked in a startlingly
loud voice. "I've been a good boy. I want my surprise now."

The tension suddenly broke as an uncomfortable titter ran
through the people waiting on the slopes. Jeryma smiled and
bent down to pick up her grandson. "Of course you can have
it, darling." She looked up then, addressing the people of
Cabradell as much as Xanda. "We should all go home. To
celebrate Glenadal's life while we mourn his death."

The pallbearers emerged from the tomb as the crowd began to disperse. Darilyn snatched Xanda from Jeryma's
arms, scolding him sharply for embarrassing her.

"He did nothing wrong, Darilyn," Jeryma said. "Leave
him be."

"What's the matter?" Laran asked, as he and Mahkas rejoined the family, obviously wondering why Jeryma was reprimanding Darilyn.

"It's nothing," Jeryma said. "Give me your arm, Laran. Let's get back to the house."

Mahkas looked at Riika as Laran led their mother down the path towards the town. "Are you all right, kiddo?" he asked gently.

Riika shook her head wordlessly, a fresh batch of tears blinding her momentarily.

Mahkas slipped his arm around her and turned her in the direction Laran and Jeryma were heading. "You'll feel better, Riika. The pain goes away. Eventually."

"How would you know, Mahkas Damaran," Darilyn snapped behind them. "You never even knew *your* father."

"But I knew yours," Mahkas replied over his shoulder. "We all got over *his* death in record time."

"Don't you dare sully my father's name—"

"Stop it!" Riika cried. "Both of you!"

She tore herself out of Mahkas's embrace and ran down the path, past Laran and her mother, past Kagan, past the people of the city come to gawk at her father's funeral. She even outran the guard.

Not that it did her one bit of good.

Because try as she might, Riika couldn't outrun her pain.

ChAPTER 24

Mindful of his pact with Dacendaran, Wrayan spent much of his time in Cabradell on the lookout for something to steal, in order to keep his promise to the God of Thieves. Stealing a trinket from the Warlord of Sunrise was going to be easy enough. Wrayan a guest in the palace with unlimited access to anywhere he chose other than the private family suites.

After several days of surreptitiously examining each room for a likely object, he settled on a small statuette of a water dragon, carved from a piece of delicate green jade. It looked Fardohnyan to Wrayan's eye, perhaps a souvenir of some trip Glenadal had made across the border in his youth. And he chose to steal it during Glenadal's wake, not because he needed the cover several hundred guests would provide, but because he was honouring the God of Thieves and there was little honour in an act that had no element of danger in it.

Besides, there was no point in half measures and Wrayan couldn't risk offending a god. If he was going to honour Dacendaran, he was going to do it properly. Stealing a statuette from the Warlord's private study with half of Cabradell present was far more daring than simply stepping into the room as soon as nobody was looking and slipping the trinket he had promised Dacendaran into his pocket.

It was late in the day when Wrayan judged the time right to honour the God of Thieves. The palace was filled with guests from the funeral. The muted buzz of conversation hovered over the public rooms of the palace, a background hum that permeated the whole building. He worked his way around the main hall all afternoon and had just excused himself politely from a discussion going on between two Cabradell matrons about the best husband for Riika Ravenspear now that her poor father was dead, when he judged the time right. With a quick look around the hall to ensure he was unobserved, he slipped inside the study, closing the door gently behind him.

Wrayan glanced around, the sudden silence after the buzz in the main hall ringing in his ears. It was a large room, with a heavy carved desk by the wall under the window covered in rolls of parchment and a low table surrounded by colourful cushions near the centre of the room, where Glenadal liked to conduct most of his business. On his left was a beautifully embroidered folding screen, done in a multicoloured geometric design which matched the cushions around the table; behind it was another, smaller writing table where Glenadal's scribe normally sat, close by his master.

The jade water dragon was on the mantel over the fireplace, which was built of polished red granite from Krakandar. Wrayan was headed across the rug towards the fireplace when the latch on the door turned. Instinctively, he dived behind the screen near the secretary's desk as the door opened and Laran Krakenshield entered the study followed by the captain of Glenadal's personal guard, Chaine Tollin.

Wrayan skidded silently on the polished floor, coming to a stop a bare hand's-breadth from the wall, breathing hard. He swore silently under his breath. There was no need for him to hide. He was a member of the Sorcerers' Collective. If he wanted to seek the solitude of Glenadal's study, then nobody would question his right to be here. Nobody but Dacendaran knew the real reason he was in the study. All he need do was step out from behind the screen and make his presence known. There was nothing to worry about. He didn't even have the water dragon on him yet. He could come back later, when they were gone . . .

"Thank you for agreeing to meet with me," Laran Krakenshield said to the captain before Wrayan could act on his decision.

"I thought it was more an order than a request, my lord," Chaine replied. The captain sounded annoyed, as if he'd had a choice when it came to an order from a member of his ruling family.

Go out there now, Wrayan told himself sternly. *Before it's too late and they find you here, lurking behind the screen, and you have to think up a reason* why *you're lurking behind the screen.*

"You have something to tell me, I assume? About the will?"

"That. And a favour to ask of you," Laran said.

"A favour?"

"When the will is read."

"You know what it says then?"

"Yes."

"Am I mentioned?" the captain asked cautiously.

"No, Chaine," Laran said. "You're not mentioned."

The captain was silent for a time, and then he swore softly under his breath. "So the old bastard refused to acknowledge me. Even at the very end."

"He had his reasons, Chaine."

"And all of them begin and end with Riika Ravenspear," the captain replied with an edge of bitterness in his voice.

"This has nothing to do with Riika. Glenadal had a far grander scheme in mind. One I'm not sure I agree with, but it does have merit, not just for Sunrise, but for the whole of Hythria."

"And for this grand scheme I'm supposed to just forget that my father refused to ever acknowledge my existence?"

"You've always been treated well here, Chaine. He made you the captain of his personal guard."

"I *earned* that rank, Lord Krakenshield. Glenadal Ravenspear gave me the job in *spite* of the fact I was his bastard, not because of it."

"Aye," Laran said in acknowledgement of the truth of Chaine's claim. "And if you recall, it was I who supported your promotion over older, more experienced men."

"For which I am grateful, my lord. But your support purchased my appreciation, not my soul."

"You have always been an honourable man, Chaine. And it's for that reason I need you now."

"Why?"

"Because Glenadal named *me* as his heir."

Chaine was silent as that news sank in. When he spoke, he sounded amused. "You'll last a week. Tops."

"That is also my assessment of the situation. Unless I have your help."

Chaine laughed harshly. "You want me to aid you in taking what should have been mine? You've got a nerve."

"I'm asking you to trust me, Chaine."

"You're asking me to turn my back on who I am. I have a right—"

"You have *no* right. Glenadal never acknowledged you, Captain. Even if your birth is an open secret, you have no proof and nobody to back your claim. Without that, you're just another mercenary looking for an opportunity."

"Then why did you call me here? To remind me of that? To gloat?"

"I brought you here to make a deal."

"What sort of deal?"

"The sort that gives us both something we want."

"I'm listening."

"Glenadal told me before he died that he would never acknowledge you. He was too afraid of causing Jeryma and Riika pain. But he did ask me to make things right, and I intend to."

"How?"

"By seeing you get what is owed you."

"And the cost of this remarkably generous act?"

"Your support. And the support of Sunrise's army."

"You have your own army."

"I'm going to need yours as well."

"And what guarantee do I have that you won't use my army for your own ends and then have me disposed of when I'm no longer of any use to you?"

"You have my word."

"And what do I get?"

"What do you want?"

"What if I said I wanted Sunrise Province?"

"I'd tell you that you were asking the wrong person. It's not mine to give."

"Of course it's yours to give," Chaine argued. "It's yours down to the last blade of grass. Even if Glenadal hadn't named you his heir, you're his only legitimate child's legal guardian. That makes this whole province and everything in it yours for the taking, my lord, and don't treat me like a fool by pretending I don't know it."

"Chaine, I will swear by any god you name that my interest in Sunrise has nothing to do with preventing you from claiming what you think is owed to you. I'm doing this because it's the only way to stop a Fardohnyan heir to the High Prince's throne. If you think your chances of ever seeing any part of what you believe is your birthright are small now, imagine what they'll be if the next High Prince is the son of Hablet of Fardohnya."

"And I'm supposed to do nothing? Say nothing? Suppose all this power you suddenly have goes to your head? Suppose once you've dealt with Hablet, you decide to turn your attention closer to home? What then?"

"Then it will be up to men like you to make certain it doesn't," Laran replied.

Wrayan waited, unconsciously holding his breath, wondering what Chaine's answer would be. There was nothing worse than a disenfranchised bastard running loose after the death of a Warlord. When that bastard had a great deal of personal support in his late master's army, the danger was extreme. Laran was very wise to take the time to warn Chaine of what was about to happen and to seek his support. Wrayan was beginning to understand why Kagan thought his nephew so capable. The knowledge gave the young sorcerer a warm feeling of provincial pride. Laran Krakenshield was Krakandar's Warlord, after all: Wrayan's Warlord (although sorcerers were supposed to eschew all loyalties other than to the Collective and the gods).

How did the old saying go? *They breed them strong and wise in Krakandar.*

"What's my alternative?" Chaine asked, although it was clear he already knew the answer. When Laran didn't reply, Chaine sighed heavily. "You'd better mean what you say about seeing justice done, Laran Krakenshield."

"I give you my word," Laran replied solemnly. "When the time is right, I will see that you are acknowledged as Glenadal's son. And that you are given your fair share of your inheritance."

"Then I'm your man," Chaine promised the Warlord.

Although Wrayan couldn't see them, he guessed the men were shaking hands to seal the deal.

Pity though, he thought, *that Chaine hadn't thought to have the transaction witnessed properly.* A handshake might be enough between soldiers, but legally, without the Sorcerers' Collective to attest to the proceedings, Laran could walk away from his promise any time he chose.

Wrayan didn't think he would. Laran wasn't that sort of man. But it disturbed the sorcerer a little to realize that with Laran's agreement with Chaine, he had effectively committed himself to following the dangerous course that Glenadal, Jeryma and Kagan had laid out for him.

And for the rest of them caught up in this whirlwind.

Because with that simple, unseen handshake, the pact was sealed and there was no going back.

ChAPTER 25

"Tell me more about men, Elezaar."

Marla paced the small sitting room of her chambers restlessly. There had been a blizzard raging for nearly three days now and she was beginning to feel claustrophobic. Unlike the large airy atmosphere of the palace chambers in Greenharbour, Highcastle's rooms were small and dingy, filled with dark heavy furniture. Thick tapestries hung on the walls in a vain attempt to lessen the heat loss through the cold stone. The dwarf *court'esa* sat on the floor near the blazing fire which was making the room almost bearable. Elezaar felt the cold much more than the heat. Lirena was gone for the afternoon, begging off with what she claimed was an unbearable headache. Marla thought it more likely the old nurse was just too cold and needed the excuse to climb under the covers of her bed and stay there until this damn blizzard had blown itself out.

"Just like that?" Elezaar chuckled, looking up from the book he was reading. "*Tell me more about men?* You would have me betray the secrets of my gender, your highness?"

"Your gender made you a slave, Elezaar. I would have you tell me their secrets because I am the one who is feeding you and clothing you and ensuring you have a roof over your head in a blizzard, in return for nothing more arduous than the pleasure of your company."

"But I'm still a slave, your highness."

"All the more reason to do as I command," Marla reminded him.

"A valid point," Elezaar agreed. He closed the book, placing a finger in between the pages to mark his place. His hands were strange, the size of a normal man's hands and out of all proportion to the rest of his stunted body. "What would you have me tell you, then?"

"How do I make a man do what I want?"

"That very much depends on whether it's something he also wants."

"What if I want something and my husband doesn't? How do I make him do what I want then?"

"That very much depends on your husband."

"You're not being very helpful, Elezaar."

"You're not asking the right questions, your highness."

"What am I supposed to ask?"

"You could ask what drives a man. Or, more specifically, how to *tell* what drives a man. Only then can you decide the best way to manipulate him."

"What drives you?"

The dwarf smiled. "The unending desire to remain in your good graces, of course."

"What about Corin?"

He wondered if he should tell her again of his suspicions about Corin being Alija's spy. In the end, he decided not to. He had no proof and, while Corin was keeping Ninane amused, he wasn't bothering them. "The need for comfort. And security."

"Then he's the same as you."

Elezaar shook his head. "No, your highness. We're quite different. Corin seeks security by trying to make himself desirable. I am trying to make myself indispensable."

"Is there a difference?"

"Most definitely."

The princess walked to the window and looked out into the swirling white of the blizzard. "Well, Ninane seems to like him. She's always coming up with reasons why she needs to 'borrow' him."

"As I pointed out to you that day on the battlements several weeks ago, my lady, your cousin is now your creature. All you need do to secure her cooperation in any venture you desire is threaten to withdraw his services."

Marla turned to him thoughtfully. "Is sex so enticing that one would willingly subjugate oneself simply to get more of it?"

He smiled at her. "I suggest, your highness, you answer that question for yourself. Once you've tried it."

"I'm not sure I want to, after seeing what a fool Ninane has become. And all over a slave I could sell any time the mood took me. I don't know I'd want anyone to have that sort of power over me."

"Then you need protection, your highness."

"Protection?"

"Knowledge."

"What sort of knowledge?"

Seeing another opportunity to make himself useful, Elezaar answered her question with a question of his own. "What is doraphilia?"

She looked at him blankly. "I don't know."

"It is sexual arousal by the touch of leather. How about formicaphilia?"

"Formica-*what*?"

"It's the act of sexual arousal by ants."

"They actually have a *name* for that?"

"You'd be surprised what they have names for. What is dendrophilia?"

"Sexual arousal by . . . *dens*?" she suggested, and then threw her hands up in defeat. "How should I know what it means? And what does it matter, anyway? What am I supposed to do? Acquire an encyclopaedic knowledge of these . . . perversions of yours, so I'll be able to say, 'Look! He's covered in ants. The man must be a formicaphile!' I can see how *that's* going to be a real big help in a Fardohnyan harem."

Elezaar rolled his eyes impatiently. "For your information, dendrophilia is being aroused by trees. And you need to know these things, your highness, because the *knowledge* is the power. Suppose Hablet turns out to have a penchant for . . . I don't know . . . say . . . feet."

"Feet?"

"You'd be surprised how common it is. If you want to manipulate him then you need to know what arouses him. If you know a man's perversions you can rule the world while he's sucking on your toes."

"That's revolting!"

"Only because it's not a perversion you share." He put the book aside, hoping to impress upon the young woman the importance of what he was trying to teach her. Marla was an intelligent girl, Elezaar had discovered, but she was a dreamer. And a romantic at heart. She still harboured futile hopes of escaping her fate. "But if you intend to do more than just survive when you get to Fardohnya, then it's vitally important you understand these things. You must learn what makes a man want you. And, perhaps even more importantly, what kills his desire. Both are very useful skills, particularly given that when you get to Fardohnya you will be living in a harem surrounded by other women, many with the ability to spot a man's weaknesses from across the room. You'll have no hope of maintaining any sort of power if some *court'esa* manages to replace you in your husband's favour."

Marla frowned. "Do you remember Welenara?" she asked, turning to look at him. "She was at Venira's the day I bought you and Corin."

"Ah, the delightful Welenara," Elezaar sighed. "A goddess made flesh and sent to walk among us."

"I didn't think she was that pretty."

Elezaar tried not to smile. "Of course not, your highness. Now I come to think of it, she was as ugly as a wagonload of old boots."

"Does she know all these . . . strange sexual practices you seem to know about?"

"Of course. She's a *court'esa*. Princess or not, without training, you'll have no hope competing against a woman like that. The difference between you and Welenara, however, is that you might learn about them, but there are many practices you would balk at, some that would sicken you, and others you would die before taking part in. Being a free woman, you have the right of refusal. A *court'esa* doesn't have that luxury. If our master or mistress wants to smother themselves in cream and have us lick it off them, we are required to perform the task with the same dedication and enthusiasm as we would if they choose to whip us with the branch of a thorn bush or dip us in hot wax because they are aroused by our screams. And I use that example deliberately. I know someone it happened to."

Marla flopped into the chair by the fire, puzzled. "Dipping slaves in hot wax? Seems an awful lot of trouble to go to for a few moments happiness."

Elezaar smiled at her. "Ah, your highness. You have a wonderful streak of pragmatism that will make you an awesome adversary when you're older."

"What do you mean?"

"I mean that when you decide what you want out of life, Princess Marla, there'll be no stopping you."

"You keep saying that like I have any control at all over my fate, Elezaar."

"You have more than you realize, your highness, but not as much as you'd like, I suspect."

A blast of cold air from the hall outside suddenly swept through the room. Marla turned to see who dared disturb her without knocking. Elezaar scrambled to his feet when he realized it was Marla's Aunt Lydia.

"Marla, what are you doing up here all alone? I insist you come down to the hall and make an effort to be part of the family."

"I'm not all alone, Aunt Lydia. I have Elezaar for company."

Lydia was a gaunt, long-faced woman, a more wrinkled

version of her daughter Ninane, both of whom bore an unfortunate resemblance to Marla's brother, Lernen. She glanced over to the slave then turned back to Marla as if he didn't exist. Marla's aunt was uncomfortable around Elezaar. His deformities made her cringe. Lydia didn't object to Corin, though. In fact, she seemed quite pleased that her daughter, Ninane, was making use of Marla's handsome young *court'esa*. A Loronged *court'esa* of Corin's quality was beyond the means of her husband, Lord Branador. This way, her daughter was getting the benefit of a *court'esa* education with none of the expense involved in providing it.

"Marla, you are being a bore. I insist you come down and join us. It's not natural for a young woman to be so secluded."

"I'm not secluded. I just don't feel like . . . being sociable."

Elezaar didn't blame the princess for avoiding her cousins. Ninane was no longer a problem since Marla had begun loaning her Corin, but Braun and Kaul were quite a bit older than Marla and seemed to derive most of their amusement from teasing her. With a blizzard raging for days and everyone cooped up inside, the boys (rather the young men—Kaul was twenty-two and his brother, Braun, almost twenty) would be feeling particularly fractious, hence the reason Marla had chosen to stay in her room today. Lydia never seemed to notice her sons tormenting her niece, and on the few occasions Marla had complained, her aunt claimed it was simply the affectionate banter of two young men who looked on Marla like a beloved little sister. Elezaar suspected it was more like jealousy. Marla was the daughter of Garel Wolfblade, after all. Kaul and Braun were the sons of his youngest half-sister, and the relationship continued through the distaff line. They were not descended from the Wolfblade family. Braun or Kaul would never have a chance at the High Prince's crown.

"Truly, my lady, I would rather stay and continue my lessons with Elezaar."

"What could the Fool possibly be teaching you that is so absorbing you're willing to forgo normal human companionship, Marla?"

With a wink at Elezaar, Marla smiled brightly. "We've been working on sexual perversions," she announced. "We're up to 'D'. We've finished learning about doraphilia, which is all about leather, and Elezaar was just explaining to me about dendrophilia, which is all about trees. Would you like to stay and listen, Aunt Lydia? Or do you know all about this stuff already?"

Lydia threw her hands up in defeat, muttered something that sounded suspiciously like a rather crude curse under her breath, and closed the door, leaving Marla alone with her slave.

"You know, I think you may be right, Elezaar," Marla mused.

"Your highness?"

She turned to him with a mischievous grin. "Knowing about these things *can* be very useful."

Elezaar smiled, remembering what he'd told the other slaves in the cells behind Venira's Emporium the night of Ronan Dell's murder. *Any court'esa worth his collar knows how to make a man or a woman want them. It's what they train us for. But to be safe, really safe, you need to be indispensable.*

Looking at Marla's conspiratorial smile, Elezaar was well pleased with the progress he was making. He wasn't indispensable yet, but Marla had just chosen his company over that of her family.

That was definitely a step in the right direction.

CHAPTER 26

Once the blizzard had blown itself out, the weather improved so dramatically around Highcastle Marla wondered if the tempest had really been just the God of Storms warning them of the harsh months to come, rather than the true onset of winter. Within a week the skies had cleared and a small thaw had set in, giving the false impression that spring was on the way.

Although the actual pass was some miles north of the fortress, Highcastle was a busy place. Deriving most of his income from taxes imposed on travellers through the pass, Marla's uncle, Lord Frederak Branador, spent much of the day dealing with irate merchants, disgruntled travellers and the large staff of customs men in his employ, most of whom lived in the town of Dakin's Rest, some eight miles east of the castle, on the other side of the Loquilarill River. The town was quite large, boasting a garrison of troops in addition to the bureaucrats and their families who lived there. Trade was so brisk these days that in recent times the population of Dakin's Rest had swelled to well over five thousand people.

Lydia decided to take advantage of the break in the weather to visit the town to do some much-needed shopping. Her daughter and her niece were to accompany her on the trip. Ninane was older than Marla by two years, a tall, gangly young woman with a long face and a ponderous intellect. Marla had despised Ninane for as long as she could remember, although there was no single incident that stood out in her mind which made her dislike her cousin so intensely. It just seemed as if she had always hated Ninane and Ninane had always hated her. That was the way life was, and nothing much was ever going to change it.

With the introduction of Corin to the household, however, the balance of power had subtly shifted in Marla's direction. Ninane was now forced to remain in Marla's good graces in order to ensure the continuing use of her *court'esa*. The change delighted Marla. And taught her a valuable lesson. She decided to let Ninane have all the access to Corin she wanted, because the ability to withdraw his services was hers and Ninane knew it. After a lifetime of torments and teasing, Marla found herself Ninane's new best friend and she delighted in the control she now had over her cousin.

"Don't smirk."

Marla looked over her shoulder at the dwarf. She was tying on her veil in preparation for the ride into Dakin's Rest. Lirena was sitting by the fire, her needles clack-clacking softly as she knitted. Elezaar had been watching his mistress get ready and had caught her smiling to herself in the mirror.

"Whatever are you on about, Fool?"

"You're smirking, my lady."

"I'm doing no such thing!"

"It never works if you smirk."

"What never works?"

"Victory," the dwarf said.

"I'm sure I don't know what you mean."

"If you climb into that carriage this morning," Lirena remarked, without looking up from her knitting, "smirking like that, Ninane is going to start to wonder *why* you're smirking."

Elezaar nodded in agreement. "It won't take her long to figure it out. As soon as she does, you will have lost any power you have over her."

"I wasn't smirking," Marla insisted.

"If you say so, your highness."

She turned to glare at him, but was disturbed by the door opening. Corin stepped into the room with a low bow. The dwarf forgotten for the moment, she turned to her other *court'esa*. "Where have you been all night?"

"With the Lady Ninane, your highness," Corin informed her, a little defensively. "You instructed me to spend as much time with your cousin as she wished."

That was true. "What sort of a lover is she?"

"My *lady*?"

"Ninane. My cousin. What sort of a lover is she?" Marla asked curiously. She couldn't imagine Ninane in the heated throes of passion. Come to think of it, there was something inherently wrong with the idea of Ninane in the heated throes of anything.

"Athletic," Corin told her tactfully. "And rather unimaginative."

Marla smiled. "That figures."

"At least she makes the effort," Lirena remarked crossly from her chair by the fire.

"What's that supposed to mean?" Marla demanded, wounded by the accusation in the nurse's voice.

"What I mean, girl, is that you're a bare three months away from getting married and all your *court'esa* has done since we got back from Greenharbour is amuse your cousin."

Marla winked at the dwarf before she answered the nurse. "I'm simply applying one of Elezaar's rules of Gaining and Wielding Power, Lirena."

"Didn't realize he had one that says 'If you want to get into trouble with your future husband, ignore all the good advice you're given'," the old nurse grumbled.

"Don't be snide," Marla scolded. "Anyway, I'm simply making use of Rule Number Eight: 'Use your enemy's weaknesses against them.' Corin is Ninane's weakness. So I'm using him."

"But Rule Number Twenty-Seven states you may think as you like, but should behave decorously, your highness," Elezaar reminded her. "Refusing to learn what is required of you is hardly the way to apply that rule."

"Isn't Rule Number Twenty-Three, 'Know when to ignore your advisors'?"

"No, my lady, that's Rule Twenty-Two. And now is not the time to apply that rule. You run a grave risk by playing this game."

Lirena nodded in agreement with the Fool. "Ignorance is a very bad look for a new bride."

"I'm not ignorant!" Marla objected. "And I'm not playing games. I just haven't been . . . in the mood."

"There's a luxury you'll not have once you're married."

"You know, in Karien a woman prizes her virginity," she informed them, turning back to the mirror to pin the veil in place. "It's considered a sin to make love before you're married."

"And a sin even after you're married for any other reason than procreation," the dwarf informed her. "But this isn't Karien, my lady, and Lirena has a point. If you're not being deliberately recalcitrant, then you're cutting it awfully fine if you plan to learn anything useful in the time you have left before the wedding."

"Maybe they'll just have to delay the wedding if I'm not properly trained," she suggested, her hopeful tone betraying the real reason for her reluctance to make use of either of the *court'esa* she had been given for that specific purpose.

"Unlikely, my lady," Elezaar told her. "The only likely outcome of such a proposal would be the death of both Corin and me for being negligent in our duties."

"But it's not your fault."

"That matters little, your highness," Corin warned.

Marla was a little surprised to hear from him. He rarely spoke up. He was always listening though. When he'd first come back to Highcastle with her, Marla had thought Corin's gifts were physical rather than intellectual. But lately she was beginning to wonder about that. He didn't miss much and, for some vague and unsettling reason, it made her nervous.

"Corin and I are slaves," Elezaar added. "Therefore, we are, by definition, responsible for any fault in our mistress."

"That's a bit harsh."

"But it's the reality of the situation," Lirena agreed, putting down her knitting to look at her mistress. "You might like to dwell on that before you send Corin away the next time."

Marla glared at the three slaves with the distinct impression they were ganging up on her. It was just so hard to explain to anyone. Marla's resistance to learning anything about the arts of seduction and love from her *court'esa* was a form of unspoken defiance. To accept that she must learn anything from Corin or Elezaar was to accept the inevitability of her fate and she wasn't ready to do that just yet. She still harboured a hope that the High Arrion had meant what he said about trying to find a way out of it. She still went to sleep at night dreaming of being in love. Of being wooed and courted; of being swept off her feet . . .

Her fantasies even had a face. Lord Nashan Hawksword of Elasapine.

When Marla closed her eyes and wished for a better future, Nash was the man who would make it happen. When she fell asleep thinking of being in love, it was Nash who walked through her dreams.

Unfortunately, when Marla opened her eyes there was nothing there but Elezaar and Corin and the harsh reality that in a mere three months she was destined to marry the King of Fardohnya and nothing short of a miracle could save her.

chapter 27

W e'll all be murdered in our beds," Laran's sister Darilyn announced petulantly.

"Don't be ridiculous," the High Arrion told her, taking a sip of wine.

They were sitting in the small family courtyard in Jeryma's chambers, enjoying the mild winter sunlight. A small fountain bubbled happily in the corner of the vine-encrusted, high-walled enclosure. The delighted squeals of Darilyn's two young sons, Travin and Xanda, who were trying to catch the goldfish in the pool with their bare hands, formed an odd counterpoint to the discussion the adults were having.

Darilyn turned on the old sorcerer. "It's all right for you! You're the High Arrion! Nobody would dare interfere with the Sorcerers' Collective. But what about my children and me? We're not above the law."

"No one has broken any laws," Kagan pointed out reasonably. "The custom of appointing new Warlords, rather than increasing the power of the existing ones when there is no clear heir, is tradition not law."

"I'm sure that will be a great comfort to my children as their throats are being slit!"

"Darilyn, your brother will not let any harm come to you

or your children," Jeryma told her soothingly. "I am surprised that you would even consider such a thought."

Darilyn turned her attention to her mother. "He is my *half*-brother," she pointed out coldly. "Had my father lived, this situation would never have arisen."

"If your father had lived, a lot of things would be different," Jeryma replied, just as coldly. "You are quite safe under Laran's protection."

"So was my husband, I recall," she noted bitterly.

"Your husband probably threw himself on a Medalonian blade to escape your whining," Kagan muttered impatiently.

Laran suspected Kagan hadn't meant the comment to be overheard, but it carried alarmingly in the still morning air. His brother Mahkas, sitting next to Jeryma, smothered a grin as Darilyn turned on Kagan.

"You unfeeling monster! How could you say such a thing? *Mother?*"

"That was uncalled for, Kagan," Jeryma scolded. "But I do think you are being overly dramatic about all this, Darilyn. Your sons will not be a target in the coming conflict."

"If you're so worried about your precious skin," Laran said, unable to bear Darilyn's whining any longer, "I'll move you to the castle at Winternest. It's the most fortified place in all of Sunrise Province. You and the boys will be perfectly safe there. Riika can go with you for company."

"You were named by my father as his heir, Laran," Riika said. "I'll stay with you here in Cabradell. I have no quarrel with his choice." She was looking tired, Laran thought, and wondered if Riika had slept much since Glenadal's death.

"Thank you, Riika," he said, genuinely touched. "But you, of all people, may be in the most danger. There is many an aspiring young warrior who thinks he could claim your father's province if he took you to wife. I'd prefer not to have that worry."

"You don't mind protecting *her*, do you?" Darilyn snapped, leaping to her feet. "What about me? Aren't you worried someone will kidnap me for the same reason?"

"If I could find some man fool enough to kidnap and marry you, Darilyn, I would have arranged it months ago," Laran said, finally losing his patience with her. "For pity's sake, stop thinking about yourself!"

Darilyn immediately sat down. Laran rarely lost his temper and even she was not fool enough to push him too far. "Very well then, I'll go to Winternest if you order it."

"I do," Laran announced. "And what's more, you will damn well stay there with Riika until I give you permission to leave. Understood?"

"Mother?" she asked pleadingly. "Is it your wish also that I be confined to the gloom of Winternest until this is over?"

Jeryma's expression was determinedly neutral. "It would be for the best, I think. And the boys have been living in Greenharbour so they've never seen snow. They'll have a marvellous time. Think of it as a holiday."

"And if the Fardohnyans attack?" Darilyn asked. "For all you know, Laran, you're not removing us to a place of safety, you're putting us in harm's way."

"Even if the Fardohnyans did attack," he replied, "you'd still be safer in Winternest than anywhere else. It's a fortress, Darilyn, and it's never been breached in recorded history." That wasn't strictly true. The fortress had been breached once, about half a century ago, when the Fardohnyans started a plague in the fort, but they had withdrawn inexplicably before they could press their advantage. "I wouldn't send you there if I thought it was a risk."

"You wouldn't send *Riika* there if you thought it was a risk is what you really mean." She stood up and smoothed down the billowing folds of her white pants. "I suppose, if I'm to be banished, I should make arrangements to pack."

Laran watched her walk towards the pool and breathed a sigh of relief when she disappeared inside with the boys in tow, protesting loudly at being taken from their game.

"I almost wish . . . no, I don't," he muttered wearily. "Mahkas, can you arrange a troop of Raiders to escort them? I meant what I said about Riika. She's in more danger than I am."

"I'll speak to Chaine."

"No!" Riika objected. "Anybody but him."

Laran and Mahkas exchanged a curious glance. "You'll be quite safe with Chaine, Riika."

"I don't care. I don't want Chaine Tollin anywhere near me. He makes me . . . uncomfortable."

"You could send some Krakandar troops with them," Jeryma suggested to Laran. "That new fellow, Almodavar, seems competent enough."

"New fellow?" Mahkas chuckled. "He's been with us since he was fourteen, mother."

"Is it that long?" Jeryma asked. "I get to Krakandar so rarely these days. It seems like only yesterday that he signed on as a Raider."

"I suppose I could send Almodavar temporarily," Laran shrugged, sympathetic to his young sister's feelings but a little annoyed she simply couldn't get over her problem with Chaine. The man couldn't help who he was and had never, in Laran's experience, treated Riika or her mother with anything less than the greatest respect. Laran wondered how much of Riika's angst towards Chaine was because she really didn't like him, and how much was just simple resentment. Chaine Tollin was living proof that Glenadal wasn't the saint his daughter liked to imagine he was.

"I'll see to it," Mahkas agreed, smiling encouragingly at his younger sister. "You know, you could name any bride price you wanted at the moment, Riika."

"I've no wish to be married to anyone, Mahkas."

"And you won't have to be, until you inform me otherwise," Laran promised.

"I know. Thank you." She stood up and sighed meaningfully. "I should help Darilyn get organised. You know what she's like."

"Only too well," Laran agreed. "You'll like Winternest, Riika. It's very pretty."

Riika smiled; the first one Laran could recall since Glenadal's death. It lit her face and for a moment she looked like the child she still was. "I've never seen snow, either. Papa always promised to take me, but he never got around to—" She stopped abruptly, unable to go on, and then turned and fled the courtyard with a loud sob.

"Riika!" Laran called after her.

"Let her go, Laran," Kagan advised. "She just needs time, that's all."

Before Laran could respond, a slave hurried into the courtyard, bowing low to his mistress. "My lady, Master Lightfinger sends word that the Warlord of Elasapine is on his way with his son and is asking for an audience with you and Lord Laran."

"Thank you, Nikki," Jeryma replied expressionlessly. "Show them to the reception hall when they arrive and see they are served refreshments. Tell Lord Hawksword and his son we will join them shortly." As the slave backed out of the courtyard, she sighed wearily. "One month today Glenadal is dead. And now it begins."

"The official mourning is over now," Kagan pointed out, rising stiffly to his feet. "I'm surprised they had the decency to wait even this long."

ChAPTER 28

The Warlord of Elasapine was a big man with a mass of thick grey hair and an equally impressive beard. He wore his ceremonial armour—the silver-chased hawk emblem of his house outlined in gold—implying that he came in peace, but his sword was big and heavy and battle-scarred, giving lie to the impression he was trying to create. Like his father, Nash was dressed in armour too; the boiled leather cuirass he wore was embossed with the hawk emblem of his Province, but his was much more serviceable than his father's.

As they entered the hall, Nash bowed respectfully to Kagan and Jeryma and then winked at Laran.

"I might have known the High Arrion would become involved in this fiasco," Charel Hawksword snapped. "Get up, fool," he added to his son. "Kagan is here to console his sister, Jeryma, not in his capacity as High Arrion. Or at least he had better be," the Warlord added ominously, glaring at Kagan.

Jeryma smiled. "Charel, do sit down."

The Warlord bowed stiffly, the ceremonial armour hampering his efforts somewhat. "My lady, I bring you my sincere condolences at your loss. And also," he said, turning his attention to Laran, "to find out what this damn fool boy thinks he's doing by accepting Glenadal's bequest!"

"Hello, Charel. Nash," Laran said.

"You stupid son of a bitch!" the Warlord declared, his rich baritone rising to a hearty bellow. "Laran, you have no more brains than a flea! Do you fancy a nice state funeral? Lots of women beating their breasts at the loss of Krakandar's Warlord?"

"Charel Hawksword! Sit down!" Jeryma repeated firmly. Looking a little startled the big man lowered himself to the cushions. Jeryma smiled. "That's better. Now, what exactly is your objection?"

Charel took a deep breath before continuing. "Laran, I've known you since you were born. I fostered you. I helped train you. I always assumed you were intelligent. What has possessed you to accept this? Isn't there some lad with potential who can marry Riika and be appointed Sunrise's Warlord? You can't think for a moment that the others will stand for this concentration of power. It's only been a matter of months since you gained your father's province. Isn't that enough for you?"

"Glenadal wanted me to have Sunrise Province," Laran replied.

"Glenadal was a sentimental old fool," Charel replied. Then he took a deep breath and assumed a much more reasonable tone. "Look, I know he was like a father to you, Laran, but you're a Warlord in your own right. Isn't being lord of the richest province in Hythria enough? What do you want? To own the whole damn country?"

"If I have to," Laran agreed.

"The gods save us all from ever having to witness another Hythrun civil war," Charel muttered, the ancient prayer something Kagan hadn't heard anyone utter in years. The Warlord turned his gaze on Kagan and the Lady Jeryma. "What is really going on here?" he demanded, suddenly wary. "What are you not telling me?"

"Lernen has arranged for his sister to marry the King of Fardohnya," Kagan told him, thinking the success or failure of this venture rested on the next few minutes. They could talk all they wanted, but without the support of Elasapine, the province that separated Krakandar and Sunrise, there was no point in even trying to make it work.

"That's old news."

"Is it? Have you thought what it means if Lernen produces no heir?"

"Is there some reason he won't?"

"Physically, he's probably more than capable," Laran agreed. "It's his choice of bed partners that places the likelihood in doubt."

"If Lernen dies childless," Jeryma added, "any son Marla bears Hablet will inherit his throne. Glenadal's greatest fear was that Hablet is planning to reunite the two nations of Hythria and Fardohnya."

"Unite them?" Charel snorted. "My lady, if anyone is planning to unite the Warlords of Hythria, it's your son! They will all be united in their desire to see his head on a spike once word of this gets out."

"Glenadal may have been sentimental," Laran agreed, "but

he wasn't a fool, Charel. Even without your help, I now command nearly a third of the armies of Hythria. Married to Marla Wolfblade, any son she bears would be the natural heir."

"It won't happen. Marla is already promised to Hablet. And even if she wasn't, it's moot. The Convocation of Warlords will never agree to you keeping Sunrise. Even if they thought you the most noble and benign soul in Hythria, the precedent is far too dangerous."

"The High Prince can overrule the Convocation," Jeryma reminded him. "For that matter, he can appoint a Warlord at his pleasure, just as he can marry his sister to whomever he pleases. The practice of the High Prince asking the Convocation to vote on the issue is a courtesy, not a law."

"You think Lernen's actually going to agree to this?"

"I believe I can make him see things our way," Kagan confirmed cautiously. "Given the right . . . enticement."

With an effort, Charel stood up and began to pace the room, tugging on his beard, as if the motion helped him gather his thoughts. The others watched him in silence as he considered the problem, knowing the man was both a friend and a potentially powerful enemy. Eventually, he stopped and turned to Laran.

"Suppose—just for a moment—I go along with this," he said thoughtfully. "I'm not, mind you, but let us suppose for a moment that I do. Have you considered the effect such a conflict would have on our northern neighbours? I can't see them sitting back and doing nothing."

"The Medalonians aren't a threat," Laran said. "They have their own internal problems to deal with."

"I agree," Jeryma added. "Since Trayla came to power, the Sisterhood seems more intent on self-destruction than expansion. One wonders how much longer they can go on."

"And the Kariens?"

"Also too self-absorbed to be a threat," Kagan concluded.

"But what of the Fardohnyans? What do you think Hablet is going to do about this? At the very least, if it comes to civil war he'll try to take advantage of our disunity. At worst he might come after you, Laran, either for the insult of stealing his intended bride or fear of the concentration of power you represent. I can assure you, Hablet of Fardohnya will have no moral qualms about ridding the world of Krakandar's Warlord."

"All of which are preferable to Hablet conquering Hythria between the open legs of Marla Wolfblade," Kagan reminded them bluntly.

"And just how do you plan to stop that?" Charel asked sceptically. "And more to the point, have you thought that while you're *trying* to stop it, the Patriot Faction will jump into the void so fast, you won't even realize they've won until you're on your knees swearing fealty to the High Prince Barnardo?"

"It's because of Alija and the Patriots that we must do this, and do it quickly," Kagan warned. "Since the murder of Ronan Dell and Marla's betrothal to Hablet, their cause has never looked better in some circles."

Charel shook his head at the High Arrion. "If you knew it was going to make things easier for Lernen's enemies, Kagan, why, in the name of all the Primal Gods, did you agree to broker the deal with Fardohnya in the first place?"

"Because it delayed them. I had to do something, Charel, or at the last Convocation we wouldn't have been meeting to vote Laran his province, we'd have been swearing fealty to a new High Prince."

Even Charel Hawksword couldn't deny the truth of that. He resumed his pacing, tugging on his beard so hard Kagan expected to see clumps of it coming away in his hand.

"Have you given any thought to the logistics of what you have planned?" he asked, as if he couldn't believe sane men would even consider such a course of action. "You'll have to get Lernen to agree. You have to somehow get your hands on Marla Wolfblade without raising suspicion. You have to marry her and make damn sure the marriage is consummated before anybody—and I do mean *anybody*—gets wind of what's going on. You'll have to move troops into place without raising suspicion to block both the pass near Highcastle and the Widowmaker Pass at Winternest, both of which will be vulnerable to attack from Fardohnya if Hablet decides to express his displeasure by using his army."

"I'll soon have Krakandar troops stationed at Winternest," Laran informed him. "They'll be there ostensibly to protect Riika, Darilyn and her boys. It won't take much to bolster their number to fighting strength."

"Which only leaves the pass near Highcastle vulnerable to attack. You need me rather badly, I think, Laran Krakenshield."

"*Hythria* needs you rather badly, Charel," Laran corrected.

"Isn't that where Marla lives?" Nash asked. "At Highcastle? Frederak Branador's wife is Lernen's aunt, isn't she?"

"Lydia is . . . was . . . Garel Wolfblade's younger half-sister. She's had the care of Marla pretty much since she was born," Jeryma confirmed. "The princess's appearance in Greenharbour for the Convocation was quite unexpected, I hear."

"Hablet wanted to see what he was buying," Kagan explained. "Once the Convocation was over, Lernen sent Marla back to Lydia and Frederak with a couple of *court'esa* and instructions to prepare her for the wedding."

"And how are you going to get her away from Highcastle without raising the alarm?"

"I could do it," Nash offered.

They all turned to look at him.

"*You?*" Charel asked his son suspiciously.

"It's not what you think! It's just . . . well . . . Marla loathes the idea of marrying Hablet. She told me that herself. She even begged me to save her from him, just before . . ." Nash hesitated and glanced at Kagan, who glared at him with a threatening scowl. He shrugged. "Just before she left the party. If I turned up at Highcastle telling her I'd found a way to save her from the marriage, she'd follow me out of there like a hound dog on a blood trail."

Jeryma smiled faintly. "Despite your son's rather colourful turn of phrase, Charel, I believe he may have the right of it. And I'm encouraged to learn Marla Wolfblade is opposed to the marriage," she added, looking pointedly at Laran. "Her cooperation in this venture will simplify it considerably."

"I haven't said we've agreed to this yet," Charel warned, glowering at his son.

"We might as well, Father," Nash replied, leaning back on the cushions. "I mean, when it comes down to it, we're either going to support the plan that will give us a Hythrun-born heir, do nothing and allow the next High Prince to be a Fardohnyan, or we let that idiot Barnardo Eaglespike take the crown, with a sorcerer calling the shots from behind the throne. I know which one I'd prefer."

"As opposed to what we have now?" Charel asked, looking pointedly at Kagan.

"I think you'll find my advice to Lernen a little less disturbing than the advice Barnardo is likely to get from Alija and her cronies."

"This is fraught with danger," Charel warned, after a moment. "The planning will have to be impeccable."

Kagan breathed a sigh of relief.

"You're with us then?" Laran asked.

Charel Hawksword hesitated for a long, tension-filled moment and then he nodded. "Aye. The House of Hawksword is with you. And the gods help us all if we fail."

CHAPTER 29

The jade water dragon was still sitting on the mantel of Glenadal's office. After his last abortive attempt at stealing it, Wrayan had decided to wait until a more opportune time. Now seemed as good a time as any. He lifted the ornament from the mantel, smiling at its delicate perfection, and then carefully, surreptitiously, slipped it into the pocket of his jacket.

". . . and we need to move at least another twenty-five centuries of Raiders to Highcastle," Laran was saying.

Wrayan glanced back at the table where Laran Krakenshield, the Warlord's half-brother Mahkas Damaran, Charel and Nash Hawksword, Chaine Tollin and Kagan Palenovar were poring over the map of Hythria spread out on Glenadal's map table.

"I'll take our troops to Highcastle," Nash volunteered.

"You'll take two-and-half thousand Elasapine troops all the way through Sunrise?" his father asked. "You don't think that's going to raise the odd eyebrow or two?"

"Winter manoeuvres," Nash shrugged. "We took twice that many into Pentamor a couple of years back to play war games with Foxtalon's army. It's not that unusual."

"I don't know . . ." Charel said doubtfully.

"It'll give Nash an excuse to be in the mountains," Mahkas added. "And a chance for one of us to speak to Princess Marla. He can tell Lord Branador and Lady Lydia they're on a training exercise. Frederak won't mind. He might even welcome it. Isn't he always complaining that nobody pays enough attention to the defence of the border passes?"

"It's one thing to bolster the border passes, but with twenty-five centuries of Raiders from a neighbouring province?" Charel asked with a raised brow. "Branador's not a fool, Mahkas. He'll know something's up."

"Which really isn't a problem provided he doesn't share his suspicions with anyone in Fardohnya," Nash chuckled.

"No," Laran announced. "If we're going to do this, then I really should go to Highcastle myself. I can't expect Nash to kidnap my bride for me."

"I don't mind," Nash told him cheerfully.

"Nevertheless, it's something I really need to take care of myself."

"Why don't you both go?" Kagan suggested. "I agree that

you need to speak to Marla yourself, Laran, but Nash is right about the troops, too. And Frederak won't think it unusual if you pay him a visit. You're his liege lord now, after all. Take Nash and the reinforcements to Highcastle with you, speak to Marla and then leave Nash guarding the pass once she's agreed."

"Suppose Princess Marla refuses to have anything to do with me?" Laran asked. Wrayan detected a glimmer of hope in the Warlord's voice. Laran was going along with this plan, but it was obvious he was a reluctant conscript. If Marla refused him, he'd be off the hook.

"Marla will do anything to avoid marrying Hablet," Kagan assured the gathering. "I even promised her I'd find a way to avoid it. You just need to tell her I sent you and this is the escape I promised."

Laran looked sceptical. "I have a feeling it's not going to be nearly as straightforward as you claim, Uncle."

Kagan shrugged, unconcerned. "Have a little faith, Laran."

"Will twenty-five hundred men be enough to hold the pass at Highcastle?" Charel Hawksword asked.

Chaine Tollin nodded. "Easily. The pass is only a few paces wide at its narrowest point. A hundred men could hold it for years, if need be."

Nash nodded his agreement. "If there's enough snow in the pass we might even be able to trigger an avalanche and block it completely until the middle of spring."

"I'll head straight for Grosburn after I leave here, then," Charel Hawksword offered. "If we can convince Bryl Foxtalon to see the merit of our plan and he brings the forces of Pentamor Province to back us, there'll be very little standing in our way."

"Which just leaves Winternest," Laran said, stabbing his finger at a point on the map that was, presumably, the location in question. Wrayan couldn't really see from his place by the mantel.

"How many men do you have there at present?" Charel asked.

"Only an extra three hundred over the normal garrison of a thousand," Mahkas answered for Laran. "I sent Almodavar with them when Riika and Darilyn left Cabradell."

"I'll need him back, though, if we're to move so many Krakandar troops through Sunrise," Laran said. "Mahkas, I want you to take the rest of the Krakandar troops I brought with me to join them."

"Wouldn't it be better to use my men?" Chaine asked with a puzzled frown. "My Raiders are used to fighting in the mountains. No offence intended, my lord, but your men are plainsmen. They don't know the mountains like we do."

"No offence taken, Chaine," the Warlord assured him. "But I have other plans for your forces."

"Perhaps you should think about moving your sisters away from Winternest," Charel suggested. "If we're facing an attack from Fardohnya, it's not going to be the safest place in Hythria."

"I thought about it," Laran admitted. "But Riika needs to be protected from abduction on this side of the border, more than anything else. Her danger isn't from Fardohnya, it's from someone in Hythria—"

"Doing to your sister what you're planning to do to Marla Wolfblade?" Chaine finished for him.

Laran studied Chaine silently for a moment and then nodded. "That's exactly what I mean, Captain. I don't have the troops to spare to send her somewhere else and provide adequate protection. Anyway, if Riika's not safe in a fortress like Winternest with thirteen hundred Sunrise Raiders in addition to a couple of thousand Krakandar Raiders surrounding her, there's few other places in Hythria that will be of any use." Laran tuned back to the map, the discussion about Riika apparently over.

There's going to be trouble with Chaine Tollin before this is done, Wrayan decided. *Laran needs to tread very carefully if he wants to keep him on side.*

"If Hablet tries to come at us," Laran continued, "I suspect he'll try the southern pass first, because it's closer to the coast

and he can sail reinforcements in through the anchorage at
Tambay's Seat. When he realizes that way is closed to him,
he'll turn his attention to the Widowmaker. If you manage to
effectively block the pass, Nash, leave a token force behind
and head for Winternest as fast as you can to support Mahkas.
If Hablet makes a concerted effort to break through, they'll
need all the help they can get."

He moved his finger along the map to a point further south.
"Chaine, I want you to bring the Sunrise troops with us as an
escort. Once we reach Warrinhaven we might need them to
hold the border against any incursion from the other Warlords
from the east or the south. They'll be our front line of defence
if anybody tries to stop the wedding from happening."

"Is that likely?"

"It depends on how soon word gets out about what we're
up to. Provided I can get Marla away from Highcastle without tipping our hand, I will meet you, Kagan, at Warrinhaven,
with the High Prince, four weeks from now. Murvyn was one
of Glenadal's oldest friends. We shouldn't have a problem
with him."

"And if we do?" Chaine asked. The captain looked a little
put out at the notion that he wouldn't be involved in any action against the Fardohnyans on the border.

"I'm sending Jeryma on ahead of us while we follow Nash
to pick up Marla. My mother should be able to handle
Murvyn. In fact, her presence should go a long way to making our forces look less threatening. But if there is any trouble, I trust you to take care of it, Captain. Preferably without
killing anyone."

Chaine smiled grimly. "You don't know old Murvyn very
well, do you, my lord?"

"I'm certain once my mother informs him the High
Prince is going to be a guest in his house, he'll start to see
reason." Laran turned to Kagan. "Are you sure you can get
Lernen to Warrinhaven in time? It's a long way from
Greenharbour."

"He'll be there. Even if I have to drag him. Which I suspect I will. The real problem will be thinking up a plausible excuse for him to leave Greenharbour that doesn't alert Alija or anyone else in her faction to what's happening."

"Surely Alija and Barnardo will have returned to Dregian by now?"

"Perhaps, but she has a spy network the Assassins' Guild would be proud of. I would count on her learning about this sooner rather than later."

As they talked, Wrayan wondered at this strange alliance of men, banding together to protect the throne of a man they universally despised. He thought he understood Laran's motives. The young Warlord was a stickler for the law and would do anything to ensure the throne stayed in the hands of the family to whom it traditionally belonged, even if he privately felt the current High Prince did not deserve it.

Charel Hawksword's motives were much less grandiose. Although a staunch Royalist, he was being pragmatic rather than loyal—protecting his province by allying with the strongest power (and the one that flanked him on two sides) whom he judged to be Laran Krakenshield. His son was in it for the adventure, Wrayan suspected. Nash certainly didn't share his father's determination to see the Wolfblade line remain in power. The idea of spiriting away a princess, however, so he could affect the succession of the throne for generations probably appealed to him enormously.

Chaine Tollin, Glenadal's unacknowledged bastard, also had his own agenda. Supporting Laran offered the only hope he had of legally securing the birthright he felt he was owed. Interesting though, that Laran had sent Krakandar troops to protect the Widowmaker Pass between Sunrise Province and Fardohnya, when it would seem far more logical to send the man whose local knowledge might presumably give him an advantage. *Was it an oversight on Laran's part?* Wrayan thought that unlikely. Laran Krakenshield didn't miss much, which meant there must be some other reason Wrayan wasn't aware of, forcing Laran to use his own men on unfamiliar mountain territory and the Sunrise army down on the plains around Warrinhaven where, clearly, the Krakandar troops would have been more effective.

And Kagan? Wrayan wondered. *What are you really doing here, you old schemer? Supporting your sister? Your nephew? Do you have some grander scheme in mind you're not sharing with me?* Or was it simply that Kagan would do anything to thwart Alija Eaglespike's ambition?

Wrayan fingered the jade water dragon in his pocket, wondering what *his* role in all this was going to be. Probably helping Kagan get Lernen safely out of Greenharbour to attend his sister's wedding in Warrinhaven—a wedding he currently knew nothing about. Kagan was right about needing to find a satisfactory reason for Lernen's absence. The High Prince rarely ventured out of his bedroom, if you believed the rumours about him. An unexplained and sudden desire to visit Warrinhaven would set alarm bells ringing all over Greenharbour.

It wasn't just Alija who ran a spy network in the capital.

I should take this opportunity to steal something from Laran Krakenshield and Charel Hawksword before we leave, Wrayan decided. *With all this talk of kidnapping and war, I may not get another chance to get close to either Warlord for a while.*

Dacendaran's price still had to be paid. How Wrayan was going to get access to the other four Hythrun Warlords was something he hadn't yet figured out, but he wasn't particularly worried. He still had eight months to complete his quest. With a conflict looming, there was bound to be a parley between the Warlords at some stage involving the High Arrion; one which his apprentice would be required to attend. Perhaps even a Convocation if this was resolved quickly enough.

"Then that just about covers it," Charel was saying as Wrayan looked back at the table. The old Warlord straightened, rubbing his back which was stiff from bending over the map for too long.

"Any questions?" Laran asked, looking around at his companions. They all silently shook their heads. The time for questions was done and everyone knew it.

"Then let's do this thing," the Warlord said.

The conspirators nodded in agreement. Wrayan resisted the temptation to touch their minds. He didn't really need to. Their feelings were written clearly on their faces and the most common emotion was fear.

Because the one thing nobody had stated aloud was the fact that if they failed in this plan, the chances were very good that they would all be hanged for treason.

CHAPTER 30

Somewhat to her surprise, Riika quite enjoyed her first few weeks at Winternest. The change of scenery, the pristine snow-laden forests, the majestic peaks, the thin crisp air, even the busy comings and goings of the merchants passing through the border post, all conspired to transport the grieving young woman to a place so far from everything familiar, she found her pain receding of its own accord. It was almost as if she had left the worst of her grief back in Cabradell.

Darilyn's sons went a long way to aiding her recovery. In the face of their unbridled enthusiasm, it was impossible to remain depressed. Travin and Xanda were such a delight, so full of life, Riika found her grief impossible to cling to. By the end of the third week she was tossing snowballs at her nephews, laughing as hard as the boys as they fought to bring her down. They built a snowman in the castle courtyard and decorated him with twigs and a helmet Travin borrowed from one of the Raiders who constantly watched over them, and then dubbed him Lord Lucky because Xanda thought it was lucky he hadn't melted before they finished him.

Predictably, Darilyn's reaction to Riika's escapades with her sons swung between gratitude that her sister was taking the boys off her hands and resentment when she realized the boys preferred Riika's company to her own. Depending on her mood, Darilyn was either fondly tolerant of their games or scathingly intolerant.

Darilyn was having one of her better days today and Riika had been able to prevail upon her sister to let her take the boys outside to the small ice-rimed stream that ran past the castle walls to see if they could find any fish. Her older sister was an accomplished musician and, after annoying Almodavar for weeks about it, had finally convinced the captain to send for her harp from home. It had arrived yesterday with one of the traders from Greenharbour. Anxious for some peace and quiet so she could tune the massive instrument, Darilyn had readily agreed to the boys going on an outing with their aunt.

Accompanied by one of Captain Almodavar's lieutenants and a dozen of his Raiders, Riika traipsed through the knee-high snow. The boys ran on ahead, telling each other of the fish they were certain they would find in the narrow water-way, even though some of the creatures they described sounded like they'd need an ocean to contain them.

Winternest loomed majestically behind them, its massive walls rising out of the mountainside as if it had grown from the very rock of the mountain, rather than being constructed there in the traditional way by men. Riika thought it might have been built by the Harshini. Its tall spires and elegant lines were certainly reminiscent of the lost race. The castle guarded the Widowmaker Pass (so named for the number of widows created during the numerous battles that had taken place there), one of only two navigable passes across the Sunrise Mountains between Fardohnya and Hythria. The other pass was much farther south, near Highcastle.

The keep served as a garrison, customs house, inn and fortress and catered to the steady stream of traffic that moved between the two countries. Commerce was the lifeblood of Fardohnya. Even when they were at war, they still tried to make it pay. Glenadal had been fond of saying the only reason most Fardohnyans didn't sell their own grandmothers was that every other Fardohnyan had already had the same idea and there was a glut on the grandmother market. Riika's eyes misted as she thought of her father. She wiped the tears away impatiently, glad to realize she could at least think about him now without breaking down completely. Maybe Mahkas was right. Maybe time would heal the pain.

Winternest was actually two castles in one, built either side of the road leading through the pass into Fardohnya. An arched and heavily fortified bridge high above the road linked the northern wing, where most of the commerce of the border post was carried out, to the southern wing, which remained the private domain of the Ravenspear family when they were in residence. There was a similar fortress on the Fardohnyan side of the border at the other end of the pass, about ten miles to the west. Although Riika had never seen it, her father had always insisted it wasn't nearly so grand or impressive as Winternest.

Her eyes began to fill with tears again. Riika stumbled on the icy ground, but a strong arm caught her before she fell.

"Careful, my lady."

Riika smiled at the young lieutenant gratefully as he helped her up. She wiped her eyes and sniffed inelegantly, hoping he would think her sniffles nothing more than a reaction to the cold air. "Thank you, Raek. I'm as clumsy as a fool today. I wish I had Travin or Xanda's ability to flit across any terrain without falling on my face."

"That's a gift owned only by little boys aged between five and seven, my lady. The rest of us have to stumble on the hard way, I'm afraid."

Riika liked Raek Harlen. He was the son of one of Laran's vassals near the southern border of Krakandar and the neighbouring province of Izcomdar. Raek had the courtly manners of a nobleman's son and the sharp instincts of a well-trained soldier. Riika always felt safer whenever he was around. She dusted the powdery snow off her skirts self-consciously and then cocked her head curiously.

"Can you hear that?" she asked.

"Hear what?" Raek replied, and then a moment later he heard it too. Horses. A *lot* of horses. "It's coming from the east."

"Do you think it means trouble?"

Raek didn't answer her. Instead, he skidded and slid down the slope towards the castle, calling to the lookouts on the bridge. At his command, one of the men high above turned his looking-glass east. After a moment he called something down to Raek, who nodded and then turned and scrambled up the slope to where Riika waited.

"Can they see anything?"

Raek nodded, a little breathless from his exertions. "It's our people, my lady. Krakandar troops, I mean. Marching under your brother's banner."

"Laran is *here*?"

Raek shook his head. "It's Lord Damaran's banner."

"Oh," she said, a little disappointed. "I wonder what Mahkas is doing here with Laran's army? Do you suppose it's started?"

"We'll know in about ten minutes," Raek suggested. "They're almost here. The lookouts have been watching them since early this morning."

"And they never thought to mention it to anyone?"

"I would imagine it was reported to Captain Almodavar as

soon as they were identified, my lady," Raek pointed out. "And Lady Darilyn."

Of course, Riika realized. *I'm the younger sister. The baby of the family. Nobody would think of reporting anything to me.*

"Would you like to return to the castle and wait for your brother, my lady?"

Riika looked up the slope where the boys had raced on ahead followed by a clutch of rather put-upon Raiders, forced to keep pace with them. Travin had reached the edge of the stream and was calling for her excitedly.

"I would love to, Raek," she sighed with a smile. "But despite the fact there is an army approaching as we speak, I suspect none of us will be doing anything until Travin and Xanda have seen their fish."

"Mahkas!"

Riika ran the length of the Great Hall, skidding to a halt on the polished floor as she reached her brother and Darilyn, who stood by the fire at the far end of the hall. Winternest was a cold, draughty place, but the bright tapestries lining the walls and the fact that Darilyn insisted every fireplace in the castle be constantly ablaze, tended to take the chill from the air.

Her elder sister shook her head disapprovingly.

"Honestly, Riika," Darilyn sighed. "It wouldn't hurt you to *walk* occasionally, you know. You can achieve just as much at a dignified pace as you can doing everything at a run."

"Oh, leave her alone, Darilyn," Mahkas ordered, embracing Riika with a grin. His leather armour was cold against her cheek. "You're looking much better, Riika. How are you feeling?"

"I'm all right," she assured him. "Some days are better than others, but . . . I'm getting by."

"Mother and Laran send their love."

"How thoughtful of them," Darilyn remarked sourly.

"Laran sent us nearly two-and-a-half thousand Raiders, too. I suppose that's because he's so certain we're in no danger from this insane scheme of his."

"Well, you know Laran. He always was the giving sort."

Mahkas was deliberately goading Darilyn. It was a sport neither of her brothers ever seemed to tire of when they were children. Riika was not sure if Darilyn was the way she was *because* of her brothers' torments, or if her nature had provoked her brothers to treat her that way in the first place. Riika couldn't really understand it, either. Both Laran and Mahkas had always treated their youngest sister with nothing but affection.

"Will you be leaving again soon, Mahkas?"

"And miss the chance to slit a few Fardohnyan throats when Hablet hears his bride has been stolen out from under his nose? I think not!" Mahkas pulled off his riding gloves and held his hands out towards the fire. "Actually, I'm here to replace Almodavar. Laran wants him in charge of the remaining troops he's taking with him to Warrinhaven."

"Good!" Darilyn declared grumpily. "The man's incompetent."

"*Incompetent?*" Mahkas asked in surprise. "He's one of the best men we've got, Darilyn."

"If he was any good, Mahkas, he'd be able to arrange a simple thing like moving a harp without causing irreparable damage to the damn thing!"

"Was your harp broken?" Riika asked, thinking it had looked just fine to her this morning when the slaves had unpacked it.

"The frame's intact," Darilyn informed her. "No thanks to those ruffians who transported it. But there are at least three strings broken. I've had it moved to my room to save it from any further damage. Where I'm going to find someone to re-string a harp out here in this god-forsaken hole, the gods only know!"

"A couple of broken strings is hardly irreparable damage,"

Mahkas told her. "And the damage is the fault of the men who brought it here, surely? Not Almodavar."

"He arranged the transport. It's his fault. He can't leave soon enough for my liking."

This had the makings of an ongoing and very unpleasant gripe. Riika smiled brightly, hoping to change the subject from Darilyn's harp. "Well, I suspect the boys will be happy to hear that you're replacing him, Mahkas."

As if to confirm Riika's prediction, a gleeful squeal interrupted them. "Uncle Mahkas!"

Travin and Xanda barrelled down the hall and threw themselves at Mahkas, who gathered them up and hugged them fondly. Mahkas was by far their favourite uncle. Laran was too aloof, too formal, to get down on the floor and tumble around with a couple of little boys. There was also a certain amount of guilt attached to Laran's relationship with his nephews, Riika suspected. It was Laran, after all, who had inadvertently sent Jaris Taranger into a Medalonian ambush during a border skirmish two years ago and robbed the boys of their father. Laran took care of them, of course. As Warlord of Krakandar he was, by default, the executor of the Taranger estate and held their inheritance in trust for his nephews. Materially, neither Darilyn nor her sons wanted for anything. But Laran still found it difficult to look at the boys without feeling some responsibility for their plight.

"We found a fish, Uncle Mahkas!" Xanda announced as his uncle put him down. "I patted him."

"Did you now?" Mahkas asked with wide eyes. He squatted down so that he was eye level with Xanda. "Was he a big one?"

"He didn't pat anything," Travin scoffed, rolling his eyes at his uncle. Being the grand old age of seven, Travin considered himself quite the little grown-up compared to his five-year-old brother. "The stupid fish swam away from him."

"I did so get to pat him!" Xanda objected, his eyes filling with tears.

"Did not."

"Did so!"

"Did not."

"Enough!" Darilyn bellowed. "For the gods' sake, stop it, both of you!"

"Did so!" Xanda whispered loudly at his brother.

"That's it!" their mother declared. "I am fed up with the two of you and your constant bickering! *Veruca!*"

Riika's old nurse must have been waiting nearby. It took only a few moments for her to appear at the entrance to the hall. She had retired here to Winternest some years ago and wasn't really supposed to be looking after the boys, but she couldn't bear Darilyn and thought her far too intolerant of her sons' boisterous natures. What had started out as Veruca trying to be helpful had graduated to her assuming almost full-time care for the children, just as she had when Riika was a child. The old nurse complained about it a great deal, but deep down, Riika thought, Veruca was rather enjoying the chance to mother a couple of small children again.

"Would you please get these boys out of here? They're giving me a headache."

"Of course, my lady," Veruca said. "Travin. Xanda. Come here, please."

With a helpful shove from Mahkas, the children complied with Veruca's request without protest, which did nothing but irritate Darilyn even more to see them so well behaved for a slave.

"Those boys will be the death of me," she complained, as Veruca took the children in hand and led them from the hall. "They lack a father's discipline."

"They're doing fine, Darilyn," Mahkas assured her, knowing his sister's comment was directed at him just as much as Laran. He'd been on the same sortie that killed her husband, after all, and he'd had the audacity to survive it. "It's just youthful high spirits."

"How would *you* know what it is, Mahkas Damaran? You have no children of your own."

Mahkas sighed, but had the good sense not to answer. Darilyn seemed to be itching for a fight. He turned to Riika instead. "I have a message for you from Laran. He said to tell you he's sorry you can't be at the wedding, but he'll try to arrange for you to meet Princess Marla as soon as possible after things settle down."

"It seems odd, Laran marrying someone the same age as me."

"It's perfectly common for a bride to be much younger than the groom," Darilyn pointed out. "Did he say when *I* would get to meet the princess?"

"I'm sure he meant both of you would get to meet her as soon as things settle down a bit," Mahkas assured them hurriedly as he realized his blunder.

Darilyn was unconvinced. "It's all right. You've no need to cover for him. I know where I stand with Laran." She pulled her shawl tighter around her shoulders. "Riika can entertain you, Mahkas. I am going to retire. I have a headache."

She stalked off without waiting for either of them to answer.

Mahkas watched her leave and then shook his head with a smile. "She'd be so much nicer if she . . . moved to . . . Karien."

"Don't be horrible," Riika scolded. "She's really not that bad."

"I'm glad you think so. I've only been here half an hour and already I want to strangle her."

"You do not! Now stop worrying about Darilyn and tell me what else has been happening at home."

"Well, the whole of Cabradell is fairly buzzing, as you can imagine. Laran and Nash Hawksword took his father's troops up to Highcastle to block the southern pass and to arrange for Marla to get to Warrinhaven."

"Is that where the wedding will take place?"

Mahkas nodded. "Kagan and Wrayan left for Greenharbour a couple of weeks ago to sort out Lernen. And here I am, ready to defend your precious little backside."

Riika studied him for a moment, wondering at his tone. "Is something wrong, Mahkas? You sound a little . . . bitter."

"Don't be ridiculous. What do I have to be bitter about?"

"You're not jealous my father left Sunrise to Laran and not you?"

"I'm always being pushed aside for Laran, Riika. I don't waste my time getting jealous about it any more."

"You *are* angry."

He smiled disarmingly. "You're imagining things. Your father did what he thought was the best thing for Hythria. How I feel about it isn't even a factor in the equation. This will work because Laran now controls two provinces. I control nothing, so even if he had left Sunrise to me, none of this would have been possible." He put his arm around her and pulled her close. "Now stop worrying about it, silly girl. I still love you. And I'm here to murder any bastard who thinks he can lay a hand on my little sister."

Riika smiled and let him hold her close, his breastplate chill against her face, unable to avoid the feeling that Mahkas was not trying to convince her that he wasn't bothered by Laran's inheritance, so much as himself.

ChAPTER 31

A lija Eaglespike much preferred the townhouse in Greenharbour to the ancient castle in Dregian Province, the traditional seat of her husband's family. With seventeen bedrooms, its own stables, accommodation for more than fifty slaves and internal plumbing to the main suites, the townhouse was far more comfortable than the tall, narrow, draughty tower of Dregian Castle with its crashing oceans, damp climate, endless stairs and impossibly ancient amenities. But even Alija couldn't delay her return home indefinitely, and it was nearly two months since she had seen her boys. She was missing them desperately.

She had no legitimate excuse to stay in Greenharbour, really. The deal with Fardohnya had been struck. Marla Wolfblade was to marry the Fardohnyan king in the spring, as soon as she turned sixteen. The young woman was back at Highcastle with her *court'esa*, learning the arts required to make her a desirable wife.

At least she should be. Alija's reports had been rather vague on that point. She had a spy among Marla's retinue, of course, and would know almost as soon as anything happened, but she didn't expect to hear much from Highcastle until the winter snows cleared. And Marla wasn't actually a problem. Just a silly girl, with no comprehension of the power she held in her foolish, innocent hands.

The Lady of Dregian was well pleased with her work. The seeds of fear and dissent among the Warlords had been sown and all that remained was for the crop to mature, which it would as soon as Marla Wolfblade bore Hablet of Fardohnya a son. Then the time would be ripe for Barnardo to make his move. Even if it took years for Marla to produce a boy, as soon as Lernen made an attempt to confirm any child of the Fardohnyan king as his heir, he was doomed. The other Warlords wouldn't stand for it. Even those aligned with the Royalist faction would move to replace the High Prince—immediately—with the only man of royal descent who could provide Hythria with not one, but two, pure Hythrun heirs.

Barnardo Eaglespike.

There wasn't much Alija could do at the Collective, either. She had long ago removed from the Collective's library any scrolls that gave an insight into the unique power she wielded as an Innate. She didn't need to be here in Greenharbour to study them. In fact, she was better off not experimenting with the scrolls here in the city, so close to the Collective, where someone might detect her working.

Kagan and his apprentice were away, so there wasn't even

her nemesis and his sidekick to keep an eye on. The High Arrion's brother-in-law had been killed recently. He was up north in Sunrise Province, consoling his sister and probably desperately trying to arrange a suitable husband for his niece, Riika Ravenspear, to keep the province in the family. If the Ravenspears arrived at the next Convocation with Riika married to some suitable but inoffensive and uncontroversial candidate, then it was more than likely the Convocation would simply ratify her new husband's appointment as the next Warlord of Sunrise Province and that would be the end of it. Alija had toyed with the idea of putting forward a husband for the child herself, but in the end settled for sending her condolences instead. There was nobody she trusted enough to place in such a position of power. Besides, the Warlords rarely interfered directly in the succession of each other's provinces. It set a bad precedent.

Let's see who the family comes up with, she decided. *I can work with whatever hand fate deals me.*

If there was one thing Alija had confidence in, it was her ability to get what she wanted out of people.

With a sigh, Alija turned from the window of her private study and glanced at the work still to be done littering her delicately carved writing desk. It was always a chore, relocating between Greenharbour and Dregian. There was the house to close up, slaves to be dispatched, others she had no further need of to be disposed of in the slave markets, invitations she must decline, others she must issue for a final soirée before her departure next week.

A thousand little details that she couldn't trust to anyone else.

She would need to make arrangements for her messages, too. The spies Alija had located all over Hythria would have no way of knowing she was no longer in residence in Greenharbour. She couldn't risk even one of those messages falling into the wrong hands.

The only person Alija trusted to take care of such things in her absence was Tarkyn Lye, the *court'esa* who had been with her since she was sixteen years old. She rarely called upon his services as a *court'esa* these days, having found him

far more useful in other areas to waste him as a pleasure toy.
Tarkyn's loyalty was one of the few things Alija was certain
of. She had delved into his mind as far as it was safe to go
without killing him and found nothing but dedication to the
mistress who had saved him from the slave pits.

Both Tarkyn and Alija knew that she had purchased him
only because it wasn't possible for her family to afford a
quality *court'esa*, but her status as an apprentice sorcerer had
demanded she have at least one, for appearances if nothing
else. A Loronged *court'esa* had been so far out of her family's reach it didn't even bear thinking about. So they had
gone to the general markets, looking for a bargain.

It wasn't uncommon for *court'esa*, even well-trained ones, to
wind up in the general markets. Slaves who had grown too old,
become disfigured or had misbehaved in some way were often
sold off at the end of their useful lives as regular house slaves.
Tarkyn had been sold for the crime of falling in love with another slave. Their master had caught the two of them sleeping
together, a crime of gargantuan proportions among slaves, particularly for those considered breeding stock. In a fit of rage, he
had Tarkyn's lover put to death and the *court'esa*'s eyes put out
for daring to look at another woman while in his wife's service
(even enraged, the lord understood Tarkyn was too valuable to
destroy out of hand). He then shipped Tarkyn off to the Greenharbour markets to recover what he could on his investment.

A blind *court'esa* seemed like a poor buy in the beginning.
But Tarkyn's blindness concealed a sharp mind and a burning
desire to seek revenge on the man who had destroyed his
lover and his sight. There was another interesting side effect
of his blindness, too. A *court'esa* required to do everything
by touch alone was an awesome tutor. And he was an astute
political advisor. It was Tarkyn who pointed out that marrying Laran Krakenshield was a waste of time if she seriously
wanted to pursue power. It was Tarkyn who had taught Alija
the skills she needed to seduce Barnardo.

And it was Tarkyn Lye who had fathered her two children,
although nobody but Alija and her *court'esa* knew it.

Barnardo was a fat, impotent fool, but with enough wine in him to goad his ego and a sorcerer wife who could invade his mind at will, the Warlord of Dregian was convinced he was a lover of quite legendary skill and stamina. Her husband doted on his sons and, as they both shared the same fair colouring, it was highly unlikely that anybody would ever suspect the truth. Alija felt no guilt over her deception. She certainly wasn't the first noble wife to pass off a slave's bastard as her husband's child.

Tarkyn had given Alija her children and, in return, she had given him the revenge he sought. Lord Parrinol, the man who had blinded him, had been found dead several years ago, apparently a victim of his own rather exotic sexual practices, strangled by a noose hanging from the chandelier in his bedroom in what everyone in Greenharbour assumed was a case of a bit of fun gone badly wrong. The practice of trying to achieve a heightened level of pleasure while being starved of breath waxed and waned in popularity among the bored and jaded gentry. At the time of Lord Parrinol's death, it was long out of fashion, although Alija heard his demise sparked a few close calls in other fools wanting to find out what it felt like to climax while suffocating. Nobody had realized he was a devotee of that particular fetish, but his *court'esa* swore he did it often and his wife was glad to see the end of him, so nobody questioned his death too closely.

It had been a very satisfactory episode all round. Tarkyn was avenged, Lord Parrinol's wife was freed of a nightmare marriage, the *court'esa* who had so earnestly sworn their Lord was fond of strangling himself for pleasure were rewarded handsomely, and Alija had gained a devoted servant who would willingly lay down his life for his mistress.

For that, it had been worth every bit of the small fortune it had cost to arrange Lord Parrinol's "accident" with the Assassins' Guild.

As if he knew she was thinking of him, the familiar tap-tap-tap of Tarkyn's cane sounded on the tiles outside in the hall. She called permission for him to enter before he had even knocked on her door.

"And to think I imagined I was sneaking up on you," Tarkyn remarked as he opened the door.

"You were," she said, smiling. "But you forget I'm a sorcerer. I wield powerful magic."

Tarkyn's once handsome face broke into a smile. Lord Parrinol had taken Tarkyn's sight with a burning brand. The skin around his eyes was puckered and scarred, the eyelids sealed permanently shut. Alija had been able to relieve his pain with magic, but restoring his sight, or even reducing his scarring, was beyond her. He wore a scarf over his eyes so as not to offend others with his hideous appearance, but rarely bothered around Alija. In fact, she barely even noticed the scars any more. He tap-tapped his way across the room to the chair in front of her desk where he knew it would be. Alija had whipped slaves for moving the furniture even a few feet from its normal position in the rooms Tarkyn frequented.

"I'm leaving you here," she announced as he sat down. "I'm expecting a message from Highcastle and I want you to be here to receive it."

"Expecting a progress report on Princess Marla, are we?" he asked, laying his cane across his knees. "I never took you for a voyeur."

"I don't care how she's getting along with her *court'esa,* Tarkyn. I want to know how willingly she's taking part in this marriage. It will help my cause no end if I can claim she was forced into it against her will."

"Why?" Tarkyn scoffed. "Most Hythrun noblewomen are forced into marriages they don't want. Nobody will think it the least bit extraordinary."

"You think like a man, Tarkyn."

"Really? I can't *imagine* how that happened."

She smiled. "What I mean is, when the time comes to bring down Lernen, those same Hythrun noblewomen who remember being forced into marriages of their own will be looking over their husband's shoulders, whispering in their ears. Some may even sway their husband's decision. Even if they're now content with their lot, they'll remember what it was like to be young and afraid and faced with a lifetime of servitude to a complete stranger. And they'll despise Lernen for forcing his sister on a Fardohnyan."

"Well, incomprehensible female logic aside, I have some news which may delay your return home."

"What news?"

"Kagan Palenovar is back."

"When?" she asked, annoyed that she was only just being told of it.

"This morning. One of our people spotted him coming through the west gate."

"Was he alone?"

"Wrayan Lightfinger was with him, if that's what you mean. But I have other news which you might find rather more disturbing."

"Then spit it out, Tarkyn. I've no time to coax it from you."

Tarkyn turned his head towards her, as if his blind eyes could actually see her standing by the window.

"Glenadal Ravenspear named Laran Krakenshield his heir."

For a brief, frozen, crystalline moment, Alija's world remained the way it had been a few minutes ago when her worst problem was the logistics involved in closing up the house in Greenharbour and heading home.

And then it shattered into a million pieces as Tarkyn's news sank in and she began to realize what it might mean.

"I'll bring Barnardo back to Greenharbour," she announced, sounding far calmer than she felt. "Now is not the time for him to be out of the city."

"I agree."

"Do we know if Laran plans to accept the bequest?"

"Nobody seems to know anything other than Glenadal Ravenspear died and left Laran his province and Charel

Hawksword rode to Cabradell as soon as he heard the news. You now know all that I do."

She stared out of the window across the flat white rooftops, but saw nothing. "If Laran accepts . . ." she said. "If he can get a majority of the other Warlords to agree . . . Gods, he'll control more than a third of the country."

"I'm sorry."

Alija looked at the *court'esa* curiously. "Sorry? For what?"

"I advised you to put Laran aside for Barnardo. Maybe I was wrong."

"There was no way to predict this would happen, Tarkyn."

"No, but there's one problem we wouldn't be facing now if you'd married Laran."

"What problem?"

"Laran wouldn't now be *unmarried*."

"What difference does that make?"

"Not a lot, I suppose," the blind *court'esa* shrugged. "I guess it will only make a difference if the good Warlord of Krakandar realizes the value of the prize awaiting him in Highcastle."

"What are you implying?"

"All I'm saying, my lady, is that if I was Laran Krakenshield, right now I'd be making my way to Highcastle as fast as my little legs could carry me, kidnapping Marla Wolfblade and marrying her so I could get her pregnant with the next heir to Hythria."

Alija shook her head. "It won't happen. Laran is far too noble to do anything so calculating. He'll petition the Collective to manage Sunrise until Riika is married to someone suitable. I know him, Tarkyn. He's not the kind to get involved in political intrigue."

"I hope you're right, my lady."

"Trust me, Tarkyn," she said with a smile. "Laran is probably trying to get out of this so fast, the thought of kidnapping and marrying a girl the same age as his beloved little sister, just to get an heir on her to thwart my plans, probably hasn't even crossed his mind."

CHAPTER 32

W e have a visitor, my lord."

The family was gathered in the main hall of High-castle at Lydia's insistence. Marla's aunt had decided they were not spending sufficient time together as a family and had ordered everyone to be in attendance this evening. Kaul was playing chess with his father, Fred-erak, on the other side of the fireplace. Ninane and Marla were working on their embroidery with Lydia and her com-panion ladies. Braun was sitting on the floor by the fire, play-ing with a hound pup he had brought in from the kennels. The room was warm and quite cosy, which was a rare thing for any room in Highcastle. Marla thought Lydia had deliber-ately seen to it that the fire was larger than normal, just to make sure neither of her sons decided to wander off in search of other entertainment in chillier parts of the castle.

Marla's Uncle Frederak was a gaunt, sour-looking man, whose features belied his genial nature. He looked up from his chess game with relief. As usual, Kaul was beating him soundly.

"A visitor? At this hour?" Frederak asked the slave. "Who is it?"

"It's Lord Hawksword's son, Nashan, my lord."

Marla's heart skipped a beat at the news. She looked up, stabbing herself with her embroidery needle in the process.

"Ow!" she yelped, sucking her finger.

Lydia shook her head disapprovingly. "Marla, you will leave blood stains on the linen. Please be more careful."

"Send him in then, by all means," Frederak ordered the

slave, glancing at his son with a puzzled look. The men in the hall looked at each other with interest. A visit from a neighbouring Warlord's son, late at night and unannounced, was a remarkable thing indeed. Marla turned to watch the door, her heart pounding, wondering why Nash was here. Had he come to visit her? Maybe even *rescue* her? Filled with anticipation, Marla gave up trying to appear interested in her needlework. She looked at the other women in the circle around the hearth. They were all sewing industriously as if nothing could distract them from so vital a task.

A few moments later the door opened and Marla thought she might faint from happiness as Nash stepped into the hall. He was wearing leather armour and a thick fur-lined cloak, his dark hair tousled, his skin ruddy from the cold. He strode across the hall as if he owned it. Frederak and his son rose to greet him.

"My Lord Hawksword," Frederak said with a respectful bow. "This is an unexpected honour."

"Please, don't get up on my account!" Nash insisted. "I've no wish to disturb your family gathering."

"The arrival of the Lord of Elasapine's son could never be counted as a disturbance, my lord," Frederak replied graciously. "You remember my wife, Lydia, don't you?"

"Of course," Nash said with a gracious bow as Lydia rose to her feet. "It's a pleasure to see you again, your highness."

"You've no need to grant me a royal title, Lord Hawksword," Lydia told him modestly. "It was my brother through whom the royal line continued."

"And continues yet," Nash replied, glancing past her aunt and winking at Marla before taking Lydia's hand and kissing her palm. He then turned to Marla with a smile that made her feel like she was melting. "Good evening, your highness."

Marla hastily threw her embroidery aside and rose to her feet, smiling coyly as she offered Nash her hand. "It's good to see you again, my lord."

"You've met before?" Lydia asked suspiciously.

"At the Feast of Kaelarn Ball," Nash explained as he kissed Marla's palm. Marla thought she might die from the lump in her throat that was sure to strangle her. "The Princess Marla stole my heart, along with the heart of every other man in Greenharbour, while she was there."

"You flatter her, I'm sure, my lord," her aunt Lydia replied, gathering up her needlework. "And now, if you will excuse us, we ladies shall retire. You obviously wish to speak to my husband."

Lydia turned her stern gaze on the other women sitting in the circle around the hearth. Her three companions and her daughter Ninane immediately took the hint and began packing away their sewing. Marla kept watching Nashan.

"Marla," Lydia called. "We must leave the men to their business."

"Thank you, but I'm staying."

Lydia glared at Marla, obviously annoyed that her niece would dare challenge her authority so casually in front of her small court. "I am sure your uncle will see fit to pass on any greetings from your brother in Greenharbour, my dear," she persisted in a strained voice.

At the mention of her brother, Marla glanced at Frederak who was studiously ignoring the exchange. Only on the subject of the Lady Lydia were Marla and her uncle in total agreement. She would be allowed to stay simply because Lydia was insisting she leave.

"Actually, I do have a message for her highness," Nash added.

"Then do I have your permission to remain, Uncle Frederak?" she asked sweetly.

"Of course," he agreed. "I would never dream of standing in the way of you communicating with the High Prince."

Marla turned to her aunt. "Don't worry Aunt Lydia, I'll let you know if it's anything exciting," she promised cheerfully.

Lydia looked set to explode. "As you wish," she said stiffly and marched out of the room with her ladies and her daughter in tow. Marla was grinning broadly.

Frederak shook his head ruefully. "Marla, I see you have yet to master the art of diplomacy."

"I'm sorry, Uncle Frederak," she said quite earnestly. "I really don't mean to upset Aunt Lydia. She's just . . ." Marla faltered, unable to describe exactly what it was about Lydia that made her so rebellious.

"I understand, Marla," Frederak said with a faint smile. "Truly, I do."

"So what brings you to Highcastle, my lord?" Marla asked, turning to look at Nash, wondering if he would blurt out the real reason for his visit (which she was convinced was to rescue her) or if he would be more circumspect in her uncle's company.

"I bring greetings from my father, the Warlord of Elasapine."

"And I return the greeting gladly," Frederak assured the young lord. "But what brings Lord Hawksword's son this far south in the dead of winter?"

"Manoeuvres," Nash informed him with a careless shrug. "Just keeping the troops on their toes. You know what winter lethargy can do to an army. Laran and I thought it would do the lads some good to march them through the snow for a bit."

"You have Lord Krakenshield with you?" Kaul asked in surprise. His face was suddenly alight with anticipation. Everyone knew he was itching to join the Sunrise Raiders, but his father had denied him permission, claiming that as heir to Highcastle, it was inappropriate for Kaul to become a mercenary, even if it was for Highcastle's liege lord.

"And several thousand Raiders. Thought we might ride up into the pass and take a look around."

Frederak looked panicked. "My lord, while I appreciate your need to keep your troops active, don't you think marching them into the pass is a little . . . provocative?"

"How so?" Nash asked.

"We are currently enjoying a rare period of stability in this region. The bandits are at an all-time low. The trade is flowing freely and therefore so are the customs levies. Is it wise to damage this current state of prosperity just to give the troops of a neighbouring province a bit of exercise?"

"I'm sure the Fardohnyans will take our manoeuvres in the spirit they're intended, Frederak."

"And Lord Krakenshield? Is he planning to visit us?"

"Of course!" Nash assured him. "He wanted to come with me this evening, actually, but I told him it was patently unfair of a new Warlord to arrive at his vassal's door unannounced so I volunteered to come and warn you that he'll be here in a day or so. You'll want to get the estate books ready, I suppose. Laran likes to look at that sort of thing."

Frederak's relief was evident. "I appreciate the warning, Lord Hawksword. We'd heard Glenadal Ravenspear was killed some weeks ago, of course. Unfortunately, due to the inclement weather at the time, we weren't able to attend the funeral in Cabradell."

"I'm sure Lady Jeryma appreciated your predicament," Nash assured him.

"Lord Krakenshield intends to keep Sunrise Province, then?" Marla asked curiously, thinking of a recent discussion she'd had with Elezaar when they'd first got the news about Glenadal Ravenspear. The dwarf was of the opinion that Laran would probably refuse the bequest. At least, he *should* refuse it—if he intended to keep his head on his shoulders.

"Of course he is," Nash replied. "Why wouldn't he?"

"Civil war?" Marla suggested.

Frederak looked at her in alarm. "Why should it cause a civil war?"

"Because he's already a Warlord," Marla told him, bringing a surprised look from the men in the room. "The Convocation will never allow one man to hold two provinces."

"Please elaborate," Frederak commanded, just a little put out by Marla's outspokenness.

Marla happily obliged, thinking that all the boring things Elezaar had been making her learn lately, like history and government and economics, were really very useful. And she so desperately wanted to impress Nash with her new-found grasp of all things political.

"Being Warlord of two provinces makes him the most potentially dangerous man in Hythria," Marla told the men in a lecturing tone. "The other Warlords will never accept such a concentration of power. With that sort of power behind him, he could take over the whole country if he wanted. He doesn't have a son, does he?"

"Not that I know of," Frederak told her, considering her analysis. "Would it make a difference?"

"The difference between life and death, I imagine. If he had a son, he'd be expendable. The child would be nominated his heir and taken to a place of safety while they obliterate the father, who immediately gets relegated to the ranks of just another power-hungry fool who must be eliminated."

"When did you become such an expert on the Warlords?" Braun asked from his place by the fire. He hadn't moved from the rug, even to greet Nash when he arrived.

"I'm inclined to ask the same question, your highness," Nash said, looking at her with new respect.

"I've been studying," Marla explained, thrilled to think she had impressed Nash with her reading of the situation.

"And what does your father think of all this, Lord Hawksword?" Frederak asked. "Is he lining up with the other Warlords, as my niece expects, to put an end to Laran Krakenshield's ambitions?"

Nash smiled. "He's concerned that one or other of the Warlords might attempt an incursion into Fardohnya for slaves to boost his wealth in the face of the coming troubles."

"Hence your arrival at Highcastle unannounced with several thousand troops?" Frederak smiled knowingly. "Are you really here for manoeuvres, my lord? Or to protect the border?"

Nash smiled. "You've found us out, my lord."

"Are your troops *here,* my lord?"

"No. They're camped across the river just outside Dakin's

Rest." Nash laughed. "We didn't want you thinking I was invading you, Frederak!"

"But you'll stay here until morning, won't you, my lord?" Marla asked anxiously. "Surely you don't intend to ride all the way back to Dakin's Rest tonight?"

"I'd be delighted to accept a warm bed for the night if there's one on offer," Nash agreed.

"Of *course* you're invited to stay, Lord Hawksword!" Frederak gushed, suddenly embarrassed. "Please, you must think me so remiss as a host! And I've not even offered you refreshment! Can I get you anything? Food? Wine?"

"Wine would be good," Nash said. "Mulled preferably."

"Of course, my lord. I'll see to it at once."

Frederak hurried off to arrange Nash's accommodation for the night and his mulled wine, leaving the Warlord's son with Marla and her two cousins. He ignored Kaul and Braun in favour of Marla.

"Perhaps while I'm here, you and I could have a word in private, your highness?" Nash asked with an innocent smile.

Marla's pulse began to race. *I was right! He really is here to rescue me!*

"I would be delighted, my lord."

He took Marla's hand and raised it to his lips once more. "Then I shall not sleep in anticipation of seeing you again."

Marla felt her face grow warm and feared she was blushing. With a curtsey and some banal rejoinder she couldn't even recall a minute later, she excused herself and fled the hall.

Once in the chilly corridor outside, Marla picked up her skirts and took the stairs to her chamber on the floor above, two at a time. She ran down the hall to her rooms, her breath a frosty mist in her wake. She threw the door open to find Lirena sitting by the fire and Elezaar and Corin playing chess. They all looked up expectantly.

"Lirena! Elezaar! It's time for you to retire."

All three of them knew better than to argue with their mistress when she started throwing orders around. Muttering unhappily, Lirena packed her knitting away while Corin moved the chessboard, with its game still in progress, to the table under the window.

"Goodnight, your highness," Elezaar said, as he waddled out of the room with his comical gait. Lirena was only a few steps behind him, however she offered no farewell. She merely scowled at Marla, obviously annoyed that she was being sent from the princess's cosy chambers to her own, far less comfortable—and much colder—quarters on the floor above.

"Not you, Corin," Marla ordered, as the *court'esa* made to follow his companions.

"Your highness?" he replied with a puzzled frown.

Marla closed the door on the other two and leaned against it. "I need you here tonight."

"But I promised the Lady Ninane—"

"I don't care what you promised Ninane. You're my *court'esa*. I want you here."

"For what, exactly?" he asked with the faintest hint of a mocking smile.

Despite all her protestations to the contrary, Marla knew Corin thought her reluctance to use his services was based on fear and not her stated intention of being uncooperative. "I need you to teach me."

"Teach you what?"

"Everything."

"*Everything?*"

"Circumstances have changed, Corin. I believe my future is about to change radically, too." Marla hesitated, thinking of everything Nash had said in the Hall. *The Princess Marla stole my heart. Could I have a word in private, your highness? I shall not sleep in anticipation of seeing you again tomorrow.*

It could mean only one thing.

And, Marla had just realized in a panic, she was totally unprepared for it.

"I have decided I require the skills you can teach me, after all," she declared, stepping away from the door. "And I'm going to need them before tomorrow morning."

Corin smiled. "I am at your service, your highness."

Marla didn't care for his tone one bit. "You're damn right you are," she warned. "And you'd better be worth every penny Lady Alija paid for you."

"I believe, your highness," Corin assured her confidently, "you'll find you have little to complain about in the morning."

"All right, then," Marla said, looking about the room, a little uncertain about what should happen next. "Where do we start?"

ChAPTER 33

Kagan thought up any number of ways of getting Lernen to Warrinhaven for his sister's wedding during the journey south to Greenharbour. Most of the plans he came up with he abandoned almost as soon as he thought of them. Given the limited time he had to convince Lernen to accompany him north—which was about a day if they were going to get to Warrinhaven on time—there was really only one sure way of doing it.

The problem, of course, was if a single soul suspected Lernen's mind had been tampered with, it wouldn't matter what happened afterwards. The Warlords would tear the Sorcerers' Collective down rather than risk such a thing happening.

For their own protection, the Collective took great pains to spread the notion among the general population that a sorcerer would rather die than invade an unwilling mind. Kagan had also done much to encourage the belief that if a person simply refused to cooperate, it provided even the uninitiated with a solid mind block that could not be penetrated without the victim being aware of it—the irony being that there were probably only two sorcerers alive who even owned the skill. That wouldn't matter, however, if he was found out in *this* little escapade. Learning the High Prince had been so easily corrupted would destroy all his hard work in an instant.

It wasn't just his own life at risk, either. If anybody realized just how easy it was for someone like Wrayan to slip into another's mind, particularly a weak mind like Lernen Wolfblade's, they would demand the young sorcerer be put to death. Kagan suspected Alija Eaglespike owned a similar talent. She was an Innate, after all, and it would account for the reason Barnardo was so pliable in her hands. Fortunately, Innates with telepathic ability usually needed physical contact with the subject before they could scan their minds. But Alija would never reveal the limits (or lack of them) of her ability, for exactly the same reason Wrayan was so coy about it.

Kagan decided not to visit the palace immediately, once he returned home. It wasn't that he had the time to spare. He didn't. It was just there were things that needed his attention at the Sorcerers' Collective and he didn't want to give the impression that he had only returned to the capital to collect the High Prince. It would raise enough eyebrows as it was, Lernen suddenly leaving the city. Kagan had no wish to contribute to the rumours by letting people think *he* was the reason behind the High Prince's hasty departure. Kagan needed to be summoned to the palace and ordered to accompany Lernen to Warrinhaven. Everybody in the city *had* to believe the High Arrion was going along with the High Prince against his will.

After deciding the only way to do this without implicating himself or Wrayan was to set the wheels in motion before they arrived, Kagan instructed his apprentice to seek out Lernen's mind while they were still two days north of Greenharbour. He was both relieved and a little disturbed to discover, even from a hundred miles away, Wrayan was able to seek out the High Prince and lock onto his thoughts.

"He's building a garden," Wrayan announced. The young man sat cross-legged by the camp fire, hands resting on his knees, eyes closed, his fire-lit face a portrait of concentration.

"Why a garden?" Kagan asked, rubbing his hands together to warm them. He hated sleeping outdoors, but couldn't risk anybody witnessing this strange scene. There was a perfectly good inn a mere five miles from the secluded camp site Wrayan had found for them. *Maybe later,* Kagan thought. *I'm going to need a drink before this night is done, I think.*

"When did Lernen get interested in botany?"

"It's more like a zoo," Wrayan corrected without opening his eyes. "He wants to stock it with creatures of legend. Nymphs and gods and Harshini."

"Really?" Kagan asked with sigh. "And where is he planning to get these nymphs and gods and Harshini?"

"He's going to use . . . Gods, Kagan, this is like wading through a sewer." Wrayan took a deep breath before he continued. "He's going to find young men and women . . . slaves, I think . . . beautiful slaves . . . and have them dress up as Harshini and gods and whatever else his twisted little heart desires. He wants them to pretend. I think he's trying to duplicate the legendary sexual prowess of the lost races. Or get a taste of it, at any rate." Wrayan fell silent for a time, then cursed softly under his breath. "I think he's trying to find a way to stain their eyes black, too, but the last few experiments with dye blinded the slaves he tried it on, so he's looking for another answer."

Wrayan opened his eyes and stared balefully at Kagan. "Are we really risking everything to keep this idiot on the throne?"

Kagan didn't answer immediately, wondering if Wrayan realized his own eyes had turned completely black as the young sorcerer drew the power he needed to reach Lernen's mind from such a distance. There was no doubt in Kagan's mind any longer. Wrayan was Harshini, whether he wanted to be or not.

"Idiot he may be, Wrayan, but his time will pass. In the meantime, the damage Lernen can do as High Prince is far less than the damage a High Prince with an ambitious Innate sorcerer for a wife is capable of. Lernen is merely the lesser of two evils, I'm afraid."

"Have you considered getting rid of both of them? Anarchy is looking quite attractive from where I sit if the choice is between Lernen Wolfblade and Barnardo Eaglespike."

Kagan smiled thinly. "I'm sure it does. Can you actually influence Lernen's thoughts from this distance, or just read them?"

"I can influence him. I just suggested he order more wine, and he did it, so I shouldn't have a problem getting him to do anything else you want."

Kagan thought on the problem and then nodded. "Plant the idea in his mind that Murvyn Rahan has the prettiest slaves on all of Hythria. Make him believe he has to go to Warrinhaven himself to select them."

"Anything else?"

"Well, it would be nice if you could suggest he needs the High Arrion along for company on his trip to Warrinhaven. But we'll add that idea to his thoughts once we're in Greenharbour."

Wrayan was briefly silent and then he opened his eyes. They had returned to their normal colour. "Done."

"Just like that?"

"What did you expect?"

Kagan shrugged. "I'm not sure. I guess I just can't get used to seeing someone wield magic without reciting a spell."

"Honouring Zymelka, you mean?" Wrayan asked with a smile.

"What?"

"It's just something Dacendaran said to me."

Kagan shook his head in wonder. "Listen to you, talking about your conversations with the gods as if it's an everyday occurrence."

"For a while there, it was."

Kagan looked at him curiously. "Have you seen any gods lately?"

"Not since we left Greenharbour."

"Well, I suppose we should call it a night," Kagan said, settling against his saddle which he was using as a back rest. "Do you want me to take the first watch?"

"Wouldn't you be happier if we saddled up and headed into that village we passed just before sunset?"

"That would add an hour to our journey in the morning."

"I know," Wrayan agreed with a smile. "But your joints won't be aching in the morning if you sleep in a proper bed, which means you might be almost bearable company."

"You'd travel ten miles out of your way, just to put me in a good mood?"

"I'd walk across Hythria barefoot, if need be. Some things are just too precious to put a price on, Kagan."

The following evening, Kagan and Wrayan repeated the same exercise as the night before. In a secluded camp site some way off the main road to Greenharbour, Wrayan penetrated Lernen's mind, reinforcing the notion that the only place in all of Hythria he was likely to find slaves of the right quality for his Harshini garden was in Murvyn Rahan's slave stables at Warrinhaven.

This time there was no village close by to take shelter in once they were done, so Kagan suffered an uncomfortable night on the ground. At first light the following day, they could see Greenharbour's white walls in the distance and the glitter of the distant harbour beyond.

It was mid-morning by the time they cantered through the gates of the city. The Sorcerers' Collective's soldiers, smart and efficient in their silver tunics, saluted as the High Arrion and his apprentice rode under the portcullis. Kagan paused to have a word with the captain in charge of the gate detail and then rode on through the city to the Collective.

They arrived at the Sorcerers' Collective to little fanfare. Kagan was hopeful he might even sneak back without anybody noticing. He was just on the point of thinking he had achieved such a remarkable feat, when Tesha Zorell marched into his quarters without knocking to inform him the High

Prince had been asking for him for days and he was expected at the palace the moment he returned to Greenharbour.

Kagan didn't have to wait a day, after all.

"My Lord Palenovar!" Lernen gushed as soon as he spied Kagan walking down the brick path laid out among the foliage so carefully planted in the roof garden of the west wing. "Come! You must see my latest acquisition!"

Wondering what folly the High Prince had indulged in this time, Kagan pushed past several workmen and the thick branches of a golden palm to find Lernen in a small artificial clearing, admiring a statue that was so new it still had the ropes attached that had enabled the workmen to manoeuvre it into place. The prince was dressed in white, presumably in mourning for Glenadal Ravenspear, unless he'd killed another slave last night. Lernen often wore mourning clothes after he did that, as if the fact he mourned his dead slaves somehow lessened the heinous nature of their deaths.

"What do you think, Kagan?"

The High Arrion examined the statue for a time, trying to think of something suitable to say. Carved from a single slab of marble, the statue depicted a larger-than-life man and woman copulating. The figure of the woman was bent over backwards and her face looked quite agonised. The expression on the man's face, however, was almost blissful.

"It's called *The Rape of Medalon*."

"Medalon is a *country*, your highness," Kagan felt compelled to point out. "Not a woman."

Lernen rolled his eyes impatiently. "I know that! But it's symbolic, don't you see? The woman represents Medalon. The man represents the overthrow and destruction of the Harshini."

"I see," Kagan replied, thinking there was nothing more gullible than a man who knows nothing about art. The statue was, as far as Kagan was concerned, simply a man and a woman copulating. Lernen obviously felt the need to put a different spin on it to justify its purchase. That could mean only one thing in Kagan's mind. "Your highness, how much did it cost?"

"Not as much as it's worth," Lernen assured him. "I'm a pretty savage haggler when I want to be."

Which meant the artist probably quoted Lernen a price three times what it was actually worth and then allowed the High Prince to talk him into only paying twice what the damn thing was worth.

"And the rest of your new . . . garden? What's that costing the Hythrun treasury?"

"Oh, do stop being such an old fusspot, Kagan! I can afford it. You heard what Hablet agreed to pay me for Marla."

"That's not a done deal until your sister is married, your highness."

"I know, but what can go wrong now, eh? You worry far too much!" Lernen linked his arm through Kagan's and led him along the path, deeper into the garden. "This will be my pleasure garden, Kagan. Here my friends and I will be able to rediscover the joys of Harshini love. Frolic with gods and goddesses. One will be able to indulge in anything that tickles one's fancy. Boys. Girls. Harshini. Nymphs. Everything here will be a delight to behold!"

"I wasn't aware one could buy Harshini or nymphs in the Greenharbour slave markets, your highness."

"Of course you can't buy them here," Lernen chuckled, obviously assuming Kagan was joking. "But I do know where to get the most beautiful slaves in all of Hythria. The most beautiful in the whole world, for that matter. You'll never guess where."

"I'm sure I won't, your highness."

"Warrinhaven!" Lernen announced with delight. "I don't know what made me think of Lord Rahan's stables. The idea just popped into my head, really. But I'm sure I'm right. In fact, I'm already making arrangements to travel there at the end of the week. Do say you'll come, Kagan. We'll have such fun."

"I have duties here, your highness."

"Nonsense! What can be more important than attending your High Prince?"

Kagan looked at Lernen, with his painted lips, his nauseating preoccupation with his own pleasure, his total disregard for his responsibilities as High Prince. *Dear gods, what am I doing? Wrayan is right. Why are we risking everything for this fool?*

Because the alternative is to put an even bigger fool on the throne, a small voice in his head replied. *One with an Innate sorcerer for a wife.*

"Your highness, I'd be delighted to accompany you to Warrinhaven," the High Arrion said. "I'm sure it will be a journey you'll never forget."

chapter 34

Marla was a complete wreck for the next week as she waited for Nash to make his move, certain she wouldn't remember a thing Corin had taught her over the last few days when it came time for her own wedding night. That her wedding—to Nash, of course—was the reason the young lord "wanted a word in private" was a foregone conclusion in Marla's mind. It was perfectly logical as far as she was concerned. The High Arrion knew how she felt about Nash. And he had promised to find an alternative to Hablet of Fardohnya. So he'd done the right thing and arranged everything as it should be.

The whole castle had been in an uproar since Nashan Hawksword's arrival. Laran Krakenshield had arrived two days after Nash and had spent the next few days closeted with her Uncle Frederak, going over the borough's financial affairs. Marla had hardly seen him, but she'd seen plenty of Nash. He'd even taken her riding once, and been very impressed with her ability to control Sovereign, the sorcerer-bred horse she'd had since she first learned to ride. Although she'd been given Sovereign as a present by her late father on her seventh birthday, it was only in the past year or so that she'd grown confident enough to control him. But Nash didn't know that. He thought she'd been born in the saddle and she wasn't going to spoil the impression by letting him know how recently she'd stopped fearing the huge golden stallion.

"How are you feeling?" Lirena enquired, as she handed Marla a cup of mulled wine. The weather had closed in again. There would be no riding today.

"Fine."

"How's Corin doing?"

"He's very informative," Marla replied stiffly, a little annoyed that Lirena wanted details.

The old woman smiled. "Informative, eh?" She glanced over at Corin who was sitting on the floor near the hearth, feeding sticks into the fire. "Did you hear that, Corin? Her highness says you're *informative*."

The young man looked up from the fire and smiled languidly. "And you're going to spend the rest of the day wondering exactly what that means, aren't you, Lirena?"

The nurse made a noise that sounded rather crude, but before Marla could scold her for it there was a knock at the door. The princess's heart began to pound as Elezaar waddled to the door and pulled it open.

Elezaar turned to Marla. "Lord Krakenshield to see you, your highness. Are you in?"

Laran Krakenshield? What was he doing here? Then Marla smiled, realising he was probably here as Nash's envoy. "Don't be silly, Elezaar. Of course, I'm here. Now invite Lord Krakenshield in and close that door before you let all the warm air out."

Laran Krakenshield stepped into the room and bowed elegantly. "I bring you greetings from the High Arrion, your highness." He glanced at Corin, Elezaar and Lirena, his smile fading a little. "Are your slaves to be trusted, my lady?"

"As much as you, my lord," she replied coolly. Although she gave the impression she was calm, Marla could barely contain her excitement. He'd said he was here with greetings from the High Arrion! That meant she had guessed correctly: Kagan had kept his promise. She wished Laran would get past the formalities quicker and tell her about the offer. *I'll bet Laran always says the right thing. The polite thing. It's probably why Kagan chose him as Nash's envoy.*

Fighting to keep her composure, she sat a little straighter in her chair. "You bring more than just *greetings* from the High Arrion, I hope, Lord Krakenshield."

"I do, your highness. I bring you the news he assures me you've been praying for." He lowered his voice a fraction. "Kagan has found a way to circumvent your marriage to Hablet of Fardohnya."

"I'm to marry someone else?"

"Yes."

"Who's she marrying?" Lirena demanded, with all the fierce protectiveness of a lioness over her cub.

Laran didn't seem to mind. "Someone who can give her a whole province to rule over some day."

He smiled warily at Marla, removing the last of her doubts. It was true. Kagan had somehow arranged for her to marry Nashan Hawksword.

Lirena didn't see things quite so clearly. She glared at the Warlord, hands on her hips, unsatisfied with his evasive answer. "That could be the son of every Warlord in Hythria, except I don't see how, unless she is to marry the Hawksword boy! Barnardo Eaglespike's sons are only little children. Glenadal Ravenspear died without an heir. You don't have any children. Rogan Bearbow has a son, but he's less than a year old. Lord Foxtalon's only son is already married and Graim

Falconlance's two boys are a couple of years younger than Marla. Gods, Kagan didn't arrange for her to marry one of them, did he?"

"You have an excellent understanding of the lineage of Hythria's noble families, mistress," Laran told her. Marla thought he was amused by Lirena. And it worried her a little. If she was to marry Nash, why not just come right out and say so . . .

And then her heart sank and the cruel truth dawned on her. "But I'm not going to marry Nash, am I?" She wasn't crying, but her eyes glistened with unshed tears.

"Nash Hawksword?" Laran asked, a little confused. "No, of course not . . . Oh, I see . . ."

Marla wiped her eyes hurriedly and stared at her slaves. "Out! All of you!"

"Marla—" Lirena began sympathetically, but she pushed the old nurse away. "I said, out! Leave me! I wish to speak to Lord Krakenshield alone!"

The slaves reluctantly did as she bade them, closing the door softly as they left. Marla rose to her feet and walked to the fire, hugging her arms around herself. Suddenly it seemed just as cold inside as it did outdoors.

"Are you privy to the identity of my future husband?" she asked stiffly.

"Yes."

"And are you at liberty to divulge his identity to me?"

"Are you sure you want to know?"

She turned on him angrily. "What sort of question is that? Of course I want to—" Marla stopped abruptly, her eyes widening in horror. "Oh, by all the Primal Gods, it's *you*, isn't it?"

"I'm sorry."

Anger replaced disappointment with lightning speed. "Sorry? You're not sorry! Why even pretend you are?"

"Your highness, if you'd just let me explain—"

"Explain what, exactly? I'm not stupid! You think you can just waltz in here and marry me now you've got two provinces and two armies to back you up. I don't *believe* this!

What's the plan, my lord? Force me to marry you and hope I have a son and then get my brother to name your son as his heir?"

"That sums it up fairly succinctly, your highness," he agreed, looking rather startled that she'd seen through his intentions so quickly. "Although I prefer to think you might come to see the merits of our plan rather than consider yourself forced into anything."

"There's more chance of the Harshini coming back!" she retorted. "Did Kagan Palenovar really agree to this?"

"Yes."

"And my brother?"

"I'm not sure he's been told about it yet. But we're expecting him to agree."

Marla paced the small sitting room furiously, her agitation wearing a track across the carpet. "But . . . Dear gods! Hablet will be furious! He's likely to invade—" She stopped and slapped her forehead, cursing her own foolishness. "Which is why Nash turned up here with you and a couple of thousand men on winter manoeuvres, isn't it? I suppose you've got the other half of your army guarding Winternest."

"Those that aren't in Warrinhaven," he confirmed, looking at her with a puzzled frown. "I must say, your highness, you appear to have a remarkable grasp of the political implications of this . . . plan."

"The dwarf is a very good teacher, my lord."

"The dwarf?"

"Never mind," she said, stopping in front of him. "Do you really want to marry me, Laran?"

He smiled faintly. "Not really."

"Then why do this?"

"Do *you* really want to marry Hablet?"

"Of course not."

"Then this is your only way out. There isn't another one, Marla. It's not as if your brother has any other options. You're the only thing he has left to sell."

"I wish people would stop saying that."

"It's not a perfect solution," Laran admitted. "We both know that. You probably think I'm an old man, and I have a sister your age I still consider a child. But given the alternative, it's the lesser of two evils."

"It's so unfair!" Marla's anger was gradually giving way to despair. "Didn't anybody think *I* might like to be consulted?"

"You're being consulted now."

"I don't want this." For a moment she feared she sounded like a petulant and frightened child. Laran might even have been fooled had it not been for her earlier lightning-fast assessment of the political ramifications of his proposal. "In fact, I refuse!"

"Very well," he agreed, turning for the door.

Marla looked at him suspiciously. "What do you mean, *very well*?"

He stopped with his hand resting on the latch. "I'm not going to force myself on you, Marla. If you truly don't want any part of this, then we'll leave things as they are. You can go to Fardohnya in the spring and that will be the end of it."

"But—"

"Yes?" he asked, looking over his shoulder.

She was fighting back tears. "All you're offering me is a choice between two husbands I don't want. What makes you so special? Hablet can make me a queen."

"Go to Fardohnya and be a queen then," he replied. "It really doesn't make that much difference to me."

Marla couldn't believe he would be so callous about it. Then Laran hesitated, and something in his demeanour softened. As if he'd suddenly taken pity on her, he turned from the door and crossed the room. Taking Marla's reluctant hands in his, he held them and smiled at her encouragingly. "Marla, if you're clever enough to work out what this means, then you're smart enough to know what will happen if you refuse to become a part of it. I don't need to threaten you or make promises you know to be insincere."

"You don't care about me. You don't even know me."

"And you think *Hablet* cares about you?"

"Of course not!"

"Then why is this offer any worse than what you've already got on the table?"

"But you're no better than Hablet," she accused. "You don't want me. You're only interested in any children I might bear."

"Until and unless your brother produces a couple of healthy sons, your highness, every man, woman and child in Hythria is only interested in any children you might bear. Surely you appreciate that?"

She pulled her hands away from his grasp and crossed her arms against the chill. "And if I don't care? Suppose I have no interest in being the repository for Hythria's dreams for the Wolfblade line?" She smiled thinly and added, "For all you know, my lord, my sympathies lie with the Patriot Faction."

Fortunately, Laran Krakenshield had a sense of humour. He smiled at the very suggestion. "A Patriot, eh? You don't look like a dangerous insurgent, your highness."

"You're not exactly what I envisaged as my husband, either, Laran Krakenshield."

"I know," he agreed. "And, believe it or not, I do appreciate how hard this is going to be for you. But in the end, either you're interested in keeping Hythria out of Hablet's grasp or you're not. That's what it comes down to."

"It's not fair."

"And it's never going to be," he said.

Marla sighed, wondering how hope could turn to despair so quickly. She'd felt the same at the ball in Greenharbour when she'd discovered she was going to marry Hablet. *You'd think, by now, I'd be used to it.*

"Do you want my answer right now?"

He shook his head. "I'll be here for another few days. You have until I leave, your highness. I trust you'll come to the right decision and leave with me."

"I'll think about it," she promised.

"That's all I ask."

Laran turned for the door, but Marla had one more question for him. "When I . . . or rather *if* . . . I leave with you, my lord, may I bring my slaves with me?"

"You may bring your nurse," he told her.

"And my *court'esa*?"

"*Court'esa* are usually sold when a woman marries, your highness. It's a husband's duty to provide new *court'esa* for his wife if she requires them."

"Suppose I've become attached to the ones I have now?"

"Are they so important to you?"

"Would it make a difference to you if they were?"

Laran smiled. "That's a very loaded question, your highness."

"You're asking me to commit my allegiance, my body and my life to you, Lord Krakenshield, because you would have me believe you're a better man than the King of Fardohnya. I think it only fair that I find a way to take your measure."

He nodded in agreement. "You may keep the nurse and one of the *court'esa*. That's a better offer than you'd get from most husbands."

"Thank you."

"I'll speak to you before I leave?"

"Most assuredly."

Laran said nothing further, simply letting himself out of the room with a courtly bow, leaving Marla alone to contemplate a future that she had thought, up until a few days ago, could not slip any more out of control than it was already.

CHAPTER 35

Alija's still here in Greenharbour."

Kagan looked up from his desk with a frown. Tesha had dumped a pile of work on him that had accumulated in his absence and he was trying to dispose of as much of it as possible before he left for Warrinhaven. He glanced out of the window, surprised to see the sun quite low on the horizon. The decanter on his desk was empty, too. He must have been at it for hours.

"Are you sure?" he asked his apprentice, stretching his shoulders painfully. *I should teach a few of the secretaries to forge my signature and hand over my seal,* he thought wistfully. *That would cut down on the workload considerably.*

Wrayan flopped inelegantly into the seat opposite Kagan's desk. "I ran into Tarkyn Lye in the Library."

"What's a blind man doing in a library?" Kagan asked suspiciously.

"Returning a scroll Alija borrowed, according to Tarkyn," Wrayan said. "It was an interesting conversation, actually. He spent most of it trying to quiz me about what you were up to, while I subtly interrogated him about Alija's movements."

"Who won?"

"Neither of us, I fear. Did you know his mind is shielded?"

"How could that be? Tarkyn Lye hasn't got a magical bone in his body."

"Well, it's Alija's work, obviously. I wonder what he knows that she's afraid somebody else will find out if they read his mind?"

"Why don't you read his mind and find out?"

"I can't," Wrayan shrugged. "At least not without giving away that I'd been inside his head."

Kagan threw down his quill and leaned back in his chair. "Do you think he's heard Lernen is leaving Greenharbour tomorrow?"

"Oh, you can count on that, Kagan," Wrayan confirmed. "And if Tarkyn Lye knows about it, you can bet Alija does."

"Damn!"

"What are you going to do?"

"I'm not sure. Don't suppose you'd like to distract her for me?"

"How?"

Kagan grinned at him with a mocking leer. "Be nice to her.

A good wine . . . nice music . . . Barnardo's probably back in Dregian and she's always had a thing for you . . ."

"Oh, you are *so* funny," Wrayan replied without so much as a hint of a smile. "And the only reason Alija has a *thing* for me is because she's afraid I'm stronger than she is and she's itching to find out."

"Is she?"

"Is she what?"

"Stronger than you?"

"How would I know?" Wrayan asked uncomfortably.

"I don't think she can be," Kagan mused, quite seriously. "I suspect even a little bit of Harshini blood gives you far more power than an Innate."

"I'm not Harshini, Kagan."

"Of course you are, foolish boy. And don't contradict me. I'm your master."

Wrayan ignored that one. "What are you going to do?"

"I have no idea. The only thing I know for certain is that Alija cannot be allowed to learn the reason for Lernen's visit to Warrinhaven. Or be in a position to follow us when we leave tomorrow."

"She's not going to let you leave Greenharbour with Lernen unremarked. She'll probably want to come along, too. At the very least, she'll try to put a spy in Lernen's retinue."

"Speaking of Lernen's retinue," Kagan asked, "got any bright ideas about how we get rid of them for a week or two? I don't want our esteemed High Prince getting distracted and there's not a chance in all seven hells of making it to Warrinhaven in time with a couple of dozen of his giggling courtiers in tow."

"Poison them," Wrayan suggested.

"*Excuse* me?"

His apprentice smiled at the look on Kagan's face. "I don't mean fatally. Just arrange to have something put in the wine the first night out that makes them puke for a few days. Lernen will think it's an assassination attempt and you'll be able to bundle him out of the camp so fast, he won't even ask where you're taking him until you're halfway to Warrinhaven."

Kagan stared at him. "You worry me sometimes, boy."

"You keep forgetting where I come from, Kagan."

"I think you keep forgetting where you *are*," the sorcerer replied with a shake of his head. "Still, it's a capital idea. Wish I'd thought of it, actually."

"Consider it my small contribution to the cause."

Kagan studied Wrayan curiously. "You don't think we should be doing this, do you?"

Wrayan hesitated before answering. "If you want my honest opinion, then no, I don't think we should be doing anything like this at all."

"Why not?"

"Why *not*?" Wrayan asked in disbelief. "Have you taken a close look at the man you're so desperately trying to keep in power? I've been inside his head, Kagan. There's not a thought in Lernen Wolfblade's mind that isn't fixed firmly on his own pleasure, and they're pretty twisted pleasures at that, let me tell you. Do you know how often they carry slaves out of his rooms in sacks? This is a man who thinks drinking the milk of new mothers and the blood of young boys will make him more virile, for pity's sake!"

"How many slaves do you think he's killed?" Kagan asked.

"I don't know." Wrayan shrugged, throwing his hand up in disgust. "A score or two, maybe more."

"A small price to pay."

"For what?"

"For keeping Barnardo off the throne."

"I don't see how he could be much worse than what we face now."

"You don't? Then think about this. You are absolutely right about the High Prince. There's *not* a single thought in Lernen Wolfblade's mind that isn't fixed firmly on his own pleasure.

But the difference between Lernen and his cousin? Lernen doesn't care about anything else. He's not going to conquer anyone. He's not going to declare war on anyone. He's not even going to interfere when the Warlords have a dispute. Lernen doesn't want to do anything but pursue his own pleasure and that's just fine by me, because while he's chasing his phony nymphs and his pretend Harshini and his fake gods and goddesses around his garden on the roof of the west wing for a bit of hanky-panky, I've got some seriously competent people running this country, making sure we stay safe and prosperous. Lernen is a figurehead, Wrayan, nothing more. He's not the best figurehead we've ever had, but the alternative is far more disturbing."

"And for the vague hope of an heir some day who'll be more than a pointless figurehead, you'll entrust a third of the country's military power and wealth to Laran Krakenshield?"

"If my nephew fathers him, I'll bet you any amount you want that the next High Prince of Hythria will be a man to be reckoned with."

"There's a word for what you're doing, Kagan."

"Nepotism?" he asked with a smile.

"Treason was the word I was thinking of. And so was every man in that meeting in Cabradell, I might add, although none was game to say it aloud."

"It's only treason if we fail, Wrayan."

Wrayan looked at his master with a raised brow. "And you accuse the *Thieves'* Guild of having an ambiguous moral stance?"

That was a charge Kagan couldn't really defend, so he decided to change the subject. "What are we going to do about Alija?"

"I don't know," Wrayan sighed, clearly unhappy that his pleas to stop propping up Lernen had fallen on deaf ears. "Distract her somehow, I suppose. And we won't even repeat your earlier suggestion about me being involved."

"But it may be the only way," Kagan said thoughtfully.

"Kagan, not in a million years would Alija Eaglespike believe that I—"

"No, you misunderstand me," Kagan cut in. "What you said earlier is the plain truth. Alija's interest in you has always been centred on whether or not she's stronger than you. Maybe it's time we found out."

"I hope you're not suggesting what I think you are, Kagan."

"You need to challenge her."

"Challenge her how? We're sorcerers, Kagan, not Warlords calling each other out over an insult."

"We need to find a way to force Alija into confronting you."

"And then what?"

"And then we'll see who's the stronger. Provided you confront her at the same time I'm leaving Greenharbour with Lernen, she'll be none the wiser about what's happening in Warrinhaven."

"And suppose it turns out she's stronger than me, after all?"

"Then I imagine you're going to have a headache that goes on for days."

"I should be so lucky. She could kill me, Kagan. Or worse, I might kill her. I don't fancy having an angry Warlord on my tail for the rest of my days seeking vengeance for murdering his wife."

"Nobody is going to die and nobody will be seeking vengeance," Kagan assured him. "Just call her out and see what happens."

"You still haven't told me how, Kagan."

The High Arrion thought for a minute and then he smiled.

"Tarkyn Lye," he said confidently. "If there is one sure way to get to Alija Eaglespike, it's through Tarkyn Lye."

CHAPTER 36

Elezaar's fragile security came crashing down around his ears as he listened to Marla inform her slaves about the substance of Laran Krakenshield's proposal. They were gathered in her small, cosy sitting room the following morning, the weather grey and uninviting outside, while the princess detailed the High Arrion's unbelievable plan to rescue her from marriage to the King of Fardohnya by marrying her to the Warlord of Krakandar and Sunrise Provinces.

As he listened, Elezaar felt that same sense of impending doom he'd experienced when Alija Eaglespike walked into Venira's Emporium after Ronan Dell's assassination. He wasn't ready for this. While Elezaar had always known the chances were slim that Marla would be allowed to keep him after her marriage to Hablet, that event was months away yet. By then, he'd planned to make himself so valuable to her, so indispensable, that he would have been in a position to beg a favour of his mistress before she married. He could have asked her to send him somewhere safe. Give him as a gift, perhaps, to another household, far from Alija Eaglespike's influence.

Laran's offer effectively ended any hope of that happening. If Marla accepted this offer, then she would marry within days and Elezaar would be right back where he was the day he watched Alija's soldiers slaughter everybody—including his brother—in Ronan Dell's palace.

"You can't be thinking of accepting him!" Lirena cried, when Marla finished telling them what Laran had offered her, echoing exactly what Elezaar felt.

"Why not?"

"You're already promised to Hablet of Fardohnya!" the old nurse reminded her. "You can't go back on your word."

"I didn't actually give my word, Lirena," Marla pointed out. "In fact, I wasn't even asked about it."

"Nevertheless, Lirena has a point, your highness," Corin said, siding firmly with the nurse. It wasn't hard to figure out why, Elezaar thought. He was Alija's creature and Laran Krakenshield's offer would stop the Patriot Faction's plans dead in their tracks. He could do nothing else but try to dissuade Marla from accepting Laran.

Which meant—by default—Elezaar had no choice but to take the opposite argument.

"I think it's a brilliant idea," he announced, after Corin and Lirena had voiced their objections.

Marla turned to him with a puzzled look. "Why?"

Picking up her wine from the hearth where it had been warming, he walked across to her chair and handed it to her with a short bow. "For one thing, it means you won't have to marry Hablet."

"Yes, but that doesn't mean her highness wants to replace him with another unwanted husband," Corin countered. "Laran Krakenshield is merely a Warlord. Hablet is a king. She'll be much better off in Fardohnya."

"Whose side are you on, Corin?" Elezaar demanded. "Her highness doesn't belong in some foreign harem with a bunch of bored wives and *court'esa* all trying to claw their way over her for supremacy. She deserves much better than that."

He glanced at Marla out of the corner of his eye as he spoke, hoping the mental image he conjured up of a harem full of enemies would be enough to persuade the young princess. Although marriage to Laran was a looming danger, at least Laran Krakenshield had promised her she'd be allowed to keep one *court'esa* if she went with him. And she *had* to believe Elezaar was the only one who understood her plight. He was gambling on the fact that if she chose Laran, and Corin opposed the union, it wouldn't be the handsome young *court'esa* who left Highcastle with his mistress tomorrow.

Marla sipped her wine thoughtfully as the slaves argued around her, apparently putting his lessons to good use. It was impossible to tell what she was thinking these days, when she set her mind to it.

"Whose side are *you* on, little man?" Corin asked. "You're encouraging the princess to renege on a deal her brother made and bring dishonour to Hythria and the entire Wolf-blade House."

"Somehow, I don't think my brother spends a lot of time agonising over the honour of the Wolfblades," Marla remarked. "Or Hythria."

"The whole thing reeks, if you ask me," Lirena grumbled.

Elezaar thought carefully before he spoke again, glancing cautiously at Corin. The handsome *court'esa* had been rather full of himself since Marla decided to make use of his services—as if sharing her bed had somehow elevated him in the pecking order. Elezaar thought it high time the young man realized that being useful in bed didn't make one particularly useful anywhere else. The dwarf had tied himself in knots befriending and instructing the princess since he'd come to Highcastle and no pretty-boy spy of Alija Ea-glespike's was going to stand in the way of his secure future. Not now. Not when it was so close he could almost taste it.

But he had to be subtle. Cautious. Marla could be a petulant child at times, but she was whip-smart when the mood took her and not easily swayed by flattery. The truth, Elezaar decided, was the only way to win this argument. Corin couldn't fight that.

"There's a lot of very powerful people in Hythria who don't wish Princess Marla's wedding to Hablet to go ahead," Elezaar told Corin, although his words were meant for the princess. "I'm not in the least bit surprised that some have come up with a way to prevent it. And Lord Krakenshield said the High Prince would be waiting at Warrinhaven. One assumes that if he's involved, then the plan is legitimate."

"I suppose the real question here is how much you trust Laran Krakenshield," Corin said.

"What do you mean?" Marla asked.

"Well, the man's obviously got ambitions far beyond your hand in marriage, your highness. If you ally yourself with him and he fails, you'll be guilty of treason, too."

"Fails in what?" Elezaar scoffed. "The man wants to marry our mistress, Corin, that's all. Hardly the stuff of treason."

"That's what he wants today," the *court'esa* countered. "But once he's married to the High Prince's sister, what then? How long before he starts eyeing off the throne?"

Marla looked at the two of them, shaking her head. "Laran suggested nothing of the sort. You're both mad!"

Elezaar turned to the princess with a grin. "Actually, probably only one of us is mad, your highness. Your job is to decide who."

She turned to her nurse, searching for some hint that would help her make the hardest decision of her life, but all Lirena could do was shrug helplessly. "Don't look at me, lass. I don't know what you should do."

"And you, Corin? You obviously think I should marry Hablet."

"Yes, your highness. I think you should honor the agreement your brother made months ago in Greenharbour. Otherwise we could be facing a war with Fardohnya."

She sipped her wine, her brows drawn together thoughtfully, before turning to the dwarf. "And you, Elezaar? You seem to think I should accept the offer Lord Krakenshield has made."

"I don't think it's an offer, your highness."

"What do you mean?"

"If your brother is waiting at Warrinhaven for you, then there's no crown awaiting you in Fardohnya any more. I think Lord Krakenshield made you an offer because he wants to give you the illusion that you have some control over your fate. What's more, I suspect if you deny him, it will make little difference. There are some powerful people behind this, my lady. They won't take kindly to you defying them."

"So you don't think it matters what I decide?"

"Not in the slightest. I think this was decided some time ago and a long way from here."

"That's silly!" Corin declared. "Why ask the princess if she has no choice?"

Elezaar shrugged. "Maybe he's just being nice."

"Do you think so, Elezaar?" Marla asked, full of hope. Even if she had no choice, the idea that the man she was being forced to marry had at least some basic human decency in him was something she needed to cling to.

"He's a Warlord," Corin reminded them. "*Nice* isn't a word you use a lot when describing the highborn. Particularly not a Warlord."

"Glenadal Ravenspear was always nice to me. He was a Warlord."

Marla sounded a little hurt. And she was starting to get annoyed at Corin. That augured well for Elezaar's future. If he kept this up, Corin had no chance of being the one she chose to take with her to Warrinhaven.

"And Laran Krakenshield is the man Lord Ravenspear chose to succeed him, your highness," Elezaar reminded her. "I think you'd be well served remembering that."

Marla nodded absently, taking another sip of the mulled wine. Elezaar wished he had some magical power, some way of reading her thoughts. Better yet, some way of influencing them.

"Leave me," she ordered abruptly. "I want to think about this some more without you all jabbering at me." The three of them rose to their feet and headed for the door, experience having taught them the futility of trying to defy the princess when she was in this sort of mood. "Not you, Fool."

Elezaar stopped, a little concerned, and returned to her chair by the fire as the other two left. She hadn't called him Fool for months.

"Your highness?"

Marla leaned back in her chair and studied him for a moment before she spoke. "Tell me what you know about Laran Krakenshield."

"What makes you think I know anything about him, your highness?"

"You hear things. I know you do. People ignore you because they think you're a halfwit, just like they used to ignore me when I was a child. Or they don't see you at all. I want to know what you've heard about him."

"Not much, your highness," he admitted, cursing his inability to have foreseen this. If only he'd known Laran might make an offer for Marla, he would have made it his business to know everything there was to know about the Warlord of Krakandar. Elezaar was a survivor, however. He knew how to turn his ignorance to his advantage. "That says something in itself, though, your highness."

"What does it say?"

"It says he probably doesn't have that many bad habits. Or if he does, he keeps them to himself."

"I don't understand."

"The slaves' grapevine is very effective, your highness. I could tell you things about some people you'd never dream of. Trust me on this. The worse the gossip, the quicker it finds its way through the slave ranks. If I've heard nothing about Laran Krakenshield, then there's a good chance it's because he's never done anything that warranted the gossip of his slaves." He smiled, as he remembered something that might help his cause. "I could tell you about his sister, though."

"His sister?"

"Lady Darilyn Taranger. She lives in Greenharbour."

"So?"

"Well, rumour has it, Lady Darilyn had a bit of an accident a couple of years ago, not long after her husband died. Had to have it taken care of rather discreetly, so the story goes."

"You mean she had an abortion?" Marla asked impatiently. "What of it? Women do it all the time when they've had a mishap."

"Lady Darilyn comes from a very wealthy family, your

highness. There's no need for an abortionist in that household. Her *court'esa* are all Loronged males. Every one of them is sterile."

"So you're saying her babe wasn't fathered by a *court'esa*?"

"I believe, at the time, the best odds were on Lord Oscarn, husband of Lady Darilyn's good friend, Lady Syble. *He's* known in the lower quarters, by the way, as 'The Hound' because according to his *court'esa* he likes to do it doggy style."

In spite of herself, Marla laughed. "You truly are the most scandalous wretch, Elezaar."

"Actually, I'm a very bad and disloyal scandalous wretch, your highness."

"Disloyal? To whom?"

"Slaves the world over, your highness. I really shouldn't be repeating our gossip to my mistress. It's considered very bad form."

That seemed to amuse her. "But it's perfectly all right to talk about your betters among yourselves in such a manner, is it? Do you have names like 'The Hound' for all your masters?"

"Most of them," he admitted.

"What do they call Aunt Lydia below stairs?"

"It would be worth more than my life to tell you, your highness."

"Do the slaves have a name for me?"

"It would be worth more than my life to tell you that, too."

"Then far be it from me to condemn you to death, Fool."

Marla rose to her feet and walked to the window. The weather hadn't improved much since they'd woken this morning. It was still a sea of impenetrable white beyond the glass. She smiled distantly, but didn't press him any further on the matter.

You will be condemning me to death if you send me away! he wanted to shout at her. But he couldn't risk it. It wouldn't do at all to let Marla know how desperate he was.

"I'd gladly die for you, my lady," he told her instead, with a courtly bow.

"Prove it," she ordered, turning to look at him.

Elezaar smiled. "Take me with you when you leave tomorrow. I promise, the first chance I get, I'll die for you."

"*If* I leave . . . I might decide to take Corin."

She's teasing, Elezaar told himself. *Please gods, let her be teasing!*

"But you *need* me, your highness."

Marla sighed heavily, downed the rest of her wine and turned to stare at the blanketing white storm outside. "What I need, Elezaar, is for somebody to cast a spell on me and turn me into a man. That way, I don't have to marry anybody."

"And if we can't arrange that by tomorrow morning? What will you do?"

Marla shrugged unenthusiastically. "Marry Laran Krakenshield, I suppose."

"Then I should start packing?" he suggested, hoping he didn't sound as desperate as he felt.

Marla turned to Elezaar and asked the one question that made him go weak at the knees with relief. "Do you think Alija would be offended if I sold her gift? I don't suppose I'm going to need Corin after this."

"Why don't you send him back to her?" Elezaar suggested, hard pressed to contain his feelings. "He's a valuable slave, after all. I'm sure your cousin will appreciate the opportunity to recoup some of her investment. She may even decide to keep him for herself."

"That's not a bad idea. I'm certainly not going to leave him here for Ninane to play with. Will you compose the letter to Alija? If we're leaving tomorrow, I don't think I'm going to have the time."

Impulsively, he grabbed the princess's hand and kissed it devotedly.

"Your highness," Elezaar replied with a beaming smile, "I speak the truth when I say there is nothing you have ever asked me to do which would give me more pleasure."

CHAPTER 37

Tarkyn was late for their regular morning meeting, which did nothing to lighten the mood Alija was in. Everything was taking far too long this morning and Tarkyn's tardiness simply added to her frustration.

Although she had dispatched a messenger to Dregian to insist Barnardo return to Greenharbour, it would be days before her husband could get here and Lernen would have left Greenharbour by then with Kagan Palenovar, heading for a destination it seemed only the gods and Lernen Wolfblade were privy to. The chances of her being invited to attend Lernen on his journey were remote. The High Prince knew Barnardo wanted his throne and was in no mood to accommodate him, or his wife.

The purpose of Lernen's journey—she had gleaned from her spies—was to buy slaves for the pleasure garden he was building on the roof of the palace's west wing. Her spies had also confirmed that Kagan had agreed to go with the High Prince with some reluctance. That made her feel a little easier. Had Kagan displayed any enthusiasm for the task, she would have been instantly suspicious.

Then again, Kagan would know that. Was his reluctance feigned for her benefit?

It gave Alija a headache just to think about it.

"My lady, Tarkyn Lye has returned," a slave announced with a bow.

"Tell him I wish him to attend me at once."

"I . . . er . . ." The young woman hesitated before continuing. "That might be difficult, my lady."

"Difficult? Why?"

"I think you'd best see for yourself, my lady."

Throwing down her quill with a very unladylike curse, Alija rose to her feet and followed the slave down the stairs to the main foyer of the house. It was a large circular chamber with a beautifully tiled floor and a domed ceiling made of frosted glass tiles that flooded the hall with light. Tarkyn Lye was standing in the middle of the foyer staring up with his blind eyes at the dome, a strange look of bliss on his face.

"Tarkyn? Where have you been?"

"See the pretty lights," he replied in a dreamy, sing-song voice.

"Tarkyn!"

"I can see the pretty lights. All the pretty lights. Pretty lights are pretty . . ."

"Are you drunk?" She turned on the young female slave who had fetched her from the study. "Do you know where he's been?"

"No, my lady. I assumed he was on an errand for you since yesterday. He hasn't been back to the house all night."

"Not drunk," Tarkyn sighed. "Pretty lights."

Concerned now rather than annoyed, Alija stepped closer to her *court'esa* and gently laid a hand on his shoulder. "Tarkyn?"

"See the pretty lights?"

"Yes," she agreed, like a mother talking to a small child. "I see them. Where have you been?"

"Looking at the pretty lights."

"But *where* were you looking at the pretty lights?"

"Wrayan showed them to me."

Alija stared at him in shock. "Wrayan *Lightfinger*?"

"Lightfinger made the pretty lights happen. He let me see them."

Without waiting for Tarkyn to explain, Alija plunged into his mind. The shield she had so carefully constructed around him to protect the knowledge he carried was gone. Whoever had done this had hunted through Tarkyn's mind like a thief rifling through the contents of a drawer looking for valuables. The damage probably wasn't permanent, but it was clumsy.

Wrayan had made no attempt to hide what he had done. Even the "pretty lights" that Tarkyn was so enchanted with had been placed in his mind quite deliberately.

It was almost as if Wrayan wanted her to know who had done this.

"I'll kill him."

"My *lady*?" the young slave gasped.

Alija hadn't realized she'd spoken aloud. Nor did the act of giving voice to her anger lessen her need for vengeance. Wrayan Lightfinger would pay for this, and pay dearly. He had violated something so close to her, something so personal, that it was almost like being raped. Trawling the depths of Tarkyn's mind, with its intimate knowledge of her thoughts and feelings, her fears and her insecurities, was a crime more heinous than rape. It wasn't just the intelligence Tarkyn might have that made him valuable. Tarkyn knew the inner workings of Alija's very soul.

Even more disturbing was the realisation that Wrayan owned such a level of skill. She had thought the High Arrion's apprentice nothing more than a bundle of raw power. Where had he learned to dismantle a shield like the one she had used on Tarkyn, without permanently damaging the *court'esa*'s mind?

But the thing that infuriated Alija the most was the notion that a mere apprentice would dare to taunt her like this. Tarkyn's condition was a blatant challenge. If Kagan—and there was no doubt in her mind that the High Arrion was behind this—had simply wanted to interrogate Tarkyn, he could have done it at any time. And could have killed the *court'esa* afterwards, making his death look like the work of cutpurses or assassins if he seriously wanted to conceal his hand in the crime. But to do this; to destroy the mind shield and then send Tarkyn back home waxing lyrical about "pretty lights"—that was more than just a goad. It was an outright declaration of war.

Alija reached into Tarkyn's mind again and he slumped at

her feet, unconscious. She couldn't let him spend the day wandering around making a fool of himself going on about the pretty lights.

"Tressa, have Tarkyn taken to his room, please. And have my litter brought around."

"You're going out, my lady?"

"There is some urgent business I must take care of at the Sorcerers' Collective. I'll be in my study. Call me when the litter is ready."

"Yes, my lady," Tressa replied with a low bow.

Alija turned towards the stairs. Her anger was like a slow-burning fire, simmering so close to the surface she wanted to scream.

You won't get away with this, Wrayan Lightfinger, she vowed silently. She would take him apart herself and then hand the pieces over to the Sorcerers' Collective for them to deal with the remainder. Wrayan had violated so many Collective prohibitions about invading another mind, they were almost too numerous to count. Even if she couldn't prove conclusively that Kagan was behind the attack on Tarkyn, Wrayan Lightfinger was finished in the Collective. She would see to that personally.

Taking a moment to calm her ragged breathing, Alija stopped at her desk and leaned on it to gather her wits. She needed to be calm. In control. Justified as she was in her anger, she couldn't risk underestimating her adversary. He'd had the skill to dismantle her shield.

Who knows what else he can do?

Once she felt a little more in control, Alija moved to the lacquered cabinet beneath the window and waved her arm across it to release the magical locks that kept its contents safe from prying eyes. She heard the faint click of the lock and opened the doors to reveal a stack of scrolls, many of them ancient and on the verge of crumbling into dust. Withdrawing one of the scrolls with particular care, she relocked the cabinet and took it back to her desk.

With the greatest of care Alija unrolled the ancient document, wishing she could read the Harshini script more fluently. But she knew enough to understand the power of this particular scroll. Knew enough to realize that with its power, Wrayan Lightfinger was no match for her, no matter how strong he was. With this scroll, she would be able to use his strength against him. The harder he fought, the stronger she would become.

"My lady," Tressa announced from the door. "Your litter is ready."

"Tell them I'll be right down," Alija replied. "Has Tarkyn been taken care of?"

"Yes, my lady. Bildon and Franken carried him to his room, and Plia said she'd stay with him until you got back."

"Good."

"Will he be all right, my lady?"

The girl sounded quite worried. Alija glanced at her for a moment, wondering if Tarkyn had been amusing himself with the young woman and her concern was that of a lover, or if he simply commanded a great deal of respect among the other slaves. She wasn't a particularly attractive girl. Alija made a point of buying plain, even downright unattractive female slaves, nor did her House own any female *court'esa*. She didn't want Barnardo getting distracted. But the girl's appearance wouldn't bother Tarkyn. He was blind. Nor did it matter. So long as Tarkyn was there whenever Alija had need of him, she really didn't care what he got up to with the house slaves.

"He'll be fine. Once I've had a chance to attend to him."

"Very good, my lady."

Alija took one last long look at the carefully inscribed instructions then rolled the document up carefully and returned it to the cabinet under the window before she headed downstairs for the inevitable confrontation with Wrayan Lightfinger.

CHAPTER 38

Wrayan waited for Alija in the main temple of the Sorcerers' Collective. He waited beneath the Seeing Stone, wondering, if Kagan's theory that he was part Harshini was true, did that mean he could use the Seeing Stone? If he stepped up to the crystal monolith and placed his hands upon it, would he connect with Sanctuary, the lost city in the Sanctuary Mountains in Medalon? Would he be able to speak to the hidden fortress that supposedly housed the last of the Harshini who had retreated there when the purge in Medalon became too dangerous for any of their number to be seen in the world of men? Would the impossibly beautiful face of a Harshini appear in the depths of the stone, smiling and serene, with eyes as black as onyx, as they were depicted in much of the artwork in the Sorcerers' Collective?

The massive crystal resting on its black marble base loomed over the apprentice. Were there even any Harshini left? Had any actually survived the purge, or was the story that the survivors had all fled to Sanctuary simply a tale put about by the Sorcerers' Collective to reassure those pagans who could not accept the peaceful race might have been so easily obliterated by a bunch of vindictive, atheist women?

The temple was empty on Kagan's command; the candles in their silver sconces illuminating the crystal had burned down quite a way, Wrayan noticed with a frown. The sorcerers who regularly came here to beseech the gods for their assistance had been told to stay out of the temple. It wasn't that they needed a large clear space for this showdown. Kagan just thought it would be better if nobody else witnessed it.

Wrayan glanced over his shoulder at the empty, cavernous temple. The geometric pattern on the tiled floor drew one's eye, quite deliberately, to the centre of the hall. But the building remained empty, as it had for hours. Wrayan was thirsty. He should have thought to bring something to drink.

Perhaps Kagan was wrong. Maybe Alija didn't care what happened to Tarkyn Lye. Or she was out when Tarkyn arrived home and didn't even know about his condition yet. Maybe all of this was a pointless waste of time because Alija was out shopping . . .

On the other hand, the chances were good that she knew something was amiss. All Wrayan's attempts to find Tarkyn in the last few hours had resulted in a puzzling silence. It wasn't that he couldn't locate and crack Tarkyn's mind shield any time he wanted; it was as if Tarkyn no longer existed.

Had Alija discovered her *court'esa* had been tampered with and killed him in a rage?

Wrayan thought that highly unlikely. Not after having rifled through Tarkyn Lye's thoughts. The blind *court'esa* knew things about Alija that were more dangerous to her than a room full of assassins. *There is no way she would allow his violation to go unavenged.*

But where was she?

Had she not taken the bait? Had she seen through the trap and decided to follow Kagan and Lernen out of the city instead of seeking revenge for the attack on her slave? Was Alija so easily distracted? Would she fall for such a transparent attempt to thwart her plans?

Doubt began to eat at Wrayan's confidence. This plan was as ill-conceived as it was dangerous. Alija was no fool. Surely she would connect the sudden and unprovoked attack on Tarkyn Lye and the departure of the High Prince.

She's not going to fall for this . . . She's not coming . . .

And then he felt her approaching, on the very edge of his awareness, even before he heard the doors boom closed as someone entered the temple. She was drawing on her power, maybe in an attempt to intimidate him. Wrayan stared up at the large crystal of the lost Harshini and wondered what a Harshini would do in his position. *Smile and do nothing probably,* he thought. *The Harshini were like that.*

"Hello, Alija," he said, without turning around.

Alija stopped behind him, her mind heavily shielded.

"Wrayan."

"Come to beseech the gods for help?" he asked, turning to face her.

She was wearing her formal black robes, the embroidered hem of her gown whispering across the tiled floor, her expression hidden by the dark hood she had pulled up to shadow her face. Alija didn't wear her formal robes often. She was wearing them now, Wrayan was certain, to remind him who was the sorcerer and who was the apprentice. Wrayan hadn't bothered to change into his robes for this. Besides being far too melodramatic, it was too damned hot in Greenharbour for the heavy woollen garments.

"*You* might want to beseech them," Alija suggested coldly, as she stopped before him. "You're probably going to need the gods' help by the time I'm through with you."

Wrayan forced a smile he really didn't feel. "Being a bit dramatic, aren't you, Alija?"

"Do you want me to show you *dramatic,* Wrayan Lightfinger?" she asked, throwing back the black hood. There was something strange about her shielded power, some element Wrayan was unfamiliar with.

"I've seen plenty of dramas, my lady," he informed her, holding his ground by sheer force of will. Power emanated from her like a furnace. He could feel it pulsing with her rage. "There are some rather interesting dramatics going on in Tarkyn's head, don't you agree?"

"You had no right to harm my slave."

"I didn't harm him. He'll be fine in a day or so." Wrayan smiled. "Once the pretty lights fade."

"Do you have any idea of what I could do to you?" Alija hissed. "Do you know how many of the Sorcerers' Collective's laws you have violated, or can't you count that high?"

"Is Tarkyn Lye really the father of your children?" Wrayan countered.

She hesitated, clearly disturbed that Wrayan had been able to penetrate her *court'esa*'s mind so thoroughly. "I will destroy you for this, Wrayan Lightfinger," she promised, her quiet confidence more threatening than if she'd shouted it at him. "And then I'll take that fool you call the High Arrion and bury him alongside you."

"You'd report my crime to the Sorcerers' Collective?" he asked, deliberately trying to draw the conversation away from Kagan. "Knowing what I've learned about you? That's an awfully big risk, Alija."

"Oh, I wouldn't worry about that too much, Wrayan. By the time I'm through with you, whatever is left of your pathetic little mind won't be in a position to reveal anything."

"You're that good, are you?"

"Let's find out, shall we?" she suggested.

Wrayan braced himself mentally, reasonably certain he could survive anything she threw at him. *Alija is bristling with unleashed power, but I'm stronger and more—*

The blast she let fly lifted Wrayan off his feet and slammed him into the base of the Seeing Stone, knocking the wind from his lungs. She blasted him again, hammering him against the black marble, cracking his head this time. White lights danced before Wrayan's eyes.

Alija wasn't trying to be subtle, or even particularly clever. She was interested only in inflicting damage on her opponent, be it physical or mental. Between trying to fill his breath-starved lungs and the pain of the fractured skull he was sure she'd just inflicted on him, it was all Wrayan could do to keep his mind shielded.

"Come on, Wrayan, why don't you fight back?" Alija coaxed with an evil smile. "Too afraid to hit a woman?"

With several deep, gasping breaths, Wrayan pulled himself to his feet. "I was waiting for you to get serious," he managed to respond. It sounded brave, but Alija wasn't fooled.

"You *can't* fight back," she concluded with malicious delight. "Can you? You can't do anything! All that power to burn and you haven't got the faintest idea what to do with it."

"Believe whatever it takes . . . to make you feel better, Alija." Wrayan was on his feet again, but his head was pounding and the white lights refused to go away. A dribble of blood trickled annoyingly down his neck as he clung to the base of the Seeing Stone for support.

"Oh, you've no *idea* how good it makes me feel," she told him, taking a step closer. "How frustrating it must be for you. You can touch the source. You can feel it. You can even draw on it now and again. But without training, you're never going to be able to do much more than what you did to Tarkyn, are you? Kagan can't teach you anything. He's got no right to even call himself a magician. And the Library's no good to you either, because anything useful in the Library about manipulating Innate power is missing, isn't it?"

"And there's no prize for guessing where that information went, is there?"

Alija blasted him again, just because she could, Wrayan thought, as his body was slammed against the Seeing Stone once more. She held him there, his feet dangling a few inches from the floor, pinned against the huge crystal, unable to move.

"Ah, Wrayan," she sighed as she stepped closer, changing her tactics abruptly to keep him off balance. "We could have been so good together, you and I. With my skill, your power . . . What a pity it's all going to end with you being thrown out of the Collective with your mind burned to a cinder."

"That's not the way the Collective works." Wrayan struggled against the power that held him, but without dropping his shield there was nothing he could do to ward off her attack. He was quite certain he could hurl Alija across the temple if he was prepared to drop his defences. Of course, the moment he did, she would be able to see into his mind and the reason for this charade would become immediately evident. He had to give Kagan all the time he could.

"It won't be the Collective who destroys your mind, Wrayan Lightfinger."

"I don't believe you'd do it," he challenged.

She stepped even closer, so close he could feel her breathing on him. She was no longer trying to cause him pain. Quite the opposite, in fact. "You don't believe I'd *do* it?" she asked in a low, menacing voice. "Or you don't believe I *can* do it?"

He was still pinned against the Seeing Stone, his feet dangling just above the intricately tiled floor, as Alija stood on her toes and pressed her body close to his. Her breath was hot on his face, her lips like a silken whisper against his cheek. On the verge of panic, he tried to pull away, but he was held fast by her power. Alija's tongue flickered over his lips, her *court'esa*-trained fingers tracing a path of delicate torment along his inner thigh.

Wrayan had braced himself for almost anything but this.

"Come on, Wrayan," she coaxed in a silky voice that seemed to have a magic all of its own. "We don't have to fight to resolve this. There are . . . other ways . . ."

"Alija . . ."

"I can teach you, Wrayan," she breathed in his ear. "Let me show you wonders you haven't even dreamed of yet . . ."

Wrayan's shielded mind screamed out its silent defiance while his body gave every indication that Alija was winning this confrontation and winning it comprehensively. There was, he noted with a sort of detached academic interest, no physical connection whatsoever between those parts of his anatomy that hungered for Alija and his brain, which was fully aware of the fact that she was simply trying to coax him into dropping his shield.

Alija kissed him then, with all the expert skill of a *court'esa*. Wrayan tried to fill his mind with thoughts of anything else as her tongue darted across his teeth and her hands set fire to his loins, but his treacherous flesh was far too interested in what it was being offered to care about what his mind wanted. Another voice in his head pointed out, quite reasonably, that his mission was to delay Alija. Distract her. And this was certainly distracting. It almost drowned out the voice screaming *"FIGHT HER, WRAYAN, DON'T GIVE IN!"*

"Oh, gods!" Wrayan moaned as he grabbed at the notion of fighting like a dying man grabbing for a lifeline in a storm.

He had to put an end to this. And he had to do it right now. With his concentration fractured into myriad pieces, he gathered what little reason he could muster and prepared to lower his shield, with every intention of pinning Alija to the ceiling, if that's what it was going to take . . .

She was waiting for him. The moment his shield wavered, Wrayan's mind was invaded. Alija attempted nothing other than damage. She didn't try to read his thoughts. She simply blasted her way through with a power Wrayan was certain had somehow been magically enhanced.

In the split second between when his shield faltered and Alija's blast, he had time to wonder how she'd learned to do that. Then Wrayan slumped to the floor, the pain beyond description.

Alija stepped away from him, smoothing down her robes. She looked at his limp body with contempt.

"Fool," she said scathingly.

The sorcerer stepped over his body and headed towards the temple entrance without looking back. He heard the hinges squeal as the massive doors opened and heard the doors boom shut behind her.

And then he lost consciousness.

CHAPTER 39

As Wrayan had predicted, within a day Tarkyn's "pretty lights" had faded. It took another day or two for him to recover completely, but it seemed Wrayan had done Alija's *court'esa* no lasting harm. By the time Barnardo returned from Dregian Castle, Tarkyn Lye was back to normal and Alija had made the decision to say nothing about the incident to her husband. She wasn't sure what to tell him anyway, because she had no proof of Wrayan Lightfinger's treachery. She had nothing at all.

Wrayan Lightfinger had disappeared.

With the High Arrion's apprentice defeated, lying unconscious on the floor of the temple (possibly even dead—Alija didn't actually take the time to check), she had triumphantly hurried from the Temple of the Gods to fetch a witness to her victory. Kagan would have no chance of defending himself against her accusations with his apprentice caught red-handed, and she intended to make the most of this blatant disregard for the Collective's rules.

The obvious choice was Tesha Zorell, the Lower Arrion and one of Alija's mentors during her apprenticeship. She had hurriedly explained what had happened between her and Wrayan (the carefully edited version, of course) as she all but dragged Lady Tesha into the temple to find the evidence of Kagan's abuse of his power as both High Arrion and apprentice master.

"I cannot believe the High Arrion was behind any attack on your *court'esa*, my lady," Tesha Zorell was saying as the doors boomed closed behind them. "And to accuse his apprentice—"

"Wait until you've interrogated Wrayan Lightfinger yourself, Lady Tesha," Alija advised. "Then tell me I'm not the victim of the High Arrion's deliberate campaign of terror designed to intimidate me and my husband."

They reached the Seeing Stone. Tesha looked around impatiently. "Well? Where is he?"

"I left him right here." For the first time, Alija began to feel uncertain. "He was . . . he couldn't have . . . someone must have moved him."

"Someone must have moved him, eh?" Tesha asked. "Another of the conspirators who are out to get you and your husband, I suppose?"

"I am not imagining things, Tesha!" Alija snapped at the older woman. "Wait until you see what he did to Tarkyn Lye!"

"If your *court'esa* came home a babbling wreck, my dear, it probably just means he spent an interesting night sampling the delights of a yakkah-pipe."

"You think I can't tell the difference between intoxication and deliberate interference?"

"I think, Alija, that you are looking for excuses to blame people for things, to fit your view of the world," Tesha informed her sympathetically. She patted the younger woman's arm and added with a smile, "I know it's been awkward for you, Alija, and I'd help you if I could, but if you haven't got one of these alleged conspirators waiting for me here, I'd like to get back to work."

Alija didn't know what to say. Tesha was her friend, but she was the Lower Arrion first and foremost. Her loyalty had always been to the Collective rather than any individual. When the Lady of Dregian wasn't able to reply, Tesha smiled sadly and turned on her heel; her footsteps slowly fading into the distance followed by the squeal of the doors and the accompanying boom a few moments later.

"This isn't over, Wrayan Lightfinger!"

Alija's shout bounced off the walls, echoing around the empty temple.

She looked around, unable to feel even a hint of the lingering magic she should have been able to sense had Wrayan been anywhere in the vicinity. Although she would make enquiries to see if anyone had seen him being spirited out of the temple, Alija knew in her gut that somehow, inexplicably, Wrayan Lightfinger had vanished so completely it was unlikely she would ever be able to find him.

Barnardo was a little peeved to be recalled, but on hearing the news that Kagan Palenovar and the High Prince had left the city for some unknown destination, he quickly got over his initial irritation. The mystery deepened, however, when the dozen or so courtiers who had accompanied the High Prince on his journey straggled back into Greenharbour looking rather forlorn and unwell a couple of days after their departure. It only took another day for the story to circulate throughout the city that there had been an attempt to poison the High Prince the first night out of Greenharbour and the High Arrion had magically transported him away to a place where they would both remain until it was determined safe for the High Prince to return.

Alija thought the rumour the most unbelievable nonsense she had ever heard. The symptoms of the poison that everyone seemed convinced had been used in this alleged assassination attempt sounded like nothing more than an overdose of stumbleweed, a purgative commonly used to clean the bowels. Nobody had even come close to dying from it. And she knew for a fact that Kagan had not "magically transported" the High Prince anywhere.

Whatever Kagan was up to, he needed Lernen involved, and this ruse with the puking courtiers was probably an elaborate show to convince Lernen he was being poisoned and make him follow Kagan without question, wherever the old charlatan wanted to take him.

By the time Alija got the news, though, Kagan had a head

start on her of several days. She had no idea where he was. No idea where he had taken the High Prince.

And Wrayan Lightfinger was still missing.

Alija's investigations into the inexplicable disappearance of the High Arrion's apprentice had yielded nothing. Nobody had seen him leave the temple. Nobody had entered the temple while she was out fetching Tesha Zorell. Nobody had seen or heard of him since. His room in the Sorcerers' Collective remained untouched. Nobody on the journey out of the city with Kagan and the High Prince had seen his apprentice with him or anywhere in Lernen's retinue. It was as if Wrayan Lightfinger had vanished off the face of the world.

Alija had tried searching for him using her mind, but had no luck there, either. Not that she was expecting to. She had blasted her way through Wrayan's mind with no care or intention of saving him from harm. She was a little annoyed at herself for doing that, in hindsight. She should have taken the time to skim the surface of his thoughts, at least. Of course, that meant she would have given Wrayan an opportunity to retaliate and she couldn't take that chance. It was hard to know how much power he had, and Alija had been fairly certain that, in a test of brute strength, he would prove stronger than she was. The only thing that had given her the edge in her battle was her speed and the scroll that had taught her the enhancement spell and given a powerful, albeit very temporary, boost to her own power.

Looking up from the accounts she should have been paying, Alija glanced at the water clock, surprised at how much time she had wasted sitting here wondering about what Kagan and that sly apprentice of his were really up to.

"Is something wrong, my lady?" Tarkyn asked, sensing her mood with unerring accuracy, the way he always did. He was sitting opposite her, waiting for her to read out the next account so that he could explain it to her. Tarkyn effectively ran the household here in Greenharbour so she always did the accounts with him present. It saved asking for clarification later.

"I was just wondering where Kagan and the High Prince were. And Wrayan Lightfinger."

"You think their disappearances connected?"

"I'm not sure," she admitted. "I'm beginning to think the whole episode with you and Wrayan was staged by Kagan to keep me occupied while he slipped out of Greenharbour with Lernen. But I don't see how he could have been in the temple at the Sorcerers' Collective helping Wrayan if he was halfway to the Sunrise Border by the time I confronted him."

They were interrupted by a knock at the door before Tarkyn could offer his opinion. Thinking it was Barnardo, Alija called permission to enter. Her slaves knew better than to disturb the lady of the house when she was alone with her *court'esa*.

"I'm sorry to interrupt, my lady," Tressa said rather shakily as she opened the door and bowed low to her mistress. "But there is someone here to see you."

"Who?"

"A slaver, my lady. He says he has something that belongs to you."

"What does he have that belongs to me?" she asked impatiently. She'd bought no slaves recently.

"Master Venira said to tell you his name is Corin, my lady."

Shocked, Alija jumped to her feet. "Corin is *here*?"

"With the slaver, my lady. They arrived at the trade's entrance about an hour ago, but I only just learned he was here. He said to tell you he knows he shouldn't have come here, but what Corin has to tell you is too important to entrust to any other means."

"Corin wouldn't risk compromising you if it wasn't important," Tarkyn agreed.

"Venira's only here for the money though," she muttered, before turning to Tressa. "Bring Corin here," she ordered. "Immediately. Tell Master Venira I thank him for his consideration and that I'll see to it he is compensated for his trouble. And tell Lord Eaglespike, when he wakes, that I wish him to join us."

"Yes, my lady."

Tressa hurried off to do as her mistress ordered, leaving Alija staring at Tarkyn with a worried frown. "If that fool has run away . . ."

"Corin's not the type, Alija," Tarkyn assured her. "He's a Loronged *court'esa*. He knows how valuable he is. He also knows his owner would spare no effort to hunt him down if he simply ran away. Besides, he's been in your service long enough now to know the consequences of disobeying your orders."

Before Alija could answer, the door opened again and Corin stepped into the study. Alija was shocked by his appearance. The normally handsome and immaculately groomed *court'esa* was unshaven and dirty. His shirt and trousers were dusty, his boots scuffed and his shirt collar pulled up to hide the jewelled metal collar that marked him as a slave. That was a crime in itself. No slave was permitted to masquerade as a free man.

"My lady," he said, with a bow.

"The news you bring had better mean the difference between life and death for someone, Corin," she warned, furious that he would arrive so openly at her home in the middle of Greenharbour in broad daylight. Although nobody would be surprised to learn she had placed a spy in Marla's entourage, to have Venira openly flaunt the young *court'esa*'s allegiance to the House of Eaglespike was political suicide. "Because, believe me, it will mean life or death to *you*."

"Never fear, my lady," Corin promised. "I believe the news I carry is worth the risk of exposure."

"Is it worth you running away from Highcastle?"

"I didn't run away, my lady. I was sent away."

"By whom?" Alija demanded. "And for what reason?"

"I was sent away, my lady, because Princess Marla is getting married and no longer requires my services."

"*What?* To whom?"

"Laran Krakenshield, my lady."

Alija sat down heavily, shocked beyond words.

"Krakenshield arrived at Highcastle unannounced with Lord Hawksword's son and several thousand troops on winter manoeuvres, so he claimed, planning to head into the border pass. He asked to speak to Marla alone while he was there and then informed her that the High Arrion had arranged for her to marry him."

"And Frederak and Lydia just let her go? When did this happen?" Tarkyn asked.

"Last Fourthday," Corin confirmed.

"Then they would be in Warrinhaven by now," Tarkyn informed Alija. "The chances are good that Princess Marla is already married."

"But to Laran Krakenshield?" Alija cried in disbelief. "He would never dare such a thing! And Lernen would never risk offending the King of Fardohnya by reneging on the wedding arrangement!"

"Perhaps he would," Tarkyn said.

"Don't be ridiculous!"

"Laran Krakenshield is now the Warlord of two provinces. He has the armies of Sunrise and Krakandar at his command. By the sound of it, he also has Charel Hawksword backing him; else Nash Hawksword appearing with troops in southern Sunrise to protect the border pass might easily be considered an invasion force. Including Elasapine's troops, that gives Laran a force of close to a hundred thousand men if he chooses to call up the reserves of all three provinces. He's Hythrun. And until the other Warlords demand he surrenders Sunrise, for the time being at least, he's as rich as Hablet. There is no other logical contender. And no other man alive that Lernen would agree to under the circumstances. By sending troops to Highcastle, he's obviously fortifying the border passes in anticipation of Hablet's reaction to the news. You can bet Winternest is just as heavily guarded. And in case it slipped your notice, he is Kagan Palenovar's nephew."

"But Laran . . . I can't believe it. You don't know him like I do, Tarkyn."

"I would suggest, my lady," the blind *court'esa* countered, "that it is you who doesn't know him as well as you think."

She turned to Corin again, refusing to accept what the *court'esa* was telling her. It wasn't possible she could have misjudged Laran that badly. "You say Marla was a willing participant in all of this?"

"Marla Wolfblade has steadfastly refused to contemplate a future as the wife of Hablet," Corin confirmed. "Even to the point of refusing my services. Once she heard Lord Krakenshield's offer, however, her attitude changed completely. I would say she was more than a willing participant, my lady. She jumped at the opportunity."

"It can't be Laran," Alija insisted, aghast that she might have read the situation so inadequately.

"There's one sure way to find out," Tarkyn suggested.

"How?"

"Go to Warrinhaven. You've got Marla's *court'esa* here, after all. It's really the only polite thing to do. Return her property to her. Tell her you couldn't dream of taking back a gift."

"If he's done this to me . . ." she began, thinking of Laran, fully aware that the moment Marla Wolfblade produced a son to a man as impeccably Hythrun as Laran Krakenshield, the chances of Barnardo ever seeing the throne went from likely to impossible.

It can't be happening. This can't be real.

"Make the arrangements," she ordered Tarkyn. "I want to leave within the hour." She turned to Corin and looked him up and down. "Get yourself cleaned up and be ready to leave with us, although if what you say is true, I suspect there will be no *court'esa* allowed in that household with any connection at all to the Eaglespike family."

Corin bowed and left the room, leaving Alija alone with Tarkyn, but before she could say a word the door opened again and her husband walked in, still wearing his nightshirt. He looked as if he had just awoken.

"Tressa said you wanted to see me," he told her, smothering a yawn, although it was almost lunch time. He blinked owlishly at Tarkyn for a moment and then looked at his wife. "You look a little frazzled, my dear. Did I miss something?"

chapter 40

In the two weeks between Laran informing her they were to be married and her arrival in Warrinhaven, Marla felt as if she'd aged a lifetime.

Neither Lydia nor Frederak had objected to Marla leaving Highcastle. Laran had, according to Ninane, taken Lord Branador aside and explained to him in no uncertain terms that if he wished to remain Lord of Highcastle, he would make no attempt to interfere in the business of his new Warlord. Marla had a feeling Frederak might have objected had he thought Marla was being taken against her will, but once she assured him she was leaving quite willingly with Lord Krakenshield to meet her brother, the High Prince, in Warrinhaven, her uncle raised no further objections.

It seemed as if her journey had taken her much further than the few hundred miles between Highcastle and the eastern border of Sunrise Province. The journey took her from innocence to disillusionment, from trusting naivety to jaded cynicism, all in a matter of a few days.

While she physically moved from the cold of the mountains to the warm humidity of the alluvial plains, her heart seemed to move in the opposite direction. Marla had left Highcastle resigned to the thought that nothing more than a cold and practical future awaited her, in which politics was the primary concern of everyone involved and her ability to breed the next generation was her most valuable asset.

Although Marla was heartbroken over the realisation that her dreams of Nashan Hawksword were nothing but her own foolish imagination, she was not so overcome that she couldn't see the merit of the arrangement. She would always love Nash, she decided privately, but he was out of her reach. She was the only sister of the High Prince of Hythria. For Marla Wolfblade there was no choice.

It could have been worse, she told herself. It *would* have been worse had she been forced to leave Hythria for Fardohnya and a life trapped in Hablet's harem. She was saved from that fate at least.

Laran Krakenshield was not the sort of man Marla would have chosen, but she accepted things could have turned out far more difficult. Laran wasn't unbearably old. He wasn't uncouth or particularly offensive. He seemed quite considerate of her circumstances. He wasn't even that ugly, although his face was too stern to be called attractive. He was probably *court'esa* trained. He was certainly rich enough to give her anything she wanted. All she had to do in return was give him a son.

Or—more to the point—give her brother a nephew.

It was raining again, as it had almost constantly since Marla arrived in Warrinhaven. The water pattered on the tiled roof and trickled down the window in little grey rivulets, until they merged into a larger puddle on the windowsill. She was wearing her wedding dress, a beautiful red silk gown embroidered in gold and seed pearls, provided by Laran's mother who had been waiting here at Warrinhaven for Marla and Laran to arrive. It was the Feast of Jashia, the God of

Fire, today. Being married on the Feast of Jashia was supposed to mean you were in for a fiery relationship, an unfortunate belief that Lady Jeryma had shrugged off as foolish superstition.

Am I in for a fiery relationship? Marla wondered. *Don't you need a bit of passion for that to happen? I have nothing. There's nothing between me and Laran but a polite distance.*

Another, more cynical voice in her mind added: *But one day you'll be the mother of the High Prince of Hythria.*

Chaine Tollin, the captain of Laran's guard, had told her that before they left Highcastle.

Marla remembered her conversation with him as she waited for the wedding to begin. It had occurred the day she was scheduled to leave with Laran. Marla had been pacing her room nervously while she waited for Lirena to return with her trunks when Chaine had arrived, along with her breakfast. He directed the house slave to lay out the meal near the hearth, dismissed the slave, then sat down and began to help himself to the honey-smothered wheat cakes.

"Sit down, your highness," he'd offered. "Laran and Nash have gone hawking with your uncle, so you have only me for company this morning, I'm afraid."

"Where are my slaves?" she'd asked, thinking it very odd that the captain of Laran's guard would act in such a familiar manner with someone who was clearly so far above his station.

"The dwarf was arguing with your nurse in the kitchen when I came through. Something about how many trunks you're planning to bring." He smiled then, and added, "It looked like they were settling in for a good long fight, so I volunteered to bring your tray up while they slugged it out. The other one . . . what's his name . . . Dorin?"

"Corin."

"He was on his way to visit Lady Ninane, I believe."

"Are you here to guard me?"

"Do you need guarding?"

Marla had wavered between being offended by the captain's rather cavalier manner and hunger. Hunger won, so she had taken the seat opposite Chaine and begun to pile her plate with the wheat cakes.

"So, the Warlord of Krakandar has Sunrise's army in his pocket as well as his own," she'd said, noting the raven embossed on the captain's cuirass.

"Actually, Laran and I have known each other since childhood," he told her. "I grew up in the Cabradell palace."

Marla didn't know that. The power at Laran's beck and call fascinated her. She could appreciate the danger Laran had brought upon himself by accepting a second province. But with the backing of Sunrise's army, he had double the forces of any other man in Hythria. And who would have thought they would follow him so readily?

"Was your father employed in Glenadal's household?"

"My father *was* Glenadal Ravenspear," the captain replied bluntly.

She looked at him curiously. "So *you're* the bastard?"

"You say that like you've heard of me, your highness."

"Just rumours," she shrugged. "Did Lord Ravenspear not acknowledge you in his will?"

"No."

Marla cocked her head. "Then why are you following Laran Krakenshield, Captain, instead of mounting a challenge against him?"

"Right now, I believe my interests and Laran's coincide."

"And when they no longer coincide?"

Chaine smiled. "We'll cross that bridge when we come to it."

"So, who else is in on this little coup?" she'd asked, through a mouthful of wheat cake. "Laran has the High Arrion in his pocket, if I'm to believe what he says about Kagan Palenovar. And obviously Lord Hawksword and his son are allies or Nash wouldn't be here." Marla said it without thinking, and then suddenly found herself swallowing down a fresh round of tears. *Oh, Nash, why didn't you say something? Why didn't you warn me?*

Chaine shrugged. "Laran has plans that even I am not

privy to. But for what it's worth, in his boots, I'd be doing exactly the same thing. Particularly with you as a prize at the end of it."

The compliment took Marla completely by surprise.

"Thank you, Captain," she said, blushing furiously. "I *think*."

"I meant it as a compliment, your highness."

Abruptly, he had put down his empty plate and risen to his feet, brushing away a few stray crumbs, then bowed and walked to the door. Marla got the impression Chaine was here for more than her company, but at the last minute he had changed his mind.

He'd hesitated with his hand on the doorknob. "Your highness," he said, a little nervously, "if ever . . . if you ever . . ." Chaine had faltered at that point, looking very uncomfortable.

"Captain?" she prompted.

"I just wanted to say . . . if you ever need a friend . . ."

Marla considered him thoughtfully. "I can count on *you*? Why?"

Chaine straightened his shoulders and took a deep breath before he spoke. "Because someday you won't be a child any more, your highness. Someday you'll be the mother of the High Prince of Hythria. I'm a baseborn son with no chance of claiming what is mine unless I have friends—influential friends—of my own."

Marla smiled. "You think I'll be influential someday?"

"A good third of the country's armed forces have been mobilised just because you're getting married, your highness," he pointed out. "That's not a bad effort to start with."

"I never thought of it like that."

"Well, the offer's there if you want it."

"Thank you, Captain," Marla had replied. Thinking back, she was left with the feeling that Chaine really meant what he said. He might have been trying to curry her favour for his own political ends, but she got the impression there was more to it than that. Perhaps, being an outcast himself, he knew what it was like to be the victim of other people's schemes and plots.

"You look lovely, my dear."

It's time, Marla thought, putting aside thoughts of political allies that she may or may not have. She turned away from the window and looked towards the door. Lady Jeryma was standing there, a warm smile on her face, her hand on the door knob.

"Will anybody care?" Marla shrugged. "It's my womb they're all interested in, Lady Jeryma, not what I look like on the outside."

Jeryma shook her head and closed the door. She crossed the small bedroom allocated to Marla by Lord Murvyn when she had arrived in Warrinhaven and took the princess by the hand. The Warlord's widow led her to the bed and sat down beside her, her expression full of sympathy and understanding.

"I've had four husbands, Marla," she said. "The first was a drunken fool. The second was like a father to me. The third was a brutish pig and the fourth was a man I grew to love dearly. You are lucky, my dear. You're starting with number four."

"Lady Jeryma, I appreciate what you're trying to do—"

"No, Marla, I don't think you do," Jeryma said. "I'm trying to tell you that this is not the end of the world. You are marrying a good man. An honourable man. And you are keeping the throne of Hythria safe from a foreign pretender."

"Only if I have a son."

"You will," Jeryma predicted confidently.

"Suppose I have half a dozen daughters?"

"Then Laran will love every one of them as if each is the most important person in the world. He's like that, Marla. Don't let childish dreams of romance blind you to the fact that your new husband is a good and decent man."

"I'll probably bore him to tears," Marla warned. "I know he thinks I'm just a child."

"You are no child, Marla," Jeryma told her. "You are a Hythrun princess. You are the future of this land. Don't belittle yourself by thinking otherwise."

"But I don't know what to *do*," she confessed, cursing the tears she'd sworn she wouldn't shed. "I mean . . . it's not like being in love, is it? Or even being with a *court'esa*. That's easy. Everyone knows their place and what they're supposed to be doing. But what do I say to Laran? What do I do?"

"Is that all that's worrying you, dear?"

"That and the fact the Convocation of Warlords will probably declare war on us as soon as they learn what's happened here today," she pointed out. The Lady Jeryma seemed to have overlooked that minor but extremely pertinent detail in her glowing recommendation of her eldest son.

"Perhaps," Lady Jeryma conceded. "But that's not your problem. As for my son, well, in my experience, he reacts better to the truth than any other kind of persuasion. If you're frightened, Marla, tell him. He's not going to punish you for it."

"I'm not properly trained, you know," Marla admitted reluctantly, as she wiped her eyes. "I was so angry about having to marry Hablet that I refused to have anything to do with my *court'esa* until a couple of nights before Laran arrived at Highcastle."

"Tell him that, too, Marla. You have nothing to lose and everything to gain."

Marla sniffed back her tears and studied Lady Jeryma curiously. "Did he send you here to reassure me?"

"Gods, no!" Jeryma chuckled. "He'd die if he thought his mother was in here with his future bride discussing the best way to bed him."

"I suppose it is a little bizarre."

Jeryma smiled and squeezed her hand comfortingly. "But necessary, I think. Don't be frightened, Marla. Be proud. We women of Hythria so rarely get to do anything that makes a difference. Don't let your chance go to waste."

"You make it sound so . . . noble."

"It is noble, Marla," Jeryma assured her, rising to her feet. "Now dry your eyes and let's go out there. As my third husband was fond of saying, just grin and bear it, girl, it'll be over before you know it."

Marla's wedding to Laran Krakenshield took place little more than an hour later, on a rainy afternoon in Warrinhaven in the hall of Lord Murvyn Rahan, the Baron of Charelle.

Marla was required to say nothing during the ceremony. In Hythrun marriages only the groom's opinion counted. All she had to do was stand there looking decorative, while Kagan Palenovar made Laran swear he would take care of his wife and any children or property she might bring to the marriage—a joke, Marla thought, when one considered she had been sold off like a brood mare.

Marla had no idea what she had been traded for—how much money, property, how many favours. Whatever it had cost, Laran Krakenshield didn't seem to mind and her brother, Lernen, appeared more than happy with the arrangement. She didn't know what negotiations had gone on between the High Arrion and her brother on the way to Warrinhaven, but the High Prince had arrived at the estate quite taken with the notion of Marla becoming Laran's wife, the deal with Hablet all but forgotten.

The High Prince looked on cheerfully during the ceremony, smiling at her encouragingly as Kagan spoke. Lernen had been well and truly bought by the Warlord of Krakandar and his cohorts, which meant he must have been offered considerably more than Hablet had offered for her hand. The High Prince must have been given some fairly substantial assurances that he wouldn't suffer for reneging on the deal with Fardohnya, too. Laran might even have offered to bear the cost of the defence of the border passes—and the gods alone knew what else—to secure the High Prince's agreement.

Laran had also gained another concession from Marla's brother she hadn't thought possible. It was something no High Prince had done in a thousand years. Lernen Wolfblade had agreed to overrule any decree from the Convocation of Warlords revoking Glenadal's will and to grant Laran Krakenshield the stewardship of Sunrise Province.

With that promise, Laran became more than just a pretender, more than just a Warlord.

He became the most powerful man in Hythria.

With a short round of applause from the men and women gathered in Murvyn Rahan's hall, Kagan Palenovar finished speaking. And, with nothing more than that, Marla Wolfblade became Laran Krakenshield's wife.

PART THREE

OF FAMILY, FRIENDS
AND TREACHERY

CHAPTER 41

The news that the High Prince of Hythria had changed his mind regarding the upcoming marriage of his only sister to the King of Fardohnya reached Hablet in Talabar a mere eight days after it happened.

On the upside, Lernen's apologetic communiqué insisted Hablet keep the delightful *court'esa*, Welenara, as some small compensation for the inconvenience the King had suffered as a result of the change in Marla's circumstances. Hablet would have kept Welenara anyway, just on principle, but he'd become quite attached to the young slave and was pleased he'd not be forced to execute her. That would have been his only recourse had Lernen wanted her back. He couldn't possibly allow her to actually return to Hythria.

What would Lernen want with a female court'esa *anyway?*

The tidings of Marla's wedding to Laran Krakenshield were delivered by the Hythrun Ambassador to Talabar, one very apologetic and nervous Lord Rene Sharroan, a cousin of the Warlord of Pentamor, whom Hablet promptly executed in retaliation for the grave insult to his royal person.

The depth of Lernen Wolfblade's treachery was unconscionable. Not only had the High Prince of Hythria reneged on a business deal (a sin more heinous than murder in Fardohnya), he had cost Hablet the one chance he had of legally redressing a forgotten and ancient flaw in the Fardohnyan laws of succession, stating that, in the absence of a male heir to Fardohnya, the eldest living Wolfblade would inherit his throne.

Lecter Turon had uncovered the ancient law while looking for something else entirely—Hablet couldn't even remember what it was any more—and had immediately brought the law to his King's attention.

There was a sound historical reason for the provision. When Greater Fardohnya (as the two southern nations had once been known) was divided some twelve hundred years ago, the split was amicable, but in an effort to assure his twin sister, Doranda, that she would always be welcome back in her homeland, King Greneth the Elder of Fardohnya had agreed that if he failed to get a male heir, Doranda's son by the newly crowned High Prince of Hythria, her husband Jaycon Wolfblade, would be the next in line for the throne. The king produced a son, however, as had every other monarch down the ages since then. The law became a forgotten piece of history and would probably remain so.

But Hablet didn't like to take chances. He'd killed every one of his father's *court'esa* and all his baseborn siblings when he ascended to the throne, even the half-brothers and half-sisters who counted him a friend, just to make certain there were no pretenders left to make trouble once he was king. On hearing of his murderous rampage, his only legitimate sister had confronted him and threatened to expose his heinous crime to the world. Hablet had been forced to have Harryat put to death as well, but he spread the story that she had selflessly killed herself so she couldn't inadvertently produce a child who might one day challenge her brother's throne. He even built a very nice shrine to honour her memory in the temple of Jelanna in the city. *Silly bitch is enjoying a much higher level of popularity as a martyr than she ever did when she was alive,* Hablet reasoned. *She ought to be grateful.*

Hablet had no doubt he would also produce the requisite son, as his ancestors for twelve hundred years had done. But it would have been nice to close the loophole that meant a Hythrun might one day rule Fardohnya if the worst happened and the incumbent king failed to get a legitimate heir. If Hablet could marry Marla and her son was the next heir to Fardohnya, the child would, at least, be Fardohnyan and it would destroy forever the danger of a Hythrun-born Wolfblade ever ruling from Talabar.

That the Hythrun shared a similar concern that their High Prince be born on Hythrun soil did not bother Hablet in the slightest. His concern for what the Hythrun wanted was on a par with his concern about what happened to those savage bitches running Medalon to the east of Fardohnya or those religious fanatics in Karien to the north. He had only one concern and that was Fardohnya. More specifically, the security of his own rule.

Anything else was, well, irrelevant.

But the first order of the day was vengeance for the insult from the Hythrun High Prince. There was an ancient Fardohnyan tradition called *mort'eda,* the fine art of seeking revenge, and Hablet intended to set a new standard in finesse and viciousness as he extracted a blood price for the insult of jilting him.

Hablet paced his office impatiently, waiting for Lecter Turon to return with news of what was happening in Hythria. The last report Hablet had received several days ago was one of great turmoil. Laran Krakenshield's acquisition of a second province, and the alliance he had hammered out with the Warlords of the two provinces that lay between Krakandar and Sunrise, meant he now had more than half the country under his control. Some of the other Warlords were talking loudly about mounting a force against him, but the odds were so overwhelmingly in Laran's favour, Hablet would be surprised if they did more than rattle their swords and curse him loudly before slinking back to their own provinces to lick their wounds.

The High Prince was back in Greenharbour, spending money as if he'd opened a vein and discovered he was bleeding gold. As far as Hablet could tell, Lernen wasn't ruling the country. He was too busy with his own entertainment to be distracted by anything so crass. Hythria was under the control of the High Arrion of the Sorcerers' Collective, Kagan Palenovar, and the people he had surrounding the High Prince. The Convocation of Warlords was relegated to the sidelines (with Laran having so much of Hythria under his control, it was a joke, anyway) and even Barnardo Eaglespike, the figurehead leader of the Patriot Faction and Lernen Wolfblade's loudest opponent, had slunk back to Dregian Castle like a beaten cur and was keeping a very low profile indeed.

Hablet's first thought had been to invade Hythria to avenge the insult, but he was hampered by geography as much as anything. The majestic Sunrise Mountains boasted only two navigable passes into Hythria and both were located in Sunrise Province. One—the Widowmaker Pass—was in the north of the province at Winternest. The other was on the coast, at Highcastle. That route was no good to him, however; his scouts reported the narrow southern pass was blocked by an avalanche (Hablet suspected quite deliberately)—which left only Winternest, a damn near impregnable fortress protected by, at last count, nearly four thousand men. Hablet could field an army a hundred times that size, but they were not much good to him if he could only feed them into the pass six abreast while the Hythrun defenders picked off the invaders at their leisure.

The door opened and Lecter Turon hurried into the room, his bald head gleaming with sweat in the humid afternoon. He spared his king a perfunctory bow before getting down to business.

"I have found Marla Wolfblade!" the eunuch announced, looking very pleased with himself.

"You're a bit late, Lecter. *Before* she was married off to someone else would have been rather more useful to me."

"No, you misunderstand my meaning, your majesty. I speak not of her value as a wife but her value as a hostage. I believe she's been hidden away against the possibility of a civil war. The Warlords of the Patriot Faction are not happy about the current situation. And they're furious the High Prince simply ruled in Laran's favour without consulting the Convocation."

"So where have they hidden her?"

"Winternest."

"Are you certain?"

"I'm making further enquiries, but it looks positive. The garrison at Winternest was reinforced with a great many additional troops around the same time as the wedding. But they're not Sunrise troops guarding the fortress. Or even Charel Hawksword's men from Elasapine, which would make sense considering how close Winternest is to the Elasapine border. They are Krakandar troops under the command of Laran Krakenshield's half-brother, Mahkas Damaran."

"That doesn't prove anything."

"On its own, no," Lecter agreed. "But coupled with the reports I have of eyewitnesses who have seen her at the castle—"

"She's been seen?" Hablet asked in surprise.

"There's definitely a young girl being guarded there. Blonde hair, about fifteen or sixteen, the whole of the southern arm of the castle sealed off and put at her disposal. I don't see who else it could be. And if Laran fears an attack from another Hythrun Warlord, he can't get Marla much farther away from danger without actually moving her across the border into Fardohnya."

"You don't think he's afraid of me, then?"

"I think Laran Krakenshield probably believes—quite rightly—that now she has been married to another man, you have no interest in Marla Wolfblade. Your issue is the insult done to you, your majesty. Marla doesn't really matter one way or the other."

Hablet shook his head. "I still don't see how the information helps us, Lecter. Winternest is the most fortified place in Hythria. How would we get her out of there without wasting half our damn army in the process?"

"By doing what we do best, your majesty," Lecter suggested with an oily smile.

"And what's that, Lecter?"

"We trade for her."

"Trade?"

Lecter nodded, looking very smug. "Everything has a price, your majesty, up to and including a Hythrun princess. Give me sufficient funds and I'll buy your princess for you. Even out of Winternest."

Hablet smiled. "It would rather get up Lernen's nose, wouldn't it?"

"Not to mention Laran Krakenshield's."

Hablet scratched at his beard thoughtfully. "He's very wealthy, isn't he? We could ransom her back for rather a lot of money, I imagine."

"Profitable *and* deliciously ironic, your majesty."

Hablet thought about it for a moment; imagined the look on that sour little pervert's face when he discovered Hablet had kidnapped his sister out of Winternest. He nodded at his chamberlain. "I think we should do it."

Lecter smiled and bowed to his king. "I will make the arrangements immediately, sire."

"You do that," Hablet said, thinking the only thing better than a *mort'eda* blood price was one that consisted of actual money.

CHAPTER 42

Alija Eaglespike was many things, but above all she was a consummate politician. She knew how to read the fickle winds of political change like others could sense a coming change in the weather.

And she knew when she was beaten. The marriage of

Marla Wolfblade to Laran Krakenshield was a done deal by the time she arrived in Warrinhaven with Barnardo and Marla's unwanted *court'esa* in tow. Consequently, her first move was to forcibly bury her anger and congratulate Laran and Marla on their marriage as if she truly meant it. Marla had no reason to suspect Alija's warm congratulations weren't genuine. Laran, on the other hand, was highly suspicious but could do nothing, in public at least, but accept her best wishes in the spirit they seemed to be intended.

It had been an awkward time for everyone and Alija planned to leave Warrinhaven as fast as they could politely get away, pleading a pressing engagement with the Earl of Glint in Dregian Province in a few days time which meant they couldn't stay longer than a day or two.

It might not have been so bad, had she not had to suffer the smug satisfaction of Kagan Palenovar. The old sorcerer, anxious to gloat over his stunning coup, caught up with her in the corridor outside Lord Murvyn's main hall after she had delivered her apologetic news about their hasty departure.

"So you're leaving us, my lady?" Kagan called after her as she headed back towards the guest quarters in the southern wing of the small palace. It was late afternoon and the sunlight streamed through the narrow west-facing windows lining the hall, striping it with lines of shadow and sparkling dust motes that danced in the still air.

"What a shame," he added with vast insincerity.

Alija composed her features into a neutral expression before turning to face him. She knew Kagan was baiting her. Her only consolation was the continuing and unexplained disappearance of Wrayan Lightfinger. There was no sign of the apprentice in Warrinhaven and although she could tell the High Arrion was burning with the need to interrogate her about what had happened in the Temple of the Gods, he could say nothing without admitting his own involvement in the deliberate tampering with her *court'esa*.

"There's not much point in remaining here," Alija shrugged. "And I imagine you'll not be here much longer yourself, my lord. You have your own problems to deal with, don't you?" The absence of his apprentice loomed like an invisible wall between them that neither could acknowledge without admitting their own guilt in the affair.

But Kagan was too sharp to even hint that he knew anything about her confrontation with Wrayan. "One of the joys of being High Arrion, I'm afraid. One is always confronted with problems. I imagine being the chief agitator in the faction determined to unseat the High Prince has its own, quite similar responsibilities."

Alija smiled, but inwardly she was seething. Admittedly, Kagan had good cause to feel smug. He knew as well as Alija did that Marla's marriage to a Hythrun of Laran's faultless breeding had stopped the Patriot Faction's campaign to put Barnardo on the throne in its tracks. With a chance that Lernen's sister would produce a male child of the Wolfblade line who might one day replace him, the High Prince's foibles would seem a lot easier to tolerate. Lernen's perversions, which a month ago were the cause of endless outrage among his peers, were already being talked about (only days after the wedding) as harmless diversions that hurt nobody—slaves not being counted as real people. Suddenly Lernen was seen as a powerless fool who nobody minded enough to do anything about.

"You won't get away with this, old man," she warned. "The Convocation of Warlords will be furious. Lernen has overridden them in the matter of Glenadal's will and arbitrarily dismissed their wishes on this issue."

"Perhaps," Kagan agreed, unconcerned. "But he's also withdrawn his earlier plan to marry his only sister to the Fardohnyan King, which rather makes his decision to grant Laran Krakenshield lordship over Sunrise Province and his sister's hand the lesser of two evils, don't you agree?"

"Marrying his sister to a Hythrun doesn't alter what Lernen is."

"And who but you cares, Alija?" the old man shrugged.

"Lernen has given your Patriot Warlords precisely what you were agitating for—a Hythrun heir, albeit one yet to be conceived. The whole basis of your push for the High Prince's crown was the fact that your husband is Hythrun, has two healthy Hythrun sons and is descended from the royal line, even though his great-grandmother was the last member of his family who carried the name of Wolfblade. None of that matters now. We will have our Wolfblade heir, born and raised a Hythrun. You and your husband—just like your faction—are irrelevant now."

"You might think so, Kagan, but you're a fool if you think the Convocation will stand by idly and let this happen."

"You underestimate how much respect Laran has among his peers, my lady. It's quite possible he's the only man in Hythria who could have gotten away with such a bold plan."

Alija nodded her reluctant agreement. Laran's standing among the Warlords wasn't accidental. She knew Jeryma had quite deliberately fostered her son with both Charel Hawksword and Bryl Foxtalon when he was a boy, so both Warlords looked upon him with almost paternal pride. His mother had also insisted Laran spend time during his youth learning the arts of war, not from their own commanders in Krakandar, but from Rogan Bearbow, the Warlord of Izcomdar, the province which bordered Krakandar to the south. "Do you think that, with three of Hythria's Warlords thinking of him as a son, the High Prince in his pocket, the High Arrion a close member of the family and direct control over another two provinces, it means nobody will dare challenge Laran?"

Kagan smiled serenely. "I rather think it does, Alija. Laran—and the High Prince, for that matter—are beyond anything you and your increasingly immaterial faction can do to them."

"For now," she agreed, wondering if Kagan thought she had abandoned her plans for her husband to eventually take the throne.

"Now is all that matters," Kagan replied, and then he turned and walked away, leaving her staring after him, wishing she could find a way to channel the helpless rage that threatened to overwhelm her.

During her short stay at Warrinhaven, Alija noted, with some concern, that Marla seemed quite indifferent to Corin's return, a situation that would not make it easy for him to become her close confidant and would limit his effectiveness as a spy. That role seemed to be reserved for the dwarf, who appeared to enjoy a much higher level of intimacy with his mistress than the handsome *court'esa* Alija had given Marla as a gift.

It had proved next to impossible to convince Barnardo to accept the inevitable. He had his heart set on the High Prince's throne and was convinced every action Lernen took simply strengthened his position in the eyes of the other Warlords. In the end, Alija used her Innate magic and changed his mind for him, effectively putting an end to his whining about it until they could return home, regroup and come up with a way to deal with this unexpected turn of events.

Marla came to see them off when Alija and Barnardo left Warrinhaven. Alija had cautiously skimmed the young princess's mind as they embraced and found nothing amiss on the surface. She seemed to accept the inevitability of her position. There was even a hint of self-importance lurking in the background. Someone had obviously planted the idea in Marla's mind that she had some noble purpose in life. That might prove a problem in the future if she ever truly came to believe it.

The only other thing Alija had been able to determine from her brief glance into Marla Wolfblade's mind was that she was still in love.

And, as Alija knew, it wasn't with her husband.

"I do hope you'll be happy, little cousin," Alija had told

her, hugging the princess warmly as Barnardo's white carriage was brought around to the front of the small palace. Trimmed with burgundy leather and gilt, it was a beautiful vehicle pulled by six matching greys, all wearing the green and gold colours of Dregian in the plumes on their harnesses. The whole outfit screamed outrageous wealth, which was exactly the impression Alija was aiming for.

Warrinhaven was really nothing more than the country seat of a fairly insignificant nobleman, but some sound investments and careful management of the borough for several generations meant Lord Murvyn enjoyed a lifestyle usually reserved for a Warlord. The palace, although small, was quite beautiful, the mosaic-tiled steps where they waited reaching down to a broad plaza and a large fountain cast in bronze that depicted the god Kaelarn.

Marla shrugged, pulling her shawl a little tighter around her shoulders. It was cool this morning. "I'll be fine."

"Don't let them bully you," Alija whispered, kissing Marla's cheek. "Especially Jeryma Ravenspear. She can be a real old cow."

"Truly, Alija," Marla assured her, "I'll be all right."

"Well, just you remember, if you need comfort, Corin is there for you."

"I'll remember."

Alija frowned, wondering if Marla would bother to call on the *court'esa* at all. Newly wed and weighed down by the burden of expectation, she probably wouldn't think of much else besides producing the heir everyone was so determined she should bear.

Perhaps I should send her another slave, Alija decided. *A female slave, this time. This girl doesn't want a lover. She needs a friend.*

"And you really should think about getting rid of that dwarf, Marla," she advised. "He's really not an appropriate companion for a Warlord's wife."

"Laran promised me I could keep him."

"He's probably just trying to be nice to you, dear. But if you care for your husband's position at all . . . well, think how it looks. A Fool like that as a *court'esa* to entertain you? What does it say about your husband?"

"I'll think about it," Marla promised, although it was clear she had no intention of doing anything of the kind.

"You do that, Marla. And if you ever need my help, for anything at all, just send for me. I will come."

Marla smiled gratefully. "Thank you."

Alija hugged her again and crossed the tiled plaza to the carriage where Barnardo was waiting for her. She allowed a slave to hand her into the carriage and waved at Marla with a smile as they drove off, surrounded by the guard of Dregian Raiders they had brought as an escort.

Almost as an afterthought, Alija released the hold she had kept on her husband's mind to prevent him saying anything stupid before they could get out of Warrinhaven.

"Are we leaving?" Barnardo asked, as if waking from a long sleep.

"Yes, don't you remember? You insisted we leave Warrinhaven immediately."

"I did?" he said, a little vaguely. "Did I say where we were going?"

"Home," she informed him. "To Dregian."

"The boys have missed you," he ventured.

"And I've missed them."

Barnardo glanced out of the window of the carriage, clearly puzzled about why he would suddenly decide to return to Dregian. "Did I mention how long we'd be staying this time?" he asked cautiously.

"Actually, you sounded quite determined to stay there for a while. I suppose that's why you wanted so many visitors."

"Did I mention visitors, too?"

"Don't you remember, dear? You were quite enthused by the idea of organising some serious hunting in the spring. You were talking about inviting Rogan down from Izcomdar to join you."

"He'd like that. Did I mention anyone else?"

"Well, it wouldn't be a proper hunting season if we didn't invite the Falconlance boys. And you mentioned bringing up a few of the sons of your vassals this year. To give you a chance to get to know them."

"That's a good idea," Barnardo said, embracing the notion as if it were his own.

"There was someone else," she told him, making a pretence of thinking about it. Then she smiled suddenly. "Of course, that was the other name you mentioned."

"Who?"

"Nash Hawksword," Alija told her husband. "You said you really wanted a chance to get to know Nash Hawksword better."

"Do you think it might help us?"

The game is still on, she reminded herself. *It's simply the field of play that's changed.*

Alija smiled at her husband knowingly. "You have *no* idea."

chapter 43

Mahkas Damaran was used to being overlooked. As the only one of Jeryma Palenovar's four children who did not inherit a substantial fortune from their deceased fathers, he had spent his whole life living on the charity of his siblings. He held his commission as a captain in Krakandar's army because of his brother. He rode a sorcerer-bred mount because his brother had given it to him. The food he ate, the very clothes on his back, were there because of Laran's charity.

And it drove him to distraction.

The frustration Mahkas felt was only compounded by his posting to Winternest to protect his sisters. Or, more specifically, to protect Riika, in case somebody decided that with the late Warlord of Sunrise Province's only daughter as their wife, they might have some chance at claiming her legacy.

There had been no such attacks. With Laran now married to Marla Wolfblade, the backing of Charel Hawksword and Bryl Foxtalon, and the High Prince agreeing to the unheard of condition of Laran taking Sunrise without the blessing of the Convocation of Warlords, there was simply nobody in Hythria who thought the idea of challenging Laran worth the effort. Even Chaine Tollin, Glenadal Ravenspear's bastard son, had decided it was easier to back Laran than oppose him.

Disappointingly, Hablet, the jilted king of Fardohnya, hadn't bothered to retaliate, either. Mahkas had been hoping for that much at least. With four thousand bored troops hanging around Winternest waiting for something to happen, it would have been nice to give them something to do. But no, even the King of Fardohnya had apparently come to the conclusion, like everyone else, that it simply wasn't worth trying to challenge Laran Krakenshield on anything.

Inaction was making Mahkas edgy. He was snapping at his nephews when their games became too rowdy and had reduced Darilyn to tears again this morning when he grew tired of her constant whining about how long it was taking for her new harp strings to get here from Greenharbour and told her to shut up. Even Riika's sweet gentleness was wearing on him. One more heavy sigh, one more wistful look into the distance when someone inadvertently mentioned Glenadal's name, and Mahkas was sure he would have to strangle his youngest sister, too.

Still, Mahkas was hopeful things would improve soon. With two provinces to administer, Laran had more than he could handle and Sunrise needed to be sorted out. Logically, Laran should head back to Krakandar to look after his interests there while his younger brother set about making Sunrise secure. Mahkas could see himself in that role. He didn't really want any more power than that. But he was certain he deserved some consideration.

Laran owed him that much, at least.

More than anything, Mahkas wanted to go home an important man. Krakandar Province might belong to Laran, but it was Mahkas's home too. He wanted to be recognised for his own achievements, not bask in the reflected glory of Laran's accomplishments. In a perfect world, he would head back to Krakandar after subduing Sunrise, marry his promised bride, Bylinda Telar, the daughter of Krakandar's most wealthy merchant family, and settle down to a life of comfort and respect.

In a perfect world . . .

Putting aside his worries about his future, Mahkas glanced up at the sky as he crossed the bridge between the southern and northern arms of Winternest Castle, thinking it might snow again later today. Mahkas spent much of his time in the castle's northern wing. It was the business end of the fort and usually filled with traders and soldiers, unlike the southern half which was filled with whining women and irritating small boys.

The Raiders on the stone bridge high above the road saluted Mahkas as he crossed over. He returned the salute and exchanged a friendly greeting with them as he passed. Mahkas enjoyed being popular among the men. It made him feel as if he was in command because the Raiders liked and respected him, not because he was their Warlord's penniless half-brother.

Once across the bridge, he jerked open the door that led to the stairwell and took the narrow torch-lit stairs down to the lower levels. Despite the fear of attack from Fardohnya once Hablet got wind of the fate of his promised bride, trade was still brisk between the two countries. With the pass further south at Highcastle blocked by snow, probably well into next spring, all the traffic was now being funnelled through Winternest, making it much busier than usual.

Nash Hawksword had been and gone. After waiting around for over a month for something to happen with his Elasapine Raiders, following their visit to Highcastle, Nash eventually decided to return home to Byamor. It had only taken a week before the first off-duty brawl had broken out. Both commanders had agreed it might be for the best to have a little space between the forces. Nash was still close enough that Mahkas could call on him and have him arrive with reinforcements in a few days if the need arose, but an extra couple of thousand Elasapine, Krakandar and Sunrise troops hanging around Winternest and nobody to fight but each other was simply asking for trouble.

The main hall of the northern side of Winternest was part customs house, part tavern and part administration post for all the commerce between Fardohnya and Hythria. As usual, it was full of people trying to get their documents processed by the rather frazzled-looking customs men whose job it was to decide what tax was payable on each load going in and out of Hythria. Mahkas didn't envy the men their jobs. Most of the merchants heading into Hythria had already been taxed on the Fardohnyan side of the border for the privilege of leaving the country. They were never happy to be taxed again a few hours later for the privilege of entering Hythria. A lot of the merchants were regulars on the route, but to hear them protest about it, you'd think the taxes had been imposed just last week instead of centuries ago.

Mahkas pushed his way through the crowded hall to the bar at the other end where a small tavern was doing a roaring trade, keeping the throats of all these thirsty merchants well lubricated. The man behind the counter saw Mahkas approach and dipped a cup of ale for him from the open barrel behind the counter, waving away any payment.

"On the house, Captain," the tavern-keeper told him with a grin.

"Thanks," Mahkas replied, as if he wasn't expecting such generosity. It was an act of course. Mahkas hadn't paid for ale all the time he'd been here. The merchants of Winternest knew how to stay in favour with their new Warlord's brother.

Taking a sip from his tankard, Mahkas made his way to the table nearest the roaring fire that warmed this end of the hall. There were two men seated at the table, both Fardohnyan merchants by the look of them. Mahkas knew the man on the left—Grigar Bolonar, a slaver from somewhere near Lanipoor. The man on his right was a stranger. He was completely bald and had the furtive air of a man trying to look inconspicuous.

"Hello, Grigar," he said, curious about the man's companion.

"Lord Damaran!" the merchant cried, jumping to his feet. "What a pleasant surprise!"

"I'm sure the sight of me has made your day," Mahkas replied with a smile. "Who's your friend?"

The bald man rose to his feet. "Symon Kuron," the man replied, offering Mahkas his hand. "I'm here in Hythria with a view to purchasing breeding stock for my slaves. The blonde colouring so common among your people is highly sought after in Talabar, you know."

"I didn't know," Mahkas replied, wondering why the man seemed so anxious to explain his presence in Hythria. He really didn't need to know his reasons for being here. Didn't care much, either. "I trust you'll find what you're looking for in Greenharbour."

"Actually, my lord, I was hoping not to have to go that far."

"Then your next best option is Warrinhaven. I hear old Murvyn keeps quite an impressive stable."

Symon Kuron smiled. "I thank you for your assistance, my lord."

"You've no need to call me lord," he replied. "Captain will do."

The merchant raised one eyebrow curiously. "But are you not the half-brother of Sunrise's new Warlord?"

"That doesn't make me a lord," he said with a shrug, swallowing down a good half of his ale in one gulp. "It was a pleasure to meet you, Trader Kuron. Grigar."

He turned away, not wishing to get into any discussion about his title, or lack thereof. And certainly not with some greasy Fardohnyan merchant.

"Do *you* have any slaves here I could purchase, Captain?" the slaver asked.

Mahkas turned back to face him. "No."

"But I saw you earlier today on the battlements with a young woman of most exquisite aspect. Is she not for sale?"

He smiled. "Absolutely not."

"Then the rumours are true?"

"What rumours?"

"That Laran Krakenshield has hidden his new wife away here in Winternest for fear of a Hythrun assassin?"

Mahkas laughed aloud at the very idea. "You should know better than to listen to rumours, Master Kuron."

"Of course, Captain." The merchant bowed with courtly grace. "Please accept my apologies for paying such rumours any credence at all."

"You've no need to apologize. Just don't repeat the rumours and give them life."

"Of course not. My lips on this matter are sealed for an eternity."

Mahkas looked at the man askance for a moment and then downed the rest of his ale. "Good," he said, slamming the tankard on the table. "See they stay that way."

A little while later, when Mahkas was returning to the southern wing of the keep for lunch, he found Raek Harlen on the bridge between the two towers, stamping his feet against the cold. He stopped and glanced down over the road then turned to look at the young man.

"Raek, have you heard the rumour that Marla Wolfblade is here in Winternest?" he asked.

"Yeah," the lieutenant replied with a short laugh. "It's been around for a while. I first heard it not long after your sisters arrived, I think."

"How the hell did it get started?"

"Riika probably."

"You think *Riika* started the rumour?"

"No. I think Lady Riika's presence here started it," Raek explained. "She's the same age as Marla Wolfblade and the same colouring, from what I hear, and few people realize that Glenadal had a daughter, he kept her so sheltered in Cabradell. Do you think it's a problem?"

Mahkas shook his head. "I think it's a joke, actually. Hasn't anybody thought to correct the Fardohnyans?"

Raek smiled. "Why bother? If everyone thinks Princess

Marla is here in Winternest rather than Lady Riika, doesn't that make it safer for Riika? Anybody looking for her will think she's still back in Cabradell."

"That's true, I suppose. I just can't believe those idiot Fardohnyans don't know the difference between Riika and the High Prince's sister."

"Maybe we all look alike to them," Raek suggested with a chuckle.

"You could be right, Lieutenant," Mahkas agreed before heading off to the southern keep and the prospect of a nice warm lunch. He thought no more about it.

ChAPTER 44

Kagan Palenovar hurried along the walkway between his room and his sister's private apartments, a brisk wind tugging at his robes. As the chill of winter gradually gave way to the promise of spring, the winds here in Cabradell increased, howling down the mountains as if they were desperate to escape the high country, making the whole valley quite unpleasant for the few months until summer's heat warmed the air and subdued the winds for a time. They didn't call the Cabradell valley the "Valley of the Winds" for nothing.

Kagan had returned to Cabradell with Laran, Jeryma and Marla Wolfblade several weeks ago and was finally satisfied that things were settling down. Charel Hawksword and Bryl Foxtalon had returned to their provinces. The High Prince was back in Greenharbour and the other Warlords had retreated in a sulk to ponder how such a strange turn of events could have come about without them knowing anything about it beforehand.

Desperately worried about Wrayan, Kagan would have preferred to return to Greenharbour straightaway to track down his missing apprentice, but there had been too much to be done, too many alliances to juggle, too many balls to keep in the air, to risk leaving things to chance straight after the wedding. The time had come for him to leave now, however. Wrayan's continued absence kept him awake at night for fear of what had become of the young man. He had to return to Greenharbour and find out what had happened to him.

The Convocation of Warlords had backed off with alacrity after Charel Hawksword was able to get Bryl Foxtalon to join their loose alliance. Once Laran had a majority of the Warlords prepared to back his plan, even Lernen's arbitrary decision to endorse Glenadal's will made little difference. Laran was going to keep Sunrise, with or without the High Prince.

Hablet had done nothing either, except behead the unfortunate ambassador charged with delivering the news about Marla. Lernen was hopeful that would be the end of the matter, but Kagan wasn't so sure. One dead ambassador seemed much too small a price to pay for an insult to a neighbouring monarch.

Marla, of all the players in this drama, had surprised Kagan the most. When she learned her unwanted marriage had been averted only by organising another unwanted marriage to take its place, he had expected a similar performance to the one he witnessed at the ball in Greenharbour. But the princess was remarkably accepting of the situation.

Kagan was suspicious of the change in her at first, but after a time, he recognised the influence of a calmer, more mature mind. It took him a while to realize who was responsible, although when he did work it out, he wasn't really surprised. Clever *court'esa* frequently managed to work themselves into positions of profound trust. Alija's first—and only—*court'esa*, Tarkyn Lye, was closer to his mistress than anybody else, including her husband. She certainly took his advice more often than Barnardo's.

The dwarf *court'esa*, Elezaar, had obviously understood the unique nature of the opportunity he had been given the

day Marla petulantly chose him over a more suitable companion and intended to make the most of it. Although he
rarely left his mistress's side, he made no attempt to win her
over with his skill as lover or a Fool. He had made himself indispensable by helping Marla navigate the dangerous political waters she was now swimming in. That might have
concerned Kagan, except it seemed it was the dwarf who had
convinced Marla that the brighter future lay along the path of
cooperation, not defiance, and with his advice, what could
have been a situation fraught with tension was working out
with remarkable ease.

Marla's sixteenth birthday passed almost without notice in
the wake of her hurried marriage to Laran. Jeryma had made
an attempt to celebrate the occasion, but they were on the
road at the time, camped for the night some eighty miles
south of the capital on their journey back to Cabradell, so the
celebrations had been haphazard at best. Kagan suspected
Jeryma was riddled with guilt about forcing the marriage between her son and the young princess and was doing her utmost to ease Marla's transition into the family, as if that
would somehow make her actions forgivable. Perhaps she
even saw herself reflected in the eyes of Marla Wolfblade.

*Or maybe she's just desperate for the princess to produce the
heir everyone is so anxiously awaiting,* he thought cynically, *and
is being so solicitous of her daughter-in-law's comfort to make
certain she's there the moment it's confirmed Marla is pregnant.*

Nobody was sure when that might happen, but they were all
expecting it sooner rather than later. Following some delicate
enquiries (Kagan had interrogated the slaves who tended the
princess), he had been able to establish that Laran and Marla
were sharing a bed. That was all he'd been able to establish,
however, and for all he knew they sat up all night arguing high
literature and had not even consummated the marriage yet.

On the balance of probability, that was unlikely. Laran was
a *court'esa*-trained nobleman married to a very desirable,
court'esa-trained princess who was under no illusions whatsoever about what was expected of her.

Kagan knocked on Jeryma's door and opened it without waiting for an answer. He was in a hurry this morning. Now he had made the decision to return to Greenharbour, he could see no point in delaying his departure for a moment longer than necessary.

"Kagan!"

Jeryma was in her small private courtyard, enjoying her breakfast in the sheltered sunlight.

"Thought I'd find you here," he said. "I've come to say goodbye."

She put down her tea and rose to her feet. "I thought you might be heading off soon. You've still no word from Wrayan, then?"

The High Arrion shook his head. "Not a whisper. Gods, I hope nothing has happened to him."

"But you fear it has," Jeryma remarked. It was a statement, not a question.

"Wrayan challenged Alija Eaglespike, Jeryma. One would think that if he survived the ordeal, he might at least have the decency to let me know about it."

"Did Alija say nothing about the incident when she visited Warrinhaven?"

"Not a word."

"Do you think he's dead?"

"Oddly enough, no. I think even Alija Eaglespike would have trouble covering up the death of another sorcerer. I'm more worried something has happened to his mind. For all I know, he's wandering the streets of Greenharbour with no idea who he is. Or where he is. Or what he is."

"It will seem so quiet once you're gone. Laran's heading up to Winternest in a few days to visit Mahkas and the girls. It's going to be so quiet around here."

"You'll have Marla for company."

His sister smiled. "I'm sure Marla would be quite happy to forgo my companionship. I'm not really the most diverting attendant for a sixteen-year-old girl."

"She seems to be doing well, though."

"Much better than I expected. I quite like her, actually. I

was expecting just a younger, more pliable version of Lernen, but I think there was a very uneven distribution of wealth in the Wolfblade family. Lernen got all the bad things. Marla seems to have inherited mostly the good."

"Only mostly?" Kagan asked with a raised brow.

"Well, she does have a rather unhealthy attachment to that dwarf."

"Take my advice, Jeryma—leave the dwarf alone. He's doing more good than harm."

"Are you certain?" she asked doubtfully.

"Not completely," Kagan admitted. "But from what I've seen so far, he's taught her more about science than sex and more about history than histrionics. I think you'd do well to simply accept the situation and worry about more important things."

"If he's teaching her more about science than sex, one wonders what's the use of him? And who is teaching Marla the things she needs to know, if her *court'esa* isn't? Last week she sent her other *court'esa* back to her cousin, Ninane, in Highcastle."

"Which proves my point, sister dear. Her other *court'esa* was a gift from Alija Eaglespike. Sending him away from Laran's household was probably the smartest thing Marla could have done with him."

"But a dwarf, Kagan."

"I'm sure Laran can cope."

"I know, but it's just not right . . ."

"Well, until either one of them starts to complain about it, I suggest you find something else to agonise over. I'm surprised that's all you're worried about. It's been nearly two months since the wedding. I thought you'd be panicking because there's no baby on the way."

"Two months is hardly reason to panic, Kagan." She smiled suddenly and linked her arm through his. "I'm sure I'll let the matter go for at least another month before I decide the poor child is barren."

"Well, whatever you do, don't make it too hard for Marla.

She's a nice girl at heart. It's not her fault she's Lernen's only sister, you know."

"I promise I'll look after her."

Kagan leaned over and kissed Jeryma's cheek. "I know you will."

"Good luck finding Wrayan. I hope he's come to no harm. I thought he was quite charming."

"You would."

She squeezed his arm with a smile. "Did you want an escort? I can arrange for Chaine and some of his Raiders to see you to the border."

"He's still fine with all this?" Kagan asked curiously.

"Laran spoke to him after the funeral. I'm not sure what he promised Chaine, but he's been the soul of cooperation and loyalty since Glenadal died. He certainly gets along well with Marla. The two of them have become very friendly."

"That's a pretty smart move for a bastard with no formal recognition of his status."

"Chaine's friendship with Marla is hardly likely to do her any favours, Kagan."

"No," he agreed. "But it can't hurt *his* cause to be counted as a friend to the High Prince's sister."

Jeryma shook her head. "You're imagining things. Marla has no power and I'm quite certain Chaine Tollin has no ulterior motives. He is simply doing what he has to, to keep his position here secure. Now did you want an escort or not?"

"Thanks for the offer, but I'll travel faster alone."

She nodded, her smile fading. "Did we do the right thing, Kagan?"

"*Now* you're having second thoughts?"

"You know what I mean."

"I do," Kagan replied after a moment's thought. "As to whether we did the right thing? Well, only history can tell us that."

Jeryma looked at him thoughtfully. "I just had a dreadful thought."

"What?"

"Suppose Marla does have a son, and we make him High Prince, and he turns out to be worse than what we have now?"

"Please don't even joke about it."

"I'm going to ask Laran and Marla to call their son Damin."

"After the first Damin Wolfblade? Damin the Wise? That's a lot to ask of a child who's not even born yet. Or probably not even conceived yet, if you want to get picky about it."

"The first Damin Wolfblade is largely credited with stabilising Hythria and leading us into a period of peace and prosperity that has been unequalled since."

Kagan shook his head at Jeryma's hopeful expression. "Do you really think a mere name will make that much difference to how the child turns out?"

"Maybe not," Jeryma said with a smile. "But it doesn't hurt to take precautions."

Kagan kissed her cheek again and let go of Jeryma's hand. "Well, I'd be careful before I announced to Marla that I'd named her child and decided what sort of man he's going to grow into, if I were you. She's still coming to terms with being married."

"Don't worry about me *or* Marla. Go find your apprentice. We'll be fine. Hythria will be fine."

"If you say so," Kagan said, thinking it would be good if he was even half as sure about Hythria's future as his sister.

chapter 45

I s he here yet?" Travin asked for the tenth time in as many minutes. Both he and his brother were cleaned and dressed in their Restday best, their hair slicked down, their boots polished to a shine. Riika thought it a bit silly really. It wasn't as if Laran had never seen his nephews dirty.

"Oh, for the gods' sake!" Darilyn muttered. "Stop asking me that! And Xanda! Get away from that table this instant!"

Slaves were laying out food on the long centre table in anticipation of their Warlord's arrival. Xanda guiltily snatched his hands back from the tray of pastries he'd been about to sample. The cooks had been baking since dawn, making delicate glazed pastries, fruit pies and seasoned skewers of cubed meat and vegetables, arranged on deep platters and kept warm by small oil burners under the silver trays. The aroma of all that tempting food was proving too much for a small boy. Riika smiled at her nephews, taking pity on Xanda as his bottom lip began to quiver at his mother's sharp rebuke.

"He'll be here soon," Riika promised. "The guards are probably opening the gates for Uncle Laran as we speak."

"Can we eat when Uncle Laran gets here?" Xanda asked, looking wistfully at the table.

"Do you think he brought us presents?" Travin added.

"Well if he has, I won't allow you to have them," Darilyn snapped. "Neither of you have been good enough to deserve presents."

"That's a bit harsh," Riika said. Travin looked heartbroken.

"Don't question my decisions in front of the children, Riika," Darilyn commanded. "They're unruly enough without you undermining my discipline at every turn."

"I wasn't—" Riika began, but before she could say anything else, the doors at the end of the hall opened and Mahkas entered with Laran at his side. The boys broke away and ran toward their uncles, their customary cautiousness around Laran tempered somewhat by the idea that he might have brought presents.

"Uncle Laran!"

"Did you bring us something?"

Laran squatted down and hugged the two boys, then reached into his pocket. He produced two small porcelain mounted knights with long blue-glazed lances and matching glazed armour with the rampant kraken of Krakandar painted on their shields.

"Look, mama!" Travin shouted with delight. "Aunt Riika!

Look what Uncle Laran brought us!" He ran back to show his mother and his aunt the present. They were beautiful pieces, probably from Walsark in Krakandar Province, the boys' own borough. It was renowned for its porcelain.

"I said they weren't to have presents," Darilyn announced, unimpressed. She glared at Mahkas. "Didn't you tell him I didn't want him coming here handing out presents? It makes them impossible to control."

"The presents aren't from me, Darilyn, they're from mother." Laran stood up, ruffling Xanda's head. Travin retreated rapidly from his mother, figuring he was better off with his uncles. "Now you two scat. And stop giving your mother so much trouble."

"Can we have something to eat?" Xanda asked hopefully.

"Help yourself," Laran invited with a smile.

Xanda and Travin snatched a handful of the small pastries from the nearest plate and with their new toys and the sticky treats clutched to their chests, bolted before Darilyn had a chance to order them otherwise, a fact which seemed to amuse both Laran and Mahkas greatly.

Darilyn didn't think it was very funny at all.

"You can wipe that smug expression off your faces," she warned. "Both of you. I'm the one who has to suffer the consequences after you've made me look powerless in front of my own children."

"Your boys are fine, Darilyn," Laran said, pulling off his riding gloves as he walked towards them. "And I hardly think two toy knights and a plate of pastries are going to cause them to fall into a life of crime and depravity." He reached the hearth where the women waited and put his arm around Riika. He kissed her forehead. "You're looking much better."

"I'm feeling better," Riika assured him with a smile. Laran's arrival at Winternest marked a turning point for Riika. She knew he wouldn't have come unless they were in dire need of reinforcements on the border or things had worked out the way he planned. As there had been nothing from Fardohnya other than an increase in trade since the southern pass at Highcastle was blocked, Laran's visit could only mean the latter.

"And you, Darilyn? How are you surviving?"

Although she was unlikely to admit it, Darilyn was just as keen to see her elder brother as Riika was. The novelty of being hidden away in a fortress under guard for her own protection had quickly worn off. Now she was just feeling trapped, Riika thought, bored witless confined here in Winternest and desperate to return to her social life in Greenharbour. As she had foolishly agreed not to leave Winternest without Laran's permission, she was anxious for him to arrive so that he could grant it. Darilyn was fed up with the cold, the snow, the lack of civilised conversation, the cold weather that was ruining her (yet to be repaired) harp—so she informed Riika on an almost daily basis—and was afraid that with nobody but Raiders and merchants' children as playmates, her boys were turning into barbarians.

Riika was more than happy to champion her sister's cause. Although she would miss her nephews, if she didn't see Darilyn again for another year, she wouldn't mind at all.

"I'm going mad," Darilyn snapped, surprising Riika with her bluntness. "I want to go home."

Laran didn't seem surprised. He smiled and turned to his brother. "What about you, Mahkas? Are you going mad with the altitude too?"

"I'm ready to go wherever you send me, Laran."

Mahkas couldn't hide the hope in his voice. He'd been looking forward to Laran's arrival almost as much as their sister, Riika thought. He was bored with nothing to do but think up ways to keep the troops fit in case it came to war. He wanted to head back to Cabradell. Riika knew he was convinced Laran would need his help governing his new province and was already making plans to bring his fiancée, Bylinda Telar, to Sunrise Province from Krakandar, rather than delay the wedding any longer. Mahkas's plans worried Riika a little. Laran had never said anything about giving Mahkas control over Sunrise, and she was afraid that if Laran didn't plan to do what Mahkas imagined, he would be even

more disappointed than he had been when Kagan read out
her father's will after the funeral and he'd realized Glenadal
had left his stepson nothing more than a couple of horses and
his fond wishes for the future.

"Good," Laran said, sounding a little relieved. "Because I
want you to stay here a little longer."

"Why, for the gods' sake?" Mahkas asked. "Nothing has
happened. Hablet got pissed off when he heard the news
about Marla, beheaded our ambassador and that was the end
of it. He's not going to invade us. I don't need to be here. Our
troops don't need to be here."

"Still, I'm keeping them here a little longer."

"And what about Sunrise?"

"What about it?"

"You need to get back to Krakandar, don't you?" Mahkas
reminded him. "If the farmers in Medalon wake up to the fact
that two-thirds of our troops are guarding the Fardohnyan
border and not their border, there's not going to be a cow, a
sheep or a goat between the Border Stream and Krakandar
City safe from their raids."

"I'd rather lose a few head of cattle to some Medalonian
farmer than underestimate Hablet of Fardohnya, Mahkas. I
need you here."

"Who's looking after things in Cabradell?"

"Mother is there. She's more than capable of administering the province during my absence. She had as much say in
governing it as Glenadal before he died. I don't see why that
needs to change."

"You're just going to leave a *woman* to run a whole damn
province?"

"She'll have my seal."

"That woman is your mother, Mahkas," Riika pointed out,
a little offended by what he was implying. "Surely, you don't
think her incompetent?"

"Of course not," he replied uncomfortably. "It's just not
right . . . a woman governing a province."

"Two women, actually."

"What do you mean?" Darilyn asked Laran.

"I'm sending Riika home. It's her province, really. I'm just minding Sunrise for her until she's old enough to choose a suitable consort to rule by her side. She can't do that if she doesn't know the first thing about administering the province, can she now?"

Mahkas stared at Laran in shock. "You're going to send Riika home to govern Sunrise and leave me here twiddling my thumbs?"

"It won't be for more than a few months. Until the end of summer, perhaps. If Hablet is going to make a move, he'll do it before then. He wouldn't be foolish enough to attempt a winter offensive. I don't want him sitting over the border just waiting for us to withdraw because we think he's no longer a threat to us, only to have him pour over our border in the summer."

"But that's insane!"

"Why is it insane?"

"Well . . . for one thing, you've got too many troops tied up on someone else's border. Our men belong in Krakandar. If you want to keep Winternest secure, then fine, secure it. But do it with Sunrise troops. Send Chaine up here with his men and let the rest of us go home."

"I'd rather keep Chaine in Cabradell," Laran explained.

"Why?"

"Because he doesn't trust him," Riika surmised, thinking in Laran's place she would do exactly the same thing. "Laran wants to keep Chaine Tollin where he can watch him. Isn't that the case, Laran?"

"Not exactly . . ."

"I don't blame you, you know. I don't trust him either."

Her brother shook his head, but didn't contradict her.

"And what about me?" Darilyn demanded. "I've had enough of this place. I'm desperate to return to civilisation."

"You can go home."

"Then you think I'm no longer in any danger?"

"I never thought you were in any danger in the first place, Darilyn. If you want to go back to Greenharbour, go. I'll send you with an escort if you wish."

"Am I not to be invited to Cabradell to meet your new bride?" Darilyn asked stiffly.

"I thought you were desperate to return home."

"What's she like?" Riika asked, before Darilyn could add anything further. "Is Marla pretty?"

"Very."

"Is she nice?"

"She seems that way."

"Does mama like her?"

"I suppose."

"I can't wait to meet her."

"Well, she's waiting in Cabradell," Laran reminded her with a smile. "And just as anxious to meet you, I suspect."

"Have you got her with child yet?" Darilyn asked.

"*Darilyn!*" Riika gasped.

"Don't look so shocked, Riika. We all know that's the only reason he married her. That's what all this is about, you know. Our Laran is going to father the next High Prince."

"You still shouldn't talk like that," Riika scolded. "You make it sound so . . . tawdry."

"It is tawdry, Riika. Because the truth is that it wouldn't matter if Marla Wolfblade looked like the back end of a horse and had the intellect of a ground slug so long as she has a functioning womb. Isn't that right, brother?"

Mahkas was trying to hide a smirk that Riika thought rather tactless under the circumstances. Laran's expression grew thunderous. He seemed about to say something they all might later regret.

"Well, I don't care. I've always wanted a real sister," Riika said hurriedly, without thinking, in an attempt to head off the trouble brewing between Darilyn and Laran. On hearing Darilyn's snort of disgust, she added apologetically, "My *own* age."

Darilyn wasn't fooled. "Yes, well, that would be so much more fun than the sister you're burdened with now, wouldn't it?"

"I didn't mean—"

"Oh, forget it, Riika. Go home to Cabradell and be best friends with Marla Wolfblade, for all I care. I'm going back to Greenharbour where at least I have civilised friends. As for you two," she added, looking at her brothers, "I really don't care if I see either of you again in this lifetime." Darilyn rose to her feet, pulling her shawl tighter around her shoulders and, with a regal toss of her head, walked away from the hearth towards the doors at the end of the hall.

"Does your desire to have nothing more to do with your brothers extend to not accepting any further funds from them?" Laran called after her.

Darilyn stopped and turned to look at him. "Of course not."

Laran nodded contemptuously. "I thought so."

"You're a bastard, Laran Krakenshield."

"Only when you're being a bitch, Darilyn."

Darilyn turned away from him and continued towards the door, leaving Riika with the bad feeling that she was, yet again, going to be the one who made peace between her warring siblings.

CHAPTER 46

Mahkas managed to keep his anger hidden the whole time he was with Laran, Darilyn and Riika. If anything, Darilyn's dramatic departure gave him a chance to deal with his feelings at Laran's dismissive attitude.

He's sending Riika back to Cabradell!

Mahkas couldn't believe it. He couldn't believe he had

been passed over again, this time in favour of his sixteen-year-old half-sister. *Laran wanted Riika to learn how to administer the province, did he? What about his only brother?* What about the man who was waiting in the wings, ready to step up and answer the call? The man who needed only a nod in the right direction to take up the career he was destined for?

Where is the return on my investment? The payoff for years of unwavering loyalty to you, Laran? To Krakandar?

Unable to tolerate the thought that he had been overlooked yet again, Mahkas made his excuses and fled. With command of the garrison still in his hands, he was able to escape the hall easily enough while Laran and Riika played catch-up on all the news since they'd seen each other last. He pleaded numerous duties to attend to and hurried across the chilly bridge between the north and south arms of the castle, down the stairs to the customs hall and straight across to the bar at the end of the room.

"Captain!" the barkeep called as he spied Mahkas approaching. "The usual?"

Mahkas nodded, accepting the tankard. He downed its contents in a single gulp then slammed the tankard down on the bar.

"Another?" the barkeep asked with a slightly raised brow.

"Another."

The man obliged, handing Mahkas a refill which he tackled with the same desperation as he had the first tankard.

"Drinking to ease your thirst, Captain? Or trying to forget something?"

Mahkas looked around at the man who had spoken. It was the slaver who'd been drinking with Grigar Bolonar a couple of weeks ago. He was sitting in exactly the same place at the table by the fire, as if he hadn't moved in the past fortnight.

"Not that it's any of your business . . . but I'm drinking to celebrate."

"A celebration?" the slaver asked curiously.

"I'm celebrating my ongoing posting to Winternest. The arsehole of Hythria!"

Symon Kuron smiled. "Just passing through, then, eh?"

Mahkas stared at the merchant for a moment and then laughed sourly. "Very funny. But I'm stuck here. You're the one who's just passing through."

"I would have thought you'd be honoured, Captain," the Fardohnyan remarked. "Guarding your High Prince's sister is nothing to be ashamed of."

Mahkas turned and leaned against the bar. "You really do think it's Marla in the keep, don't you?"

"I'm not a fool, Captain. You have the southern wing of this keep more heavily guarded than King Hablet's harem. And guarded with Krakandar troops, I notice, not Sunrise's own forces. And now Laran Krakenshield himself is here to visit. Say what you will, Captain, but I can draw my own conclusions."

Mahkas picked up his tankard and walked to the table. He should probably put the slaver out of his misery and simply tell him who Riika was, but he wasn't feeling particularly generous this evening. Besides, Riika's presence, while not exactly a state secret, was still not something Mahkas wanted bandied around. Laran's reasons for sending her here to Winternest were sound, even if he had now changed his mind and decided to take her home to Cabradell.

"And what if it is Marla Wolfblade?" he asked curiously, taking a seat opposite the Fardohnyan. "What would you do?"

"Me? Why nothing, Captain," Symon Kuron assured him innocently. "If I wanted to make myself a rich man, however . . ."

"I never met a Fardohnyan merchant who *didn't* want to make himself a rich man," Mahkas noted sceptically. "What are you on about?"

"The insult done to our king when your High Prince married his sister to a Warlord was most heinous, Captain," the merchant pointed out. "The man who was able to help our great and beloved leader redress such a grave insult would be looked upon most favourably at court."

"Meaning *what*, exactly?"

"Let's just say that there are certain . . . shall we say . . . *interested parties,* who would pay a great deal to get their hands on Marla Wolfblade."

"Well, that's not very likely, is it? She's not even here."

The slaver nodded, tapping the side of his nose with a knowing smile. "Of course, Captain. I understand."

Mahkas shook his head helplessly. No matter what he said, the man refused to believe that anybody other than Marla Wolfblade was currently resident in the southern arm of the keep.

"I'm curious, Trader Kuron. Suppose these *interested parties* of yours managed to get their hands on Marla. What exactly would they do with her?"

"Ransom her back to her husband, of course," Symon Kuron replied. He seemed astonished that Mahkas had even had to ask. "Or to the High Prince. Whichever has the most money, really, so I suspect it would be Laran Krakenshield rather than Lernen Wolfblade. There is no question that our King would want her for any other purpose. Not now that she's been married to another man. But the financial arrangements to secure her return would go a long way to easing our King's grief over this matter."

"I'm sure your King will get over it eventually," Mahkas said, rising to his feet. "Without the need to kidnap anybody."

"You know, the man who made such an arrangement possible, would find himself quite richly rewarded, Captain."

Mahkas looked down at the man in surprise. "You're not suggesting *I* might aid you?"

"Of course not, Captain! I would never think of insulting you so! I was merely speculating on the opportunity for some young fellow with limited prospects to make a moderate fortune. Enough, perhaps, to set himself up free of his . . . family's . . . *charity*?"

"You'll find no such man here," Mahkas claimed. The trader was dreaming. *Who in Hythria would do such a thing?*

"Of course not," Symon Kuron replied, clearly sceptical. "It was just an idle thought in any case."

Annoyed by the trader's smug assumption that a traitor might be so easily found in the ranks of his men, Mahkas glanced down the hall to where the on-duty guards stood near the customs table. He snapped his fingers in their direction then turned to the slaver with a contented smile. "Well, you'll have plenty of time for idle thinking behind bars. I'm arresting you, Master Kuron, for plotting to kidnap the High Prince's sister."

"You can't arrest me for what I was thinking!" the slaver complained as the guards surrounded him.

"No, but I can arrest you for saying it aloud," Mahkas replied. "Get him out of here," he ordered the soldiers, and walked back to the bar for another ale as they dragged the loudly protesting slaver from the hall.

By the time Mahkas returned to the hall much later that evening, Laran and Riika were both gone. Darilyn was there, however, collecting her embroidery basket. She looked up when she heard the doors open.

"They've gone to bed," Darilyn announced, tucking the basket under her arm as she straightened. "Which is where I'm headed, too. I have to start packing in the morning. And I have to arrange for my harp to travel with me. I'll not make the mistake again of entrusting it to somebody I don't know."

"You're going back to Greenharbour then?" he asked.

"It's bad enough that I have to live on Laran's charity, Mahkas. Unlike you, however, I don't feel the need to stay around and have my nose rubbed in the fact."

"Laran's never rubbed our noses in the fact that we live on his charity," Mahkas pointed out, even now feeling the need to defend his older brother.

"He doesn't need to, Mahkas. His mere presence is all it takes. I can't touch a rivet of my sons' inheritance and he knows it. He doles out a living to me a piece at a time, making me beg for every morsel."

"He doesn't make you beg, Darilyn."

"Oh, yes, he does. Not openly, perhaps, but he's got me dancing at the end of his strings, just like you." When Mahkas didn't answer, Darilyn knew she'd hit the mark. She smiled knowingly. "He's really got to you, hasn't he? Leaving you here in the middle of nowhere while he takes Riika back to Cabradell to learn how to rule the province that could have been yours if only you'd thought to suck up to Glenadal a bit more when he was alive. Gods, how *that* must hurt."

"You have no idea what you're talking about," Mahkas scoffed, surprised at how close to the truth she was.

"Riika's always been everyone's favourite, you know," Darilyn continued mercilessly. "Mother loves her best. Glenadal thought the sun rose and set in her. And Laran was prepared to send thousands of our own troops into the mountains to protect her. He wouldn't have done the same for you or me."

"They all think it's for Marla," Mahkas remarked.

"Who thinks that?"

"The Fardohnyan merchants who pass through here," he explained. "Most of them don't even realize Laran has a younger sister. They all think the blonde girl in the southern keep is Marla Wolfblade. I just arrested a slaver who suggested I could make a fortune handing her over to the Fardohnyans so that Hablet can ransom her back to Laran."

Darilyn stared at her brother thoughtfully. "How much?"

"How much would the ransom be?" he asked. "Gods! How would I know?"

"No, I mean how much is a fortune? How much did he offer you for the girl he believes to be Marla Wolfblade?"

Mahkas stared at her in shock. "You can't be serious!"

"Think about it, Mahkas. You're stuck here guarding the Widowmaker Pass while Laran ignores your years of loyal support for the sake of a spoiled sixteen-year-old girl. You've backed him without question since we were small children and he's repaid you by kicking you in the teeth. I don't know about you, but I'm sick of it. I'm fed up with living on his mercy. With enough money, we could both be free of him."

Her words were an eerie and disturbing echo of the slaver's suggestion.

"Dead isn't exactly the type of freedom I had in mind, Darilyn. And that's what would happen to us. Laran would kill us both."

"Only if he knew we were involved."

"I can't believe you're standing there suggesting we hand our own sister over to the Fardohnyans!"

"Where's the harm in it? They won't hurt her. All they want is gold. They'll take her over the border, keep her locked up for a bit and wait for Laran to cough up the ransom. Even if they find out she's not Marla, what's the worst they could do? They'll probably just ask for a smaller ransom."

"You're mad, Darilyn."

"Well, I wouldn't expect you to do anything that might upset dear brother Laran, anyway," she said scathingly. "And the gods know, we mustn't ever do anything to harm poor little Riika."

He shook his head, as if he was shaking away the temptation. "It would never work. Laran would find out we were involved. He'd know."

"Not if we were careful."

"But what if you're wrong? What if something happened to Riika?"

"It would break my heart," Darilyn replied unsympathetically.

"I won't do it."

"Fine."

"I mean it, Darilyn. I refuse to be a party to anything so treacherous."

"You said that already."

"She's our own flesh and blood, for the gods' sake!"

"Fat lot of good that did either of us when Glenadal died."

That hurt. Darilyn knew it, too.

"I won't do it," Mahkas repeated, as much to himself as his sister.

"As you wish."

"It's too dangerous."

Darilyn smiled coldly. She could tell he was weakening; trying to convince himself, not her.

"You're probably right," she agreed, shifting her embroidery basket to the other side. "It's not something either of us would seriously contemplate."

Mahkas breathed a sigh of relief.

"But hypothetically speaking," Darilyn added thoughtfully, "how much do you think we could get for someone the Fardohnyans believe is Marla Wolfblade?"

ChAPTER 47

The departure of Marla's husband for the fortress at Winternest gave Elezaar the opportunity to relax. He didn't like Laran Krakenshield, not because of anything he'd done to Elezaar in particular; the Warlord was quite civilised in his dealings with his wife's *court'esa*. It was the influence he could see Laran gaining over his mistress that concerned the dwarf.

Laran was the sort of man others instinctively turned to. People sought his good opinion without even realising they were doing it and Marla was no more immune to his personality than any other courtier. With Laran Krakenshield as her husband, with him guiding and aiding Marla as she matured, Elezaar could already foresee a time when he would become superfluous.

Having gone to all this trouble to ingratiate himself into

Marla's confidence—the effort he'd expended getting rid of Corin, all the work it had taken to convince Marla she couldn't decide *anything* without first seeking his counsel—well, the last thing he needed was for her to start getting attached to her husband. The strength of Elezaar's relationship with Marla lay in her belief that she had no more true and loyal friend in the world than her *court'esa*.

Unfortunately for Elezaar, Laran had proved to be much less daunting than he'd hoped. He didn't mistreat his young wife or force himself on her. Marla had been treated like the royalty she was since arriving in Cabradell. Her every whim was catered to. Her every request treated like a royal decree. Foods she liked had been brought in especially from the coast, her dislikes banished from the palace menus. Her sorcerer-bred mount had been brought from Highcastle and stabled in his own private accommodation. Her nurse had been given the status of a senior slave in the household. Marla had more clothes than she'd ever dreamed of owning and a steady stream of visitors who came to kneel before her and swear their fealty to her and to her husband. Even her mother-in-law, Jeryma Ravenspear—reputedly one of the most fearsome and powerful women in all of Hythria—had bent over backwards to make Marla feel welcome, and now Laran was promising to return from Winternest with his sister, Riika, a young woman the same age as Marla (who, if you believed the gossips around the palace, was the sweetest and most likeable creature the gods had ever breathed life into) so that Marla would have a friend her own age to keep her company.

Elezaar's job would have been much easier, he decided peevishly, if they'd been sent to Fardohnya, after all. At least there, surrounded by enemies, Marla would have needed a friend.

Still, things were not all roses and cream. Laran treated Marla with due deference, but they had little in common other than their mutual desire to produce an heir for Hythria.

Laran didn't take the time to find out if Marla was interested in anything else, leaving her to her own devices each day, with nothing but her mother-in-law and the women of Jeryma's court to entertain her.

Marla very quickly grew bored and frustrated by the assumption that she was good for nothing but lounging around the palace. And it was clear that Laran's belief that she was neither interested nor capable of taking an active part in the governance of his realm did not stem from the misogyny so common among the ruling men of Hythria. Jeryma had an enormous say in the running of Sunrise and Laran frequently spoke of the plans he had for Riika when he brought her back from Winternest, leaving his wife with no choice but to conclude that Laran's assumption that her purpose was purely decorative was because he thought her incompetent.

She sought Elezaar's advice, and he told her to do nothing, assuring her that things would get better once people got to know her better. In truth, he was afraid that if Marla mentioned her concern to Laran, he would immediately see the error of his ways and offer to involve his young wife more closely in his affairs. Elezaar couldn't risk that happening. He had no doubt that Marla was more than capable of taking on such a role, but he simply couldn't risk her finding her feet so soon. His safety lay in her uncertainty. The last thing he needed was Marla discovering that her opinion carried weight. Or worse, spending so much time with her husband that respect turned to admiration, or like turned into love.

Women in love had a bad habit of sending their *court'esa* away.

Jeryma didn't like him, Elezaar knew, but for reasons he couldn't quite fathom, she left him alone and didn't try to discourage Marla from keeping his company. He was often called upon to entertain the ladies of her court with poems or comedic recitals which always left them in peals of laughter and reinforced the idea that he was a Fool. Marla didn't approve of him playing the Fool for the entertainment of

Jeryma's court, thinking it demeaning for him. Elezaar almost cried when she told him that. No master he had ever known had cared that he was being humiliated. Some of them had *owned* him for that purpose. His affection for his young mistress solidified into a deep and abiding love that day and he was determined never to be separated from her, no matter what it took.

"Elezaar!"

The dwarf climbed down from the window seat in the sitting room and hurried into the courtyard in answer to his young mistress's summons. Like Lady Jeryma's quarters, Marla had a small private courtyard with a high wall surrounding it just outside her suite of rooms. It was sheltered from the wind, with a small fountain in the corner, so Marla frequently ate breakfast in the open air, a novelty she was unused to after a lifetime in the mountains.

"Your highness?"

Marla looked up from her breakfast and pushed the plate away unenthusiastically. She was wearing a light robe against the chill, a priceless purple silk dressing gown threaded with something that looked suspiciously like real gold filament. The wealth of these people—and their casual acceptance of it—left Elezaar gasping at times.

"Is the food not to your liking, your highness?"

Marla frowned. "I always worry about how fresh the fish is here. We're a long way from the coast."

"Perhaps the fish comes from one of the nearby rivers?"

"It's blue-finned arlen," she said, shaking her head. "It's a saltwater creature. I don't know how they get it here before it turns rancid."

"Snow," Elezaar explained.

"Snow?"

"They bring the catch into Greenharbour from the far southern waters of the Dregian Ocean, move it north as fast as they can, and then pack it into snow-filled wagons for the rest of the trip here. Most of it melts by the time they reach Cabradell, but what's left of the snow gets tipped into the cisterns in the palace to help cool the water."

"How do you know all these things, Elezaar?" she asked with a puzzled look. "I swear, you have an answer for everything."

"I listen, your highness. And I learn."

"Aren't you breaking your own rules?" she asked with a smile.

"What do you mean?"

"Rule Number Thirteen? Doesn't it say you should never appear too bright or too clever?"

"Actually, I was applying the Seventh Rule."

She thought for a moment before she replied, obviously trying to recall what Rule Number Seven was. "Make others seek your aid? I wasn't seeking your aid."

"No, but by making you believe I have an answer for everything, who else are you going to turn to?" Elezaar could always make Marla laugh and it concerned him a little when all she did was smile distantly. "Is something wrong, your highness?"

"Not really."

"You're not unwell, are you?"

"No."

"But something is amiss."

She hesitated then blurted out, "How will I know when I'm pregnant, Elezaar?"

He stared at her curiously. "Do you think you might be?"

She shrugged. "I don't know."

"You've been sharing a bed with Lord Krakenshield for nearly three months now," he reminded her. "One can safely assume he's been diligently undertaking the necessary steps to create our next High Prince?"

She laughed this time. "One could safely assume that, yes."

"Then you might well be, your highness. When was your last bleed?"

"About three weeks ago."

"Then it's far too early to tell."

"But aren't there other symptoms? Aren't I supposed to get sick?"

"Not all women get morning sickness. Some get tender breasts, some get no symptoms at all until their belly starts to swell." He glanced at her discarded plate and nodded in understanding. "Let me guess. You couldn't bear the thought of fish for breakfast this morning and wondered if that meant you were pregnant?"

"Something like that."

He patted her hand comfortingly. "You're young and healthy, your highness. There's no need to fret just yet."

"If I'm not with child, then I hope Laran's not away too long," she sighed.

"Are you now so committed to your husband's cause that you've become a willing participant?"

"I'm bored, Elezaar. At the very least, a child will give me something to do."

Elezaar bit back the temptation to remark that no poor woman ever thought such a thing. Instead he smiled, looking for a way to distract her. "We could resume our lessons until your husband returns, my lady."

"To what purpose, Elezaar?" she asked miserably. "Nobody cares if I know anything other than how to spread my legs."

"A game, then," he suggested brightly.

"What game?"

"How about . . . 'If I Was Ruling My Own Province'?"

"That's not a game."

"We could make it one," he said. "We'll use the chess pieces and rename them. Laran would be the king. You could be the queen. Captain Tollin would be a knight. Captain Almodavar the other one."

"Lady Jeryma's the queen around here," she pointed out with a frown.

"Very well. You could be the tower then."

"And Laran's precious little Riika can be the other tower," she added.

"That's the idea! Lord Kagan and Lady Tesha would be the bishops . . ."

"And the people of Sunrise would be the pawns."

"Now you're getting the idea! You think about who the opposing pieces are going to be and I'll fetch the board."

Elezaar hurried out of the courtyard to get the chess set, thinking this was a wonderful way to keep her amused, educate her and play on her fears all at the same time while Laran was away. He even felt a little guilty for doing it.

It was unfortunate, but Elezaar's security lay in Marla's insecurity. Perhaps, after she had her child, he would be able to establish himself as teacher and confidant to the next High Prince of Hythria.

Maybe then, Elezaar decided, he would finally be safe.

ChAPTER 48

Darilyn's foul mood eased up a little after a few days. The boys tiptoed around her, terrified of incurring their mother's wrath. After a few days, however, with the preternatural understanding common to all children, they worked out who had the real power in the family. It took them very little time to discover Laran could (and would) overrule Darilyn if they asked nicely, so they started going to him for permission to play outside or go over to the northern keep to play with the children of the merchants and customs officials who lived there. Laran wouldn't authorise an excursion outside the walls of the keep, however, even when they tried begging, unless Darilyn agreed to it, so they appealed to Riika to intervene on their behalf to take them to the stream to see if the ice had started to thaw yet.

Much to Riika's surprise, Darilyn agreed readily to the notion. Riika figured she was getting sick of the boys underfoot and was glad of the chance to be free of them for the day. Raek Harlen agreed to accompany them and arranged for a squad to escort Riika and the boys to the stream. It had iced over completely early in the winter and both Travin and

Xanda were concerned about what might happen to the old pike who lived there, whom they had unofficially adopted as a pet.

Everything was set to go, when, at the last minute, Mahkas ordered his lieutenant and two-thirds of the squad back to the keep and offered to escort Riika and the boys himself. Travin and Xanda were thrilled by the notion their beloved Uncle Mahkas was coming on their picnic, although Riika was a little disappointed. She liked Raek Harlen, much more than she probably should, considering she was the daughter of a Warlord and he was just a Raider, albeit the son of a minor noble. She'd been looking forward to spending the day with him, having him help her up the slope or catch her when she stumbled. Mahkas would do the same for her, of course, and just as willingly, but it wasn't the same as having a handsome young Raider at her beck and call.

"Why so glum?" Mahkas asked, as they followed the boys up the western slope of the mountain away from the southern keep on the Fardohnyan side of the castle. The border itself was a few miles further west, right in the Widowmaker Pass. Travin and Xanda were shouting excitedly as they ran on ahead, their cries echoing over the steep mountain slopes.

"Was I looking glum?"

"Like your best friend just died."

"I was just thinking about something."

"Well, cheer up," Mahkas ordered. "This is supposed to be fun."

Riika smiled. "I hope you remember that when you have to wade into an icy stream to fetch one of your nephews out of it. And when you have to explain to Darilyn afterwards why her boys are wet and freezing to death."

"Now you're spoiling *my* day."

"You didn't have to come, Mahkas."

"I wanted a day off. Laran's here. Let him deal with all the insanity that goes along with running Winternest for a day and see how he likes it."

"He says you've done a good job," Riika told him, hoping

to cheer her brother a little. For a man supposedly on a family picnic, he was rather morose.

"Does he? He never told me that."

"Laran wants you to stay here in command of Winternest," she pointed out, puffing a little with the exertion of negotiating the snowy slope. "Doesn't that tell you something? I mean, if he didn't like the job you're doing, he would have sent you back to Cabradell by now. Maybe even home to Krakandar."

Mahkas looked at her oddly. "Is that what you think?"

"You've nothing to worry about, Mahkas," she assured him. "In fact, I'm sure if you asked him, Laran would make your posting here permanent. He says you're really good at dealing with the merchants. He says you have the common touch."

"Laran thinks I'm *common*?"

Riika laughed. "Oh, Mahkas, look at your face! It was a compliment! He meant you're really good at dealing with the common people."

"Oh, sure, he meant it as a compliment," Mahkas replied, clearly not convinced. "But if Laran is so damned impressed with my *common* touch, why leave me stuck up here on the border? I was more use to him fighting off Medalonian cattle thieves than I am collecting taxes off a bunch of greasy Fardohnyan caravan drivers."

Riika detected a note of bitterness that seemed more than just a young man feeling a little put out over something trivial.

"Perhaps you should talk to Laran when we get back, Mahkas."

"Perhaps I will," Mahkas muttered unhappily, striding on ahead of her and effectively putting an end to their conversation.

With the stream still iced over and no sign of Zag, the name Xanda had given to their missing fish, Mahkas suggested after lunch that his nephews might like to take a walk even further from the castle, into the woods. Under the shelter of the trees closer to the pass, the small stream was still flowing.

Mahkas thought the boys might have more luck finding Zag upstream and they happily agreed to the suggestion. Riika wasn't sure it was such a good idea to stray so close to the border, but figured that if Mahkas thought it was safe, there was nothing to be concerned about. Once he'd made the suggestion, there was no chance of getting out of it anyway. Travin and Xanda were determined to find their fish and, with an ally as influential as their Uncle Mahkas, they knew there was little chance of Aunt Riika overruling his decision.

The air grew colder as they walked under the trees. The boys bounded on ahead, as usual, calling for Mahkas to catch up with them. Mahkas had left the guards back by their picnic things, claiming (out of his nephews' hearing) that there was no need for everyone to traipse through the forest upstream trying to find one not-very-large fish that probably wasn't there anyway.

Mahkas hurried on ahead to catch the boys. He stopped after a few steps and turned to look at Riika. "Come on, slow coach!"

"It's all right for you," she called after him. "You're not wearing a skirt!"

The snow was deeper here in the shadow of the trees where the shade stopped it from melting in the weak winter sunlight. Riika trudged through it doggedly, wishing she'd decided to stay back with the guards and their picnic.

At least she'd had the sense to wear an old outfit, even if it was a little tattered and ragged; she knew it'd be messy and wet trudging around in the snow with her nephews.

Mahkas laughed and turned to follow the boys. Within a few steps he was hidden by the trees, only the sound of Travin and Xanda's distant laughter reminding Riika that she wasn't totally alone in the world. Smiling at the boys' obvious delight and at Mahkas's generosity in humouring his nephews, Riika slowed her pace a little. She wasn't really needed. Mahkas and the boys were having plenty of fun without her. It must be something about boys—little boys as well as big ones—this idea that floundering around in knee-deep snow looking for a fish probably long gone in an icy stream in the dead of winter was entertaining.

Riika's next step plunged her into a small gully, where the snow went from knee-deep to thigh-deep in the space of a single step. Cursing, she struggled out of the depression, looked in the direction Mahkas had disappeared with the boys and threw her hands up in defeat. They didn't need her and she was going to be soaked to the skin. At least, back at the picnic site, they had a small fire going. Riika turned and headed back to where the guards waited with the remains of their lunch, shivering as she tried to shake the powdery snow from her skirts before it began to melt.

As she trudged back towards the camp, the sound of the children's voices faded away to nothing and the silence under the canopy of the forest began to feel unnerving. Riika looked around, wondering why she hadn't noticed how far into the treeline they had wandered. She wasn't afraid of getting lost. Her footprints, along with those of Mahkas and the children, were clearly visible heading back towards the small plateau where the guards waited. There were other footprints too, she noted, that ran parallel to theirs. Perhaps the guards Mahkas left back at the picnic site had shadowed them into the forest for a way, to make certain they were safe. There wasn't a Raider in Winternest who wanted to be the one to face Lady Darilyn and break the news that something had happened to one of her sons.

The sharp, unexpected crack of a breaking twig made Riika jump. At the sudden sound a large bird roosting in the trees was also disturbed. It launched itself from the branches overhead with a raucous squawk, showering her with snow.

This time she let out a short, involuntary squeal and then, her heart still pounding, she laughed at herself for being so foolish.

Shaking the snow from her hair, Riika followed the footprints back the way she had come, scolding herself for being an over-imaginative idiot. Despite the blanketing silence, it was broad daylight and there was nothing in the forest to be concerned about. In front of her lay her brother's guards, left minding their picnic lunch; behind her nothing more sinister than Mahkas and his nephews hunting an old pike in a frozen stream.

Riika saw the edge of the trees ahead and increased her pace, hoping she didn't look too bedraggled. Between trudging through the snow, falling into that damn hollow and having a bird take off over her head, she'd received quite a dousing in the past half hour. Suddenly, she was glad Raek Harlen had been sent back to the keep. She wouldn't want him to see her looking like—

Emerging from the trees, Riika took in the scene before her with an uncomprehending stare. The cheery little fire was trampled into the snow. The four guards Mahkas had left behind lay on the ground, the snow stained dark and bloody beneath them. To a man their throats had been slit with a single slash, as if they had been attacked from behind. There was no other sign of a struggle. No sign of who had done such a dreadful thing. No reason for it that Riika's paralysed mind could grasp.

It took only seconds for the implications to register, but it felt like a lifetime before she was able to scream. Even then, Riika wasn't sure if it was a warning or a primal cry of terror that she let loose.

She had barely opened her mouth before she was grabbed from behind. Her screams intensified with fear, echoing across the slopes. They could probably hear her back at the castle, but it did her little good. The man who held her was much stronger than she. He lifted her clear of the ground as another man grabbed her feet and bound them securely around the ankles. As soon as he had, the man holding her dropped her to the snow, where a third man jumped on her and bound her wrists in a similar fashion to her ankles and then produced a gag. She wriggled helplessly, screaming as loud as she could, tossing her head from side to side to avoid the gag, but the man who had tied her ankles simply grabbed her head and held it still while the other man secured the gag. They were Fardohnyans, she realized as the dirty cloth smothered her screams. The swarthy man who had first grabbed her pulled her to her feet.

"*Riika!*"

Mahkas's cry echoed across the slope as he emerged from the trees at a run, his sword drawn. There was no sign of Travin or Xanda behind him, but that was probably a good thing. Mahkas would have easily outdistanced his young nephews when he heard his sister's screams. He rushed at the men holding her with a wordless yell of fury. The man who had tied her ankles drew his own sword and stepped forward to face this new opponent. The man who held Riika didn't pay the duelling pair any attention. He just spun Riika around to face him, breathing hot, foul breath on her before pulling a dark hood down over her head.

A few seconds later she heard Mahkas cry out and the sound of clashing blades suddenly fell silent.

"Let's get out of here," the man holding Riika ordered.

Without ceremony, she was picked up and thrown over the shoulder of one of the men, tears of fear and grief saturating the suffocating blackness of the hood as she was bounced and thumped along the steep mountain slope.

West.

Towards Fardohnya.

ChAPTER 49

Does it hurt, Uncle Mahkas?"

Laran turned away from his discussion with Raek Harlen and glanced at his brother sitting by the fire in the main hall of the southern keep. The firelight glistened off the sweat on his brow as Travin and Xanda looked on with concern while Darilyn stitched the long wound in their uncle's arm.

"I'll be all right," Mahkas assured Travin, wincing as Darilyn tugged on the stitches. "Your mama will fix me."

"Perhaps the boys should be thinking about bed?" Laran suggested to Veruca, who was watching over her charges as if they might vanish at any moment. Like their mother, the old nurse seemed afraid to let them out of her sight.

"Will they be safe, my lord?" she asked nervously.

"Here in the keep?" he asked. "Of course they'll be safe."

"You thought they'd be safe out on a picnic, too," Darilyn pointed out as she snipped another stitch with her embroidery scissors. "I want them to stay here with me."

Laran shook his head. He wanted a council of war, not a nursery.

"Will you be much longer?"

"I'm almost done."

"Good," he said, turning back to Raek. On Laran's orders the young lieutenant had had his men scouring the slopes for any sign of Riika since they'd heard her screams just after midday, but nothing had been found. It was dark now. Between that and a recent snowfall that had obliterated any tracks, there was little chance of finding anything useful until morning. "Have every man you can spare ready to leave at first light," he ordered Raek. "Riika may still be out there somewhere."

"Of course she's not still out there somewhere," Darilyn scoffed, plunging the needle back into Mahkas's arm. "She'll be over the border and in a fast carriage for the Fardohnyan inland by now. You might as well sit back and wait for the ransom demand, Laran. There's nothing else you can do."

Laran was furious that Darilyn was so unconcerned about Riika's fate. He'd been simmering on the edge of unreasonable rage since learning of the death of four of his Raiders and his youngest sister's abduction. Darilyn might well push him over the edge if she made another comment like that.

"And if it was slavers who killed the guards and took Riika?"

"What slaver in his right mind attacks someone so well guarded?" Darilyn shrugged. "Anyway, we haven't had any slave raids at Winternest the whole time we've been here. Mahkas said the slavers usually concentrate their raids on the Highcastle pass because it's closer to the coast."

"The Highcastle pass is closed," Laran reminded her.

"Still, Darilyn has a point," Mahkas added, wincing at her heavy-handed doctoring. "They haven't been a problem around here for years."

"Well, they seem to be a problem now," Laran snapped.

"Will the bad men hurt Aunt Riika?" Travin asked with concern.

"You don't think they'll find Zag and hurt him too, do you, Uncle Laran?" Xanda asked in alarm. "They might catch him and eat him!"

"No, I don't think the bad men will eat your fish," Laran told him brusquely. "Veruca, get the boys out of here. Now. Raek will see there is a guard on their door tonight, but I want them gone."

"I want them here," Darilyn insisted.

"Too bad," Laran told her unsympathetically. Anxiously, Veruca glanced between the Warlord and the mother of her charges and apparently decided Laran's orders carried the most weight. She bustled the boys together and hurried them from the hall. With a jerk of his head, Laran indicated Raek should accompany her and see the boys were safe. The young lieutenant saluted and followed the nurse and Laran's two rather subdued nephews from the hall.

Darilyn glared at him. "You have no right to order my slaves around."

"She's not your slave, Darilyn. She was Riika's nurse, not yours, and belongs to the Ravenspear family. Your use of her while you're here in Winternest is a courtesy only. So if you don't like me telling *my* slaves what to do with your children, find your own to order around."

Darilyn tied off the last stitch on Mahkas's wound with a jerk, making her brother yelp, before she turned to look at Laran. "Don't take your frustration out on me, Laran Krakenshield. I'm not the one who couldn't protect his family with half a damned army here to watch over them."

"Well, now, you see there's the problem, Darilyn, I *had* half a damned army ready to watch over my family and Mahkas sent them back to the keep."

"It was a stupid thing to do," Mahkas admitted as Darilyn began to bandage his arm. "I'm sorry, Laran. I just didn't think there'd be any danger so close to the castle. I'll ride out with you in the morning. We'll find Riika. I promise."

"You can't hold a sword," Laran reminded him, pointing to his wounded right arm.

Mahkas glanced down at the long cut reaching from his bicep to his wrist that Darilyn had so neatly stitched. Laran thought him lucky that the tendons hadn't been cut and so lost the use of his sword arm completely. Squaring his shoulders manfully in the face of what must have been considerable pain and anguish, Mahkas looked back at his brother with determination. "This won't slow me down."

"No, but it will slow me down," Laran told him bluntly. "I'm sending the bulk of the troops out to scour the hills tomorrow, just in case this was simply on opportunistic raid by Fardohnyan bandits. They may have taken what they wanted—"

"You mean they may simply have raped Riika, of course," Darilyn cut in.

"Yes, I mean that," Laran agreed, with a dangerous expression. "And if they did, they may have left her for dead somewhere in the mountains."

"And if they haven't?" Mahkas asked.

"I'm taking Raek and a small troop with me into Fardohnya to see if I can track her down."

"You're just going to ride into Fardohnya with a troop of armed Raiders?" Darilyn asked in horror. "Are you mad, Laran? Even if they do have her, the Fardohnyans will consider that an act of war."

"Kidnapping my sister was an act of war, Darilyn. I am simply responding in kind."

"Why don't you just wait?" she insisted reasonably. "Give it a few days. See if we get a ransom demand. Gods, it's not as if you can't afford to pay to get her back. And it's a damn sight more logical than you, Raek Harlen and a handful of vengeance-seeking Raiders declaring war on Fardohnya."

"Is that all you think this is?"

"No, it's not what I think," she replied harshly. "What I think is that this is just another example of how you are prepared go to any lengths for Riika, even if it endangers the rest of the family. Only in this case, you're endangering the rest of Hythria."

"How is rescuing Riika endangering Hythria?"

"You're asking *me*?" she laughed scornfully. "Gods, Laran. You just turned the whole damn country on its ear by marrying Marla Wolfblade so you can get us an heir we can all be proud of. A Hythrun heir, remember? So what are *you* planning to do? Instead of staying at home like any sane man would do and making certain your new bride conceives our precious Hythrun heir, you're going to gallop off on some damn fool rescue mission that is totally useless, given that you can probably buy Riika back any time you want, even if it was slavers that took her."

Laran stared at Darilyn for a moment, too angry to trust himself to speak. That she could so callously disregard Riika's fate was more than he could comprehend. That she might have a point about a ransom demand only made things worse.

"I will do whatever it takes to get our sister back," he announced. "And I will take as long as I have to, with as many men as I need. I am not going to pay for something that is rightfully mine."

"Your stubbornness will be the death of me, Laran," Darilyn accused.

"I should be so lucky," Laran muttered angrily.

CHAPTER 50

The following morning, at first light, Laran led Raek Harlen and a squad of twenty Raiders out of Winternest and turned them onto the road leading to the Widowmaker Pass. The air was crisp, their horses' breath frosting in the early morning light as they cantered west toward Fardohnya.

Laran wasn't expecting any trouble. At least, not until they reached the keep on the other side of the ten-mile pass that cut through the Sunrise Mountains separating Fardohnya and Hythria. Once they reached Westbrook, Laran figured his problem would be the Fardohnyan customs officials rather than armed resistance, and he was certain he could buy them off. It was pretty much a given in Fardohnya that you didn't hold any sort of public office if you *couldn't* be bought off.

Thanks to Fardohnya's endemic corruption, Laran expected to learn all he needed to know for the cost of a few bribes. Within hours he would know who had brought Riika through the pass, or, indeed, if she had been brought through at all. He would know the names of the traders, know the identity of their wives and children and probably what they had eaten for breakfast this morning.

By dinner time, if he didn't have Riika back, he expected to know where to find her and to be making plans for her recovery.

Their early departure meant they avoided traffic in the pass, for which Laran was grateful. Parts of the natural chasm were barely wide enough for a wagon to pass through and traffic jams were common, as were fights between the caravan drivers about who got there first, who should have right of way and who should back up—another reason it was known as the Widowmaker Pass.

Glenadal had long advocated the need for some road rules through the pass, but every attempt to negotiate a set of viable rules had ended in failure because the Fardohnyan officials, given the right incentive, could so easily be convinced to turn a blind eye to any infractions. Chaos remained the rule of law and Laran's only hope of avoiding it was to cross the border before any of the caravans camped on either the Fardohnyan or Hythrun side of the border last night got too deep into the pass this morning.

The gods were with him, it seemed. They encountered no traffic, although the road was boggy and rutted with the passing of so many wagons. Glenadal had also spoken on a number of occasions of paving the road through the pass, but had been reluctant to undertake such a feat because of the disruption to trade while the road was built and the huge cost involved. Laran wondered if it was still worth doing, though. They could charge a toll to help offset the cost, it would speed up the journey between the two countries, and they could build rest areas in a couple of the wider parts of the pass which would allow caravans travelling in the opposite direction to pass each other without coming to blows. He could probably even get Hablet to agree to bear half the cost of construction if he offered him half the tolls in return.

Assuming Hablet was still speaking to him, of course. There was that unfortunate issue of Laran stealing Hablet's bride that might yet prove an insurmountable barrier to any meaningful negotiations with Fardohnya.

"There's the keep."

Laran gave up wondering about the feasibility of paving ten miles of high mountain pass at Raek's warning and looked into the distance. A rather less impressive version of Winternest, Westbrook was built to a similar scale, although it lacked a bridge over the road linking the two arms of the keep. But it was still a solid, almost impregnable fortress and Laran didn't fool himself for a moment that he could take it by force. Certainly not with the twenty Raiders he'd brought with him. Despite what Darilyn thought, the Fardohnyans would not consider Laran and his men riding to Westbrook an act of war. A Warlord and twenty Raiders attacking the keep would be treated as a joke.

They rode into the bailey of the northern keep just ahead of a long caravan heading out, its wagons filled with barrels of wine, large clay jars of oil, bolts of cloth and two loads of muscular male slaves, probably destined for the mines near Byamor in Elasapine. The slaves were seated in the wagons, covered with blankets against the cold but otherwise unrestrained. The trader was obviously an astute businessman. The slaves would arrive in Byamor in peak condition. There would be no infected sores from chafing chains, no cramped muscles or wasted limbs. They would be fit and ready to work and worth five times a slave who needed to recover from his transport to the mines. There was little chance the slaves would attempt to escape. They were naked and barefoot under the blankets. They'd be lucky to survive more than a day or two in the mountains without shelter.

Laran dismounted as the caravan trundled out of the gates, the caravan driver yelling at the following wagons to keep up. A few moments later a figure emerged from the hall of the main building. He was bald and stocky and wore a large chain and medallion around his neck that indicated he was the Plenipotentiary of Westbrook, an archaic title that dated back to the early days of the new nation of Hythria, when the Fardohnyan border garrison commander was authorised to negotiate with the full power of his king, to save time by not having to constantly refer decisions back to Talabar. The first High Princess of Hythria had been the Fardohnyan King's beloved twin sister, after all, and her husband, Jaycon Wolfblade, one of his most trusted vassals. King Greneth the Elder had anticipated no unreasonable demands from the new nation and had confidently delegated the responsibility to an underling. That was over a thousand years ago. The Plenipotentiary of Westbrook's authority had been eroded considerably since then by ever more distrustful kings. The man now wielded no more power than the average captain in the Fardohnyan army, but the title was prestigious and he got to keep the impressive gold medallion when he retired.

"There's a marker about three miles up the road," the man remarked in fluent Hythrun as he approached. "It says 'Fardohnya'. I'm guessing you boys don't realize that means you can't ride into my keep armed to the teeth and looking for trouble."

"I'm Laran Krakenshield."

"Ah," the man replied. He looked him up and down with a considering expression, his eyes stopping on Laran's beaten silver cuirass, and then shrugged. "Well, I suppose that makes the circumstances a little . . . extenuating. I am Symon Kuron. What can I do for you, Lord Krakenshield?"

"A member of my family was kidnapped yesterday."

"How tragic. Why are you telling me?"

"She was kidnapped by Fardohnyans."

"Are you certain?"

"Yes."

"I see."

"I hope you *do* see," Laran warned. "Because if she was brought through here and you let her pass without question, Plenipotentiary, I'm going to be *very* angry with you."

Kuron glanced over Laran's twenty-man escort with a faint sneer. "You frighten me, Lord Krakenshield. I'm positively quaking in my boots. Twenty Hythrun Raiders! Gracious, what will I do?"

"I have a few thousand more where these came from," Laran pointed out coldly.

"I know," Kuron agreed with a sigh, "but you see, here's *your* problem, Lord Krakenshield. They're not here, are they?" Symon Kuron snapped his fingers and suddenly they were surrounded. The Fardohnyan guards on the wall-walk had their crossbows trained on Laran and his troop, the soldiers in the bailey had their swords drawn.

Laran held up his arm to halt Raek and his men drawing their own weapons and sparking a bloodbath.

"A wise move, Lord Krakenshield," Symon Kuron remarked when he saw the gesture.

"We're expected." It was a statement, not a question. Riika's kidnapping obviously went a lot higher than a few slavers stumbling over an opportune target.

The Plenipotentiary of Westbrook nodded. "Yes, my lord, you were expected. Your recent actions have rather disturbed my king and he would very much like a word with you."

"And for this you kidnapped an innocent girl?" Laran asked as the Fardohnyans moved in to disarm the Hythrun. "Why not just send me a message asking for a parley?"

"Because there's no profit in *that*," Kuron said, as if Laran was a little dim for even having to ask the question. "In the meantime, may I offer you some breakfast, Lord Krakenshield? It will be some time before your escort gets here."

"Escort?"

"You don't expect the king to come to you, do you, my lord?"

"Where are you taking me?"

"Not far."

"And where is my lady?" Raek demanded, unable to contain himself any longer. Laran glanced at him and shook his head. Despite their virtual captivity, there was a good chance he could negotiate their way out of this. If Hablet wanted to talk to him, and had simply kidnapped Riika to get his attention, then it was highly likely he would let them both go once he'd had his fun.

Hablet wouldn't kill him, Laran was certain of that. No matter how fractious the Warlords of Hythria were normally, nothing would unite them faster than the death of one of their number at the hands of the Fardohnyan king and Hablet didn't want a war with Hythria. He'd wanted their princess as a wife.

"Her highness is safe and well," Kuron promised. "And will remain so, while ever Lord Krakenshield is being cooperative."

"It'll be all right, Raek." He turned to the Plenipotentiary. "I'll want *my* men to accompany me, too."

"Of course."

Laran nodded and watched as his escort was herded away. The Plenipotentiary of Westbrook stood back and politely gestured that Laran should follow him inside. It was only as they entered the hall and the smell of freshly cooking bacon wafted over them from the fires at the other end that Laran thought to wonder why Symon Kuron had referred to Riika as "her highness".

ChAPTER 51

Mahkas's arm ached abominably. He was horrified by how close the Fardohnyan slaver's man had come to causing him permanent injury, but he could hardly complain about it to anyone. The agreement was that he would be wounded convincingly in the attack, and he had been. Laran *had* to be convinced Mahkas had endangered his own life trying to rescue Riika. The slightest hint that he hadn't done his utmost to save her might be enough to cast doubt on his story.

Mahkas just hadn't realized it would hurt so much.

He hadn't counted on the Fardohnyans killing the guards either, but there was no way he could take Symon Kuron to task for it now. He'd sent Raek and the rest of the guards back to the castle for the simple reason of reducing the number of men who would need to be subdued in order to take Riika captive. He'd inadvertently saved their lives, not realising the Fardohnyan definition of "subdued" was his definition of "dead".

Mahkas felt as if he'd done a deal with some evil god, intent on turning him from everything he knew to be good and decent. He wasn't sure if the evil god was made flesh in the form of the Fardohnyan, Symon Kuron, or in his own sister, Darilyn.

She was the driving force behind this unconscionable betrayal of both Laran's trust and Riika's. A few weeks ago he wouldn't have imagined himself capable of such a thing. But a few weeks ago, Laran hadn't passed him over for a position of great responsibility that he patently deserved simply because he thought their sixteen-year-old sister more worthy of the trust. A few weeks ago Mahkas had been facing a future with some sort of promise, not a future stretching before him filled with always being someone's second-in-command.

None of that excused what he had done, of course. But he was on this path now and there was no turning back. He was responsible for the deaths of the four men killed in the raid and, to himself at least, did not try to shift the burden to anyone else. But guilt and conscience were two different things. Just because he felt bad didn't mean Mahkas wasn't prepared to go the distance. He knew that should his involvement ever come to light he would be ruined. Laran would probably kill him and that would be the kindest fate that could befall him if his treachery were exposed. The thought of others knowing of his betrayal and having to live with their recriminations was more than he could bear to imagine.

With Laran gone, even for a short time, he was able to breathe a little easier. Mahkas didn't expect his brother to get far with the Fardohnyans. *He'll be back by tonight with nothing to show for his little expedition across the border.* The Plenipotentiary would probably just laugh when Laran confronted him. Mahkas didn't know who held the post at present. He hadn't really thought to ask. The less he knew about this dangerous enterprise the better. All he knew was that Symon Kuron had assured him the Plenipotentiary of Westbrook was willing to negotiate and would ensure that "Princess Marla" would come to no harm while awaiting her release.

Of course, the slaver had no idea that Riika wasn't Marla Wolfblade. And that was Mahkas's protection. Even if someone told Laran outright that his brother had arranged to have Marla kidnapped, Laran wouldn't believe him. Marla was back in Cabradell, so whoever set this plan up was obviously someone who didn't know Mahkas and Laran had a younger sister. It couldn't have been a member of the family. Darilyn was quite adamant on that point. Laran simply wouldn't believe it, she had assured her brother. Of either of them.

Now, it was just a case of waiting for their share of the ransom. He had done well in the negotiations. Darilyn and Mahkas were to receive twenty-five per cent of whatever the Fardohnyans managed to get for Riika. Symon Kuron had spoken of a figure in the millions. Even if they found out who Riika really was and the ransom demand became more reasonable, their share of the loot was still likely to be a six-figure amount. With that much money he could buy himself a decent holding in another province, be a very wealthy man and no longer beholden to Laran's whims.

He didn't give a fig for what Darilyn planned to do with her share of the ransom, although her alibi was probably even more convincing than Mahkas's excuse. Laran would never believe she would willingly endanger her own children.

The only problem he really had was coming up with a plausible reason for his sudden and unexpected wealth. Perhaps he could claim a forgotten legacy from his father? Probably not a good idea. Jeryma knew his late father's business affairs too well. A gift from a deceased friend? Mahkas didn't have that many close—or more to the point—wealthy friends. Better to claim the money came from Bylinda's family. His fiancée's father was a rich merchant. It wasn't inconceivable that he might want to set his future son-in-law up in the manner to which his daughter was accustomed.

But that was a problem for another day. Mahkas cut a lonely, tragic figure as he paced the bridge over the road, his arm in a black sling, waiting for word about his missing sister. The search parties had turned up nothing, as he knew would be the case. Mahkas interrogated each troop anxiously as it returned and sent them out again as soon as possible, swearing he wouldn't rest until Riika was found.

When Laran returned from Westbrook, he would hear about Mahkas's dedication, his obvious distress and his desperate attempts to find Riika. And he wouldn't suspect a thing.

But it was cold out here on the bridge and his arm was aching. Night was falling rapidly. The last of the search parties had returned but there was no sign of Laran. He may have decided to stay at Westbrook for the night and return in the morning. Stamping his feet against the cold, Mahkas turned towards the entrance of the northern keep. He consciously kept his thoughts on his fiancée, Bylinda; her dark hair, her wide green eyes, her smile, even the freckles that lightly dusted her nose. He kept the picture of her in his mind. Refused to let anything dislodge it. That way he didn't think about Riika and what she might be going through.

There was no point being out on the bridge any longer. They would be closing the gates to the northern keep soon anyway. Mahkas said goodnight to the guards on bridge duty and headed downstairs for a cup of ale before he went home.

The customs hall was uncharacteristically subdued and the tavern-keeper's greeting much less ebullient than usual. Mahkas drank his ale down, noticing how every other eye in the hall was desperate not to catch his. None of them knew what to say. The common belief around Winternest, he knew, was that Riika had been taken by slavers and was probably on her way to the markets in Talabar by now. They felt for Mahkas; sympathised with his plight. He had tried to save his sister against overwhelming odds (Mahkas had put about the story that there were at least six of them) and failed. And he had the wounds to prove it.

But along with their sympathy came a healthy dose of caution. Nobody was sure if Mahkas should be hailed as a hero for trying to save his sister, or a cur for not being able to, and until the people of Winternest figured which way the wind was blowing, they preferred to avoid the young captain.

Realising there would be no joy here tonight, Mahkas swallowed his ale, refused a refill and headed back to the stairs that would take him up to the bridge and over to the southern keep. Maybe tomorrow, when Laran returned from Westbrook, things would settle down a bit. Maybe tomorrow the ransom demand would come and they could get to work on assembling the money.

Maybe tomorrow he wouldn't feel like this.

Maybe tomorrow he would wake up and be able to find some small measure of merit in what he had done.

"A messenger has arrived from Cabradell," Darilyn announced, looking up as Mahkas entered the hall. The fire was lit and it was almost cosy in the normally draughty chamber. Quite an accomplishment when one considered the size of the hall. The boys were absent, probably getting ready for bed, given the hour.

Mahkas was glad they weren't here; he was in no mood for Travin or Xanda this evening.

"A messenger?" he asked, taking a seat in front of the fire. He relaxed back into the cushions, wishing there was something he could take for the pain in his arm. Or maybe it simply needed to be warmed. The air was icy out on the bridge and he'd been up there most of the day.

"The messenger had a letter for Laran," Darilyn told him. "From mother."

"What does it say?"

"It was addressed to Laran."

"That wouldn't stop you reading it."

Darilyn scowled. "It says that it doesn't matter what we do, dear brother Laran always manages to come out on top."

"What do you mean?"

"She's pregnant."

"Mother is *pregnant*?"

"No, you idiot!" she snapped. "The future heir of Hythria has been conceived, just as Laran planned. He's single-handedly quelled the Warlords of Hythria and now he's proved his manhood. Mother is thrilled, as you can well imagine. We will find ourselves bowing at the feet of our own nephew some day, Mahkas. Won't that be fun?"

"What are you *talking* about, Darilyn?"

She held up the letter with its broken seal, shaking it at him. "She's pregnant, fool. Marla Wolfblade is pregnant."

ChAPTER 52

Shivering a little in the weak winter sunlight, Marla sat on the edge of the fountain in Jeryma's private courtyard, trailing her fingers in the chilly water, waiting for Jeryma to finish her discussion with Delon Grym, the Ravenspear family physician. Originally a *court'esa*, Delon's skills as a medic had kept him in Jeryma's household long past the time a *court'esa* would normally expect to remain in service. Like Elezaar, Delon had other talents to offer his mistress that had secured his place in her household on a permanent basis. In his sixties now, with a head of thick white hair, a quick mind and an arthritic limp, he had delivered all four of Jeryma's children and was probably the only man Jeryma trusted to deliver her grandson, too.

It was no surprise to Marla that news of her pregnancy had
spread through Cabradell, almost before she was certain of it
herself. She had been watched with eagle-eyed enthusiasm
by everyone in the palace from the first day she had shared a
bed with Laran; and by her mother-in-law most of all.

Marla understood the position she was in and knew, in her
heart, that this was as good as it was ever likely to get. This
plan to save her from a marriage to Hablet was Jeryma's idea,
Marla realized. Either Jeryma or her late husband, Glenadal
Ravenspear, had thought it up, at any rate. She didn't fool
herself for a moment that it had in any way been motivated
by the notion that Marla would rather have died than be sent
to marry Hablet in Fardohnya. Their plans centred entirely on
the desire for a Hythrun-born heir to her brother's throne.
Saving Marla from Hablet was merely a by-product of their
scheme.

Laran was not a volunteer. He had been conscripted to
their cause, Marla decided, after a few weeks of marriage to
him. He was not the type to launch a coup without reason.
Laran could see the sense in the plan, was prepared to do
what he had to, to ensure its success, but it was clear that he
would rather have found a way to achieve his political goals
without taking a wife. Particularly a wife almost half his age
with whom he had nothing in common.

Marla had not been much help in the early days, either.
Still smarting over the harsh realisation that she was, essen-
tially, a walking womb on offer to the highest bidder, she
didn't really have much enthusiasm for fulfilling her duties as
a wife. Besides, she was in love with Nash Hawksword. It
seemed like a betrayal to even think about sleeping with another man.

She had come to her marriage bed the night of her wedding as drunk as a victorious warlord, and had passed out before anything happened. The second night she had been
drunk again—Hythrun wedding receptions went on for
days—but this time, instead of passing out, she threw up all

over the bed, effectively putting an end to anything remotely romantic for the rest of that night, as well.

On the third night, she began to feel a little guilty that she wasn't being fair to Laran. She made a new resolution to herself. *Stop putting it off. Get it over with. Do what Hythria needs you to do . . .*

So, full of wine and good intentions, determined to do what she must to honour the bargain her brother had made in her name, Marla let herself into Laran's room. She draped herself alluringly over the chaise near the fireplace, her long hair unbound, dressed in a sheer gown that offered a tantalising glimpse of the bare flesh beneath, and waited for her husband.

Laran arrived a few moments after Marla. He looked at her in surprise. "You're conscious," he remarked coolly. "And appear to have kept your dinner down, as well."

"I'm sorry about . . . last night," she said. "And about the night before."

Her apology probably would have sounded more heartfelt if she hadn't hiccupped loudly at the end of it. Laran took the chair opposite the chaise near the fire and studied her curiously.

"How much have you had to drink tonight, Marla?"

She shrugged. "One or two . . ."

"Glasses?"

"Decanters."

He shook his head. "And this drinking problem you appear to have developed in the past three days. Is this something you're planning to continue, or can we expect you to sober up any time soon?"

"I'm not a drunk!" she protested.

"No?" he asked with a raised brow.

"It's just . . ."

"You can't bear the thought of sleeping with *me*?" he concluded.

Marla couldn't tell whether he was angry or disappointed or simply making an observation. Laran was good at not giving away things like that. "You've had two *court'esa* at your disposal for months, Marla," he pointed out, a little puzzled by her reluctance. "Surely there are no surprises awaiting you?"

"I know . . . but . . ."

"What?"

"Well, Elezaar might be a *court'esa,* but you really don't think that I . . ." Her words trailed off as she squirmed uncomfortably under his gaze. "Anyway, Corin was . . . helpful, but I was so angry at Lernen for promising me to Hablet, I only used him . . . a bit."

"So what's the problem?"

"I'm afraid you'll think me . . . I don't know . . . stupid, or something . . ."

"Coming to my bed drunk each night is going to convince me of your stupidity, Marla, much faster than you admitting you're afraid or inexperienced."

She hadn't thought of it like that. "I'm sorry, Laran, truly I am. It's just . . . I don't want to let anyone down. Not you, or my brother. Even your mother and the High Arrion. I know what everyone wants of me. I understand what's riding on it. I can even see the logic of it—"

"When you're sober?" he cut in, with the ghost of a smile.

She pulled a face at him. "All right . . . when I'm *sober.* I'm just so afraid of not being what everybody expects of me. Suppose I don't have a son? What if I'm barren? Or suppose—"

"Marla!" Laran said sharply, cutting her off mid-sentence.

"What?"

"Go to bed," he ordered. "Your *own* bed. Tomorrow, when it's *you* talking and not the wine, we'll talk again. I'm sure we can work out a way to deal with this then."

"You're not angry with me?"

"Not this time," he assured with a smile. "Too many more nights watching you stagger inebriated from the dinner table, however, might start to wear on my patience a little."

Marla smiled in remembrance of his words, thinking that was the moment she began to *like* Laran. She didn't love him. She loved Nash. But Laran was likable and, when all was said and done, if you had to be married to someone, it rather helped things along if they were tolerable company.

"Well," Jeryma announced, putting an abrupt end to Marla's reminiscing as she dismissed the physician and walked back out into the courtyard. "Delon says you're fit and well."

"I suppose I'm to be packed away now," Marla sighed. "And coddled like an invalid until it's born?"

"Gracious, child, whatever makes you think that?" she exclaimed. "You're pregnant, not suffering some terrible disease. Besides, how do you expect your child to become vigorous and healthy if you're spending the next few months lying about like a slug?"

"I thought that's what happened when noblewomen get pregnant. They're confined like well-kept prisoners until their child is born for fear of damaging the precious heir they carry."

"And it's half the reason so many of those precious heirs don't thrive," Jeryma said, sitting beside Marla on the edge of the pool. "If you were a farmer's wife, Marla, you'd be out working the fields until your water broke and be back at the planting the very next day, your baby strapped to your back."

"Do you think Laran will be pleased?" Marla asked. "Or just relieved?"

Jeryma smiled. "Both, I suspect. Once he gets my letter informing him of our happy news, I'm sure he'll come straight home from Winternest. And he'll bring Riika back with him. It will be good for you to have a friend your own age here."

"I hope she likes me. I've never had a real sister before. It'd be a bit tragic if we discover we can't stand the sight of each other."

Jeryma looked at her with concern. "Are you unbearably lonely here, Marla? I could send for your cousin, Ninane, if you wish."

"No," Marla replied hurriedly. "I'd really be quite happy if you didn't send for Ninane."

"Well, if there's anything you need . . ."

"Was it difficult for you, Lady Jeryma?"

"Was what difficult, dear?"

"You've had four marriages to men you never knew. Didn't you ever wonder what it was like to be in love?"

"All the time," Jeryma admitted with a rueful smile. "I don't think I ever was, although there was a young man once—"

Marla was shocked. *"Really?"*

"It was while I was married to Mahkas's father. My husband was much older than me, forty years older, actually, so we didn't have much in common. Thelen was one of the Krakandar Raiders the Collective assigned to protect Laran when he was a small boy."

"Were you in love with him?"

Jeryma chuckled softly. "In lust with him would be a better description, I think."

"And you actually had an *affair*?" Marla found the idea that the perfectly proper Lady Jeryma had ever done anything so . . . risky . . . almost beyond comprehension.

"For a while. It was after Mahkas was born and I was feeling rather . . . unattractive, I suppose. Thelen made me feel like a goddess. It didn't last long; couldn't last, realistically. Affairs like that are doomed to fail. Phylrin could turn a blind eye for a time, but if the news had ever leaked out, the scandal would have been much worse than the few moments of pleasure that precipitated it. Trust me, Marla, if you need that sort of comfort, stick to a *court'esa*. They're actually better at it and they don't come with all the risks attached to one's own class."

"Do you think Laran would turn a blind eye if I took a lover?"

Jeryma looked at her in alarm. "Are you planning to?"

Marla smiled. "Hypothetically."

"Let's not find out, shall we?" Jeryma suggested.

"I was only joking, Lady Jeryma."

"I'm sure you were, my dear," her mother-in-law agreed. "But right now we've just confirmed that you are pregnant with the next High Prince of Hythria. Let's not muddy the waters by wondering aloud about what your husband's reaction would be to you having a lover, yes?"

"Yes," Marla agreed with a smile.

Jeryma patted her hand, looking rather relieved. "There's a good girl."

There's a good girl, Marla repeated silently with a sigh.

I wonder if she'll still be saying that if I don't give birth to a son.

ChAPTER 53

By the time her captors removed the hood, Riika knew she was well over the border into Fardohnya. She had been bundled away to a place some miles from the picnic site where Mahkas and the others lay dead, and then thrown over the back of a sturdy mountain pony. The three men responsible for her kidnapping had ridden hard through the forested slopes for the rest of the day, their efforts at concealing their tracks helped considerably by a short, savage snowstorm that obliterated all evidence of their passing. They sheltered in the lee of a shallow cave while the storm blew itself out and then moved on until they finally entered the Widowmaker Pass about two miles from Westbrook. Once they were on the road, their speed increased considerably and they were safely behind the walls of Westbrook before nightfall.

Just on sunset, Riika was handed over to the Plenipotentiary of Westbrook, confirming her suspicion that this was no random attack by slavers. These men were too well prepared, too organised and too nonchalant about their fate to be acting without high-level government sanction.

"Your highness," he said with a bow, as her hands were untied and she was lifted from the back of the mountain pony. "I am Symon Kuron, the Plenipotentiary of Westbrook."

"I demand you return me to Hythria at once!"

"We intend to, your highness," the Plenipotentiary promised. "As soon as your brother pays your ransom."

"You're mad if you think you can blackmail my brother," she scoffed.

"We'll see," Symon Kuron shrugged. "In the meantime, I've made arrangements for your accommodation here. You'll be moved further inland in the morning. I'm sure you understand how foolish it would be for us to keep you so close to the border until an agreement has been negotiated for your release. I would like your word you won't try to escape."

"And if I refuse to give it?"

"Then instead of the room we have prepared for you, your highness, with a nice fire and a warm bath, a feather bed and complete privacy other than a guard on the door outside, I will be forced to incarcerate you in the keep's dungeons among the thieves, murderers, rapists and runaway slaves we normally hold down there. Unfortunately, we're a bit crowded at the moment, so I won't be able to offer you a private cell."

"You wouldn't dare throw someone like me in a dungeon full of murderers and rapists!" she gasped, quite certain that nobody intending to collect a ransom on a noblewoman would be so stupid. It was an unwritten but well-understood rule that when you held a prisoner of rank for ransom, particularly a female prisoner, you made certain they remained unmolested.

"This is the frontier, your highness," the Plenipotentiary said. "We're a long way from Talabar and really not renowned for our skill in the niceties of court politics. If you do not give me your word that you won't attempt to escape— and please note I said *attempt*, because there is no way you could succeed—then I have no choice but to confine you to the most secure, albeit most dangerous and uncomfortable, place in my fortress. You see, I have orders to hand you over to my superiors. They didn't actually stipulate you must be unharmed."

Riika studied the man in the fading light, wishing she could tell if he was bluffing. Surreptitiously crossing her fingers against the lie, she nodded. "Very well, then. You have my word. And you don't have to keep calling me 'your highness', you know. My lady will do."

"If that's what you prefer, my lady," the Plenipotentiary replied. "This way."

Riika followed Symon Kuron inside, looking around hopefully, but she hadn't been taken to the northern keep, where, like Winternest, most of the trade of the border post took place. She was led into the southern keep, through the bailey and the dingy main hall, up a dark narrow staircase and into a room that contained—as Symon Kuron had promised—a fire, a bath already drawn and a comfortable-looking feather bed. She stepped into the room and looked around before turning back to face the Fardohnyan. "Am I to be fed, or is starving me also part of your plan?"

"Your dinner will be brought up shortly, your highness. Once you've eaten it, I suggest you get some sleep. You have a long journey ahead of you tomorrow and you'll be leaving before first light."

"Where are they taking me?"

"I'm not at liberty to say."

"You mean you don't know," Riika guessed.

The Plenipotentiary of Westbrook smiled faintly. "Goodnight, your high—I mean, my lady."

Riika turned to watch him leave. "You know, my brother is just as likely to declare war on you for this," she warned as he opened the door. "He won't want to pay any sort of ransom."

Far from worrying him, Symon Kuron seemed to find the threat amusing. "Won't, or can't?" he asked. "Still, he can always borrow the money from your husband. The gods know *he's* rich enough. Goodnight."

The Plenipotentiary of Westbrook closed the door and locked it before Riika had a chance to point out that her brother was probably the richest man in Hythria and she didn't actually have a husband for Laran to borrow anything from, anyway.

Three days later, Riika was exhausted but a little less frightened than she had been. No longer tied hand and foot, she had been given a beautiful dun gelding to ride and, with an escort of thirty men—making no attempt to hide the fact that they were Fardohnyan army troops—she was taken west at a hard pace, leaving before first light each morning and pushing on until after dark each night.

The officers of her escort treated her with courtesy and the deference due the daughter of a Hythrun Warlord. It was clear the Fardohnyans intended to treat her as a prisoner of rank. Riika breathed a huge sigh of relief. Laran would get a ransom demand in a day or two, she supposed. He'd be furious that his sister had been kidnapped, but he wouldn't hesitate before ordering the gold brought to Winternest and the exchange could take place shortly after. With luck, Riika calculated she would be in Fardohnya no more than a month before she was on her way back home.

Of course, Laran may not be satisfied with simply paying a ransom to get her back. Mahkas might be dead, too, and Laran would demand vengeance for that. Riika clung to the hope that he wasn't dead. Perhaps he'd just been badly wounded and the Fardohnyans mistook his injury for a fatal one. She kept telling herself that. In between imagining what had become of her nephews.

Every time Riika closed her eyes she saw those guards ly-

ing by the trampled fire, bleeding into the snow. And prayed
Travin and Xanda hadn't finished up lying there beside them.

Their destination proved to be a large estate in eastern Fardohnya called Qorinipor. It was also known as the Winter
Palace, King Hablet's Summer Palace being his main residence in the capital, Talabar, located on the coast some
twelve hundred miles north of this place. Although she was
saddle-sore and weary from the long ride, she was impressed
by the palace as it came into view, nestled in the spectacular
foothills of the Sunrise Mountains.

Built of polished pink marble on a small island, it rose
majestically out of a broad crystal-blue lake, linked to the
mainland by a bridge that looked as if it had been crafted of
cake icing. The scrollwork was so delicate, it seemed impossible that it had been carved from anything as crude as stone.
As they rode across the bridge, Riika couldn't help but wonder what it had taken to build such a place. Perhaps the
Harshini had had a hand in Qorinipor's construction. The
place seemed too beautiful to have been wrought by human
hands.

They rode into the main courtyard of the castle and halted
at the foot of a set of broad steps that reached up to a large
open area in front of the palace itself. The paving was made
of alternating light and dark stones in a pattern that wound
around each other like snakes swallowing their own tails.

There was a man waiting for them at the top of the steps.
He wore a long, elaborate robe of red and gold silk and his
head was shaved in the manner common among eunuchs. Riika guessed who he was. Even in Cabradell, they'd heard of
King Hablet's chamberlain, the eunuch, Lecter Turon. Riika's last doubts about her fate vanished as he walked down
the steps to greet them. If Lecter Turon was here to meet her,
she was right. This plan to kidnap her went as high as it could
go. Right up to the King of Fardohnya.

"Who is that?" the eunuch asked, jerking his head in Riika's
direction as the captain of her escort dismounted. She didn't
know his name. He'd never bothered to introduce himself.

"That's the hostage, Lord Turon. The Princess Marla."

The Chamberlain stared at the man for a moment and then cursed. Riika stared at him in shock, too. Suddenly it all made sense: the Plenipotentiary of Westbrook's comments about her brother borrowing money from her husband. Calling her "your highness" all the time . . .

Oh, by all the Primal Gods! They think I'm Marla Wolfblade!

"That is not Marla Wolfblade, Captain."

"*Sir?*"

"I don't know who you have there, Captain, but I met Princess Marla when I was in Greenharbour and I can assure you, that's not her." The eunuch walked over to where Riika waited astride the dun. "What's your name, girl?"

"Riika," she replied cautiously. Until she worked out what was going on, the rest of her name was a secret she preferred to keep to herself.

"And are you a princess? The sister of Lernen Wolfblade, perhaps?"

"No."

The Chamberlain turned to the captain and shrugged. "There. You see, captain. That's all it took to establish that this girl is not Marla Wolfblade." Then he added at a yell only inches from the captain's face, "*All somebody had to do was ask!*"

The captain flinched at Lecter's tone, but stood his ground. "I'm sorry, sir. But this is the girl the Plenipotentiary of Westbrook handed over to us with the assurance that she was Marla Wolfblade."

"The gods *forbid* you'd think to use a bit of initiative and establish that for yourself! Look at her!" he shouted furiously, making Riika wince. "She's dressed like a galley wench! Didn't *that* alert you to the fact that this might not be a *princess*?"

"I'm sorry, my lord."

"Not as sorry as the Plenipotentiary of Westbrook is going to be," Lecter promised savagely.

"What are your orders, Lord Chamberlain?"

"My orders, you *moron,* are to get that idiot Symon Kuron here from Westbrook, before the King arrives, so that he can explain to our esteemed monarch how he mistook a chamber-maid for the High Prince of Hythria's sister!"

Riika opened her mouth to protest that she was no cham-bermaid, but the words froze in her throat as another thought occurred to her. If the Fardohnyans didn't realize who she was, they might simply let her go. Granted, there was a cer-tain level of protection in being a hostage, but she was more determined than ever to escape. It was a much better idea than sitting around waiting to be rescued.

Lecter Turon turned away, heading back into the palace.

"What did you want me to do with the Hythrun girl then?" the captain asked his retreating back.

The eunuch stopped and turned to glance uninterestedly at Riika over his shoulder before fixing his gaze on the captain. "Kill her."

Riika gasped as the captain saluted in acknowledgement of the order.

"No . . . wait!"

Lecter Turon continued walking back into the palace. The captain turned to face her, drawing his dagger from his belt as he did so.

"But you don't realize who I am," she began, as he moved towards her. All of a sudden, her silence seemed foolish, not clever. Two other soldiers closed in on her from behind and Riika was dragged from the saddle. She screamed, her heart pounding so hard she couldn't speak. Blood rushed through her ears so loudly she couldn't hear herself think. Her knees collapsed as she hit the ground. The captain drew closer. Ri-ika screamed again, paralysed with terror. They intended to carry out Lecter Turon's indifferent order for her execution right there and then.

Tell them who you are! a small voice in her head shouted at her urgently.

With a burst of terror-inspired strength, Riika found the will to struggle against the hands that held her down, but with two strong men pinning her to the ground, she had little hope of fighting them off. The words that might save her—*I am Glenadal Ravenspear's daughter. Laran Krakenshield's sister*—couldn't get past her terrified screams.

The Fardohnyan captain hesitated for a moment, looking down on her with a hint of pity, giving Riika a brief glimmer of hope. But it lasted only an instant before the blade came down, cutting off her cries of protest and ending any chance she had to explain that she wasn't some nameless chambermaid.

After a sharp, brutal pain there was a sudden feeling of warm, sticky wetness as the blade sliced across her throat; more pain, shock—and a refusal to believe this was really happening—all filtered through the gauze of her unintelligible terror.

The world went dark. Riika Ravenspear's blood spilled unhindered onto Qorinipor's delightful chequerboard paving.

And then the pain stopped and there was nothing. Not even darkness.

ChAPTER 54

Kidnapping Marla Wolfblade had seemed a wonderful idea to Hablet, right up until he arrived at the Winter Palace to taunt Laran Krakenshield with his victory, only to discover he had nothing to bargain with.

Hablet was just about ready to kill someone, starting with that idiot Symon Kuron and ending with his chamberlain who'd come up with this crazy scheme in the first place. He should have just invaded Hythria, razed a few villages, captured a couple of hundred slaves, slaughtered the odd town square full of unarmed peasants and been done with it.

He was pissed off with Lernen Wolfblade for reneging on their deal. Massacres were good for making a point like that.

Instead he'd let himself be talked into this stupid, convoluted plot, which was unravelling faster than he could comprehend. He'd arrived in Qorinipor to find their hostage was no hostage at all. Lecter had killed her without bothering to find out who she was if she wasn't actually Marla Wolfblade, and now Laran Krakenshield was on his way to negotiate for . . . well, Hablet wasn't really sure *what* the Warlord of Krakandar and Sunrise wanted.

If they hadn't kidnapped his wife (and presumably he knew that) why was Laran coming here? Were the men killed in the raid his four best friends? Or was the dead girl a particularly favoured slave? Just to be on the safe side, Hablet had ordered his chamberlain to prepare her body properly and lay it out in the temple, in case Krakenshield wanted to see it and assure himself the girl was really dead. If he didn't care about her one way or the other . . . well, there was no harm done and it would please the gods if she got a decent burial. Hablet was a devout man, after all.

Lecter Turon speculated that the girl so well (and so blatantly) guarded in Winternest had actually been a decoy, put there by Laran Krakenshield to deliberately confuse the issue. Hablet knew there was a younger sister somewhere, and for a while had been worried that was who the dead girl was, but Lecter scoffed at the suggestion. Their contact in Winternest had been a member of Laran's own household, perhaps even a family member, according to the intelligence sent by Symon Kuron prior to the kidnapping. (Privately, Hablet thought that unlikely. If there was a traitor, it was more likely a disgruntled servant or slave in the employ of the family.) The problem with that theory was that slaves, even free servants, who got that close to the family were too well cared for to betray one of their own and risk finding themselves back in the slave markets of Greenharbour. Marla was a newcomer to the household, so it was easier to believe their spy had no loyalty to her.

The trouble was, it was even easier to believe that the spy

who had betrayed the girl that looked so suspiciously like
Marla Wolfblade had done so at the behest of his or her master, and that Hablet was the victim of this charade, not the
other way around.

The door at the end of the hall opened and Lecter walked
in, his silks hissing softly as he walked. Except for the half
dozen bodyguards Hablet insisted on having here for the
meeting with the Hythrun Warlord, he was alone in the glori-
ously gilded throne room, pacing the podium in front of his
throne while he waited for Laran Krakenshield to get here
from Westbrook.

"They've arrived."

"What does he look like?"

"Who? Laran Krakenshield? Well, he's a tall man, really;
rather lean and—"

"I mean, does he look angry, you *idiot*? Murderous?
Smug? *What?*"

"I couldn't really say," Lecter shrugged.

"Maybe we should have met with Symon Kuron first."

"That would give the impression we have something to
hide, your majesty."

"Oh? And we *don't*?"

"Trust me, your majesty," Lecter urged. "And if anything
goes wrong, just follow my lead."

"We're being played, Lecter," Hablet warned. "I can feel it."

Before the chamberlain could respond the doors opened
again and a herald dressed in a loose red robe and turban
stepped into the hall.

"His grace, the Warlord of Krakandar and Sunrise, Lord
Laran Krakenshield and the Plenipotentiary of Westbrook,
Symon Kuron."

Laran was already striding through the hall before the herald had a chance to finish announcing him. Hablet didn't
think that was a good sign. The Hythrun looked quite . . .
peeved.

"Lord Krakenshield."

"Your majesty."

The Warlord and the king sized each other up for a long, tense moment. Although they had met before, Hablet had paid little attention to Laran Krakenshield while he was in Greenharbour. The Hythrun was young, only just ready to inherit his province, and in Hablet's view was going to be relatively ineffectual for years yet while he grew into his power and made the alliances one needed to become any sort of effective power broker.

How wrong about one man can another man be? Hablet thought, looking Laran up and down. Older than Hablet, the Hythrun was lean and tall, with the physique of a man who lived by the sword. The king made a mental note not to goad Laran into making any sort of personal challenge. Hablet's bulk was mostly the result of good living. If Laran called him out, he'd be obliterated.

"How nice of you to pay me a visit," Hablet said with an insincere smile.

"You didn't really leave me much choice," Laran pointed out.

"May I offer you wine?"

"I want to see Riika," Laran replied. "Once I know my sister is safe, then we can bother with the social niceties."

Hablet glanced at Lecter Turon, whose face wore an alarming look of dawning comprehension, then looked back at Laran blankly. "Pardon?"

"My sister, Hablet. Bring Riika to me so that I can determine for myself that she has been well treated, and then we can talk about the terms for her release."

Hablet turned to stare at the Plenipotentiary of Westbrook who had suddenly gone very pale.

The chamberlain stepped forward into the uncertain silence. "His majesty did not bring you here to negotiate, Lord Krakenshield, but to offer his deepest regrets and, hopefully, to avoid an armed conflict."

"What?" both Laran and Hablet said simultaneously.

He pointed to Symon Kuron. "Arrest this man!"

"*Eh?*" the Plenipotentiary of Westbrook cried. Hablet was almost as confused, but he trusted the eunuch as he trusted no other person in Fardohnya.

"You heard him!" Hablet shouted. The guards rushed forward and grabbed the garrison commander, who was looking as confused as Hablet felt.

"Both you and my king have been the victim of a foul plot, Lord Krakenshield," Lecter continued, as the Plenipotentiary struggled against the guards who held him. "This man, hoping to use his position as the Plenipotentiary of Westbrook to enrich himself, devised an evil plan to kidnap your sister from Winternest. Like you, my unsuspecting king was also duped. Claiming his foul deed was not a kidnap but actually a rescue, Kuron sent a message to his majesty in Talabar some weeks ago, stating that Marla Wolfblade was being held prisoner in Winternest and had managed to smuggle a message out with one of our traders, begging King Hablet to rescue her. The message spoke of her undying love for my king and the pain she had suffered when her brother reneged on the marriage he had previously agreed to and married her to you instead."

"That's a lie!" Symon Kuron protested. "The orders came from—" His words were cut off abruptly by a mailed fist in the mouth from one of the guards. Spitting blood and teeth, the Plenipotentiary wisely fell silent.

"As I'm sure you understand, with no reason to suspect the lie, his majesty had no choice but to respond to the desperate plea from a damsel so obviously in distress."

Hablet was fascinated by the eunuch's gift for mendacity. *He* almost believed him and he knew every word of this fabulous tale was a lie. *The man's a genius.*

"Marla has never left Cabradell," Laran pointed out. "Didn't your agents inform you of that?"

The chamberlain looked at Laran, aghast at the implications of his question. "Surely you're not suggesting that we have spies in your court, Lord Krakenshield?"

"Of course not," Laran replied sceptically.

Lecter ignored the Warlord's tone and continued his story. "His majesty sent orders to the Plenipotentiary of Westbrook asking him to do whatever was necessary to expedite the rescue of the woman he believed to be Marla Wolfblade, which, as I'm sure you're aware, resulted in the inadvertent abduction of your sister." Lecter sighed heavily. "Unfortunately, this is where the truly heinous nature of this crime becomes apparent. Fully aware that it was your sister and not Marla Wolfblade whom he had abducted, Kuron planned to hold her to ransom and demand payment from you for her return, take his money and be gone across the border into Hythria before anybody realized what was going on. However, when he learned King Hablet was on his way to the Winter Palace and had demanded that Marla be brought to him, he realized his scheme was about to unravel. With one glance, the king would know the woman he had kidnapped was not Marla Wolfblade and he would be exposed."

Lecter stopped and glanced at Hablet before saying anything more.

"And?" Laran demanded in the long silence that followed.

"You must understand, Lord Krakenshield, that my king is innocent of anything other than the noble desire to rescue the woman he loved. Perhaps, the charge of a lack of good judgment in appointing such a recalcitrant to a position of power as the Plenipotentiary of Westbrook might also be levelled at him—"

"Where is my sister?" Laran asked.

"She is dead, my lord," the chamberlain announced heavily. "Symon Kuron had her killed in an effort to cover up his crime. He sent a message to the king informing him that Marla had been unavoidably delayed but he would be bringing you here to negotiate her release, knowing his own guard had been ordered to kill her as soon as they were out of sight of Westbrook. The order was carried out, my lord, on the side of the road some ten miles south of the border fortress the morning after she was kidnapped. Several of the soldiers on Kuron's murderous escort proved to be loyal Fardohnyans. Instead of fleeing into the mountains to join the bandits, they brought her body here to their king and confessed their part in the crime in the hope of gaining leniency. They did not, of course. All of them, with the exception of this man," he said, pointing to the shocked Plenipotentiary of Westbrook, "have been executed."

Hablet watched Laran Krakenshield closely, acutely aware that the man was armed and very good at wielding the blade he carried. But Laran didn't look vengeful. He looked stunned, as if he couldn't comprehend what the eunuch was telling him. The Plenipotentiary's expression had changed from outrage to a certain resigned inevitability. He could tell he was being set up to take the blame for Riika Ravenspear's death. And could clearly see the futility of trying to rail against it.

"Riika is *dead*?"

"I would give half my kingdom to bring her back," Hablet swore, with a touching catch in his voice. "Whatever ill feeling there might have been between us over the matter of Marla Wolfblade, Lord Krakenshield, if petitioning the gods themselves could undo this heinous crime, I would do it."

"Name your reparation," the chamberlain added (which Hablet thought was going a bit far—the man might ask for anything). "Fardohnya will do what it must to redress the wrong done to you and your family."

"I want to see my sister," Laran said, his voice choked.

"Of course!" Lecter snapped his fingers and two of the guards not holding down the Plenipotentiary of Westbrook stepped forward. "Take Lord Krakenshield to the temple where Lady Riika's body is laid out."

Without another word, Laran turned on his heel and followed the guards from the throne room. As soon as the doors closed behind him, Hablet turned to Lecter. "Well, he seemed to take that quite well."

"Your majesty . . ." Symon Kuron began. "Please . . ."

"Shut him up," Hablet ordered impatiently. He turned back to Lecter as a guard used his mailed fist to remind the Plenipotentiary of Westbrook why he should remain silent. "What happens now?"

"We buy him off."

"I thought the whole idea was that *he'd* have to pay *me*?"

"That was before this fool kidnapped the wrong girl and we accidentally killed her. We've no choice now but to distance ourselves from this as fast as we can. Enough coin and Symon Kuron's execution should do the trick."

"Your majesty, *no*!" Symon cried, despite the blow he received for opening his mouth again. Hablet ignored him.

"Her death was no accident, Lecter. You had her killed."

"An error of judgment for which I shall never forgive myself, your majesty."

Hablet shook his head. "This feels all wrong. Laran Krakenshield was supposed to come to me on his knees, begging for his wife back. Now we're on our knees to him, offering him anything he wants for killing his sister. Why don't I just kill him, too?"

"Because Hythria would declare war on us."

"So? My army is as large as theirs."

"Your army is scattered all over Fardohnya, your majesty. A good portion of Hythria's forces, however, are currently sitting just across the border. They'd be in Lanipoor before we could mobilise and in Talabar by the end of spring."

"None of which you seem to have thought of before you talked me into this foolish plan."

"My plan was not foolish, your majesty. I simply lacked the appropriate resources to carry it out."

"Oh, so now it's *my* fault Laran Krakenshield has me by the balls?"

"You are, as you so frequently remind me, sire, the king."

"This is going to cost me a fortune."

"There will be a chance to recoup some of the costs."

"How?"

"The Plenipotentiary of Westbrook's position is about to

become vacant. There's a tidy sum to be made selling that honour to the next incumbent."

Hablet looked across at the man who had, until a few minutes ago, been his first line of defence on the border. Symon's face was distraught and there was moisture on his cheeks that Hablet suspected came from tears of terror. Hablet smiled. All was not lost if he could still make a man sob with fear.

"Should I kill him, or let Krakenshield do it?"

"I'm sure Lord Krakenshield would like the pleasure of killing his sister's murderer himself, your majesty, but I suggest it would be unwise to allow him to interrogate the prisoner first in case certain . . . *inconsistencies* . . . in your story come to light."

"Then I'll make him a gift of Symon Kuron's head," Hablet decided, ignoring the former Plenipotentiary of Westbrook's terrified whimper. "And his balls, too. That should convince him I'm innocent of anything to do with his sister's death."

"An excellent idea," Lecter Turon agreed.

Hablet nodded, feeling a little better. The Plenipotentiary of Westbrook's head on a platter should please Laran Krakenshield. It would certainly please Hablet.

And, in the end, that was all that mattered, really.

ChApTER 55

Riika's body had been laid out with care. It lay on a carved bier in the centre of the small Qorinipor temple under a shroud. Glittering dust motes hung in the cool winter sunshine from the narrow line of windows that circled the base of the domed ceiling. Laran approached the bier cautiously, hoping there had been some mistake, but knowing with sick certainty that there wasn't. Riika was gone and the girl who had been kidnapped was dead. It couldn't be anybody else.

The body was covered with a thin cloth embroidered in gold. Laran hesitated before touching it, knowing that when he did, he would no longer be able to keep his grief at bay. His last chance to pretend this wasn't happening was about to be taken from him, the moment he lifted that shroud and confirmed Riika was dead.

Cursing his own cowardice, Laran snatched at the corner and jerked it from the body.

They had dressed her in a simple white gown, its high neck almost, but not quite, covering the wound on her throat which had obviously been washed clean when the body was prepared. Riika's expression was lifeless; rigor mortis had long passed. Her face was not frozen into a terrified rictus of fear. It simply looked dead, the bloodless flesh so pale it was almost translucent.

How could this have happened?

A few days ago, Riika was playing in the snow with her nephews. Today she lay dead, her young life snuffed out before it even began. Laran had seen plenty of death in his time, but this seemed so senseless. It was the opportunity lost that made him want to scream with outrage. The life that never really got a chance to start.

And for what? Because Riika had the misfortune to share the physical description of my wife?

He could imagine the rumours. *"There's a girl at Winternest."* *"She's only fifteen or sixteen. Pretty. Blonde."* *"And guarded by Krakandar Raiders."*

He had sent Riika into a death trap without even realising it, thinking any danger to her would come from Hythria. It never occurred to him that somebody in Fardohnya might mistake Riika for Marla.

Although he believed that much, Laran was fairly certain the rest of Lecter Turon's tale was an outright lie. He couldn't prove it, though, and in the end, even if he could, what good would it do Riika? He couldn't bring her back to life. He couldn't undo what had been done. Hablet was obviously fearful of his reaction. Lecter Turon's continued assurances of their innocence was enough to prove Hablet both culpable and willing to pay his way clear of his guilt.

There would never be a better time, Laran realized, to make Hablet come to the negotiating table. With so many troops massed on the Hythrun side of the border and Fardohnya so patently unprepared for war, Laran could force Hablet to sign a treaty. He could probably demand he pay for the construction of a paved road through the Widowmaker Pass, for that matter, so anxious was the Fardohnyan monarch to absolve himself of any blame in the affair.

Laran looked down on Riika's lifeless form, another wave of guilt washing over him for thinking of politics at such a time.

"I'm so sorry, Riika," he whispered in a choked voice. "I should have taken better care of you. I promised Glenadal I would and—"

Laran couldn't go on. His own guilt in putting Riika in harm's way was intolerable. *What marvellous conspirators we've been.* Laran, Glenadal and Jeryma; Kagan and Charel Hawksword, Nash, Mahkas, even Chaine and eventually Lernen Wolfblade. *All our noble sentiments about helping Hythria; all our great plans and schemes seem trivial now.* All of it seemed so trite now the price had proved so high.

Riika was an innocent bystander. She shouldn't have had anything to do with this at all.

The door opened at the end of the hall and booted footsteps echoed across the tiled floor, stopping a few paces from the bier. Laran looked up to find Raek Harlen standing there holding a covered tray. The young lieutenant's expression was set and hard as he forced himself not to look down at the body of his former mistress.

"What's that?" Laran asked, fairly certain the young man had not brought him refreshments.

"It's a gift from the King of Fardohnya, my lord." Raek knelt on one knee to place the tray carefully on the floor, then rose again, lifting off the cover. "The head and the balls, believe it or not, of Symon Kuron."

The Plenipotentiary of Westbrook's freshly severed head stared sightlessly up at Laran, who almost gagged. The bloodied objects either side of the head didn't bear thinking about.

"With all due respect, Hablet's a sick bastard, my lord," the young man remarked.

"He's pretty good at covering his arse, too," Laran noted.

Gently, Laran drew the cover back over Riika's body before turning to the lieutenant. He looked down at Symon's grimace of terror and shook his head.

"Fardohnyan justice is quick, I'll grant Hablet that much."

"What do you want me to do with it?"

"Give it back to Hablet. I'm not interested in keeping any man's head as a souvenir."

Raek nodded and bent to pick up the tray that was awash with blood draining from the severed skull. He paused for a moment, studying the head curiously.

"I recognise him from somewhere, you know. I thought that the first time we met him in Westbrook. I'm sure I've seen him in the customs hall a few times. I thought he was a slaver."

"Do you know if he spoke to anyone?" Laran would find out who betrayed Riika if it was the only thing of import he ever did in this life.

"I can't recall. But it'll come to me. Eventually."

"I want to know as soon as it does, Lieutenant. In the meantime, get your men organised to depart. We're leaving at first light tomorrow."

The young man rose, holding the tray, and looked down at the covered bier. "We're taking Lady Riika home, sir?" he asked, his voice thick with emotion.

Laran nodded, feeling his heart was made of lead. "Yes, Raek. We're taking Riika home."

"Would you object if I posted a vigil here tonight, sir?"

Laran looked at him in surprise.

"She shouldn't be left alone. Not in this place."

"Thank you, Raek. I think Riika would like that."

"I don't suppose we're going to be allowed to murder every one of these Fardohnyan bastards for doing this before we leave, are we, sir?"

Laran smiled humourlessly. "I appreciate the offer, Raek, truly I do. And you have no idea how much I'd like to take you up on it. But we have the head of the man who kidnapped Riika, a plausible excuse for how it happened and the sworn promise of a king that he had nothing to do with it."

"Even though you know he's lying?"

"Yes."

"That isn't justice, my lord."

"I know," Laran agreed heavily. "But without a war that's going to kill thousands of other innocents for no good reason—both Hythrun and Fardohnyan—we're going to have to settle for it, I fear."

They left Qorinipor at first light the following morning. Along with Riika's body laid out in a beautifully lacquered carriage Hablet had donated for their journey home, Laran was taking back a guarantee from the Fardohnyan king that there would be no further recriminations regarding Lernen's broken promise about Marla. He had also extracted a guarantee that there would be no unauthorised incursions into Sunrise Province for at least the next ten years. And a promise of three million Fardohnyan gold rivets towards paving the Widowmaker Pass.

Laran had no idea of the cost of the venture, but three million had sounded a nice round number and he would never again have Hablet in such a cooperative mood. He had also secured a separate payment for Jeryma to compensate her for the loss of her daughter of another five hundred thousand gold rivets. As Hablet agreed to each of his increasingly absurd demands with barely a murmur of protest, Laran became more and more convinced of the Fardohnyan king's guilt in Riika's death.

He learned one other thing that disturbed him; something that, even now, he wasn't sure he should believe. As they were preparing to depart the Winter Palace, Lecter Turon had sought Laran out and drawn him away from his men. They stopped under an archway between two of the palace outbuildings near the bridge linking the palace to the mainland, where they were out of earshot of the rest of his troop and the Fardohnyan guard of honour Hablet had laid on for their return to the border.

Both suspicious and curious about what the eunuch wanted of him, Laran waited for Lecter Turon to speak.

"There is one other thing I wish to give you, Lord Krakenshield," the chamberlain told him, looking around furtively.

"You don't give *anything* away, Chamberlain Turon."

"That's true," he conceded with a thin smile, fixing his gaze on the Warlord. "Think of this as a favour then; a favour you might be able to repay someday."

Laran wasn't sure if owing Lecter Turon a favour was a good idea, but he was really curious now. "What have you got for me, then?"

"Some intelligence, my lord."

"About?"

"About the spy in your household who told Kuron's men where and when they would find your sister in the mountains."

Laran snorted sceptically. "You'd expose your own spy?"

"The spy was never mine, Lord Krakenshield. He or she—and I honestly don't know which it is—was the Plenipotentiary's creature."

"If you don't even know the gender of this spy, Chamberlain, how do you know their identity?"

"I know only what the Plenipotentiary of Westbrook confessed before he died, Lord Krakenshield. The spy who betrayed your sister—according to Symon Kuron—was a member of your own family."

"That's impossible."

"Well, that's a judgment I'll leave to you, my lord. I just thought you might like to know what he said." The chamberlain bowed and walked away, leaving Laran to ponder his words.

And ponder them he did. He had thought of little else since leaving Qorinipor.

The chances were good that the eunuch was lying and had simply suggested such a dreadful thing hoping to eat away at Laran's confidence in those closest to him. Or it might be true. And if it was, who in his family hated Riika enough to wish her harm?

No closer to an answer when Westbrook came into sight than he had been when they rode out of Qorinipor days ago, Laran sent Raek and two other Raiders on ahead with a letter to Mahkas—the one person Laran trusted implicitly—to warn him they were coming home and of the terrible burden they brought with them.

Laran made only one promise to himself. Once he had arrived at Winternest, he would find out who had betrayed Riika and, when he did, the Plenipotentiary of Westbrook's fate would seem merciful in comparison.

ChAPTER 56

Well," Hablet sighed heavily as he stood on the wall-walk of the Winter Palace of Qorinipor watching Laran Krakenshield and his escort as they crossed the delicately wrought stone bridge connecting the palace to the mainland. The lake glittered in the early morning sun, almost too brightly to look upon in places, and the air was crisp this high up, the wind snatching at his cloak with greedy, grasping fingers.

The carriage carrying Riika Ravenspear's body was at

the centre of the column, surrounded by the twenty-man guard Laran had brought with him, who were, in turn, escorted by another hundred men Hablet had assigned to accompany the Hythrun Warlord back to the border. He wasn't just being polite. Hablet wanted to make *sure* Laran Krakenshield went home. The hundred-man guard was there to persuade him it would be dangerous to think of doing anything else.

Hablet was going to miss that coach, too. Exquisitely lacquered with the royal insignia inlaid in real gold on the doors, it had cost a small fortune and he'd only used it once.

He turned and glared at his chamberlain. "Your 'Let's Kidnap Marla Wolfblade and Make a Fortune' plan turned out to be a complete waste of time and money, Lecter."

"It didn't turn out exactly as I envisaged," the chamberlain conceded.

"Three and a half *million* gold rivets, Lecter! Where am I going to find that sort of money?"

"Where you find most of your money, sire," the eunuch suggested. "In the coffers of your subjects."

"I could impose a tax for paving the Widowmaker Pass, I suppose," the king mused. "In fact, come to think of it, I probably *should* impose a tax. It's the merchants using the pass who'll get the most out of this. They should contribute at least part of the cost."

"Not to mention how popular it will make you," Lecter reminded him. "There's been talk of doing something about the Widowmaker Pass for years. Now that Glenadal Ravenspear is dead and you have been able to force his successor to the negotiating table, the long overdue construction can finally begin."

"But it wasn't my idea, Lecter. Krakenshield forced *me* into it."

"The general population doesn't need to know that, sire."

Hablet smiled. "And there's nothing like major capital works to make the people think I care about them."

Lecter Turon nodded. "Of course, now that Marla Wolfblade is no longer a viable option as your wife, we do have the problem of finding you another, your majesty."

"Who did you have in mind?" Hablet asked, certain Lecter wouldn't have raised the issue if he didn't have at least one candidate he'd accepted a bribe to promote.

"Princess Shanita, sire."

"Who?"

"The only daughter of Prince Orly of Lanipoor," Lecter informed him. "The family's royal lineage dates back before Greneth the Elder. It is a very ancient and noble line."

"Is she pretty?"

"Very, so I'm led to believe."

"Yes, well, Orly would say that, wouldn't he? Is she educated?"

"Not excessively."

"Good. There's nothing worse than a bored wife with an educated mind. How much is he paying you?"

"Enough that I feel compelled to raise the matter with you, your majesty."

Hablet smiled. "That much, eh? What about her dowry?"

"I believe Orly mentioned a figure in the vicinity of three hundred thousand, sire."

"As a dowry?" Hablet asked in surprise. "Is she cursed and turns into a monster after sundown, or something? Nobody offers that sort of money for a dowry. Not for a princess, anyway."

"The offer was first made some months ago while you were still considering Princess Marla. I believe Orly was trying to make a more attractive offer than Lernen."

"That wouldn't have been hard. Lernen was expecting *me* to pay *him*. Which, I might add, thanks to your bungling, I ended up doing anyway and still don't have anything to show for it."

"It is the nature of a gamble that one sometimes loses, sire."

"Interesting that you've *now* decided it was a gamble," Hablet remarked. "*After* I lost three and a half million gold rivets. You claimed it was a sure thing when you first proposed the idea. And the only reason it didn't work, I might add, was because you had the girl killed. I should take the cost of this disaster out of your hide, Lecter. If you'd left Riika Ravenspear alive we could still have got a ransom for her. Maybe even as much as for Marla. The Warlord of Krakandar actually *felt* something for his sister. Lernen Wolfblade's sister means little more than a rather expensive *court'esa* to Laran, I imagine." Hablet laughed suddenly, as he pictured the frivolous young girl he met in Greenharbour and the serious, dour Warlord of Krakandar trying to hold a meaningful conversation.

"Don't despair, sire. There are other ways of making sure a son of the Wolfblade line can never take the throne of Fardohnya."

"And how much is it going to cost me?"

"One simply has to ensure that no child of Marla Wolfblade's ever reaches maturity. If there are no heirs, there is no problem."

"Krakenshield threatened to turn Fardohnya into a killing field if I even *thought* about harming another member of his family, Lecter. What do you suppose he'd do if he found out I'd killed a son of his?"

"Are you afraid of Laran Krakenshield, sire?"

"Of course I am!" he declared. "The man has the two most dangerous qualities possible: the innate belief in the righteousness of his opinions and unlimited power to back them up. I'd be a fool not to fear him."

"Then my way is infinitely better, sire. Children die all the time. Provided it's the result of childhood illness, or can be disguised as an unfortunate accident, you need never be connected to the tragic loss of such an important child."

"Childhood illness?" Hablet scoffed. "Don't be ridiculous! Who ever heard of anything as idiotic as trying to use diseases to kill people deliberately? How would you control it? How would you stop your own people getting caught in an epidemic?" He put his hand on the eunuch's shoulder. "Don't let your imagination run away with you, Lecter. If you're looking for a new innovation in assassinations and warfare, you should talk to my engineers when we get back to Talabar. They tell me there might be a way to turn the powder used in fireworks into something more . . . dangerous."

"But, sire, Fardohnya's last successful incursion into Hythria during the time of your great-grandfather was only fruitful after he lobbed plague-infected body parts into Winternest Castle, forcing them to open the gates."

"Yes," the king agreed. "But what did it get him?"

"Control over the border?" Lecter ventured cautiously.

"It got him a visit from a very irate Brakandaran the Half-breed, Lecter. That was back in the days before the Harshini disappeared completely. I remember my father telling me about it."

"Surely you don't believe such fairytales, your highness? Stories of dangerous halfbreeds and the Harshini demon child are simply something we tell children to frighten them into behaving themselves."

"I'm pretty sure the whole demon child thing is a crock," Hablet conceded. "But I'm not so sure about Brakandaran. Even the nice stories about him claimed the Halfbreed was a dangerous bastard. And by all accounts, Brakandaran was not amused about what went on at Winternest. Damned Harshini."

"They claimed to be incapable of violence," Lecter pointed out.

Hablet snorted. "Didn't stop them letting the Halfbreed off the leash every now and then when they got their noses out of joint."

"What did he do?"

"The Halfbreed? I've no idea. Even my father never found out exactly what Brakandaran threatened my great-grandfather with to make him toe the line, but we ended up having to withdraw from Winternest *and* pay compensation to Hythria."

"Even so, the Harshini are long gone, your highness," the eunuch assured him. "And even if he ever actually existed, Brakandaran the Halfbreed is long dead, too. I don't think you need worry on that score."

Hablet shrugged. "Maybe. But I think—for the time being, at least—I'll restrain myself. There'll be a chance later to deal with any Wolfblade heirs. They have to be born first. And, after all, this only becomes a problem if I don't have a son, eh?"

"Exactly, your majesty."

"Has she got good hips, this daughter of Orly's?"

"Broad and true, your majesty."

"And she's *court'esa* trained?"

"Naturally."

"Speak to Orly then. I need to start taking some wives and getting a son of my own. Then it won't matter how many brats Marla Wolfblade pops out. Tell Orly I'll take the wench off his hands."

Lecter smiled. "I will, your majesty. Although, perhaps not quite in those words."

The eunuch bowed and turned to head back down to the gardens.

"One other thing, Lecter," Hablet told him as he walked away.

"Sire?"

"I want my coach back."

"Pardon?"

"Give it a few days—we don't want to appear disrespectful—but send a message to Lord Krakenshield and tell him that after he's done with it, I want my coach back."

"Is that really necessary, your majesty? It's only a coach."

"It's the principle of the thing, Lecter."

Lecter bowed deferentially. "As you wish, your majesty."

Hablet turned back to watching the column wend its way up the road toward the foothills and the border, thinking he was right to stick to his principles.

The King of Fardohnya was—in his own mind, at least—a very principled man.

CHAPTER 57

One of the advantages of relentlessly prowling the bridge spanning the road between the northern and southern keeps of Winternest—other than the tragic figure he portrayed—was that it gave Mahkas an excellent view of the road leading into the Widowmaker Pass. When Laran appeared in the pass, Mahkas was confident he would know of it first. When his brother returned, he would get to Laran before anyone else could, which meant he would find out what Laran had learned about Riika in Fardohnya and be in a position to allay any suspicions he might have, be suitably outraged at the ransom they were demanding for her return, and be there to offer his aid in whatever capacity Laran needed him. All of which, he knew, would simply strengthen his position in his older brother's eyes.

In light of this, Mahkas was furious to learn that on one of his rare absences from the bridge to answer the call of nature, Raek Harlen and a small advance party had returned from Fardohnya bearing dispatches from Laran. By the time he emerged onto the chilly walkway, Raek had already left the bailey and entered the southern keep to deliver the messages he carried.

Mahkas hurried across the bridge to the southern keep, desperate to intercept the letter from Laran before Darilyn got her hands on it. She wouldn't care who it was addressed to. Darilyn was itching to get her share of the ransom and a letter from Laran was likely to contain the details of any payment he had negotiated for Riika's release.

When he threw open the door to the main hall, he was surprised to find only Veruca by the fire, her knitting nee-

dles clacking rhythmically as she warmed her toes in front
of the fire.

"Where is Lady Darilyn?"

"In her room," the old slave replied. "Those strings she's
been waiting on for her harp arrived this morning. She's been
there all day, cussing and swearing like a trader trying to fix it.
Won't do those boys any good to hear that sort of language—"

"One of Laran's Raiders just arrived from Fardohnya with a
letter from Lord Krakenshield," Mahkas cut in. "Where is he?"

"I sent him to Lady Darilyn."

Mahkas cursed and all but ran the length of the hall.

"Won't do those boys any good to hear that sort of language . . ." Veruca called after him grumpily.

Mahkas knocked and opened the door of Darilyn's room
without waiting for permission to enter. His nephews looked
up from their game.

"Hello, Uncle Mahkas," Travin said cheerily. They were
sitting on the floor near their mother, playing with the porcelain mounted knights that Jeryma had sent them. "Did you
want to come play with us?"

"I can't at the moment, Travin, I'm busy."

Darilyn was sitting on the stool by her harp, still as a rock,
holding Laran's unopened letter on her lap.

"Darilyn? I believe that's addressed to me."

His sister looked up at him blankly for a moment. Then
she reached into her lap and tossed the folded parchment at
him. It landed at his feet. Mahkas stepped forward cautiously
to pick it up.

"Travin, Xanda," Mahkas said, deliberately keeping his
voice level, "why don't you go find Veruca? She's in the main
hall. Tell her I said you could have a treat."

"What sort of treat, Uncle Mahkas?" Xanda demanded.

"Anything you want."

"Is something wrong with mama?" Travin asked.

"Just leave, Travin."

The boys didn't need to be told again. They dumped their porcelain horses on the table beside their mother's tools and the wires, bits, levers and pegs she'd taken off the harp and ran from the room, already arguing about what constituted a treat. Mahkas closed and locked the door behind them and turned to face his sister.

"This is it, Mahkas," she said, her voice barely containing her excitement. "They say fortune favours those who take risks."

"Shut up!" he ordered impatiently, unfolding the letter. He read it aloud, mostly to stop Darilyn talking. "My dear Mahkas, it is with a heavy heart that I must report that our beloved sister Riika is dead—" He looked at Darilyn in shock. "*Dead?* How can she be *dead*?"

Darilyn shook her head wordlessly, clearly not believing what she was hearing.

"It appears she was kidnapped," Mahkas read, "in the mistaken belief she was Marla Wolfblade, a tragic error that cost Riika her life. When it was established that she wasn't the sister of the High Prince, the Fardohnyans executed her out of hand, without waiting to establish her true identity." Mahkas stopped reading, feeling physically ill. "By Zegarnald, Darilyn, what have we done?"

"Dear gods!" his sister gasped, covering her mouth with her hands in horror.

Mahkas turned his attention back to Laran's letter. "It is my belief that Hablet himself was involved, but I cannot prove it. He and that leech, Lecter Turon, had a very plausible story worked out—one that lay the entire blame on the Plenipotentiary of Westbrook, a man named Symon Kuron." Mahkas almost dropped the letter; his hand was shaking so hard. "Symon Kuron? But he was the slaver . . ."

Mahkas held the letter in both hands to stop the parchment from shaking before he continued. "Hablet gave me Kuron's head and balls as a gift, to apologise for the misunderstanding and agreed to several million gold rivets in compensation, but none of this will bring Riika back or ease the pain I know we share at the loss of our beloved sister. I am bringing her body home and expect to be back by next Fourthday. Will you arrange to have everything ready? I intend to head straight for Cabradell after a night's rest. Jeryma will want her daughter buried in the family vault next to Glenadal."

Mahkas couldn't bring himself to look at Darilyn as he took a seat near the table before reading any further; his knees no longer had the strength to hold him. "I have another favour to ask of you, brother," Mahkas read on, his voice shaking almost as much as his knees. "Before I left Qorinipor, Lecter Turon informed me this monstrous plot was made possible because of a traitor in our midst. His exact words were 'a member of your family'. It may be that he was just trying to cause disharmony in the family, and besides, I cannot bring myself to contemplate the notion that Darilyn would stoop so low as to betray her own sister. I would appreciate it if you could investigate who in the household had reason to turn on us, and, although I am loathe to think ill of a member of our own family, a few subtle questions to establish Darilyn's involvement (or lack of it) in this terrible business would also be prudent.

"I trust you'll see this letter does not fall into the wrong hands, and that we can root out the traitor in our midst without causing any more grief to the family. I'll see you soon. Yours in sorrow, Laran."

Mahkas hung his head in shock for a moment before he looked up and stared at Darilyn. "He thinks you're involved."

"But not you," she pointed out angrily. "How convenient."

"I loved Riika," Mahkas reminded her. "You've always resented her. And made no secret of the fact."

Darilyn swung her foot around the big gilded harp until she was facing him on the stool. She had such big, ugly feet, he thought idly. A bit like her personality. "You hypocrite!" she hissed. "This was *your* idea, Mahkas Damaran! *You* set it up! And now *I'm* to be blamed for it? I don't think so!"

"We need to deal with this carefully," he advised.

"*Carefully?* You mean in a manner that keeps you looking innocent, don't you?"

"Laran doesn't really think you're involved," he tried to assure her. "The letter says—"

"The letter says: *a few subtle questions to establish Darilyn's involvement!*"

"Yes, but I'm sure—"

"I'm not going to take the blame for this, Mahkas," she warned. "Not on my own."

"You certainly don't expect me to confess *my* part in it, do you?"

"Gods, no!" she snorted scathingly, jumping to her feet. "Mahkas Damaran take the blame for something he did? Perish the thought!"

Mahkas watched her pacing back and forth with a growing sense of panic. To save her own neck Darilyn could—and would—expose his participation in the plot to kidnap Riika the moment their elder brother stepped into Winternest. Although she derided him at every opportunity and blamed him for the death of her husband, Darilyn was more than a little afraid of Laran and the power he wielded over her. Without Laran she was penniless. Without Laran she had no protection, no status in life other than that of a minor nobleman's widow whose sons would inherit their father's estate but to which she had no access. Her fear of alienating Laran guided most of her actions, Mahkas knew, and her actions from now on were all going to be directed at shifting as much of the blame as possible to Mahkas, to spare her own neck.

But Laran still trusted Mahkas. That was obvious from this letter to him questioning Darilyn's motives. Preservation of that trust was the most important thing in Mahkas's mind. He studied his sister carefully for a moment, aware that her desire to shift the blame in this affair was probably just as strong as his desire to remain untarnished by it.

"I'll tell Laran you had nothing to do with it," he promised, hoping that would silence her. "I'll just have someone executed before Laran returns tomorrow and then you'll be exonerated."

"And suppose he wants proof your dead body really is the perpetrator of this crime?"

"I'll . . . I'll claim the person confessed."

Darilyn nodded anxiously. "Yes, he might believe that. Who?" *"Who?"*

"Who will you kill? I suppose it will be easier if it's a slave. But which slave? It will have to be a house slave. Nobody else would have known where Riika was going to be."

"Veruca?" he suggested, caught unawares by her question. Mahkas had no intention of killing one of the slaves. He abhorred unnecessary bloodshed and, in reality, only those who knew of his role in this disastrous affair were a danger to him. One of them was the Plenipotentiary of Westbrook, Symon Kuron, and he was already dead.

"No! Not the nurse," his sister objected, wringing her hands nervously. "Find someone else. I need her to look after the boys."

He nodded, thinking the only other person who could expose him was Darilyn. Mahkas needed to silence *her* more than anyone else.

"I'll think of someone," he promised. "Would you like me to have your dinner sent to your room?"

"What?" she asked, confused by the abrupt change of subject.

"I think it might look better if you stayed here in your room," he explained. "Once word gets out about Riika, nobody will think it strange that you've retired to deal with your grief in private. I'll get Veruca to take the boys for the evening. And I'll make sure you've nothing to do with my investigations, too. When I find our culprit, you won't be anywhere near the scene so nobody can later accuse you of perhaps coercing a confession from an innocent to protect yourself."

"You'd better make this look good, Mahkas," she warned. "If Laran has even a moment of doubt about the guilt of the dead slave you present him with, he'll go back to thinking I'm to blame. And trust me, if he does, I won't be taking the blame alone."

Mahkas rose to his feet and stepped in front of Darilyn to stop her pacing. He put his hands on her shoulders and smiled encouragingly. "It'll be all right, Darilyn. I'll fix this. You don't need to worry about it." He put his arm around her and guided her to sit on the chair by the table he had just vacated. "Why don't you sit down and stop pacing. You're making me tired just watching you."

Darilyn let him sit her down, still wringing her hands. "Maybe it would be better if we told him what we did. He'll be angry, of course, but if we—"

"We can't tell him, Darilyn!" Mahkas cried, shocked by the mere suggestion. "There's no forgiveness for this, no easy way out."

"Laran would never make an orphan of his nephews," she reasoned. "He might be angry, but he wouldn't kill me. He feels guilty enough about Jaris being killed. He wouldn't take away the boys' mother as well as their father. And it wasn't as if I actually did much. I mean, you were the one who brokered the deal . . ."

Darilyn's reasoning frightened Mahkas. As he paced the room in her stead, he realized that in her own selfish, self-absorbed mind she was already distancing herself from him; heaping the blame at his door. At this rate, by the time Laran got back from Fardohnya, she would have talked herself into believing that she'd had nothing to do with it at all.

He looked at her, thinking her more threatening at that moment than any man he had faced in open combat. He was behind her now, the small round table between them.

"Laran won't be thinking of your boys, Darilyn," he tried to warn her. "Right now, the only thing he's thinking of is Riika."

Darilyn dropped her head into her hands and started crying again. Mahkas was certain it was for herself and not the sister she'd helped to kill.

"I can't do this, Mahkas," she sobbed. "It's one thing to make a bit of money. But this is murder. I can't live with it."

Nice of you to decide that now! he thought angrily. He realised then that he was going to have to silence Darilyn, one way or another. The danger she posed to him was extreme. One hint that Laran suspected either of them was involved in Riika's death and she'd blurt out everything. On the table between them lay the pieces of her partially dismantled harp, the wire she'd been waiting on for so long to fix the broken strings and the two small horses with their proud riders that Laran had given the boys.

"You're going to *have* to live with it, Darilyn," he told her unsympathetically. Still standing behind her, he glanced up at the beam that supported the ceiling. *Would it hold her weight?*

Darilyn kept sobbing but didn't answer him. She wasn't crying for Riika, he knew. There was no room in Darilyn's self-obsessed mind for grief. Riika's demise meant only the danger of being exposed as a conspirator in her death.

Darilyn is a bad person, he thought, wondering how long the coil of harp wire was, and if he could get to it without alerting Darilyn to his intentions. Mahkas and Laran had both understood instinctively how shallow and selfish she could be from the time they were small children together. She cared for nobody but herself. Even her children ranked a poor second to her own desires.

"I swear, Mahkas, if you—"

He cut her off mid-sentence with a loop of the harp wire. Tossing it around Darilyn's neck he pulled back with all the force he could muster. The thin wire sliced like a razor through her larynx before she could cry out, sending a spray of blood across the room as he pulled back on it. Pulling the wire even tighter, he clambered onto his knees on the table behind her for better leverage, his wounded arm crying out in protest as he strained against the stitches. A fountain of blood spurted across the rug from her severed arteries, some splashing so far Mahkas could hear it hissing as it hit the fire. She thrashed maniacally on the chair, unable to get her hands under the wire as he squeezed the life from her. With the last of her strength, Darilyn reached behind her, flailing wildly. Her right hand knocked the tools from the table and finally closed on one of the boy's porcelain horses. She slammed it down, hitting his wounded arm more by luck than anything else. Mahkas ignored the sharp pain and pulled the wire tighter. *Dear gods, how long was it going to take her to die?*

Not much longer as it turned out. After a few more moments of uncontrollable thrashing, Darilyn slumped in the chair, her almost severed head lolling backwards on the table. Mahkas jumped clear of her open, accusing eyes, gasping for breath and knocking the table over in the process. His heart pounding with fear, his blood racing with the thrill of death, he glanced down to check his clothes. Miraculously, by staying behind her, he had escaped the torrent of blood, but the rest of the room was awash with it, already reeking with a sickly stench as the blood on the hearth began to steam.

He didn't have much time. Forcing himself not to think about what he'd done—what she'd *forced* him to do, he corrected self-righteously—Mahkas grabbed one end of the wire still embedded in Darilyn's throat and tossed it over the beam. He caught the other end and hauled on it until Darilyn began to lift from the chair. Then he encountered another problem. The wire cut through human flesh as if it was butter and the dead weight of her body was causing the harp string to slice so far into her neck he was in danger of decapitating her. Cursing, he had to let her down again. He'd have trouble convincing anyone she'd committed suicide if that happened.

Mahkas hauled on her again, lifting her more slowly this time, the wire sawing through the beam and Darilyn's throat with almost equal ease. After a few minutes of careful lifting, though, he finally got her feet clear of the floor and the puddle of blood that had dripped down from her severed head and pooled beneath her. Hurriedly, Mahkas tied off the wire on one of the hat-pegs by the door, then, with infinite care, he tiptoed around the bloody floor to the door, making sure he left no footprints to betray his presence during Darilyn's death throes. He refused to look at her too closely. The force of the wire had dislocated her jaw and her face was misshapen and grotesque beneath the veil of blood she wore.

Mahkas took several deep breaths and checked his clothes once more before opening the door. The only evidence he'd been in a struggle was a slight tear in the sling and a small bead of blood on the sleeve of his shirt, easily explained away by his wounded arm bleeding from overuse.

Lifting the sling back into place and forcing his face into an unconcerned expression, he let himself out of Darilyn's room and walked down the candle-lit corridor to the main hall where his nephews were probably still trying to convince Veruca that Uncle Mahkas had promised them a treat.

In a little while, he'd send the boys to say goodnight to their mother and her tragic suicide would be discovered. That would further strengthen his story when he faced Laran tomorrow. No man in his right mind would send two young boys to discover what was awaiting them in Darilyn's room.

But that was all right, he mused, because Mahkas was starting to wonder if he'd lost his mind anyway.

CHAPTER 58

Winternest came into view late on the afternoon of Thirdday. Laran had never been so glad, yet so tormented, at the idea of coming home. Not that Winternest was his home. No place in the whole of Sunrise Province really felt like a home to him. It was familiar, certainly, and comforting to be back, but it was the red granite walls of Krakandar that Laran considered his true home.

When he spied the castle he noted the flags were all flying at half-mast, a sure sign the news about Riika had reached the border post already. Laran considered himself something of a coward for breaking the news about their sister's death to Mahkas and Darilyn in a letter rather than in person. *But what did one say at a time like this?* Mahkas was probably blaming himself. Darilyn—assuming she was innocent of any involvement in the affair—was probably just as torn with grief. Once they found the traitor in their household, things would be a lot easier to deal with, he reasoned. Their anger would have a focus. Their need for vengeance would have something concrete to fix itself to.

Laran clung to that thought as he led the funeral procession into Winternest. He had dispensed with Hablet's escort, leaving the Fardohnyan guard of honour back at Westbrook. Only the Krakandar Raiders were given the honour of bringing Riika home.

Mahkas was waiting for him in the bailey of the southern keep, his arm still in a sling, his expression grave. The boys were with him, standing either side of their uncle, but there was no sign of Darilyn in the welcoming party.

Laran dismounted, handed his reins to one of the grooms then waited until the carriage bearing Riika's body had come to a complete stop before he turned to greet his brother.

"This is a sad day for our family, Mahkas."

"Sadder than you realize," his brother agreed. He glanced at the coach with a shake of his head. "I've made room in the main hall for her. I thought it would be more . . . comforting, than what passes for a temple here."

Laran nodded, and signalled the Raiders to bring Riika's body inside. The boys watched solemnly as their aunt was lifted out of the coach and carried towards the keep.

"Mama won't be so lonely now," Travin announced. "Not with Aunt Riika for company."

Laran looked down at his nephew in confusion. "What?"

"Veruca!" Mahkas barked sharply. "Take the children inside, please." As the nurse hurried forward, Mahkas laid his hand on Laran's arm. "There's something you need to see."

Puzzled, Laran followed Mahkas into the hall in the wake of the guards carrying Riika. The room was ablaze with candles and a trestle had been set up near the fireplace to take Riika's stretcher. Next to that table, another body was laid out, covered with a funerary cloth of gold, similar to the one that covered Riika.

Laran stared at the second body for a moment then strode forward, impatiently throwing back the cover. His shock at finding Darilyn lying on the second trestle left him speechless. Mahkas dismissed the guards and turned to Laran as soon as they were alone.

"She intercepted your letter," he explained, walking the length of the hall to stand at the head of Riika's trestle. "I swear, I had no idea she was involved, Laran. Not until I was told Raek Harlen had come back early and I went looking for the dispatch you sent with him. She was distraught when I found her, in tears over Riika's death, I thought, at first. But then she started babbling about how she hated you and how she had no control over her life and how things would have been so much better once she had money of her own . . ."

"How did she die?" Laran's voice was flat and lifeless.

"She hung herself," Mahkas informed him. "After I spoke to her and realized the depth of her infamy . . . well, she knew I was furious. And I *had* to leave at that point, Laran, I swear, because I was ready to kill her myself for what she'd done. Anyway, I'd confined her to her room while I considered what I should do next, when I heard Veruca scream. She'd taken the boys in to say goodnight to their mother and they found her hanging from a beam . . . It was awful, Laran. She used the wire from her harp. I've never seen so much blood."

"Did the boys see her?"

"Travin did, but I'm not sure if he realizes what he saw. Fortunately, Xanda was pulled away by Veruca before he could get a good look at her."

Laran pulled the cover back a bit further. Darilyn's arms were crossed, resting on her chest. He pulled down the high collar of her gown to find that Mahkas spoke the truth. Her neck was severed almost to the point of decapitation.

"Are we being punished, Mahkas?" he asked, as he gently laid the cloth down. "Is this the price the gods have extracted for our arrogance?"

"Perhaps," Mahkas agreed. "It seems rather a high price, though."

Laran shook his head, unable to comprehend the tragedy that had brought both his sisters to such untimely deaths. He discovered he wasn't angry at Darilyn. He was still too numb to be capable of rage. He just felt weary. And old.

"What do I tell Jeryma?"

"The truth," Mahkas suggested. "It's always better when you tell the truth. Much less pain in the long run."

Laran shook his head sadly. "I can't believe she would do such a thing . . . her own *sister*? It's . . . it's almost inconceivable."

"Don't judge her too harshly, Laran."

Mahkas's words made him feel rather ignoble, but Laran couldn't find it in himself to forgive this. Not yet. It was too raw; too painful for forgiveness. "Your generosity of spirit is far greater than mine, little brother. I doubt I will ever be able to forgive her."

"Neither of us could ever really know what drove her to such an act," Mahkas said. "But you know she's always been resentful of Riika. And of the fact that you controlled her wealth."

"I never denied her, Mahkas. Not once."

"But you *could* have," Mahkas reminded him. "It was the possibility that drove her mad, I think, not the facts."

Laran glanced down at Darilyn once more then pulled the gold funerary cloth back over her head. "It doesn't seem right, leaving Riika here in the same room as her murderer."

"Don't think of them as victim and assailant. They were family first."

"Family don't arrange to have each other kidnapped and murdered, Mahkas."

"Nor did Darilyn, I suspect. She would have thought only of the profit to be made from a hefty ransom you were sure to pay, not of any other consequences."

Laran looked at Mahkas, whose face seemed carved out of grief in the flickering candle-lit hall. "You're far more charitable towards her than I'm feeling right now, brother."

"One shouldn't speak ill of the dead," Mahkas replied.

Laran nodded. "Do the boys understand . . . ?"

Mahkas shrugged. "I'm not certain. Travin's old enough to realize what's going on, but Xanda? Who knows? Which brings me to another matter. I was thinking . . ."

"What?"

"Well, someone has to take care of them now. Mother has done her time raising children, and Marla's going to have her hands full with the new babe. Perhaps, when Bylinda and I are married, they could come and live with us?"

"It's my responsibility to see my nephews cared for," Laran replied. Mahkas was making this far too easy for him. "Not yours."

"And how is placing them in a loving home with their own uncle not discharging your duty, Laran? I care for those boys as much as you do."

Laran nodded, conceding the wisdom of Mahkas's suggestion. "Perhaps they should stay with you, then. If you're sure Bylinda won't mind."

"She loves the boys as I do."

He shook his head uncomprehendingly. "How typical of Darilyn to worry only about her own fate, and not care for the future of her orphaned sons."

"Selflessness was never a virtue of hers," Mahkas agreed.

Laran sighed heavily. "It's a sad journey we'll be making back to Cabradell."

"I've made arrangements for us to get away first thing in the morning," Mahkas informed him. "With the immediate threat of reprisals from Fardohnya no longer an issue, I'm not needed here any longer."

Laran nodded in agreement. "We'll take the girls home in the morning."

"Then I'll leave you to your own devices for a time, if that's all right? I have a few more things to arrange before we leave and I promised the boys I'd tell them a story before they went to sleep."

"You'll spoil them."

"They need a little spoiling at the moment."

"No wonder you're their favourite uncle."

Mahkas smiled faintly. "They love you, too."

"Not as much as their Uncle Mahkas. You have far more patience with them than I do. You'll make a fine father when you have your own sons."

"So will you, Laran," Mahkas assured him. "I'll see you at dinner?"

"Yes."

Mahkas turned and headed towards the entrance to the hall, leaving Laran between his two sisters. He was almost at the door before something else Mahkas had said worked its way forward into Laran's consciousness.

"You said Marla would have her hands full with the new babe?" Laran called after his brother. "What did you mean?"

Mahkas stopped and turned to him. "I'm sorry, Laran. With everything that's gone on these past few days it completely slipped my mind. A letter arrived from Cabradell the day after you left for Westbrook. Marla is with child."

"Already?"

"You're obviously a quick worker," his brother noted with a hint of a smile.

"How strange to be thinking of a new life in the midst of so much death."

"The gods never let the balance falter for long," Mahkas pointed out.

Laran nodded, thinking that was the most logical thing he'd heard anyone say for the past few days. The rest of it didn't seem real. Riika and Darilyn were dead and Marla was pregnant. It felt like he had stepped into a whirlwind that was gradually picking up speed, and that any minute now he would be flung off in some random direction that only the gods could predict.

"So all is not lost," Mahkas added. "We have our heir to Hythria."

"And all it cost was the lives of our two sisters," Laran replied.

chapter 59

For the second time in almost as many months, Kagan presided over a funeral on the crowded slopes of the Cabradell valley as his youngest niece was laid to rest beside her father. It was the most heartbreaking thing he had ever done.

In contrast to the sombre gathering, it was bright and sunny—a glorious spring day that cared little for the sad duty they were performing under a cloudless, cobalt sky. He stepped back and waited as the family placed their parting gifts on the bier then moved forward again to beg Death's sympathetic consideration for this pure and unsullied soul when he welcomed her into his realm. As Kagan said the final prayer and stepped back again to allow the pallbearers to lift Riika onto their shoulders he glanced at his sister. Veiled in mourning white, Jeryma stood beside Marla Wolfblade who held Darilyn's two boys by the hand. She looked shattered.

There were only four pallbearers. Riika's slight body required no more. Laran and Mahkas took the front, Chaine Tollin and Raek Harlen the rear. The young lieutenant had begged the boon from Laran en route from Winternest. They carried her into the vault, taking with them the hopes of a whole province. Kagan wasn't sure what effect the death of Glenadal Ravenspear's only child was going to have on the people of Sunrise Province, but whatever it was, he doubted it would be a good one. Laran was going to have to tread very carefully these next few months.

It was hard not to feel partly responsible for Riika's death. And Darilyn's death, too. Like his nephew, Kagan suffered from an uneasy feeling of guilt. The additional loss of Wrayan still weighed on him like a constant pressure on his chest that made it difficult to breathe.

All this time without word from his apprentice could only mean one thing. The boy was probably dead; he had accepted that. Whether Alija had killed him, or he had been wounded in his confrontation with her and died later, remained a mystery. Tesha claimed Alija was quite shocked to find Wrayan gone when she dragged the elder sorcerer into the temple to bear witness to his alleged crimes, but that could have been an act for Tesha's benefit.

The only thing Kagan was certain of was that there was no chance Wrayan was out there somewhere, hale and hearty, having simply decided not to return to his master. Unfortunately, months of investigation had left Kagan no wiser than he had been when he first returned to Greenharbour.

It was another life lost to Glenadal's plan.

Funny how we're all calling it that now—Glenadal's plan—as if that absolves the living conspirators because it wasn't our idea.

But he was just as guilty as Glenadal Ravenspear. Kagan had wanted to avoid a Fardohnyan heir to the High Prince's throne as badly as any other Hythrun. Thinking of their precious heir, his eyes rested on Marla for a moment. She showed no physical sign of her condition yet, other than that indefinable air of smug superiority all pregnant women seemed to acquire. *It has something to do with being able to create and nurture life,* Kagan thought. As if Jelanna, the Goddess of Fertility, endowed every pregnant woman with a sense of serene and total confidence in their ability to bring a child into the world. He'd first noticed the phenomenon when Jeryma was pregnant with Laran and had observed it in every pregnant woman he'd met since.

The pallbearers emerged from the vault, signalling the end of the ceremony. Kagan noted, without surprise, that there was not a dry eye among the young men who had performed the heartbreaking duty of laying Riika Ravenspear to rest.

But what happens now? he wondered. They were due to leave Cabradell in a few days to perform the same ceremony for Darilyn in Krakandar Province, where both her father and her husband were interred. She was to be laid beside her husband, Jaris, in the Taranger family vault in Walsark, the northernmost borough in Krakandar on the border between Medalon and Hythria.

Another funeral procession. Another young life snuffed out prematurely. Kagan was uneasy with the manner of Darilyn's death. He hadn't thought her the suicidal type. Selfish, certainly. Shallow even. But not suicidal. Her wound disturbed him, too. Her throat was sliced to the bone. He couldn't imagine how she had inflicted such injuries upon herself unaided.

"My lord?"

"Yes?" he replied, putting aside his disturbing train of thought. He turned to Marla, thinking she had coped better than all of them with this tragedy. But then she wasn't as close to it as they were. To Marla, Riika Ravenspear and Darilyn Taranger were simply names—the sisters of the husband she barely knew. She had never met them and, while she understood the grief of those around her, she remained untouched by it.

"Would you see Lady Jeryma back to the palace?" Marla asked.

"Of course," he replied, chiding himself silently for having to be asked. Jeryma had taken the loss of her daughters so close on the death of her husband very hard. "Will you keep an eye on the boys, your highness?"

"They'll be fine with me," she assured him. She was still holding each of Darilyn's sons by the hand and they seemed content with her company. Xanda clutched at the porcelain horse Jeryma had sent him. It was broken now, shattered as Darilyn kicked the table over when she hanged herself. Mahkas had apparently retrieved all the pieces but one, and glued them together for the child before they left Winternest, a remarkably generous act given the circumstances. The horse and its knightly rider were complete, except for the tip of his lance. There had been no chance of finding a piece so small in the chaos Darilyn left in her wake. Jeryma had tried to relieve Xanda of the horse before the funeral, but he'd refused to relinquish it and a mighty tantrum had ensued. Marla restored the peace in the end by promising to let him keep it— perhaps the first time in her life Jeryma had been overruled by another woman in her own home. But Marla was probably the only member of the family who wasn't so wrapped up in her own grief that she couldn't take the time to understand the distress of two young children who had just lost their mother.

"Thank you," Kagan said, pleased with the way Marla was dealing with all of this. The potential for her to grow into nothing more than a spoiled, profligate wastrel had been high, particularly given the family she came from. Perhaps the isolation of a childhood at Highcastle, away from the corruption of her brother's court, had done her good. She was certainly dealing with the current situation with a dignity the High Prince seemed incapable of.

Grateful that at least one part of this increasingly costly plan appeared to be successful, Kagan laid his hand on her shoulder in a silent gesture of appreciation. Marla nodded in acknowledgement of his thanks then turned and led Travin and Xanda down the slope towards the palace.

It was several days before Kagan began to fully appreciate the potential of Marla Wolfblade. Like every other person involved in this scheme, he had thought of Marla as little more than the instrument of their hopes. She was the vessel who would carry their Hythrun heir and he'd really not given her much consideration beyond that.

Kagan and Laran were in Glenadal's old office, going over the arrangements for the management of Sunrise after Laran returned to Krakandar, when Marla knocked on the door and admitted herself without waiting for permission to enter. They both looked up at her approach, Laran with a hint of impatience.

"Is something wrong?"

"No," she assured him. "I just wanted to talk to you about something."

"Can't it wait, Marla?" Laran asked. "I'm very busy. There's a great deal to be done before we leave tomorrow."

"Well, it's sort of about that."

"What about it?"

"Can I suggest something, Laran? About Sunrise Province?"

"If you're quick about it."

"I know it's not really any of my business . . . but I think you should make Chaine Tollin the Governor of Sunrise, and let him run the province for you."

Kagan wasn't sure what startled him most: the suggestion that Chaine be given Sunrise or the fact that Marla had proposed it. The young woman who stood before them now was nothing like the dramatic and emotional girl who had wailed so pitifully about her cruel lot in life at the ball in Greenharbour less than a year ago.

Laran didn't seem nearly so surprised by the change in her. He simply leaned back in his seat and studied her curiously. "Why?"

"Because this is his home, Laran. He knows the people of Cabradell, the people of Sunrise, and they know him. More importantly, they respect him. And he backed you to the hilt after Glenadal died at a time when he might just as easily have challenged you, with an excellent chance that—with the army behind him—he could have got away with it. He's capable, he's loyal and he's done the right thing by you. It's time to do the right thing by him."

Kagan was astonished. "Who's been whispering in your ear, Marla?"

"What do you mean?"

"Did Chaine ask you to speak to Laran on his behalf?"

Marla looked a little hurt by the notion that without someone else pushing her, she had no care or understanding about what happened in the halls of power. "Don't you think I'm capable of thinking about something like this on my own?"

"I'm really not sure what you're capable of, Marla," he told her, quite honestly. "And Laran has already arranged for Mahkas to look after things here in Cabradell."

Marla shook her head and turned to Laran. "You mustn't. And it's not because I don't think Mahkas capable of administering Sunrise as well as any man. I like Mahkas. But he's *your* brother, not Glenadal Ravenspear's son."

"Neither is Chaine Tollin," Laran pointed out.

"That's just an excuse, Laran. Everyone knows he's Glenadal's son, even if it's never been formally acknowledged. Lord Ravenspear never recognising the fact doesn't stop the whole world knowing the truth. Gods! I knew about him and I'd never even been to Cabradell before I married you."

"And you don't think handing all that power to Glenadal's unacknowledged bastard wouldn't be flirting with danger?" Kagan asked.

"I think you've all been flirting with danger from the day you fixed it so that Laran would inherit Sunrise Province," she countered, surprising Kagan with her willingness to argue the point. He was quite sure it was Elezaar who made Marla pay attention to politics, but she spoke with real conviction. Marla wasn't repeating something learned by rote. She had thought this through.

"Do you now?" Laran said, rather more tolerant of Marla's

interference than Kagan was. The High Arrion's only thought at that moment was: *why couldn't Lernen have even a fraction of the brains his sister apparently has?*

"I think the only things keeping the population of this province from revolting against your rule," she continued, "are that, firstly, you've a reputation for being a reasonable man, secondly, Chaine backed you after Glenadal died and, thirdly, you were Riika's guardian. While that situation remained, there was always the chance you would either acknowledge Chaine or hand back Sunrise to Riika when she married. Either way, there was hope that Sunrise would stay within the ruling family. That's all changed now. There's no stability. The Ravenspear line is broken. Their Warlord's only legitimate child is dead. You're Glenadal's *stepson*, Laran, and so is Mahkas. And to add insult to injury, you're the Warlord of another province located at the opposite end of Hythria. You will never be able to convince the people of Sunrise that you're prepared to put their welfare ahead of Krakandar's. Placing Mahkas in charge will only exacerbate the feeling and give rise to charges of nepotism, regardless of how capable an administrator he proves to be. Chaine Tollin is the only man you can appoint as governor and return to Krakandar certain you won't be back here in six months trying to put down an uprising."

"Don't you think Mahkas would be rather upset if I took Sunrise Province from him only hours after awarding it to him?"

"You're a Warlord, Laran," she reminded him bluntly. "Your job is to look after everyone in the province, not just your brother."

Kagan stared at her in surprise, realising, for the first time, that Marla was probably the only Wolfblade born in several generations who actually had some inkling of what it meant to be a prince.

Laran turned to Kagan thoughtfully. "She does have a point, Kagan."

"She does," Kagan agreed cautiously.

"You'll do it, then?" Marla asked.

"I'll think about it," Laran conceded.

"You'll see I'm right."

"Yes," Laran said with a hint of a smile, "but gloating about it won't help your cause."

Marla smiled suddenly, which cost her the air of solemn dignity she had worn a moment ago and turned her back into a sixteen-year-old girl anxious for praise from someone whose good opinion she was obviously keen to foster.

"I should go then, shouldn't I?"

"Yes," Laran agreed, "you should."

"But you *will* think about it?"

"I promised I would."

"I'll see you later then." She dropped into a small curtsey in Kagan's direction. "Lord Palenovar."

"Your highness."

When she had closed the door behind her, Kagan turned to Laran with a shake of his head. "Does your wife often drop by to tell you how you should rule your provinces?"

"Given that we haven't been married more than four months, she's not really had the time." Laran seemed a little bemused by his young wife, but not upset by her audacity. He smiled humourlessly and added, "But I do detect a disturbing trend emerging. It's my mother's influence, I think. Between Jeryma and that damn dwarf . . . I swear, Kagan, Marla must own the only *court'esa* in all of Hythria whose main function seems to be teaching her about politics rather than sex."

"Must make for some interesting pillow talk," Kagan observed dryly.

"It does," he agreed, without offering any further explanation. "Do you think she's right about Chaine?"

"I fear she might be."

"Mahkas won't like it."

"He'll understand," Kagan replied. "And even if he's a little upset, the one thing you can rely on is Mahkas's willingness to do the right thing by you. He'll take it on the chin. Besides, he's itching to get back to Krakandar and marry

Bylinda. Once he gets over his initial disappointment, I'm sure he won't mind."

Laran nodded. "I'm lucky to have a brother I can trust so well. I only wish—"

"That Riika was still alive so you didn't have to even consider the problem?" Kagan finished for him.

"She was too young to die like that, Kagan. I'm still half-tempted to raise an army and lay waste to Fardohnya."

"You did the right thing, Laran."

"I know," he sighed heavily. "But it would have felt so much better if I'd spilled some blood."

"You cost Hablet money, Laran. For him, that probably hurt *more* than shedding blood. Anyway, enough lives have been spent in this ill-fated quest for a Hythrun heir. Let's not drown your unborn son in a bloody legacy of eye-for-an-eye that has no end."

"I know," Laran agreed, turning back to the list of appointments they had been going over before Marla interrupted them. "I'm just saying that Riika is dead and vengeance for that unforgivable crime would have felt better if there'd been more blood spilled than gold."

PART FOUR

LEGENDS, LIES AND LEGACIES

CHAPTER 60

For a long time Wrayan Lightfinger knew nothing but blinding pain, as if his head had exploded and left his brains splattered all over the inside of his skull. He couldn't move; might never be able to move again. He couldn't see. He couldn't feel his legs. Or his fingers.

He knew he'd been hurt; probably beyond help.

Time lost all meaning. Wrayan drifted in and out of consciousness so often it became his whole existence. Sometimes there was blessed peace for a while, but the relief was temporary. Other times he woke to agonising pain. Sometimes he felt as if he had drifted out of his body and was looking at the world from above it. He had flashes of memory on occasion. And dreams. Dreams that seemed too real to be a work of imagination. And there were faces. Beautiful faces. Beautiful, silent strangers with eyes as black as onyx, inhuman in their whispering serenity.

I'm dying, Wrayan decided.

Whatever had happened to him, the pain burned through his brain, damaging him physically as well as mentally. Through the ache he could feel the hand of Death on his shoulder, waiting to lead him into the afterlife.

Only the beautiful strangers held him at bay.

There was a story Wrayan had heard as a child; a story about how when Harshini died, unlike mortal men, Death took them body *and* soul. *Have I got enough Harshini in me for Death to want both my body and my soul?* Wrayan wondered during a rare bout of lucidity. He looked around him but nothing was familiar. Everything was white. Blurred. As if he was looking at the world through an oily lens. Wherever he was, it was no place he had seen in the mortal world. He drifted off and the dream came back again. The dream that lingered just out of reach, with the answers to all his questions. The dream that served only to confuse him more . . .

"*Wrayan.*"

He always wanted to open his eyes to see who was calling his name, but even in his dream only a part of him remained anchored to his corporeal body. The rest of him was in retreat, hiding from something fearful. He couldn't speak; couldn't even indicate that he'd heard someone calling his name.

"*He's too far gone,*" the unknown voice of his dream remarked. "*And I'm no healer.*"

The dream always started like that. Disembodied voices talking about him as if they were unaware he could hear them.

"*But he needs help,*" a younger voice always replied.

"*Then call Cheltaran. This boy needs the God of Healing.*"

"*He'll claim I'm interfering with the natural course of events.*"

"*That's because you are.*" The older voice sounded impatient, irritated.

"*He needs magical help to heal him. Besides, you can't let him die,*" the younger voice insisted. "*He hasn't finished honouring me yet.*"

It was Dacendaran, Wrayan always realized at this point. *I sold my soul to the God of Thieves.* He didn't know how he knew that, but somehow he did. *Or maybe I'm delirious and this is my final madness-filled nightmare.* Wrayan had heard your life was supposed to flash before your eyes just before you died. He'd never heard of anybody having bizarre dreams involving gods and unnamed strangers, though. But then, he'd never really had a conversation with someone who'd just died, so he'd never been in a position to interrogate anyone about it.

"*I should do the lad a favour and let him die,*" the other voice replied heavily. "*Do you have any idea what you're asking, Dace? I don't even know if I can get through the Gateway with a human.*"

"*He's Harshini.*"

"*Not enough for it to matter to the Gatekeeper.*"

"Look, if you don't want to help, Brakandaran," Dace pouted, *"just say so."*

"I don't want to help."

At this point, Wrayan always became convinced this was some muddled-up montage of everything he'd seen and heard in his long forgotten past; his broken mind's last-ditch attempt to scrape up some hope of salvation before it gave way to oblivion.

"But you have to!" the God of Thieves insisted. *"He's dying!"*

"The lad's as good as dead, Dace," the Halfbreed pointed out with callous practicality. *"His mind has been scoured. Even if you could fix it, without Cheltaran's direct intervention, it would take months, maybe years."*

"The Harshini could fix him."

"Why would they want to?"

"Lorandranek likes humans."

"A minute ago you were claiming the lad was Harshini."

Lorandranek, the Harshini King? Wrayan wished he could see the people in his dream more clearly. He wished he could put a face to the man he knew only from legend. There were a lot of names for Brakandaran. The Halfbreed. The Death-maker. In Medalon they called him the Sister Slayer, because of the death he'd meted out during the first Purge, but that was more than a hundred and fifty years ago now. The Sisters of the Blade probably thought Brakandaran was dead. For that matter, even in Hythria and Fardohnya, most people thought Brakandaran was dead.

Wrayan wasn't sure why he could remember such detailed historical information yet was able to recall little more of his own past than his name.

"Well, he is Harshini. A bit."

In his dream, Brakandaran fell silent for a time at this point and, even though he'd dreamed this scene a thousand times, Wrayan always worried the Halfbreed would refuse to help him.

"All right then," Brak replied after an agonisingly long pause.

"You'll take him? And you'll promise to make him better? So he can finish honouring me?"

There was silence for a time. Wrayan wondered if the dream was over and if, this time, the voices had stopped because he was about to die.

But it wasn't over yet. *"Someone's coming,"* Brakandaran warned.

"It's the Innate who hurt him," Dace replied. *"And another human. A woman."*

"An Innate did this?" Brak asked, sounding concerned. *"Maybe we didn't clean the Library out as thoroughly as we thought?"*

"I could come back later and steal some more scrolls," Dace offered brightly.

"That may not be a bad idea," the Halfbreed agreed. *"But right now, let's just get your boy out of here."*

In his dream, someone scooped him up from the floor and carried him away from the base of the Seeing Stone. Wrayan heard more voices in the distance. Female voices. But he could never make out what they were saying because, at that point, he was always swallowed by the blackness, only to dream the dream once more and puzzle over the inhumanly beautiful faces of the silent, black-eyed guardians who watched over him.

In time, however, the dream occurred less often, until eventually it stopped completely and even the details began to fade from Wrayan's memory. The pain receded and finally faded away completely. The silent, black-eyed guardians became less ephemeral, more real; until they resolved into Boborderen and Janarerek, the two Harshini healers who had nursed him back to health. The blurry whiteness took form and became the white walls of a palace.

And the voices he barely remembered from his dream acquired faces and bodies, and Wrayan awoke to discover he was in Sanctuary, the fabled, magically concealed hideaway of the last of the Harshini.

Wrayan remembered little of his life before Sanctuary. There was a hole in his memory, filled with blurry, half-formed images from his former life that never seemed to resolve themselves into coherent memories. Wrayan knew he was human. He knew he'd been hurt—badly—by magic, but he couldn't grasp who had done this to him, or how he'd wound up in a battle with another sorcerer in the first place.

The Harshini assured him his memory would return in time. *These things have a way of healing themselves,* Boborderen and Janarerek promised. *You just have to be patient.*

Patience was proving a gift far more common among the Harshini than among humans. Wrayan was desperate to fill those holes in his past that would complete the picture about who he was and how he came to be living among the Harshini.

There were many things he couldn't recall from his time before Sanctuary, but he was certain of one thing. The Harshini were supposed to be dead, eradicated by the Sisters of the Blade in Medalon during their regular purges to rid the world of anything smacking of magic or religion. Like most of the people living in Hythria and Fardohnya, Wrayan liked to believe the Harshini were merely in hiding until the day they could make a triumphal return, but after nearly two centuries without a sign of them, it was easier to believe they were extinct.

Clearly, they were not. Wrayan had woken to this realisation several months after losing consciousness in the Temple of the Gods of the Sorcerers' Collective in Greenharbour, following a battle with an assailant he couldn't name for a reason he couldn't guess.

Today, however, he would take a step closer to resolving his past. It was the first day of spring and for the second time since Wrayan had been here in Sanctuary, Lorandranek, the King of the Harshini, would return the hidden settlement to real time, to allow the Harshini and their settlement to catch up. Perhaps, this time, some of the memories Wrayan had lost would catch up with him, as well.

For most of the year, Sanctuary remained hidden out of sight and out of time, so the Sisters of the Blade—or, more specifically, their frighteningly well-trained military arm, the Defenders—would think the Harshini dead and gone, and, lately, to hide from the growing number of Xaphista's priests in Karien to the north who shared the Sisterhood's desire to rid the world of the magical race. Every spring, Lorandranek released the spell hiding Sanctuary and allowed the settlement to return to the present. Without it, Sanctuary would stagnate and eventually die. Suspended as it was out of time, nothing grew or was replenished. Children could not grow, nor even be conceived. It was a false security, being hidden away out of time. Each day was repeated with the same fragile optimism—the hope that the next time Lorandranek brought them back, it would be into a world where the Harshini might once more be welcome.

Coming back into real time also meant that Brak was coming home. The Halfbreed didn't spend a lot of time here in Sanctuary, Wrayan had learned after he woke up in this magical place and realized who it was who had saved him (*from whatever it was that I had needed saving from,* he added silently to himself). When Sanctuary was hidden out of time, Brakandaran preferred to roam the cities and towns of the human world. It wasn't that he couldn't cross the barrier when Sanctuary was hidden; Brak had assured Wrayan that he could feel the pull of Sanctuary no matter how far from home he was, and that if one knew where to find it, one could cross over provided the Gatekeeper allowed it. It was just that he felt he was more use to his people roaming the human world.

Lorandranek often jokingly referred to Brak as the "Self-Appointed Head of Harshini Intelligence", a phrase he had picked up from the Halfbreed when he was trying to explain the military hierarchy of the Defenders to a king who couldn't even contemplate swatting a fly.

It would have been an interesting discussion to sit in on, Wrayan often thought.

Brak's forays outside were more than just the unsettled journeys of a restless wanderer. Brak kept the Harshini up to date on what was happening in the world of humans. He kept watch over the Sisters of the Blade and their army of Defenders. He kept an eye on the growing power of the Incidental god, Xaphista the Overlord, in the north. And he kept a paternal eye on the people of Hythria and Fardohnya, even going so far, on one occasion, as to reveal himself to the King of Fardohnya some years ago when Lorandranek felt the king had overstepped the mark, even for a human, by trying to start a war using plague-infected body parts.

Brak had what the Harshini euphemistically referred to as a "troubled soul". Wrayan worked out eventually that it meant Brak had something of a temper. The Halfbreed—as strong a magician as any full blood—lacked the one thing that marked a true Harshini. He was capable of violence.

And he could wield magic while he was angry.

Only one thing frightened the Harshini more than that, Wrayan had discovered, and it wasn't the Sisterhood, or Xaphista, or any other external threat to their precarious existence. It was the idea that a member of the té Ortyn family— King Lorandranek's family—might conceive a half-human child like Brak. A demon child.

While Brak's "troubled soul" was of concern to the Harshini, he was descended from the té Carn family. He could wield the power of the gods as well as any other Harshini, but it meant he was limited in what he could draw on without actively seeking the cooperation of the gods. The king, however, along with his niece and nephew, Shananara and Korandellen, could, if he wanted, draw on the power of all the gods simultaneously—an ability that wasn't really a problem when you were incapable of even thinking a violent thought. It was a whole different story, however, when you added human blood to the mix. Human blood cancelled out the Harshini prohibition against violence.

Brak's temper was something of an inconvenience. A demon child having a tantrum could, conceivably, destroy the world.

Lorandranek, the Harshini King, was a cheerful fellow, but then all the Harshini were cheerful. They were incapable of any other emotion. He was also fascinated by humans in a manner that reminded Wrayan disturbingly of a bug collector studying a particularly interesting colony of ants. Wrayan's arrival in Sanctuary more than two years ago had been the highlight of the nine-hundred-year-old king's last century, it seemed. He sent for the young human almost every day and spent hours questioning him about the ordinary lives of humankind. They had become friends over time. Despite the danger humans represented to the king and his family—or perhaps because of it—Lorandranek, and his niece, in particular, spent hours with their human guest, questioning him, teaching him, and sharing the delights of Sanctuary.

The beauty of Sanctuary had overwhelmed Wrayan at first. And it wasn't just the impressive white-spired fortress, with its scores of beautifully crafted balconies and terraces. Inside, the settlement encompassed an entire valley with a rainbow-tinted cascade that supplied the settlement with water and tinkled musically across the valley in a fashion too perfect to be a mere accident of nature. Everything here was steeped in happiness, almost to the point that Wrayan sometimes wanted to run through the halls screaming at the top of his voice just to see if he could dent their inhuman calm.

He didn't, of course. Instead, he anxiously awaited Brak's return. Brak would take him out of the settlement for a while and let him breathe the air of the mountains, where he could scream and curse and get into a fight if he felt the need. It wasn't that Wrayan actually felt the need. It was just the idea that he *could* that appealed to him, even if only for a short time.

"Did you feel it?"

Wrayan turned from the balcony. Princess Shananara stood by the door to his room in the elegant, loose white robes favoured by her people. He'd spent a great deal of his idle time over the past two years fantasising about Shananara té Ortyn. She was the most stunning creature Wrayan had ever laid eyes on. She was very tall, with a statuesque body and long dark red hair. Her eyes were her most startling feature, and the single most obvious trait that betrayed her inhuman ancestry. They were completely black with no white surrounding the pupil to relieve their piercing intensity. He had no idea how old Shananara was. She looked no more than twenty, perhaps twenty-five at a stretch but she was probably four or five hundred years old. Wrayan didn't dare ask. He knew better than to question any lady about her age.

"Are we back in real time already?"

She nodded and crossed the airy, spacious room to stand with him on the balcony overlooking the picturesque valley. "Perhaps your senses are not as refined as mine," she suggested diplomatically. "My uncle released the spell about an hour ago."

"I didn't realize," he admitted, thinking "refined" was a very polite way of saying "nowhere near as powerful". In Wrayan's muddled memories he heard a voice sometimes, telling him how powerful a magician he was. The disembodied voice was wrong, he knew now. Compared to even an average Harshini, Wrayan was like a day-old kitten—blind, deaf and completely helpless. And compared to Shananara, her brother and her uncle, even the average Harshini wasn't much better off.

"Is Brak back yet?"

Shananara shook her head. "We've only been back in real time for an hour, Wrayan. It could be days before he gets here. He may not even be in the mountains yet."

"Oh," he said, trying to hide his disappointment. "Can't the demons tell how far away he is?"

"Only if they feel like it," she chuckled. "Besides, Brak tries to discourage the demons from following him around in the human world. They have been known to cause mischief on occasion."

"I can imagine," Wrayan agreed, wondering how Brak prevented the shape-shifting little creatures from trailing him. Here in Sanctuary they were everywhere, the counterbalance to the Harshini's pacifist natures. The little grey demons were everything the Harshini were not, their mischievous spirits tempered by their blood bond with the Harshini. At first, Wrayan had thought the relationship between the Harshini and their demons to be that of master and slave. He realized eventually that it was more like different sides of the same coin.

"I hope he gets here soon."

The princess took his hand in hers and smiled even wider. "Am I such terrible company, Wrayan?"

"Of course not!" he hurried to assure her, acutely conscious of her silky, seductive touch. "It's just . . ."

"Brak is part human, like you?" she suggested with an arched brow. She let go of his hand, which allowed Wrayan to breathe a little easier. "I suppose you're itching to get out of here and go do strange human things with a like-minded fellow of your own race. Or is it just a male thing?"

"A bit of both," he admitted. "Brak promised the next time he was here we'd go—" He was going to say "hunting" but thought better of completing the sentence. Wrayan's Harshini blood was diluted enough that their strict vegetarian diet left him craving meat; a craving he couldn't give voice to without upsetting his hosts. The Harshini abhorred violence. To express a need or, worse, a desire to kill any animal (even if the carnivorous part-humans planned to eat it afterwards) would offend Shananara greatly.

"Well, I'm sure he'll be here soon. In the meantime, if you need to get out of Sanctuary that badly, my uncle is planning a foray into the mountains shortly. I'm sure he wouldn't mind if you joined him."

Wrayan smiled. The suggestion he accompany Lorandranek into the mountains had more to do with keeping an eye on the king than Shananara's desire to allow Wrayan a chance to stretch his legs. Lorandranek had a tendency to wander off. Last spring he'd announced he was going out for a walk in the mountains and didn't come back for several weeks, and even then he only returned because Korandellen sent Brak after him to bring him home.

The Harshini king was a tormented man, torn between the need to preserve the last of his own people by hiding them out of time and mourning the human lives he knew had been lost as the world tumbled slowly but inexorably into anarchy, because the Harshini were no longer there to guide them down the path of peace. He maintained a jovial exterior, but everybody from the newest demon to the oldest Harshini in Sanctuary knew that the irresolvable conflict was tearing Lorandranek apart.

"Perhaps I will join him," Wrayan agreed, pushing off the balcony. "If you're sure he won't mind."

"Of course he won't mind," Shananara assured him. "He'll enjoy your company."

"I'd better go then. I don't want to miss him."

"Don't let him wander too far."

"I won't."

She smiled, and touched his face lightly with her hand. The intimate gesture sent a shiver down his spine. And alarmed Wrayan a great deal. He was suddenly afraid she had read his thoughts. But even if she knew how he felt about her, until that moment Wrayan had been convinced there was no chance of the princess ever looking at him as anything other than a novelty, because he had far too much human blood in him for safety.

"I'll miss you," she told him softly.

Breathe, damn it! Just keep breathing!

"I . . . really, *really* . . . should be going, your highness."

With a hint of regret, she lowered her hand and stepped away from him. Even from that distance Wrayan could sense her desire radiating off her like heat from a small sun. There were legends about the Harshini and the effect they had on humans. If you believed the rumours, the Sisters of the Blade cult had started because a few Medalonian women had been afraid of the effect Harshini lovers had on their menfolk. Some people believed the purges the Sisterhood periodically launched to wipe out the Harshini were prompted by jealousy as much as a grab for power. Fighting back the almost irresistible urge to take Shananara in his arms, Wrayan thought he understood what the Sisters of the Blade were afraid of.

The princess took a deep breath and another step back from him. "Yes, Wrayan," she said with a rueful smile. "I think perhaps you should go."

Without another word, Wrayan bowed hastily and fled the room, thinking he didn't need a walk in the mountains right at that moment so much as a very cold shower.

CHAPTER 61

The air in the Sanctuary Mountains was crisp. Winter
might be officially over, but the season clung tena-
ciously to the slopes, reluctant to relinquish its grip.
The higher peaks remained covered in snow and even
on the lower slopes only a few brave trees dared show
their spring foliage yet. The evergreens were still weighed
down by their winter dressing of ice, too, but the air smelled
like spring in some indefinable way that Brak could not explain.

The Halfbreed stopped for a moment and smiled as he felt
Sanctuary return. The pull towards home was always there,
but when Sanctuary was out of time it was muted and dull.
The moment Lorandranek let go of the spell that kept the settlement hidden, however, Sanctuary blazed like a beacon in
Brak's mind, calling him home with an irresistible compulsion. *Lorandranek must be feeling particularly restless this
year,* Brak thought as he trudged upward through the snow-
covered trail. *It is barely the first day of spring and already
Sanctuary is back. The king must be itching to escape his
self-imposed imprisonment so he can roam his beloved
mountains again.*

Maybe, this time, he wouldn't wander too far, although it
was probably an idle hope. Lorandranek hated being locked
in Sanctuary for most of the year, even though he knew it was
the only way to protect his people until the reign of the Sisterhood was at an end. For that matter, none of the Harshini
was really thrilled with the idea, with the possible exception
of the King's nephew and heir, Korandellen, who seemed to

have no trouble at all with his enforced confinement. Brak was lucky he had a choice, but for his full-blooded cousins it wasn't as easy. So many had been killed in the purges over the last two hundred years, and since they lacked the ability to defend themselves, they had little choice but to hide.

The trouble was, Brak thought as he continued on his way, over the past hundred years, as humans cleared ever more land for farming, the logging villages in the mountains had been moving higher and higher until there were now several human settlements within a few days of Sanctuary. It was an alarming trend that Brak often wondered if he should try to reverse. Rumours abounded among the humans in Medalon about the haunted Sanctuary Mountains. With a bit of magic, it wouldn't take much to scare the settlers off. On the other hand, if news reached the Citadel that the villagers had seen or heard anything that might indicate there were Harshini in the vicinity, the Sisterhood would send the Defenders to investigate.

Perhaps it was safer to leave well enough alone.

"Brak is back!" a high-pitched voice suddenly squealed delightedly. Before he had a chance to react, a small missile launched itself at him from the concealment of the trees, followed by another creature who threw itself at him so hard that, together, they knocked him off his feet.

"You're back! You're back! You're back!" one of the little demons shrieked, jumping up and down on his chest.

"Eyan! Elebran! Get off him at once!" a stern female voice commanded.

The demons jumped off Brak hurriedly, fortunately before they broke any ribs, and allowed him a chance to sit up. An elegant hawk stood on the path in front of him. It stared at him for a moment then began to change form until it was replaced by a small grey demon.

"Lady Elarnymire," Brak said with a smile.

"Lord Brakandaran."

"You didn't have to come and meet me."

"I didn't," the little demon informed him curtly. "I was after these two fools. Eyan and Elebran are the ones who thought you deserving of a welcoming party."

The little demons stared at him cautiously as he climbed to his feet, dusting off the snow he was now covered with before it could melt and soak his clothes. "Next time, warn me before you do that," he ordered crossly.

Elebran's ears drooped and Eyan's bottom lip trembled. Brak took pity on them and smiled. The little demons shrieked with glee when they realized he wasn't really mad at them and threw themselves into his arms, almost choking him with the strength of their embrace.

"All right! Enough!" he cried, pushing them off. "Here, carry my pack. That should keep you out of trouble for a while." He unshouldered his heavy pack and tossed it on the ground. It was bigger than both demons put together and they immediately began squabbling about the best way to lift it. Brak ignored them and turned back to Lady Elarnymire, the matriarch of his family's demon brethren.

"Sanctuary is back early this year," he remarked.

"It's spring."

"Only just."

"I am not responsible for the actions of the Harshini king, Brakandaran."

"If you were, he'd be much more organised, I'm sure," Brak replied with a smile.

The demon grinned and turned to the squabbling pair who still hadn't figured out how they were going to lift Brak's pack off the ground. "Oh, for the gods' sake, you two!" she snapped impatiently. "One of you must change into a sleigh and the other can drag it!" She shook her wrinkled grey head in frustration. "This happens every year. The young demons spend too much time cooped up in Sanctuary, and then when they do get a chance to escape they're too ignorant to do anything. We don't meld often enough any more," she lamented. "Not into the really big melds. We can do the small things while Sanctuary is out of time, but some of these younger demons are only a hundred years old. They've never even seen a dragon meld, let alone taken part in one. There's just no way for them to learn what they need to know."

"Maybe we can meld a dragon while I'm here?" he suggested.

The little demon sighed wistfully and began walking back up the path. Brak fell into step beside her. Behind them, Elebran had managed to change into a rather lopsided-looking sleigh onto which Eyan was pushing Brak's pack with a great deal of grunting and groaning and quite a few protests coming from the sleigh.

"Do you remember what it was like in the old days, Brakandaran? When we melded into dragons and flew the length and breadth of the continent? We ruled the skies, once. Do you remember what it was like to be a Dragon Rider?"

"I remember."

"Do you think those days will ever come again?"

"Not while the Sisterhood rules Medalon," he warned. "And Xaphista's getting a bit full of himself lately. I suspect we'll have more trouble from that quarter some day, rather than the Sisters of the Blade."

"Bah! Xaphista!" Elarnymire scoffed. "What would that self-important, overrated demon know?"

"He knew enough to transform himself from a demon into an Incidental god," Brak reminded her.

"*I* know how to do that, Brakandaran. Having a few thousand followers believing you're a god is all it takes."

"Yes, but you can count Xaphista's followers in the millions these days, my lady, not the thousands. That makes him *very* dangerous."

"Perhaps," the demon conceded reluctantly. Xaphista's defection from the demon brethren still rankled with some of the older demons who remembered him from when he was just a pup. Fifteen hundred years since the rogue demon and some of his halfbreed kin had left the Harshini to establish their own cult in Karien had done little to dampen Elarnymire's fury over the matter. "But that's a matter for the Primal Gods, not us. Do you have news?"

"Plenty of it," he promised. "But I think I should wait until we get back. I hate repeating myself."

His words were prophetic; they rounded a small bend in the path to find Lorandranek and Wrayan Lightfinger, the young human Dace had insisted Brak save from the Temple of the Gods in Greenharbour, heading down the path towards them.

"Brak!"

As soon the Harshini and the human spotted Brak and the demon they scrambled down the path. Lorandranek arrived first, his dark red hair in disarray, his black eyes glistening, his golden skin flushed with the exertion. Wrayan was only a few steps behind him. Both were dressed in quite ordinary human clothes. Although Lorandranek was the older of the two by almost a millennium, oddly, it was Wrayan who looked the elder.

"Brak! You're back already!" Lorandranek cried. "This is excellent!"

"Your majesty," he said, bowing respectfully to his king.

"Yes, yes, enough of the formalities. You remember Wrayan, don't you?"

"I'm hardly likely to forget him," Brak pointed out, offering the human his hand. "Hello, Wrayan."

Wrayan shook it warmly. "My lord."

"You heard the king," Brak said with a grin. "Enough of the formalities. You've not wasted any time escaping, have you? I only felt Sanctuary reappear a little while ago. Who was it who couldn't get out of there fast enough? You, Wrayan, or our great and glorious king?"

"Princess Shananara sent me out to keep an eye on him," Wrayan admitted.

"The cheek of her!" Lorandranek cried, but he was amused rather than offended. When you weren't physically capable of feeling anger, there weren't many other emotions left to you. "Do you have news, Brak? Or have you spent the past months sitting in a cave somewhere, contemplating your navel?"

"I have news," he assured the king.

"Then tell me everything you know!"

"Wouldn't you rather we got back to Sanctuary first?"

"Gods, no!" the king declared. "We only just got out of there! Here is good enough." He waved his arm and three overstuffed, human-sized armchairs appeared in the clearing, accompanied by a small padded stool for Lady Elarnymire. "There, that should be comfortable enough." The king hesitated and looked past Brak with a puzzled frown. "What *are* those demons doing?"

Brak glanced over his shoulder and laughed. Eyan was dragging Elebran up the slope, but the pack kept sliding off, so Elebran's sleigh had grown two sets of arms which were wrapped around the pack in an attempt to keep it secure.

"Just ignore them, your majesty," Lady Elarnymire advised.

"As you wish," Lorandranek replied with a shrug as the demons grunted and groaned their way painstakingly forward. "What news, Brak?"

"Hablet of Fardohnya has taken another wife," he announced, taking a seat in the chair Lorandranek had provided for them. The air felt warmer too, as if the king had heated this small area for their comfort.

"Didn't he get married last year?" the king asked.

"That was to Lady Sharel Hellene. The year before that it was Princess Shanita of Lanipoor. His new wife is Lady Sybil of Tarkent."

"What happened to his other wives?" Wrayan asked.

"They're still in the harem, I suppose," Brak replied. "But nobody has given him a son yet and Hablet's not a patient man. Mind you, according to the gossip in the Talabar marketplace, the reason he never gets his legal wives with child has more to do with the time he spends with his *court'esa* than any fault on their part."

"And Hythria?"

"Well, there at least, the succession is quite clear."

"The High Prince has a son?" Wrayan sputtered in surprise. He might not remember much about his past, but he knew he was Hythrun and his High Prince's reputation for pederasty was something that had survived even his partial amnesia.

"A nephew," Brak corrected. "Lernen's sister, Marla, is married to Laran Krakenshield, the Warlord of Krakandar and Sunrise Provinces. They had a son just over a year ago. Lernen adopted the boy as his heir on his first birthday. His name is Damin, I think."

"Then let us hope the child lives up to his namesake," Lorandranek said. "The first Damin Wolfblade was known as Damin the Wise."

"I wouldn't hold out too much hope," Brak warned. "Not if he grows up in Lernen's court."

"I remember something about that," Wrayan said, as the names seemed to resonate in his mind.

"About Damin the Wise?" the king asked.

"No. About Princess Marla marrying Laran Krakenshield."

"I'm not surprised," Brak shrugged. "It was about the same time Princess Marla got married that Dace asked me to bring you to Sanctuary."

Wrayan shook his head. "It was more than that. This doesn't feel like something I just happen to know. It feels like it was something I was involved in."

"Then perhaps the mystery of how you came to be injured will soon be answered," Lorandranek suggested hopefully.

"Actually, I may finally have an answer for you about that. Or part of an answer, at least," Brak suggested, wondering how the young man would take the news he'd picked up in Greenharbour. He'd promised Wrayan he would try to find out what he could during his travels but had not really expected to come up with anything so substantial. "Does the name Kagan Palenovar mean anything to you?"

The lad nodded. "It sounds vaguely familiar."

"It should," Brak agreed. "He's the High Arrion of the Sorcerers' Collective."

"And that's where you found me, isn't it? In the Temple of the Gods at the Sorcerers' Collective?"

Brak nodded. "It seems the High Arrion had an apprentice once, who went missing about two years ago. Everyone thinks he's dead."

"I was the High Arrion's *apprentice*?" Wrayan gasped in shock.

"Unless there are a few more magic-wielding Wrayan Lightfingers out there," Brak told him with a smile.

"Well, that makes perfect sense!" Lorandranek declared, clapping his hands together. "You have a limited ability to wield magic, which I suppose would have seemed quite re-markable to your human friends. And, as you say, Brak found you in the temple of the Sorcerers' Collective. Who else would you be?"

"And everyone thinks I'm dead?"

"Not an unreasonable assumption considering the condi-tion you were in when I found you."

"Do I have a family?"

"I'm sorry, Wrayan. I didn't learn much more than the name of the High Arrion's missing apprentice," Brak apologized.

"But that's a start," the boy said, leaning forward excitedly. "I have to go back!"

"You can't."

They all turned as the God of Thieves suddenly appeared in their midst, dressed in his normal motley array of mismatched clothes. Dacendaran's preferred mode of dress had always both-ered Brak, until he finally came to the conclusion that divinity didn't come with any sort of predisposition for good taste.

"Divine One!" Lorandranek cried, jumping to his feet. "How nice of you to join us!"

Brak was immediately suspicious. It was never a good sign when a god just popped up like that. He scowled at Dacen-daran. "Why can't he go back, Dace?"

"You know, you really should call me Divine One, Brak. Everybody else does."

"They don't know you like I do. Why can't Wrayan go back to Hythria?"

"Because he's mine," the god informed them.

"What do you mean, he's yours?" he asked.

Dace crossed his arms and glared at Brak, rather put out that he was being asked to explain himself. "The Sorcerers' Collective can't have him, Brak. He swore an oath to honour me."

"I remember. That's the reason you wanted me to save him."

"Well, he didn't keep his oath. He promised me seven trinkets from the seven Warlords of Hythria and he had a whole year in which to do it. He didn't, so he owes me."

"The lad was unconscious for nigh on half that year," Lorandranek pointed out. "That doesn't leave much opportunity to fulfil an oath, Divine One."

"I don't care," the God of Thieves announced petulantly. "I don't care who he is, where he's from, or where he wants to go. He swore an oath. Wrayan Lightfinger is mine. He's all better now and I want him."

"For what?" Brak asked, a little alarmed about what some oath Wrayan couldn't recall might demand of him. *Seven trinkets from the seven Warlords of Hythria? What was the boy thinking?*

"What do you *suppose* I want, Brak," the God of Thieves replied, rolling his eyes impatiently. "I *want* him to be a thief. The greatest thief in all of Hythria. That's what he promised me."

ChAPTER 62

The banquet hall of the Krakandar Palace could seat three hundred people—or so the steward of the Krakandar palace insisted. Marla stood behind Laran's chair at the high table, chewing on her bottom lip thoughtfully as the slaves moved the tables around, wondering where she was supposed to fit them all. Perhaps the last time they'd had three hundred guests for dinner in Krakandar, they'd all been midgets. Or maybe the old man was remembering a birthday party from when Laran was a child and the guests had all been small children.

She really had no idea how she was going to accommodate three hundred adults.

"Are you sure we're going to be able to fit all of them in, Orleon?" she asked doubtfully, as the slaves brought in another trestle table and stacked it next to the others.

"It will be cosy, my lady," the old steward agreed. "But not unduly uncomfortable. We have catered for three hundred guests before."

"When?"

"I believe the last time was at Captain Damaran's wedding, the year before last," he reminded her. "You were here for that event, as I recall."

"And there were really three hundred people in here?"

"Give or take," Orleon agreed.

"It didn't seem like that many."

"Lady Jeryma has a knack for making these affairs seem effortless," Orleon replied, leaving Marla with the uncomfortable feeling that the old man was censuring her efforts as a hostess.

"Well, the Lady Jeryma has returned to Cabradell for the spring," Marla reminded him with a frown. "You'll just have to put up with me running the show."

Sensing that he had offended the princess, the steward bowed his white head apologetically. "I did not mean to imply that you were not as competent a hostess as the Lady Jeryma, your highness. Simply that she has more experience in these sorts of things."

"You helped Jeryma when she first came to Krakandar, didn't you?"

"Most assuredly."

"Don't I deserve the same sort of help?"

"You need only to ask, your highness."

I shouldn't have to ask, she thought in annoyance, but

knew better than to voice her opinion aloud. Laran's servants could be quite intransigent when the mood took them—which seemed to be almost any time she tried to take charge of anything to do with running the palace. Elezaar said she needed to be firmer with them, but Orleon in particular had a way of looking down his nose at her that made her want to run and hide in the cellar.

Marla was not *unbearably* miserable as the mistress of Krakandar. But neither would she have claimed to be happy, had anyone bothered to ask. Everyone treated her with the respect and courtesy due a princess of the blood and the wife of their Warlord, but nobody in Krakandar had really tried to befriend the princess. Mahkas's wife, Bylinda, was probably the only one who still bothered to make the effort. She was a nice enough girl, about three years older than Marla, but she was a merchant's daughter who was so overawed by Marla's exalted rank that she would probably never be comfortable enough around her sister-in-law to ever really call her a friend. There were other ladies at court, too, who might have been friends, but most of them suffered from the same problem as Bylinda. Not one of them could see past the fact that Laran's wife was the sister of the High Prince and the mother of his heir.

After a while, Marla had given up trying to make friends. She had Elezaar and Lirena for company. Her old nurse insisted on looking after Damin, and Veruca was here in the palace, too, having come out of retirement in Winternest to look after Darilyn's orphaned sons. Travin and Xanda also lived with them, ostensibly in the custody of Mahkas and Bylinda, but in reality everyone seemed to take a hand in their care.

Marla was lonely rather than unhappy. Laran was away a lot, either off fighting cattle raiders on the border with Medalon or launching his own cattle raids in retaliation. When he was home, he was usually so busy Marla didn't see much of him. It wasn't easy. She knew everyone was expecting her to bear another son. Just because she had provided Hythria with an heir didn't mean her duty was discharged. Now Krakandar needed an heir to inherit the Province.

Marla wondered if Bylinda was hoping she would deliver a boy and that Laran might make Mahkas's son his heir. Her brother-in-law's wife was due to give birth any day now and was firmly convinced she was carrying a son. For that matter, every woman in the palace had an opinion about it. Some claimed she was carrying the child high, so that was sure to mean a boy. Others claimed they could tell by the colour of her cheeks, the size of the half-moons on her fingernails and—Marla's all-time favourite—by the amount of meat she had consumed during her pregnancy. It was no secret that Mahkas was desperate for a son. For all their sakes, she hoped Bylinda was able to give him what he wanted. Then he could petition Laran to make his son the heir to Krakandar and Marla would be relieved of the need to provide an heir herself.

As it was, only Marla's child made everything bearable.

The sheltered young princess had been unprepared for the feelings of love and protectiveness that swamped her the first time she held her son. She had expected to feel little more than relief when the midwife announced she had delivered a healthy boy. But she would never forget the moment they laid him in her arms. And she would never let any harm come to him. She had promised him that as she held him, still slick and bloody from the womb. *"I will never let anyone hurt you, my darling,"* she had whispered softly. *"I swear it."*

Not that her son seemed to need much protecting. Surrounded by guards who would give their lives to protect him, he was a strapping boy who had suffered none of the risky childhood fevers that stole so many babes from their mother's breast before they made it through their first year. Damin had thrived. He was a sturdy toddler, with a laugh that cheered everyone in the palace and an eye for mischief that Marla suspected was going to be the cause of a great deal of trouble when he grew older. She didn't care, though.

There was nothing about her son that Marla could find fault with. He was fair-haired, blue-eyed and blessed by the gods, as far as she was concerned, and she didn't care that everyone thought her a silly, pathetic girl, blind to her son's failings. As far as Marla was concerned, Damin *had* no failings.

As promised, Lernen had made Damin his heir when the boy turned one year old. Her son was officially named Damin Wolfblade now, having taken his uncle's family name to continue the Wolfblade line. It was an adoption in name only, however. Following the ceremony, Marla had returned to Krakandar with Laran and their son. Damin was to be raised away from Greenharbour, at least until he was much older. It was an arrangement that suited everyone. Marla didn't want to leave her child; Laran wanted to keep his son close and safe; and Lernen had no desire for a toddler running loose in the Greenharbour Palace, getting in the way of his other amusements.

Marla glanced out of the tall windows that opened onto the balcony overlooking the gardens of the inner compound of the city and realized it was almost time for Damin to wake from his nap. She liked to be there when he woke. Let Orleon figure out the best way to arrange the tables to fit in three hundred guests for the Feast of Kalianah. He probably thought her incapable of organising the function, anyway.

She was about to announce her intention to leave everything to the steward when a commotion at the entrance at the far end of the banquet hall caught her attention. Several armed men pushed their way into the hall over the protests of the slaves. Her initial stab of fear vanished when she saw the swooping hawk escutcheon on the soldiers' breastplates. Marla's frown turned into a cry of delight as she realized who it was.

"Nash!"

The young lord looked at the head table and immediately began heading towards her with his escort following close behind. With rather unladylike haste, Marla dropped the steward's carefully detailed seating plan on the floor and hurried to meet them halfway, almost colliding with Nash when she reached them as her slippers failed to find any traction on the highly polished floor.

"I swear, your highness, you're even more beautiful than the last time I saw you," Nash declared, catching her smoothly as she all but crashed into him. He steadied her with a laugh, took her palm and kissed it gallantly, then indicated the men who stood behind him. "Allow me to introduce Captain Sawen, your highness, and the captain of Elasapine's Household Guard, Captain Darenne. Gentlemen, allow me to introduce her highness, Princess Marla of the House of Wolfblade, the Lady of Krakandar, mother of Hythria's true heir and the most beautiful woman in all of Hythria."

"Your circle of female acquaintances must be severely limited, Lord Hawksword, if you think I'm the finest example of Hythrun womanhood," she laughed, blushing at his introduction. Elezaar had taught her a great deal over the past few years, not the least of which was how to deal with outrageously flirtatious compliments. Marla wasn't the same girl who had swooned over Nash on the balcony overlooking the ballroom of Greenharbour palace. She still felt her pulse race whenever she laid eyes on Nashan Hawksword, broke into a sweat whenever he touched her, no matter how innocently, but at least now she knew enough not to advertise the fact to all and sundry. She smiled at the captains graciously. "Please, present yourselves to Almodavar down at the barracks," she told them. "Tell him I sent you. He'll see you and your men are taken care of."

"Almodavar's not with Laran and Mahkas?" Nash asked in surprise as the captains saluted and took their leave of the princess.

Marla shook her head. "Almodavar is captain of the Palace Guard now. Laran's still rather touchy after what happened to Riika at Winternest. He doesn't take his most trusted captain with him over the border any more. These days he leaves him at home to look after his son."

"And his wife?"

Marla smiled. "I think if it came to a choice, Almodavar would save Damin before he lifted a finger to save me."

"And the rest of the guests? Have they arrived yet, or do I have you to myself for a few days?"

"The High Arrion sent word he was on his way," she informed him. "We're expecting him about the same time Laran and Mahkas get back from the border. But Jeryma's gone back to Cabradell for the spring. She worries Chaine is becoming too popular. She likes to remind him that he's Governor of Sunrise at Laran's whim, I think."

"Is Laran's whim likely to change?"

"I don't see why it should. Chaine's done a fine job these past couple of years."

"And the High Arrion is coming too? It's a long way for Kagan to travel," Nash remarked. "Just for the Feast of Kalianah."

"Laran mentioned some urgent business," she shrugged. "Who knows what the High Arrion really wants, though."

Nash looked her up and down and sighed. "Motherhood agrees with you, Marla. You look ravishing."

The compliment was not misplaced. Motherhood had left Marla with a much more curvaceous figure. She *felt* like a woman now, even if she was only just eighteen. "I'll bet you say that to all the girls," she laughed.

"Only the ones that have children," he conceded with a grin. "The others tend to get a little upset, for some reason, if I start complimenting them on their maternal qualities and they're still unmarried."

Marla slipped her arm through Nash's and led him towards the entrance to the banquet hall. "Well, I'll suffer your pathetic attempts to flatter me because you're Laran's friend. But you'd better stop once my husband gets home or I'll have to have him run you through."

"For you, it would be worth it."

Marla laughed. "Nash, you really are incorrigible."

"Incorrigible, eh? It sounds contagious. Where is Laran, anyway? The border, you said?"

"He and Mahkas have gone to liberate some cattle for the celebration."

"When are you expecting them home?"

"Any day now," she informed him as they stepped into the main foyer of the palace. "If they don't get back soon with our 'liberated' cattle, we won't have time to slaughter and drain the beef properly."

"Liberated?" he asked with a chuckle.

"Apparently the Medalonians get upset if you call it stealing."

"I can see how they might."

"Anyway, according to Mahkas it's not really stealing," she explained as they walked through the foyer towards the grand staircase that wound its way impressively to the upper floors. "Rumour has it all this raiding started a score of years ago when some cheeky Medalonian farmer stole one of Krakandar's best bulls and took him back over the border to service his herd. Being a Krakandar bull, he was naturally of above average stamina and virility . . ."

"Naturally," Nash agreed solemnly.

". . . so he covered most of the cows in the region during his sojourn over the border. Consequently, if you believe my brother-in-law, stealing Medalonian cattle isn't stealing at all, because all their cattle are descended from our bull, so technically that makes them ours, anyway."

"Sounds perfectly reasonable to me," he laughed.

"I'm not sure the Medalonians agree with you," she warned. "They have a new Lord Defender in Medalon. Laran says since Lord Korgan took over the Sisterhood has been sending more and more Defenders to protect the border."

"You see," Nash sighed, shaking his head. "That's what happens when you let women rule a country. Medalon has the best damned army on the continent and they're going to waste it fighting off cattle raids."

"What would you rather they did, Nash? Invade us?"

"Of course not. But surely, they could declare war on *somebody*, every now and then. For the practice, if nothing else."

Marla smiled. "For the *practice*? Really, Nash, why do you get so excited about the idea of going to war?"

"I follow Zegarnald," he shrugged. "What else is one supposed to do to honour the God of War?"

"Good point," Marla agreed with a laugh. They reached the foot of the grand staircase and stopped. "I've had the Green Room made ready for you." Nash had been a frequent enough visitor to the Krakandar palace that he didn't need a guide to find his way to his room.

He turned to look at her, lifting the arm she had linked through his to kiss her palm and then her wrist, smiling at her, his eyes never leaving hers. "Are you sure you wouldn't like to show me the way?"

His words whispered against the skin at her wrist, causing goose bumps along her arm.

"You know the way, my lord," she replied, with commendable calm.

"Yes, but it would be so much more . . ." He hesitated and searched her face for a moment. "Are you happy, Marla?"

"Why wouldn't I be?"

"You just look a little . . . forlorn."

"This is the first time I've organised anything on this scale without the Lady Jeryma watching my every move," she said, more than a little uncomfortable that Nash might suspect her true feelings. "I'm nervous, not forlorn."

"You don't have to be alone, Marla," he said, as if he could read her mind.

Marla smiled faintly, wondering if Nash had any idea how tempted she was by his offer. He flirted with her quite openly now she was safely married to Laran, in a manner he would never have dared when she was single. "Perhaps it's a good thing I'm going to the nursery to see my son, and you're going to your room, Nash."

"There's nothing wrong with honouring the Goddess of Love," he told her in a low, seductive voice.

"Then I'll have one of the *court'esa* sent to your room, shall I?" she suggested, pretending ignorance about what he was really proposing.

Nash lifted her hand to his lips again and smiled. "You're a cruel woman."

"The cruellest," she agreed, extracting her hand carefully

from Nash's grasp before she did something likely to embarrass them both. "Now go. I'll see you at dinner."

Nash smiled regretfully and bowed before taking the stairs two at a time to the upper floor. Marla watched him leave, a part of her wishing she was brave enough to follow her heart instead of her head. Nash was always joking about making love to her. Even when Laran was around. Marla was never sure if he was just doing it to tease her, to get a rise out of Laran, or if he was testing her in some way. Perhaps even at Laran's behest . . .

I've been listening to that damn dwarf too much, she told herself as she headed across the foyer to the south wing where the day nursery was located. *I'm seeing plots in everything these days.*

Nash flirted with Marla because he flirted with every woman he met. Marla had seen him flirting with Jeryma. At Damin's adoption ceremony in Greenharbour, she'd heard him telling old Lady Foxtalon, the incumbent Warlord of Pentamor's great-grandmother, that she was the most stunning woman present. It was what Nash did. It was his nature. Marla was wise enough now to realize that believing anything else would simply lead to heartbreak.

Unfortunately, all the mature common sense in the world couldn't stop her longing for what might have been.

CHAPTER 63

Mahkas waited anxiously with Laran for the scouts to return from across the Medalonian border. Their small camp was hidden in the trees a few hundred paces back from the Border Stream which marked the line between Medalon and Hythria. Their fires were low and carefully shielded, even though they had seen no sign of any Defender patrols on the Medalon side of the border. That didn't mean they weren't there. It might just mean the patrol was particularly good at hiding any sign of their passing.

It was just on dusk and the slight breeze was chilly, even though spring had officially started several weeks ago. Mahkas shivered, hoping it was the weather and not some terrible premonition that made him feel so jittery. They had expected the scouts back over an hour ago. Laran seemed unconcerned, more interested in preparing his dinner. The scouts had found a young straggler the day before yesterday that had wandered away from its herd on the other side of the stream. The steer was barely a yearling, the meat tender and sweet. They'd butchered the carcass and eaten like kings for the past few days.

"Stop pacing, Mahkas," Laran ordered, as he adjusted the haunch of beef over the fire to make the most of the flames. "They'll be back."

"They're late," Mahkas reminded his brother. "Aren't you worried?"

"Not particularly," Laran shrugged. Then he smiled. "Or maybe it's not overdue scouts that have you so edgy."

"I'm not edgy."

"We'll be home in a couple of days," Laran assured him. "You'll see Bylinda soon enough."

Mahkas frowned, wondering if he'd been so obvious that every man in the troop knew he was fretting about being away from home. "Suppose she gives birth while I'm away?"

"Your wife wouldn't dare give birth to your son without you being there," Laran chuckled. "I'm quite sure she has her legs firmly crossed."

"We *are* going home after this raid, aren't we?" Mahkas demanded of his brother. "No more reconnaissance? No more detours? No more 'just checking on the strength of the Defenders'?"

"Yes, Mahkas," Laran promised. "We're going home after this raid. I need to get back for Kagan, anyway."

Mahkas stopped his pacing and came to sit opposite Laran by the fire. "The High Arrion is coming to Krakandar for the Feast of Kalianah this year?"

"A letter arrived from him just before we left," Laran confirmed, feeding some more sticks into the fire. "He said he had something urgent to discuss with me."

"He probably wants money," Mahkas suggested with a humourless laugh. "Perhaps he wants to build a monument to himself before he dies and figures his nephews should be the ones to pay for it."

Laran shook his head. "He said it had something to do with Darilyn's death."

On the other side of the fire, Mahkas froze warily. In the past two years he had aged ten, living in terror of the day when someone realized he had murdered his sister. He felt bad about having done it. Really bad. And Mahkas had tried to make amends. He treated Darilyn's sons like his own. Loved them like a father. He insisted that Bylinda treat them as her own too, determined to see the boys didn't suffer for want of a mother. But not a day went by that he didn't think about it. Not a day went by that he didn't expect to be caught out in the lies. Not a day went by when he didn't rub the sore spot on his arm that for some reason refused to go away. He couldn't leave it alone, either, rubbing it raw when he was tired or worried about something.

Remarkably, nobody had ever discovered the truth. Laran had believed him. Jeryma had believed him. Even Kagan, after expressing a few doubts, had come to believe his version of events. Until now.

Is that why Kagan is coming to Krakandar? Has he discovered the truth?

Forcing himself to stay calm, Mahkas enquired casually, "Oh? Did he say what he wanted to tell you?"

"No. Just that some information had come to light which needed to be dealt with urgently. I can't imagine what he'd think was so important after all this time, but it must be fairly serious to bring him all this way. He's barely left Greenharbour since Wrayan went missing."

Mahkas jumped on the chance to change the subject. "Has nobody ever discovered what became of his apprentice?"

"Not that I'm aware of. I know Kagan thinks Alija Eaglespike was behind Wrayan's disappearance, but he can't prove it. For that matter, without a body, he can't even be sure that Wrayan didn't just suddenly decide to take off from the Sorcerers' Collective and return to his former life as a thief."

"That's a bit unlikely, isn't it? After ten years?"

"That's what Kagan thinks. I'm interested to hear what he has to say about Darilyn, though."

"Don't worry about it," Mahkas advised with a remarkably steady voice. "We'll know what news he has for us in a few days." *A few days.* The words rattled around Mahkas's head like a threat.

That might be all the time he had before Laran learned the truth.

Did Kagan really know what had happened? Had he finally figured it out? He'd been suspicious of Darilyn's wounds after he'd viewed her body in Cabradell after Riika's funeral. What should I do?

What would Laran do?

Mahkas hesitated. There was really no question about what Laran would do to Mahkas if he discovered who was responsible for Darilyn's death. And worse, if his older brother discovered the motive behind Darilyn's killing, Laran would also learn that Mahkas was responsible for Riika's kidnapping and death at the hands of the Fardohnyans, and he would be doubly damned.

And what if we're late back home? What if Kagan arrives in Krakandar before us and has time to tell someone else his theory about who was really responsible for the death of his two nieces?

"Mahkas!" Laran said sharply, jerking him out of his horrifying train of thought. His older brother was still squatting on the other side of the fire, turning the haunch of beef. The flickering light on his angular features made him look like the face of Judgment.

"Yes?"

"What's wrong with you? I thought you'd suddenly gone deaf." Laran wiped his hands on his trousers as he stood up and pointed north towards the border. "No time for day-dreaming, little brother. The scouts are back."

Several other Raiders were gathered near the edge of the camp, bows raised and pointed into the darkness in case the scouts were being pursued. The two men sent to find the most likely herds to raid tomorrow slipped into the camp, stopping near the closest fire to shed their weapons and share their intelligence. Mahkas didn't know how long he'd been sitting there, staring into the fire, wondering what would happen when Kagan spoke to Laran. He prayed none of his guilt or fear was showing on his face. Scrambling to his feet, he forced his features into a grin.

"Then let's go plot the recovery of some prime Medalonian beef for the Feast of Kalianah, eh?" he announced with a strained laugh.

"And let's honour Dacendaran while we're at it," Laran laughed, turning towards the other fire.

Mahkas followed close behind—just one of the boys, the Warlord's loyal younger brother—thinking the only thing he was interested in at the moment was not stealing Medalonian cattle or honouring any god.

All Mahkas cared about was finding a way to stop Kagan Palenovar and Laran Krakenshield discussing anything to do with the death of his sisters.

chapter 64

After dinner, Nash joined Marla and Bylinda for a walk in the gardens. Enclosed on three sides by the palace walls and the high granite defensive wall on the fourth side, the carefully laid out palace gardens were the only slice of greenery to be had in the inner circle of the city.

Having grown up at Highcastle with the majestic Sunrise Mountains all around her, Marla found the gardens the only real escape in the palace and treasured any chance she had to lose herself among the scattered grottoes. Jeryma had also enjoyed the gardens when she was mistress here and spent quite a bit of her late husband's money having them redesigned and maintained. Before leaving for Cabradell she had made Marla promise to ensure the gardens would not be let go in her absence. Jeryma had put so much emphasis on her precious gardens, Marla got the impression she could allow almost any other calamity to befall Krakandar and her mother-in-law would forgive her, provided the gardens remained unscathed.

Nash offered Bylinda his arm with a sympathetic smile as they stepped out of the solar onto the lawns. "Allow me," he said, helping her down the steps.

Bylinda blushed. Marla couldn't help but smile. Nine months pregnant and awkward as a beached water dragon, yet Nash still managed to make Bylinda think she was worthy of a man's attention.

"Thank you, Lord Hawksword," her sister-in-law muttered self-consciously.

"The pleasure is all mine," Nash assured her. "And it is I who should be thanking you, my lady. How often does a man get to stroll around the Krakandar palace gardens in the starlight with a stunning woman on each arm?" He smiled at Marla and offered her his left arm. "Shall we?"

Seeing no harm in it, Marla took his arm and fell into step with Nash and Bylinda. They walked along the gravelled path between the flowerbeds, enjoying the crisp spring evening. An earlier breeze had died down, leaving the air sharp and clean.

"How much longer until your confinement, Lady Bylinda?" Nash enquired after a few moments of companionable silence.

"The midwives say any day now."

"Well, if my opinion counts for anything, I think you'll make a wonderful mother," he told her. "You have that glow about you."

"What glow?" she asked, obviously flattered.

"You know, that . . . that glow women get about them when they become mothers. It's very attractive, I can tell you."

Marla nudged Nash warningly.

"What?" Nash asked with an innocent look.

"Don't listen to him, Bylinda," she ordered. Bylinda was heavily pregnant and very vulnerable at the moment. She didn't need a man teasing her, even if he meant no harm by it. "Lord Hawksword is an outrageous flirt and he's just trying to embarrass you."

"You wound me, your highness," Nash declared.

Bylinda laughed. "I think she's right, though. You are a terrible flirt, Lord Hawksword."

"And now she has turned you against me, too!" he wailed, as if he'd just learned his best friend was dead. "What am I to do?"

"Shut up, for starters," Marla laughed. "Or you'll bring the guards out wondering what is going on down here."

Nash opened his mouth to object but before he could say a word, Bylinda doubled over with a sharp cry.

"Bylinda?" Marla cried, hurrying to her side. "Has it started?"

The young woman shook her head, pushing both Nash and Marla aside. She ran into the bushes and a few moments later the unmistakable sound of someone throwing up announced what was wrong with her.

Nash shook his head in amazement. "And women do this? Get pregnant, I mean? On purpose?"

"It's your sex that makes us that way," Marla reminded him, as the sounds of Bylinda retching in the bushes continued.

"Will she be all right?"

Marla nodded. "She's been doing this for the past month or so. Bylinda's carrying the child very high and it's pressing on her stomach. If she has a big meal . . ."

"Poor girl. What should we do?"

"Let her be until she's done and don't make a fuss," Marla advised. "She'll be embarrassed enough without you making it worse."

A few moments later, Bylinda emerged from the bushes, wiping her mouth. She looked down at her spattered skirts with an expression of utter humiliation. Marla hurried to her, but the young woman pushed her aside. "No. I'm fine, Marla, really. Why don't you continue your walk with Lord Hawksword. I'll go back to the palace and get changed."

"Are you sure, Bylinda?"

She nodded and picked up her skirts, fleeing the scene as fast as she was able. Marla watched her leave, shaking her head, then turned to Nash. "Poor thing. She's not having a very good time of it."

"As I recall, you were quite the opposite when you were having Damin. I remember thinking you looked very . . . robust."

Marla smiled and slipped her arm through Nash's as they walked on. "You tell Bylinda she's glowing and I'm *robust*? Some flatterer you turned out to be."

Nash glanced over his shoulder before answering, perhaps checking that Bylinda was truly out of earshot. Then he took

Marla's hand and drew her off the path into the shelter of the tall bushes. He took both her hands in his and raised them to his lips.

"Would you like me to tell you what I really think of you, Marla?" he asked in a voice laden with promise.

Acutely aware that they were in a very public place, albeit hidden from view temporarily, she tried to extricate her hands from his. "I think, Nash, that it might be better for both of us if you *don't* tell me."

"What are you afraid of?"

"Nothing."

"Then why are you trembling?"

"I'm cold. Please let me go, Nash."

"Do you love me, Marla?"

His question startled her sufficiently that she found the strength to break free of him. "*What?*"

"Alija seems to think you love me."

"She had no right to say something like that!" Marla gasped, infuriated that her cousin would spread such vicious gossip. "And when were you talking to Alija Eaglespike, anyway? I thought you didn't trust her."

"It seems I'm on the summer hunting season guest list in Dregian Province these days," he shrugged. "But that's not the point. Is it true?"

"Don't be absurd!" she snapped, crossing her arms and turning her back to him.

Nash came up behind her and slipped his arms around her. "It's the Feast of Kalianah, Marla," he whispered in her ear. "There's nothing wrong with honouring the Goddess of Love."

Trying very hard to ignore the shiver his words sent down her spine, she turned to face him, pushing him away and stepping out of his embrace. "Making love to you wouldn't be honouring the Goddess of Love, Nash. I'd be honouring the God of War. Because that's what there'd be if Laran thought I was having an affair with his best friend."

"Laran doesn't care if you have an affair," Nash scoffed.

"He probably expects it. You both know the reason you married and it had nothing to do with love. Hell, he lets you keep your own *court'esa*, doesn't he?"

"Elezaar hardly constitutes a threat to him. For one thing, he's a Loronged *court'esa*. For another, I've never . . ." She hesitated, thinking it was really none of Nash's business who she shared her bed with. Just so long as it wasn't Nash, no matter how much she might wish otherwise. It wasn't moral strength that stayed her hand. It was Elezaar's voice in her head reminding her of the Rules of Gaining and Wielding Power. Rule Number Ten to be exact. *Your reputation is like a virgin—once violated it can never be restored.* Marla couldn't risk damaging her reputation. Not when she was still so uncertain of her place here in Krakandar.

But Nash was not so easily deterred. "Not even Laran expects you to deny yourself love just for the sake of Hythria's throne, Marla. Why impose such a burden on yourself? You're only eighteen years old, for the gods' sake! Are you going to spend the rest of your life in a loveless, gilded cage?"

"I have all the love I need," she retorted. "I have my son."

"That may do you for now," he agreed. "But some day your son will leave the nest. He'll find someone of his own to love. Then where will you be?"

"Content that I didn't betray my husband."

"But I haven't asked you to betray Laran, have I? I'm not asking you to leave him. Or publicly embarrass him. All I'm asking is 'do you love me', Marla? And if you do, why should the inconvenient fact that you're married to one of my oldest friends get in the way of you being happy?"

Marla suddenly smiled. "Are you serious, Nash? Gods! What goes on in that head of yours that you can see things so . . . conveniently?"

He stepped closer to her and took her hands in his again. "Kiss me."

"No."

"Just once," he insisted. "Kiss me once, and then I'll walk away and never mention it again."

"I don't believe you."

"I promise," he said seductively, drawing her near. "One kiss and I swear by Kalianah herself, I'll never mention anything about loving you again."

"Really?" she asked sceptically.

"Not unless you bring up the subject first," he promised softly, his voice like liquid velvet.

"See, already you're putting conditions on your word."

"One kiss," Nash whispered, their lips hovering a hair's breadth apart. "Just one kiss that won't mean a thing if you truly don't love me."

The reasonable part of Marla's mind was screaming that this was both dangerous and futile, but it was drowned out by the roar of blood in her ears. All the logic, all the reasoning in the world, seemed a pale shadow compared to the notion that Nash wanted her. He wanted her kiss. *Just one little kiss that wouldn't mean anything,* she told herself. And then she could stop wondering. She could stop trying to imagine that Laran was Nash when she lay with him. Stop living with the torment of being married to one man whilst loving another . . .

After this, he said he would leave me alone, she quickly convinced herself. One kiss and then Nash might stop looking at her the way he did. Maybe he'd stop smiling at her in that intimate way. Stop visiting the palace when he knew Laran would be away . . .

Don't be stupid! she told herself firmly. *He flirts with every woman he meets, remember?*

"Just one kiss?" she asked, horrified to hear her voice come out in a tremor. "And then you'll leave me alone?"

"If you want me to," he promised.

Marla nodded, unable to speak without betraying her inner turmoil, and then she closed her eyes, thinking it was better this way.

Nash kept her waiting a tantalisingly long time before she felt him gently brush her lips. When he did finally lower his face to hers it wasn't a kiss. It was the mere whisper of a promise. She whimpered in protest. Then he brushed her lips again, taking her face in his hands. Then he kissed her lightly again. And again. Each time a little more desperately. A little more urgently. Every time she felt his lips on hers, she leaned closer until Marla thought she might go mad with the torment. He was making her want him. And it wasn't as if she didn't know what he was doing. She was *court'esa* trained. So was Laran. In fact, like most noblemen in Hythria, her husband was an accomplished lover. So, it seemed, was Nash.

But this was different to kissing Laran. This wasn't the considerate caress of a thoughtful husband wishing to do his duty. This was dangerous. It was wrong. It was wanton. It was everything Marla had ever dreamed of and like nothing she had imagined all in the one breath. It was torment. It was ecstasy . . .

And then he let her go.

Marla staggered with the suddenness of his withdrawal, her breath coming in ragged gasps. Nash stared at her, waiting, perhaps even hoping. But there was a glint of something in his eyes. Was it triumph? Was his smile just a little too smug?

He knew the effect he'd had on her. And, she realized with despair, he was gloating about it, ever so slightly. Nash didn't love her. He was doing this because Alija had told him that Marla was in love with him and he wanted to see if it was true.

"You bastard," she said, rubbing away his kiss, sorry now that she'd ever let him lay a hand on her.

"Marla . . ." he began, holding his hand out to her.

"Don't touch me!" she hissed and then she fled the clearing and that smug, self-satisfied smile and ran back towards the palace as if she could somehow outrun her destiny.

ChAPTER 65

The day nursery of Krakandar Palace took up much of the ground floor of the south wing and opened onto the gardens. Brightly painted with glorious Harshini murals on the walls and a tiled floor that was a puzzle in itself, it was a wonderful playground and school-room for the children of the palace. When Marla arrived it was just past breakfast. Travin and Xanda should have been at their lessons with Elezaar; Damin quietly playing with his toys. Instead, she arrived to find Travin and the dwarf on their hands and knees being ridden by Damin and Xanda wielding toy wooden swords, the four of them locked in a mock battle that seemed to involve a great deal of yelling, screaming, falling about and laughing. There was no sign of either Lirena or Veruca, the two nurses responsible for the boys.

As soon as Elezaar spotted her, he guiltily scrambled to his feet. Travin glanced over his shoulder and pulled his cousin off his back, hastily standing up when he saw his aunt's expression. They made an odd pair, standing side by side, the dwarf and the boy. At nine, a handsome, slender lad, dark and olive-skinned like his mother, Travin towered over Elezaar. Xanda and Damin seemed much less concerned that they might have been caught doing something they shouldn't. Xanda was still laughing as he climbed to his feet.

Not even two years old yet, Damin was the least concerned of all. He spied his mother and ran to her happily. "Mama! Mama! Tabin horsey! Tabin horsey!"

Trying very hard not to smile at his baby talk, she picked

him up and glared at the *court'esa*. "Is this your idea of education?"

"Would you believe we were studying . . . *battle* tactics?"
Elezaar ventured with a cautious smile.

"You're supposed to be teaching the boys about history
and politics, Elezaar. I don't pay you to teach them the arts
of war."

"I'm a slave, your highness," the dwarf reminded her with
an insolent grin. "You don't actually pay me at all."

Marla frowned. "You're a bigger child than they are,
Fool."

"But at least I've stopped growing," he pointed out reasonably.

There was really no answer to that. She kissed Damin's
fair curls and set him down. "Go play outside with your
cousins for a while. I need to talk to Elezaar."

"Tabin horsey?" he enquired.

"Yes, I'm sure, if you ask him nicely, Travin will play
horsey."

She glanced across at her elder nephew, who understood
immediately. He nodded and held out his hand to Damin.

"Come on, Damin," he said. "You too, Xanda. Let's play
outside for a bit."

Damin trotted off happily with Travin and Xanda each
holding one of his hands. Elezaar turned to her, nodding approvingly. "Travin is going to turn into a fine young man,
some day."

"I suspect you're right," she agreed. Then she added
sternly, "Of course, he'll be illiterate, because his tutors only
taught him how to play horsey, but I'm sure that won't hold
him back."

Elezaar smiled. "My, we're in a bit of a mood this morning, aren't we?"

"I could have you flogged for speaking to me like that."

Realising he might have pushed her too far, the dwarf
bowed apologetically. "Forgive me, your highness. How may
I be of service?"

Marla hesitated, suddenly unsure about confiding in the *court'esa*. But who else did she have? This was hardly something she could discuss with Bylinda. And it was certainly not a subject she could comfortably raise with Laran when he got home. Hugging her arms across her body, she walked to the window. Damin was chasing Travin and Xanda across the lawn. His older cousins were letting him almost catch them and then darting away at the last moment. Damin was squealing with laughter, caught halfway between delight and frustration.

"I let Nash Hawksword kiss me last night."

Elezaar didn't answer immediately. Marla still had her back to him so she couldn't see the expression on his face. She wasn't sure she wanted to see it, anyway.

"Did you enjoy it?"

"That's not really the point."

"I'll take that as a 'yes'. What did you do afterwards?"

She turned to look at him. "He was gloating. I called him a bastard. And then ran away."

"You say you *let* him kiss you? Then you insulted him and fled?"

"Yes."

"There's a name for girls like you."

"I'm in no mood for your jokes, Elezaar."

"Actually, I wasn't joking. What do you want from me?"

"I want you to tell me what I should do."

"Why, your highness, when it's clear you've already decided?"

"What do you mean?" Marla was quite certain she hadn't decided anything. All she'd done was lie awake all night, tearing herself apart in a torment of guilt, desire and indecision.

"If the way was clear, you wouldn't need my advice to do anything," he said. "You want my advice because you've decided to take the riskier path, and if I tell you it's a good idea then it'll be *my* fault when it all comes crashing down around you, not yours."

She was horrified by what he was implying. "You think I'm planning to betray my husband?"

"I remember leaving Highcastle, your highness. I remember you demanding Corin teach you everything he knew, because you thought Nash Hawksword was waiting for you. So I wouldn't be too concerned about betraying your husband, if I were you. You've been betraying him in thought since the day you married him," the dwarf pointed out. "It doesn't seem that big a step to do it in deed, as well."

Marla leaned her head against the cool glass, glancing out over the lawns. Travin was on his hands and knees, letting Damin play horsey again. They were chasing Xanda now, who stopped every few paces to let them catch up.

"Nash said Laran wouldn't care if I had an affair. He said he's probably expecting it. He said Laran doesn't expect me to turn away a chance for love just for the sake of Hythria's throne."

"It's in the interest of any man trying to seduce a woman to have her believe it's inevitable. That doesn't make it true, your highness. Or untrue, either, for that matter."

"Do you think Laran expects it?"

"I'm not in a position to guess the mind of a Warlord," he replied evasively.

"Nash called my marriage a loveless, gilded cage."

"Which is not an unreasonable assessment."

"So you think I should—"

Before Marla could finish, the door to the nursery opened and Almodavar stepped into the room. That in itself was not unusual. He was responsible for the security in the palace, after all. What was remarkable, however, was that in his arms he was holding a dirty, thin child with saucer-sized eyes who seemed about three years old. Rather than the stern expression the Raider captain usually wore, he looked quite uncertain.

"Er . . . your highness?"

"Yes?"

"This is the child we spoke of."

"The what?" she asked in confusion.

"I mentioned him the other day, your highness," he reminded her. "When you went into the city? I mentioned I might know of a child who would be suitable to be fostered in the nursery?"

Marla remembered now, wishing that Almodavar could have found a better time to bring the child to her. Like all noble houses, it was common to raise a number of children in the nursery of the same age and gender as the heir, in the hope of foiling an assassin should one find their way through the palace defences. Laran had been at her for months to find some appropriate children with which to surround Damin, but as she thought the practice quite cruel—unless the child of palace functionaries or staff, the poor things would rarely see their own families again—she'd had little interest in doing anything about it. A few days ago, Almodavar had mentioned that he knew of a suitable child. She had told him to bring the child to the palace so that she could check him over. *But why now?*

"This is the child?" she asked with a sigh.

"Yes, your highness," he said, bringing the boy closer. He was an underfed, scrawny-looking thing, with fair hair and bright blue eyes. He smiled at Marla then buried his face in the armoured shoulder of the Raider.

"He looks half starved. What's he called?"

"Starros."

"That's an odd name. Does he have a last name?"

"No, ma'am. His mother was a working *court'esa.*"

Working *court'esa* was the polite euphemism for whore, Marla knew. She wondered what Laran would think if the first "suitable companion" she chose for their son was some whore's bastard that Almodavar had picked up off the streets of the Beggars' Quarter.

"And what's your interest in this child, Captain?" Elezaar asked with a canny look.

"Pardon?" Almodavar looked startled that the slave was questioning him.

"There are a thousand homeless orphans out there, Captain. Why do you think this one deserves to be raised in the palace?"

"His mother died recently. Was killed, actually, quite brutally. By one of her customers. The boy has nowhere else to go."

"A sad tale, but hardly an exceptional one. Why do you care what happens to the child?"

Almodavar glared at the slave and turned to Marla with a pleading look, but she was just as interested as Elezaar in the captain's answer. Realising he would get no help from that quarter, he shrugged uncomfortably. "There is some chance . . . a *good* chance, that the child is . . . a relative of mine, your highness."

Marla smiled. *So Almodavar has a bastard.* It seemed everyone had a secret lover, even the stern and loyal Almodavar.

"Of course he can stay," she told him, thinking it would be much easier to convince Laran that Starros was suitable if he knew the child was Almodavar's. "Although he'll need a good bath and some decent clothes. How old is he?"

"Nearly five, your highness."

"But he's so small!" she exclaimed. "He's hardly much bigger than Damin."

"And therein lies the difference between a prince's diet and a pauper's," Elezaar remarked. He waddled over to Almodavar and held his arms out to the child. "Come, young Starros. I think I've got some friends outside you're very much going to like to meet. Although I'm not sure what the Witches of Krakandar are going to have to say about this."

Almodavar set him down beside the little man and, remarkably, the child went to the dwarf without hesitation. The two of them headed out into the gardens.

"The Witches of Krakandar?" Almodavar asked.

"That's Elezaar's name for Lirena and Veruca."

The captain smiled. "Thank you for this, my lady."

She returned his smile, feeling quite proud of herself. It wasn't often Marla got to make a decision that might make a real difference in someone's life. "Well, we can't have a *relative* of the captain of the Krakandar Raiders begging on the streets now, can we?"

"The boy doesn't . . . he thinks I was just a friend of his mother's," the captain explained uneasily. "I'd prefer it if he kept believing that."

"As you wish."

The captain bowed. "You've done a good thing this day, your highness. I'll not forget your kindness."

Almodavar departed the nursery, leaving Marla looking after him thoughtfully. The door to the gardens opened and Elezaar waddled back in. She glanced over his shoulder when she realized he was alone.

"Where's Starros?"

"Playing horsey with his new best friends," Elezaar explained. "That was very well done, by the way. One of the most influential men in Krakandar's army now owes you a very big favour. A classic application of the Twenty-Fifth Rule of Gaining and Wielding Power."

"The Twenty-Fifth Rule?"

"Be merciful when it doesn't matter; ruthless when it does."

"I'm sure you make these damn rules up as you go along, Elezaar."

He raised a brow at her and assumed a mysterious air. "You'd like to think that, wouldn't you?"

She smiled wearily and glanced out at the boys playing in the gardens. Starros had evened the numbers up and now Xanda was on all fours with the newcomer on his back. Damin was laughing so hard he almost toppled off his cousin's back as he and his faithful "horsey" Travin chased the other pair around the lawn.

"What am I going to do about Nash, Elezaar?" she sighed, taking a seat on the windowsill.

"I can't advise you, your highness," the dwarf replied, coming to stand beside her where he could watch over his charges.

"Why not?"

"Because you're not asking the right questions."

"You're always saying that."

"Ask me if I think you have a right to be happy and I'll answer, of course you do. Ask me if I think Nashan Hawksword is the man you should find that happiness with and I'll tell you I don't know. Ask me if I think you should consider if he has another motive in pursuing your affections, and I'd answer, absolutely. But ask me what path you should take and I really couldn't say. I know you're not happy. But neither are you married to a man who beats you, or forces himself on you, or even takes that much notice of you."

"So you're saying I shouldn't risk a lifetime of mediocrity for a few moments of bliss?"

"No," he replied, shaking his head. "I'm saying you need to think about whether those few moments of bliss are *worth* the lifetime of mediocrity you could be throwing away in pursuit of them."

"A moment in the sun or a lifetime in the shadows. That's my choice, isn't it?"

"Pretty much."

The door opened before she could respond. It was Almodavar again, making Marla wish she'd found a better place than the day nursery to discuss anything so private and sensitive with her *court'esa*.

"You haven't had second thoughts about Starros already, have you, Captain?"

"No, your highness," he replied. "I bring news you've been waiting on."

"My husband has returned?" she asked hopefully, thinking that would put an end to her dilemma very smartly. If Laran was home there was no decision to make. No question of what she should do . . .

It was then that she realized Elezaar was right. She had already made up her mind.

"Unfortunately not," Almodavar said with the faintest of smiles, no doubt thinking her anxious question was prompted by affection for her lord and husband. "But it's news almost as important. I've just received word from the Captain of the Outer Ring, your highness. The High Arrion, Lord Palenovar has arrived."

CHAPTER 66

By the time Laran led the raid over the border into Medalon to "liberate" the cattle they needed for the Feast of Kalianah, Mahkas had worked himself into a frenzy. The more he thought about it, the more convinced he was that Kagan Palenovar had discovered how Darilyn had died and had come to Krakandar to expose him.

Mahkas lay awake all night, rejecting excuses that might explain away any accusation the High Arrion could level at him. He intended to claim someone else murdered her and that he was merely an innocent—duped, like everyone else, into believing it was suicide.

Or perhaps there was a witness. That was probably more easily taken care of than any other problem. *I am the trusted brother of the Warlord of Sunrise and Krakandar Province. My word is worth ten times more than some slave or castle flunky who may have seen more than they should.*

But there *was* no witness, Mahkas was certain of that. He'd been so careful. There was no way anybody could have seen him hauling on that harp string.

Of course, he may have made an error when he used the harp wire. Kagan had expressed some concern over the depth of Darilyn's wounds when he examined her body before they buried her.

He'd been so careful not to get any blood on himself, too, as if by remaining untouched by it, he was somehow guiltless.

But feeling guiltless wouldn't help Mahkas much if the first thing Kagan did when they arrived back in Krakandar

City was to announce to Laran and Mahkas that he had proof their sister was murdered.

Mahkas needed to find a way to stop Kagan and Laran speaking with each other, although how he could arrange such a thing, stuck out here in the wilderness, was beyond him. Had he been at home, he could have engineered a message, recalling the High Arrion to Krakandar. Or he could have arranged for Laran to be urgently needed in Cabradell. There were any number of diversions he could have arranged. But he was powerless. There was no chance to do anything . . .

Except he *did* have a perfectly good excuse to go home. All the Raiders in the troop had been mocking him about how nervous he'd been this trip. Mahkas had heard every expectant father joke known to man at least three times in the past week. Laran had even suggested before they left that Mahkas might want to stay in the palace this time and wait for his wife to give birth, rather than take part in a raid. But the idea of listening to Bylinda heaving up every meal until she delivered the brat seemed a poor choice when faced with a chance to do a bit of cattle thieving. A trip away had seemed just the thing. Therapeutic, almost.

Until he heard the news about Kagan . . .

Did Laran keep that from me? Deliberately?

"What do you think, Mahkas?"

He snapped his head up at the mention of his name and realized he was so wrapped up in his own woes he'd not heard a word Laran said. Mahkas quickly looked down at the diagram Laran had sketched in the dirt, then glanced around the circle of twenty stubbled, grubby faces staring at him, waiting for him to offer his opinion. The sun was just on the rise and Mahkas was looking into it, so he couldn't see the expression on his brother's face, but he guessed Laran would be annoyed if he thought Mahkas—of all people—wasn't paying attention.

"Are we certain there are no Defender patrols nearby?" he

asked, fairly sure he was on safe ground. The Hythrun
Raiders made a point of not attacking when the Medalonian
Defenders were in the vicinity. In fact, nobody in their right
mind tackled the Defenders when there was a chance to avoid
them. With a well-trained standing army and an officer corps
who started their training at the age of thirteen, they were not
a force to be trifled with.

There is honouring the War God, Zegarnald, after all, Glenadal used to say, *and then there is just plain stupidity.*

"They're headed back into Bordertown," one of the scouts
assured him, turning up the collar of his cloak against the
chilly spring dawn. "They left a couple of days ago."

"That's the patrol we *know* about," Mahkas warned. "If
Jenga's out there, that could just be the one they wanted us to
see. What about the patrol that didn't make quite as much
noise?"

Palin Jenga was probably the most feared Defender captain on the border. He was both a fearless soldier and a clever
one, commanding begrudging respect even from his Hythrun
enemies. Laran often claimed Jenga would be Medalon's
next Lord Defender after Korgan, a state of affairs that
Mahkas was actually looking forward to. It meant the bastard
would be recalled to the Citadel and would leave the border
region, making it a safer place for everyone.

"Weren't you listening, Mahkas?" Laran asked. He sounded a
little annoyed to be repeating himself. He pointed to the diagram
on the ground. "They're here. Watching the Border Stream."

"Then how do we get the cattle away? That ford is the only
level crossing between here and Bordertown."

"Didn't you hear *anything* I just said, Mahkas?"

"Probably dreamin' of his missus," one of the Raiders
chuckled.

"Well, he's been daydreaming about something," Laran
agreed. "So let's go over this again, shall we? For the benefit
of those who were asleep the first time. We're going to cross
the border further north, here, across the Bardarlen Gorge

and then double back once we've found our cattle. We want about ten head, no more. They'll be too hard to keep together when we drive them across the stream, otherwise."

The Bardarlen Gorge was a narrow cutting some ten miles north-east of their current position. Although deep and treacherous, at its closest point it could (theoretically) be straddled by a man on horseback. A Hythrun horseman could jump it, at any rate. With their sorcerer-bred mounts and their far superior skills in horsemanship, the Hythrun Raiders were able to make what the Medalonians considered to be a dangerous if not impossible leap across the gorge from Hythria into Medalon. They were so convinced it wasn't possible to breach Bardarlen Gorge that it had still not occurred to the Defenders how the Raiders managed to cross the border when they watched the known passes so closely.

Of course, it wasn't possible to return that way. No steer would attempt to jump the gorge, but it was a quick and easy way into Medalon that allowed the Krakandar Raiders the chance to miss the Defender patrols and gather the cattle they wanted, leaving them fresh and ready to fight their way back into Hythria at the Border Stream where the Defenders were undoubtedly waiting for them.

"The Bardarlen Gorge it is then," Mahkas nodded, glancing at Laran.

"And no killing," Laran added. The orders weren't prompted by any particular nobility on Laran's part. It was a coldly practical decision. The Defenders might try to stop the Hythrun raiding their cattle, but while nobody died it was just an irritation. Once over their own border, the Defenders tended to let them go, not pursuing the Raiders much further than a couple of miles into Hythrun territory.

If they started killing Medalonian civilians, however, the Defenders got rather peeved. They started taking Hythrun lives in retribution. Hythrun farms became the target of Defender reprisals, and because Laran couldn't allow any attack on his citizens to go unavenged, it wouldn't take much after that to plunge them into a full-scale war.

They all knew Laran didn't want a war. He just wanted a few head of cattle for the Feast of Kalianah and it had become something of a tradition for Krakandar to serve Medalonian beef at the feast.

"Mount up," Laran ordered, after glancing around to make certain everyone knew what they were supposed to be doing. The Raiders hurried to their horses while Laran kicked over the sketch in the dirt, obliterating it. Then he glanced at Mahkas, a little concerned. "Are you all right, brother?"

"Of course. Why?"

"You seem a little . . . I don't know . . . distracted?"

"I guess I can't stop worrying about Bylinda," he shrugged. "I keep thinking I should have stayed with her."

"Women don't want their menfolk hanging around at a time like this."

"But still, I was thinking, Laran . . . maybe I should go back . . ."

His older brother slapped him on the shoulder comfortingly and led him towards his waiting mount. "She's in good hands, Mahkas. The midwives know what they're doing and, between them, Lirena and Veruca have probably delivered half the noble-born babies in Hythria. You've no need to worry."

"But Laran—"

"Stop fretting," Laran said with a laugh. "And that's an order. Your wife will be fine. She's as healthy as a horse and strong as an ox. So forget about Bylinda and let's go honour Dacendaran with some prime Medalonian beef."

Mahkas nodded unhappily and swung into the saddle. He gathered up his reins and turned his horse to follow the others towards the Bardarlen Gorge, thinking things were just going from bad to worse.

The best he could hope for now, Mahkas thought miserably, was that Laran misjudged the jump at the Bardarlen Gorge, saving Mahkas from having to face his brother's wrath when he learned the truth about Darilyn and Riika.

Which gave Mahkas another, even more terrible idea . . .

CHAPTER 67

The High Arrion looked exhausted when he arrived at the palace. After a perfunctory greeting for Marla, Bylinda and Nash, he retired to his rooms almost immediately. He wasn't at dinner that night or at breakfast the next morning. Marla was quite worried about him. He was an old man, after all, and it was a long way from Greenharbour. Perhaps the journey had taken more out of him than he'd expected. Kagan had sent a message asking not to be disturbed so she ordered Orleon to see that his every need was catered for and went to check on Bylinda.

Her sister-in-law was having an uncomfortable time of it this morning and had stayed in bed. It was obvious she must give birth any day now, but the child seemed reluctant to leave the warmth and security of the womb. Marla hoped it didn't mean it was going to be a difficult birth. Even for a woman as well cared for as Bylinda, childbirth was a dangerous time. But the midwives seemed unconcerned, assuring their young mistress that the babe would come when it was good and ready. So Marla left Bylinda with the midwives and went looking for Nash.

"Lord Hawksword took Master Travin and Master Xanda into the city just after breakfast," Orleon informed her when she couldn't find him in the palace.

"Why?"

"Do you expect me to question the comings and goings of every visitor in the palace, your highness?"

"I expect you to know why my nephews were allowed to leave in the care of a stranger."

"Lord Hawksword is hardly a stranger, my lady, and he took a full guard with him. The young lords will be quite safe."

Marla remained silent, having learned that a glare was sometimes the only way to deal with the steward.

"I believe they mentioned something about puppies, your highness," he added after a moment.

"And you couldn't just *tell* me Lord Hawksword had taken the boys into the city to buy them a dog?"

Nash had promised the boys he'd get them their very own fighting dog the day he arrived, even though Marla thought them much too young to own anything so potentially vicious.

Orleon had the sense to look a little shamefaced. "I apologize, your highness."

Marla had the feeling that Orleon wasn't in the least bit sorry, but there wasn't much she could do about it. "I would like to be informed as soon as they return. I have matters I need to discuss with Lord Hawksword."

"As you wish, your highness."

"I'll be in the nursery."

"Very good, your highness."

"Very good, your highness," she muttered sarcastically under her breath as she walked away, her slippers silent on the perfectly polished floor. If it was "very good, your highness", she shouldn't have to ask these things at all.

As it turned out, Marla didn't need to wait on Orleon to advise her of Nash's return. Nash brought Travin and Xanda back to the nursery himself just before lunch—fortunately without a puppy. There had been nothing available that Nash had liked the look of, he claimed, so the boys had returned empty-handed. Marla was quite relieved. The task of choosing any sort of companion—canine or otherwise—for Laran's nephews should have been left to Laran or Mahkas, she thought.

"Orleon mentioned that you wished to speak to me, your

highness," Nash remarked casually after the boys had finished their excited tale about the terriers they'd been to see.

She nodded, handing Damin over to Lirena. Starros stood near the old nurse, hiding behind her skirts. He was still wary of all these new faces, but had taken the change in his circumstances with remarkable equanimity. Marla suspected the child was too street-smart to question his sudden good fortune. He was simply riding this unanticipated wave of prosperity while it lasted, probably expecting it to come to an end at any moment. After tut-tutting about the notion of allowing a working *court'esa*'s bastard into the nursery, Lirena and Veruca had taken the child under their collective wing and set about making him look more like a suitable companion for a prince. Starros was scrubbed this morning, his hair trimmed and combed neatly, and he was dressed in a shirt, trousers and boots that had once belonged to Xanda. He was really quite a presentable-looking child when he was clean.

Marla spared the child a quick, reassuring smile, kissed her son and then took a deep breath before turning to face Nash.

"Yes, I *would* like a word with you, my lord," she agreed, trying to sound formal and aloof. "Would you take a turn around the gardens with me?"

"I'd be delighted."

Leaving the children in the care of Lirena, Marla waited for Nash to open the door for her then stepped out onto the terrace which led down to the lawns. Nash fell into step beside her as they walked away from the palace.

Neither of them said a word until they were out of sight of the terrace, at which point Nash took her arm and led her into one of the sheltered grottoes scattered through the gardens. Surrounded by a tall hedge which was covered in jasmine climbing across from the nearby wall, there was a small love-seat in the grotto beside a fountain sculpted in the shape of Kalianah, the child Goddess of Love, pouring water into the small pool through an earthenware pitcher. Marla glanced around with a frown. Of all the places she *didn't* want this conversation to happen, Kalianah's grotto was probably the top of the list.

Another day had given Marla a chance to think things through, and she realized the folly of what she had been contemplating. It didn't matter what she felt about Nash. She gave up any hope for something between them the day she married Laran. What was it Jeryma had said back in Cabradell when she confessed her own dalliance? *Affairs like that are doomed to fail.*

It would break Marla's heart to give up the only man she had ever truly wanted, or loved, but she had her son to think of. And the danger was very real. A cuckolded husband was quite within his rights to put aside an adulterous wife. And he could deny her any access to their child. Her mother-in-law was right. *If you need that sort of comfort, stick to a court'esa,* Jeryma had advised. *They're actually better at it and they don't come with all the risks attached to one's own class.* Keeping a slave for pleasure wasn't considered cheating. Slaves were possessions, after all, not people. A wife could only be accused of cheating if she indulged in an affair with a free man.

Filled with a sense of righteousness, Marla took a deep breath before she spoke.

"I wanted to talk to you about the other evening," she began as she pulled away from Nash and put the small fountain between them.

Nash didn't answer her. He simply waited for her to continue. His expression was hard to read, but he had learned one lesson. He wasn't looking in the least bit smug.

"There can be nothing between us, Nash. You know that."

"I see," he replied in a voice that betrayed no emotion at all.

"I mean it," she added sternly. "I don't want you to even suggest such a thing, ever again. What happened must be forgotten."

"As you wish."

She glared at him suspiciously. "So you agree?"

"If that's what you want of me . . ."

"It is."

He nodded. "Very well."

This was too easy. She felt a stab of disappointment. Nash had capitulated to her wishes far too readily. Maybe he never really loved her at all. Maybe that's why he raised no objections to her insistence that he stop pursuing her. He didn't care . . .

Marla swallowed hard in an attempt to lubricate her dry mouth. She was suddenly aware of every little detail—the cobalt sky, the warm spring air with a hint of jasmine on it from the hedge. The birds chirping in the branches of the milkwood trees near the outer wall. She could feel the silk of her gown against every pore, even the leather on the soles of her slippers.

"Well," she said uncomfortably. "That's taken care of that, then."

She squared her shoulders and walked back around the fountain towards the small arch in the hedge which led back to the path.

"Marla . . ."

She turned back to him impatiently. *"What?"*

"I'll always love you."

She was three steps away from Nash. And three small steps away from the path outside the grotto and doing the right thing. Marla hesitated for barely a moment before turning her back on every good excuse and reason she'd thought up in the past two days for not following her heart. With those four words Nash undid every good intention she aspired to.

Hearing that simple admission, Marla discovered she didn't care about anything else.

Marla was in Nash's arms before she had time to question the lunacy of her decision. He lifted her off the ground, kissing her hard and hungrily. She kissed him back ferociously, wrapping her legs around him, wishing she could treasure this moment, this feeling, forever.

For the first time since she rode out of Highcastle more

than two years ago, Marla felt like she was doing something for herself—not for her brother, or for Laran or for Hythria, but for *herself*.

Ignited by a moment of madness, her ardour had no bounds. There was no need for words. Nash stumbled backwards and Marla landed astride him on the small patch of lawn. Neither of them had the breath or the wit to speak. Perhaps it was this place. Here in this grotto dedicated to the Goddess of Love, reason and duty dissolved into mist. Only pleasure mattered. Only love prevailed.

Marla didn't even realize her gown was gone until she felt Nash's lips on her breast, his hands between her thighs. She was so consumed by the heat of her desire, she didn't even notice that he'd unbuckled his belt. Nash didn't bother trying to undress completely, for which Marla was extremely grateful. This was urgent and the awkwardness of high boots and tight trousers was something she had no time to deal with. She was still tearing at his shirt when she felt him enter her. Arching her back, she cried out—a moan of sheer ecstasy. Nash pulled her head down and silenced her with a kiss, perhaps still aware enough of his surroundings to understand that anybody strolling past the grotto through the gardens might hear them. Marla didn't care. She just wanted Nash. She wanted this to go on forever; wanted this moment of bliss to last a lifetime.

Marla wasn't sure how long it was before they were spent. She knew only that nothing in her life, not all the lectures from Elezaar, or demonstrations from Corin, or even the considerate ministrations of her husband, had prepared her for this.

It was, she decided, worth everything it might eventually cost her.

"Why don't they warn you it's like this when you're in love?" she murmured dreamily as she rolled onto the grass beside Nash, breathing hard.

"That would take all the fun out of it, I suppose," he answered, gathering her into his arms. Marla snuggled into his embrace and looked up at the sky. The sun had barely moved but the world had shifted significantly since she'd last glanced at it a few minutes ago.

"I love you, Nash," she sighed. It felt so good to say it aloud. And she needed to say it. She needed him to know she loved him; that this wasn't some tawdry way to pass the time because she was bored and lonely as Laran's wife and the Mistress of Krakandar.

"And I love you," he replied, kissing her forehead tenderly.

"I just wish . . ."

"What?"

"I don't know . . . that it could always be like this, I suppose. Or that we could do it in a real bed." She smiled suddenly. "This grass is going to make me itch like crazy."

Nash laughed softly and sat up, making Marla do the same.

"Get dressed," he advised.

She felt suddenly cheapened by his practicality. She wanted to lie here in his arms forever.

"I can come to your room tonight," he offered as he tucked in his shirt.

"No, you can't risk it!"

"Why not?" he asked, reaching for her gown. He tossed Marla the garment which lay abandoned on the grass a few feet away.

"Are you insane?" she gasped as she slipped the rumpled gown over her head. "How long could we keep this a secret if every slave in the palace knows you've been sneaking into my room at night?"

"I'll use the slaveways."

"The *what*?"

"The slaveways," he explained. "The tunnels between all the suites. Some distant ancestor of Laran's had them built. Seemed he didn't like the idea of his slaves walking the same halls as their masters. They connect all the main suites with the kitchens and the other service areas of the palace."

"You mean there are secret tunnels all through Krakandar Palace?" she asked in astonishment.

"Well, I'd hardly call them secret," he laughed, doing up his trousers. "We used to play in them all the time when I was fostered here as a child. Some of them are still in use, as far as I know. It's the quickest way from the kitchens to the main banquet hall, that's for certain. And the only way to get the food to the guests before it cools. I thought Laran would have told you about them before now."

"He never said a word."

"Well, he probably didn't think them worthy of mention," Nash shrugged. "Anyway, it means our rooms are connected. I can come and go as often as you please."

She smiled at him, thinking that to answer that comment would only prove how wanton she had become. "You'll come to me tonight?"

"Nothing short of death could keep me away," he promised, climbing to his feet. He held out his hand to her and pulled her up. In the distance they could hear voices. Female voices. Some of the palace ladies taking a turn around the gardens before lunch, probably.

Nash kissed her quickly, furtively, and then smiled, pulling a twig from her hair. "You're a real mess. You'd best get back to the palace and get cleaned up. And hope you don't meet anybody on the way back."

"What will I tell them if I do?"

"The truth," he suggested with a soft laugh. "That way nobody will believe you."

She kissed him again hungrily as the voices drew nearer. "Tonight?" she whispered. "Promise?"

"I promise," he said, peeling her arms from around his neck. "Now *go!*"

Checking the path outside the grotto, Marla slipped away. She blew Nash a kiss as she left, wondering why, of all the emotions she was feeling at the moment, not one of them felt like guilt.

CHAPTER 68

Built on a small hill, the Krakandar palace commanded a view of the entire city, which sprawled across the surrounding slopes with geometric precision. The city was constructed of the local dark-red granite, which was quarried not far away and was one of the province's major exports.

Krakandar's population numbered close to twelve thousand, they guessed, and had been growing steadily for a number of years now, so consistently, in fact, that Mahkas had suggested to Laran on a number of occasions that he should take a census to find out what the current population was exactly. The city was laid out in concentric rings and looked—even to the inexperienced eye—almost impregnable, but that wouldn't mean much if a shantytown grew up outside the walls, as had happened in so many other cities when their ruling lords gave little thought to planning for the future.

There were two rings in the city, each one protected by progressively more complex defences. The inner ring housed the palace and most of the government buildings. It also contained a huge grain store that each year at harvest time was filled as insurance against a siege. This close to the northern border, they couldn't risk complacency. Prior to the annual harvest, the Krakandar stewards distributed the past year's grain to the poor and, come harvest, the warehouses were filled again for the following year. The outer ring contained the markets and industries of the city and housing for the bulk of the population, the residences growing progressively more affluent the closer one got to the inner ring.

The men rode through the massive iron-reinforced gates
into the outer ring of the city, the guards on the gate recognising Mahkas on sight. Little fuss was made of their return,
although a few speculative gazes followed the troop as they
rode by.

There was a good argument for building an outer ring and
moving the city's industries and markets away from the inner
ring, Mahkas thought, as they rode through the city. It would
mean freeing up a good half of the existing outer ring and
making it available for housing. An additional ring would enhance the city's defences, too, but it would cost a great deal.
Still, it wasn't really as if they couldn't afford it. The Warlord
of Krakandar was richer than a god, now he had access to
Sunrise's revenue as well.

I'll have to do something about that, he decided. The people needed the room, and even with slaves doing the bulk of
the physical labour, the city would benefit from the employ-
ment such an undertaking would generate. *I'll bring a level
of prosperity to Krakandar the likes of which have never been
seen before . . .*

As they rode on towards the inner wall, however, Mahkas's
idle musings about vast capital works to improve Krakandar
were no longer able to offer him a diversion. He began to feel
ill. He was bringing home more than just cattle for the Feast
of Kalianah and his burden weighed on him like the weight
of the entire world.

They had delivered the cattle taken in the raid to the abat-
toir in the city's outer ring earlier this evening. It had been a
very successful raid in some respects. They'd got away with
nearly thirty head of cattle—three times what Laran had estimated they would need. But the cost had been prohibitive.
The Defender patrol they'd encountered on the return journey had been commanded by Captain Jenga, just as Mahkas
had feared. They'd had no hint of the ambush waiting for
them at the Border Stream, although they probably should
have suspected something. But there had been so little sign of

the Defenders—during and after the raid—that even Laran had been convinced that, for once, they might get away cleanly.

Mahkas consoled himself with the notion that it had been Laran's error that had cost them so dearly. Laran was the one who judged it safe to cross the border. It really wasn't Mahkas's fault. He'd simply taken advantage of the situation.

You couldn't hang a man for that . . .

The patrol Mahkas led towards the palace was made up of the remainder of the troop that had left for the border more than ten days ago. They were few in number—barely twelve men left of the twenty who had ridden out of the city—so not many people marked their passing. A few curious souls cast a glance over the horse he led, but nobody really understood the significance of the covered bundle tied to the saddle.

It was almost dark by the time they reached the inner ring. The guards waved them through without stopping them. Inside, the road opened out into a vast courtyard surrounded on three sides by buildings. To the left and right of the square were the government buildings, three storeys high, gracefully symmetrical and uniform in their construction. In front of them lay the sweeping steps of the palace itself, which rose up majestically, commanding a view of the entire city. Mahkas saw the palace as he'd never seen it before, with an air of possession he'd never dreamed possible until now.

Because now, there was nothing standing in his way but a child not yet two years old, his mother, a slip of a girl still in her teens and the High Arrion of the Sorcerers' Collective, his uncle, Kagan Palenovar.

Orleon came out of the palace to greet them, holding a torch high against the gloom. Mahkas remembered thinking as a child that the steward had some sort of magical power. It didn't matter what time of the day or night it was, Orleon *always* seemed to know when somebody arrived at the palace and was there to greet them. He walked down the steps a short way, recognised Mahkas, then looked around with alarm in the fading light when he couldn't see Laran among the other faces in the troop.

Orleon's eyes alighted on the horse Mahkas held by a lead rope and he shook his head in disbelief as understanding slowly dawned on him. "Surely not . . ."

Mahkas dismounted, his expression grim, as Orleon hurried down the steps.

"By the gods," the old man muttered. "It cannot be . . ."

Mahkas stood back to let the steward look at the bundle tied to the pack horse, then glanced over his shoulder at Raek Harlen, who was still mounted. "Find Almodavar," he ordered quietly. "Tell him what's happened."

Raek nodded and wheeled his horse around, heading for the barracks. Mahkas turned back to Orleon, who had untied the cloak covering the corpse tied to the pack horse. Laran's body was not a pretty sight. His face and limbs were swollen and black where the blood had pooled after death. Orleon just stood there, shaking his head.

"It cannot be . . ." he repeated, too stunned to think of anything else to say.

"I share your shock and grief, Orleon," Mahkas said, placing a comforting hand on the old man's shoulder.

His words seemed to galvanise the steward. Orleon squared his shoulders and looked at Mahkas. His eyes glistened with unshed tears. "I will arrange to have my lord laid out in the appropriate manner, and begin to make the funeral arrangements. Do you wish to inform her highness?"

"I suppose I'd better. Is my uncle here yet?"

Orleon nodded. "The High Arrion arrived two days ago from Greenharbour. Lord Hawksword is also here."

So Nash was here. That was a good thing. He was friendly with Marla. With another shoulder to cry on, Mahkas wouldn't be required to console his sister-in-law. He still had enough honour left to consider himself the worst kind of hypocrite if he stood there sympathising with a young woman, when his actions (or lack of them) had made her a widow. Mahkas pushed the thought away. Now was not the time to start reliving the gory details of Laran's death. He had a lifetime to do that.

Or he would have provided Kagan hadn't shared his news with anyone. Mahkas was still hopeful. Orleon had come to meet him alone. If Kagan had told anybody what he knew about Darilyn, there would have been a troop waiting to arrest him.

Orleon sent a Raider into the palace to get some help while he supervised the other men unloading Laran's body. It wasn't an easy task. Laran had been a big man and, with Orleon crying out in horror every time he thought them too rough in their handling of his dead lord, it was no mean feat getting him off the horse and laid out whilst trying to be respectful.

Mahkas watched the proceedings with a heavy heart. It should never have come to this. But the die was cast and he would see it through. And it really wasn't his fault.

Laran had led them into that ambush, stampeding the cattle ahead of them. The arrow that had knocked him off his horse wasn't even fatal. It had taken him in the right shoulder, making his sword arm useless, but leaving him very much alive and able to fight. The red-coated Defenders had closed in on Laran with alarming speed. He'd struggled to free his sword with his left hand and then turned to face his attackers. The first man fell to a wild, undirected blow. Laran staggered. He was losing blood, but was still a formidable enemy. Another Defender attacked. Laran fought him off valiantly, but couldn't know there was yet another coming up behind him. Mahkas cried out a warning. With his hands reaching for his short bow and an arrow, Mahkas used his knees to turn his mount. He charged across the small battlefield, desperately trying to reach his brother before those Medalonian bastards could take him down . . .

And then the world seemed to slow down around Mahkas. The sounds of the battle faded away to nothing. He no longer tasted the dust, could no longer smell the blood. The lowing of the panicked cattle, the squealing of terrified horses, the grunts and cries of the soldiers, the sound of metal on metal—all of it dimmed to a distant background noise that made little impact on him.

Mahkas slowed his mount almost unconsciously, lowering his short bow with its black-fletched arrow that was nocked and ready to fly. With the instrument of his brother's salvation resting across his lap, he watched Laran fight off the Medalonian. In a state of detached numbness, he watched his brother take a knife in the back from the other Defender who attacked him from behind.

Through it all, Mahkas did nothing. He didn't raise his bow; didn't attempt to stop the Defenders attacking his brother. And he could have. Like most Hythrun Raiders, Mahkas was an excellent marksman. He'd made the rank of captain on merit, not simply because he was Laran's half-brother. In his heart, he *knew* he could have stopped the man three paces from Laran. But it seemed easier this way. Less complicated . . .

And then the battle seemed to come alive around him again. A Defender charged at him, screaming at the top of his lungs. Mahkas calmly lifted the bow, drew back the arrow and took the man through his left eye. Then he fought his way through the mêlée to Laran's side, determined to recover the body.

It was important, after all, that he bring Krakandar's Warlord home.

chapter 69

They gathered in Laran's study as soon as word got around: Kagan, Bylinda, Mahkas, Nash and Marla. *They all look so shocked,* Marla thought. *So blank and uncomprehending.*

It wasn't that nobody here had experienced death before. It was just that nobody expected it. Not like this. Laran had been on a hundred cattle raids across the border. They were a sport among the Krakandar Raiders. There were rarely any casualties. Three or four a year perhaps. To lose Laran to something so ordinary was too bizarre to be real.

It was simply unbelievable.

It had not really registered yet with Marla that she was a widow. She was too shocked even to shed a tear. Instead, she had retreated into practicality. She had ordered the flags lowered to half-mast. She had cancelled the feast and ordered the banquet hall cleared so that Laran's body could be laid out in state. She'd ordered the Raiders to select an honour guard to watch over his body until the funeral. She'd also arranged for notices to be posted throughout the city, advising the citizens of Krakandar their Warlord was dead and that they should place a candle outside their doors to light his soul on its way to the underworld in case it wandered down their street.

Marla had been issuing orders like a little general ever since Orleon had interrupted dinner to break the news.

It was all she could think to do.

Mahkas looked terrible. He must be tearing himself apart with guilt and grief, she realized. That he had been there on the border and unable to save his brother was an almost unbearable torment. As he told them of the battle, he kept apologising, as if he could somehow make amends for something that was plainly not his fault. Bylinda tried to comfort him, but there was little she could say to her husband that would console him. Mahkas had lost both his sisters and now, just when things appeared to be settling down, he had lost his only brother.

Kagan was just as devastated. The High Arrion looked old, as if the loss of so many of those close to him had beaten him down, a little at a time, until he almost seemed to be stooping. Marla had asked him to compose the letter to Jeryma informing her of Laran's death and requesting her immediate return to Krakandar.

Marla would take care of informing the High Prince herself.

Nash's reaction was harder to gauge and she didn't dare look at him. Laran had been his closest friend, but that hadn't stopped him coveting his best friend's wife. If he was feeling even half the guilt that Marla was currently burdened with, then Nash would be ready to throw himself on his sword.

A moment in the sun or a lifetime in the shadows.

That had been her choice.

Well, you had your moment in the sun, she told herself harshly. *And look at the price you've been asked to pay for your folly.*

Laran's death, she suspected, was the beginning of her long descent into the shadows.

"Has anybody thought to let Jeryma know?" Nash asked in the uncomfortable silence that followed Mahkas's tale of Laran's last moments.

"I've asked Lord Palenovar to take care of it," Marla replied tonelessly.

"The High Prince will need to be informed, too," Bylinda pointed out unnecessarily.

"I'll take care of that."

Mahkas glanced around the room, wiping away the tears he had tried to hold back while relating his version of events. "I know this will sound harsh at a time like this, but have we thought about Chaine Tollin?"

"What about Chaine?" Marla asked, thinking that the last person she would have thought a problem at this dreadful time was Glenadal's bastard.

"We have two provinces without a Warlord," Mahkas pointed out. "Chaine may finally decide to take what he thinks should be his."

"He's been content to act as Governor of Sunrise Province up until now," Nash pointed out.

"That's because defiance meant facing a Warlord. Do you think he'd baulk at facing an army under the command of a toddler?"

"The Collective will assume control of Krakandar," Kagan said heavily. "As we did when Laran's father died."

"No!" Marla said, without even thinking about it.

Everyone looked at her in surprise, particularly Mahkas who looked astonished.

"Why not?" Kagan asked.

"The Sorcerers' Collective only needs to assume responsibility for a province when there's nobody else to rule it because either the heir is too young or there is no clear heir at all. Damin is the heir to Krakandar and he has an uncle more than capable of ruling as his regent. Mahkas will look after things for Damin until he inherits."

"Damin is the High Prince's heir, Marla," Nash pointed out, as if she didn't understand the way these things worked. "He can't inherit Krakandar, too."

"He is Laran's only son."

"Yes," Kagan agreed, siding with Nash. "But we never intended for him to be the Warlord of Krakandar, Marla. The province, by rights, should have gone to Laran's second son."

"Laran has no second son."

"Actually, he doesn't even have a *first* son," Kagan added. "Lernen adopted the boy. Your son is Damin Wolfblade, your highness. He's legally not even a member of the Krakenshield family any longer."

"That doesn't matter," Marla insisted. "He's still Laran's only son."

"The High Prince will never agree," Nash warned.

"The High Prince is my brother," she reminded them. "He'll do whatever I want of him." She wasn't actually sure such a boast was true, but the others didn't need to know that.

"The Convocation won't allow it," Kagan declared.

"My brother has already overruled the Convocation of Warlords once, Lord Palenovar. At your behest, as I recall. He can do it again."

She turned to her brother-in-law for support. If Mahkas didn't back her on this, she would look like a fool. But she needed to do this, she knew with a certainty that bordered on illogical. Her job was to secure her son's inheritance. And she had no intention of letting anybody outside the family have a hand in Damin's fate. Admittedly, Kagan was Damin's great-uncle, but he wouldn't always be High Arrion and it was more than twenty-eight years until Damin could inherit his birthright. She intended to make certain it was kept safe for him. It was hard to tell what Mahkas was thinking, though. He was looking at her with something akin to awe.

"What say you, Mahkas? Will you become the Regent of Krakandar until Damin comes of age?"

"I would be honoured," Mahkas replied without hesitation.

"Mahkas," Nash began, appealing for reason, "think about what you're taking on."

Laran's younger brother shook his head determinedly, refusing to be swayed. "Marla is right. Damin is Laran's heir and I will fight all of you, if need be, to keep that inheritance safe for him."

She smiled at him, relieved that she had at least one person she could rely on totally. Laran had always trusted Mahkas and Marla was beginning to understand why. He was a stalwart in a sea of uncertainty; a solid and dependable bastion in a world that was suddenly crashing down around her. Anyway, she needed Mahkas's support more than he realized. As a widow, Marla would have little power and even less say over her own future. Without Mahkas on her side, life might get very awkward indeed.

"But Mahkas," Kagan said, adding his objections to Nash's, "if you only thought about it—"

"Do you *mind*?" Bylinda cried angrily, jumping to her feet. "Laran's body has barely even cooled down! Could we argue over the best way to divide up his legacy *after* we've buried him?"

Everybody stared at her, looking shamefaced. Bylinda so rarely raised her voice that her outburst was all the more remarkable for its ferocity.

"And in case anyone is interested," she added with a quiver in her voice, effectively putting an end to the discussion, "I think I'm about to have the baby."

It was past midnight before Marla found her bed, and even then she discovered it was impossible to sleep, so she paced the room in darkness, hugging her arms around her against the slight chill.

Despite Marla's fears of it being a difficult birth, Bylinda had delivered a healthy baby girl about an hour ago. Mother and child were fine, although Mahkas was disappointed, Marla could tell, but he covered it well in front of his wife and made all the right noises about how beautiful she was and what a sterling job Bylinda had done in having the baby so easily.

But on the way out of the birthing room with Marla, he had let some of his disappointment show, even if only to her.

"Perhaps next time a boy, eh?"

"Perhaps," she agreed, noncommittally.

"I was going to call him Laran," Mahkas told her, a catch in his voice.

She squeezed his arm comfortingly as they walked down the hall together. "It's all right, Mahkas. You mustn't keep blaming yourself."

"I know . . . it's just . . ." Mahkas hesitated for a moment, before adding, "I can't help but wish Kagan had picked a better time to visit."

"In hindsight, he couldn't have picked a better time," Marla replied sadly.

"Has he said why he came all this way?" Mahkas asked casually.

"Something to do with Darilyn's will," she told him. "She'd made some fairly specific requests about what she wanted to happen to the boys, should anything happen to her. Apparently, she expressly stated she didn't want them raised in Krakandar. The High Arrion was going to talk to Laran about it when he got back. He thought if Laran appealed to the High Prince, my brother would overrule the will and leave the boys here, where they were obviously happiest. I suppose we'll still have to deal with that, too, even with everything else that's happened."

Mahkas had gone deathly pale. Perhaps the shock of the past few days had finally caught up with him.

"And that's all he wanted?" Mahkas asked, his voice choked.

"It seems so trivial really," Marla agreed. "Although now you have a child, I suppose you'll need to think of making the same sort of provisions for your daughter."

"Bylinda wants to call her Leila," he said in a strangled voice, as if it was all he could do to hold back his grief. "After her mother."

Marla's heart went out to him. "It's a lovely name."

He glanced down at Marla then and smiled distantly. "Perhaps Leila can marry Damin someday, eh?"

"Let's wait for her to grow up a little before we start sending out the wedding invitations, Mahkas."

"Of course . . . I don't mean to be insensitive, Marla. With all this happening . . . with Laran dying . . . you must be distraught."

She *was* feeling distraught, but not for the reasons Mahkas imagined. "I'll get by. We Wolfblades are hardier than we look."

Marla could see him battling to contain his emotions.

"Thank you."

"For what?"

"For asking me to be your son's regent."

"You are the only one I would consider for the job, Mahkas."

"I know. It's just sometimes . . . well, I don't think Laran ever truly saw me as anything other than his little brother."

"I chose you because you're the only one I can truly count on."

He nodded, and lifted her hand to his lips. "And you *can* count on me, Marla. I promise."

Thinking back over the conversation, Marla wondered if Mahkas's determination to take on the mantle of regent was his way of compensating for the guilt he felt for letting Laran die. And it was obvious he believed it was his fault. When he was telling them about it earlier, he'd kept on saying, *if only I'd been faster, if only I'd turned around sooner, if only I'd advised Laran to wait a little longer* . . .

Poor Mahkas. To be burdened with such guilt must be appalling.

Almost as bad as the guilt Marla was trying to deal with.

"Deep in thought?"

Marla jumped with fright at the unexpected voice and turned to find Nash standing behind her. He held out his arms to her, but she pushed him away, aghast.

"How did you get in here?"

"I told you this morning. Through the slaveways. The one in this room comes out behind the mirrored panel in your dressing room."

"Then you can leave the same way," she told him coldly, turning her back on him.

Nash reached for her again, ignoring her attempts to fight him off. He pulled her close and held her until she stopped struggling and finally relaxed against him.

"There, there, my love," he crooned as she began to cry. All the tears she'd been unable to shed earlier suddenly seemed to catch up with her. "It's all right."

"This is all our fault," she sobbed into his chest.

"It was an accident, Marla," Nash told her gently, stroking her hair. "You have to believe that, or you'll go crazy."

"No, it's our fault," she insisted. "The gods are punishing us."

"Kalianah *rewards* lovers," he reminded her. "Only the Kariens up north believe that nonsense about sinning and paying penance for honouring one god over another. Laran was a follower of Zegarnald, Marla, and the War God only takes his favourites in battle."

She sniffed loudly and looked up at him. "And that's how you expect me to look at this, I suppose? I should be happy that while I was honouring the Goddess of Love with his best friend, my husband was honouring the God of War with his life?"

"Stranger things have happened, my love."

"Don't call me that."

Nash smiled faintly. "You were fine with it this morning when you thought your husband was still alive. Do you really think it all right to cheat on him in person, but somehow wrong to betray his memory?"

"You're twisting things around," she accused.

He kissed her forehead and pulled her close again. "I'm sorry. Did you want me to stay with you tonight?"

Yes. I want you to stay. I want you to make love to me again like you did in Kalianah's grotto so I can forget this is happening. I want to . . .

"No," she said, pushing him away. "I don't want you to stay. Not now. Not tonight."

"Are you sure?"

"Positive."

He nodded, accepting the wisdom of her decision if not the reason for it. "I'll see you in the morning, then?"

"Probably."

Nash kissed her again, this time on the mouth, leaving her hungry for more, and then he turned and walked back into the dressing room without another word. When Marla heard the panel sliding shut a few moments later she returned to her pacing, thinking the chances of her getting any sleep this night had just moved from unlikely to impossible.

If she couldn't bring herself to sleep with Nash, she had no chance of sleeping with her guilt.

CHAPTER 70

The Feast of Kalianah was celebrated in Sanctuary like no other place in the world. The Harshini were, after all, the only race alive to whom violence was an anathema, so they didn't have a lot to choose from when it came to celebrating with the gods. Their natural aversion to violence meant they couldn't really commemorate the Feast of Zegarnald, the God of War, the way he would have liked, although they did offer him their praise and honoured him like any other guest whenever he came to visit.

Kalianah, on the other hand, was a particular favourite. The goddess treated the Harshini like they were her own people, even though (in theory) the Harshini had no favourites and treated all the gods with equal respect. The Harshini didn't worship the gods, though. They spoke to them on a daily basis, they begged favours of them when they wanted something, and they even disagreed with them at times.

The Harshini drew on the same source of magic as the Primal Gods. They had been created by the gods for just that purpose—a race specifically designed as a safety valve to prevent the immortals from tearing each other apart when the balance of their powers became unstable. But it was only humans who worshipped them.

And only humans from whom the gods drew their strength.

Dacendaran appeared on the path beside Brak as he headed down to the concert. The god was looking a little peeved.

"Well, if it isn't the King of Larceny. What brings you here, Dace?"

"Hello, Brak," the boy replied miserably. His motley clothes hung on his slumped shoulders as if he'd just thrown them on and hoped he wouldn't miss.

"What's the matter?" Brak asked with a sigh, knowing that when he used that tone, Dacendaran was looking for sympathy.

"I'm just feeling a little . . . unwelcome tonight."

"It's the Feast of Kalianah, Dace. This is Kali's time, not yours."

"Why don't they have a festival for me?"

"They do," he reminded the god.

"But not like this one."

"That's because thieving isn't as much fun as a bit of un-bridled lust," Brak told him with a grin.

Dacendaran was not amused. "I think it is."

"Yes, well, you would, wouldn't you?"

"Is Wrayan going to take part?"

"I suppose."

"But he belongs to me."

"Not while he's still here in Sanctuary," Brak reminded the god. "You can't get your larcenous little claws into him until he goes back into the human world, *Divine* One. So stop whining about it. Go visit the Grimfield, or something. It's a prison town so there are lots of thieves, I hear. I'm sure *they'd* be happy to worship you."

"But the Grimfield is in the middle of Medalon. They're all atheists now."

"If they're thieves, Dace, what do you care?"

"Oh," Dacendaran said, suddenly brightening with the prospect of finding some new worshippers. "I'll see you later then."

The god vanished abruptly, leaving Brak shaking his head. It was the god's own fault, Brak thought, that Wrayan wasn't quite as devoted to him as Dacendaran would have liked. It was Dace, after all, who had introduced Wrayan to Kalianah. The God of Thieves and the Goddess of Love were strange but frequent companions. It had little to do with their areas of divinity. Brak speculated it was a power thing. Depending on what was happening in the human world at any given time, Zegarnald generally had the advantage over Kalianah and Dace. He grew stronger with each new conflict the humans managed to embroil themselves in. He was not the strongest, though. Not by a long way. If you didn't count Xaphista the Overlord, who wasn't actually a Primal God (although lately his power was starting to rival the combined strength of the other gods), then Voden, the God of Green Life, probably held that honour. If not him, then Brehn, the God of Storms, or Kaelarn, the God of the Oceans, were just as likely candidates for the title. Kalianah and Dacendaran, and even Zegarnald, had to work at it a little harder.

As humans were much more efficient at making war than love, the War God tended to keep one step ahead of Kalianah, who considered herself Zegarnald's self-appointed nemesis. Dace hung around the other two, Brak was certain, because with no chance of ever being as strong as them, he liked to bask in their reflected glory.

The Goddess of Love favoured the form of a child, although she could assume any aspect she wanted. Kali believed that everyone loved children and chose to appear in that form more often than any other. Her first question was invariably "Do you love me?" and she could sulk for days if one was foolish enough to answer in the negative. On her feast day, however, in the Harshini settlement "Do you love me?" became the greeting of the day. To further mark her divinity there was to be a concert tonight, followed by a feast and then the Honouring.

"Wrayan!"

The young human stopped and turned at Brak's call as the Halfbreed strode down the path behind him. Tall and dark-haired, dressed in the traditional white robes of his people, were it not for his blue eyes the lad looked almost like a full Harshini.

Wrayan waited until Brak caught up with him, standing aside to allow two Harshini to pass. The man and the woman were holding hands and smiling—the Harshini were *always* smiling—as they passed the young human. They stopped for a moment and the woman turned to look at him with her totally black eyes.

"Do you love me?" she asked.

"Sure," Wrayan agreed. "Do you love me?"

"Of course," the woman laughed. She dropped the hand of her companion and took Wrayan's face between her slender, long-fingered hands and kissed him, tenderly and lingeringly.

"Put him down, Sam," Brak ordered as he caught up with them. "You don't know where he's been."

The woman let Wrayan up for air and laughed. "Do *you* love me, Brak?"

"You know I do."

"We'll see you at the concert?"

"Wouldn't miss it for all the fanatics in Karien," Brak assured her.

Seemingly content with that, she smiled at them both, took the hand of her companion again and headed off down the path. Wrayan watched her leave with a thoroughly bemused expression then turned to Brak.

"How come she didn't kiss *you* like that?" he asked.

"Who? Samaranan? She's my sister."

"That woman is your *sister*?" Wrayan asked in shock.

"I know," Brak shrugged. "Hard to credit, isn't it? Still, she's never seemed too upset that I got all the looks in the family."

Wrayan adjusted his robes uncomfortably as Brak fell into step beside him. "Well, too many more greetings like the one she just gave me and I'm going to end up doing something really embarrassing before the evening is over. Are they always like this on Feast Days?"

Brak nodded. "On Kalianah's Feast Day, they are. You would've still been recovering from your little bout of Almost Being Killed during the last one, I suppose. But yes, this is pretty usual. Kali's fairly popular around here."

"That's because the Harshini love me," a voice announced smugly. The men stopped and looked back to find the goddess had materialised on the path behind them. She was dressed in an airy waif-like tunic and appeared to be no more than five or six years old, with fair hair and an angelic face. You could feel Kalianah's power from ten feet away. The compulsion to love her when she was this close was almost irresistible.

"Pick me up, Brak," she demanded, holding out her arms to him. "I don't feel like walking."

"You're a goddess, Kali," Brak pointed out. "You can fly, if you want."

"I know that, but it's not the same. Oh, hello, Wrayan."

"Divine One."

"Do you love me?"

"Of course."

She turned back to Brak and held out her hands again. "Pick me up."

"Wrayan loves you so much, why don't you ask him to carry you?"

"He belongs to Dace."

"But it's your Feast Day, Kali," Brak reminded her, and then added with a smile, "I'm sure Dace won't mind."

"I suppose." Kali held out her arms to Wrayan. "Pick me up."

Unlike Brak, Wrayan wasn't nearly so certain of himself that he could deny a direct order from a god. He lifted her into his arms and she sighed contentedly, resting her head on his shoulder. Brak knew she weighed almost nothing, but he could see Wrayan was having a hard time thinking of anything else but the need to cater to every whim of this adorable child.

"And let the poor bastard breathe," he ordered.

Kali sighed heavily, but the overwhelming desire Wrayan felt to do whatever she wanted faded into something more manageable.

"Are you going to the concert?" she asked, as they resumed their trek down the path towards the amphitheatre.

"No, we're heading this way because we want to build a shrine to Zegarnald and we thought your Feast Day would be the best time to do it."

Kali spluttered indignantly for a moment before halting her tirade and staring at Brak suspiciously. "Oh, I see. That was you trying to be funny, wasn't it?"

Brak looked over Kali's head at Wrayan. "You'd think with all that power at their beck and call, somebody might have thought to endow immortals with a sense of humour."

"It's very rude to mock the gods, Brak," the goddess told him sternly.

"But so much fun," Brak replied, unrepentantly.

Obviously deciding Brak was no longer worthy of her attention, Kalianah deliberately turned her back on him and fixed her attention on Wrayan instead. "Have you decided who you'll honour me with this evening, Wrayan?"

"I'm still not even sure *how* I'm supposed to honour you tonight, Divine One."

Kali rolled her eyes impatiently. "I'm the Goddess of *Love*, Wrayan. How do you *suppose* the Harshini honour me?"

Brak laughed as he saw the blank look on Wrayan's face. "Oh, dear! They didn't warn you, did they?"

"Warn me about what?" The young man thought for a moment and then blushed an interesting shade of crimson. "You mean the Harshini . . . they all . . ."

"Every one of them. You don't think I come home every spring just for the food, do you?"

Wrayan stopped and lowered the little goddess to the ground. "What about me?"

"What about you?" Brak shrugged. "This is a chance not many humans get these days, Wrayan. Make the most of it."

"But . . ."

"I think he's shy!" Kali laughed delightedly.

"Kali, just go away for a while, would you?"

The goddess rolled her eyes. "Fine! I'll go find somebody who *wants* to talk to me."

She vanished almost before she'd finished speaking, leaving Brak and Wrayan alone on the path. Below them, Brak could already hear the Harshini orchestra tuning their instruments.

Wrayan looked at Brak desperately. "I don't know what to *do*."

"*How* old are you?" he asked with a raised brow.

"No! It's not that! I mean, I *know* what to do . . . it's just . . . Gods, Brak, how does this work? Do I approach someone? Do I wait until somebody finds me? Will I *survive* it?"

"You're a guest here," Brak advised. "Wait until you're asked. And yes, you'll survive it, although if you left behind a human lover in Greenharbour, you might find it difficult to look at her the same way after you've been with a Harshini. They're fairly famous for ruining humans for any other lovers."

"Well, if I left behind a lover, I don't remember her," Wrayan shrugged. "Suppose nobody asks me?"

"On the Feast of Kalianah? Not a chance."

"Is it really everything they claim?" he asked curiously.

"And then some," Brak agreed with a smile. "And you've got just enough magic in you to mindlink at the same time. Trust me, Wrayan. It'll probably take you several days before you can even speak coherently again." He laughed at the young man's expression and slapped him on the shoulder. "Come on, we'd better get a move on or we won't be able to find a seat at the concert and we'll end up sitting with the demons."

chapter 71

The music of the Harshini was an ethereal, unearthly sound. Even though Wrayan had heard their haunting music almost every evening for months now, it still caught him off-guard and tears welled in his eyes as the inhuman harmonies filled the valley, striking a resonant

chord in the soul of every living creature who experienced it.
At some point during the performance, two small demons appeared beside Wrayan and crawled into Brak's lap, where
they sat listening with rapt attention. Brak didn't seem to notice his uninvited companions and made no move to dislodge
them. Kalianah had reappeared at Lorandranek's side further
up the rows of tiered seating to listen to the music, although
she fidgeted as if she was bored. Music was the province of
Gimlorie, after all. Kali had little interest in music unless it
was doing something to further the romance she craved.

Once the concert was finished, the stage was cleared and
tables were set up, laden with food. Everyone mingled about,
laughing and smiling, helping themselves to the abundance
of perfectly grown fruit and vegetables, seasoned with spices
Wrayan had never even dreamed of before coming to Sanctuary (confirming his suspicion that he hadn't been a cook in
his former life). The wine was sweet and heady with the
faintest hint of pepper and left him feeling light-headed so
quickly, he wondered if it had been spiked with something to
enhance the mood of the evening. He lost track of Brak for a
while and then found him again when the Halfbreed appeared with a stunning Harshini woman—was there any
other kind?—on his arm.

"Wrayan, this is Andreanan, Sanctuary's librarian."

Andreanan had totally black eyes, like all the Harshini,
flawless golden skin and a body that no librarian in Wrayan's
experience had ever been in possession of, which her thin
white robe did little to disguise. Like most of the other
women here, she looked no more than thirty but had probably
lived ten or twenty times that many years. She smiled at him
warmly. "I've heard about our young human visitor. You must
come and visit our library soon. There is much there we
could teach you."

"I'd like that very much."

"Do you love me, Wrayan?"

"It seems I love everyone tonight, my lady."

She laughed delightedly. "I hope you find much happiness, then." She smiled at the Halfbreed and took his hand. "Come along, Brak. Lorandranek has returned us to real time so we actually *don't* have forever."

"I'll catch up," Brak promised. Unconcerned, Andreanan nodded and walked off toward the tables. Brak turned to Wrayan with a frown. It was probably the only frown in the whole of Sanctuary this night.

"One more bit of advice," Brak said. "While you're finding 'much happiness' tonight, don't make the mistake of thinking you're in love."

"What do you mean?"

"These are the Harshini, Wrayan, and they might look mostly human, but it's the 'mostly' that sets them apart. They don't love like humans. They're not monogamous. They don't understand jealousy or the concept of adultery. They have no grasp of faithfulness and think the human desire to remain with one partner for life to be ridiculous in the extreme. The woman you make love to in the next hour might be making love to me an hour after she's done with you and another woman an hour after that. Don't read more into this than really exists. You're the only one who'll be hurt because the Harshini will just think you're crazy."

Having delivered his dire warning, Brak headed off in the direction Andreanan had disappeared. Feeling even more confused than he had been before Brak offered his advice, Wrayan wandered among the food-laden tables, returning the smiles of the Harshini as they laughed and chatted to themselves in their own language. It had never really occurred to Wrayan until now that the Harshini didn't speak Hythrun among themselves. They spoke his language when they addressed him, and were never rude enough to exclude him by falling into a conversation in another language when he could overhear, and, of course, speaking mind to mind involved no language as such, just feelings and pictures. But to hear their musical voices surrounding him, and not know what they were saying, left Wrayan feeling quite alone.

For the first time since waking up in this magical place, he felt like a foreigner.

Wrayan finished his wine with a gulp and was looking around for another when his glass magically refilled itself. Shrugging over this unexpected bounty, he wandered aimlessly through the party, smiling and returning greetings whenever he was offered them, being kissed into oblivion by a series of unbelievably beautiful women who then passed him over for their own menfolk, but as the evening wore on, and his glass kept refilling itself, no stunning Harshini came forward to present herself to him for anything more than that; no vision of loveliness stepped across his path and did more than kiss him, smile and move on. Disappointed and more than a little drunk, Wrayan headed away from the tables. He staggered through the amphitheatre, his head spinning from the potent wine, and stumbled down the valley towards the waterfall that supplied Sanctuary with its water. At the edge of his senses he could feel something strange going on, something he couldn't understand, but in his current inebriated state, he didn't have the wit to figure it out.

The path to the pool beneath the waterfall was deserted, although a few times Wrayan passed couples in the bushes who had been heading for the pool perhaps, but had not made it that far before being overtaken by their desire to honour the Goddess of Love. Wrayan found their presence disturbing. It wasn't that he was particularly prudish—he'd grown up in a society where *court'esa* were the norm—it was just that every couple, or trio (or whatever the Harshini found entertaining) he stumbled past reminded him that everyone in Sanctuary was honouring Kalianah this night but him.

It just didn't seem fair.

By the time he reached the pool beneath the cascade, Wrayan was burning up. His skin was hot and dry and his head was spinning like one of those little fireworks they nailed to a wall and set alight on the Feast of Jashia, the God of Fire, back in Krakandar. He was starting to think he was sick. He didn't even notice that he'd remembered something from his childhood that had, up until a moment ago, been lost to him.

Wrayan reached the pool and stripped off his robes, plunging naked into the cool water. The shock left him gasping, but he forced himself deeper into the crystalline water until his feet no longer touched the bottom. The water seemed to clear his head a little. He rolled onto his back and stared up at the sky, a narrow strip of star-sprinkled darkness far above the valley where Sanctuary was hidden. The cascade tumbled ceaselessly down the rocks above the pool from some three or four hundred feet above at the top of the valley. Floating on his back, Wrayan closed his eyes and let the calm water and the chilly spray from the waterfall cool his fevered body.

"It's time, don't you think, Wrayan Lightfinger," a voice whispered seductively behind him, "that you and I got to know each other a little better?"

Wrayan turned around with a splash to find himself face to face with Shananara té Ortyn. She was treading water a mere hand-span from him, the crystal-clear droplets beading on her skin like condensation, her long hair floating out around her like a dark red cloud. The Harshini princess swam closer. She took his hand and raised it to her lips with a smile that promised a glimpse of paradise.

"Can you feel it?" she asked softly.

Wrayan was feeling a great deal, but he wasn't sure if his . . . *feelings* were quite what the princess was enquiring about.

"Feel what, your highness?" he asked, a little nervously.

"Close your eyes," she told him.

Wrayan did as she commanded, with the realisation that the cool water no longer seemed very cool at all. It seemed to have been warmed by the heat of their bodies.

"Your highness—"

"Shh," Shananara whispered. "Feel."

Wrayan wasn't sure what she meant, but after a moment he became aware of the odd feeling that had followed him from the amphitheatre. It was bliss, ecstasy, rapture and delight all rolled into one. His skin began to burn hotter and hotter the more aware of it he became and he realized, with some alarm, that in addition to the heat, his body was reacting to the strange stimulus in a way that was impossible to hide in the crystal-clear water of the pool.

"What is it?" he asked in wonder, opening his eyes to look at her.

"Kalianah's gift to the Harshini." She smiled at his expression. Reaching out to him, she touched his face, wiping away the water drops that lined his upper lip with a feather-light touch of her thumb. "You can feel the Harshini, Wrayan. We're linked to the same source. What you can feel is that joy being channelled. Humans can't feel it normally. They're aware of it, and it makes us seem irresistible to them, but they don't understand what they're feeling. Not consciously."

"But I can feel it."

"That's because you're part Harshini."

And that, it seemed, was enough for Shananara. She slid her hands around his neck and pulled him to her. Wrayan was too stunned to object. Her mouth tasted like the cool water of the pool mixed with the headiest wine—the taste of all his wildest fantasies distilled into the essence of pure hunger and desire. And then she embraced him with her mind as well as her body, her magic keeping them afloat, and Wrayan thought he might die.

He quickly lost all sense of where he was, only the cold water caressing his inflamed skin and the hot touch of Shananara's lithe and slender body against him seemed to register in the maelstrom of his befuddled mind. He felt her breasts against his chest as she wrapped her strong legs around him. He tried to pull her even closer, wishing there was some way to devour her whole. Wrayan had never experienced anything so intense or so consuming. This wasn't just making love. This was much, much more. This was agony. It was bliss. This was where paradise and hell collided with each other.

The world blurred around Wrayan as her touch became flame on his already-burning skin. Desire was all he could think of, blended with the sheer rapture of all the other Harshini sharing their experiences as well; the air crackled with lust, and joy, and a thousand other emotions that Wrayan was in no condition to identify.

He couldn't say later how long it lasted. It might have been a few moments or it might have been hours. All he knew was that when it was over, he could barely breathe and his body felt like it had been wrung out and tossed aside to dry. He staggered out of the water, a little surprised he hadn't drowned, and collapsed onto the grassy shore. Shananara followed a moment later and sat down beside him, much more in command of her faculties than Wrayan was. He tried to sit up, but she smiled and drew his head down into her lap.

"There, there, my love," she whispered softly, stroking his damp hair. "Sleep now. You'll feel better once you've rested."

Wrayan lacked the strength to answer her. He closed his eyes and, as he let fatigue overtake him, a thought wormed its way unbidden into his consciousness. What was it Brak had told him? *You'll be incoherent for days.*

Smiling, he let sleep steal over him, exhausted and spent in a way he had never imagined possible. Shananara held him while he fell asleep, crooning to him like a mother comforting a frightened child, and he drifted off into a world of misty veils and whispering kisses that seemed to have no end . . .

And then his dreams were rudely shattered as he was shaken roughly awake. He blinked owlishly, squinting in the harsh sunlight that had risen over the rim of the valley. Wrayan had no idea what time it was but he was cold, a rock beneath his hip had left him with a stone-bruise, his head was pounding and his mouth felt drier than a Karien nun's beer garden.

Shananara was gone, as if she'd been nothing more than a dream.

It was Brak who had woken him. The Halfbreed loomed over him, his pale eyes furious, his whole body radiating contained rage.

"Wha—what?" Wrayan stammered in confusion.

"Get dressed," he ordered, tossing Wrayan's discarded robe at him.

Wrayan caught the white Harshini robe reflexively and struggled to sit up, pulling the garment self-consciously over his head. "Is something wrong?"

Brak didn't answer him. He just stood there, waiting for Wrayan to get dressed, glowering at him.

"Brak? Is something wrong? What's happened?"

"You happened," Brak informed him coldly.

As soon as Wrayan was clothed and standing—albeit rather shakily—Brak pushed the young man ahead of him along the path back towards the fortress.

"What do you mean, *I* happened?" Wrayan demanded, speaking over his shoulder as he stumbled up the path. "What have I done?"

"What have you *done*?" the Halfbreed repeated incredulously. He shook his head in disgust, as if Wrayan should already know the answer.

"But I didn't do anything!"

The Halfbreed didn't seem impressed by his protestations of innocence. "You're an idiot, Wrayan Lightfinger," Brak told him unsympathetically. "A reckless, thoughtless, towering bloody idiot."

Wrayan stopped and turned to confront the Halfbreed, determined to uncover his obviously dreadful—and completely baffling—mistake before they took another step closer to the fortress. "I don't understand, Brak! What have I *done*?"

"You slept with Shananara."

"I know, but—"

"She's a té Ortyn."

"I know, but—"

"Don't you realize what that means?"

"*No!*" he cried, wishing Brak would simply explain it to him.

Brak sighed heavily. "There are more than a thousand women here in Sanctuary, Wrayan, and the *only* one you shouldn't have gone near last night was the king's niece."

"Is he angry?"

Brak ground his teeth in frustration. "You just don't get it, do you? Lorandranek isn't angry. He isn't capable of it. But you . . . you're about ninety per cent human, by my reckoning."

"So?"

"Sleeping with a member of the royal family is forbidden for humans. Didn't anybody tell you that?"

"Well, yes, but I didn't hurt her, Brak," he protested. "Anyway . . . well, it was Shananara who started it."

"I don't care who started it, Wrayan. You slept with a té Ortyn Harshini, you fool."

"How much trouble am I really in?" he asked sheepishly, remembering the friendly, but stern warning Lorandranek had delivered the first time the king noticed the way Wrayan looked at Shananara.

"Provided nothing comes of it, you're in no trouble at all," Brak informed him, which relieved Wrayan a great deal.

And then the Halfbreed ruined everything by adding, "But if Shananara té Ortyn is pregnant, Wrayan, well, then you've just fathered a demon child."

chapter 72

The death of Laran Krakenshield caught Elezaar unawares and once again threw his future into doubt. It also left him suspicious about the circumstances of the Warlord's unexpected death. After Marla related the details of his fall in battle, Elezaar began to wonder about the train of events that had taken Mahkas Damaran from penniless half-brother with a brother and two sisters to the wealthy sole ruler of two provinces and the only one of his siblings still alive, in the space of a little more than two years. There was an unfortunate trend emerging around the new Regent of Krakandar and Sunrise Provinces. It worried Elezaar a great deal. If there was some curse on Mahkas Damaran that placed his family under threat, Marla and her son—Mahkas's sister-in-law and nephew—may also be in danger.

And if anything happened to them, that was the end for Elezaar, too.

Elezaar didn't know Mahkas well. As far as possible, he avoided contact with the other members of the household, and Mahkas in particular. The dwarf was Marla's slave and content to remain so. He had taken on the role of history tutor to Travin and Xanda because that would put him in the nursery on a daily basis. And it had paid off handsomely. Not only was Elezaar genuinely fond of Darilyn Taranger's orphaned sons, but over the past two years he'd become so much a part of Damin Wolfblade's world that nobody would think of taking him away from the child.

His position was—*had been*—almost secure. But Laran Krakenshield was dead and his brother, Mahkas Damaran, was going to be ruling in his place until Damin came of age, which meant they were playing a different game now and Elezaar still hadn't figured out the new rules.

Elezaar wished Marla had consulted him before offering Mahkas the regency, although even if she had, there was little he could have done to prevent it. Marla was right about that much. There really was nobody else to take over the provinces and the only alternative was to place it in the hands of the Sorcerers' Collective. That meant Kagan Palenovar now, but one day it might mean Alija Eaglespike and Elezaar hadn't come this far just to fall under her influence again by default when the old High Arrion died.

Marla had averted *that* potential disaster by insisting Mahkas assume the regency, but Elezaar still wasn't happy about it. There was something about Mahkas Damaran that Elezaar didn't like; some darkness in his soul lurking just beneath the surface, indefinable, vague, but somehow *wrong*. It niggled at Elezaar like a pebble in his shoe, so much so he felt compelled to raise the issue with his mistress a few days after she told him what she had done about Mahkas and the regency.

"Are you sure it was wise to appoint your brother-in-law as Damin's regent, your highness?" he asked as she was preparing to retire one evening, a few days after the news about Laran had reached them. He was leading his mistress into her dressing room, holding the large candelabrum to light her way, when he posed the question, as if it had only just occurred to him and was not something he'd been stewing on for days.

"Even if it wasn't wise, Elezaar," she said, as she sat down at her dressing table to unpin her white mourning veil, "what other choice is there? Do you think I should let the Sorcerers' Collective into Krakandar?"

"Absolutely not!" he agreed, lifting the heavy silver candelabrum onto the table so that his mistress could see her reflection in the gilded mirror. "But it's an awfully big responsibility for one man."

"Laran seemed to manage it quite well."

"Your late husband was an exceptional man, your highness," Elezaar told her, thinking it would do no harm to speak well of the dead, even though he had often questioned Laran's decisions privately to his mistress in order to keep her believing that she needed her *court'esa*'s counsel. "While Mahkas Damaran is capable, he's not his brother."

"Are you saying he won't cope?"

"I think he'll do well enough."

"But?" she asked, turning to face him.

She looks tired, Elezaar thought, *even in the candlelight.* It had been a trying few days for the princess and was not likely to get any easier for a while yet. "Why do you think there's a 'but' involved?"

"I can tell, Elezaar," she told him. "You just say things like that and let them hang, like you haven't finished speaking yet. There's a 'but' in there somewhere. Tell me what it is."

"Very well," he said, climbing onto the stool beside her dressing table. His feet didn't touch the floor, but with the princess sitting down, he was almost eye level with her. "I don't think you should try to keep both provinces. And I'm not sure Mahkas will be able to, anyway."

"Why not?"

"Laran Krakenshield was the legitimate heir to Krakandar, highly respected and well thought of among his peers. His brother is none of these things. If anything, he has a reputation for being a bit reckless. The Warlords accepting Laran ruling two provinces is a world away from them accepting his half-brother."

"But I'm going to ask Lernen to confirm it. Do you think the Warlords will defy my brother?" She began to remove the pins from her hair, dropping them into a small crystal dish on the dressing table that Laran had given her as a gift on the first anniversary of their marriage. "I can have Lernen make this a decree, you know."

"I'm quite sure you could make the High Prince decree the sky is pink, your highness," he informed her as the pins dropped with a metallic "plink" into the dish. "But that's not the point. Your brother got away with confirming Laran as the heir to Sunrise because Laran was capable of doing the job. Laran held on to Sunrise Province and Krakandar because the other Warlords quickly realized he had no territorial ambitions beyond holding those two provinces. He gave Hythria the Hythrun-born heir she so desperately needed—"

"Excuse me, but *I* gave Hythria the heir she so desperately needed," the princess corrected testily.

Elezaar smiled. "Your husband kept his word, your highness. And he kept the peace with Fardohnya which meant he kept the trade routes open."

"And when Laran made Chaine Tollin—Glenadal's

bastard—Governor of Sunrise Province," Marla concluded, nodding in understanding, "he also gave rise to the hope that he might one day cede the province to a Ravenspear, even an illegitimate and unacknowledged one."

"Exactly."

"So you're saying I should ask Mahkas to keep Chaine Tollin on as Governor?"

"I think you need to go further than that, your highness. If the Warlords don't like the current arrangement, they could easily step in and make their own changes. And they may not be changes that suit you. Far from remaining an ally, Sunrise could end up in the hands of a Warlord sympathetic to the Patriot Faction. The revenue from Sunrise will be lost. There will be nothing you or Mahkas, or even Lady Jeryma, can do about it, either. Glenadal Ravenspear made Laran his heir and the High Prince confirmed him as the Warlord of Sunrise. There was no provision in there for his half-brother to take his place, even as regent."

"But that would mean giving away half Damin's inheritance."

"There is no inheritance for your son in death, my lady."

"What do you mean?"

"Damin is the High Prince's heir, your highness. You're going to have enough trouble convincing the Warlords he's entitled to inherit Krakandar. You don't seriously think they will allow a High Prince to hold direct lordship over two provinces as well, do you?"

"Rule Number Eleven," she said suddenly, shaking her long hair free.

Elezaar nodded, pleased with her quick assessment of the situation. "Do the unexpected."

"Mahkas won't be happy."

"Your job is to protect your son, your highness, not nurse your brother-in-law's tender ego."

"But what if Chaine Tollin can't be trusted?" she asked, picking up the silver-backed brush.

"Has he given you any reason to believe that he can't be?"

"No," she replied, tipping her head to the side. She began

to brush her long fair hair with slow, deliberate strokes. "But that doesn't mean much. He may be simply biding his time and plans to make his move as soon as he thinks the way is clear for him to grab power."

"Then perhaps you should give it to him, your highness, before he has a chance to grab it. Then he'll be forever in your debt. That's preferable to having an enemy in Sunrise controlling the trade routes from Fardohnya."

"Which is all very well, Elezaar," she said, tipping her head the other way so she could brush the left side. "But I'm not really in a position to give anybody anything."

"No. But your brother is. As you're so fond of threatening, my lady, have the High Prince make it a decree."

"I suppose I can make it look like it was Lernen's idea," she mused. "That way nobody will think I'm to blame. But won't the Warlords object if he does that again? They weren't too happy when he ruled on Laran."

"Make Glenadal's son the Warlord of Sunrise Province—a man who's already proved himself capable—and nobody will object. Leave Mahkas Damaran in charge and just watch the fun begin."

She stopped brushing her hair and looked at him curiously. "You don't like Mahkas much, do you?"

"It's not my place to like or dislike him, your highness," he replied evasively.

"That's not what I asked you, Elezaar. Why don't you like him?"

The dwarf shrugged. "I'm not sure."

"Has he mistreated you in any way?"

"No."

"Then I don't understand your dislike of him. Mahkas is about the only person around here, besides you, who I feel I can trust."

The dwarf shook his head in despair. "Then you have forgotten the Fourth Rule, your highness."

Marla put down the hairbrush and looked at him thoughtfully. "Trust only myself? Does that include you, Elezaar?"

He smiled crookedly. "Always."

Marla stared at him doubtfully for a moment, not sure if he was joking, then she sighed wearily. "Don't tease me, Elezaar. Not tonight."

"Trust in this, your highness," he said, jumping down from the stool to stand before her, his hand on his heart. "With my dying breath I will defend you and your son's right to the Hythrun throne."

Marla smiled at him fondly. "I may hold you to that some day, Fool," she warned.

Elezaar returned her smile, a little alarmed to realize that, given the nature of Hythrun politics and having tied his fortunes so closely with Marla Wolfblade and her son, the chances were rather high that Marla was right and he might well be called upon one day to fulfil his rash and foolish promise.

chapter 73

I've been a very naughty girl, haven't I?"

Brak stared at Shananara, shaking his head in wonder. She was sitting on the window seat in her room overlooking Sanctuary's picturesque valley (hiding, no doubt) while poor Wrayan bore the brunt of the recriminations for a deed that was—in truth—Shananara's fault.

"Why did you sleep with him, Shanan?"

"I didn't," she protested, and then she smiled coyly. "Well, there wasn't a lot of *sleep* involved, anyway."

"You know he's human."

"He's very pretty."

"So is every Harshini male in Sanctuary. That's no excuse."

"I like him."

"Neither is that."

"He's part Harshini."

"Which part?" Brak asked scathingly. "His big toe?"

"Are you angry?" she asked curiously. "I can never really tell. What does it feel like?"

Brak ignored her blatant and rather pathetic attempt to change the subject. "What's Lorandranek going to say when he finds out?"

She smiled at him sweetly. "He's not going to find out."

"You think I won't tell him?"

"You didn't tell him the last time I *slept* with a human—that's a very misleading expression, by the way. Why would you betray me this time?"

"Because your fascination for humans is getting dangerous."

She smiled. "Don't exaggerate. I've made love with two human men in the past two hundred years. Well, three, if you count you. But then you're only half human, so I suppose you don't really count. My point is, Brak, one human a century hardly qualifies as dangerous. Besides, I like human boys. They're so . . . innocent."

"In case you've forgotten, Shanan, the last time you indulged your taste for pretty human boys, we wound up with the bloody Sisterhood."

"That's not *entirely* true . . ."

"Isn't it?" he asked pointedly.

"You think I'm the only Harshini who likes humans?" she asked, climbing off the window seat and crossing the room to confront him. "Where was Lorandranek the last time Korandellen sent you to find him, Brak? Where is he now? Communing with the God of Green Life? Discussing the weather with the God of Storms? Or lurking around near that human village—what do they call the closest one to us? Haven, isn't it?—watching a small town full of humans go about their ordinary daily lives, because he's just as taken with them as I am. It's all part of the burden we té Ortyn carry. The gods' idea of a joke, I think. They made it dangerous beyond words for us to love a human, and then made us totally captivated by them, just to torment us."

"Your brother doesn't seem to have much trouble fighting off the urge," Brak reminded her, wondering if there wasn't some truth in her claim that her fascination for humans was a curse laid on her by the gods and not simply her wilful nature.

"Korandellen hasn't stepped foot outside Sanctuary in almost two hundred years," Shananara replied with a smile. "That's how he deals with it. He simply refuses to put himself in temptation's way."

"Don't you know what the gods will do if you're having a child?" he demanded of her, wishing there was some way to drive home the seriousness of her folly. "They will kill it, Shanan. The gods won't allow a demon child to exist."

"Please don't speak of killing, Brak."

"All right, how about insanity?" he asked. "Has it ever occurred to you that one of the reasons you're not supposed to fraternise with humans is because the mere act of bearing a demon child would drive you mad?"

"New life could never drive me mad."

"If you're carrying Wrayan's child, Shanan, then you're going to unleash a force on his earth that's capable of anything. A demon child could kill a god, if the mood took him. You can't even step on a bug. The conflict would drive you crazy."

"Even if I conceded that you might be right, it's unlikely I'm with child, Brak," she shrugged. "It's not possible to conceive when Sanctuary is hidden out of time."

"But we're not hidden," he reminded her. "Sanctuary is here for anybody to find. And you're just as capable of creating a child as any other woman."

Shananara sighed wistfully. "If only that were true. This constant jumping in and out of time has played havoc with our people. Did you know there were only twelve Harshini born this year when we came back into real time? And the

demons are starting to be affected, too. Korandellen specu-
lates we have less to fear from the Sisterhood in Medalon and
the Overlord's priests in Karien, than we do from our own
cowardice."

"What do you mean?"

"Hiding from the danger may prove to be the biggest danger of all," Shanan sighed, and then she stepped up close to
him and touched his face. "Don't be angry at me, dearest."

She smiled languidly then stood on her toes and kissed
him and, for a glorious, dangerous moment, he let her. Being
kissed by Shananara té Ortyn was a gift rarely bestowed and
he was still human enough to crave her affection, even though
the Harshini part of him knew she was really just doing this
to prevent him reporting her indiscretion to her uncle or her
brother.

Brak revelled in it for a few perilous seconds before he
pushed her away. "Don't think you can get out of it that easily,
Shananara. What you did was stupid. And unbelievably risky."

"What are you going to do?" she asked, realising she
hadn't won him over with her charms. She looked a little
puzzled by that. Shananara didn't understand anger, so she
couldn't work out why her attempts to quell Brak's fury were
having so little effect.

"I won't tell Lorandranek, this time. Although the gods
know, I probably should. But I'm taking Wrayan home,
Shanan," Brak told her. "Back to the human world where he
belongs."

"But it's not safe for him out there!"

"If I leave him with you much longer, he'll be in just as
much danger here. I think he'd rather risk an unknown human assailant than having all the Primal Gods pissed at him."

"Are you sure you can't leave him here, Brak?" she
begged. "If I promise to be good? Once we're back out of
time, it won't matter, anyway. I can't conceive *any* child, let
alone a demon child, when we're out of real time."

"He's not a *thing*, Shananara," Brak retorted crossly. "And

I'm not going to leave the lad here so you've got something to play with to relieve the tedium."

"That's unfair, Brak."

"So is you making any human believe they have a future with you," he replied harshly. "If I leave him another year, he'll be so in love with you he won't be able to think straight. And then he'll grow old and die and you won't have aged a day. How long will you want him anyway, once he's no longer so pretty? Humans only get a short life, Shanan. They haven't got the same room for mistakes that you and I have."

Shananara had the decency to look a little shamefaced, but that didn't mean Brak was getting through to her. The Harshini really didn't understand humans. That the gods had created them to look like the most perfect human specimens ever imagined was simply a cruel jest. And Brak knew the Harshini. He could think like one when he had to. Although the world was a much different place now, he had grown up among these people. His childhood companions in the Citadel were Shananara and Korandellen. He had played with gods and Harshini princes as a child.

But it still didn't make it any easier to explain to a Harshini anything about humans when they simply didn't have the words in their vocabulary to explain concepts they were, literally, incapable of grasping.

"You make me sound quite cruel, Brak," Shananara accused, looking wounded by the thought. "I'm not supposed to be capable of hurting anything."

"And you're not," he assured her. "Not deliberately, anyway. You just have to trust me on this, Shanan. If I leave Wrayan here, you'll inflict more hurt on him than you're able to imagine."

She nodded, probably accepting his request that she trust him rather than showing any true understanding of what he meant. "I'm sorry if I have caused you pain, Brak. Or young Wrayan."

Brak smiled, thinking Shananara knew the word but didn't understand remorse any more than she understood anger. "I'd better go and break it to our house guest that he's being evicted."

"You'll do it gently, won't you?"

"Yes, Shanan," he sighed. "I'll do it gently."

"And you must promise to guard him. In the human world."

"He doesn't need guarding."

"Yes, he *does*!" the princess insisted. "He came here because someone hurt him very badly, Brak, and he doesn't know who that person is. If it's my fault that Wrayan must leave the protection of Sanctuary, then I'm going to ensure he's safe in his own world. I am *commanding* you to go with him. And you're to *stay* with him until he was recovered his memories, or the threat to him is gone."

Brak looked at her in horror, unable to believe what she was demanding of him. "But Shanan . . . that could take years!"

"Years *you* have, Brak," she pointed out, suddenly all regal. "As you just reminded me, humans only get a short life. I cannot knowingly make Wrayan's life any shorter by denying him protection when I have you here to do my bidding."

"You're assuming I'm going to do your bidding, Shanan."

She smiled at him again, her black eyes shining, and slid her arms around his neck. "I could make you," she whispered against his lips.

He smiled at the unashamed offer and, ignoring the very real temptation to give in to her, deliberately lifted her arms from his neck and held them by her sides. "I think not."

"You think I couldn't make you, Brak?"

"I think you've had all the human flesh you're going to taste for a while, your highness."

She smiled even wider, seemingly unconcerned that he had refused her. Perhaps because she knew she could count on having him again eventually. "Eventually" was almost a certainty in a lifetime that spanned several thousand years.

"I command you, then."

"What do I tell the king?"

She shrugged, unconcerned. "Ask Jakerlon. The God of Liars is always good for things like that."

"You're effectively exiling me for something *you* did," he accused.

"Then think of it as doing me a favour."

"That would imply you're giving me a choice."

"Then do it because you love me."

Brak shook his head in defeat, realizing that she still had no idea. She had Kalianah's unyielding faith in love without any concept of the other emotions that went along with it.

"All right," he agreed reluctantly. "But only because I love you."

After he left Shananara's room, Brak headed to the Gateway, thinking he needed some time outside of Sanctuary's suddenly claustrophobic walls before he visited Lorandranek and informed him he was leaving with Wrayan. He knew this mess wasn't the young human's fault. Brak could barely fight off Shananara when she was trying to seduce him. Poor Wrayan would have had no hope. He'd probably been too hard on the lad this morning, but Brak couldn't get angry with the Harshini. They barely knew what anger was, anyway.

"Ah, Lord Brakandaran!" Jerendenan exclaimed when he saw Brak heading for the Gateway. The Gatekeeper was probably the oldest soul in Sanctuary and could name every single being who had passed through his gate in the past few thousand years. "I was just about to send for you."

"You were?" he asked curiously. "Why?"

"We may have a problem."

"What sort of problem?"

Jerendenan beckoned Brak closer. Near the huge arch of the open gate stood a shallow bowl of water balanced on a white marble pedestal. The bowl was used by travellers to refresh themselves when they stepped across Sanctuary's threshold. But it also doubled as a scrying bowl, and when the old Harshini began to draw on his power and waved his arm over the water, Brak realized that was what he was doing now.

Brak looked into the water which resolved itself into a picture of the mountains outside the fortress. Spring was firmly in command now and the forest was burgeoning with new life. After a moment he spied several dark-clothed and well-armed men sneaking—that was the only word for it— through the trees in Jerendenan's scrying bowl. There seemed to be about six of them, followed, Brak saw with alarm, by a tall man wearing a long black cassock who carried a staff topped with a golden star intersected by a silver lightning bolt.

"That's a Karien priest!"

Jerendenan nodded solemnly. "That's why I was going to call you. Those men you see in the scrying bowl are only a few hours away."

"What?"

"This is the problem I spoke of, Brakandaran," the Gate-keeper told him heavily. "The Karien priests have found us and I believe that, within a day, Sanctuary may be under attack."

CHAPTER 74

Wrayan paced his room anxiously for several hours after Brak left him there, envisaging all sorts of dreadful fates about to befall him. He had never imagined the night he'd spent with Shananara—which had seemed so wondrous at the time—might be the cause of so much trouble. What if Shananara really *had* conceived a child? Would the gods kill him? Would Brak? Would Shananara have to die too, or would the Primal Gods simply demand the child be killed in the womb? And how would the Harshini manage such a thing, anyway? They couldn't hurt a fly.

He had an even more immediate problem, however, than the wrath of the gods. What would Lorandranek do? Would the king have him thrown out of Sanctuary? Was there some punishment for breaking the taboos of the Harshini that he didn't know about?

And why am I wearing the blame for this anyway? Shananara came to me!

The door to his room opened and Brak strode in without knocking. He was dressed not in the white robes of the Harshini, but in close-fitting dark leathers that seemed moulded to every inch of his tall, muscular body. He was carrying a bundle in his arms of similar material and tossed it to Wrayan. Wrayan couldn't tell if the Halfbreed was still angry. But he certainly didn't look happy.

"Get changed."

"What's this?"

"Dragon Rider's leathers," Brak explained.

"We're going *dragon* riding?" Wrayan asked in alarm.

"Unfortunately, no. You ever killed anyone?"

"Not that I recall."

Brak shrugged. "Well, you're about to learn how. It's frighteningly easy, once you get the hang of it."

"This is a joke, right?"

"Do I look like I'm joking?" Brak asked him coldly. "Get changed. I'll meet you down by the Gateway in half an hour. I need to find out what those damn demons did with my pack. It had all my weapons in it."

"But Brak—"

"Not here," the Halfbreed warned. "I'll explain when we get outside. And shield your mind until we leave. If anybody around here picks up on you thinking about killing, they'll be distraught and this will just get infinitely harder for everyone."

As promised, Brak was waiting for him by the gate, his pack slung over his shoulder and the two demons, Eyan and Elebran, scampering around his feet. The Gatekeeper bowed as Wrayan approached, smiling as always.

"Good afternoon, young sir. You'll be joining Lord Brakandaran on his trip into the mountains?"

"So it would seem, my lord," Wrayan agreed warily, looking to Brak for his cue.

The Halfbreed nodded and shouldered his pack a little higher. "Don't wait up, Jerendenan," Brak advised, heading out through the arch.

Wrayan hurried to catch up with him, feeling strange in the dark Harshini leathers. He didn't know what type of leather they were made of, but they were as comfortable as his own skin and allowed a freedom of movement Wrayan had never experienced when wearing simple human garments.

Brak strode on ahead into the dense forest that was budding with the wild regrowth of spring. It was a glorious day, cool but clear, and the mountains seemed to be teeming with new life. Wrayan followed Brak without saying a word until they were several miles from the fortress. There Brak stopped in a small clearing and tossed the pack to the ground. When he squatted down to open it, Wrayan was astonished at the array of weapons concealed inside.

"They're all *yours*?" Wrayan asked, as Brak began to unpack the weapons. "I thought the Harshini couldn't kill?"

"I'm a halfbreed, remember? My human side doesn't have any trouble with it at all." He lifted out a beautifully crafted Fardohnyan dagger in a dark leather scabbard and tossed it to Wrayan. "Know how to use a knife?"

Wrayan balanced the dagger in his hand for a moment. It felt comfortable. He nodded cautiously. "I think so."

"Good. Because we're going to have to do this quietly."

"Might I enquire about who we're going to kill?"

Brak sat back on his heels and looked up at the young man. "Jerendenan spotted a Karien priest and a small guard of Karien soldiers heading toward Sanctuary. We have to take them out before they find it."

"But Xaphista's a god, isn't he? Doesn't he know where to find it anyway?"

"Only the Primal Gods can feel it. The others have to be told."

"But even if he's an Incidental god," Wrayan mused, testing the weight of the knife absently in his other hand, "surely he can find it, even when it's hidden out of time? I mean, the demons come and go as they please. So do you, for that matter."

"The demons can't find Sanctuary. It's the Harshini inside it they can feel. Xaphista took all his clan with him when he left the Citadel, so there's nobody there he can sense. Anyway, Sanctuary was built after he abandoned the Harshini, so when it's hidden he's as blind to it as any human." Brak glanced up with a wry smile. "Or did you think Lorandranek goes to all the trouble of hiding a settlement of several thousand Harshini every year just because he gets a kick out of it?"

"I suppose not. But why doesn't Lorandranek simply send Sanctuary back out of time until the danger passes?"

"He's not there."

"Where is he?"

Brak shrugged. "Roaming the mountains, I suppose. He hates being cooped up in Sanctuary. When it's back in the real world he spends as little time there as possible. And he's not the only one. A good third of the Harshini are probably wandering around these woods at the moment. Like I said, we have to do this quietly."

"Did Jerendenan have any idea what you were planning when we left?"

"He might have suspected," Brak replied, sliding a vicious Hythrun blade down the side of his boot. "But he won't allow himself to dwell on it. As far as he's concerned, we've gone out for a stroll in the mountains."

"They're pretty good at turning a blind eye to things they don't want to know about, the Harshini, aren't they?"

For the first time, Brak seemed amused. "You have no *idea*

how good they are at it, Wrayan," he agreed. "You can't even imagine. It's how they survive."

He tossed a small pouch to Wrayan and tucked a similar one in his own belt. Wrayan emptied the contents into his hand and looked at it curiously. It was a weapon of some sort—a piece of coiled wire about a foot-and-a-half long, with a small bone handle at each end.

"What's this?"

"A Fardohnyan garrote."

"What's it do?"

Brak stood up and held out his hand. Wrayan gave him the garrote. The Halfbreed shook it out and took a bone handle in each hand. "You sneak up on your victim," he explained, walking around Wrayan until he was standing behind him. "And then you do this."

Before Wrayan realized what was happening, the wire was round his neck and Brak was pulling on the handles so hard he thought his head would be severed from his body. The wire sliced sharply into his throat, white lights danced before his eyes and he couldn't breathe. Wrayan had just enough time to think this whole thing had simply been a ruse for Brak to get him out of Sanctuary so he could kill him, when the Halfbreed let him go with a shove and the air rushed back into his lungs.

"Works pretty well, actually," Brak continued in a conversational tone as Wrayan bent over double, wheezing. "It's quiet. Easily concealed. Only trouble is, it's rather messy. But your victim can't raise the alarm. The larynx is the first thing to go and a garotte'll slice through that like a hot knife through butter."

Wrayan glared at Brak, but decided not to ask for any more weapons demonstrations. He may not survive the next one. "How . . . how did a troop of Karien soldiers . . . and a priest . . . get this far into Medalon, anyway?" he gasped instead, rubbing his neck.

Brak shrugged. "The Sisters of the Blade have a treaty with

Karien, and it's held for nigh on a century and a half now. There's nothing on their northern border but an old ruin. It wouldn't have been difficult for the Kariens to simply walk into Medalon and head for the mountains. I'm sure the Defenders would take a very dim view of them being here, but the chances are pretty good they don't have a clue about it. All the Kariens had to do was keep a low profile and nobody would have even noticed them. They couldn't have got here this quickly from Karien this spring, though. I'm guessing they came over the border last spring and have been hanging around the mountains, waiting to feel Sanctuary come back, since last year."

"They can feel it?"

"Like a beacon in the night," Brak confirmed. "The priests can feel the Harshini, at any rate. Xaphista lets them drink his blood when he initiates them. It creates a link with him through their staff and lets them wield a bit of magic. Not enough to seriously threaten the Harshini, but enough to be an irritation. And speaking of magic, if you get near the priest, don't touch his staff. Or let him touch you with it."

"Is it a weapon?"

"It might as well be. It reacts to anybody who can wield magic. One touch of a Karien priest's staff and you'll be on your knees begging for mercy, sobbing like a little girl. And don't try to use your own power, either, while we do this."

"Why not?"

"Because the Karien priest will feel it. Even worse, so will every Harshini between here and Sanctuary, and they'll know what we're doing. It would destroy them to think we were killing anyone—even a Karien priest—to protect them."

Wrayan stared at Brak with sudden understanding. "You've done this before, haven't you? Taken out a danger to the Harshini without them even knowing about it?"

"More times than I care to count."

Brak had laid out the rest of his weapons while he spoke, slapping away Eyan and Elebran's curious little hands as the demons tried to help. It was an awesome array. There was a Hythrun short bow, waiting to be strung, with a full quiver of black-fletched Hythrun arrows. There were two swords. One was a curved scimitar, like those favoured by the Fardohnyans. The other was a long, well-made, and very serviceable looking Defender blade, along with sundry other throwing knives, another couple of garrotes and a savage-looking mace.

"Didn't you grow up in the Citadel with the Harshini?" Wrayan asked curiously.

"Yes."

"Then how come you know so much about killing people?"

"When I was about seventeen, I got a little . . . fractious," Brak explained, rising to his feet. "A hot temper, coming into my power and the Harshini didn't sit very well together. My mother sent me to live with my father while I grew out of it and settled down a bit. He was a Medalonian human. I stayed with him until I was nearly twenty-five."

"He was a soldier?"

Brak shook his head. "Medalon didn't have soldiers in those days. This was long before the Sisterhood came to power. He was a farmer. One evening in winter we were bringing home the sheep to pen them for the night when we were attacked by bandits. They killed my father and left me for dead. It was a rude awakening. I discovered that day not everyone believed in the sanctity of life the way the Harshini did. So after that I made a point of learning how to defend myself. And my people." He smiled grimly. "I've been around a long time, Wrayan. I've had plenty of opportunity to learn."

"Is your mother still in Sanctuary?"

"She was killed in the Sisterhood's first purge."

Wrayan wasn't sure how to respond to that so he tactfully changed the subject. "If the priest can only wield a minimal amount of magic, why is it so important to stop him finding Sanctuary? He couldn't do it any damage, surely?"

"The staff links him to Xaphista, although, granted, the Overlord would have to be watching at the right moment for him to learn anything useful. But if the priest finds Sanctuary, you can bet everything you own on him calling to his god. If Xaphista learns where Sanctuary is, we'd probably have time, this year, to get it hidden before they got here, but by next year there'd be an army waiting in these woods to tear the place apart, stone by stone, the moment Sanctuary returned."

"I thought the gods created the Harshini?"

"The Primal Gods did. But Xaphista's an Incidental god. The Overlord—he gave himself that name, by the way, which should tell you something—is just a puffed-up demon really, who's managed to acquire most of the powers of a god because he's got several million believers."

"So why does he have it in for the Harshini?"

"Because they worship *all* the gods. And when they're around humans, they tend to encourage them to do the same. Xaphista's trying to create a world in which he's the only god."

"Can't the Primal Gods do something about him?"

"You'd think," Brak agreed. "But Xaphista's probably as powerful as most of the Primal Gods combined, these days."

"So they just leave it to you?"

Brak smiled grimly. "It's not so difficult. The Harshini are safe provided Xaphista never learns where they are."

Wrayan knew Brak was right. And that the Harshini had faced this threat before. He could do no less than the Half-breed in protecting them. Besides, after the Feast of Kalianah, it seemed he had some fences to fix with Brak and saving the Harshini from extinction seemed a fairly useful way of mending them.

"How do we do this?"

"That's where these two troublemakers, Eyan and Elebran, come in," Brak said, pointing to the demons, who both puffed up self-importantly at the mention of their names.

"We're going to help save the Harshini," Eyan announced proudly—or was it Elebran? Wrayan could never tell them apart.

"We do stuff like that all the time," the other demon added.

Wrayan looked at Brak doubtfully. "They're going to *help*?"

"The demons and Zegarnald," Brak replied. He grinned at

the horrified expression on Wrayan's face. "Now here's the thing, Wrayan, m'boy," he added, tossing the scimitar to the young man then buckling the Defender sword around his own hips. "There's really not much use in being Harshini with no aversion to violence if you can't call in a favour from the War God every once in a while."

chapter 75

The God of War appeared at Brak's summons, barely larger than a normal man, dressed in an elaborate suit of archaic armour wrought in gold that was even more tasteless than Dacendaran's motley garb. Brak was glad to see Zegarnald looking quite diminutive. At his most powerful he would tower over them, his polished helmet, with its tall golden plumes, brushing the tree tops.

"Looking a bit seedy today, aren't we, Divine One?" he asked with a grin. Zegarnald annoyed the hell out of Brak and he enjoyed seeing the god like this, even though they both knew it was only temporary. "Ah, but that's right! It was the Feast of Kalianah last night. The whole world was making love not war. How is your delightful little sister, Kali, this morning? Has she been around to gloat yet?"

"What do you want, Brakandaran?"

"Why, nothing more than the chance to honour you, Divine One."

The god stared at him suspiciously. "You are my most reluctant disciple, Brakandaran. You rarely honour me willingly."

"But you must admit, Zegarnald, that when I do, it's usually in style."

"Say what you want of me," the god snapped impatiently. "I have better things to do than listen to your pathetic attempts at flattery."

"There's no need to be so testy. I just thought you might be interested to know there's a Karien priest and six of Xaphista's followers in these woods about to stumble over Sanctuary," Brak announced, a declaration which instantly got the god's attention. "I thought you might like to help in making sure they don't get out of here alive. And it would be nice if you made certain the priest doesn't get a message back to Xaphista before I kill him, too."

"*Seven* of Xaphista's believers?"

"In the flesh."

"You have a plan, I take it?"

"Don't I always?"

"And the thief?" Zegarnald asked, glaring at Wrayan, who had wisely remained silent and unmoving throughout the exchange, as had the demons, who were uncharacteristically subdued in the presence of the god. "What part will Dacendaran's lackey play in this?"

"For the purpose of this little enterprise, Wrayan Lightfinger belongs to you, Divine One. Just as I do."

Zegarnald smiled. "Dacendaran will be most put out."

"And you look so upset about that."

Actually, the god was positively gloating, but so long as he did what was asked of him, Brak really didn't care.

"Do what you must to protect the Harshini, Brakandaran," Zegarnald ordered with a decisive nod. "No magical force will be able to penetrate these woods until the deed is done."

"And the Harshini will know nothing?"

"As usual, they will remain ignorant of your activities," Zegarnald promised. "I know how much it distresses them when you honour me."

Zegarnald vanished, leaving Wrayan staring at Brak with a puzzled look. "As *usual*?"

"As you so astutely remarked earlier, Wrayan, this is not the first time something like this has happened." He turned to the demons without waiting for the young human to answer. "You know what to do?"

"I'll be the bird," Eyan offered. "And Elebran can come back to you with the message when I've found them."

"No!" Elebran objected. "I'm the bird and *you're* the messenger."

"I'm the bird!" Eyan insisted, stamping his little foot soundlessly on the needle-covered clearing. "I said it first!"

"But you always get to be the bird."

"That's 'cause I'm better at it."

"But I want to be the bird, this time!" Elebran demanded. "Can I be the bird, Brak? Please? Please?"

"Oh, for the gods' sake! Take it in turns!"

"Then I'm going first!" Eyan announced petulantly, and without giving his companion a chance to argue about it, changed into a large and ungainly sparrow.

Elarnymire is right, Brak thought, shaking his head. *These demons don't get to meld with the older demons and learn from them nearly enough any more.*

"He calls that a *bird*?" Elebran scoffed. The unlikely sparrow twittered at him angrily in response. "He'll never get off the ground."

Despite the little demon's prediction, the sparrow flapped its wings furiously and finally, after a few false starts, lifted in the air and headed through the trees, ducking and weaving between the branches in a rather alarming manner.

"Follow him," Brak ordered Elebran. "And I promise, you can be the bird next time."

A little put out that he hadn't won the argument, Elebran vanished without another word. Still shaking his head at the young demons' foolishness, Brak picked up one of the throwing knives and tossed it to Wrayan, who was looking bemused. He caught the knife, however, with an impressive display of quick reflexes.

"Ever used a throwing knife?"

"Don't know."

"See that knothole? Try hitting it."

With a shrug, Wrayan changed his grip on the blade and threw it at the tree trunk Brak indicated. It landed with a solid "thunk" about an inch from the knothole.

"Beginner's luck?" Wrayan asked, almost as surprised as Brak that he had come so close to the mark.

"Try again," Brak suggested, handing him another knife.

This one landed even closer to the knothole than the first. Brak looked at the young man speculatively. "You may not remember much about your past, Wrayan Lightfinger. But I can tell you one thing about it. You're more likely the son of a criminal than a nobleman."

"Why do you say that?"

"Dacendaran's unhealthy interest in you notwithstanding, you didn't learn to throw a knife like that in between dancing lessons with your *court'esa*."

Elebran suddenly reappeared at Brak's feet, jumping up and down excitedly. "We found one! We found one! Can I be the bird now?"

"Where?"

"This way," the demon said, scampering off into the woods. Brak quickly gathered up the remainder of his gear and shoved it back in the pack while Wrayan retrieved the knives from the trees. He kept the Hythrun short bow out, however, and the quiver of arrows, before hurrying after the demon.

They followed the demon for a few hundred yards before they heard the sound of movement in the trees ahead. Brak stopped and waited for Wrayan to catch up.

There's two of them, he told the young human, as he quickly and expertly strung the bow. *Over there. Can you see them?*

Wrayan nodded. *Where's the priest?*

He'll be coming up at the rear. Brak knew that from experience. Karien priests weren't the type to lead their troops into battle. Or anywhere for that matter. *Which one do you want?*

Does it matter?

I'll take the one on the left then, he told Wrayan, nocking an arrow as they squatted behind a low bush that was struggling for room to grow under the canopy of the forest. *Reckon you can take the one on the right?*

Wrayan glanced down at the throwing knife he still held and nodded warily. If the boy had taken a human life before, Brak thought, it was certainly one of the memories he'd lost. It was clear the lad wasn't sure about this at all.

It's them or the Harshini, Wrayan, he reminded him. *Try to picture Shananara as a broken and bleeding corpse. That should help.*

The young man paled a little, but Brak could see his resolve firming. Telepathy was an inexact form of communication at the best of times, but it had been easy for Brak to force the lad to imagine the unthinkable.

Take him in the throat, Brak added with cold practicality. *We don't want him calling out a warning to his friends.*

With a final hesitant nod of agreement, Wrayan changed the grip on the throwing knife and stood up. At the same time, Brak rose from the covering of the bush, drew back on the string and let fly in the direction of the Karien furthest away from them on his left. When he looked across at the other soldier, the man was toppling silently to the ground, Wrayan's knife embedded to the hilt in his throat.

Brak nodded his approval and looked around with a frown. *Where have those damn demons got to?*

"Psst!" A loud hiss came from the bushes to his left. Back in demon form, Eyan was crouched beneath a flowering alpine bitterpea, waving his arms at them. In a low crouch Brak and Wrayan ran to the demon and peeked over the top of the bush. Barely three feet away, one of the Kariens was relieving himself against the bole of a tree with his back to them, while his companion stood guard about ten paces further on, both of them blithely unaware of any danger.

I'll take the one having a leak, Brak told Wrayan. *You take out his friend over there.*

This time, Wrayan didn't hesitate. He threw the knife with

the same unerring accuracy he had the first time. The Karien dropped silently as Brak expertly garrotted his companion, letting the body slide to the ground as soon as the Karien stopped struggling and Brak was certain he was dead.

They didn't need the demons to tell them where the next two were. Wrayan barely had time to pull the blade from the neck of the soldier he'd killed before they heard the other soldiers and the priest, who was making no attempt to sneak anywhere. Brak quickly rolled the body of the man he'd garrotted into the bushes and waited for the Kariens to arrive. Wrayan kicked some leaves over the man he'd taken down, hiding the throwing knife behind his back just as the last two soldiers and the priest emerged from the trees.

"Good evening, sirs," Brak said cheerfully to the startled Kariens. "Lovely evening for a walk in the forest miles from the nearest civilisation, don't you think?"

Wearing Harshini Dragon Rider's leathers, there wasn't much hope that the Karien priest wouldn't quickly realize what Brak and Wrayan were, despite their human eyes.

"It's them!" the priest screeched, raising his staff as Wrayan threw his blade. He was aiming for the priest but the throw went wild. The soldier on the right charged at Wrayan, almost at exactly the same time as Brak pulled the long Hythrun blade from his boot and stepped into the path of the other soldier who rushed at him, driving the steel up under the man's ribcage and into his heart. He pushed the dead man backwards off the blade in time to see Wrayan go down under the onslaught of the Karien soldier. The priest was still standing, chanting desperately under his breath as he scrambled backwards calling for his god, but Wrayan was in immediate danger of having his throat cut, holding back the blade of the man astride him by sheer desperate strength. Reluctant to save his human companion by drawing on his magic and risk alerting the Harshini of the conflict, Brak cursed under his breath and pulled the garrotte from his belt. Turning his back momentarily on the priest, he looped it over the head of the Karien and pulled hard. A dark spray of blood splashed over Wrayan's face as the Karien went limp. With a grunt, Brak pushed the man aside and, ignoring the young human's desperate scramble to get clear of the fountain of blood gushing from the dead soldier, he turned to face the priest.

"Back, evil creatures of the night!" the Karien cried, brandishing his staff before him, desperately looking for a place to run to, but with two Harshini in front of him and the demons closing in behind, he had nowhere to go.

"Evil creatures of the *night*?" Brak repeated, with a wounded look. "How can we be evil creatures of the night, for the gods' sake? It's the middle of the afternoon!"

"Your sinister charms will not work on me!" The priest was sweating profusely and panting with fear. "I call on Xaphista to vanquish you!"

"Xaphista actually can't hear you right now, old son," Brak told the babbling priest with a deliberately evil leer. "Got a few gods on our side, too, you know."

"There are no other gods!" the priest declared bravely. He lifted his staff even higher. "Wither and die, servants of evil. You cannot harm me!"

"Did Xaphista tell you that?" Brak asked, noticing that Wrayan had come up beside him and was advancing in step with him on the terrified priest. The Halfbreed was as tall as any Harshini. Wrayan was not much shorter. Dressed in their dark leathers, looming over the priest and with Wrayan bathed in blood from Brak's kill, he supposed they really did look quite terrifying.

"No other gods, eh? Boy, are you in for a shock when you die."

The priest fell almost as soon as Brak had spoken, Wrayan's knife protruding from his right eye. The Halfbreed turned and stared at the young man in shock. He hadn't expected him to learn *that* quickly. Wrayan couldn't meet his gaze, though. Brak suspected the young human would have quite a bit to deal with later, once his blood cooled down. He stepped forward and kicked the priest's staff clear, staring down at the dead man unsympathetically.

"How do we get rid of the bodies?" Wrayan asked in a surprisingly calm voice.

"The demons will take care of it."

"*Those* two?" he asked sceptically, indicating Eyan and Elebran who had run past the fallen priest and were now standing on top of the body Wrayan had brought down earlier, squabbling over a shiny buckle they'd found on his belt.

Brak shook his head, smiling at the very idea. "Gods, no. I'll get Elarnymire and the older demons to deal with them."

"What about the staff? Can the demons take care of that, too?"

"No more than we can," Brak replied, squatting down to examine it more closely. The staff was made of a black metal and, in the fading afternoon light, seemed to suck in all the illumination around it. The head of the staff was made of gold; shaped like a five-pointed star intersected by a lightning bolt crafted of silver. Each point of the star was set with a crystal and in the centre was a larger stone of the same crystal.

Brak studied it for a moment longer then looked up. "Zegarnald!"

The War God appeared almost immediately—noticeably larger than he had been the last time they'd spoken to him. The blood of seven Kariens had given him a much-needed boost after Kalianah's Feast, which had drained him considerably.

"What can I do for you, evil creatures of the night?" the god asked, sounding rather amused, which Brak thought strange because Zegarnald had no sense of humour at all.

"You thought that was funny, I suppose."

"As much as I care about anything being funny, I suppose it was."

Brak stood up and pointed to the staff lying on the forest floor. "Can you get rid of that?"

The War God nodded and the staff vanished—gone to the gods alone knew where . . . quite literally.

"Thank you, Divine One."

"Thank *you*, Brakandaran," Zegarnald replied gravely. "As usual, despite how much you profess to dislike it, you are there when the Harshini need you most."

"Which was more good luck this time than anything else," Brak warned. "The Primal Gods need to do something about Xaphista, Divine One. And soon."

"We are considering it," Zegarnald conceded.

"Well, consider faster. The Harshini may not survive you lot taking your time on this."

Zegarnald didn't answer the warning; he merely vanished, leaving the humans alone in the clearing with the squabbling demons. Brak turned to the young man, who was looking pale and rather ill under all that blood now he'd had a few moments to consider what he'd done.

"You all right?"

Wrayan nodded uncertainly. "I think so."

Brak looked around the woods at the bodies lying there, dead because he had taken it upon himself to protect his people, no matter what.

Some things never seem to change, he mused sadly. And then he clapped his hand on Wrayan's shoulder and smiled wearily.

"Come on, Wrayan," he said. "Don't start whipping yourself. You did what you had to and the Harshini are safe."

"I killed three men, Brak."

"I know."

"It was easy."

"Sometimes it is."

"Too easy."

"Well, it seems you are an 'evil creature of the night',

after all," Brak reminded him with a faint smile, trying to divert the young man from where he knew he was going with this.

"Come on, there's a stream up ahead. You can wash the blood off there."

"Are you sure I was an apprentice magician, Brak? I might have been an assassin. A cold-blooded killer . . . you said yourself I couldn't have learned to throw a knife like that if—"

"Stop it!" Brak commanded. "There's no point in this. And if you don't get it under control, every Harshini in Sanctuary is going to know what we've done here today. You need to worry about *that* more than the lives of seven men who were planning to bring about the total destruction of the Harshini."

Wrayan nodded, accepting the wisdom of Brak's advice. He kneeled down and pulled the knife from the priest's eye and wiped it on the grass before handing it back to Brak. "Was it difficult for you? The first time?"

"The first men I ever killed were the bandits who murdered my father, Wrayan," Brak told him, accepting the knife. "It wasn't difficult at all."

ChAPTER 76

It was unthinkable that Laran would be laid to rest before Jeryma returned home, so the funeral was delayed long past the normal time for burial. Fortunately, the hot weather hadn't set in yet, so it wasn't really a problem, but Marla had ordered the embalmers to do what they could to preserve the body, in the hope that when they finally got around to interring Laran in the family vault the cadaver still bore some resemblance to him.

The delay meant that many people who would not normally have been able to make it this far north for a funeral were able to attend. That included the High Prince, the Warlords of Pentamor and Izcomdar and the Warlord of Dregian, Barnardo Eaglespike, along with his sorcerer wife, Alija. Jeryma arrived last of all, escorted by Chaine Tollin, his wife and his eight-year-old son, Terin. By then Marla's grief was all but done. Her guilt, however, seemed to have a much longer shelf life. Laran was finally laid in the family vault almost six weeks after he was killed on the border.

Six weeks, Marla had discovered, was a lifetime in politics.

Some of her problems were easily fixed, and the first thing she did after the official mourning period was over—which was almost as soon as Laran was buried, as the customary duration was only a month—was to settle the issue of Sunrise Province, once and for all.

Laran had hung on to Sunrise by a thread, she knew, aided only by Chaine Tollin's willingness to bide his time and the fact that Laran hadn't instigated any new taxes or changes radical enough to cause the population to revolt. Elezaar was right. She couldn't hold the province without a fight. Their province in the hands of a foreign Warlord was hard enough for the people of Sunrise to stomach. Their fate in the hands of a foreign Regent, however, when their true Warlord's only remaining heir (unacknowledged bastard or not) was relegated to the role of Governor, would be intolerable.

Marla was aware that as Laran's widow she had little real power, but she wielded considerably more as the mother of Hythria's future High Prince.

Despite what others thought of Lernen's lifestyle, he and Marla had always gotten along well. Lernen wanted as little trouble in his life as possible and Marla had been hardly a problem at all. She had grown up quietly at Highcastle, not made too big a fuss over that awkward business with Hablet, married Laran Krakenshield (a deal Lernen had profited from considerably) without complaint and then thoughtfully provided him with the heir he needed and had no inclination to produce himself. She was confident she could extract a few favours from her brother that would allow her to secure Damin's inheritance as much as was possible in the volatile world of Hythrun politics.

Marla asked Chaine to take a turn around the gardens with her one morning several days after the funeral, deliberately steering him away from Kalianah's grotto, where the memories of her tryst with Nash were still too raw to deal with. They wandered, instead, along the path near the outer wall, their footfalls silent on the rain-washed gravel. An overnight shower had rinsed from the trees the dust laid down during a long dry winter and the garden sparkled with the onset of summer.

"It was good of you and your family to come all this way for the funeral," Marla told him as they strolled along.

"Laran was my friend as well as my Warlord, your highness. And I could not, in good conscience, allow Lady Jeryma to return to Krakandar without an escort."

"Even though she despises you?"

"She despises what I represent, your highness. I think, given enough wine, she finds me tolerable enough personally."

Marla smiled. She liked the fact that Chaine made no secret of his status as a bastard. And that, as yet, he hadn't played on it. For his forbearance, Marla intended to see he was rewarded.

"Have you heard that Mahkas is to become Regent of Krakandar until Damin comes of age?"

"It was my understanding that he was to become Regent of Sunrise, too. Or are we soon to be absorbed into your province so comprehensively that we'll be known as little more than Southern Krakandar?"

"Southern Krakandar," she repeated thoughtfully. "That has a nice ring to it, Chaine. Now why didn't I think of that?"

He smiled when he realized she was teasing him. "That's *not* the fate you have in mind for Sunrise?"

"I *was* going to petition my brother to let you have it," she told him. "But I really like the sound of *Southern* Krakandar."

He stopped and stared at her in shock. "You're going to just *give* me Sunrise Province?"

"Well, I was. But now you've given me this wonderful idea about Southern Krakandar . . ." She smiled at the expression on his face. "I think we need to clear something up at the outset, Chaine Tollin. I don't intend to *give* you anything. You'll pay for the privilege, believe me."

"And the price?"

"Two things. You will swear fealty to my House and promise to fight to the last man standing in Sunrise Province to see that Damin becomes the next High Prince of Hythria."

"Suppose your son grows up to be an incompetent fool?"

"That will never happen," she declared flatly. "I won't allow it."

Chaine smiled. "I believe you wouldn't. And the second thing?"

"When Laran spoke to Hablet after Riika died, he negotiated a deal for three million rivets to pave the Widowmaker Pass at Winternest."

"I know. We've had surveyors up in the pass all spring working on it."

"I want a guarantee that all the building material used in the construction of the pass comes from Krakandar. I want my share of that three million."

"I can get granite cheaper, and faster, from our local quarries. Even Elasapine travertine would be less expensive than transporting red granite all the way from here, and arguably a better material for the job. And then there's the other costs involved. The weight of the wagons alone would mean construction of new roads, new bridges and the gods know what else between here and Sunrise."

Marla knew that, although it had been Elezaar who pointed it out to her. It was much of the reason she was making this demand. Ensuring Krakandar was a major trading partner in the Widowmaker Pass construction meant a great deal more to Damin's province than selling a lot of red granite.

"That may be the case, Chaine, but think for a moment of what I'm giving up by surrendering your province and all the wealth that goes with it. Sunrise controls the only two navigable passes from Fardohnya into Hythria. This might cost you, but you certainly won't starve from it. If you want Sunrise, that's my price."

He studied her for a moment, then shook his head in wonder. "If you don't mind me saying so, your highness, you've changed a great deal since that morning we spoke in Highcastle."

"The day you offered to be my friend?"

"You remember?"

"I never forget a kindness, Chaine. No matter how small."

"And I appreciate the sentiment, truly I do, but can you deliver, your highness? Do you have the power to grant me this?"

"I believe I do."

"And you would trust the word of a baseborn son?"

"I trust the word of a Ravenspear, Chaine."

"I'm not a Ravenspear, my lady. Glenadal denied me that, even in death."

"Then you should start your own dynasty," she suggested, slipping her arm companionably through his. "Why not pick a different name? One that is truly your own and not a legacy of the man who refused to acknowledge you."

Chaine frowned thoughtfully. "You would allow me to do that?"

"Perhaps."

"What does 'perhaps' mean?"

"It means that unless I have your word, you'll never find out, because I'll not say a thing to my brother about the lordship of Sunrise Province without it."

He barely even hesitated before he nodded his agreement. "Then you have my word, your highness."

"On what, exactly?" she asked, determined to do this right from the outset.

"Fealty to the house of Wolfblade from me and my descendants," Chaine promised. "And Krakandar becomes the major supplier of construction materials for the Widowmaker Pass."

It was as easy as that.

Sunrise Province, however, proved to be the least of Marla's woes. Lernen agreed to her proposal with surprisingly little argument. Despite the profit he'd made allowing it to happen, he'd never really been happy with letting one Warlord rule two provinces, and neither had the other Warlords who were not part of Laran's original alliance. It was an open secret that Chaine was Glenadal Ravenspear's bastard; he had a good reputation as a soldier and had done a competent job as governor these past two or more years. Nobody was really surprised when Lernen announced he was granting Chaine the province and elevated him to the status of Warlord, except perhaps Jeryma, who seemed quite taken aback by the arrangement, accepting it with ill grace. Chaine adopted Lionsclaw as his House name, and although there were a few rumblings that he should have taken the name Ravenspear, they were minor gripes, in the face of an overwhelmingly popular decision. The only other person who really objected was Mahkas, who was furious when he heard the news. Marla tried to explain it to him, but in the end decided it best not to mention that Lernen had rewarded Chaine at her request. He seemed a little too upset to take the news as calmly as she'd hoped he might.

There was an even more urgent problem looming on the border, in which—oddly enough—Marla's gender actually aided her for once. Several days after Laran died, Raek Harlen and a few of his Raiders had taken another party over the border, this time to seek vengeance for the death of their Warlord. They had killed several Medalonian civilians and burned a number of farms before heading home full of self-righteous bravado.

Marla was furious when she heard of the attack; even more so when the notorious Defender, Captain Palin Jenga, led a retaliatory expedition over the Hythrun border and burned several of their farms, firing the crops and poisoning the wells.

It just got worse from there. With the Krakandar Raiders' blood up and the Defenders itching for a fight, the border skirmishes were rapidly escalating into a full-blown war. That didn't bother the men of Krakandar one bit, Marla noted with concern. They worshipped the God of War above all others and thought it a wonderful idea to honour him with as much Medalonian blood as possible.

And then, just at the point where Marla thought the whole disastrous mess might get completely out of hand, the Medalonians sued for peace.

Mahkas claimed it was simply further proof that women shouldn't be allowed to rule a country, but in private the women of Krakandar breathed a collective sigh of relief. The letter from the First Sister, delivered under a flag of truce, demanded the Hythrun send an appropriate woman of rank (Lady Trayla refused to deal with the High Prince, or any Hythrun male for that matter) to meet with the First Sister at a rendezvous in Bordertown, some four weeks hence. In the meantime, there would be a cessation of hostilities until a suitable agreement could be negotiated.

The offer of a truce sparked a power struggle the likes of which had not been seen in Hythria before. At least, not among its women.

Jeryma wanted to be the one to lead the delegation, desperate for an opportunity to spit in the eye of the woman responsible for the Defenders who had killed her son.

Alija Eaglespike, who had been remarkably demure until the letter arrived from the First Sister, demanded that she be the one to represent Hythria, as the only female member of the Sorcerers' Collective available. Jeryma pointed out that if the Sorcerers' Collective wanted to send a delegate, then the highest-ranked female sorcerer was not Alija, but

Tesha Zorell, the Lower Arrion, and that four weeks was plenty of time for her to get here.

Marla finally got sick of listening to the others argue about it and offered to go herself. She was the High Prince's sister, after all, and outranked the whole damn lot of them. Rather to her surprise, Lernen readily agreed to the notion. Elezaar suggested the real reason Lernen agreed was that the Hythrun weren't big on peace treaties at the best of times. Kagan had probably advised the High Prince that any agreement negotiated by his young and inexperienced sister was going to be fairly easy to weasel out of if the need arose at a later date.

As the date for the meeting drew closer, Marla had more and more visitors, each of them full of advice on what she should and shouldn't agree to when she met with the First Sister of Medalon. One day she would be advised to cede them nothing; the next to give the Medalonians whatever they wanted if it meant keeping the peace. Elezaar attended all the meetings—nobody objected; people rarely thought him anything other than a Fool—and he and Marla discussed her options long into the night, examining and discarding ideas, until they finally had what they believed to be a workable offer that kept Krakandar secure and didn't cede too much to Medalon in the process.

Marla didn't share her plans with Lernen, or the High Arrion, Jeryma or Alija, or any of the visiting Warlords who kept offering her their wisdom and refusing to go home with such an important meeting on the horizon. She simply nodded in meek acquiescence to anything they suggested and kept her own counsel.

Besides, Marla had another problem that overshadowed the threat of invasion from Medalon, and this one wasn't going to be solved by clever politics, sly manoeuvring or slippery diplomatic tactics.

Because, several weeks after Mahkas brought her husband's body back from the Medalon border, Marla realized she was pregnant, and that Laran Krakenshield couldn't possibly be the father of her child.

CHAPTER 77

The closest human settlement to Sanctuary was a small logging village called Haven, some three days down the mountain to the south of the Harshini fortress. Brak planned to make their way down past Haven and across the plains of central Medalon to the city of Testra, then take a barge south on the Glass River to Bordertown, where they would cross into Hythria and make their way south to Greenharbour.

Brak and Wrayan left Sanctuary the same day they killed the Karien interlopers. Wrayan knew that Brak considered him too inexperienced to shield his mind from the Harshini and was determined to get the young human out of Sanctuary as fast as he possibly could, before Wrayan could betray their dreadful deed—no matter how well intentioned—to his gentle hosts. That was the excuse Brak gave for their hasty departure at any rate, but Wrayan knew it was much more complicated than that. Brak wanted the young human gone from Shananara's tempting presence more than he feared Wrayan's inability to shield his thoughts. So, with a few hasty goodbyes and little ceremony, Wrayan found himself back in the real world, his brief sojourn among the magical Harshini at an end.

As a travelling companion, Brak was excellent. He wasn't particularly talkative, but he answered any question Wrayan put to him and knew the Sanctuary Mountains in a way that only a man with several lifetimes to roam their tall slopes could come to know them. With Wrayan heading back into the human world to fulfil a promise he still couldn't recall making—to become the greatest thief in all of Hythria—Dace often tagged along, nattering away cheerfully as they walked, annoying Brak with his ceaseless questions. Eyan and Elebran insisted on accompanying them too, despite the fact that Brak ordered them back to Sanctuary every time they appeared. The young demons always complied, their ears drooping miserably, when Brak told them to scat, only to appear a few hours later hoping Brak might have forgotten his earlier command that they return home.

It was just on sundown on the third day after they'd left Sanctuary, with the evening chill setting in rapidly, when Dace disappeared mid-sentence. Puzzled by his abrupt departure, Wrayan and Brak rounded a curve in the faint game trail they were following and found themselves face to face with a tall, balding woodsman carrying a large and lethal-looking axe. Standing with him was a boy of about twelve, similarly armed. The woodsman glared at the two men, both of whom were still dressed in their Dragon Riders' leathers, and blocked their path, hefting his axe in a decidedly threatening manner.

"Who would you two characters be?" the man demanded suspiciously.

Brak smiled disarmingly. "Greetings, friend. I didn't think we were so close to a settlement yet."

"You're not," the big man snarled. "Where did you come from? Don't know of any strangers around here lately."

"Ah," Brak said, glancing at Wrayan. *Let me deal with this,* he told the young man silently, before smiling even more broadly at the woodsman. "I see. Well, my associate and I are from the Citadel. We are here on a mission for the Sisterhood to investigate reports of Harshini hiding in the mountains around here."

"The Harshini are all dead," the woodsman replied bluntly.

"A circumstance I am happy to say we now concur with," Brak said. "In fact, having come to the same conclusion, we were just heading back down the mountains. My name is Brak Andaran," he added, offering the man his hand. "And this is Wrayan Lightfinger."

"J'shon Warner," the woodsman replied, warily accepting the handshake. "This is my boy, G'ret."

The child stared at them, but he seemed more curious than frightened.

"Maybe they've seen J'nel, Pa," the boy suggested, glancing at his father.

"What's a J'nel?" Wrayan asked.

"Who, not what," J'shon corrected. "She's a little girl. Six years old, 'bout this high, dark hair, big eyes. Been lost for about two days now."

"Would you like our help finding her?" Brak offered.

The woodsman eyed them up and down and then smiled sceptically at the suggestion. "Appreciate the offer, Master Andaran, but I don't know what a couple of pretty city boys in fancy dress could do when some of the best woodsmen in Haven haven't been able to find her."

"Well, we'll keep an eye out for her, all the same."

"You do that," J'shon said. "Come, G'ret. We've still got time to check the ridge up near Hopper's Gap before sunset."

Wrayan and Brak stood back and let the woodsman and his son pass, waiting until they were out of sight, and out of earshot, before they spoke.

"Pretty city boys in fancy dress?" Brak scoffed, looking quite offended. "I think I preferred being an evil creature of the night." He dropped his pack and let out a low whistle, to which Eyan and Elebran immediately responded. The Half-breed glared at the demons as they materialised in front of him with hopeful expressions on their wrinkled little faces. "I thought I told you two to go home?"

"But you just called us back," Elebran or Eyan—who could actually tell?—pointed out smugly. "So you can't get mad at us."

There was no arguing with that sort of logic. "There's a little lost human girl around here somewhere," Brak informed them. "Go find her."

"Can I be the bird?" the other demon asked quickly, determined to get in first this time.

"You can both be the bird," Brak told them impatiently. "Just find her. She's been out here two days and the sun's going down. Now scram!"

Oddly enough, it was easier to tell the demons apart when they changed form. Eyan melded into his large, ungainly sparrow, while Elebran turned into a speckled crow with a vivid purple plumage Wrayan was certain no self-respecting crow would ever have willingly owned. As the birds flapped and squawked and flew off in opposite directions, Brak relaxed against the bole of a large pine and took a swig from his water skin, before tossing it to Wrayan.

"Will they find her?" Wrayan asked, after he'd drunk his fill.

"I give them less than an hour," Brak predicted confidently. "If she's still alive, mind you. They're no better than you or I at finding inanimate objects."

"What happens if they find her?"

"We'll see her home and then continue on our way," Brak replied. "Why? What did you think was going to happen?"

"I don't know," Wrayan shrugged. "I suppose you never struck me as the type who takes time out to be a hero."

Brak smiled grimly. "Just your average, ordinary, everyday halfbreed Harshini killer, eh?"

"That wasn't what I meant."

But Brak didn't seem offended. "There's a balance in this world, Wrayan, and the gods like to keep it that way. We kill a few Kariens; we get to rescue the odd little girl. Keeps things nice and even." He pushed off the bole of the tree as Elebran's embarrassingly garish crow flew towards them. He alighted on the branch over Wrayan's head, changed back into demon form and promptly fell out of the tree. "See, I told you it wouldn't take them long."

"I found her! I found her! I got there first!" the demon cried excitedly as he righted himself on the ground.

"Where?" Brak asked.

"Follow me."

*   *   *

The child was lying beneath a massive elm almost half a mile away, but close enough to her village that they could smell the wood smoke from the cooking fires. Obviously she'd almost made it home before exhaustion overtook her. She was unconscious and blue with cold, a pretty, waif-like little thing with dark hair and long slender limbs. Brak examined her gently then looked up at Wrayan. "She's suffering from exposure, but she should be all right." He smiled down at the little demon and rubbed his head fondly. "You did good, Elebran."

"Does that mean I can stay?"

"No."

Brak's eyes darkened and Wrayan felt him drawing on his power. While he was wielding magic, Brak looked as Harshini as Lorandranek, his eyes totally black and alien. He placed his hand on the child's forehead and slowly her colour began to return. After a few moments her eyes fluttered open. They were an unusual shade of violet, and when she stared at him Wrayan felt she was seeing beyond his flesh and blood outer skin and into his very soul.

"Are you the fairy people?" she asked, unafraid. Wrayan supposed they must look odd to a child in their dark dragon leathers.

Brak smiled at Wrayan and nodded to the little girl. "I suppose we are. Your name's J'nel, isn't it?"

She nodded, sat up and looked around the clearing. "Where am I?"

"On your way home," Brak told her. "It's just down there. Through the trees."

"Did you want to come with me? Aunt B'thrim makes a really good rabbit stew."

"Thanks, but we'll be fine, J'nel. Besides, your aunt might not like the idea of entertaining fairy people."

She climbed to her feet and brushed the leaves off her skirts before leaning forward and placing a kiss on Brak's cheek. "The shining soldier was right."

"Shining soldier?"

"The one in my dream. Last night, when I couldn't find the village, I started to cry and then I went to sleep, I think, and the shining soldier came and told me the fairy people would find me."

Brak frowned. "Did he have a helmet on? With tall red plumes?"

"And a golden shield," she confirmed. "Do you know him? Is he one of the fairy people, too?"

"Oh, yes, Zegarnald is most definitely one of the fairy people."

"Well, he said the fairy people would find me and help me get home safely. And he was right." She glanced up at the rapidly darkening sky with concern. "I should be going now."

"Goodbye, J'nel."

"Goodbye."

The child darted off between the trees and was lost to sight within moments. Brak stared after her thoughtfully and then turned to look at Wrayan.

"Did she really dream about the God of War?" Wrayan asked.

"Sounds more like Zegarnald appeared to her," Brak replied with concern, shouldering his pack once more.

"Why would he do that? He's more interested in killing than saving lives, isn't he?"

"Usually," Brak agreed. He turned and started walking back towards the game trail they'd been following before meeting the woodsman. Their plan was to circle around the villages in the mountains as much as possible. Strangers were too often remarked upon out here where there were so few of them. Besides, now the Karien priest was dead, until they reached the more populated areas of Medalon they were free to use as much magic as they wished, so food, shelter and warmth were hardly a problem.

"Zegarnald is up to something," Brak added after a while.

"That's probably not a good thing, is it?"

"Definitely not," he said, leading the way. Elebran had disappeared, presumably to find his companion and brag that he'd discovered the little girl first. "And where does he get off calling us 'fairy people', anyway?"

"It's better than 'pretty city boys in fancy dress'," Wrayan pointed out as he followed the Halfbreed into the gloomy trees. It was almost completely dark. He hoped J'nel had found her way home safely.

"I think I'm starting to actually *like* 'evil creatures of the night'," Brak grumbled in reply. "At least it's got a bit of dignity."

"It's scary, too," Wrayan agreed with a smile.

Brak strode on ahead, irritation driving him, it seemed. Before long the darkness enveloped him completely, only the sound of Brak angrily muttering, *"fairy people, indeed!"* guiding Wrayan in the direction he should go.

CHAPTER 78

Nash used the slaveways to visit Marla after she had Elezaar deliver a message, asking him to meet her in private. She had every intention of making her lover stand on the other side of the room while she delivered her news, and then inform him dispassionately that he had until she returned from Bordertown, in about ten days time, to make up his mind regarding what he planned to do about it. He could claim the baby or not, she intended to tell him. It wasn't too late to say Laran had left her with child. Perhaps only Elezaar could accurately bear witness to the last time Marla had lain with her husband, and she was confident he would lie for her if she asked him to.

It wasn't what she wanted, of course, but under the circumstances, she had little choice but to honour the God of Liars if Nash let her down.

The decision about her unborn child's fate had to come from Nash. She would offer him a chance, just once, to claim his child. After that . . . well, if he didn't want her or their child, she'd deal with that when it happened.

But Marla's good intentions remained just that. Nash was in her room and she was in his arms and they were on the rug in front of the fire, tearing at each other's clothes, before she got a word out. It was only later—much later—after they had moved to the bed and made love a second time, that Marla got a chance to tell him why she wanted to see him.

She was lying in his arms in the darkness, the room lit only by the dying fire, exhausted and replete, her guilt, for the moment, fading into the distance, drowned out by her love for this man. She remembered what he'd said the night she found out Laran was dead, when he'd come through the slaveways the first time.

Kalianah doesn't punish lovers.

Perhaps, Marla thought, in a rare moment of cynicism, *she leaves that job, not to Death, as I thought the night Laran died, but to Jelanna, the Goddess of Fertility, instead.*

"I've missed you so much, Marla," Nash murmured into her hair as he held her close, his finger tracing a line between her breasts and down to her navel and then back again to circle her nipples.

"I've missed you, too."

"Don't make me stay away so long again," he begged, taking her breast in his hand and bending down to kiss it. "I couldn't bear it."

"I'm pregnant, Nash."

He stilled warily and let her go, propping himself up on one elbow to stare at her thoughtfully. "Are you sure?"

"Yes."

"Is it Laran's child?"

"No."

A slow smile crept across his face. "It's mine?"

"No, Nash," she snapped impatiently. "I've slept with so many men since my husband died that I'm working my way through them alphabetically until I come up with one willing to take responsibility!"

He laughed delightedly. "You're pregnant!"

"I just said that."

"But that's marvellous!"

She was shocked by his obvious delight. "It is? I thought you'd be . . . a little . . . I don't know . . ."

"But I'm thrilled!" he cried, placing his hand on the round mound of her belly. Although the child didn't show yet, after having Damin she'd never fully regained the flat stomach she'd had as a girl. Not that she minded. The faint lines of faded stretch marks and the curves of womanhood were a thing to be prized in Hythria. It was proof a woman was favoured by Jelanna. "Can you feel him yet?"

"You're assuming it's a boy."

"Of course it's a boy!" He placed his ear on her belly and smiled. "I can hear him calling me . . . *Daddy . . . Daddy . . .*"

"You're an idiot, Nash," she said, pushing him off and struggling to sit up.

"But I'm the idiot who loves you," he reminded her. "We'll have to get married, of course. Right away."

"I can't marry you, Nash! My husband has been dead for barely two months!"

"Which is scandalous, I agree, but not nearly as scandalous as it would be if he were still alive," he pointed out reasonably. "My father adores you. He won't mind."

"What about my brother?"

"He adores you, too. Anyway, if you can negotiate a treaty with the First Sister of Medalon that means he doesn't have to stay away from his playground in Greenharbour for a moment longer than necessary, I'm sure he'll give you anything you want."

"And my son?"

"Damin? What about him? I love the child like he's my own."

"But he's *not* yours, Nash. He's Laran's son and heir to the throne of Hythria. I won't marry you unless I know that you'll respect that."

"Laran was my best friend, Marla," he reminded her. "I would never permit any harm to come to his son."

She allowed herself to start hoping, at that point. All the terrible futures she had imagined were suddenly no longer going to happen. Nash loved her. He loved their child and had sworn to protect Damin as if he was his own. He wanted to marry her.

Things didn't get much more perfect than that.

Things stayed perfect for the rest of that night and right up until she spoke to Lernen the next day, who flatly refused her permission to marry anybody, let alone another Warlord or his heir.

"But *why*?"

"I only let you marry Laran because Kagan forced me into it," the High Prince reminded her, as they walked arm in arm through the gardens. "I'm not going through all that again, Marla."

"But you made a fortune from my marriage to Laran. You told me that yourself."

"That doesn't mean I'd be as lucky a second time. What happens when you have another child? There'll be another contender for my throne, for one thing."

"*Damin* is your heir, Lernen," she told him firmly. "There is no question that any other child I have will be anything other than his father's son."

"You say that now," he grumbled. "But a few years from now . . ."

"I won't let that happen, Lernen. I give you my word."

He patted her forearm paternally. "And I'm sure you mean it, dearest, but what is it worth, the word of a woman?"

"That's not fair, Lernen! Why is my word any less valuable than a man's?"

He smiled at her ignorance. "You wouldn't understand, dear. Now put this silly notion out of your head. You weren't all that thrilled about being married off to Laran Kraken-shield, as I recall. Well, the fates have seen to it that you're rid of him. Be thankful for it. You have your son. You must settle down and enjoy a quiet life from now on, and put all these notions of remarriage aside. It doesn't suit me to have you married again so soon."

"You can't be serious! I'm only *eighteen,* Lernen! And you're telling me that's *it*? Settle down and raise my son? That's all that's left to me?"

"Don't raise your voice, Marla, it's unseemly."

"I'll raise my voice as much as I want!" she retorted, and then, realising she sounded like a testy child, she hesitated. What was Elezaar always telling her? *Don't look for the plot before you've eliminated the obvious reason?*

"You want the bargaining power I represent," she concluded after thinking about it for a moment.

He looked at her in alarm. "What?"

"That's why you don't want me to remarry," she explained. "You learned the lesson very well when I married Laran, didn't you? While you have a sister you can dangle as a prize, you can wheedle and deal and get whatever you want out of men who think that if they pander to your bizarre tastes enough, there's a chance you'll make them a member of the High Prince's family."

"Marla, that's a callous thing to suggest," he said, refusing to meet her eye. "Do you honestly believe I would use you in such a manner?"

"You've killed three house slaves for fun since you've been here in Krakandar, Lernen," she reminded him bluntly. "And you know you can get away with it, because you're the High Prince of Hythria. If you can abuse your position in such a manner just to satisfy your carnal needs, why would I think you have any conscience at all?"

"It's not the same thing," he objected. "And I'll see you're compensated for the slaves."

"It's not about the slaves, Lernen. I want to be *happy* and you're denying me the only chance I've got for it. You owe me this. I married Laran and gave you the heir you needed. Damn it! You've still got your throne because I let you use me. Now it's time to do something for *me*. I want you to let me marry Nash, and I want you to do it soon."

"And if I don't?"

"Then I'll find out who your worst enemy is and claim the child I'm carrying is his," she threatened.

Lernen stopped walking and stared at her in shock. "You're pregnant again?"

"Yes."

"And Nashan Hawksword still wants to marry you? Even knowing you carry another man's child?"

"I'm carrying Nash's child, brother, not Laran's."

He frowned at her disapprovingly. "How long has *that* been going on?"

"That's not the issue. Do I have your permission or not?"

He hesitated, chewing on his bottom lip uncertainly. "Kagan isn't going to like this. I should probably consult with him—"

"Oh, no you don't! You're not consulting with anybody. I'm *your* sister, Lernen, not the High Arrion's and not anyone else's. This is between you and me."

"But Marla—"

"I'm no good to you in this condition anyway, Lernen," she pointed out, thinking he would understand lust, even if he couldn't comprehend love. "What man is going to be interested in a woman all fat and bloated with another man's child? I'm not the prize you thought I was. Let me marry Nash, and I promise, if I ever become a widow again, I'll let you dangle me all you want. I'll marry a dozen times to help secure your throne. But just this once, let me be happy."

"With my luck," he grumbled, "Nash will live to be ninety."

"With my luck," she countered with a smile, realising she was on the verge of winning, "if my first marriage is anything to go by, I'll be doing well if it lasts two years."

"This is very inconsiderate of you, Marla," he complained, "getting yourself pregnant like this. Didn't that *court'esa* of yours show you how to take precautions?"

"Does that mean yes?" she asked hopefully.

He shook his head and sighed heavily. "Promise me I won't regret this, Marla."

"I promise, Lernen," she said, kissing his cheek. "There is nobody in Hythria who loves you more than I do, right at this moment."

"That wouldn't take much, Marla. It's been a long time since anybody in Hythria really loved their High Prince."

"Don't be absurd! Look at what Laran and the High Arrion and Charel Hawksword and even Glenadal Ravenspear did to secure your throne and give you an heir. They could have just made *you* marry, you know."

"Their concern was for Hythria, not me," he warned. "The Warlords want a High Prince they can mould themselves. And they will, you know. Your son will have more offers of fosterage than any other child in Hythria's history as they all try to influence the boy. That's why I'm really not happy with you marrying Nash Hawksword, Marla. This arrangement will give Charel Hawksword far more power over your son—and my heir—than is healthy."

"Then I'll refuse to live in Byamor," she shrugged. "Would that make you feel easier about it?"

"You can hardly stay here," he pointed out. "Not with Mahkas Damaran as Krakandar's regent."

"Then we'll reside in Greenharbour," Marla decided. "At least until Damin is old enough to be fostered. And I promise, I'll not let him spend more than a year in any one province. In fact, that's probably the safest way to do it, anyway. That way none of the Warlords can accuse you of favouritism or influencing Damin unduly."

The High Prince smiled at her, looking a little puzzled. "First you solve the problem about what to do with Sunrise Province and now this. You know, you really have quite a good head for this sort of thing, dearest," he remarked, making Marla swell with pride.

And then he spoiled the moment by adding, "For a girl."

CHAPTER 79

Bordertown was the southernmost town in Medalon, located close to where the borders of Fardohnya, Hythria and Medalon converged. Brak and Wrayan arrived at the beginning of summer on a shallow-draughted barge, crewed by a dour Medalonian and his seven brothers, all of whom seemed to resent their elder brother, the captain, enormously, making for an unhappy time for everyone on board. Not having any money when they arrived in Testra, Wrayan had picked the pocket of a fatuous-looking woman in a blue robe who was, Brak informed him afterwards, one of the notorious Sisters of the Blade. There was enough in the purse for a good room at an inn, an excellent meal and two rather ordinary berths on the barge travelling to Bordertown.

Lapped by the broad silver expanse of the Glass River, the busy docks were north of the town and echoed with harsh shouts and muttered curses as the sharp smell of fish permeated the hot, still air. It was mid-morning when they docked and the wharves were thick with sailors and traders, riverboat captains and red-coated Defenders, all of whom seemed to have business there.

They walked towards the centre of the town, Wrayan's head swivelling with curiosity, past wagons and elegant pol-

ished carriages, beggars and rich merchants, whores and fine
ladies, all shoving for space on the cobbled streets. Bordertown's buildings were almost all double-storeyed establishments with red-tiled roofs and balconies overlooking the
shops below. Many of them were festooned with washing
hung out to dry. The closer they got to the centre of town, the
greater the number of rickety, temporary stalls with tattered
awning covers set up in the gaps between the shops, selling a
variety of food, copper pots and exotic Fardohnyan silks and
spices. They were manned by impatient and obsequious merchants, who fawned over potential customers and screeched
at the many beggars to move on for fear they would drive
away business—often in the same breath.

Wrayan found the assault on his senses overwhelming.
Two years spent sheltered among the gentle Harshini had left
him unprepared for the raw verbosity of a place like Bordertown. There was nothing gentle or soft here. No friendly
smiles. No guarantee of a welcome. Everybody was a
stranger. Nothing was certain. And nothing could be taken
for granted.

Brak wanted to head for a good tavern and a nice long
bath. They had shed their Harshini Dragon Riders' leathers
back in Testra, and they were now tucked into the bottom of
their packs. Both men were dressed in ordinary clothes and
boots, making them no different from any other travellers in
the town. Wrayan's accent marked him as Hythrun, but that
mattered little in a town that seemed to have just as many
Hythrun residents as it had Medalonian and Fardohnyan.
Brak looked Medalonian—which wasn't hard to understand,
given his father was a Medalonian human—and he blended
in as if born here.

Wrayan envied Brak his composure. But then, he'd worked
out over the past weeks as they travelled together, that Brak
was probably about seven hundred years old, although he
looked barely thirty-five. One had plenty of time to work on
one's composure, he supposed, when one had lived that long.

As they jostled their way through the markets, Wrayan passed stalls selling just about anything he could name. He passed raucous chickens stacked in cages, bleating sheep, sloe-eyed goats and squealing piglets, their cries so pathetic and heartbreaking that Wrayan began to understand why the Harshini were so opposed to eating meat.

A tall fountain in the shape of a large, improbable fish, which spewed forth a stream of water from its open mouth into a shallow circular pool, dominated the town square. On the other side loomed the Defenders' Headquarters, located in a tall, red-bricked building with a rather grand arched entrance that led into a courtyard in the hollow centre of the building.

"Is it my imagination," Wrayan asked, as they watched a troop of smartly dressed, red-coated Defenders ride under the arch of the building, no doubt returning from a patrol, "or is this place crawling with an awful lot of Defenders?"

Brak nodded and looked around. "There do seem to be more than usual in the town. Maybe someone in the Dog's Hind Leg will know why."

"The Dog's Hind *Leg*?" Wrayan repeated doubtfully.

"Great little tavern," Brak assured him. "Good food, cold ale . . . and a few other enticements that set it above your average Medalonian establishment."

"It's a brothel, I suppose?"

Brak looked at him in surprise. "You've been there?"

"No. I'm just starting to figure you out, that's all. You're not the same person at all that you were in Sanctuary."

"That's because when I'm in Sanctuary, I'm Har—" Brak hesitated, looking around the crowded street, where it seemed every third man was wearing a red jacket, and changed what he had been going to say. "An evil creature of the night," he amended with a wry smile. "Out here in the human world, I'm human."

"Doesn't that get confusing?"

"Sometimes."

"Wouldn't it be easier to just decide to be one or the other?"

"I tried it once. Didn't work. How much of that money have you got left?"

"Not much, why?"

Brak pointed to a corpulent man who had stepped out of a shop a few paces ahead of them. His brocaded waistcoat was stretched over a belly that it must have taken years to construct. Hanging from his belt was a fat purse that clinked with the weight of coin in it. "Our friend there looks like he could lose some weight."

Wrayan smiled and stepped sideways as they passed the fat man, bumping into him. He apologized profusely, helped the man pick up his hat and then scampered after Brak, who had kept walking as if nothing had happened.

"Not bad," Brak remarked when Wrayan produced the stolen purse for his approval. "You're pretty good at this, aren't you?"

"Not as good as my pa," Wrayan replied without thinking.

"You remember your father?" Brak asked.

Wrayan shook his head, desperately wishing he could recall more of his past. These odd, inexplicable flashes were driving him crazy. "Not really. I don't even know why I said that. This is *so* frustrating, Brak! It's like it's all there—everything that makes me who I really am—but it's just out of my reach!"

"It'll come back to you, Wrayan."

"I wish it would happen sooner."

"These things always take time," the Halfbreed assured him. "You just have to be patient."

Brak arranged for rooms and a bath for them both at the Dog's Hind Leg and then announced he wasn't going to budge until he'd soaked away the top few layers of skin. Too restless in this new and strange place to relax, it was less than an hour before Wrayan had washed away the grime of the past few weeks, changed into clean clothes and headed back into the town for a proper look around.

He learned the reason for the increased Defender presence from one of the whores working in the Dog's Hind Leg. The First Sister was in town, she explained. Something to do with a treaty she was negotiating with Hythria. The whore had little interest in politics and no time for the Sisterhood, apparently, since she followed her news about the First Sister with a tirade about the taxes one had to pay these days and how if the First Sister thought she deserved thirty per cent of every trick the whores of Medalon turned, then perhaps she should get on her back, open her legs, cop the odd black eye, and find out what it felt like to earn some of it herself.

Wrayan escaped the righteous indignation of the *court'esa*—which was what Medalonian whores called themselves, although they were nothing like the trained professionals in Hythria and Fardohnya—and went for a walk.

Now the streets were, unexpectedly, a lot less crowded—almost deserted, in fact—which seemed strange for the middle of the day. He stopped a young boy hurrying past carrying a faggot of firewood and asked him what was going on.

"Everybody's gone to the East Road to see the Hythrun princess," the boy explained, barely halting his hasty pace.

"Hythrun princess?" Wrayan asked, but the boy hurried on and didn't answer him. Curious, Wrayan wondered if they meant Marla Wolfblade. He couldn't recall if there were any other Hythrun princesses around, but he knew of her, thanks to Brak's update about what was happening in the real world when he had first returned to Sanctuary. Something about her name had tugged at a long-buried memory. Perhaps, if he saw her again, it might come back to him. Perhaps the sight of her would lift the veil that surrounded his life before waking up among the Harshini.

When the boy had said "everybody's gone to the East Road to see the Hythrun princess", Wrayan hadn't realized he was telling the literal truth. Every one of Bordertown's seven thousand or so residents seemed to be lining the eastern ap-

proach to the town to watch the long line of Hythrun
Raiders escorting the princess to the negotiating table with
the First Sister. There was a large pavilion set up on the
open ground outside the town and close to a thousand red-
coated and very smartly turned-out Defenders arrayed
around it, both to protect the First Sister and hold back the
curious crowd.

Wrayan arrived just as the Hythrun Raiders—near a thousand of them, he estimated—halted on the road outside the
pavilion. In the centre of the column were two women, the
younger of whom was obviously the princess. She wasn't
particularly tall, but she was remarkably beautiful, with long
blonde hair braided with gold ribbons down her back, finish-
ing just below her waist. She rode a magnificent golden stallion and wore an elaborate costume, also of gold, that
seemed as much mist as it did actual cloth. It appeared to be
made of layer upon layer of fine silk, so light that it stirred in
the faint breeze created by her movement. The dress must
have been hell to ride in, Wrayan guessed, but if she was
planning to overwhelm her Medalonian audience, it was just
the ticket.

Then the second woman dismounted and Wrayan turned
his attention to her—and the world suddenly shifted focus.
She was fair, slender and beautiful. Her green eyes were
framed by lashes so long they looked as if they couldn't be
real and her hair was arranged in an elegant cascade of curls.
She managed to make the formal shapeless robes of a sorcerer look almost as attractive as the dress of the princess beside her. The woman glanced around the crowd with a
superior smile, her eyes sliding over Wrayan without seeing
him, and then she nodded to the princess and followed her
inside.

"My name is Wrayan Lightfinger!"

Brak didn't appreciate being disturbed in his ablutions. He
was immersed, neck deep, in a large tub of steaming, soapy

water, his eyes closed blissfully, obviously enjoying the attention of the young *court'esa* who was washing his back.

He opened one eye balefully and looked at Wrayan. "I know that."

"I was born in Krakandar," he announced. "My father's name was Calen Lightfinger. He was a pickpocket. Still is, for all I know."

Brak sighed and looked over his shoulder at the whore with a rueful smile. "I think we're going to have to finish this later, my sweet," he sighed.

The girl glanced at Wrayan and nodded reluctantly. She climbed out of the tub, wrapped a thin robe around her dripping, naked body and smiled warily at Wrayan as she let herself out, thoughtfully closing the door behind her.

"You've got your memory back," Brak noted as soon as they were alone.

"I used to be a pickpocket," he continued excitedly. "That's why I'm so good at it! And why I can throw a knife like I can. My pa made me learn how. Made me practise it for hours. Said I needed to know how to defend myself, but only a fool got into a fight at close quarters. He said it was best for a thief to throw a knife and run. I remember it all! And you were right. I was the High Arrion's apprentice. I was caught doing tricks in the Krakandar markets by the Lower Arrion, Tesha Zorell, when I was about fourteen and she took me back to Greenharbour. Kagan used to think I was an Innate, but eventually he worked out that I must have been part Harshini."

"Slow down!" Brak ordered, shaking his head at Wrayan's tirade. "What happened? What made you suddenly remember all of this?"

"Alija Eaglespike."

"Who?"

"Alija Eaglespike. She's the wife of the Warlord of Dregian Province. And a sorcerer. An Innate."

"Dace said it was an Innate who wounded you," Brak confirmed. "But I could never understand how an Innate could wield that sort of power. Even I'd be taking a risk channelling enough force to burn out someone's mind."

"But that's what happened!" Wrayan told him. "It was just after the Warlord of Sunrise Province died. He left his province to his stepson and we were trying to arrange for Marla Wolfblade to marry Laran Krakenshield. Alija's husband had been pushing to claim the throne for himself and Kagan didn't want her to know what was going on, so he asked me to distract her while he got the High Prince out of Greenharbour for the wedding. Gods, Brak! I can remember every little detail! I waylaid her *court'esa*, Tarkyn Lye, and pulled down the mind shield she'd built around him, and then made him see these pretty lights—it was a joke, you see, he's blind—and then Alija came after me for interfering with her *court'esa* and we met in the temple and she had all this power . . . she was so strong, Brak . . . I couldn't do anything but shield my own mind from it. And then she made me drop my shield and that's the last thing I remember before waking up in Sanctuary."

"How did an Innate *make* you drop your shield?" Brak asked suspiciously.

Wrayan suddenly blushed as that memory came back to him, too.

Brak saw his face redden and smiled. "Idiot."

"It was . . . well, it was an unfair tactic."

"In my experience, there's no such thing," Brak replied. "What sparked this sudden rush of memories, anyway?"

"She's here."

"Who?"

"Alija Eaglespike. That's why all those Defenders are in town. The First Sister is here to negotiate a treaty with the Hythrun. I just saw her. She's part of the Hythrun delegation."

"Is she now?" Brak asked thoughtfully.

"Yes! No more than half a mile away! What are we going to do?"

Wrayan waited anxiously, expecting the Halfbreed to leap out of the tub. Brak would be very interested in learning how Alija had been able to wield all that power, he knew. He had sworn to

Shananara that he'd help Wrayan find out what had happened, after all. Shananara had told him that before he left Sanctuary.

"Well, I don't know about you, boy," Brak announced, settling back into the steaming water and closing his eyes, "but I'm going to finish my bath. Send my little friend back on your way out, would you?"

"Brak!"

"Patience, Wrayan."

"The woman who tried to kill me is right here!"

"And she's surrounded by a couple of thousand troops," Brak pointed out with maddening calm, opening his eyes to look at him. "Defender *and* Hythrun. Let's not do anything rash, lad."

"What am I supposed to do in the meantime?"

"Get drunk," Brak advised, closing his eyes again. "You certainly look like you could use a drink."

CHAPTER 80

The thing that surprised Marla most about the First Sister of Medalon was her age. She was expecting an old woman, but Trayla Genhagan was only just in her forties, Marla guessed, a stern and humourless woman with dark hair severely pulled back into a bun and a gorgeously embroidered, high-necked white gown, which was—according to Elezaar—proof that she was a member of the Quorum, which, as best as Marla could tell, was the equivalent of the Hythrun Convocation of the Warlords.

Trayla seemed just as taken aback by Marla's age, obviously not expecting a girl young enough to be her daughter.

The meeting was held in a large pavilion set up on the outskirts of Bordertown. The Defenders had constructed it for the sole purpose of hosting the treaty negotiations. Their first suggestion—that the meeting be held in Bordertown in the Defenders' Headquarters—was met with a flat refusal by the Hythrun delegation. Marla's escort was intimidatingly large, and matched, almost man for man, by the Defenders.

"So, Francil," Trayla remarked in her own language to her companion, another woman dressed in white, after looking Marla up and down critically. "This is the High Prince of Hythria's legendary sister, eh? The great beauty who almost brought Hablet of Fardohnya to his knees and damn near caused a civil war in Hythria?"

The women obviously didn't realize that Marla spoke their language.

"Hardly what we were expecting," Francil agreed. "She's no older than a Probate."

"These Medalonians seem little more than bitter and rather masculine-looking old women," Marla announced to Alija— in Medalonian, just to make certain the First Sister understood her. "*Exactly* what *we* were expecting."

Trayla bristled at Marla's words and turned to face her. "Don't think you can come here and insult me, girl."

"Then do not attempt to insult *me*," Marla advised calmly, in fluent Medalonian. "And you may address me as 'your royal highness' or 'your highness.' 'Ma'am' or 'my lady' is also appropriate, but usually only among familiars. I believe the correct term of address to a First Sister is 'your grace,' is it not?"

"It is," Trayla agreed. And added a moment later, "Your royal highness."

"This is my advisor, Lady Alija Eaglespike. You may address her as 'my lady.' "

"She's a sorcerer?"

"She is."

"Sorcery and religion are forbidden in Medalon."

"Then I shall ask her very nicely to refrain from turning you into a toad," Marla replied with a smile.

Trayla was not amused. "You've a pretty smug attitude for a supplicant at *my* table, your highness."

"Medalon sued for peace, your grace," Marla reminded her. "Not Hythria. My Raiders are quite happy to continue avenging the death of their Warlord."

"Your damn Warlord wouldn't need avenging if he'd stayed on his own side of the border."

"That *damn* Warlord was my husband, your grace."

Trayla took a deep breath, as if trying to control her temper, and forced a smile. "I think, perhaps, that we're getting off to a bad start, your highness. Let's have a seat and some tea, and begin this again, shall we? We are women, after all, and there's no need for us to bicker and puff out our chests like men."

Marla nodded and allowed the First Sister to escort her to a small table, where only two chairs were arranged, one on each side. Their advisors, it seemed, would have to stand.

Once they were seated and had been served tea in delicate porcelain cups (Hythrun porcelain from Walsark, Marla noted with interest), Trayla put on her very best diplomat's smile and studied the young woman across the table.

"I think you will agree, your royal highness, that it is in the best interests of both Medalon and Hythria to cease this conflict. Peace is always more profitable than war."

"Not if you're a swordsmith," Marla responded, taking a sip from her tea. It was awful—some foul, bitter green concoction—but the First Sister seemed to think it was drinkable.

"The Defenders tell me you've stolen more than a hundred head of cattle in the past year."

"Cattle that would not even exist had not your farmers stolen one of our bulls and had him cover every cow in a fifty-mile radius of the border, your grace. Those cattle come from Hythrun seed. Can you blame us for taking back what was stolen from us in the first place?"

The First Sister shook her head in disbelief. "You can't be serious! The incident you refer to happened more than two decades ago!"

"Do you have some strange law in Medalon that says one may steal a thing and claim legal ownership of it, your grace, provided one manages to keep possession of it long enough?" Marla enquired with a raised brow. "What a quaint custom. And you say Medalon eschews honouring the gods? I'm sure Dacendaran, the God of Thieves, would greatly approve of such a law."

"There is no such law, your highness, as I'm sure you're well aware. I was simply referring to the fact that, in some cases, the cattle your Raiders are stealing are five generations removed from the incident you speak of."

"The men your Defenders killed, starting with my husband, are not removed from anything, your grace. They all left families who grieve them. I have a son not yet two who will never know his father. There will be no peace without some reckoning for that."

"Your husband was killed raiding inside Medalon, your highness. We are not the ones at fault here."

"But you are the ones who wish to put an end to it," Marla reminded her. "So what are you offering?"

"An immediate cessation of all hostilities," the First Sister told her. "And an agreement from you that all cattle raids by your soldiers will cease immediately, and forever."

"And in return?" Marla asked, knowing the First Sister would not have come all this way, or demanded the Hythrun meet with her, simply to tell her that.

"We will negotiate a price and agree to sell you the cattle you seem to so desperately need each feast day, your highness. At a reasonable rate, of course."

"You want us to pay for what is rightfully ours?"

"Those cattle are not rightfully Hythria's," the First Sister insisted. "We are never going to resolve this if you keep insisting that they are."

"Even if I were to concede the ownership of the cattle in question, your grace, your Defenders reacted in a brutal manner out of all proportion to the crimes they were supposedly avenging. Our Raiders took cattle. They only killed those attempting to stop them. They didn't poison any wells, First

Sister. Your red-coated thugs destroyed the livelihoods of countless Hythrun farmers along the border with their wanton barbarism. There must be some reparation for that."

The other Sister of the Blade, Francil, leaned forward and whispered something into the First Sister's ear. Alija took the opportunity to do the same to Marla.

"You're doing very well, little cousin," the sorcerer assured her softly, speaking close to her ear. "But it's the poisoning of the wells where we have the moral high ground. Keep pressing that point. And make sure any agreement to cease raiding specifies 'troops in the colours of the High Prince of Hythria'."

"Sister Francil informs me that there were only three wells affected by the raid you speak of."

"Three wells that supplied all the water for a dozen or more farms in the district," Marla informed her coldly. "Should I send someone back for the black, bloated bodies of the children who died when they innocently drank from those wells, First Sister? Did you want to see the scores of birds who lay dead on the ground? Can you imagine the lowing of poisoned cattle? The squealing of dying pigs? Will you sleep well tonight, your grace, or will the tormented keening of mothers who gave their children what they thought was a life-saving drink of water, only to discover they delivered death to their own, haunt your dreams?"

"Don't overdo it, Marla," Alija warned softly in Hythrun behind her.

The First Sister looked rather taken aback by Marla's graphic descriptions. "I can assure you, your highness, the men responsible for such a heinous crime will be brought to justice."

"I'm glad to hear it. Because I want them for that very reason. I believe Hythrun justice to be more appropriate in this case."

"Out of the question! It is against all the rules of war to hand over one's own soldiers to one's enemies."

"Perhaps," Marla conceded, "if I saw you take sufficient action to bring these miscreants to justice, I might be convinced."

"What do you want?"

"I want them all put to death, of course."

The First Sister stared at her in shock.

"However, I am willing to acknowledge that you're unlikely to grant me this, so I will settle for the following. Hythria will grant your request regarding the cessation of hostilities. The Raiders of the High Prince of Hythria will guarantee never to raid across the border again. We will also, in an act of extreme generosity, compensate the farmers for the thirty head of cattle taken in the raid that killed my husband. You, on the other hand, will agree to compensate those Hythrun farmers ruined by the poisoning of their wells—a sum of some two hundred and fifty thousand gold rivets, we calculate—and agree to the demotion by one rank and the transfer from the border to other places in Medalon, I don't care where, of all the Defender officers who took part in or planned the raids that involved the use of poison."

"A quarter of a *million* gold rivets?" the First Sister gasped. "Those farms would barely be worth a fifth of that!"

"Is that what you're offering?"

The First Sister glanced at her companion with a shake of her head then turned back to Marla. "Seventy-five thousand, and not a copper rivet more."

"One hundred and fifty thousand and I may still be able to convince my brother that he shouldn't raze Bordertown to the ground."

"One hundred thousand," the First Sister replied, "and if you don't like that, your highness, for all I care, you can raze the whole of Medalon, all the way to the Citadel, and be done with it."

"Take it, Marla," Alija advised. "That's much more than Lernen expected, anyway."

The First Sister didn't know what Alija had said, and the sorcerer's tone betrayed nothing about the direction of her advice. Trayla glanced at Sister Francil with concern then turned to await Marla's decision. Marla frowned, making a great show about considering the offer, forcing her delight to stay hidden. Lernen had sent her into Medalon with orders not to give anything away. She would be coming home with much more than he bargained for.

"Very well, your grace," she said heavily, as if she'd just conceded something hugely valuable and gotten nothing in return. "I think I can probably convince my brother to agree to that."

After that, it was all just procedure, really. Trayla ordered more tea and they discussed inane and safe topics until the treaty was brought back for Marla and Trayla to sign. Trayla enquired politely about Marla's son, and she, in turn, asked if Trayla had any children (she had two daughters) and they filled in the rest of the time talking of motherhood and children.

When she was handed the final draft of the treaty, Marla read it through carefully, asking for clarification on a few words she was unfamiliar with, consulted with Alija on several paragraphs and asked that the scribes change the wording from "Hythrun Raiders" to "soldiers of the High Prince". The change didn't mean anything really, she assured the Medalonians. It was just semantics.

When the amended treaty was ready, she signed both copies with a flourish, followed by Trayla and then Francil and Alija as witnesses. Princess Marla of Hythria's first—and probably only—official role as a Hythrun diplomat was successfully concluded.

PART FIVE

AWAKENING

CHAPTER 81

Marla didn't allow her children near the Greenharbour palace often. The atmosphere there was decidedly unhealthy and she didn't like to expose her children to it unless it couldn't be avoided. She never left the children alone with their uncle, either, or any of his "friends". Lernen had acquired a coterie of sycophants who were just as depraved as her brother, but much less likely to care that her children were of royal blood. It was easier to simply keep the children away from the palace than to deal with such things.

Marla had accepted what her brother was, and provided he didn't do anything that endangered Hythria, provided he confined his twisted pleasures to slaves and those members of the nobility who seemed to share his bizarre tastes, Marla had no argument with him. She just made certain that when Lernen was doting on his beloved niece and nephews, she was there to supervise it.

But some weeks ago, the High Prince had brought in a troupe of travelling puppeteers from Fardohnya, famed throughout both nations for their amazing repertoire, although they were most renowned for their lewd and graphic adult entertainment, which Lernen and his increasingly decadent court were anxious to see. The trouble was, even the children of the household slaves had heard of the Lanipoor Players, and Damin—egged on by Starros, no doubt—begged his mother to let them see a performance. Finally, at Marla's request, the puppeteers had put on a special show for her children, one in which the content was adjusted so it was much more appropriate for a younger audience.

The puppeteers were very good, well deserving of their reputation. They had done several pieces, mostly about the gods, and one very funny piece about a stupid demon child who thought he was a teapot on a mission to destroy Xaphista, and ran around Karien trying to drown the Overlord in tea. The older boys, Damin and Starros, had laughed themselves silly over it. The twins had laughed too, but mostly at the boys' antics. Kalan and Narvell were just two years old and, while they liked the pretty colours, were much too young to really appreciate the humour.

Lirena was holding Kalan in her arms. Marla sat next to Narvell, while Damin and Starros sat beside them, squabbling over who was going to look out the window of the carriage.

They were heading back toward the house she and Nash had purchased not far from the palace in the better part of Greenharbour. Starros, the young fosterling Marla had taken in as a favour to Almodavar, was almost unrecognisable now. He would never be as big as Damin, but he had filled out considerably since coming to live in her household. Two years older than her own son, he and Damin were the best of friends, although when they got into mischief together—which was more frequently than she liked to recall—it was hard to say who was the leader and who was the follower. There should have been more fosterlings, she knew, but Marla had her hands full with the twins and she never seemed to get around to finding other, suitable children to introduce into the household.

Marla told Damin and Starros to stop arguing and smiled at Kalan's drooping eyelids as the carriage clattered over the cobbled streets. She was a beautiful child. The twins both favoured their father in looks. Kalan had Nash's eyes and Narvell had inherited a great deal of his father's charm, as well as his facial features. Kalan was the older twin by a mere twenty minutes, but it had been a fraught twenty minutes,

Marla recalled with a smile, Nash standing there with a crest-fallen expression, thinking Marla had given him a daughter rather than the son he craved.

When Narvell was born a few minutes later, however, rather than reject the daughter he had seemed so disappointed over, Nash had embraced her as his favourite (perhaps out of guilt for ever thinking he didn't want her) and now shamelessly spoiled the child. Marla was forever trying to explain to Nash that he was going to ruin her completely. It was bad enough that Kalan had two brothers and a foster brother to spoil her. It wasn't right that her father did it, too.

"They'll sleep well, tonight," Lirena remarked, as Kalan laid her head on the old nurse's shoulder.

"The twins will," Marla agreed. "I wish I could be so sure of these two little terrors. More likely, they'll be so excited, they won't sleep until midnight." She shifted Narvell onto her lap and turned to pull Damin away from the carriage door, where he was leaning out precariously, waving to passersby who would then wave back to him.

"Damin! I won't tell you again!" she growled, pulling him backwards by his shirt. This happened every time she took him out in a carriage lately. "Stop leaning out that window!"

It was her impatient jerking of Damin that saved his life. The sudden "thunk" just above Starros's head made Marla jump. When she realized there was a crossbow bolt protruding from the leather upholstery a bare inch from the child's head, she screamed, alerting her escort who were, until that moment, blissfully unaware of any attack on the passengers in the carriage.

Lirena saw the bolt at the same time as her mistress and threw herself down on the floor of the carriage, grabbing Kalan and Starros and shielding them with her body. Marla did the same for her sons. The captain of their escort rode up alongside the coach, took one look at the women crouched over the children on the floor and the crossbow bolt in the back of the seat, and let out a yell. Immediately the speed of the carriage picked up and the escort closed in around them, beating back anybody who got in their way. Another two Raiders jumped from their horses to either side of the carriage, clinging to the roof as they rode on the narrow steps, shielding the open windows with their bodies.

Despite the quick response of her guards, the rest of the short ride back to their house was the most harrowing Marla had ever experienced. The carriage lurched dangerously as it sped through the streets; Narvell squirmed uncomfortably under her, with no concept of the danger, while Damin laughed aloud, thrilled at the sudden increase in the speed and the way the carriage tilted as they took the corners much too fast for safety.

When they finally reached the house and the carriage was hauled to a stop in the courtyard, Marla wanted to sob with relief. The door flew open and the guards bustled them from the carriage, anxious to get their mistress and her children inside, in case another attack was waiting for them outside the house. The children were snatched from her grasp and she was almost carried herself, until they were safely inside.

"Where is Lord Hawksword?" Marla demanded, as soon as they were all inside. She squatted down to comfort Narvell who had started to cry, frightened by the rough handling of her bodyguards.

"I don't know, ma'am," Rowell Cahmin, captain of Nash's household guard, informed her.

"Find him."

"Of course, your highness."

Marla hugged Narvell and looked up at Lirena who was still holding Kalan. "Is she all right?"

"She's fine," Lirena assured her.

"And you two?" she asked, gathering Damin and Starros to her, neither of whom seemed in need of comfort.

They wriggled free of her embrace and grinned at her. "Can we do that again?" Damin asked, his blue eyes glittering with excitement. "That was *fun*."

Marla frowned at him. "Somebody just tried to kill you, Damin."

"But did you see how fast we were going?" he asked, blithely ignorant of the threat to his life. "You *never* let them drive the coach that fast any other time, Mama."

"Damin!" she said sharply. "This is no laughing matter. We were almost killed today!"

Her tone, if not her words, warned Damin to contain his glee. "Can Starros and me go play, now?" he asked.

"Starros and *I*," she corrected automatically. "And no, you can't. I don't want you out of my sight until your stepfather gets home and we decide how to deal with this."

Exactly how they were going to deal with this, however, was something, right at that moment, Marla had no notion of. She turned to Lirena, falling into practicality, as she seemed to do every time she was confronted with a crisis. "Could you arrange to have the children fed, Lirena? They can eat in here with us. And send Elezaar down to me. I want a message sent to the palace, too. Damin is Lernen's heir—an attack on him is an attack on the High Prince. The High Arrion will need to be informed, also. We'll need the Sorcerers' Collective to provide us with additional guards until we can get more of our own people here from Elasapine. For that matter, I might send to Krakandar for Almodavar. He's the best there is and would give his life for Laran's son." Then she glanced at Starros and added, "And his own."

"I'll see to it," the old nurse promised, looking at Marla with concern. "Are *you* all right, my lady?"

"Just a little shaken. I'll be fine."

Lirena handed Kalan to her mother, bowed arthritically and walked from the room, leaving Marla holding her precious daughter with the sick realisation that the past two years of relative bliss had abruptly come to an end. Someone had tried to kill her eldest son, which meant somebody didn't want him to be the High Prince's heir. She tried to run through the possible enemies of the throne in her mind, but the list started with Hablet of Fardohnya and finished with any number of abused and discarded slaves with a grudge against her brother—and considering the life he led, *that* number might be in the thousands.

Who could do such a thing? she wondered. *Who could be heartless enough to order the assassination of a four-year-old child?*

She couldn't imagine anybody being so callous. She could, however, imagine a limitless array of very painful and cruel things she would cheerfully do to the perpetrator of this crime when he was caught. And he *would* be caught. There was no question in Marla's mind about that. She was the High Prince's sister and had the resources of a whole nation at her disposal if she decided to mobilise them. What was it Elezaar had taught her? One of his damn Rules of Power. Number Nineteen, if she remembered correctly. *Be merciful when it doesn't matter—ruthless when it does.*

Where is the dwarf, anyway?

Nobody threatened one of her children and lived to boast of it. Nobody.

And where the hell is Nash?

· CHAPTER 82

After two years in Greenharbour, Wrayan Lightfinger probably wasn't able to claim he was the greatest thief in all of Hythria just yet, but he was certainly well on his way to earning that title.

Wrayan had chosen not to follow in his father's footsteps and become a pickpocket. As Brak pointed out, there was far too much risk involved for too little reward. So Wrayan chose a career as a burglar, instead. Thanks to his family name and connections—Calen Lightfinger was a respected member of the Krakandar Thieves' Guild, Wrayan discovered—he had been granted leave by the Greenharbour Guild to pursue his chosen career, provided they got twenty per cent of all his takings. Brak thought the figure offensive, but Wrayan accepted it philosophically as the cost of doing business here.

Besides, the alternative was to go it alone and risk a visit from the Doorman, resulting in broken kneecaps (or worse) as a warning from the Guild about the perils of freelancing.

Dressed in his dark Harshini leathers, Wrayan blatantly used his magic to aid him in his chosen career. He'd been uneasy about that to start with, questioning the ethics of using magic to enhance his criminal activities, until Brak reminded him, that by stealing anything he was honouring the God of Thieves. The Harshini never judged any of the gods as good or evil. Even the concept of right and wrong was a little bit foreign to them, so there was nothing he was doing that would particularly bother them. On the Feast of Jakerlon, the God of Liars, the Harshini spent the day thinking up the most outrageous lies they could imagine for the entertainment and amusement of their god. Or at least, they tried to. For a race to whom lying was not a natural skill, telling any falsehood was something of a chore for them. Still, any race that celebrated a liar and a thief with the same enthusiasm as it honoured the Goddess of Love wasn't going to be offended by the judicious use of a bit of magic to stop a worshipper from being caught in the act of honouring his god.

Wrayan travelled the flat rooftops of Greenharbour like a shadow, flitting from one pocket of darkness to the next. With his magically enhanced Harshini senses, he knew when there were people in a room and if they were sleeping or awake. He could feel somebody coming down a hall long before others could hear them. No dog barked at his approach, no startled cat betrayed his presence. Even when his handiwork was discovered while he was still in the vicinity, the city guards never saw him, their eyes sliding over him as if he wasn't really there—a useful trick Brak had taught him that required astonishingly little power.

He didn't rely entirely on his magical skills, however. There was always a risk, however small, that someone from his former life might recognise him, so he regularly bleached his dark hair to lighten it and had grown a moustache to disguise his features.

Rather to his surprise, Wrayan discovered he enjoyed what he did. There wasn't much risk involved, but there was a great deal of entertainment to be had watching those around him wonder how he managed to be so successful. He was living quite well, in rooms he shared with Brak in a boarding house on Lemon Street, a few minutes walk from the main markets in the merchants' quarter. Their neighbours thought them cousins, staying in Greenharbour to squander the inheritance left to them by an elderly uncle.

Wrayan had wanted to go straight to the Sorcerers' Collective and see the High Arrion when he first reached the city, but Brak had persuaded him not to. Although the former apprentice now remembered most of the details of his previous life, they still had no idea how Alija had been able to amplify her power the way she had. Until they discovered that, Brak thought it better if everybody continued to believe that the High Arrion's apprentice was dead.

The deal Wrayan had with the Halfbreed was quite straightforward. Wrayan kept his bargain with Dacendaran—he remembered making it now—and kept them in relative style, while Brak, posing as a Fardohnyan scholar researching a book on the ancient Harshini kings, worked his way through the massive library of the Sorcerers' Collective.

Brak knew what he was looking for. Andreanan, Sanctuary's voluptuous librarian, had told him about some of the ancient scrolls the Harshini had not been able to recover from the Sorcerers' Collective library before retreating into hiding. There were ways, she assured him, of amplifying even an Innate's power temporarily. One just needed a little bit of raw power, the right scroll and the ability to read it.

Brak was worried about those scrolls, fearful they might fall into the wrong hands. Wrayan was pretty sure he didn't give a fig about Alija, but the idea that a Karien priest might one day find a way to amplify his meagre power to a point where he might be able to hurt the Harshini was motive enough for the Halfbreed to keep looking for them as long as he had to. And he didn't mind how long it took. Brak was almost immortal. He had the time to spare.

It was for Brak that Wrayan was going out across the rooftops again tonight; not on a mission to steal anything, but to investigate the house of Alija Eaglespike. An exhaustive search of the Sorcerers' Collective library had convinced Brak the scrolls he sought were simply not there. He was guessing the next best place to look was Alija's house. It was unlikely, he surmised, that she had memorised the spell back in her home in Dregian Province and simply invoked it when she was in Greenharbour. Such a spell was long and complicated and absolutely useless if you got so much as a syllable wrong. She had to have the scroll nearby, Brak reasoned, and the most logical place to keep it would be in her house.

"You know what to look for?" Brak asked, as Wrayan finished getting dressed. The Harshini leathers had never been cleaned the whole time he owned them, yet they looked as fresh as the day Brak had handed them to him in Sanctuary. They were dark, comfortable, silent in a way normal leather never was, and left him free to climb and run as if he was wearing nothing at all.

"Scrolls?" Wrayan suggested as he bent down to tug on his boots, which were made of the same strange leather as the rest of his clothes.

Brak glared at him.

"Locked away in a cupboard somewhere," Wrayan added with a grin.

"Check for magical locks as well," Brak advised. "If I were trying to keep something so valuable safe, I'd have them bound with every warding spell I could think of. Just don't touch anything she's warded magically."

"Are they dangerous?"

"Are they *dangerous*?" Brak repeated with a baleful glare. "Have you learned nothing from me? If you trigger a warding spell accidentally, it might kill you, idiot! No wonder you were Kagan's apprentice for ten years! It's a miracle you've learned anything at all!"

"Sorry. That sounded a lot more stupid than I meant it to be. I was just thinking . . . would she really risk anything so dangerous? She has children in the house."

"Then the best that can happen is Alija will know instantly if someone tries to tamper with her wards."

"I'd like to tamper with more than that bitch's wards," Wrayan declared, rising. He bounced on the balls of his feet a few times, feeling ready for anything. Odd how dressing in the Harshini Dragon Riders' leathers made him feel invincible.

"Not tonight, lad," Brak warned. "I just want you to have a look around and tell me if there's anything there that's warded or otherwise magically protected. If those scrolls are in her house, let's find a way to get a close look at them without getting ourselves killed, eh?"

"If you insist," Wrayan sighed, as if Brak was spoiling all his fun.

"I do," Brak replied. "Now go. I'll meet you at Fuller's Basket when you're done and you can tell me what you've found over a well-deserved ale."

"I could tell you while I'm in the house, if you want."

"Too risky. You don't know if Alija will be home. And if she is, you don't know if she'll detect someone drawing on the source in her vicinity. She might even be able to pick up

on any telepathy. In and out, Wrayan. Nice and clean. And no
magic."

Alija's house was on the other side of the city, in the most exclusive part of Greenharbour. It took Wrayan more than an
hour to get there, and then another hour watching the house,
waiting to make sure everyone was asleep, before he judged
it safe enough to go on. He was being unusually cautious tonight. He couldn't draw on his magic to aid him for fear of
alerting Alija to the presence of another magician, so he was
going to have to do this the hard way.

It was almost midnight before Wrayan was finally satisfied
that the entire house was asleep. A little stiff from being
crouched for so long on the roof of a neighbouring mansion,
he nimbly jumped across the small gap between it and Alija's
house and ran silently along the flat roof to the other end of
the main wing. He reached the edge and leaned over, pleased
to find a balcony a small drop below him, from which he
could then swing across to the balcony beside it. That would
enable him to check most of the rooms on the second floor
without having to go inside.

He lowered himself over the edge of the roof and landed
without a sound, then gently tested the diamond-paned glass
doors that looked as if they led into a deserted sitting room.
Not surprisingly, the doors were locked.

He jumped across to the next balcony, which accessed
the same room as the first. The next one led into a bedroom, and this time the door was partially open against the
heat of the muggy Greenharbour nights. He gingerly
eased it open a little wider and slipped inside, halting just
inside the door behind the curtains, reaching out with
every human sense he owned to determine if the room was
empty. After a time, he realized the room was humming
with the deep, sonorous snores of the occupant, but he
could sense nothing that felt like magic in the room, so he

slithered back through the door and jumped across to the next balcony.

This room was also occupied, he discovered when he cautiously entered through the open door. Although wrapped in darkness, he could just make out low, intimate voices, talking in the dark. Holding his breath, Wrayan backed up cautiously. He was still behind the curtain, so the couple in the bedroom had no idea he was there, but it would take as little as a scrape of his boot to betray his presence.

"I should be getting home," a man's voice remarked softly. Wrayan froze. He knew that voice.

"Don't leave on my account," Alija replied, with the languid tiredness of a sated lover. "I gave Barnardo a draught. He'll sleep like the dead until tomorrow's lunch is served."

"I know. But . . . well, I was thinking . . . maybe . . . I shouldn't visit for a while." The tantalisingly familiar voice sounded a little concerned.

A bit late for that suggestion, Wrayan thought, *for a man obviously cheating with another man's wife.*

"Why?"

"Things might get . . . a little awkward, that's all."

"You'd raise suspicion if you changed your routine now," Alija pointed out reasonably.

Risking a glance, Wrayan opened the curtains a fraction. The man's face was turned from him, so he couldn't see who Alija's lover was. But he knew that voice. It was driving him crazy that he couldn't place it.

"No, it wouldn't," the man replied with a hint of scorn, in between kissing Alija. Wrayan's eyes had adjusted well enough to the dark to make out the two figures entwined on the bed, oblivious to anything but each other. Alija's lover appeared to have started at her neck and was working his way down towards her navel. "She adores me . . . I can do no wrong."

"Does she suspect nothing?" Alija asked, obviously amused, but whether by the ignorance of her lover's spouse or what her lover was doing to her with his tongue, Wrayan couldn't tell. "Even after all this time?"

"Not a thing," her lover confirmed.

Wrayan let the curtains fall closed and the voices fell quiet for a long time. The silence was torment. That voice was so familiar; he felt he ought to know who owned it instantly. But a name eluded him.

This is crazy, he told himself sternly. *It doesn't matter who Alija's lover is. I'm supposed to be looking for those damned scrolls.*

Alija moaned with pleasure and then laughed softly into the darkness. "I thought you were going home?"

"Just one more time," the man replied and there were no more words, just the sound of their lovemaking.

Putting aside the very real temptation to draw on his power to find out who the man was, Wrayan backed carefully away from the window, silent as a cat, and swung across to the next balcony to continue searching the house.

He was between one balcony and the next when it came to him. Wrayan's foot slipped and he almost fell as the realisation hit him. He scrambled over the railing and sank down onto the balcony, not sure which had frightened him most—his near fall or the identity of Alija's lover.

Because the voice that had seemed so tauntingly familiar belonged to a man Wrayan had once counted among his best friends.

CHAPTER 83

It was after midnight before Nash got home. The children were long abed, surrounded by a small army of nervously alert troops from the Sorcerers' Collective and another contingent sent by the High Prince for the protection of his heir. Marla was frantic by the time she heard Nash in the hall, afraid that the assassins who had tried to kill her son had her husband in their sights as well.

He walked into the main sitting room, pulling off his riding gloves, a puzzled look on his face. "Did you declare war on someone while I was out this evening, darling? There's Sorcerers' Collective troops all over the—" He stopped abruptly when he noticed they had guests. "Lord Palenovar. And your highness," he said with a short bow to Kagan and Lernen who were sitting opposite Marla on the cushions around the low table in the centre of the room. "To what do we owe this unexpected honour?"

Marla ran to her husband and threw her arms around him, finally able to shed some of the fear she'd been keeping to herself since the attack this afternoon. "Oh, Nash! They tried to kill Damin!"

"What?" he demanded, hugging her close. "What are you talking about?" He looked across at the High Arrion over Marla's head. "What's she talking about?"

"Someone took a shot at young Damin with a crossbow on the way back from the palace this afternoon," Kagan explained. He made no attempt to rise. He'd not been well of late and every movement seemed an effort these days.

"Someone tried to kill my heir," Lernen added unnecessarily.

"Who would do such a thing?" Nash said, obviously shocked, as he led Marla back to the cushions with his arm around her tightly.

"Anybody who thinks they might benefit from the death of the High Prince's heir," Kagan shrugged. "Let's start with the King of Fardohnya and work our way down."

"Are the children all right?" Nash asked anxiously. "They weren't hurt, were they? What about Kalan? And Narvell?"

"All the children are fine," Marla assured him. She smiled wanly, wiping away her tears. "Damin thought it was fun."

"He would."

"I've loaned my sister a platoon of palace guards and Kagan has chipped in with some Sorcerers' Collective troops to protect them," Lernen told him. "We were waiting until you got home before we decided what we should do about this."

"You should have sent a message," he scolded, kissing Marla's forehead. "You shouldn't have to go through this alone."

"We tried to," she said. "But you weren't at the cock fight. They said you'd been and gone. We had no idea where you were."

"I'm so sorry, Marla," he told her, helping her to sit down. "I never even gave it a thought. A few of us went back to Barnardo's house for a game of dice. I just completely lost track of the time."

Lernen wasn't pleased to hear where his brother-in-law had been. Or with whom. "You actually *associate* with that bloated pretender? *Willingly?*"

He still resented Barnardo's push for the throne before Damin was born, even though the Patriots had been very quiet of late, and neither the Warlord of Dregian Province, nor his wife, had displayed even the slightest hint of defiance since accepting the inevitability of Marla's marriage to Laran Krakenshield. They lived not far from the Hawksword town-house here in Greenharbour and Alija was a frequent visitor when she was in town. Despite everything the men claimed she had done, Alija had never been anything other than kind to Marla. She often brought her own children, Cyrus and Serrin, to visit, insisting that the cousins should get to know one another, even though the blood relationship was quite distant and her sons were closer in age to Travin and Xanda than Damin and the twins.

Lernen turned to Kagan, adding, "If you're looking for assassins, the House of Eaglespike would be as good a place as any to start."

"It'd be a waste of time," Nash declared. "Barnardo's long ago accepted he doesn't have a claim on the High Prince's throne, your highness, and as a loyal subject *and* a member of your family, I would never associate with him if I thought he did. No. We need to look further afield for our culprit, I think."

"And quickly," Kagan agreed. "They've made one attack. Whoever is behind this won't want to lose momentum. There will be more. And they'll be sooner, rather than later."

"Then I'll move the children to my father's fortress in Elasapine," Nash announced. "Let them see how far they get throwing themselves at the walls of Byamor."

"But getting them there would be far too dangerous," Marla objected. "Byamor is four hundred miles from here."

"That's four hundred miles of open road where they'd be vulnerable to attack," Kagan agreed. He really didn't look very well at all, Marla thought with concern. "We're better off leaving them here where they can be protected. Although I do think you should move them to the Sorcerers' Collective."

"You think the sanctity of your Collective will stay an assassin's hand?" Lernen asked sceptically. "I would far rather you just found the assassins, Kagan, and removed the threat completely. For all you know, once they've taken the child out, they'll be coming after me!"

Marla could have slapped Lernen for being so selfish at such a time. "They won't be killing anyone, brother. I won't permit it."

"Admirable sentiments, my dear," Kagan said. "But unless we can discover who's behind this attack, not much more than that, I'm afraid." He was sweating profusely, despite the late hour. Although Greenharbour was notorious for its humidity, at this time of the year it was not hot enough to evoke such a response.

"Why don't we ask the Assassins' Guild who's paying them?"

The men looked at her as if she was insane.

"Well, why not?" she asked defensively. "If someone has hired an assassin to kill my son, I want to know who it is."

"You can't just march into the Assassins' Guild and demand to know who hired them, my love," Nash tried to explain.

"Why not?"

"Because it would be commercial and political suicide on their part," Kagan told her bluntly. "They make their money killing people, Marla, not betraying their employers."

"Their *employers* just tried to kill the heir to the High Prince's throne, Lord Palenovar! Since when do the concerns of a commercial guild outweigh the security of the nation?"

"Marla, be reasonable," Nash urged soothingly. "Attacking the Assassins' Guild's right to protect the identity of their clients is attacking the very fabric of our society. It would destabilise the whole nation."

Marla pulled away from Nash, hurt beyond words that he would take such a stance. He should be calling out his guards and preparing to march on the Guild himself, not patting her on the head and telling her there was nothing to be done.

"I wasn't aware the whole nation was in the habit of employing the Assassins' Guild," she retorted coldly. "I thought that was something only disgruntled noblemen did in order to settle scores they're not man enough to deal with any other way."

"Nash has a point, Marla," Kagan said.

She turned to her brother to see if he agreed with the others.

"They probably wouldn't tell us anything useful, anyway," Lernen added, avoiding her accusing glare. As usual, Lernen went along with anything Kagan said.

She climbed to her feet, her anger a warm, living thing. "And this is your idea of a council of war? You're going to sit here and do nothing but debate the best place to hide?"

"Marla . . ." Nash began soothingly, "you're distraught. Come. Sit down, darling. I'm sure—"

"Of what, Nash? What are you sure of? That there'll be another attack on my son? One that might succeed the next time? And you!" she accused, turning on the High Prince. "You spineless fool! How dare you sit there and wail about the danger you might be in! Someone tried to kill your heir, Lernen, not you! It's your job to retaliate, not sit there worrying about them coming after you next. Gods! If it were up to me, I'd have sealed the city by now. I'd be turning Greenharbour upside down looking for the conspirators with the gall to threaten my child. But no . . . you're just going to sit there and talk about it like old women. On second thought, I take that back. Even old women would have done something by now!"

Without waiting for any of them to respond, Marla stalked from the room, shaking with fury.

If her husband, her brother and the High Arrion weren't going to do something about the attack on Damin, she would.

"How do I get to the Assassins' Guild?" she demanded of Elezaar as soon as she reached her room. The dwarf woke with a jerk and scrambled to his feet. He'd been waiting for her for hours, guessing that she would seek his counsel eventually.

"It's just near the palace," he said, looking a little puzzled. "It's a tall building, with green marble—"

"Not literally," she snapped. "How do I threaten them? How do I make them tell me who hired them to attack Damin?"

"You're assuming it is the Assassins' Guild who is responsible, then?"

"Who else would have the balls to attack the High Prince's heir in broad daylight?"

"Someone who wants you to think the Guild is behind it?"

"What do you mean?"

"In my experience, the Assassins' Guild tries to stay away from political assassinations, your highness. They tend to stir up a lot of trouble, upset the wrong people and draw unnecessary attention to themselves, none of which is particularly good for business."

That made sense. It also gave Marla an idea. "Then if the Guild believes the High Prince holds them responsible for the attack on his heir, they might cooperate simply to ensure their business activities are able to continue uninterrupted."

"Quite possibly," the *court'esa* agreed. "But what's the point? If they're not involved, then how can they help? They can't tell you who hired them if they weren't hired in the first place."

"No. But they can find the people who *are* involved for me, Elezaar," she explained, pacing the room impatiently. "The gods know, none of those fools downstairs are ever going to find out anything useful. They're still arguing about the best place to cower in. Even Nash agrees with them! Can you believe he actually suggested moving the children to Byamor?"

"Hire an assassin to find an assassin," Elezaar said thoughtfully. "That may even work." He frowned then, shaking his head. "And no, I can't believe Lord Hawksword would suggest that. I always thought him smarter than that."

"Well, it doesn't matter, anyway," she declared. "Tomorrow I'm sending you to Krakandar. I want you to come back with Almodavar and three centuries of Raiders. I can bring that many troops into the city without asking anybody's permission."

"If Mahkas will permit you to have three centuries of Krakandar Raiders, your highness," he reminded her.

"That's why I'm sending you. I'll write Mahkas a letter for you to pass on, but if he hesitates in the slightest, I want you to impress upon him the danger Damin is in. Point out that if his nephew dies, he's out of a job. The province will fall under the protection of the Sorcerers' Collective. That should convince him to release the troops I want. And then tomorrow, I will pay the Assassins' Guild a visit. It's time they demonstrated where their loyalties lie."

Elezaar studied her in the candlelight, his expression one of almost paternal pride. "It will be as you command, your highness. Although I am curious about one thing."

"What's that?"

"What do you think your husband will have to say about all this?"

"Right now, Elezaar," she told him determinedly, "I'm too angry to care."

CHAPTER 84

ou were right," Wrayan told Brak in a low voice as he took a seat opposite the Halfbreed in the almost empty tavern where Brak was waiting for him. "They're in a cabinet in a study on the second floor."

"You found them?" Brak asked in surprise. He signalled the tavern-keeper for ale for his companion. Wrayan waited until it had been delivered and he'd taken an appreciative sip from the tankard before he answered. The Fuller's Basket was a popular place and it was unusual for it to be so quiet, even at this late hour.

"I found a cabinet warded so heavily it damned near glowed in the dark," he told him. "Not big on subtlety, is Alija."

"Can you get me into the house?"

"With or without using . . . our special talent?" he asked, deciding it might be a little unwise to use the word magic in such a public place.

"Without, preferably. I'd like to get a look at those scrolls before I do anything rash."

"It'll be difficult," Wrayan said. "Particularly tonight. I don't know what's going on, but the streets near the palace were crawling with Sorcerers' Collective guards on the way back."

"But it's not impossible?"

"*Almost* impossible."

"Well, that's all right then," Brak said with a smile.

"I nearly walked in on her, you know," Wrayan told him, after taking another good swallow of the ale. "Alija and her latest lover."

"You told me she had a *court'esa* she was particularly fond of."

"This wasn't Tarkyn Lye. This was a sleazy bastard cheating on his wife while Alija's husband slept in the next room."

"It's not our place to judge others, my son," Brak replied, with a solemn air of entirely false wisdom.

"I wasn't judging her," Wrayan shrugged. "I don't care who she beds. It's just . . . damn it! I recognised him, Brak! Or his voice at least."

"Forget about it," Brak advised. "It's got nothing to do with our little problem, so let's leave well enough alone."

Wrayan nodded, knowing Brak was right. He glanced around the tavern with a slight frown. "It's quiet in here tonight. What happened? Did someone find a dead rat floating in the beer barrel again?"

"No. Apparently there was an assassination attempt on the High Prince earlier today. Or something like that, anyway." He smiled. "The rumours are getting pretty wild, the longer the night goes on, and you know how hard it is to sort fact from fiction at a time like this. At one stage there, I believe we were being invaded by Fardohnya."

Wrayan smiled, thinking Brak had probably had a very enjoyable evening listening to the panicked rumours flying around the city in the wake of an assassination attempt. "That would explain the guards near the palace then. I wonder who's behind it this time."

Brak shrugged uninterestedly. "I care even less about who wants to remove that disgusting little pervert you call a High Prince right now, Wrayan, than I do about who our Innate is sleeping with. Reckon it's worth going back there tonight? I'd really like to get a look at those scrolls as soon as I can."

Wrayan shook his head. "It's not a good night to be out on the streets, Brak. You can't move in some quarters at the moment without bumping into a soldier. Let's wait until the fuss dies down over the assassination attempt. Then we'll have a clear run at the place."

"In that case," Brak announced, swallowing the dregs of his ale, "I think I'll have another drink."

While Wrayan was tossing and turning in bed later that evening, he finally accepted that he couldn't simply ignore what he'd seen in Alija's house. Even if he wasn't seething over the idea that a man he'd once called a friend was cheating on his wife with the woman who tried to kill him, the political ramifications were too important for him to simply shrug off the identity of Alija's lover. There was too much at stake.

Wrayan had deliberately kept out of the way of his old companions since returning to Greenharbour, in order to maintain the fiction he was dead. But his desire to remain anonymous hadn't stopped him keeping up with what had become of them. Laran Krakenshield had been killed, Wrayan knew, in a border raid in Medalon not long after his only son was born and Marla Wolfblade had remarried with almost indecent haste. To Nash Hawksword.

Nash and Marla lived in Greenharbour now, in a house not far from Alija's mansion, and had two children—twins if he remembered correctly, a boy and a girl—in addition to Damin, Marla's son by Laran, who was the High Prince's long-awaited (and much-anticipated) heir. Wrayan still remembered the girl he'd accidentally frozen on the wharf outside the palace as she begged Nash to save her from a fate worse than death. He also remembered that saving Marla from the magic he'd accidentally wrought had cost him a life dedicated to Dacendaran. She'd been such a pretty, delicate little thing, Marla Wolfblade. He'd felt quite sorry for her. And it seemed Nash had come to her rescue, after all.

But if he was married to Marla, what was he doing in Alija Eaglespike's bed?

"It's pretty bloody obvious what he was doing in her bed,

Wrayan," Brak pointed out grumpily, when Wrayan bashed on his door to discuss the issue.

The Halfbreed didn't think the identity of Alija's lover nearly as problematic as Wrayan did and was rather peeved that Wrayan had woken him out of a sound sleep to tell him about it. Considering the man only slept about every third day, Wrayan thought it a bit rude of him to complain. Any other night, Brak would sit up reading until dawn, or he stayed down at the Fuller's Basket winning at dice. And he blatantly cheated at that, too.

"But what am I going to do?" Wrayan asked, desperate for some guidance, even if it was from a dice-cheating, halfbreed Harshini. He was torn by divided loyalties. Nash had been his friend. But Marla was the High Prince's sister. The mother of Hythria's heir. She was the innocent victim here, not Nash, who patently knew better. The princess deserved more than this.

"How about going back to sleep?" Brak suggested pointedly.

"Should I tell her?"

"Who? *Marla?* Don't be absurd! What are you going to do? Turn up at the princess's door and announce her husband is sleeping with Alija Eaglespike? She doesn't know you from a hitching post. She'd never believe you."

"She'd remember me, though, I'm certain," Wrayan insisted. "I met her when I was Kagan's apprentice."

"And you're dead, remember? Unless you're planning to make a very loud comeback, old son, I suggest you stay that way."

"I can't just do *nothing*!"

"Oh, yes, you *can*," Brak countered. "Anyway, for all you know, Marla knows all about the affair and is quite happy to send the bull over to another pasture for a couple of nights a week. She might enjoy the rest."

"She doesn't know," Wrayan told him confidently. He remembered watching Nash working his way down towards his mistress's navel while he bragged about Marla's ignorance. *She adores me* . . . Nash had boasted between kisses. *I can do no wrong.*

Does she suspect nothing? Alija had asked. *Even after all this time?*

Not a thing.

"Trust me, Brak, she hasn't got a clue."

"Then more fool her, Wrayan."

"I have to do *something*."

"Go back to bed."

"But suppose . . ."

"What?"

"Well, suppose . . . suppose it has something to do with this latest attack on the High Prince?"

"How do you figure *that* one?" Brak asked sceptically.

"Well, Alija's already made one attempt to put her husband on the throne. If Lernen were to die now, then Damin would become the next High Prince, and because he's only four or five, the chances are good that, as his stepfather, Nash Hawksword would be a likely contender for regent . . . Maybe a lover as regent is almost as good as a husband as High Prince."

Much to Wrayan's relief, Brak didn't dismiss the idea out of hand. "It's possible."

"It's more than possible, Brak. I mean, everyone knows it's Kagan, not Lernen, who's running the show. Perhaps Alija thinks she can do the same thing for Nash Hawksword?"

"That could well be the case," Brak conceded.

"Then I should go to Princess Marla, shouldn't I? And warn her?"

"No."

"But Brak—"

"Stay out of it, Wrayan," Brak warned. "You'll do nothing but hurt the people you're trying to help if you interfere. You're in Greenharbour to honour the God of Thieves, remember? Not the God of Interfering Fools."

"I didn't realize there *was* a God of Interfering Fools," Wrayan said with a puzzled look.

"There's not. But there'll be one for certain if you keep this up."

"But—"

"Good*night*, Wrayan."

Brak closed the door firmly in his face, leaving the young thief standing in the darkened hall wondering only one thing.

When did he start listening to Brak's advice, anyway?

CHAPTER 85

Kagan's mysterious illness had crept up on him unawares. It had begun several months ago, with the odd ache here, the odd pain there, followed by an unexplained drowsiness that had never really left him since. After a time he lost his appetite, and then the nausea set in, the bone-wearying fatigue . . .

Each day seemed to be longer than the next, each chore a little harder, each action requiring a little more effort than it had the day before. He was often confused, plagued by headaches and stomach pains, and lately he'd started having fainting spells.

The healers could find nothing wrong with him. He figured he'd drunk every herbal concoction known to man in the past few months, but nothing seemed to make an impression. His decline was slow but implacable and he knew it was taking him down, ever so relentlessly, towards death.

And there was simply nothing he could do about it.

He'd accepted that there wasn't much he could do about dying, but there was still time to put his house in order, Kagan decided. He'd been to visit Jeryma in Cabradell and said his goodbyes to his sister, although not in as many words. She was living in the palace there, an uneasy houseguest in the new Warlord's domain. Chaine Lionsclaw was always unfailingly polite to her, and would never dream of turning out his late father's widow, but it was obvious he would prefer it if she chose to retire some place other than under his roof.

Kagan had suggested to Jeryma that she should think of moving to Greenharbour to be closer to her grandson, Damin. He wasn't very hopeful that she would take his advice. Jeryma seemed far less worried about how Marla and Nash might be raising her grandson than she was about how Chaine was looking after her other grandchild—Sunrise Province. Maybe she didn't want to be too far away from Riika. Whatever the reason, Kagan was impressed by the noble and patient way Chaine was dealing with the dowager Lady of Sunrise and hoped Chaine's young son, Terin, turned out half as well as his father.

He'd come home via Krakandar and said goodbye to his last remaining nephew, too. Mahkas was doing a good job in Krakandar. He'd started work on the addition of another ring to the city's defences, which would enable the population to spread out without a shantytown springing up outside the city walls. The Krakandar Raiders continued to raid into Medalon with the same frequency and enthusiasm they had done in the past, despite the treaty. Marla's insistence on changing the wording to restrict the prohibition on raiding to the High Prince's troops meant the Krakandar Raiders were free to plunder at will. On the frequent occasions when the First Sister complained about the raids, Mahkas sent reply after reply assuring the First Sister that the High Prince's troops had not left Greenharbour and that while he appreciated her frustration at the ongoing raids, they were, under the treaty signed by both parties, perfectly legal.

Mahkas's wife, Bylinda, had fallen pregnant twice more, but had miscarried both times, so he still lacked the son he craved. Leila was growing into a pretty little thing, with her mother's eyes and a wild streak that Kagan thought her parents might have some difficulty taming in later years. Travin and Xanda doted on their little cousin, and the three of them kept poor old Veruca run off her feet, but it was, generally, a happy household in Krakandar. Mahkas had arranged for Travin to be fostered with Charel Hawksword when he turned thirteen and the lad couldn't wait for his chance to get out into the big wide world.

Kagan saw his other great-nephew, Damin Wolfblade, much more frequently, so he hadn't felt the need to say good-bye to him, just yet. Although not quite five years old, Damin seemed to possess all the qualities Kagan had hoped for in a prince, and he hoped Marla was able to foster them without breaking the boy's spirit. Their gamble seemed to have paid off. Marla had proved to be so much more than any of them had expected, and Damin was a bright child, personable and charismatic, intelligent and charming—everything Hythria needed in a prince.

Kagan smiled at his own foolishness. *The child is not even five yet,* he told himself sternly. *For all you know, he's going to grow into a tyrant.*

Assuming he lived long enough to turn into a tyrant. The attack on Damin had taken Kagan completely by surprise. There were no plots afoot that he knew of. The Warlords had been quiet ever since Marla delivered a son and Lernen adopted him. The country was running smoothly. Several good seasons had ensured bumper crops. Famine had never been further away. Hablet was quiet, dealing with his own woes in Fardohnya, mostly the inability of any of his wives to give him a live child. Several children had been born to Hablet, Kagan heard, both legitimate and bastard, but none had survived more than a few hours. There was no reason to suspect that any plot against the High Prince or his heir came from further afield, either. The Medalonians were interested only in keeping Medalon free of religion and magic. The Kariens to the north of them were even more self-absorbed, caring only for the wishes of their damned Overlord.

To attack now wasn't just puzzling. It was downright illogical.

Kagan shifted on the bed and realised he'd been dozing, even though it was only late afternoon. A few months ago he would have laughed if anybody had told him he wouldn't be able to get through the day without a nap. Now it seemed his periods of wakefulness were simply interrupting his sleep time and he was coming to resent every moment he was forced to remain conscious.

It wouldn't be long, he knew, before Death came for him and led him into the longest sleep of all . . .

"No, I have to stay awake," he muttered aloud, forcing himself to sit up. *Lernen needs me*. Kagan remembered his lost apprentice questioning his dedication to Lernen once. It was on the road to Greenharbour. The time he'd made Wrayan reach out for the High Prince's mind from a couple of hundred miles away. Or was it a hundred miles? Or ten? Kagan could no longer remember. He remembered Wrayan, though. He often thought about the young man these days. He often wondered what had happened to him. Had he died in unbearable agony? Where had Alija dumped his body? He felt guilty about the lad's death, certain he had let the young man down. Alija had killed the boy; there was no doubt in Kagan's mind about that. But he'd done nothing about it. That he had no proof, that there was nothing he *could* have done, was little consolation. He should have tried.

Kagan opened his eyes again, astonished to discover it was dark. He wasn't sure how long he'd slept or what had woken him, but he cursed his own weakness. He should have been up hours ago. He was expected at the palace. Lernen would want to know what he was planning to do about this attack.

"Kagan?"

A black shadow flitted across the window, softly calling his name. *Death has come for me*, he thought. *I am ready*.

"Yes, lord?" he replied, not sure if that was the correct way to address Death. Perhaps he should have called him "Divine One".

"Kagan! It's me!" the shadow hissed. "Wrayan."

Kagan was quite sure he was dead now, or well on the way to the afterlife. It had been such a painless transition too . . .

Then the lamp flared brightly and Kagan discovered the man holding it was Wrayan Lightfinger.

"*Wrayan?*"

"Sorry about coming through the window," the young man said, putting the lamp on the table beside the bed. He sat down beside Kagan, his weight pressing on the mattress. He was dressed in some sort of close-fitting leather outfit, but other than his strange clothing, he was as solid as any other object in the room. "I just thought it might be easier this way."

Kagan stared at him in shock. "You're real!"

"Well . . . yes."

"But we all thought you dead, lad! Where have you been?"

"Proving you right, actually," the young man told him with a smile.

"I don't understand . . ."

"It seems I really am part Harshini. A very small part, I have to say, but a part, nonetheless."

"But where have you *been*?"

Wrayan smiled knowingly. "Sanctuary."

"Surely not!" Kagan gasped. "How?"

"After I fought with Alija, she sort of fried my brain. Dacendaran came looking for me and he fetched Brak, who took me back to Sanctuary, where they healed me."

The boy said it so matter-of-factly, Kagan nearly choked. "You met *Brakandaran*?"

"And Lorandranek," Wrayan added. "And a whole bunch of other Harshini I thought were just legends."

"But . . . how could this be? Why would the God of Thieves come looking for *you*?"

"That's a story for another day," Wrayan told him. "When we've got more time."

"Why . . . why didn't you let me know you were still alive? I've been out of my mind with worry!"

"For much of the time I couldn't remember who I was. I mean, I knew my name—Dacendaran had told the Harshini that—but everything else was fairly hazy for a while. Dace knew I was a member of the Sorcerers' Collective, but I don't think he understands the hierarchy enough to appreciate what it meant to be your apprentice. According to Brak, he said something along the lines of, 'He's part Harshini. An Innate hurt him. Fix him up for me, would you.' He didn't give Brak much more to go on. I only really got my memories back properly a couple of years ago."

"And you couldn't come to me then? You had to wait *years* before putting an old man out of his misery?"

Wrayan's smile faded. "Brak thought it would be better if everybody continued to believe I was dead. He claimed it was so we could find out how Alija was able to enhance her power sufficiently to burn my mind out, but in truth, I don't think he wanted me making it public that I'd been to Sanctuary. The Harshini are supposed to be long gone, remember. In fact, he's going to be a little pissed at me when he finds out I've been to see you."

"Brakandaran is here?" Kagan gasped. "In Greenharbour?"

Wrayan nodded. "He's spent almost every day for the past couple of years going through your library."

This was almost too much to take in. Kagan shook his head, as if that might clear it. "Why would your visit to me anger him?"

"He thinks I should still be playing dead. But I saw something, Kagan. And I want to do something about it. Brak thinks I shouldn't interfere."

"You're defying the advice of the Halfbreed?" Kagan asked, a little awestruck by the notion.

A brief smile flickered over Wrayan's face. "It happens more often than you think."

"What did you see?"

"Alija has a lover."

Kagan leaned back against the pillows. "Alija always has a lover. She's slept with half the men in Greenharbour."

"Apparently she's started on the other half."

"What do you mean?"

"She's sleeping with Nash Hawksword," Wrayan told him.

"And I got the impression it's been going on for quite a while."

Kagan shook his head. "Impossible!"

"I saw them, Kagan. And Nash wasn't tied to the bed against his will. Actually, he was boasting about how his wife didn't suspect a thing."

"I do not believe it!" Kagan scoffed. "Nash is one of the High Prince's most loyal supporters. He was one of the men who helped us thwart Alija when she was trying to put Barnardo on the throne. And I know for a fact that Nash is madly in love with his wife. I see him two or three times a week! He is a devoted husband and father. He would never do something like that to Marla."

"I saw them, Kagan," Wrayan insisted. "Nash and Alija. In her bed. Together. While poor Barnardo slept in the next room."

"You must have been mistaken."

"Nash was a friend of mine," Wrayan reminded him. "I know him. And I'm not mistaken. You have to believe me, Kagan. You have to warn the princess. It may even have something to do with this recent attack on the High Prince."

"There was no attack on the High Prince," Kagan said, looking a little confused. "Unless you mean the attack on young Damin."

"The High Prince's heir? The rumours on the street say the High Prince was attacked." Wrayan shrugged. "The prince or his heir, what's the difference?"

"You expect me to believe Nash Hawksword is involved with Alija Eaglespike in a plot to assassinate his four-year-old stepson? That's absurd."

"Is it?" Wrayan asked. "Who's the most likely heir if something happens to the current one, Kagan?"

"Marla's second son, probably," Kagan replied.

"The one Nash fathered?" the young man asked pointedly.

Kagan shook his head, aghast at what Wrayan was implying. "No. You're wrong. Even if I thought him capable of treason on such a scale, Nash Hawksword would never plot the murder of an innocent child just to see his own son elevated."

"Nash wouldn't," Wrayan agreed. "But Alija would. In a heartbeat."

Kagan was still trying to digest that when a noise outside in the hall alerted them to the approach of someone. Wrayan was instantly on his feet, poised warily, listening with every sense he owned, including his Harshini senses.

"It's Tesha," Wrayan whispered. "She's come to see how you are." Then he grinned and added, "I didn't realize she cared about you so much."

Wrayan was at the window, climbing over the balcony before Kagan had time to react.

"Wrayan! Wait!" he hissed loudly. "How can I find you again?"

"Try the Thieves' Guild."

"*What?*"

"I'm the greatest thief in all of Hythria," he whispered with a grin.

And then Wrayan was gone and Tesha was there, bending over him with a look of genuine concern on her face. Kagan was suddenly confused. *Was it a dream? Was Wrayan really here, or have I finally fallen into senility?*

"You're sleeping far too much," she scolded, placing a cool hand on his forehead. "And you missed dinner again. I think I should get the healers—"

"Help me up!"

"You look like death, Kagan. I really think you should—"

"Help me up!" the High Arrion ordered. "I need to get dressed. I have to visit Princess Marla."

"It's long past polite visiting hours, Kagan."

"It doesn't matter, Tesha. I have to see her. Now."

The Lower Arrion stared at him for a moment and then shook her head with a heavy sigh. Tesha did as he asked with a look that spoke volumes.

And what she was saying was: *Who am I to deny the wishes of a dying old man?*

CHAPTER 86

A late-night visit from the High Arrion worried Marla a great deal. As she rubbed the sleep from her eyes, tied her robe and hurried down the stairs to see him, she tried to imagine what would prompt him to visit at this hour. *Has he found out who was behind the attack on Damin? Does he have news of another threat?*

The slaves opened the door to the main sitting room for her as she approached. Kagan was pacing the floor, looking bent and ill. He was sweating profusely and seemed to be having trouble breathing. Marla hurried to his side with concern.

"My lord? Come, sit down, please! You look ill!"

"No, if I sit down I fear I'll not be able to get up again. Where's Nash?"

Marla shrugged. "Some of his father's Raiders are in town, so he's gone out to show them the city." She smiled fondly. "Just between you and me, I think he's enjoying the excuse to visit a few establishments a respectable married man shouldn't be seen in."

"Two days after his stepson is attacked he goes out for a night on the town?" Kagan asked disapprovingly.

"This has been planned for some time, my lord. He offered to stay home, but I insisted he go."

"And are you sure that's where he is?"

The question puzzled her. "Are you suggesting he might be somewhere else?"

The High Arrion began pacing again. Marla didn't like the look of him at all. He looked agitated. Frantic, almost.

"Do you remember my apprentice, your highness? You met him the night of the ball when you first met Hablet."

Marla nodded at the memory. "I remember you lecturing me about growing up. I fainted that night as I recall, too. And I do remember Wrayan, although I don't remember seeing much of him after that. He went missing around the time I married Laran, didn't he?"

"Yes. And all this time I believed him dead."

"And he isn't?" she asked, wondering what this had to do with Nash.

"He's been . . . away," the High Arrion told her. "But now he's back. At least I think he is. Parts of it seem like a dream."

"And what part of your dream brings you to my house in the middle of the night asking if I know where my husband is, Lord Palenovar?"

"You will think me a crazy old man if I tell you," he warned, wiping his streaming brow.

Marla laughed softly. "I think you're a crazy old man now, my lord. Don't let that stop you."

"Wrayan is some sort of thief now, I gather," Kagan began as he paced.

"A *thief*?"

"There was . . . an accident," he explained. "Wrayan lost his memory. So he fell back into what was familiar, I suppose. His father was a pickpocket, so his choice of profession is not that hard to comprehend."

"And this has exactly *what* to do with me?" Marla asked, a little impatiently. She was tired and Kagan seemed to be rambling.

"In his travels, Wrayan saw something, your highness. Something that concerned him enough to break his silence about where he's been these past five years. Something that concerns you."

"You have me intrigued, my lord. What is this great mystery he saw?"

Kagan stopped and turned to her, taking a deep breath before he replied. "He claims he saw your husband, my lady. In the bed of Alija Eaglespike."

Marla laughed. "Oh, that's ridiculous!"

"That's what I said, your highness," Kagan replied, resuming his pacing with even greater frenzy, "but Wrayan was adamant. He and Nash were good friends once. He's not likely to mistake him for another man. He claims it couldn't have been anybody else. He also maintained that it appeared to be an ongoing affair of some significant duration."

"I never heard anything more preposterous in my life!" Marla told him, still laughing at the absurd notion that Nash was sleeping with any woman other than her. "And I can't believe you gave it credence enough to wake me in the middle of the night to tell me of it."

"Believe me, your highness, if I could dismiss this out of hand, I would have. But Wrayan was convinced. And given the events of the past few days, there is reason to be suspicious."

Marla's amusement was rapidly turning to anger with what the High Arrion was implying. "Surely you're not suggesting this has something to do with the attack on Damin?"

"If Damin were to die, your highness, Lernen would have no choice but to adopt Narvell as his heir or get married and produce his own. You know the likelihood of the latter as well as I. Damin's death will result in Nash Hawksword's son becoming the next High Prince of Hythria."

"Nash loves Damin as if he were his own son."

"But his own son is Narvell, not Damin, my lady."

Marla shook her head. "It's not possible. I would know if my husband was having an affair."

"Are you sure?"

"You think I wouldn't notice the change in his behaviour if he was suddenly cheating on me?"

"If the affair has been going on for some time, as Wrayan believes, if it predates your marriage to Lord Hawksword, your highness, how would you tell?"

"Now I *know* you've lost your mind," she declared. "You're implying that Nash and Alija have been lovers for . . . what? Three or four years? That's so absurd, it's laughable. Alija has a husband, you know. Surely he would have suspected something if that were the case?"

"I could give you the names of a dozen men who've slept with Alija Eaglespike, your highness, and Barnardo hasn't got a clue about a single one of them. Don't rely on the Warlord of Dregian's powers of observation for your peace of mind."

"It's not possible, my lord," she insisted, shaking her head. "Nash loves me. He loves Damin. And he's not a traitor. You will have to look elsewhere if you hope to find my support in bringing your nemesis down."

Kagan stared at her, obviously distraught. "You think I'm doing this to get at Alija?"

"I don't know why you're doing it, Lord Palenovar. And to be honest, I don't even care that much. But I do know that you've always hated her. Alija told me that herself. You resent her power. You know she'll be the next High Arrion after you and are desperate to discredit her. She told me once that you lie awake at night, thinking up ways to get at her. I thought she was imagining things, but now I'm not so sure."

"But your highness—"

"I love my husband, my lord, and Alija Eaglespike is my friend. She has never done anything to hurt me; never offered me any advice that wasn't sound. You, on the other hand, arranged to have me married off to the King of Fardohnya, then reneged on that deal and had me married to a complete stranger, simply so I could bear an heir for my brother with enough Hythrun blood in him to make you happy. And now, when I am finally married to the man I love—and who loves me, I hasten to add—you feel the need to drive a wedge between us by coming here in the middle of the night with your wild tale about a dead apprentice sorcerer who has become a thief appearing to you to tell you that he's seen my husband in bed with one of my best friends."

"Your highness, you misunderstand—"

"I know you're not well, my lord," she added, a little more sympathetically, "but please, don't bring your fevered dreams to me without proof. I will not be a party to your scheme to manipulate the succession of the High Arrion from beyond the grave. When you die, the Sorcerers' Collective will choose the most likely candidate to replace you, and you will have no say in the matter at all."

Kagan opened his mouth to object further, but then he shook his head, as if it wasn't worth the effort. He bowed awkwardly instead. "I apologize, your highness, for disturbing you at such a late hour. Please forgive my rudeness."

Without waiting for her to dismiss him, Kagan strode from the room. A sick and pathetic old man, Marla thought, desperate to win at all costs, even though everyone in Greenharbour knew he was dying.

It was the early hours of the morning before Nash climbed into bed beside Marla. She was still awake. Kagan's preposterous claims had planted a seed of doubt in her mind, making her feel like a traitor. But even though she was sure in the deepest part of her being that Nash was true to her, the niggling doubt refused to go away.

Once planted, the seeds of distrust took root quickly, Marla discovered.

"I'm sorry, darling," Nash whispered, as he slid into the bed beside her and realized she was awake. "I didn't mean to disturb you."

"Did you have a good night?" she asked, turning to look at his face in the darkness.

He smiled. "It was excellent. But I won't kiss you. I must smell like a barrel of ale."

"You smell just fine to me."

Nash didn't take the bait. He snuggled down beside her and gathered her into his arms. "You're too good to me, Marla. Most wives would yell at a man for coming home drunk in the wee small hours after a night out with the boys."

Nash didn't sound drunk. Or smell it either. He smelt clean and wonderful, the way he always did. *As if he'd bathed before he came home,* a traitorous little voice in her head whispered.

"Make love to me, Nash." In all the time they had been married, she'd never had to ask him that. Not once.

"Now?"

"No, next Fifthday!" she laughed softly. "When did you think I meant? Of course, *now.*"

"It's awfully late, my love. And I'm very tired."

Worn out from your mistress, are you? the traitor in her head asked.

Stop this! Marla told herself angrily.

But she couldn't help herself. "Don't you want me any more?"

"I always want you. You know that." He kissed the top of her head and closed his eyes, determined to sleep. "But can't a man be tired *once* in a while?"

Of course you can be tired. But why tonight, Nash? Why, on this night, of all nights, couldn't you just take me in your arms and make me believe there's nobody else?

"I'm sorry."

Nash didn't respond to her apology. He was feigning sleep, she was certain. Nobody lost consciousness that quickly without a blow to the head.

"I love you, Nash," she told him softly.

"I love you, too," he murmured, pulling her closer.

After a time, his breathing became deep and even and Marla knew that he really was sleeping this time. She lay awake in his arms until dawn, wishing she hadn't sent Elezaar away.

But then, even if the *court'esa* were here and she had someone to confide in, all he could have done was remind her of the Fourth Rule of Gaining and Wielding Power.

Trust nobody but yourself.

CHAPTER 87

A few days after he'd been to visit Kagan, a messenger from the Thieves' Guild was waiting for Wrayan at the boarding house when he got home in the early hours of the morning after relieving a dour matron on Durony Street of most of her jewellery. The message bearer was a scrawny lad of about nine who sat on the top step outside the boarding house, cleaning his filthy fingernails with a wicked-looking blade while he waited for Wrayan to appear.

"You the Wraith?" the lad asked as Wrayan approached. It was still dark although the air was balmy. Summer was fast approaching and with it Greenharbour's notorious humidity.

Wrayan stopped and stared at the boy, puzzled by the question. "The what?"

"Wrayan the Wraith," the boy explained. "That's who Gillam told me to wait for."

"Wrayan the *Wraith*?"

"Hey, don't blame me," the child shrugged. "And it could be worse. Last chap I delivered a message to was called Taryn the Turd. Nice threads, by the way," the boy added, looking Wrayan's leathers up and down with a covetous eye. "Bet you could go just about bleedin' anywhere without bein' seen, dressed like that. Where'd you get 'em?"

"They were a gift from the Harshini," Wrayan told him.

The boy scowled at him. "Fine, don't tell me then. Make you look like a bleedin' fancy boy, anyway."

"What does Gillam want?" Wrayan asked.

"He wants to see you."

"Did he say why?"

"Do I look like his bleedin' secretary?"

"Did he say when?"

The boy rose to his feet and dusted off his filthy trousers. "Now."

Franz Gillam was the head of the Thieves' Guild in Green-harbour. He was a nondescript little man, with white hair and a slow smile that sent a shiver down the spine of any man reckless enough to cross him. He was the sort of man you could walk past in the street and never even notice—one of the qualities that made him such a good pickpocket. Although Wrayan was a burglar, being the son of a well-respected pickpocket made him quite a favourite with the old man. It didn't hurt that he'd been making a tidy fortune for the Guild since arriving in the city, either. Gillam got a cut of everything the Guild earned, so, in a way, Wrayan was responsible for his current prosperity.

Although not as blatant as the Assassins' Guild, who actually had a sign outside their building a couple of blocks from the High Prince's palace, the Thieves' Guild made no secret of their headquarters. It was a two-storey, red-brick building down near the wharves with a rather pretentious marble portico out the front and a doorman—known only, oddly enough, as The Doorman—who wore the livery of a nobleman's slave and had the ability to break a man's kneecaps with his decorative staff on little more than a nod from Franz Gillam.

Gillam smiled as Wrayan walked into his office, furnished entirely with items stolen from all over the city. The head of the Guild liked to lead by example, he claimed. The comfortable leather sofa had once belonged to the High Prince, it was rumoured, although how anybody could manage to lift something so large and cumbersome and sneak it out of the palace was beyond Wrayan. He suspected the story was either an outright lie or Gillam had acquired it by deceit rather than theft. Neither would have bothered the little man. It was a given that if one honoured Dacendaran, one frequently honoured Jakerlon, the God of Liars, in the same breath.

"I hear old Widow Saks is missing some rather valuable trinkets?" the thief said as Wrayan took a seat on the High Prince's sofa.

"She hardly goes out any more," Wrayan shrugged. "Seemed a pity to leave all that nice jewellery lying about the house gathering dust."

"You see!" Gillam declared with an approving nod. "That's what people just don't get about us, Wrayan. We're actually performing a civil service for the citizens of Greenharbour. We've saved her *how* many hours a week dusting that stuff? Cleaning's such a chore, too."

"And it's so hard to find decent slaves these days," Wrayan agreed with a grin. "What did you want to see me about?" He thought it couldn't be too bad. Gillam would have sent The Doorman, not a lad, to collect him if Wrayan had transgressed against the Guild's rules in any way.

"Had someone down here looking for you yesterday."

"Really?"

"Someone real important."

Wrayan waited for Gillam to go on, but the man seemed disinclined to continue. After a moment's pregnant silence, Wrayan threw up his hands. "Well? Are you going to tell me who, or is this a guessing game?"

"Why didn't you tell me you knew the High Prince's sister?" Gillam replied, watching him closely.

"Princess *Marla* came here looking for me?"

"You been takin' more than the silverware from the Princess's place?" Gillam asked with a raised brow.

"Taking more than the silverware" was a euphemism in the Guild for sleeping with the lady of the house while out on a job. Wrayan knew of a few thieves who thought it fun. He

thought it absurdly dangerous. While the understanding was
that the woman must be a willing participant in what was considered, in some circles, a harmless if somewhat titillating and
certainly risky game, a serious problem arose when the lady's
husband (father, master . . .) inadvertently walked in on a
thrill-seeking burglar helping himself to "more than the silverware". Everyone involved (with the exception of the thief) invariably cried rape. The woman would never admit that she
was so jaded she got a thrill out of letting a perfect stranger
have his way with her; the man of the house would never admit
that his womenfolk were so dissatisfied with his efforts to
please them that they might *invite* a perfect stranger to have his
way with her. So of course it was rape. And that meant death to
the thief and a great deal of trouble for everyone else involved.

Wrayan shook his head. "I've never even done over the
Hawksword place. Too risky. Too many guards."

"Well, she knows you. She asked for you by name."

"Did the princess say what she wanted?"

"She wants you." Gillam slid a folded piece of parchment
across the desk.

"What does it say?" Wrayan asked, knowing full well that
Gillam had read the note.

"It's just a time and a place."

"And you'll be there watching me, of course?"

"You don't get to deal with someone as important as the
mother of the next High Prince without us knowing what's
going on, lad. You shouldn't need me to tell you that."

"Maybe she wants me to do a job for her."

"Well, whatever it is," Gillam warned, "I want to know
about it."

"I'll keep you posted," Wrayan agreed as he rose to his feet.
He took the folded piece of parchment, knowing there could
only be one reason why Princess Marla wanted to see him.

Kagan must have delivered his warning about Nash and
Alija Eaglespike, after all.

* * *

Marla had arranged to meet Wrayan in the temple dedicated to Zegarnald, the God of War, in the centre of the city. It was by far the largest temple in Greenharbour, outside the Sorcerers' Collective, where the massive Temple of the Gods dominated the city skyline. As Hythria probably had more followers of the War God than any other nation on the continent, his temple was always a busy place and it was a good place for a thief and a princess to rub shoulders without raising suspicion.

He didn't recognise her at first. The princess was wearing a white veil that shadowed her face and concealed her rich clothing. In the crowded temple, where it was customary to prick your finger on the spikes near the door so that you honoured the God of War with a blood sacrifice before departing, she looked like just another widow come to beg the God of War's protection for the soul of her lost husband.

"Wrayan Lightfinger."

He turned at the sound of his softly spoken name to find the princess standing behind him. She had matured a great deal since he saw her last, which was, he realized, over five years ago. She had lost the coltishness of youth and had blossomed into a truly beautiful woman.

"My lady," Wrayan replied, with a short, polite bow, guessing she no more wished to be identified in public than he did.

"I appreciate you answering my summons," she said, coming to stand alongside him. "I hope I didn't get you into too much trouble by appearing at your Guild."

"Just a few questions about how I know you," he assured her. "Did Kagan tell you how to find me?"

"No. He just mentioned that you were a thief now. I figured the Guild was the best place to start."

"He told you then," Wrayan surmised. "What I saw."

"Yes. But I didn't believe him. I don't believe you."

"Then why are you here?"

"Because I have to be sure, Wrayan," she said, in a flat

voice devoid of all emotion. "Someone tried to kill my son. I can't afford to leave any stone unturned, even if I'm certain there is nothing under the stone but good clean soil." She hesitated for a moment then added, "Tell me what you saw, Wrayan. All of it."

So Wrayan told her. They stood in the temple of the God of War, side by side, as if they were simply two strangers praying, while Wrayan explained in a low voice exactly what he'd seen in Alija's house.

"And there is no doubt in your mind that the man was my husband?" she asked when he was finished. "Even though you never saw his face?"

"No doubt at all, my lady."

"And why should I believe you?"

"I have no reason to lie, my lady."

"Don't you? Where have you been these past five years, Wrayan? Kagan thought you gone forever. Why should I believe anything from the mouth of a thief who abandoned his master and let everyone think he was dead?"

"I was injured, my lady. Very badly. I've spent much of the past few years with the Harshini in Medalon. I came back to fulfil a vow I made to the God of Thieves."

Marla glanced up at him with a faint smile. "I find that harder to believe than your story about my husband."

"But it's the truth. I can even prove it if you want," he offered, wondering what Brak would make of such a suggestion. "Although I'd prefer not to do it in quite so public a place as this."

"I may yet ask that of you, Wrayan Lightfinger," she replied, but if she said anything else after that he couldn't hear it. The temple bells began to toll, along with the bells from every other temple in the city, the metallic chorus led by the massive bronze bells of the Temple of the Gods. Marla, along with every other person in the temple, looked around in confusion. Like them, she was puzzled by what the sudden tolling of every bell in the city meant.

Wrayan didn't need to ask. He knew the last time the city bells had tolled like this was some ten years ago, just after Tesha Zorell brought him to the Sorcerers' Collective. Then it was because Garel Wolfblade, the High Prince of Hythria, had just died, leaving the way open for his son Lernen to inherit.

The only other time in Greenharbour's history that all the bells tolled in unison was on the death of a High or Lower Arrion.

With a heavy heart, Wrayan recalled the sick old man he had visited only a few days ago in his room at the Sorcerers' Collective, and knew with certainty that Kagan Palenovar was dead.

CHAPTER 88

The funeral and the appointment of the new High Arrion were held simultaneously, in a practical, if somewhat irreverent, case of "out with the old and in with the new". Marla was shocked when she learned the Sorcerers' Collective had met to decide their new High Arrion the very night Kagan had died. She was even more disturbed, although not really surprised, to learn his successor was Alija Eaglespike.

Alija had handled herself very wisely these last few years. From a pariah whom half the Warlords of Hythria were willing to band together to defeat, she had become acceptable, even accepted. Once Barnardo stopped making noises about becoming High Prince, and the fear of a sorcerer behind the throne had abated, the Royalists had relaxed a little. Only then did they have time to notice that a sorcerer behind the throne was exactly what they'd wound up with anyway. Lernen Wolfblade was a figurehead. The heir to the throne was a small child. Hythria was, in reality, being governed by Kagan Palenovar and all their posturing about the separation of religion and state seemed rather pointless in hindsight.

Alija had won the support of everyone, sorcerer and Warlord alike, by promising to do the exact opposite of what they had once feared was her ambition. She would not, she promised, attempt to interfere with the governance of Hythria. That was the High Prince's job. Kagan spent so much time at the palace, he had his own suite of rooms there, she complained. This would not happen any more. Lernen must govern the nation as High Prince. The High Arrion was responsible for the health of the nation's soul; he or she should not be expected to do the work of a lazy, perverted despot as well.

Marla was dressing for the ceremony, putting on the mourning veil she had worn when she went to meet Wrayan Lightfinger, when Nash came into the dressing room. He kissed her behind the ear and smiled at her in the mirror. "You look gorgeous."

"That wasn't actually the look I was aiming for," she replied with a frown. "This is a funeral, Nash."

"And a celebration," he reminded her. "We have a new High Arrion, don't forget." He smiled and added cheekily, "And she's a damn sight better-looking than the last one, I have to say."

Marla turned to look at him curiously. "Do you like Alija, Nash?"

"I suppose," he shrugged. "I never really thought about it."

"You've known her for a long time, haven't you?"

"I knew her back when . . ." He hesitated, looking a little uncomfortable.

"What?"

"When she and Laran looked like they might be . . . an item."

"I didn't know about that."

"Alija passed him over for Barnardo. He didn't like to talk about it much."

Marla desperately wanted to ask him more. She wanted to ask him if he was sleeping with Alija. *How long has it been going on? Since before you met me? After? Why? What did I do wrong?* But she said nothing, still clinging to the hope that it wasn't the truth. Still desperate to believe that a common thief everyone believed had been dead for the last five years had simply made up the whole thing for—

And that was where her reasoning failed her every time. There *was* no reason for Wrayan to lie, which left only the intolerable notion that he might be telling the truth.

"We should get going," she suggested, pinning the veil into place. "We don't want to be late. Alija might be offended."

He nodded his agreement and opened the door for her. If he noticed the bitterness in her voice when she mentioned Alija's name, he studiously ignored it. *Because it's all a lie,* she told herself firmly.

Then the traitor's voice in her head added, *Or because he's had so much practice in lying to you, he doesn't even need to think about it any more.*

The ceremony to lay the old High Arrion to rest and elevate the new one into his place seemed to go on for hours and Marla was desperate to be gone from the Sorcerers' Collective by the time she was finally able to escape. Despite a copious banquet laid out afterwards for the guests, Marla could barely look at the food. She'd drunk a little too much wine, too, which didn't help her unsettled stomach.

I've haven't felt this light-headed since I tried to get drunk the first night I was married to Laran, she thought.

It really was time to go home, Marla decided. She looked around for Nash, but couldn't see him anywhere. Instinctively, she looked for Alija, her heart sinking to the bottom of her ribcage when she realized the new High Arrion was missing, too.

Would they dare it? Here in the Sorcerers' Collective? At Kagan's funeral?

Why not? Marla thought bitterly. *He made love to me the first time in broad daylight in the gardens of Krakandar Palace and that didn't bother him at all. Nash gets a kick out of flirting with danger.*

Noticing it was dark outside, Marla wondered if they were on the balcony, the darkness offering the lovers some protection. She was headed that way when she saw Alija standing in a small group of people by the main entrance. Nowhere near the balcony. Nowhere near Nash.

"This is ridiculous!" she whispered to herself, under her breath. And it had to stop. She was tearing herself to pieces for no good reason.

"Are you all right, darling?" Nash asked, coming up behind Marla and taking her arm. "You look quite pale."

"Can we go home, Nash?" she asked. "I need to ask you something."

"If you want," he shrugged. "It's late enough that we can get away without offending anyone, I suppose. Are you sure you're feeling well?"

"Just take me home, Nash."

"Are you having an affair with Alija Eaglespike?"

Marla blurted it out in the carriage before she could stop herself. They weren't even through the gates of the Sorcerers' Collective. She wanted to die for asking such a thing. But as soon as she took her seat in the carriage she saw the tear in the upholstery where the crossbow bolt had landed. The bolt aimed at her son's head.

She had to know before the doubt and the fear drove her insane.

Nash laughed at her foolishness. "Whatever gave you that idea?"

"I have a witness, Nash. Someone who saw you in Alija's bed."

"As we're not in the habit of inviting an audience, my love, I don't see how you *could* have anybody who saw us."

Marla stared at him in shock.

Nash took a few seconds to realize what he'd said, and then he shrugged philosophically. "That came out rather more . . . honestly . . . than I planned."

"It's true, isn't it?" Marla asked, surprisingly calm.

He looked out of the window into the darkness, unable to meet her eye. "If you insist on knowing the sordid details, then yes, my love. It's true."

"Stop calling me that!" she snapped, the only outward sign of her torment. "How long has it been going on?"

"Marla, there's really no need to—"

"How long?"

"Long enough."

"How long? A week, a month? A year? Two years? Five? Ten? How *long*?"

He sighed and stared out into the darkness again. "The first time was the year you married Laran. Barnardo invited me to Dregian for the Summer Hunt. I took a spill from my horse one afternoon and went back to the castle early. Alija and I got to talking . . . one thing led to another . . . you know how it is . . ."

"Actually, I don't know how it is, Nash. Why don't you explain it to me?"

"Marla—"

"And when you came to Krakandar? Was it really to visit Laran? Or to woo me? Did Alija put you up to it? Is that why you said you loved me, Nash? Because Alija ordered you to?"

"Marla, don't do this to yourself—"

"I want to know, Nash!"

"Alija told me you were in love with me. I suppose I wanted to see for myself."

"So you *seduced* me? Just to see if I was in love with you? You unbelievably arrogant *bastard*!"

"Don't sit there getting all self-righteous on me, Marla, my love," he retorted, starting to lose patience with her. "You didn't take a whole lot of seducing, as I recall. And you were still married to Laran when you jumped me in that grotto in Krakandar Palace. Check if your own sheets are dirty before demanding that I change mine."

"I wasn't cheating on Laran. I was a widow. He was already dead when I slept with you the first time, Nash."

"But you didn't know that, your highness," he pointed out harshly. "So don't start looking down your royal nose at my transgressions. You've a few of your own, you know."

Marla couldn't believe he was just sitting there so calmly, as the carriage jolted along, not denying a thing. It was almost as if he was proud of it.

Or tired of waiting, the traitor in her head suggested. *Alija is High Arrion now. Perhaps he's simply had enough.*

"Did you have anything to do with the attack on Damin, Nash?"

She expected him to deny it, but instead he smiled unpleasantly. "My, we really do have the knives out tonight, don't we?"

"Answer the question."

"Does it matter?" he shrugged. "You seem to already know if I'm guilty or not. Why should I add to your entertainment by confirming your suspicions?"

"You should be denying them."

"Would there be any point?"

"Please tell me you didn't try to have Laran's son killed so Lernen would make your son his heir." She hoped desperately that she didn't sound like she was begging. It *felt* like she was begging.

Nash was silent for a long time before he answered. When he did, his answer took her completely by surprise. "You will ruin Damin with your coddling long before he can become High Prince, Marla. If I choose to do what I believe is in the best interests of Hythria, I don't expect you to understand. Damin cannot be what you want him to be; what Hythria *needs* him to be. He's a wilful, spoilt little monster and your smothering love will only make him worse. I can't stand by and watch another Wolfblade like Lernen sitting on the throne."

She was aghast at his reasoning. "For *Hythria* you would murder my son?"

"I'm a Patriot, Marla," Nash replied coldly. "For Hythria I would do *anything*."

As the carriage rolled to a stop outside their house, Marla, numb with grief and despair, recalled wondering on the day of the attack: *Who could be heartless enough to order the assassination of a four-year-old child?*

Apparently, she had her answer.

CHAPTER 89

All her life, Marla had had someone to whom she could turn to make the hard decisions for her. Lydia and Frederak were there all through her childhood, then Lernen decided who she should marry, and then Laran was there. Then Nash . . .

All her life there had been a man to tell her what to do. Until now.

Force of habit sent Marla to the palace to seek her brother's counsel after she'd confronted Nash, feeling sick to the stomach at the idea she'd been so grandly deluded. She knew it was her own fault. Nash had been playing to a very willing audience. On the way to the palace, she remembered a conversation with Kagan at the ball in Greenharbour the night she first met Nash. What had he said? *Don't be stupid, girl! You met him for less than five minutes and wove an entire fantasy around a misunderstanding. You don't know him; you don't know anything about him.* If only she'd taken that advice. But her youthful arrogance didn't allow for the possibility that she might be wrong about Nash Hawksword. *I happen to be an excellent judge of character,* she'd told the High Arrion that night.

Ah, yes, Kagan Palenovar had replied. *The lady who decided she was in love based on a conversation consisting of two whole sentences.*

Marla wanted to be in love—and to be loved—so badly that she would have believed anything Nash told her, if it meant fulfilling her fantasy of finding true love and living happily ever after.

Well, there is no happily ever after. Marla realized that now. All that was left was vengeance. And to protect her children.

With Kagan dead—not that she would have asked his advice anyway—and Elezaar on his way to Krakandar, the only man left in Greenharbour who she might trust with the burden of her grief was her brother. She wasn't hopeful of getting much sense out of him, but he *was* the High Prince. That ought to be worth something.

When she arrived at the palace, the seneschal informed her that the prince was about to retire to his garden on the roof of the west wing. Marla had no intention of visiting him in that revolting den of iniquity, so she ordered the man to bring her brother to her. Lernen and his disgusting little friends had far too many games going on in the roof garden for her to deliberately place herself within their reach. There seemed to be some sort of unwritten rule that said if you stepped into the garden, you were willing to play the game. She wasn't, so she sent the seneschal to demand her brother be brought to her and that she would be waiting in his private audience chamber.

Marla stared at the walls, shaking her head, as she stepped into the chamber. The silk hangings had been removed and the room was in the process of being redecorated with several very explicit murals. The uncompleted diagrams seemed to involve a lot of nymphs, Harshini and other creatures of fable, a lot of very handsome young men with a startling resemblance to Lernen and a number of sexual positions that Marla was sure were physically impossible.

The table in the centre of the room was scattered with scrolls. She glanced at them, a little concerned. This was the work normally done by Kagan, she suspected, when he visited the palace each day. And yet it was sitting here neglected, while Lernen played in his garden.

Muttering a curse at her brother's recklessness, she moved a little closer to examine the drawings on the walls, tilting her head until her ear was resting on her shoulder, trying to figure out how one could get *that* part of one's anatomy into *that* part of another person's anatomy from *that* angle, whilst standing on a pedestal with one foot in the air.

"A friend of mine tried that once," Lernen told her as he walked up beside her. He examined the diagram and laughed. "Put his back out quite badly, as I recall."

"I'm not surprised," Marla remarked. She turned to look at him and frowned. He was wearing a short loincloth, a pair of stag's antlers tied to his head, and his face was heavily made-up, his eyes outlined in kohl, his lips reddened with berry paste. He looked like a fool.

"Where have you been?"

"I was just going out into the garden," he told her, a little defensively. "With my friends."

"Your idea of mourning, I suppose?"

"Kagan wouldn't have wanted me to stop living, just because he's dead. Life goes on, you know, Marla."

"And what about all this?" she asked, waving a hand in the direction of the cluttered table.

Lernen shrugged. "Kagan used to deal with it."

"Kagan's dead," Marla pointed out bluntly.

"Then perhaps the new High Arrion—"

"Alija? I don't think so!"

"I thought you liked her?"

"I've changed my mind."

Lernen shrugged helplessly. "I'm not very good with this sort of thing, Marla. Kagan never made me deal with anything I didn't have to."

"You're the High Prince of Hythria, Lernen. You *should* be dealing with all of it!"

"I know," he sighed. "What did you want to see me about?"

Help me! Marla had been planning to say. *I need your advice. I know my husband is cheating on me. He's as good as admitted that he arranged the murder of my son. I'm not sure, but I think the new High Arrion is also in on the plot. What should I do?*

But she hesitated. Perhaps, for the first time in her life, Marla looked at her brother and saw him for what he really was. And at that moment, she realized just how alone she was. There was no help to be had here. Lernen wasn't going to advise her. He was just going to whine about the amount of work he was burdened with and let Hythria fall into wrack and ruin. Marla might not have approved of Kagan's method of dealing with the High Prince, but for the first time she thought she understood it.

She forced a smile. "I came to offer my help."

"What?"

"I thought you might like my help," she repeated. "With all this stuff Kagan left you to deal with. I thought maybe I could come to the palace each morning for a few hours and sort through it for you. You know, weed out the stuff you don't need to see and just save the important bits for you. I mean, you need the help obviously, and Alija certainly won't offer to aid you."

Lernen smiled, delighted by the idea. "Would you do that?"

"It's the least I can do, brother," she said. "And perhaps, when he's a little older, I can bring Damin along and he can start to learn about the responsibilities of being the High Prince."

"That's an excellent idea!"

She smiled and leaned forward to kiss his rouged cheek. "I'll come back tomorrow then," she said. "You go and . . . do whatever it is you do in your garden. I'll take care of everything for you, Lernen."

"I'll see you're rewarded for your kindness, Marla."

Kindness has nothing to do with it, you idiot, Marla felt

like telling him. *This is about power, and if you don't know
what to do with it, then I do.* She remembered what it felt
like, sitting opposite the First Sister of Medalon and negotiating that treaty after Laran died. She'd enjoyed that. Better
yet, she'd been good at it. She belonged in the halls of power.
She had the ability—and, more importantly, the will—to
govern that her brother lacked.

So be it. She was the mother of Hythria's heir. Marla had a
duty to her son. Damin deserved a legacy that wasn't falling
into decay. And she was the High Prince's sister, so nobody
could deny her the right.

Except her husband.

But that wasn't going to be a problem for much longer, she
decided coldly, realising what she must do to protect her children. Her husband was guilty of so many crimes she could
barely begin to list them all. Treason, adultery, attempted
murder . . .

A snap of her fingers and he would be made to pay.
Vengeance was as close as her brother, standing there in his
ridiculous stag horns. There was a name for what was wrong
with her brother—his latest fetish, anyway. Elezaar had made
her learn about it long ago, when she was a silly girl in Highcastle dreaming of that elusive "happily ever after". Pseudo-
zoophilia, they called it. The sexual fascination for creatures
of myth. *Of course, I could fill an encyclopaedia with a list
of all the other bizarre fetishes my brother has,* Marla
thought. But so long as she was not required to indulge in
them, so long as Lernen left her to do as she wished, he could
do what he wanted in his garden on the west wing roof and
she didn't give a damn.

Elezaar was right about that, too. Knowing what made her
brother tick was going to be the only way to handle him.

No, vengeance may be only a step away, but Marla wasn't
going to take that route. She wasn't going to drag Nash's
name through the dirt. She wasn't going to hurt Kalan or
Narvell by leaving them a legacy of treason and mistrust.
They would grow up believing their father was a good and

noble man. She didn't want Nash's father cowed either, with the shame of learning his son had betrayed the Hawksword name with his treachery. Nash would be remembered as a wonderful father; a dutiful son.

Marla had a much more effective, much more direct plan for dealing with Nashan Hawksword.

All it was going to take was money.

After all, that's what we have an Assassins' Guild for, isn't it?

"I'll come back tomorrow," she said, smiling at Lernen comfortingly.

"There's an awful lot there," he pointed out, obviously relieved that she was going to take some of the burden from him. "Are you sure you wouldn't like to get started today?"

This is your fault, Kagan, she lamented silently to the old man's ghost. *Lernen might not have been the intellectual giant you wanted as High Prince, but you didn't do any of us any favours by keeping him away from his duties.*

"I can't I'm afraid," she told him. "I have another appointment. Something very important I have to take care of. But I'll be here first thing tomorrow."

"Promise?"

"I promise, brother," she told him with a reassuring smile. "You can always count on me."

Accept what you cannot change—change that which is unacceptable.

It was Elezaar's Second Rule of Gaining and Wielding Power.

Marla made a detour on the way home that meant she was late for lunch. By the time she arrived, the twins were down for their afternoon nap. She kissed their unlined foreheads, cautioned the guards standing over their beds to remain silent and not disturb her children, and went to find Damin. He and Starros were in the nursery with Lirena who was knitting by the window while the boys played with a puzzle Elezaar had found for Starros in the markets for his sixth birthday.

"Look, Mama!" Damin cried as she knelt beside him. "We fixed it!"

"You broke it," Starros complained. "That bit doesn't go there!"

"Does too!"

"No, it doesn't!" Starros insisted, moving an incorrect piece into the correct place, not the least bit intimidated by his young companion.

"Listen to Starros, Damin," Marla ordered. "Wanting to be right doesn't make it so. The piece goes there, where he said it did."

Damin tossed the last piece he was holding down in annoyance. "It's a stupid puzzle, anyway. You wanna get the swords, Starros?"

The young fosterling calmly finished the puzzle then looked at Damin thoughtfully.

"I'll let you get the first hit in."

He thought about it for a moment longer then looked at Marla questioningly. "Is that all right, your highness?"

"Of course it is. Off you go, Starros. Damin, come here and give me a kiss before you go."

Damin brushed her cheek hurriedly and then ran outside to find the wooden swords one of the guards had fashioned for the boys. Damin was much more excited about it than Starros, who was far more studious than his foster brother.

"He's going to be a handful, that one," Lirena remarked sagely from her chair by the window.

"Who? Damin?"

"Doesn't like to lose," the old nurse noted with a slight frown.

"That's not a bad quality in a prince, Lirena," Marla pointed out.

"No, but it's going to make him a right pain in the buttocks until he grows into his crown," the old nurse declared knowingly. "Just you wait and see."

CHAPTER 90

The new High Arrion of the Sorcerers' Collective, Alija Eaglespike, was many things, but patient had not always been one of them. It had been a hard lesson, learning to wait for what she wanted.

But learn she had—the hard way—that, in the end, those who endured won the prize as often as those who fought for it.

When her plans for Barnardo to take the throne had been so comprehensively quashed by Laran Krakenshield and his cohorts, Alija had known the only choice she had was to regroup. Despite thinking it was disastrous at the time, Laran Krakenshield's coup had been a blessing in disguise. Things were turning out even better than she could have hoped, and the best part was, unlike her last unsuccessful bid for power, this time nobody was even aware she was involved.

She had attended the wedding of Marla and Nash Hawksword in Krakandar, thinking nobody had any concept of what this seemingly innocuous union meant. Marla was deliriously happy. Even without touching her mind, Alija could tell that from across the room. Her love for Nash hadn't faded in the slightest in the years she'd been married to Laran, and the fact that she was now being allowed to marry the love of her life meant the young woman positively glowed with contentment. Alija was happy for her. She had no personal gripe against Marla and was glad the girl would have a chance to be with the man she loved. It was more than Alija had ever had.

And she was pregnant; that had been the best news of all.

Nash had let it slip after they returned from Bordertown and his happiness was almost equal to Marla's, although for quite different reasons.

Poor Marla, Alija remembered thinking at the time, feeling genuinely sorry for the girl. *You really have no idea, do you?*

Alija had been having an affair with Nash even then. They had a lot in common, she and Nash. They both believed they should be wielding power. They both had to wait for their chance. They were both impatient. It had been surprisingly easy to make Nash see the opportunity within his grasp. He had always known that Marla liked him, although, until Alija brought it to his attention, Nash had no idea the girl was in love with him. The idea amused him at first. And then he began to see the possibilities.

After that, there was no stopping him.

Nashan Hawksword was a common enough phenomenon among the sons of Hythria. Born when his father was barely twenty, Nash was over thirty now, with a hale and hearty father not yet fifty years old, who showed no signs of slowing down. Unless killed in battle or by accident, Charel was likely to live a good while yet and Nash might be middle-aged or older before he got to inherit Elasapine. It was an awkward situation for an ambitious man who loved his father and wished him no harm.

But married to the sister of the High Prince, Nash's horizons had suddenly been broadened. Why hunger after a province when a chance for the whole country lay within your grasp?

Laran's death in a border raid had been a boon Alija couldn't have planned better if she'd tried. To have Marla pregnant and married to Nash so quickly was something neither of them had imagined possible. It was really only a matter of time after that. Nash's son was almost two, having weathered the first, and most dangerous, year of his life. Any time now they could kill Damin and replace him with Nash's son. Both children were the fruit of Marla Wolfblade, after all.

Once Damin was dead, Lernen would have no choice but to adopt his only other nephew, Narvell Hawksword, as his heir.

It didn't bother Alija unduly that the first attack on Damin had failed. Even surrounded by guards, nobody could protect Damin from Nash, or would suspect his beloved stepfather was responsible. When she seriously wanted to remove him, it would be easy enough to poison the child. This attack had been little more than a feint, really. Just testing Nash's resolve. While the whole of Greenharbour was up in arms about the threat to the High Prince's heir, Kagan had quietly slipped away and Alija had been able to step immediately into his position; the need was so urgent to replace him at such a critical time, that nobody had thought to object.

And now . . . well, it was quite straightforward, really. Once Damin was gone and his brother named heir, the High Prince would die—an illness would be easy enough to arrange. Foxglove was such a wonderfully virulent poison. And she knew it worked. One only had to look at Kagan to see how effective its leaves were. Young Narvell would become High Prince with his father, Nashan Hawksword, as his regent—conditional, of course, on Alija's eldest son, Cyrus Eaglespike, being named as Narvell's successor. Then it was just a matter of time. Nash could rule in his son's name until Cyrus was old enough to rule in his own right. At that time, she could remove Narvell in some terrible and tragic accident, and her son would become High Prince.

It was a roundabout route, she thought, opening the door to her study, *but an effective one.* She'd learned her lesson the last time—

Alija stopped just inside the door and looked around the room in shock. It was a shambles. The drawers of her desk had been upturned, their contents scattered on the floor. The shelves on her left had been emptied onto the floor as well, the pictures torn from the walls, the silk screens slashed to ribbons.

But the worst devastation was to the lacquered cabinet by

the window. The doors were wide open, the magical locks gone, and the contents nothing more than a heap of smoking ash.

Then she noticed the man sitting at her desk. He was very tall, dressed in black leathers, with dark hair and a smug look on his face. He was leaning back in her chair, his boots resting on the desk's polished surface. Angrily, she reached for her power, drawing every scrap she could handle, and hurled a blast at the presumptuous stranger, thinking the fool had no concept of who he was dealing with.

But her angry blast dissipated into nothing. Shocked beyond words, it was then that she noticed the stranger's eyes were black. Totally black. There was no white in them at all.

"Lady Eaglespike, I presume?" the man said, with the faintest hint of a sneer.

"Who are you?" she hissed, looking around for a weapon. There was nothing nearby. The best she could hope for was to use some of the scattered debris as missiles, but when she reached for her power again, she couldn't find it. She could feel it, just out of reach, but there was something holding her back. The stranger looked amused as he felt her struggling against the invisible barrier.

"My official title among the Harshini is Lord Brakandaran té Carn," he announced calmly, picking up a stick of sealing wax from the desk and turning it over curiously in his hands. "You might know of me by my other name, though. Brakandaran the Halfbreed?"

"Brakandaran is a legend!" she spat at him.

He smiled. "Why, thank you, my lady. I like to think so."

"Who are you really? How did you get in here? How did you . . ." She stared at the cabinet and then looked at the man who claimed to be the Halfbreed. Perhaps he was. She couldn't imagine anybody else being able to break the wards on the cabinet.

"What do you want?" she asked, a little more cautiously.

The Halfbreed made a great show of thinking about it be-

fore he replied. "Hmmm . . . what do I want . . . world
peace . . . a nice little place in the countryside, perhaps . . . a
tavern where the beer is free . . ."

"What do you want of *me*?" she demanded angrily.

"Ah, now that's a little more complicated. You've been a
very naughty girl, Alija."

"What are you talking about?"

He tossed the stick of wax onto the desk and stared at her.
"You hurt a friend of mine, lady. Very badly. And you did it
using Harshini magic. I take a rather dim view of that."

He knows about Kagan. Alija desperately wanted to glance
over her shoulder to check the distance to the door, but realized it was an idle hope. If this really was the Halfbreed, she
would have no hope of making it out of the room before he
caught her. He could probably flay her alive with a thought.
She remained silent, just hoping he hadn't tried reading her
mind.

"And now you're High Arrion, I hear."

"I deserve to be High Arrion," she informed him, sure of
that, at least. "I'm the only one in the whole damn Sorcerers'
Collective with any sort of real power. The rest of them are
just faking it."

"There was another contender," Brak reminded her. "Until
you tried to kill him."

"Who?" she scoffed. "There's not been anybody since—" Alija stared at him in shock. "That's your *friend*? Wrayan *Lightfinger*?" The relief she felt was indescribable. He didn't know about
Kagan. He knew about Wrayan, but he had no idea she'd killed
the High Arrion. She might even survive this confrontation.

Brakandaran was not looking pleased, however. "I don't
like people who hurt my friends."

"He hurt my slave."

"You tried to *kill* him. I'm not sure if that lesson escaped
you at all during your long apprenticeship, my lady, but the
Harshini frown upon that sort of thing."

"The Harshini are gone."

"*Are* they?" he asked pointedly.

"Is that why you're here? To kill me?"

Brakandaran smiled. "Despite what you may have heard about me, Alija, I actually don't go around killing people without a good reason. As it is, Wrayan survived your attempt to cauterise the inside of his skull, and he's none the worse for it, so I'm going to let you off with a warning—this time."

"Wrayan is *alive*? Where is he?"

"Closer than you think. But entirely out of your reach," the Halfbreed replied cryptically. "He's no concern of yours any longer. Wrayan won't be back to bother your ambitions. The gods have another fate in mind for him."

"What's going to happen to me?"

"Not a thing," Brakandaran said. "Provided you behave yourself and I don't catch you using any more Harshini enhancement spells."

Her eyes strayed to the cabinet in dismay. Just a smoking pile of ashes.

"And I don't think that's going to be a problem any more, is it, Alija?" he asked confidently, seeing the direction of her gaze.

Alija wanted to weep at the loss of the contents of that cabinet. "Those scrolls were irreplaceable!"

"For you, perhaps," he shrugged. "I can get copies any time I want."

He swung his feet to the floor and stood up. He was very tall. Dressed in his dark leathers, he really was as impressive as the legends claimed. For a fleeting moment, Alija's fear waned and she thought of the possibilities.

What could I achieve with a man like Brakandaran at my side?

She began to get an idea when he held out his arm and she found herself walking towards him, even though she desperately tried to resist him. He moved around the desk to meet her, forcing her across the room until they were standing toe to toe.

The Halfbreed leaned forward until his lips hovered beside her ear and she could feel his hot breath on her skin. "Now,

I'm going to tell you this just once, Alija," he said softly, silk-
ily, in a voice that sent a shiver of fear down her spine, "so
listen, and listen well. If I *ever* have to come back here and
scold you again for misusing the gift the gods have given
you, trust me, you *will* regret it." He leaned back and smiled
at her then and Alija thought her life was about to end.
Brakandaran's smile wasn't the warm smile of a benign
Harshini. It was the cold-blooded smile of a killer. "Do we
understand each other?"

Alija nodded dumbly, too frightened to speak. This close,
she could feel the power he commanded, like the heat from a
forge. It was more than she believed possible. More than she
had drawn to herself with the enhancement spell. More than
the raw power she had felt in Wrayan. It was more than she
had imagined one person could wield. It was terrifying.

And then he let her go with a careless flick of his wrist and
she collapsed onto the rug, sobbing with fear. It took her a few
minutes before she was able to think again, to get the surge of
terror under control. Cautiously, she opened her eyes and looked
up at him, only to discover she was alone in the ruined study.

Brakandaran the Halfbreed was gone.

chapter 91

Several days later, long after civilised people were abed,
Marla received a visitor. The man was in early middle age,
dark-haired and nondescript, except for his eyes which
seemed to take in everything at once. On his left hand he
wore the raven ring of the Assassins' Guild. He didn't offer her a name, but she knew who he was and was expecting
him. She opened the door to him herself, having dismissed
the guards and the slaves in preparation for this appointment.

Marla hardened her heart as the man bowed to her, his features shadowed by the single candle she had lit in the main reception room.

"Well?" she asked, surprised her voice wasn't trembling.

"It is done, your highness."

"How?"

"Are you certain you want the details, your highness?"

Marla squared her shoulders grimly. "If I have the courage to order this thing, sir, I believe I should have the courage to hear how it was done."

The man nodded his agreement. "As you wish."

"Will it look like an accident?"

"A tragic accident, your highness."

"Where did it happen?"

"In the slave quarter. Your husband frequented some of the brothels there with his friends on a fairly regular basis."

Marla wasn't surprised. Not all households kept *court'esa*. Those lords and ladies who liked a bit of variety often preferred to visit Greenharbour's countless brothels rather than go to the expense of purchasing their own *court'esa* and then having to buy a new one when they tired of them. "How did you know that?"

"It's our job to know these things, your highness."

"What happened?" she asked, determined to hear this through. Marla wasn't being morbid. She had to know she had the stomach for what lay ahead, and if she couldn't bear the details of her first unpalatable act, then she was never going to be able to make the everyday decisions necessary to rule Hythria the way it needed to be ruled—ruthlessly and without fear.

"He spent some time with a *court'esa* named Lora. She's serviced him before. During the evening, she offered him wine, which he drank. It was laced with a soporific."

"You drugged him?"

"He would have struggled otherwise, your highness, and you specifically requested we leave no marks of violence upon his body."

"I also told you I didn't want him poisoned."

"And he wasn't, your highness. The wine merely made him sleepy. After he was finished with the *court'esa*, she suggested he bathe before coming home, an offer he accepted. Whilst in the tub, it appears Lord Hawksword fell asleep and tragically slid beneath the water. The *court'esa* will raise the alarm in an hour or so."

I feel nothing, Marla thought, a little surprised. *No guilt. No grief. Not even relief.* "You've done well."

"We aim to please, your highness."

"How many people know of this transaction?"

"Only you, me and the *court'esa* who performed the task, your highness. Only I know that it was you who arranged the contract."

"And what will it cost to ensure your silence?"

"One of your sons, your highness."

Marla stared at him in shock. "You can't be serious."

"I'm sorry," the man replied, "that came out all wrong. I don't mean the sons you have now, my lady. Both your sons are heirs to empires that far outweigh the benefits of my profession. But you're young and have just become a widow. You'll marry again. You'll have more children, step-children perhaps, even fosterlings. I want one of them. To train as an apprentice, nothing more sinister."

"Why?"

"Because I like the idea of having someone in the Guild with the ear of the High Prince, your highness."

Marla thought about it for a moment and then nodded. "Very well," she agreed, thinking it was a deal she could delay indefinitely. For that matter, she may never even have another son.

The assassin bowed and smiled at her. "It's been a pleasure doing business with you, your highness."

Marla showed him out herself, locked the door and then climbed the stairs slowly. She didn't go straight to her room. Instead, she walked down the hall a little way, nodded a greeting to the guards standing outside the children's room as she let herself in. There were guards inside, too, silent and alert, watching over her sleeping children. She checked on each one of them herself, guided by nothing more than the starlight coming in from the open window where yet another silent guard stood to attention.

Damin slept on his back, sprawled across his bed as if trying to claim as much of it as possible. He looked like an angel when he was asleep, a fair-haired vision of sweetness and innocence that was at complete odds with the noisy mischief-maker he could be when he was awake. In the next cot lay Kalan, sleeping on her stomach with her thumb in her mouth, so serene and secure. So unafraid of life she could sleep peacefully in a world where assassins lurked in every corner. *In a world where her mother had arranged to have her father killed . . .*

Marla pushed the thought away. Thinking like that would drive her crazy. Beside Kalan in the cot was Narvell, lying in almost the same position as his sister—a mirror image of his twin. A murmur from the last bed in the room caught her attention. She glanced over at Starros, who was curled into a tight ball as if he was cold. Marla moved to his side and gently pulled the light cover over him with a smile and he unconsciously relaxed a little.

What have I done to you, my darlings? she wondered, glancing at the twins again. *Will you be better or worse for never having known your father? Should I have killed him? Or should I have stood by and waited for him to kill your brother?*

When she thought about it like that, there was really no question that she'd done the right thing. Nash was old enough to make his own choices and he'd made the choices that led to death.

Funny thing is, Nashan, my love, I would have given everything to you had you asked. You never needed to take anything from me . . .

And Alija? How much of this was her doing? And how would she react to the news her lover was dead? She certainly couldn't accuse Marla of anything. Not without betraying herself. But that was a problem to be faced tomorrow. And the day after.

And the day after that.

From this moment on, nothing would ever be the same for Marla Wolfblade.

Marla sighed and turned away from her children. They were safe now. Safer than they'd been for a very long time. Nobody would ever be allowed to threaten them again like that, she silently vowed.

And Marla intended to make certain of it, even if it meant taking the throne of Hythria herself.

As she stepped into the candlelit hall, Marla wished Elezaar was here, thinking the dwarf would know what to do. But then, she'd done all this without him. Perhaps she'd finally reached the point where she no longer needed his counsel. Marla smiled at the thought, imagining the panicked look on Elezaar's face if she even hinted that she might no longer have a use for him. She wasn't blind to the dwarf's desperate need to stay at her side. It puzzled her at times and she was determined to get to the bottom of his inexplicable devotion to her some day, but for now it was time she retired to her room.

It was very late and she was going to need a good night's sleep, because tomorrow morning the city guard would be banging on the doors at some ungodly hour to inform her that, tragically, her husband was dead.

EPILOGUE

*F*rom the balcony overlooking the great staircase of the
Greenharbour Palace, you could see tomorrow ...

Marla remembered thinking that the last time she stood here in her dressing gown, waiting for the ball to start. Memories of that innocent and foolish child seemed to belong to someone else. The ruthless young woman who stood here now found it hard to credit that she had ever been so innocent, so naive.

She looked down at the preparations for the Feast of Kaelarn Ball with a wistful smile. *You couldn't see as far as tomorrow, but you could see right across the hall, and get a very nice view of the handsome and smartly dressed young men who had come for the ball this evening.*

In a way, she missed that girl; the one whose most pressing chore was to decide which of those handsome and smartly dressed young men would be her husband. Marla was thinking along the same lines again, but she was no longer content to choose a young man for his looks or his smile. She'd fallen for that once and the cost had proved more than she was willing to pay. No, the next time Marla got married it would be for far more tangible things in life. Money. Power. Influence.

The sixteen glorious cut-crystal candelabra showered their warm yellow light over the guests. The musicians in the corner were tuning their instruments discordantly and barefooted slaves hurried back and forth from the kitchens, piling the long tables with exotically displayed foods and countless flagons of the fine imported Medalonian wines for which the palace was so famous. The thirty-two fluted marble columns no longer looked as if they could support the weight of the entire world in Marla's eyes. These days they were just another unique architectural feature in a palace that was full of unique architectural features.

Marla pushed her long fair hair off her face, remembering the gesture as if she had somehow stepped back in time. As she had that evening so long ago, she knew that somewhere down there, amid the sea of faces, polished boots and slicked-down hair, was her future husband. She had no idea who he was, but he was sure to present himself at some stage this evening. These days, she didn't care if he was handsome, but he *would* be wealthy, probably old. She had promised Lernen she would marry whoever he wanted the next time and she meant to keep her word.

She would never marry for love again. That was certain.

The chances were high that her next husband wouldn't be the son of one of the many noble houses. Lernen needed friends in the increasingly affluent and influential merchant class and they were looking equally attractive to a princess wishing to acquire material wealth. Marla already had two sons who were the heirs to two different provinces and the High Prince's crown. She did not intend to complicate matters further by adding a third heir to the mix.

"Is something wrong, your highness?"

Marla turned as Elezaar approached. He'd arrived back several weeks ago with Almodavar, who was now responsible for the security of her children. She was sleeping much better since he had arrived from Krakandar with three hundred battle-hardened troops.

"No. I was just reliving old times."

"Old times?"

"I stood here once, Elezaar, a lifetime ago, trying to imagine what my husband might look like. That was the night I met Nash. And Laran. Wrayan, too, now that I think about it."

"Sounds like quite an eventful evening."

"It was."

"And are you still determined to marry again?"

"More than ever," Marla told the dwarf. "As a widow, I'm powerless. As a wife I have much more freedom."

"Is it only freedom you want, your highness?"

Marla smiled thinly. The dwarf saw through her so easily. "I want power, Elezaar. I want people to think twice before they harm me or mine again. I want the men of this land to think about what they could gain by harming my sons, and then consider what they might lose if they fall out of favour with me. I want the power to ruin, not just to kill. Any man with enough coin can hire an assassin to redress a wrong he feels has been done to him. I want the serious wealth it takes to destroy a man's livelihood and his family's future. That's the kind of wealth and power I want. I'll need it, if I'm to keep my children safe."

"Will you keep them here in Greenharbour with you?"

She shook her head. "I'm too busy with my work at the palace and too frightened for their safety. I'm sending them back to Krakandar. Almodavar will watch over them. And he'll teach them to look after themselves. Far better than I could. Besides, with Mahkas and Bylinda there, it'll be just like a real home. Leila and Xanda are there too, although Travin's gone to Elasapine with Charel now. Anyway, I don't want my children growing up in this cesspit. If Lernen wants to be a doting uncle, he can do it from a distance. I won't let Damin or the twins be corrupted by him."

"Have you thought about asking the Sorcerers' Collective to manage Krakandar until Damin comes of age?"

"With Alija in control? I think not. Besides, Mahkas has done a good job as regent so far. I see no reason why his stewardship of Krakandar shouldn't continue."

"And what of Alija?"

"What of her?"

"You're just going to let her get away with everything she did?"

"I have no proof she was involved in anything, Elezaar, other than sleeping with my husband. Besides, she's High Arrion now. Unless I want to take on the whole Sorcerers' Collective, there's no way I can confront her without incontrovertible proof that she was involved in something illegal. I put an end to Nash's push for the throne. For the time being, we'll have to be content with that."

"She turned him against you."

Marla was silent for a time, then she shrugged philosophically. "Did she? If Nash ever really loved me, Elezaar, Alija couldn't have made him betray me the way he did. Decent men don't arrange to have babies murdered to further their own ambition."

"Wrayan believes she was behind it all."

"Wrayan also claims he speaks to the gods and that he's been living among the Harshini in Sanctuary for the past few years, Elezaar. You don't believe that, too, do you?"

"I'm not sure I *don't* believe him."

"And that's why I'm sending him back to Krakandar, too."

"Almodavar *will* be busy."

Marla smiled. "Look at it this way. Either Wrayan is crazy, which means that with Almodavar watching over him in Krakandar he can do very little harm, or he really *can* speak to the gods and wield Harshini magic, in which case I'd much rather have him where he can watch over my children."

"And the High Prince?"

"What about him?"

"Will you do nothing about your brother?"

"I will fight to keep him on the throne with my dying breath. Damin deserves that much from me."

"Even knowing what he is?"

Marla sighed. "Kagan told me once that Lernen's greatest virtue was his total obsession with his own pleasure. He's not interested in anything else. I believe he was right. Lernen can do what he pleases, Elezaar. I will look after Hythria until my son comes of age. And then Hythria will have a High Prince it can be proud of."

"I think Hythria already has a princess it can be proud of, Marla Wolfblade."

She looked down at the twisted little man fondly. "Do you remember telling me once that your only purpose in life was to remain in my good graces, dwarf?"

"I do, your highness."

"Keep coming up with comments like that," Marla replied with a smile, "and you may yet get your wish, Fool."

From Jennifer Fallon
and Tor Books

WARRIOR

Now available in hardcover!
Turn the page for a preview. . . .

PROLOGUE

Damin Wolfblade wasn't sure what had woken him. He had no memory of any sound jarring him into instant wakefulness; no idea what instinctive alarm had gone off inside his head to alert him that he was no longer alone. Straining with every sense, he listened to the darkness, waiting for the intruder to betray his presence. He had no doubt it was an intruder. Uncle Mahkas or Aunt Bylinda had no need to sneak around the palace. Any other legitimate visitor to his room at this hour of the night would have announced themselves openly.

It might be one of his stepbrothers, Adham or Rodja, looking for a bit of sport, Damin thought, as he inched his hand up under the pillow, or even his foster-brother, Starros, trying to frighten him. Maybe his cousin, Leila, or one of the twins had sneaked into his room via the slaveways, hoping to scare him. It wouldn't be the first time they'd tried. There was a great deal of amusement to be gained by sneaking up on an unsuspecting brother and making him squeal like a girl. Then again, it might not be one of his siblings. It might be an assassin.

It certainly wouldn't be the first time in Damin's short life someone had tried to kill him.

Damin's fingers closed over the wire-wrapped handle of the knife Almodavar insisted he keep under his pillow, the hilt cool and reassuring in his hand. There was still no betraying sound from the intruder, a fact that made the boy dismiss the idea the trespasser was simply one of his friends looking to play a joke on him. There would have been a giggle by now; a hissed command to be silent, a telling scuff of a slipper on the highly polished floor. But there was nothing. Just a heavy, omnipresent silence.

Not even the sound of someone breathing.

Damin opened his eyes and withdrew the dagger from under his pillow with infinite care, the thick stillness more threatening than the shadows. There should have been a guard in the room. For as long as he could remember, Damin had slept with subtle sounds of another human presence nearby. The faint creak of leather as a watchful guard moved, the almost inaudible breathing of the guardian who stood over him as he slept—they were the sounds he associated with the night. With safety. With comfort.

And they were gone.

Was that what had woken him? Had they already killed his bodyguard? Any assassin worth his fee should be able to take out a single guard silently, Damin knew. It also meant there was little point in trying to raise an alarm. His room was large—a suite fit for a prince—and the nearest guards would be out beyond the sitting room in the hall. Even if a palace patrol was in the vicinity and they heard him on his first cry, the chances were good he would be dead long before they were able to get through the outer room and into his bedroom.

There was no help from that quarter. Damin was going to have to deal with this himself. Alone.

Forcing his breathing to remain deep and even, Damin cautiously brought the knife down under the blanket and ever so carefully changed his grip so the blade lay against his forearm. He flexed his fingers and wrapped them around the hilt again, to make certain he had a good grip. Then he froze as the faintest sound of leather on polished stone whispered through the darkness.

It was close. Very close.

There was no longer any doubt in Damin's mind. There was an assassin in the room and his bodyguard was probably dead.

How he had got into the palace was a problem Damin had

no time to worry about right now. He judged the man to be almost at the bed, which meant he had only seconds before the assassin's blade fell. *Do the unexpected*, a voice in his head advised him. It was one of Elezaar's infamous Rules of Gaining and Wielding Power, but the voice sounded suspiciously like Almodavar, the captain of Krakandar's Raiders, his weapons master, instructor and mentor.

Where is he now? Damin wondered. *When I actually need him?*

Another barely audible scuff of leather against stone and Damin realized he had no time left to wonder about it. He felt, rather than heard, the intruder raise his arm to make the killing stroke. With a sharp, sudden jerk, Damin threw back the covers, tossing them over his assailant, blinding him. Then he rolled, not away from the assassin and his blade, but towards them, slicing the man with all his might across where he thought his midriff might be, before kicking his legs up and ramming them into the space where he thought the assassin's head was located. It was impossible to tell if his aim was true between the darkness and the man fighting to get clear of the bedcovers.

The pounding of his pulse seemed loud enough to be heard in the hall.

Damin's blade had sliced across hardened leather and made little impact on his assailant's chest but the boy was rewarded with a satisfying grunt as his heels connected with something solid, presumably the assassin's head. He sliced with his arm again, this time a little higher, hoping to wound the man. The intruder leaned back to avoid Damin's blade and momentarily lost his balance.

His blood racing, filled with a strength born of desperation and fear, Damin threw himself at the assassin, knocking the man off his feet. He landed on top of the killer, slamming the man's head into the stone floor with one hand as he changed the grip on his knife with the other and raised it to plunge his dagger into the throat of his assailant. He drove the blade downward, his heart hammering . . .

Then he stopped, a whisker away from killing his attacker, "*Almodavar?*"

The man beneath him relaxed, smiling as Damin recognised him in the darkness.

"Not bad," the captain said.

Lowering the blade, Damin sat back on his heels, breathing heavily, still astride his would-be assassin, and grinned broadly. "See, I told you . . . I could look after . . . myself."

"Aye, you did, lad," the captain of Krakandar's guard agreed. "Pity you're so damn cocky about it, though."

As he spoke, Almodavar gathered his strength beneath him and threw Damin backwards, his blade slicing across the boy's throat as he lashed out. Damin landed heavily on his back and skidded on the polished floor, coming to rest against the wall. He scrambled to his feet, blade at the ready, stunned to discover blood dripping from his wounded neck.

"Ow!" he complained, gingerly touching the long thin cut across his throat.

"That was a stupid mistake, boy."

"But I beat you!" Damin protested.

"I'm still breathing," Almodavar pointed out, as he climbed to his feet. "That's not beaten, lad. It's not even close."

"But I'd won! That's not fair!"

"What's not fair?" a voice asked from the doorway.

Damin turned to find his Uncle Mahkas striding into the room holding a large candelabrum, his face shadowed by the flickering light of half a dozen candles. Mahkas was still dressed, so he hadn't been called from his bed, nor had the room suddenly filled with guards, as it should have done following an attack on the heir to the throne.

Which meant Mahkas knew about this little training exercise, Damin realized; had probably sanctioned it. It might have been his uncle who had suggested it. Mahkas did crazy things like that sometimes.

"Almodavar attacked me!" he complained. "After I'd won."

"If you'd *won*, Damin, he shouldn't have been *able* to attack you," Mahkas pointed out unsympathetically. "Always finish your enemy, otherwise he'll finish you. You should know that by now." He turned to the captain of the guard with a questioning look. "Well?"

Almodavar sheathed his knife and nodded. "He'll do, I suppose."

His objections about his unfair treatment forgotten, Damin glanced between his uncle and the captain, as he suddenly realized what this meant. "I'll do?"

"You'll do," Mahkas told him, with a hint of pride in his voice. "If you can take down Almodavar, there's not much else that's a threat to you around here."

"Really?" Damin couldn't hide his grin. "You mean it? No more sleeping with a bodyguard in my room?"

"No," his uncle agreed. "You're almost thirteen and I promised we'd dispense with the guard when you could prove you were able to look after yourself. If Almodavar is content you can, then I'm happy to accept his word on it."

"Just wait 'til I tell the others!"

"You can tell them in the morning," Almodavar informed him. "After you've done forty laps of the training yard. Before breakfast."

Damin stared at him in shock. "Forty laps? For *what*? I took you down, Almodavar! I won!"

"You hesitated."

"You think I should have *killed* you?" Damin asked, a little wounded to think Almodavar wasn't thanking him for staying his hand; instead he was punishing him for it. He'd come awfully close to killing the most trusted captain in Krakandar's service, too.

"How did you know I hadn't *really* come to kill you, Damin?"

"You're the senior captain of the guard."

"That doesn't mean anything."

"There's a comforting thought," Mahkas muttered with a shake of his head.

Almodavar glanced at Mahkas, a little exasperated that Damin's uncle was making light of his point. "He needs to understand, my lord. I might have been subverted. For all any of you know, my family has just been taken hostage by your enemies and I came here willing to kill even the heir to Hythria's throne to save them."

"But you don't have a family, Almodavar," Damin pointed out. "Except for Starros."

The captain ignored the comment about Starros. He always did. "You have no way of knowing the mind of every man in your service, Damin. And any man who can get near you is a potential assassin. You shouldn't hesitate just because you think you know them."

"I *could* have killed you," Damin insisted. "If I really wanted to."

"Why didn't you?"

"Because I knew you weren't really trying to kill me."

"How?"

"You sliced the blade across my throat. If you were serious about killing me, Almodavar, you would have stabbed me with it. Straight through the neck. Up into the brain. Splat! I'm dead."

"He's got a point," Mahkas agreed with a faint smile, and then he glanced at the thin cut on Damin's throat. "Although you came close enough."

Almodavar shrugged. "The lad needed a scare."

Mahkas squinted at Damin in the candlelight, shaking his head. "Let's hope that slice has healed without a scar before his mother gets here. Seeing Damin with his throat almost cut is a scare I'm not sure Princess Marla is ready for."

"He'll be fine," Almodavar promised Mahkas. "Anyway, it'd take more than a cut throat to put Laran Krakenshield's son down."

A part of Damin wished he'd had a chance to know the father Almodavar spoke of so admiringly. All his young life, he'd heard nothing but great things about Laran Krakenshield, so much so that Damin sometimes wondered if he would ever be able to live up to his father's legacy.

"That's true enough," his uncle agreed with a fond smile. "For now, however, I suggest we try and get some sleep. Well done, Damin."

"Thank you, sir."

Mahkas left the room, taking with him the only source of light. It took Damin's eyes a few moments to adjust to the darkness again. He turned to Almodavar, grinning like a fool, his blood still up from his close brush with death.

"I *could* have killed you, you know."

The captain nodded. "I know."

"So do I really have to do forty laps?"

"Yes."

"I *should* have killed you," the boy grumbled.

Almodavar smiled at him with paternal pride. "If you've worked that out, lad, then you may have learned something useful from this little exercise, after all."